Reasonable Maniacs

Novels of Northern Ireland Series

Reasonable Maniacs

For the Love of Northern Ireland

Monty Miles

Writers Club Press
San Jose New York Lincoln Shanghai

Reasonable Maniacs
For the Love of Northern Ireland

Published by Writers Club Press
an imprint of iUniverse.com, Inc.

For information address:
iUniverse.com, Inc.
620 North 48th Street
Suite 201
Lincoln, NE 68504-3467
www.iuniverse.com

ISBN: 0-595-01106-3

Printed in the United States of America

To Joe. Thank you for making everything possible.

"*You don't negotiate with someone who marches into another country, devastates it, killing whoever stands in his way. You get him out, you make him pay, and see he is never in a position to do these things again. Dictators can be deterred. They can be crushed, but they can never be appeased.*"

—British Prime Minister Margaret Thatcher

"*The right of the Irish people to the ownership of Ireland and to their unfettered control of Irish destinies is a sovereign right, and the sooner British generals and politicians convince themselves of our absolute determination to assert that right through force of arms until final British disengagement, the better for all. They will not, and cannot prevail.*"

—the Irish Republican Army

Preface

Year after year, Northern Ireland's Troubles persist. Peace has been promised but not delivered, dialogue has been squandered. The loyalists continue their campaign of intimidation; nationalist houses and churches are burned, nationalist men are beaten to death, nationalist lawyers are blown up in their cars. The police still terrorize nationalist communities. Hundreds of nationalist files are in loyalist hands, suggesting collusion between loyalists and the crown forces. The British soldiers haven't withdrawn, they continue fortifying the border. The IRA has silenced its guns, but they haven't surrendered or disarmed. Because history has shown the Catholics of Northern Ireland are most vulnerable and abused when they are stripped of their ability to fight back; remember Bloody Sunday. If there is to be peace, it must be equitable, all sides must decommission their weapons and demands for dominion. This includes the British Army and their loyalist factions. Until then, a ceasefire is but a respite and Ireland remains unfree. And the *Reasonable Maniacs* go on.

Acknowledgments

Thank you to all my friends and relatives in Belfast who taught me the joys and sorrows of being Irish. And many thanks to everyone from the New Lodge to New Barnsley who gave me guidance and Guinness and inspiration. *Síocháin libh.*

Chapter One

How It Began.

"Slow sex in the back seat of a Rolls Royce. That's mine."

"My fantasy," Reason confided, "is making love in long, soft grass and tappy rain."

"Tappy?" Wilder thought he misunderstood.

"Tappy rain is that soft, fine mist that rubs like mink against your skin. I'd like to be nude, drenched in tappy rain, and madly in love."

Wilder imagined Reason disrobing. He could see her, lush and glorified in transparent black, leaning back in the back seat of a Silver Cloud. "Aren't you madly in love with Reid?"

"I've known him for so long I can't remember," Reason joked.

But Wilder didn't laugh. "You're wasted on that man."

Rain drifted against the windows. Standing in the doorway, Reason watched the storm. "Sometimes rain makes me feel homesick even though I know I'm home. For some reason it reminds me of sad good-byes."

"It's the Irish in you, Reas. There's a part of you pining for Ireland."

"I'm not Irish."

"I've always just assumed you were. How can you not be Irish with a name like McGuinness?"

"Maybe centuries ago someone in my family came from Ireland, but both my parents and their parents are from Connecticut. Greenwich, Connecticut," Reason added as if to make some point.

"Do you have something against the Irish?" Wilder couldn't figure why she acted put off.

Reason hadn't been to Ireland but she had grown up hearing the Irish maligned. Her mother never missed an opportunity to voice her contempt. To be Irish, specifically Irish Catholic, was to be dirty, violent, stupid and drunk. The Irish were little better than apes, or so Reason had been told. And while she tried to ignore her mother's prejudice, she had no desire to claim a vulgar heritage. She knew Wilder was from Belfast, but he was more American than Irish, and he was an exceptional exception. "I don't think it matters where you come from as long as you're a good person," she answered carefully.

"Well, I'm Irish and proud of it."

"Wilder, you left Ireland years ago. You're an American now." Reason joined him on the sofa. "Living here has had a good effect on you."

"You say that like there was something wrong with me before America had its 'good effect.' What if I'd just gotten off a plane from Belfast? Would you think less of me?" He awaited her reply, thinking it might be best if she said "yes." He was far too enamored of his housemate's fiancée.

"Who says I think of you at all, O'Neill?" Reason laughed. "Wow, look at the time! It's after midnight. Reid promised he'd be home by ten."

"He probably got called back into surgery."

"He should have phoned then. I've been waiting for him all evening. No doubt you've had enough of me."

"I'll never get enough of you, Mac."

Reason slugged Wilder's arm. "Don't call me 'Mac!'"

"Whatever you say, Mac," he laughed then frowned. "I can't believe your wedding is Saturday. In six days you'll walk out of my life...are you sure you want to marry Reid?"

"I don't have much choice. It's too late to change my mind."

"Are you having second thoughts?" Wilder hoped.

"I think everybody does this close to their wedding. It's such a big commitment. And I'm not sure I'm ready, or that Reid's even right...there are days I just feel like running away from the whole thing."

"Do you think about running away with me?"

"Of course not," Reason lied. The fantasy had crossed her mind. "Why would I!"

"Because for the past few months you've spent more time with me than you have with Reid and we've become really close."

"Reid's been busy with his residency…"

"I've been busy with mine too but, unlike Reid, I always have time for you. Won't you miss sharing your life with me?"

Realizing she gazed too long upon Wilder, Reason lowered her eyes. Then glanced back. Even after two years she had a hard time not staring at the Irishman; swarthy and tall with compelling blue eyes. But something about those Irish eyes inspired a sense of loss; in his gaze, as in the rain, she felt homesick again. "We'll just have to find new things to share," she said.

"There won't be much time. I'll finish my residency next year and go home to L.A."

"Ah, that's right," Reason teased, "you'll officially become one of the prima donna glamour boys. A thoracic surgeon. Lah-dee-dah."

Wilder wasn't listening. He focused on Reason, taking in the sight of her sitting close beside him. "A week from tonight you'll be on your honeymoon. In Baltimore! My God, that's the worst. What happened to Reid's promise to take you to Antigua?"

"He has an interview at Johns Hopkins, so it's more convenient."

"A 'convenient' honeymoon? Oh, now *that's* romantic. If I married you," Wilder grazed a knuckle along Reason's cheek, "I'd take you to a castle above the Irish Sea. By day we'd sit on the white cliffs and plan our future. By night we'd lie in our bed and listen to the wind off the surf, and our souls would entwine like the waves blending into the ocean. Sound good to you?"

"It sounds…" Reason raised her eyes to Wilder's, "…like you've read too much poetry."

"This isn't a joke!" His affection betrayed him. "I've seen you every day for 700 days…how can I let you go? Don't marry him, Reas…"

She flew to her feet. "Oh, Wilder, don't say that! I'm engaged to Reid, I've been with him for five years…"

"And you've been with me for two years."

"But you and I are just friends."

"No, Reason, we're liars. We haven't been honest about our feelings, and time is running out."

"It's already too late. Maybe if I'd met you first…but I didn't."

On impulse, Wilder jumped up and turned Reason around. He caught her chin in both hands and lifted her mouth to his, and though she knew she should, she didn't resist him. She weaved her fingers through his hair, kissing him with passion. She told herself it was for friendship, a one-time caprice, just to feel his lips upon hers. Just once, a first and last kiss. His arms tightened around her, she melted against him, and the telephone rang.

Reason cringed to see Wilder's joy to be hearing from his sister in Belfast sicken. As Merry relayed the news of their older brother, Wilder fell back on the sofa and covered his eyes. "Brendan's dead," he uttered as he hung up the phone.

Reason moved to comfort him but he declined her touch. She wrapped her arms around him anyway. "What can I do to help you?"

"Nothing…anything…Jesus, nobody should die like that. They hunted him down…and his death won't be thought of again. A Catholic son of a bitch got what he deserved, case closed." Wilder struggled to his feet in a failed attempt to regain composure. "Members of a loyalist murder squad waited for him at his house. They handcuffed him to his bed and shot him in the head…but not before they cut off his penis, wrapped his rosary around it, and crammed it down his throat."

"Oh my God!" Reason cried. "Oh…my God."

"But the sickest part is that the security forces in Belfast gave Brendan's name and address to the loyalists, knowing full well what they'd do with the information."

The security forces, loyalist murder squads, Catholic sons of bitches…Reason didn't understand what Wilder was telling her. She only knew it was horrific, and it was nailing him to some long-standing cross.

"I should be going over there to take care of Merry, to carry on for Bren," Wilder anguished. "I should have gone back years ago."

Reason towed him back to the sofa. "Wilder, your life is here now. The war in Ireland isn't your fight."

"Not my fight?" A faint smile softened his face. "My grandfather spent his whole life fighting British rule, and he never forgave my father for bailing out of Belfast, *never.*" He brushed tears off his eyes. "I should have gone to see him. I knew Brendan would never come to America…just like my grandfather, he thought my dad sold out. But I should have gone to see him."

Without another word he strode to the door and jerked on his coat. Stashing a pint of whiskey in his pocket, he dipped into the rain-damp night.

Reason grabbed her jacket and ran to catch him. "Where are you going?"

He shook her off and walked to his car.

Reason blocked his path. "I'm not letting you drive."

Her expression was Wilder's invitation to be touched and consoled, and he looked down at her, not knowing whether to crush her to him or thrust her aside. He wanted her, he needed her, but she belonged to Reid. "Leave me alone."

"I'm not leaving you when you're this upset. I don't care how late it is or how far we go. Do you want to drive around Denver, do you want to go up to Vail? I'll drive you anywhere you want."

He turned away from her.

"Let me be with you, Wilder," Reason pleaded. "Tell me where you want to go."

"Away. Just away. I want to put the top down and go faster than reality, faster than this pain," he touched his heart, tears ran down his cheeks. "Can you drive me that fast, Mac?"

She plucked the keys from his fist. "Try me."

As Reason shoved the convertible in gear and flew west towards the highway, Wilder settled back with a drink of whiskey. The wind off the mountains lashed his face, each gust was a slap of reality and remorse. He should have gone home. But he didn't. He considered the moon breaking through clouds, raindrops flicked his cheek, and his eyes turned to Reason. Like they always did. How he admired and loved her.

Reason was fearless, passionate. As an architect, art was her life, and life was her art. Every day was a canvas, her space to play, to dream, to create and inspire. And inspire Wilder she had, with bold eyes Donegal-blue, flowing blonde hair, and an easy smile yielding dimples to a face of strength. It was her strength he admired most; strength he'd seen before. In the women of Belfast. In Reason, Wilder sensed the essence of Northern Ireland; a courageous, unfettered spirit. Even her name recalled his homeland where girls were named Róisín. But he liked Reason's name; the name her father gave her because she was his reason for living. Reason, vital Reason. And after months of friendship, Wilder found himself aching to possess the woman he couldn't have.

Now, as Reason pressed the accelerator down and conquered the Rockies, as the pain of Brendan's murder burned in his breast and Belfast was worlds away, Wilder writhed between grief and desire. "Most people are afraid to drive this fast," he called as Reason sped faster, deeper, higher into the hills.

"I have nerves of brass," she said. "Weren't you born to be wild, Wilder?"

"No, I'm the sensible O'Neill. The one who stayed safe in the States with my dad."

"Does he know about Brendan?"

Wilder nodded, whiskey to his lips.

"You rarely talk about your father."

"Old habit. I've spent years ducking the press."

Reason knew Wilder's father worked somewhere in Hollywood. "What does he do?"

"In the four years I've been here in Colorado I haven't told a soul who my father is. His stage name is Sumner Steed."

"*Sumner Steed?*" Reason's eyes flew huge. "He was the funniest, sexiest actor around until…" she caught herself.

"Until he had a rip roaring nervous breakdown and trashed his career? Yeah, Desmond O'Neill was one of the greats." Wilder glanced away, making it clear he wouldn't discuss his father.

"Will you and he go to Brendan's funeral?"

"Dad won't. I should. But I'm not ready to take on what's waiting for me in Belfast."

Reason cocked her head. "What's waiting for you?"

Wilder stared at the passing mountains, filling his silence with sips of whiskey.

"You've never told me much about Ireland." Reason encouraged Wilder to talk. "What was it like growing up there?"

"It's been seventeen years since I left Belfast and I still remember every inch of it."

Belfast. Images of bombs and bloodshed stained Reason's mind. "Is Northern Ireland pretty?"

"It's gorgeous."

"I can't imagine your childhood with the war."

"It was unlike your pampered life in Greenwich that's for sure. I grew up in a place called the New Lodge." Wilder laced his fingers behind his head and savored fond memories. "We lived on Upper Forest Street; it ran downhill to the docks. The name always killed me. It was a forest all right, of rowhouses. One house faced another and in between were asphalt and concrete. There wasn't a tree or garden in sight; a real desert of deprivation. We were poor, but we knew all the neighbors, and our families were close. We kids grew up happy. Are you freezing? We could stop and put up the top."

Reason was warm in her raincoat and continued speeding. "What did you do for fun?"

"Raised hell. I spent my youth in the confessional, kept the priests busy I did," Wilder grinned. "The New Lodge was built across the street from a Protestant neighborhood called Tiger's Bay; the enemy's camp. We Catholic kids were Fenians for sure. We loved hurling rocks and insults across the street at the Prods, and they'd holler and pitch rocks back at us. But then rocks became bullets and it wasn't fun anymore."

"What's a Feen-yan?"

"An Irish warrior, and we lads were warriors. When we weren't taunting the Prods, we played football on an asphalt playground, and I remember the Ra was big there. The Ra, that's the IRA."

"Weren't you afraid of them?" Reason gasped.

"Nah. We'd all grown up together."

"I can't believe you knew terrorists." Reason shook her head. "It's beyond me how the IRA can hate England."

"Obviously you've never read Irish history."

"No, but the British are so civilized and decent, surely they've been good for Ireland."

Tears scorched Wilder's eyes. "Those 'civilized and decent' Brits just murdered my brother!"

"Oh, Wilder, I'm sorry. There's so much I don't know." Reason laid her hand on his arm. "Why don't the Irish just kick the British out like we did?"

"They've been trying to do that for 800 years." Wilder tipped the whiskey to his mouth again. "And that's what's waiting for me in Belfast."

Steeped in Yankee showbiz and memories of Ireland, thirty-year-old Wilder was an Irish warrior and an American deserter. Six feet of strength and prowess topped with jet hair, he could have joined his father in Hollywood's glare; he was certainly as handsome as Desmond O'Neill. They shared the square, determined jaw and brilliant blue eyes, the slender nose, quick smile and slightly clefted chin. They shared the lazy curls that swept back off their faces. And within both Irishmen beat mad romantic hearts. But Wilder had chosen medicine over the stage, medicine over Brendan and Merry and Belfast. Medicine, an honorable profession. And still he feared he, like his father, had betrayed the O'Neills.

"Brendan never left Belfast?" Reason broke the silence.

"Never. He was like my grandfather, a politician who lived to free Ireland. Merry went back when she was nineteen. She hated me for not going with her. 'You joined the IRA all right,' she yelled at me, 'only in your case it means 'I Ran Away.' I didn't let on how much her words hurt, and maybe she's right. Sometimes I think it's time I go home."

"California's your home."

"But every day I miss Belfast…every day I think of who I left behind."

"Who do you miss the most?"

"I miss Merry, but I also miss my cousin. Kieran McCartan. We were inseparable as kids…now we've lost touch. I'll never forget the morning I told him I was moving to America. He thought I was kidding, and when he realized I wasn't he just stood there with this crumpled smile on his face. Then all of a sudden he tackled me and started crying and pounding my chest. 'Promise you won't become a Yank, promise!' he kept yelling. And I was fighting to get free and not cry myself. 'I won't become a Yank if you promise not to join the Ra.' 'I won't join the Ra, no way, no way,' he swore. But by the time he was seventeen and I was sixteen, he had joined the Ra and I'd become a Yank. I'm sure Kieran hates Dad and me for bailing."

"Do you think your father sold out leaving Ireland?" Reason asked as they crossed the Continental Divide.

"No. But you have to understand my grandfather Liam. Every morning he got up ready to die for Ireland. And with him, it was all or nothing; either you were a republican or you were wrong. He did nothing but hard-sell the armed struggle against the Brits to us kids and my dad. But Dad didn't want to pick up a gun, he wanted a microphone and a monologue. It wasn't that he didn't support the cause, he just wasn't willing to die for it. That's why Liam and Bren never forgave him, and that's what flings my dad to the shrinks. He feels guilty for leaving Belfast and guilty for loving America. He sold himself out by denying his old home and denying his new home until he had nowhere left to be except miserable. And what worries me is that I'm just like him, running away from my history only to trip over it again and again. I want to be Irish, but I don't…and I'll be damned if I don't feel guilty every day of my life."

In three hours they had outlasted the night and driven deep into the Rockies. Wilder told Reason to turn left off the interstate and directed her up a dirt road to the banks of a furious stream. Frothing white and loudly rushing, the water erupted over boulders and rumbled down a scree to the valley below.

"Let's park and watch the sunrise," Wilder suggested.

"Obviously you aren't in surgery today."

"I don't have another patient for four days! This is the first time I've had Memorial Day off in three years. Memorial Day," Wilder's smile faded.

"Will you tell me about Brendan?"

Wilder shook his head. "I'd rather you tell me more about you. You asked if I was born to be wild, were you? Or were you Daddy's little angel?"

"I was Daddy's big headache!" Reason chuckled. "I used Wesley's credit cards like pocket change, I was mad for older boys and fast cars, I skipped school and drank…oh! I was the rebel with no cause other than being outrageous. I swear I didn't mean to be bad, there was just something in me that was born to be a devil." She lifted her honey hair off her shoulders and grinned across at Wilder. "There still is."

But all Wilder saw was the chic, successful architect with a seraphic smile. "Obviously Wesley was a good stepfather because you turned out all right."

"He's been the best. I'll always think of him as my dad. But what's weird is, even though my real father died when I was three, Mom wouldn't let me change my name. She hated the man, and I don't remember him, but she's insisted I keep his name. In school I hated being a McGuinness when Wellworth-Howell is one of the best names in New England."

"And that's important to you?"

"When you live in Greenwich it is."

"But earlier you said it doesn't matter where you're from as long as you're a good person."

"Well, a good pedigree can't hurt," Reason said not entirely in jest.

"I'm anxious to finally meet these Wellworth-Howells. I thought I'd drop by your parents' house tomorrow and…"

"No!" Reason looked startled then hastily declared, "They're busy, very busy, with the wedding." She hated herself for what she was thinking.

Wilder knew Reason wasn't being honest, but it hadn't occurred to him why. "I won't stay long. I was just going to drop off some wedding gifts."

"Now isn't a good time. You can give the presents to me." Reason averted her face. "You'll meet everyone at the rehearsal dinner."

"Well, OK," Wilder shrugged. "But it seems like every time I want to meet your family, they're 'busy.'"

Reason felt sick understanding what she had just done, but she knew the consequence if Wilder strolled in to greet her family with that damning Irish accent. She could see her mother's face staring coldly upon him as if he were filthy and cheap, staring the colder upon her daughter for inviting an Irishman above the salt. No better than apes. She watched the river leaping to its fall. "I love Colorado," she finally said, "and I'm glad my family moved here, but I miss the ocean."

"Me too." Wilder hopped from the car. "Help me fold the top up."

"I just have this thing about the sea," Reason continued, lending a hand. "I must take after my father. He loved sailing…that's how he died." She glanced across the car at Wilder, and that vague sense of loss pricked her heart. "Are you feeling any better?"

"No, but if you hadn't come with me, I'd be feeling a lot worse." He gave the top of his car a slap and shoved his fingers in his pockets. "Are you up for a walk along the stream?"

"Sure."

The rising sun fanned orange rays beyond the mountains and speckled the water with rainbows. There wasn't a sound to be heard over the ebullient flood. Pretending he was a pitcher, Wilder hurled rocks across the water, causing a flock of cedar waxwings to take flight through the trees. "Hey, what's wrong with that bird?" He pointed to the opposite bank where a waxwing floundered and lifted its wings. "See how she's struggling? She can't get off the ground."

"Oh no, Wilder, look. Her feet are tangled in plastic. There's nothing we can…" To Reason's horror Wilder was already up to his ankles in the water, surmounting the rocks and teetering boulder to boulder across the stream, "…are you *insane?* Wilder, *stop!*"

The whiskey had stolen his sense and replaced it with daring. "I'm going to tear that stuff off her feet."

"No! You can't save her. Don't go out any further! *Don't!*"

"Reason, I can't just stand by and watch the poor thing suffer. Don't worry, the water isn't deep."

"But it's fast! Wilder, stop! *Stop!* You're drunk for God's sake!"

"I'm not drunk, I'm heroic," he laughed and wobbled precariously. "Aw, relax, Reas, I'm nearly across. It's just a hop," he hopped rock to rock, "skip," he skipped, "and a jum…" *whooosh.* He flipped backwards into the racing water, smacking his head on the rocks as he fell, and went bobbing downstream. Only his foot snagging between two boulders spared him a ride over the waterfall. Barely keeping his head above water, he managed to pull himself forward to hug the rock. "My foot's stuck! Shit, I can't reach my shoe to untie it." A fallen tree lay to his right but its branches were just out of reach. "If I can get my ankle loose, I think I can lean over and grab that tree."

"Don't do anything! If you free your foot, you'll wash over the waterfall."

Wilder appeared to be blacking in and out. Reason feared he'd lose hold of his rock, fall backwards and drown. She dashed into the water and crawled up onto the fallen tree; a lodgepole pine denuded of bark. Bending forward like she was climbing a horizontal pole, she crept out across the rapids. "Just hold onto that boulder, Wilder, hold it like it's your life!" *Don't let him die, don't let him die.* "And don't pass out, OK? Keep saying my name so I know you're conscious. Say it a thousand times."

Wilder strained to hear her. The roar in his head was louder than the roar of the stream. All he heard was "Promise me…saying my name," and he would promise Reason anything. Her name was a thousand life rafts. "ReasonReasonReason," wouldn't let him drown. He was thinking of Brendan one shot to the head, of the cold blast of water pounding his neck, of the waxwing thrashing on shore. Waxwing. Like Icarus. *Oh Bren, I'm so sorry…* Wilder's arms felt weak, the current pushed him and lured his release; still he clung to the boulder.

Slowly Reason moved along the log keeping her eyes on Wilder. And as water splashed around her she remembered the first time she had seen him. Two summers ago in July. A garden hose spewing water every direction had greeted her. She had just moved back to Denver after finishing graduate school. Wilder was washing his car in the driveway of the house he shared with Reid. Dark glasses masked his eyes, and he didn't speak when Reason approached.

"You must be Wilder," she recalled saying nicely.

"I must be," he had acknowledged without interest and ignored the fact his hose was sprinkling his guest.

Reason had then extended her hand in greeting and Wilder had passed her a wet sponge that dripped dirty water all over her Bruno Magli shoes. "Toss that in the bucket for me, will you, love?" he'd said with the Belfast accent he'd never lost. Reason had marched away thinking him rude. But since that day she had warmed to him and his irreverent Irish ways, and with Reid's blessing they had spent time together and become friends; friends who grew closer each day. Closer, closer. *Don't let him drown.*

After what seemed an eternity Reason came to the end of the fallen tree, close to the boulder pinning Wilder. There was less than three feet between him and the tree, but in that gap the stream boiled, flinging anything in its path down the scree. Stripping off her jacket Reason tied one sleeve around a branch. Then lying flat, hoping she didn't fall into the stream, she stretched her hand through the racing water to pass Wilder the other sleeve of her jacket.

"Grab the coat, and when I get your shoe untied, pull your foot out then pull yourself over to the log. Can you do that? Careful, careful!" With the stream slapping her face, gripping the log with her legs, Reason hung down and ripped loose the laces on Wilder's shoe. Once his foot was free, using the sleeve to stay anchored, he was able to reach one of the tree's branches and pull himself out of the water. For twenty minutes he and Reason sat on the log in the sunshine catching their breath. "I ought to kill you for being so stupid," Reason panted.

"You just had your chance."

She gave Wilder's back a rub. "You hit your head pretty hard. Do you need to go to a hospital?"

"No."

"Can you make it back across the log? I don't want you passing out."

"I'll be fine…but what about the waxwing?"

"Wilder, forget the damn bird! Come on, let's get out of here. You go first and I'll slide along behind you."

He glimpsed back over his shoulder. "So you can catch me if I fall?"

"Oh sure, then we'd both be swept away."

Inch by painstaking inch they crawled back to shore.

Thanking God for solid ground, Wilder sprawled in the grass.

"Are you sure you're all right?" Reason worried.

"Yeah. Just let me lie here awhile," he sighed, exhausted. "What did you think you were doing rushing into the water like that? You could have been killed."

"You'd prefer I'd let you drown?"

"Better to let me drown than risk your own life to save me, love," he said quietly.

Liking his low voice, liking his calling her "love," Reason stroked Wilder's hair. "You shouldn't have been in the stream risking either one of us. My God, Wilder, what were you thinking?"

"I just wanted to cut the bird free. Hobbled like that, the poor thing will die."

"*You* nearly died. I nearly lost you!"

Wilder heard the affection in Reason's voice and smiled. "Silly girl, you just saved my life." Where Brendan lay bleeding in his heart, Reason sprang forth; fair lily from desecration. "Now you'll never lose me."

Reason lay back in the sunshine and stared up at the clouds. Wilder's words were sweet but they were just words. She would lose him. In five days. Still her heart beat wildly, not from the rescue but from desire. To kiss and be kissed by Wilder, to hold him like a wave to the ocean with their souls entwined. He was right, she hadn't been honest. She'd been swept away by his kiss and his smile and his body and mind. But it was too late.

"It's amazing how suddenly death can come," Wilder said, sitting up. "As a physician I see death all the time, but this is the first time it's come so close to me. If I'd died in the stream, that would have been it, just one smack to the head and lights out. No pain, nothing. That's so easy. I wish Brendan's death had been as easy...I'm never going to forgive those bastards for what they did to him...and I'm never going to fear dying again."

"Wilder, look! The waxwing...it worked itself free."

They watched the bird open her wings and take flight.

"It's a miracle," Reason marveled as the bird disappeared.

"It just goes to show you, Mac, even when things look impossible, you can't give up hope."

"Have you thought any more about going to Brendan's funeral?" Reason asked as they drove into Wilder's driveway.

"I know I should be there but I have exams next week. Plus I've always had this feeling, if I went back to Belfast, I'd get sucked in..."

"You make the place sound like quicksand."

"It's my grandfather's spirit that would grab me. God, how he wanted me to be like him." Wilder laughed at the thought. "Can you see me toting a rifle and stalking Brits? Thanks, but I'll take angioplasties and a house on the beach."

"But wouldn't it be nice to see your sister?"

"What, are you trying to get rid of me? If I leave town now, you'll marry Reid and be gone."

"And what if you don't leave?"

"I have five days to steal you away."

"Fat chance, O'Neill."

"If that waxwing can break free, so can you."

Reason checked her watch. "I have the final fitting for my wedding gown in an hour. Do you think they could do it while I'm asleep?"

Wilder didn't comment. "Are you and Reid still going to the residents' party tomorrow night?"

"You think Reid would miss a chance to suck-up? The chief of staff will be there. Of course we're going. How about you? Do you have a date?"

"No." Wilder smiled at Reason. "You're the only woman I want."

"Will you stop saying things like that? I'm marrying Reid."

"Hey, I'd let the matter drop if you hadn't kissed me last night. You could have pushed me away but you didn't. You pulled me closer."

"It was just a kiss, Wilder."

"We'd be lovers by now if Merry hadn't called."

Reason didn't contradict what she feared was true. What would have happened if they had made love? She smiled to imagine then shuddered to think. The consequences of loving the best man instead of the groom were too daunting to consider. She jerked open the car door. "I have to go."

Wilder caught her hand. "Be like that bird, Reas, and untangle your feet. Reid's the wrong man, you know he is. You've known it for months. So have I."

"*You're* wrong. All wrong."

"He appreciates nothing about you, you're old news. I've seen you two together. There's no passion. He's taking you on a honeymoon to *Baltimore!*"

"Wilder, I can't just cancel a $50,000 wedding."

"How much will an unhappy marriage cost?"

Reason marched to her car. "Tell Reid I'll call him tonight."

"And you'll tell him good-bye?"

"I'm telling *you* good-bye!"

"Only until tomorrow, Mac." Wilder tossed her a kiss. "Thanks for the rescue."

Chapter Two

Reason had one goal in mind for the evening, to prove Wilder wrong. She'd show him how attentive her fiancé could be. She dressed in black strapless with a bustier bodice and full, short skirt. Her hair fell across her shoulders, a single diamond graced her throat, and the perfume of jasmine sweetened her skin. All long legs and soft breasts she arrived to sweep Reid off his feet.

"He's not here," Wilder called when Reason walked into the house.

She went back to Wilder's bedroom. "He told me to meet him here."

Wilder stood stripped to the waist before his closet. "Whoa!" He turned to see Reason, passing his eyes over her breasts and hips down her legs. "Lady, you've sure got a whole lotta legs. You're looking too hot not to handle tonight, Mac."

"Thanks. So, where's Reid?"

"Doing an emergency C-section." Wilder flashed Reason a grin, "So, as his best man, I offered to fill in. I said I'd drive you to the country club and keep you company until he shows."

"Forget it. I'll go by myself before I'm going with you."

"What's the matter, Mac? Afraid something will happen? Something spontaneous and hot?"

She watched Wilder sort through his shirts, hating herself for liking his body. His back was broad and tan, his skin smooth, muscles slid over bone, he was vigorous and strong, and she imagined gliding her hands from his shoulders to his thighs. *Oh God, this can't be happening!* She strode from his room. "I'll meet Reid at the club."

An hour later Reid arrived at the party. He gave Reason an apology and a perfunctory kiss but he didn't compliment her appearance. He seemed immune to her silky hair and bare shoulders and sensuous skin. Wilder was right; Reid barely saw her. But he did see the chief of staff, and off he hurried to advance his career. Over dinner it was the same. Reid talked to his colleagues, giving Reason the occasional peck on the cheek or pat on the knee. And Wilder sat across the room watching her be patronized and ignored.

He let her suffer awhile then strolled over. "You don't mind if I steal Reason away, do you, Reid?" he asked with an innocent face. "For a dance."

"Not at all," Reid glimpsed up at Wilder then continued conversing, "And I've never seen an ovary that large…"

Reason accepted Wilder's hand but the minute they were away from the table she warned, "Say one word and I'll smack you."

"You mean like I told you so?" Wilder laughed.

"OK, so he takes me for granted. But it wasn't always this bad," she said as Wilder took her into his arms. "Reid and I used to have fun, we were in love…"

"What happened?"

"We've just been so busy for the last two years, him with his residency, me with launching my career…I guess we stopped seeing each other. But I thought for sure he'd notice this dress…".

"I noticed," Wilder was quick to point out. "From the moment you walked in tonight I've wanted to touch you…I've never seen you looking more beautiful. You know what you're like? A jack-o-lantern."

"A *pumpkin*? Gee, thanks."

"You're like a jack-o-lantern because its best part is its inner light. Sure you have a pretty face and a knock-out body, but it's what burns inside you that makes you shine…you're beautiful, like truth, it touches your soul, and shakes you with its power."

Reason looked into Wilder's eyes. Blue as the wild Irish bluebells. And in those eyes she felt homesick and at home, like he was a place from a former life, like she'd seen those eyes before. And she felt a sense of loss and fear, and still she drew him closer. "That's the nicest thing anyone has ever said to me."

Around the torch-lit terrace they danced. Possessively he held her, his fingers strayed along her shoulders, he spoke close to her ear, and when his lips came within a breath of hers, she wound her arms around him. All she felt was happiness.

"I'll take over now," Reid interrupted, drawing Reason away, leaving Wilder standing alone.

"You could have waited until the music stopped," Reason objected.

"You and Wilder were a little too close."

"I'm surprised you noticed."

"I think he's forgotten you're my wife."

"Not yet I'm not!" Reason snapped.

"Oh, Reason, what's the matter with you? You've been impossible for weeks."

"No, Reid, I've been invisible. Do you want to touch me, do you want to kiss me…no, you want to discuss ovaries!" She backed away from him.

"Reason! Where are you going?"

"Home. I need time to think."

"About what?"

"Obligations and passion and waves on the sea and," she caught her breath, she felt strangled, *"Baltimore!"*

Reason left the terrace and headed onto the golf course. Her parents' house was off the tenth hole. The night was lit by a full, rising moon, and the air smelled of roses; June roses, the sweetest of summer. She stared up at the sky and thought of Wilder, how good he'd felt in her arms, so close she could feel his body's heat, and her heart yearned for a life that couldn't be. Everything had made sense until he kissed her. But that kiss shattered her illusion that they were just friends, and she felt like Sleeping Beauty aroused by the wrong prince. She was supposed to love Reid, and she had tried. But it was Wilder, always Wilder. She didn't want to love him. To have a relationship with him would be to sacrifice her wedding, her sense, five years with Reid, thousands of dollars, and worst of all her mother's respect. Wilder was profane. The moment he spoke with his brogue, Reason's troubles would start. "They make English sound dirty," her mother would say. But Reason thought the Irish made English sound happy. And the Irish made her happy. And heartsore. Once she'd been a rebel, but never against stakes so high.

She pushed through the back gate and hiked up the stone path, but she didn't go to the house. She walked through the trees to the gazebo; a sanctuary entangled in roses. She sat on the day bed and listened to the still of the night. Her engagement ring caught the light of the moon and she told herself life with Reid wouldn't be bad. Surely calling off the wedding would be worse. But then she looked up. Wilder stood in the doorway. "What are you doing here?"

"I followed you. I wanted to make sure you're all right."

Reason's heart began to pound. The sight of Wilder was torture, she had to let him go, but how attractive he was in the moonlight, how glad she was to see him, and how she longed for more of him than one kiss. "I got so mad at Reid I had to leave."

Wilder stepped into the gazebo and sat down across from Reason. "I like this place."

"Thanks. I designed it. I always come here when I need to think."

"And what are you thinking?"

"About my wedding of course." She glanced around. "Isn't this space romantic? See how the moonlight wraps its arms around the gazebo and blue shadows emerge like we're in a dream? There's darkness around us, but this place holds light. We're safe here."

"From what?"

"Reality. In here time stops. I designed this gazebo for lovers. Look how the moonlight spills across the bed. I put the day bed precisely here because there's nothing more beautiful than bare skin in the moonlight. And smell the air, hundreds of roses. White roses, the symbol of eternal love."

"You and Reid have made love here I suppose."

"Actually n…"

Wilder didn't let her finish. "God, how I hate the thought of him touching you. For two years I've had to put up with knowing he could do what I couldn't. You'd spend the evening with me, turning me on, then he'd come home and take you to bed. And then tonight, I had you there in my arms, and it felt so good and so right, and he cut in…" Wilder couldn't stand it. He had to know, "So are you going to marry him?"

"Wilder, I…"

He could see the answer in her face. "Don't tell me you've chosen Reid!" He leaped to his feet. "Reason, if you marry him, part of me will die. I love you. Why did you save my life yesterday if you were going to kill me today?"

"Wilder, I can't just blow off my wedding! What do you want me to say?"

"The truth, for once just tell me the truth! Say you love me."

"I do love you. I honestly think you're my soulmate. But we met too late."

"It's only too late if you tell me good-bye."

"Well, that's the problem. Soulmates can't say good-bye. They're bound, heart-to-heart. Forever." Reason got up to leave but Wilder caught her shoulders with no intention of letting her go.

"Then give me forever."

She put her hand on his chest to push him away and he jerked her against him, kissing her with kisses too long withheld, kisses deep and hard, demanding reward. And Reason surrendered, because this was what she wanted. She knew it was wrong, but in that moment she didn't care. She slipped Wilder's jacket down his arms, letting it drop behind him. "I can give us tonight."

She unknotted his tie and loosened the buttons on his shirt. Savoring the feel of him, she rubbed her hands along his arms, down his back, inside his shirt, across his chest. His skin was hot, her kisses hotter. She reached behind her and unfastened her dress. Wilder threw off his clothes and pulled Reason down on the bed. His hands slid upon her reverently, ravenously, and easing on top of her, he folded her to him in joy. Joy. He hadn't known it before this warm night in June. As Reason wrapped her legs around him and her moan was his name, his wish was granted. There could be no peace, no rapture higher than this.

And Reason was thinking this was what God had in mind when he made the puzzle of woman and man. Wilder's body molded to hers, a perfect fit. Tenderly he stroked her, but he wasn't restrained. With abandon he touched her and tongued her then softly kissed her and gripped her to his heart. And he promised to be hers forever. In a fever they flooded together. Reason ground her fingernails into Wilder's spine and relished each thrust, each orgasmic gasp. And she knew no matter who she married, from now until her last breath it would be Wilder, always Wilder, who possessed her.

After midnight they returned to Wilder's house. Reid had been called to the hospital. Wilder gave Reason a hallelujah grin and danced her into his bedroom. "We have the house to ourselves for *24 hours!*" He searched her face. "You aren't sorry we made love, are you?"

"No. I love you, Wilder. I love you with all my life!" She fell into his arms.

And so it went until the next night, and after each time they made love, Wilder played Reason a different Irish love song on his flute. The Celtic Pied Piper. Leading her head and her heart astray.

"You'll really shake things up when you marry the best man instead of the groom," Wilder said, cuddling Reason to his chest.

She barely listened. All she felt was panic. *How could I have been so reckless?* Her entire family and Reid's family were in town for a wedding, two hundred invitations were sent, two hundred gifts had arrived, she had given her word to Reid…and her body to Wilder…and Wilder was Irish…and *Oh my God,* her mind raced. She didn't want to hurt anyone, and in her intemperance she had hurt everyone. She looked at Wilder and saw a stranger. *I must have been mad.* Flames engulfed her world and she had thrown the match! How hungrily his hands clasped her, demanded her, pinned her to his heart. She thought of the waxwing tangled in plastic and she felt as ensnared, in love, in lust and confusion.

"How are we going to explain this to Reid and your parents?"

Reason slammed back to reality like hitting a wall. "We...won't."

"You can't put this off, love. We have to tell them about us today."

"There is no 'us,'" Reason choked out, barely able to speak. "I said I'd give you one night, and that's all we had."

Wilder sat up. "Reason, I want you to marry me."

"Marry you?" she cried in shock. "I can't just change everything and marry you instead of Reid. It wouldn't be right."

"Who cares? We're in love. Everyone will see that."

"No, they'll see you're Irish and Catholic," Reason blurted too bluntly. "My family would never forgive me, or you."

"There's nothing wrong with being an Irish Catholic," Wilder said, thunderstruck.

"There is if you're a Wellworth-Howell."

"You're a *McGuinness!*" Wilder knocked his knuckle under Reason's chin and wished she wasn't slamming her eyes. He didn't understand what was happening. "Reason, we made love. We committed ourselves to each other."

"All I've committed here is a mistake." She felt cornered, and fear inspired her to say the worst, "I'm sorry, Wilder, but you simply won't do."

"What?" He reeled out of bed and pulled Reason up to stand before him. "I simply *won't do?* Well, forgive my filthy hands, your highness!"

"You were born in a ghetto, you're Irish...everyone will say you aren't good enough," Reason stumbled on, causing more damage.

"Who gives a damn what they say?" Wilder yelled.

"I do! Marrying you would break my mother's heart."

"So you'll break mine? Is this why you've made sure in two years I've never met your family? You're ashamed of me? Because I'm *Irish?*"

Reason shied from Wilder's glare, thinking if she truly loved him, she'd find the courage to defy convention and go forward, but no such courage came. She was afraid to cancel her wedding, afraid to face Reid and her family's censure. And she was afraid of Wilder. But it had nothing to do with his being Irish; that was an easy excuse. His intensity and her electric response overwhelmed her. He asked for everything, demanded every part of her, and he opened himself up to her with a greedy, grasping heart. In reply, she gave and she gave and ran willingly into his arms. But as she poured herself into his hands, she feared she would lose herself to him forever, that they *would* blend like waves into the sea and become one soul from two. And to be so enthralled wasn't romantic like she had thought. It terrified her. And she realized that's why Reid had seemed so appealing. For all he didn't require.

Wilder yanked Reason's head up, forcing her to face him. "Why did you go to bed with me if I'm so beneath you?"

"I just did it, like you rushing into that stream, I didn't think. I wanted to be with you once, just once, but I never dreamed you'd want to *marry* me. You haven't wanted to marry any of the other women you've known."

"Gee, Reason, could that be because I didn't love them? I've loved you for two years, and I swear to Christ I never thought you'd say you want me and love me, then say I won't do. You are the cruelest woman I've ever met."

"I do love you, Wilder, but love doesn't always make sense, and it doesn't guarantee a happy end. Oh, can't you see this was all too sudden, too intense? We were friends and now we're...screwed up! We went too far, I need time to get my head straight, to understand what's happened, to figure out what to do!" She stroked Wilder's hair and stared into his unhappy eyes. "Please, try to understand..."

Wilder brushed her aside and hastily dressed.

"Wilder, it wouldn't work out! My family would never accept you. They'd make our life miserable..."

"Oh, I understand," Wilder laughed gruffly. "For the first thirteen years of my life I was punished for being an Irish Catholic, I just never thought I'd be punished in the States as well. But I don't think that's what this is about. I know you, Reason. You'd tell your family to fuck off if you wanted to be with me. But you don't. You're using this prejudice as an excuse because you're too afraid to dump Reid and stick with me. That's all I see in your eyes now, fear. I love you, and I made love to you like a madman, you didn't expect that passion in me, or in yourself, and it scares you to death. So much for us being 'soulmates.'"

Reason drew her robe close to her chest. The room felt cold as love fell burning. "OK, yes, there's something about you that scares me. Sometimes I look in your eyes and I see my self, and sometimes all I see are good-byes; either way I feel lost. You want too much. Making love with you was like drowning in you."

"I gave you my *soul!*"

"In exchange for mine! You want to possess me."

"Not anymore. Not ever again." Wilder's heart lay in ruins beside his trust. He had surrendered himself to Reason, and surrender was anathema to Irishmen. He thought of Liam. *"Lie down once, lad, and you're lost. Never lie down. And never forget."* So roused the warrior, so began Wilder's war. "Just tell me this, Reason, was I good enough in bed? Did this dirty Irish Catholic get you off?"

"Nobody is ever going to feel that good again," she admitted faintly.

Her reply made Wilder laugh but cut him the deeper. She was flinging aside the beautiful and good. "So what are you going to do now? Marry Reid like nothing's happened?"

"Why are you smiling like that? You're not going to say anything to him, are you? Oh, Wilder, please don't. Let me handle this."

"Relax, Mac," he was sarcastic. "My lips are sealed."

Reason finished dressing and joined Wilder in the living room. "I never meant to hurt you, Wilder. This just happened so fast...I know you think I'm horrible but I'm really confused. What we did was wrong." She reached for his hand but he didn't want her.

"You don't matter enough to hurt me. Get out."

Reason stole one last glance at her Irishman. Gone were the gentle eyes and soft, lover's smile. Hatred hardened his face. Turning her back, she walked out. But not before hearing his curse, "Coward."

The next morning Reason returned to face Reid.

"Did you get all your thinking done after you left me?" he asked.

"Reason didn't take time to think," Wilder walked into the room and hijacked the conversation. Reason fired a look of "Don't do this," but Wilder just laughed. "We spent Tuesday night and all day yesterday together in bed. It was the most incredible sex I've ever had. How many times did we make love, Mac? I lost count, didn't you? She was fantastic, Reid, the best I've ever laid."

Reid gaped upon Reason in disbelief. "Is this true?"

"You bastard," she said to Wilder as her cheeks drained white. She dropped her engagement ring on the coffee table and made for the door. But Reid nabbed her by the neck, spun her around and slipped her the back of his hand.

Reason rocked on her feet and turned to Wilder in tears. "Is that what you wanted to see?"

"Hey, I'm sorry he thought of it first."

Reason was getting into her car when Wilder skidded up to her. "Gee, Mac, your blood looks mighty red for a Wellworth-Howell blue-blood," he ridiculed her split lip. "At least now you won't have to cancel the wedding. Reid will do it for you. That's what you had in mind all along."

"You really are an Irish pig," Reason wept. "What did you expect to gain by telling Reid about us?"

"If I couldn't have you, I wanted to make damn sure he couldn't either. Hey, one day you'll thank me."

"That'll be the day you drop dead. I'll hate you forever for this."

"Fine with me, Reason, just keep me in mind. I'd rather you hate me than forget me."

"I've already forgotten you, *taig!*" She slammed the car door and started the engine.

That jarred Wilder like he'd heard the banshees keen. "Where did you learn that word? Tell me where? *Where?*"

"How should I know?" Reason shoved the stick into reverse. "Get off the car," she screamed then sobbed, "Let me go. Just let me go!"

"Good thing you're an architect, Mac," Wilder taunted as she revved away. "You're going to need that degree to rebuild your life!"

Chapter Three

Two Years Later.

How could it be June again? At thirty, Reason was a partner with Morrissey and Yeats in Manhattan, and she had one more day of vacation in Denver with her family before facing her latest challenge.

June. How it provoked recollection. Two years was time enough for a heart to heal, Reason tried to convince herself, but she still thought about him. From her bedroom she saw the gazebo. Even now she could see the moonlight, and Wilder, always Wilder…

"Reason love? Are you all right?" Her mother peeked in. "I thought I heard you crying."

Reason stepped from the window. "It's too hot to sleep. What are you doing up?"

"I haven't slept a wink since you announced you're going to Belfast. Of all the dreadful places! Isn't there any way you can get out of your assignment over there?"

"I don't want to get out of it, Mom. They're sending me to design the new wing of the Grosvenor Hospital. It's an amazing opportunity."

Anna took one look at the fire in Reason's eyes and covered her face. "You've a mad spirit like your father…it's boldness that killed him…" her voice crystallized like it always did when she mentioned Reason's father. "Oh, I have a bad feeling about this, Reason. Please don't go."

"Mom, it's OK. I'll be staying with Mrs. McKee and her son, I'm sure they'll look out for me. Oh, before I forget, what does the word 'taig' mean?"

"Taig?" Anna looked blank. "I've never heard that word before."

"Yes, you have. I remember one time a package came for you addressed to Anna McGuinness. You took one look at it and said, 'That spiteful old taig,' then you burst into tears and threw the box in the trash."

"I don't recall a box or any such outburst. You must have me confused with someone else."

"That's funny, I could have sworn it was you. Oh well, it doesn't matter. I just blurted the word out once like it was some sort of curse."

"Well, be a lady, dear, and don't say it again until you know what it means." Anna snapped off the light. "Get some rest."

"Mom, why do you dislike the Irish?"

Anna's reaction was instant, and it hadn't softened over the years. "Because they're filthy, they're ignorant, and they're careless…they rush to their deaths, their almighty country matters above all…they've bled the love and brains right out of themselves."

"Was my father Irish? His name was McGuinness."

"Heavens no!"

"Well, have you ever even known any Irish men?"

"A few."

"You must have had some horrible experience to be so biased. Not all Irish people are bad."

"All the ones I knew were. Growing up we had Irish servants. They were dirty, drunken liars and thieves, and they did nothing but cause us grief. You be careful of Irish men, Reason. They're the serpents of Ireland. Snakes, every last one of them."

"Don't worry, Mom, I'm not afraid of snakes," Reason laughed.

"You're not afraid of anything and that's what scares me."

"I was afraid of someone once…it was all in his eyes. Tell me something, did my dad have blue eyes?"

"Yes…why?"

"Because lately I think I've had memories of him. He had midnight blue eyes and dark, curly hair, and I think I remember his funeral. It was raining, and I had a little green handkerchief or something, and I was really scared and really sad."

Anna looked stunned. "What on earth has made you remember this?"

"I knew this man named Wilder and I think there was something about him that reminded me...I think that's why he scared me...I loved my father, didn't I? And then he died and I felt lost. I think his death affected me more than I realized."

"If you loved him, it was only because you were too young to know him."

"Was he really that bad? You married him. You must have loved him."

"Oh, Reason, don't remind me of this!"

"Why won't you *ever* talk about him?"

"Because the man is dead and gone and we're better off for it."

"Then why wouldn't you let me change my last name?"

"Some questions have answers you don't want to know. Now go to sleep." Anna hurried into the hallway before Reason could see her cry. Later she returned to her daughter's room. "When you go to Belfast don't be bold like your father," she whispered as Reason slept. "Promise me you won't be bold."

Chapter Four

Belfast wasn't like Reason feared. As the plane circled to land, she saw patchwork fields holding cattle and sheep not paratroops and tanks. Green as Iowa, rolly as Pennsylvania, the size of Connecticut, there was nothing threatening about the little country; at least not from the air. Arriving in the airport, Reason spotted a petite, copper-haired woman, about fifty years old, waving a small American flag with Reason's name printed on it. Reason introduced herself and Fiona threw open her arms and kissed Reason's cheeks.

"Hello, dear! Och, you must be exhausted. I'm Fiona McKee, and we're thrilled, just thrilled to have you staying in our home. We've fixed up a lovely room for you."

Fiona grabbed Reason's two suitcases, and against Reason's protests, hauled them out to the car. Besides being overwhelmed by the woman's effusive personality, Reason was shocked at Fiona's thick accent. Having listened to Wilder's Americanized brogue for two years, it had never occurred to her there would be a language barrier. But a rapid-fire tangle of R's and *ochs* was all Reason heard without concerted listening.

"Och, it's a brilliant day for your arrival, pet. June can be dodgy, sun or rain." Fiona's words inflected up-down-up; her speech sounded hilly. "I do believe you brought the good weather with you."

Reason surveyed her new home as they sped along a country road lined with Georgian farmhouses and pastures of sheep. The winds were fresh from the south, knocking several degrees off the sixty-degree day, and the sun was more illusion than bright; its light strained through knitting clouds and cast a dismal haze across the green fields. A sizable hill rose north above Belfast, and Reason noticed its resemblance to the head of a reclining man. She thought the profile resembled Abe Lincoln with its plateau forehead, flat rocky nose, puckered rock lips and bushy chin; his head then flowed into a chain of tree-studded mountains that swept down and around and clasped North and West Belfast in its curl.

"That's Cave Hill," Fiona introduced the manly mountain. "Belfast is in a bowl you see. When we get to the top of this hill you'll be looking over the city, and you'll see it's surrounded on three sides by mountains, and on the fourth side is the Belfast Lough which runs into the Irish Sea."

Over the rise and there it was. Belfast, a sea of slate roofs and red chimneys. The countryside dwindled and row after row of brick houses began. And there to the east was the lough, shimmering green-grey and calm with its massive shipyards. "The Titanic was built there," Fiona declared.

It only took a number of miles before Reason realized the docks were visible from most parts of the city.

Curving down the Antrim Road, the lanes were clogged with cars, delivery trucks and buses. The sidewalks bustled with shoppers and schoolchildren. Ordinary life hummed along with the harmony of any small city. Where was the oppression, the aggression, the evidence of arms? Where in this teeming metropolis was the 800-year-old war? As Fiona parked in front of her three-story flat with its manicured garden and rose-covered fence, Reason decided Wilder had been out of touch.

Fiona's street, Duntroon Drive, ran parallel to the Antrim Road on the north side of Belfast. Along Duntroon's cracked sidewalks, oak trees lined rows of red-brick, attached and identical houses. The houses were narrow and tall with sheer gables. Each had a bay window off the parlor, and a mahogany door with a fanlight. Upstairs was another bay window draped in lace curtains. The third floor was an attic. A patch of grass or a garden brightened the little front yards, and protruding from each black, mossy roof was a slim brick chimney and a television antenna that looked like a rake.

"Would you like a cup of tea, Reason?" Fiona already had the kettle on. "Your room is upstairs, front room, second floor; the one with the lovely big window. You go relax, love, and I'll bring you your tea and a sandwich."

Before heading to her room Reason looked around. The downstairs had three rooms; the parlor, a back family room and a small kitchen. All were decorated with pastel, flowery wallpaper and draperies to match. Fringed shades capped the lamps; Chippendale furnishings showed Fiona's fine taste. Photographs of her late husband, children and grand-children covered the walls, and figurines cluttered the tables. Towing her suitcases up the steep steps, Reason was glad to be staying in a gentle home untouched by the purported war.

"We're not much of a family anymore. My husband Sean took a stroke and died two years ago," Fiona said as she perched on the bed and watched Reason unpack. "My daughters moved to Australia in '89, and my oldest boy, Vincent was shot dead in '91. Swore up and down he wasn't a Provie, but he was. But I still have my son Ruairi. You'll meet him later."

"What's a Provie?" Reason inquired innocently.

"Och lord love, you'll learn soon enough! Provies, Provos, republicans are all names for members and supporters of the Provisional IRA. Now then, I work around the corner, just up the Antrim Road at the pastry shop. I own it with my brother Eamonn. You'll have to pop over and try our wee scones." Fiona admired Reason, inquiring, "Where did you get that glamorous blonde hair? We don't see many blondes here, at least not true ones."

"From my mother," Reason laughed, amused by the word 'glamorous.'

"So, you're here to enlarge our Gov…everybody calls Grosvenor Hospital 'the Gov.' Both my boys were born there. It's a grand old place."

"I can't wait to see it. Tell me, Fiona, from where I am now, am I near a place called the New Lodge?"

"Aye, love, it's down the Antrim Road. My Sean and I lived there for over ten years."

"I knew a man who was born there. I'd like to see where he grew up."

"You know Sumner Steed, the actor? He's from the New Lodge. I knew him," Fiona boasted.

"You knew Desmond O'Neill?" Reason opened her mouth to tell Fiona about Wilder, but Fiona charged forth in her bumpity speech.

"*Everyone* knew Dessie. He'd stand on the corner of Duncairn Gardens and the Antrim Road and tell jokes to anyone who'd listen. Tried to make a living for his family that way. They were so poor, it sickened the heart of me because there was no one sweeter than Dessie and his wee wife Frances."

"Were they really that poor?"

"Oh aye. Dessie never had a job, Frances worked as a seamstress, and they had three children to tend. Most times they didn't have proper shoes or coats or more than bread and beans to eat. Two of the kids were awfully shy, but the youngest was a wee devil. Rain or shine, he'd come to the corner with his da and hold out a cap for donations. And whenever someone dropped a coin in his cap, he'd grandly bow and say, 'Thankee, thankee, gods bless ye.' Anyway, you walk straight down the Antrim Road, and when you come to a side street called Duncairn Gardens turn left. That'll lead you to the New Lodge. Och, you look shattered, love. I'll let you take a rest."

Reason was tired from the flight, but her desire to see Wilder's birthplace overruled jet lag.

Late afternoon brought a shroud of clouds that discarded two hours of steady rain. Armed with her umbrella and trench coat, Reason headed out. At once she smelled dust and diesel and heard the city's roar. The traffic zoomed non-stop, and above the din was *Bap, Bap,*

Bap, like a beating drum. Looking up, Reason saw the helicopter. She thought it would fly away but it hovered like a kestrel.

Dodging loose dogs and pigeons, Reason studied the natives as she walked; aged, stooped ladies in worn wool coats; young, earringed men in t-shirts and jeans; ivory-skinned, sweet-scented girls in tight skirts and spiked heels; old men in tweed caps, baggy sweaters and polyester slacks. Many of the women were striking beauties with thick and tumbling black curls and brilliant blue eyes; most men as well were blue-eyed, dark-haired, thin and not tall. At five-foot-eight, Reason was taller than most people she passed. Here and there idle young men huddled around shop fronts, some drank from green bottles of wine, most of them smoked. And many of the young women pushed prams with one hand while leading a toddler with the other.

As Reason progressed down the hill, the evidence of strife became more apparent. Belfast appeared to be a world decaying and a world resurrecting; construction, destruction it was all the same rubble. It was like the old town built itself up to devour itself. There were rows of bricked-up houses, stores caged behind chain-link screens, and to the left and right of the road tumbled walls of brick and glass not long bombed or burned or torn to the ground. At the intersection of Duncairn Gardens, Reason departed the Antrim Road to walk along the flashpoint between Catholic New Lodge and Protestant Tiger's Bay. Cracked and heaved sidewalks led into dim, littered alleys. Wine bottles stood upright like flowers; cigarette butts were like grass. More walled-up rowhouses, more decay, more cages and windows behind iron bars lined the street. She recalled Wilder laughing about his old home on Upper Forest Street and now understood what he'd meant; New Lodge was a stretch of concrete desolation and there were few trees in sight.

She peered down the trash-speckled streets to the buildings beyond. Multi-story housing projects occupied the background, and red-brick rowhouses sandwiched together in uncomfortable rows ran east and west like identical dominoes. There were no porches, no yards, there was nowhere to sit or seek shelter; just strings upon strings of flat facades on bleak, crooked streets. But the harsh man-made places were softened with graces of lace curtains and silk flowers in the homes' tiny windows. Children, pigeons and dogs dominated the open spaces while forgotten laundry on clothes lines dominated the air. Disarray and privation made the projects depressing, but the children didn't care. They raced around merrily in the rain, and Reason could imagine Wilder running wild with a gang of six and a dog on his trail.

Raising her eyes above the laundry and chimneys, she saw a green, white and orange Irish Tricolour flag waving atop one of the seven-story projects. "IRA" was scrawled beneath it in blue paint. Above it two helicopters circled. And Reason couldn't miss the Army command post built on top of one of the projects; surveillance cameras were aimed at every window, every door, every alley, every inch of the New Lodge. Reason looked down and there on the street before her stood six British soldiers. Decked in camouflage greens and thick helmets, they prowled up against the rowhouses, close to the walls; their long, black rifles and sharp looks darted her way. Then they ignored her. The six men loitered in doorways, squinted in the New Lodge windows, glanced left glanced right, and using the children as targets, adjusted the sights on their weapons. Startled, Reason hurried away. And she noticed a spray-painted wall as she fled; **Irish youths demand British murderers off our streets now. Stop Killing Us.** The invisible war had begun to show its fist.

Crossing Duncairn Gardens, Reason entered Tiger's Bay. As Wilder had said, it looked as deprived as its Catholic neighbor, but the Army and its electronic eyes and ears were nowhere in sight. Tiger's Bay was poor but unguarded. She was reading the bold proclamation painted on a brick wall, **You Are Now In Loyalist Tiger's Bay** when she collided with a man carrying an armload of groceries.

"Are you fucking blind?" he howled, watching his groceries roll down the wet sidewalk. "Look what you've done! You better pray you didn't bruise my bananas."

"I'm sorry." Reason helped collect the man's cans and bags of bread. "I was looking at that wall over there and..."

"Are you a Canadian?"

"No, I'm from New York."

"A Yank?" The fellow lightened up. "What are you doing in Belfast? Aren't you afraid you'll get *killed?*"

"No," Reason answered uneasily, "but then I've only been here a few hours."

"What are you doing in this part of the city?"

"I wanted to see Tiger's Bay and the New Lodge. Do you live here?"

"Fucking no way. I live over in the Shankill. I'm only here to bring my granny her groceries."

"What's the Shankill?"

"A loyalist neighborhood off the Crumlin Road in West Belfast. Best part of Ulster it is."

"What's a loyalist?"

"Don't you know anything?" the thirty-year-old fellow gawked at Reason, insulted. "A loyalist is a Protestant, a *British* Protestant. Look at this, you bruised my bananas! You got a quid to pay for the damage?"

Reason was almost afraid to ask, "What's a quid?"

"Bloody hell, it's a coin! A pound coin. You do know what a coin is, don't you?"

She fished in her pocket and pulled out a quid. "Here."

He checked the gold coin carefully to make sure she'd gotten it right. "What's your name?"

"Reason."

"Reason what?"

"McGuinness."

"Reason McGuinness. A Roman Catholic, are you?"

"No! And I'm not Irish either."

The orange-haired fellow approved. He had crooked, tea-tan teeth behind a sly smile. "You're all right then. Not hard on the eyes either. You want to go out for a pint some night?"

Reason considered the short young man with the scalped-to-fuzz hair. Though plain, he was potent. Hard, sculpted muscles defined his wiry torso, and an intimidating swagger guaranteed he had no fear. Tattoos dotted his hands; a red hand of Ulster and a dagger dripping blood. In a fake leather jacket, torn jeans and metal-toed boots, with a cigarette hanging off the corner of his grin, and a silver bullet earring strung from his ear, he looked Doberman-tough. He had the eyes of a con man, shifty and shrewd, made the more unsettling by his stained smile. His face was milky with gaunt, ruddy cheeks and a nose hooked like a hawk's, and above his mouth the hint of a mustache resembled flecks of orange mold sprouting on cheese. "I don't even know your name," Reason said, inching away.

Wiping his palm on his trousers, he offered Reason his hand. "They call me 'the Knack,' Duggie Knack. You want to go out?"

"No, thanks. I have too much work to do."

"What do you do?"

"I'm here to work on the Gov's new wing."

"I was in the Gov last summer. Got shot in the stomach by a taig. I fucking nearly died."

There was that word again. "What's a taig?"

"You don't know anything at all, doll!" Duggie snorted. "What's a *taig?*" he repeated in a shout and stared across the street. "A *taig's* a fucking white Irish *nigger*, a fucking Roman Catholic *pig*," he aimed his insults towards several young men loitering in front of the New Lodge, "like those *pigs* across the street."

Before Reason knew what was happening, a shower of rocks and garbage competed with the rain and pelted down around her and the Knack. Duggie immediately pitched aside his groceries, without concern this time, and returned fire with several empty bottles conveniently stowed in the gutter. In no time a crowd of young men swarmed on both sides of the flashpoint and a riot was on. Using her umbrella as a shield, Reason took off running but not before a fistful of orange peels pounded her knees.

"You throw like a girl, ye scum," she heard Duggie shout as she sprinted back to the Antrim Road.

Later, Reason lay in bed with a knot in her heart. She couldn't believe she had called Wilder a "fucking white Irish nigger." No wonder he had reacted so strongly. Where had she learned such a mean word? She knew now it wasn't from her mother, who'd never set foot in Ireland much less use profane Irish slang, so who taught her that curse? Who?

Chapter Five

"Fiona, are the Protestants and Catholics here fighting over religion?" Reason wondered as she made herself breakfast Monday morning.

"Och no, pet. The problem isn't which church we support, it's which country. The words Catholic and Protestant identify what tribe you're in. Catholic says 'I want the Brits out and I'm for a unified Ireland,' and Protestant says 'I'm a loyalist loyal to the British Queen.'"

"So when someone asks me whether I'm Catholic or Protestant, what they're really wanting to know is 'are you for or against our side?'"

"That's right. But around here people are quite clever about finding out what side you're on without asking about faith. They can tell by your clothing…och, you won't see a loyalist wearing a Gaelic football jersey…and they can tell by what road you walk up, what bus you take, what taxi you hail, even your name can give you away. They'll ask about your school or your address or even what country you consider your-self to be living in. If you call Northern Ireland 'Ulster,' that says for sure you're a Protestant. If you call it 'the Six Counties' or 'the North of Ireland,' that says you're a Catholic."

"'The Six Counties?'"

"That refers to the six counties the Brits have partitioned from the rest of Ireland. You watch yourself when you answer questions about where you live, Reason love. This is a Catholic neighborhood. Tell a loyalist your address and you might be a sorry critter." Fiona gazed in the mirror and smoothed her auburn curls. "I'm away for the shop then. Cheerio!"

As Reason was leaving, Ruairi McKee came into the kitchen. He resembled Fiona with bright blue eyes, a pale complexion and rusty hair. But unlike his dainty mother, he was five-foot-nine and solidly built.

"So, you're the notorious Reason. I'm Ruairi." Pleased to meet her, he kissed both her cheeks then poured himself a bowl of cornflakes and lit a cigarette. "What do you think of Belfast?"

"It's not like I imagined," Reason hedged, unsure what to say.

"You were expecting Beirut, right? I hear you caused a riot in the New Lodge yesterday." Ruairi shook his head. "You didn't waste any time getting into it, did you?"

"Uh, no," Reason blushed. "It all happened so suddenly."

"That's how everything happens here. Get used to living on your nerves, love."

Reason smiled uncertainly. "Well, I'm off for the Gov. Someone should be picking me up soon."

"Do you know about West Belfast where the Gov is?"

"No. Why?"

"No reason, Reason," Ruairi smiled. "It's just that it's different. You'll see what I mean."

The wind was brisk but the morning was warm when Reason stepped into the semi-sun. As her driver swung to the curb to collect her, Reason heard the *Bap, Bap, Bap* and peered up. Another helicopter hovered.

"Yoo hoo, Reason, hello! I'm Gillian Paradise, but everyone calls me Jillie," Reason's driver popped out of the car and introduced herself. "I've been assigned to be your executive assistant while you're here. I can do everything."

"That's good," Reason said, trying not to stare.

A stunning young Irishwoman, Gillian Paradise sported metallic red streaks in her frizzed, auburn hair. She had blue fingernails and wore green feather earrings. A blue leather jacket, a blue leather skirt, blue fish-net stockings and ruby spiked heels comprised her unusual outfit, and her big violet eyes were circled in kohl. She was four inches taller than Reason, nearly six feet, and model-thin with muscle-tone like a puma. Despite her jolting veneer, her manner was graceful and self-assured; she was fine-boned and pretty. Erect of spine, shoulders back, head high, she moved as though she glided on ice.

"Reason McGuinness. What an odd name." Jillie stepped into her car. "Shall we go? The Gov isn't far."

Before Reason even had her door closed, Jillie was speeding up Duntroon Drive, spouting her life story.

"I don't always dress this way, but I'm so many different women I can't keep up with myself. Some days I feel romantic, other days wild and rebellious. The hospital staff freaks when I show up like this, but the patients love it. I visit all the wards. Everyone likes me." Jillie spoke quickly in a deep, satin voice. Her Irish accent bumped together and bumped apart in a collision of high and low sounds that bounced off Reason's ear. "Before becoming an executive assistant I was a hairdresser in Dublin; that's where I'm from. But Dublin got boring, and Belfast sounded marvelously self-destructive. I moved here last summer." She swerved in and out of traffic along the Antrim Road.

"Och, it's a splendid morning. June's my favorite time of year. Warm days, cool nights...oh hi, Danny," Jillie waved out the window to a passing jogger then turned back to Reason. "I was born in June, I'm twenty eight years young, but I'm *very* worldly...Nora!" Jillie careened around a roundabout, slammed on the brakes and called to an elderly woman walking a poodle. "Look who's here in the car. A terribly famous architect. She's come all the way from America to salvage our Gov!" Popping the clutch, Jillie plunged on down the road towards the city centre. "Not a pretty sight, is it?" she referred to the neighborhood. "Everything here is pitifully sincere, but och! Such bad taste. This entire city reminds me of pink plastic flamingos."

Reason saw empty, shattered windows shedding light on empty, shattered homes. It was misfortune and strife, not bad taste, rumbling the walls down, but she wasn't fast enough to comment.

"There's intense emotion in these ruins. They describe the situation here without saying a word. Now where was I? Oh yes, I like soft music and hard sex. I drink wine not Guinness, I don't smoke, and I don't believe in God, so don't ask me if I'm Catholic or Protestant." She fondled her crucifix necklace. "I'm Catholic of course, but...Owen!" Another acquaintance hailed Gillian from a passing bicycle. "I jog on Tuesdays, swim on Wednesdays, and Monday and Thursday evenings you'll find me studying modern art at Christ Church College. I'm hooked on expressionism...isn't everyone?"

Reason thought Jillie had stopped, but she was pausing only long enough to shove a wad of gum in her mouth.

"I have a steady boyfriend. He says I'm the perfect woman...ha, he's right," Jillie larked with a sweet little laugh. "Trouble is he's poor, so I see other men. I'll see any man who dedicates his time and money to pleasing me." She laughed again, and Reason couldn't tell if she was kidding. "I'm the most candid person you'll ever meet. If I don't like you, I'll tell you straight to your face, but I like you already. You have kind eyes." Jillie finally paused. "Now, tell me what's interesting about you."

"Well," what could Reason say to this whirlwind girl, "I..."

"Here's the Falls Road." Jillie swooped right onto a congested, four-lane street rushing uphill towards green, rocky hills. "Up ahead there are Black Mountain and Divis Mountain."

Reason glanced up with interest. Announcing the Falls Road to the right was a large sky-blue mural painted on the wall of a hostel. An alabaster Madonna cradling her child was skillfully depicted. A dove flying over blue waves decorated the mural's background, and over the Madonna's head swirled peaceful clouds and a star. Announcing the Falls on the left was a Gothic cathedral with two spires jutting into the air like the two-fingered peace sign; Saint Peter's.

"The Falls runs all the way up to Milltown Cemetery. Milltown is where a lot of the Catholics are buried. And it's where the IRA funerals are held," Jillie informed. "I live over there." She motioned to the right to yet another bland strand of rowhouses. "It's wonderfully close to the hospital, and I love my neighbors, but I do get sick of being stopped by the squaddies. The Gov's just up the road. You can't miss it, it looks like a prison. A real eye bruiser."

Jillie wasn't kidding. One view of the massive hospital and Reason thought of Stephen King. Behind a ten-foot wall of brick topped with barbed wire sat six stories of sooty red brick with rows of black windows like rows of beady black eyes. English ivy clung to the bricks like cobwebs, and where there wasn't ivy, there was moss. Irish moss, mortaring everything from the red tile roof to the flag pole flying the Union Jack to the cracks in the front steps.

"There's where the Gov's new wing will be built," Jillie indicated a large lot to the left of the hospital. "Until last month it was a string of wee shops. See the big pile of bricks? That used to be the world's best butcher shop. Now it's to be the trauma center...don't see much difference, do you?" Speeding around the hospital, Jillie screeched into a parking lot, flashed the security guard a grin, and as soon as the gates lifted, she parked the car and hopped out.

"I'll run ahead and get your office looking magic. You go on in and meet the Gov's gov. His name is Bernard Thunder. He's expecting you."

"I'll be there in a minute. I want to look around." Feeling like Henry Higgins, Reason walked the Grosvenor grounds. The hospital and its clinics covered two blocks. No attempt had been made to landscape. Here and there an elm tree grew, dandelions pushed through thin grass, moss filled any void. The entrance to the hospital, through the outer brick wall, was an arch with a caduceus keystone. It led to a concrete courtyard with a pigeon-splattered statue of King George V. Up seven steps lay the Gov's revolving doors; doors in perpetual spin. A steady stream of people entered and left.

Beside the Grosvenor was the Falls Road. Brakes hissed and squealed, cars revved, it seemed nobody had mufflers, and diesel clouded the air. There were grocers and butchers, flower shops and pubs. Like denim tumbleweeds, unemployed men collected in corners. Pretty women strutted along. As in the New Lodge, children and dogs played, neighbors chatted. But unlike New Lodge, which just looked poor, the Falls

Road looked angry. Brightly painted IRA slogans, **Onward to Victory, We Will Never Leave,** and anti-Brit murals showing Irishmen in chains colored the walls. **Brits Out Brits Out Brits Out** cried the graffiti. Protesters carrying placards decrying British terror tactics stood shouting in the center of the street. And the people didn't lower their eyes as they passed, and they didn't smile. They stared defiantly at strangers; there was resilience on every face.

Up the road, Reason saw a police station armed with cameras, antennae, metal walls and fanged wire; a similarly barricaded Army barracks flaunting a huge British flag towered nearby. Both had watch-towers poked like periscopes into the air to monitor life on the Falls. And Reason had found it. Here was the 800-year-old war. Left and right, she saw squads of soldiers, looking too young to shave, patrolling the streets with their assault rifles poised. Charcoal Land Rovers and green Army tanks prowled with two armed squaddies popped up through the open roofs, prepared to shoot. Here too the buzzard helicopters whacked away any chance of tranquillity and circled in search of rebel-lious seeds. And Reason saw the people of West Belfast staring through the British Army. The Falls Road *refused* to be occupied.

Chapter Six

Touring the hospital with chief-of-staff Bernard Thunder, two words came to Reason's mind: overcrowded, outdated. One after another, she passed through generic wards chock-full of patients in 50-year-old beds pushed against peeling, painted walls that hadn't been white since the Victorian age. Children cried, televisions blared, intercoms paged, and like silence, privacy was left at admissions; thin curtains partitioned the beds. But what the Gov lacked in ambiance was made up by its quality care. A dedicated staff kept the old place running, and everyone Reason met said the same thing, "Believe it or not, you'll like it here."

At the end of a long morning she found her office adjacent to the critical care unit on the sixth floor. While not spacious, there was a reception area for Jillie, and inside Reason's office were a desk, a drafting table and a computer, and a view of the Falls Road.

Jillie was waiting with flowers. "I arranged everything in here myself." She handed Reason a dozen pink daisies in a vase. "I put your drawing table over there so you can look out the window, and I picked out those draperies…gee, I hope you like the colors."

Reason could live with hot pink and mustard flowers. At least they weren't faded like every other square foot of the Gov.

"Now, Reason, you sit down and relax. I'm fixing you a cup of tea. What else can I do? I have my own computer and…what's the matter?"

Reason called Jillie over to the window. "That soldier down there just kicked a little boy in the stomach."

Jillie was unfazed. "Happens all the time."

"Why did he do that?"

"Just to be mean," Jillie shrugged.

"Well, someone ought to report him for being abusive."

"To whom?" Jillie laughed at Reason's naïveté. "The RUC is worse."

Reason didn't understand. She saw the boy pick himself up and resume walking. But he kept glaring over his shoulder at the jeering soldier, and his fists were clenched. "What's the RUC?" she asked.

"The Royal Ulster Constabulary. They're the police here. Och, you look shocked. You've just learned the first lesson of Belfast. What seems abnormal to an outsider is normal here…stay here long enough, and you'll be 'normal' too. Now what shall I do first?"

"I think I'll have that tea," Reason watched the boy disappear around a corner, "then you can help me organize my schedule."

Jillie rolled her chair into Reason's office. "Tell me all about the Gov's new wing…oh, but first tell me about the design team. I thought this was your project."

"Oh no, no. The Board of Directors hired me as the principal architect, but I'll be working with engineers and other architects and construction crews, plus the Gov's physicians and the Board. For the next year or so we'll be a little family, meeting once a week to fight over revisions and budgets. Luckily, you won't have to attend any of those."

"Have you met our illustrious Chairman of the Board yet?"

"Hunter Cromwell? Not yet, why?"

"He's a Brit; an aristocrat." Jillie turned up her nose. "He's only in Belfast a few days a month, but for the past year I've been his assistant. Thank heaven Bernie Thunder reassigned me to you! Och, H.C. treated me like a wench. You watch out for that one, Reason. I had a crush on his son last fall, he was my professor at CC, but when I mentioned it to Hunter, he tried to have me fired. He doesn't want his purebred English progeny within a mile of an Irish girl."

"Oh dear," Reason sympathized, but noting Jillie's zombie-punk demeanor, she could understand a father's objection. "Now then, I need the specs on…"

Jillie paid no attention. "If you had to choose, would you marry a rich man you didn't love or a poor man you adored?"

"Oh, Jillie," Reason wagged her head, "I'm the last person you should ask about marriage."

"I love dating interesting men, but I need to be practical. After all," she slapped her fish-net thigh, "I'm not getting any younger. Oh, why did I have to fall in love with a pauper? I would have been wiser falling for Decky, but stupid Cupid didn't make it happen that way. Decky's my rich man. We meet twice a week for dinner and sex." She fluffed her hair and smiled. "He say's I'm a perfect woman too."

"Decky?" Reason laughed. "It sounds like the name of a chipmunk."

"I'll tell him you said that," Jillie cracked up. "He's dreadfully full of himself. Do you think I should pursue a rich man and forget the poor man? I mean, Decky's a good catch…that is if you can catch him. He's completely heartless, but then so am I. I know he'll never love me, he can't love anyone he says, but he gives me anything I want…and he does live out the Malone."

"The Malone?"

"That's the road that runs past CC; Christ Church College. It's one of the main roads through South Belfast where the posh Prods live. It's the prettiest part of this city. So, do you think I should forget the pauper?"

"I'd stay with the man you love."

"Love!" Jillie pressed her hand to her brow. "Och, love is such pain. Maybe I should be a nun. I tell you what, come with me to the pub tonight. You can meet my friends. I'll introduce you to everyone I know. And you can tell us about the Gov's new wing. How about it?"

"Some other time, Jillie. I'm way too tired."

Before falling to sleep, Reason kept seeing the squaddie driving his boot into that little boy's gut, and it occurred to her she didn't know why the Army was in Belfast. In America it was assumed the Brits were there to keep the peace, but there was nothing peaceful about that soldier's kick.

"Originally they did come to restore order," Ruairi explained over breakfast. "In 1969, the violence between the loyalists and nationalists was wild…nationalists are what we call the Catholics here. The nationalists wanted equality and tried to gain civil rights by peaceful marches. But the Catholics wanting equal employment, equal housing and equal say in the government was the ultimate threat. To hire Catholics meant there would be Protestants who didn't get jobs. To give fair and equal housing to the Catholics meant there would be Protestants who didn't get houses. And to share power with *Catholics?* Great Mother of God, next thing you know the Pope would be ruling a unified Ireland!

"So the Prods started their own marches…into Catholic neighborhoods to terrorize the 'taigs.' In turn, the Catholics drove out any Protestants living nearby, and these confrontations led to one riot after another. The situation exploded in Belfast in August '69, when Protestant gangs went on a rampage up the Falls Road and burned down more than 200 Catholic houses. The police showed up in tanks and raced up and down the Falls with machine guns. But besides firing random bullets at nationalist targets, the cops did nothing to stop the Protestants from burning down houses and attacking the Catholics. Needless to say the British Army arrived the next day to restore order, and for a moment, the Catholics thought the Brits had come to save the day."

Reason still didn't get it. "So why was that soldier kicking a little boy?"

"That wee boy is the enemy. Working alongside the police…the 'peelers' we call them…the soldiers were quick to adopt the peelers' anti-Catholic sentiments. Because the police are Protestants and consider themselves to be British, the troops consider them allies, while the Catholics are Irish traitors and a threat to sovereign England. Funny how you can be a traitor in your native land. Anyway, by 1970, the Army refused to respond to pleas from the Catholics when their communities were ransacked and burned by Protestant gangs. It didn't take long for the

Catholics to see the Army was just another arm of British oppression. The Prods, on the other hand, see the Army as their assurance the North will stay British and the Catholics will be kept in their place."

"Are all the soldiers from England then?"

"Och no. A lot of the ones you see on the streets are from right here in the Six Counties; Protestant Irish-Brits they are. There are plenty of English soldiers about, but in the 80's the Army began recruiting Ulster Prods to do England's fighting. So, there you go, love," Ruairi smiled, "you know it all."

"Could I ask you one more question? Is the Irish Republican Army a good thing or a bad thing? I really don't understand what's what around here."

"The IRA wants the British out of Northern Ireland. To some people that's a good thing, to others it's diabolical."

Reason just shook her head and pushed from the table. "I'd better get ready for work."

"Before you go," Ruairi spoke up, "I hear you'll be supervising the hiring for your project at the Gov."

"I'll have some say in it…who said I was supervising it?"

Ruairi smiled another nice smile. "I met Jillie at the pub last night."

"You know Gillian?"

"Everyone knows Jillie. When you're hiring construction engineers, I'd like to apply."

"I didn't know you were an engineer."

"Yeah," Ruairi nodded shyly. "After I got out of prison, my mum put me through school. But I haven't been able to find a job." Reason's shocked face prompted him to say, "Thirteen years ago I was lifted right here in my own front yard for possessing a pair of rubber gloves; the RUC called them 'implements for the purpose of terrorism.' They said I used them when I made bombs. Actually I wore them to prune the roses. I was held on remand in the Crumlin Road Jail for two and a half years. When I finally got my trial, the judge threw out the charges. And why wouldn't he?" Ruairi simmered. "I hadn't done anything wrong."

"Come in and fill out an application," Reason said, thinking Belfast most strange.

Chapter Seven

Fifty artists had been invited to submit samples of their work to be juried by the Grosvenor's architects, but only one artist would be selected to create a masterpiece for the hospital's new atrium. After work on Thursday, Reason walked around the Gov's cafeteria judging the submissions; watercolor street scenes, metal sculptures, tapestries, and her personal favorite, a tile mosaic of an Irish meadow with winged sheep wearing mantles of stars. She and the other architects would vote in the morning.

"I like those little tile doodads. How do you suppose the artist gets them to stick in there?" a deep voice inquired behind her. "Perhaps he uses gum."

Reason turned to greet a man in a navy blazer, linen slacks, and an electric green tie. He was about her age, maybe a year or two older.

"I've come to see your artwork," he explained, taking stock of Reason. "I heard it was on display."

"That's right," she nodded, wishing the attractive man had come looking for her.

"What do you call a thingamajig like this?" he asked, still ogling Reason.

"It's a mosaic," she laughed.

"Ah," the man nodded blankly and followed Reason across the room. "Do you like it?"

"Yes. Do you?"

"It's certainly unique. That sort of thing would cheer the patients up, don't you think? Especially the kids."

"That's what I like about it. All these other works are so serious. As if being in the hospital isn't serious enough. And it's approachable. You can get close to it and touch it…imagine an entire wall like this."

"I wouldn't make it too approachable," the man cautioned. "Around here somebody's likely to paint 'Brits Out' on it." He trailed Reason display to display, watching her every move. "Here's an interesting photograph. Look at the play between shadow and light."

Reason cocked an ear. "You sound like Alistair Cooke."

"The curse of good breeding," the man revealed his smile. "I like this sculpture's texture and tension and you have beautiful eyes."

Reason gazed up at him. "Thank you."

"And you don't look like a blood-sucking witch," he added brightly.

"Well…good. But that's the strangest thing a man has ever said to me."

The man was pleased to hear that. "Makes me hard to forget, doesn't it?"

He had warm brown eyes and a five o'clock shadow. He wore the clean scent of vetiver. English, well-dressed and affable, with his honey-pale hair precisely cut and falling upon his neck, with his feet bare in Chinese thongs, he personified a hip aristocrat; tall and able-bodied, he grabbed Reason's attention like an eruption of church bells and sparks.

"This tapestry is nice," Reason stroked the wool threads, "but not very practical."

"What's that thing?" The man pointed to a sculpted mother and child. "It looks like a pair of penguins. Does that child have *flippers?* Aw hell, who am I to criticize? Do you have any idea the number of talented artists who give up art because of the cruelty of critics?"

"True artists can't give up their art," Reason disagreed. "They're driven to create. Driven mad."

"To know that you must be an artist yourself."

"I'm an architect."

"And are you driven mad?"

"Yes, by budgets and schedules."

"There's the rub; reconciling art to reality," the man was at once provoked. "You can't harness passion with the wallet and watch. That's like demanding a forest fire confine its burning!" With that he threw up his hands and strode from the cafeteria. Five minutes later he was back with his fists full of dandelions. "Next time I'll give you violets," he promised Reason then walked away.

*   *   *   *   *   *

Jillie had worked late every night without complaint, but at five o'clock Friday afternoon she was at Reason's door with keys in hand. "I have a date and I want to look hot. May I leave?"

"Did you get all those applications filed?"

"Alphabetically, skill by skill just like you asked. I swear I now know every contractor and engineer in the Six Counties. It's all in the computer, plus I made two back-up copies."

"That's it for today then."

"Oh, before I go," Jillie paused, "who won the art competition? The mosaic man?"

"Yep. Our decision was unanimous. Only I don't know his name. He signed his work as 'Mr. X.'"

"Well, whoever he is I'll bet he's over the moon about winning." Jillie tapped her lips in thought. "You're working late again I see."

"Only a few more hours."

"Would you do me a favor? Meet me at the pub later. C'mon, Reason, you're working way too hard, and I want you to have some fun. Please say you'll come, *please*."

"If I can, I will."

"The pub is called Albie's. It's way up the Falls on the darkest side street in all of Ireland." Jillie wrote down the address. "I'll expect you there by eight thirty."

At seven o'clock he appeared beside her desk with three dozen violets in a teacup. "Did you miss me?"

Reason glanced up from her computer, at once smiling to greet the distinguished Englishman in a black raincoat. "Well, I did hope we'd meet again."

"Here I am then!" He slid forth with the violets. "These are from my garden. Their leaves are heart-shaped, see? I'm Cain Cromwell."

While delighted to see him and his indigo flowers, the name meant nothing to Reason.

"I'm the Gov's new artist."

"You're Mr. X?"

Happily he nodded. "I used that Mr. X thing so the jury wouldn't be prejudiced. I know several of your colleagues here and didn't want them accused of favoritism. I'm a professor in CC's fine arts department."

"You did that mosaic and didn't tell me?" Reason cried.

"I didn't want my good looks to sway you." Cain noticed Reason had saved the dandelions in a vase on her desk, and he thought her very sweet.

"And here I thought you were artless." Then it registered. She would be working with this man. Her attraction heightened. "Calling things doodads and thingamajigs, you must be an interesting professor."

"I do my best," he stated modestly.

"I'm Reason McGuinness by the way."

"I knew who you were last night. Your reputation preceded you. I read the article about you in yesterday's news. And are you reasonable, Reason?"

"Terribly," she smiled, showing her winsome dimples.

Studying Reason again in his private-eye, probing way, Cain appeared baffled. "I can't get over it. You aren't at all like I expected."

"What did you expect?"

"Warts and a broomstick," he chortled under his breath.

"What?"

"Oh, nothing. I have to be going, but I wanted to pop in and thank you for selecting my work. This project for the Gov means a lot to me."

"Why's that?"

Cain grew somber. "It's my chance to do something right for a change. When do you want to see my designs for the mural?"

"I need to settle in and get my own designs together. How about next month?"

"I'll look forward to it." He walked to the door, stopped, and came back. "Do you paint?"

"Yes, though the Gov is going to keep me too busy to do any recreational art for awhile."

"Pity. Well, goodnight." Cain revisited the doorway. Then he swung back. "You're welcome to come to one of my classes at Christ Church and try your hand."

"Thank you, but my schedule is so crazy..."

"I understand." He bowed once more for the door. "Cheerio." But he returned. "Thursday is my night class. Will you come next week?"

"Maybe."

"Maybe is for cowards, Miss McGuinness. Have you seen much of Belfast?"

"Only the highway between here and the Antrim Road."

"Then you've seen nothing. I'll pick you up here next Thursday at six and show you an hour's worth of sights. We'll get better acquainted." He passed his eyes over Reason again. Not an ice maiden this slayer of men, but a woman who saved dandelions. A woman quick to be cordial, quick to entice a man's ease, a man's pleasure. She was pleasing. But there was something else about her, something behind her eyes; the light of an unblemished soul. "I'll be damned if I don't like you, Miss Reasonable McGuinness."

He held her eyes then her hand before finally departing, and Reason liked this English artist.

Before returning to her sketches, she scanned the Falls Road below. How far from home and alone she felt. How foreign this place. She was alien to every aspect of the city. She wasn't Irish, she wasn't British, but it was more than that. Everywhere she turned something reminded her of Wilder. The coal-haired, blue-eyed men, the charming brogues, the tappy rain, the little boys on twisty streets in the New Lodge which she passed daily en route to work…this was his city, and being alien to Belfast, Reason felt the more estranged from Wilder, and lonely. So lonely. How now, steeped in his essence, was she to forget him? Homesick and growing depressed, she hoped Albie's would cheer her.

At first Reason wasn't sure Jillie had given her proper directions. She wouldn't have known Albie's existed if it weren't attached to Albie's Funeral Home. A block off the Falls, the pub was the fourth, two-story duplex in a chain of ten duplexes. It was surrounded by boulders and protective caging to deflect gunmen and bombs. No sign indicated it was Albie's, and when Reason reached the door she had to step into the cage and ring a buzzer to be screened. After several seconds an anonymous sentinel allowed her inside.

The interior was loft-like with brick walls, an open-beamed ceiling, and a scattering of tables on a black checkered floor. Cigarette smoke clouded dim lights; stout and musk perfumes scented the air. A soccer match on the television boomed over the din of the customers, and many of the customers were gruff-looking men. Being a stranger, Reason attracted inquisitive eyes as she picked her way across the room, and feeling exposed, she breathed a sigh of relief to nab a stool at the bar. She'd been seated less than a minute before the bartender served her an Irish whiskey.

"Compliments of the lads playing snooker," he said. Seeing Reason's hesitation the barman patted her hand. "You're all right, love. The boys here are gents. They just want to say welcome."

Wishing Jillie would hurry, Reason took a sip of the whiskey and stared around at the pub's patrons. Long-haired men in black boots and leather jackets; skin-headed men in faded jeans; clean-cut men in t-shirts and chino. They cavorted with best mates and lovers. Captivating lovers these Irish women. Red-haired, raven-haired, dyed blonde, pretty fair-skinned, slender women, boisterously chatting. Nearly everyone was smoking and knocking back pints and shouting to be heard, paying scant attention to the screeching TV.

Focusing through an archway, Reason saw an unruly-coifed and bearded man playing snooker in the back room. He was tall, a novelty among most Irish men. He appeared healthy and fit, and he wasn't drinking or smoking like his companions. His corduroy slacks and black sweater were plain but well-tailored, and he wore fashionable Nikes. As if sensing her scrutiny, he raised his eyes from his cue, fired Reason a grin, and returned to his game. *Bang,* he plugged her straight through the heart with that quick-draw smile; that unforgettable lover's smile she'd seen on a warm summer's night. Wilder.

Reason leapt off her perch and rushed towards him. If he was surprised to see her, he didn't show it; when she finally reached him, he insisted he didn't know her.

"Wilder, it's me. Reason," she persisted with embraces of joy.

Pushing her off him, the man was displeased. "My name is not Wilder," he snarled with a thick Belfast accent and went on playing snooker.

"But of course it is." Reason knew she couldn't be wrong. She knew his voice, his eyes, his body by heart.

"I'll tell you what, sweetheart," he made a sarcastic face that caused his comrades to howl, "if you want to call me Wilder, that's fine with me. What did you say your name was? Treason Reason?"

For two years she had prayed to hear his voice saying her name again but had long ceased to listen for that which never spoke, never called. Now reminded, its richness was bitter, sweet. "I don't understand." Her enthusiasm waned. "Why are you acting like you don't know me?"

"Because I *don't* know you. Would you move so I could make my shot?"

"Well, if you're not Wilder, who are you?"

He drummed up another familiar smile. "I'm Declan."

"*Deck*-lan?" She had never heard such a name and scowled with doubt. "You turned my life upside down. You think I don't recognize you?"

"Look, honey, I've never seen you before," he fired back snidely.

"But it's just too extraordinary." Reason stared at the stranger's face. "You look exactly like him." He appeared to be ignoring her, and with his friends gawking and making jokes, Reason felt ridiculous. "Sorry for troubling you then. But," she just had to add, "I still say you're Wilder."

"Hey, blondie, what if I were this Wilder?" He watched her long legs as she left. "What would you do?"

She turned back and looked him in the eye. "Too bad you'll never know."

Reason rushed out as Jillie waltzed in; a drastically transformed Jillie. She wore a white cotton sundress with lace and pearl buttons. Gone was the zombie make-up, revealing high cheekbones, a squarish face and an upturned nose. She wore cherry lip gloss on her wide, cheery lips, and her natural hair was rich ginger spilling over sleek shoulders. With her fair skin and violet eyes, she was even more jolting than her punk alter-ego.

"Jillie," Reason dismayed, "you look…beautiful!"

"Aye, so I do. I'm glad you decided to come. Look who I found out walking the Falls. Reason," she slapped her arms around her companion, "this is my pauper. Kieran, this is my new boss Reason McGuinness. You weren't leaving were you, Reason? Of course you weren't! There's a booth back here where we can sit." She pushed Reason toward the snooker room. "You don't want to go out now anyway. An IRA sniper just opened fire on a brick of squaddies."

"Might as well get a few pints in before all hell breaks loose," Kieran suggested jovially.

"I hear Decky is here. Did you meet him?"

"I met a man named Declan."

"That's him." Jillie looked around. "Did he leave?" she asked one of his snooker mates.

"Yeah. Out the back. He got called to the Gov."

"He's always getting called away," Jillie huffed. "I wanted you to get to know him. Oh well." She plopped down and pulled a mirror out of her purse. "My hair is shocking! I'll be back." She left Reason staring at Kieran.

"So, you're the infamous Reason." He pumped her hand and welcomed her to his country by offering her a Guinness stout and a cigarette. She accepted another whiskey. "I hear you're living with Ruairi McKee."

"You know Ruairi?"

"Aye. I warned him to be careful of you," Kieran joked, giving Reason a tickle under the chin. "I told him what England couldn't do in a few hundred years, you managed to do in one night."

"What's that?" Reason warmed at once to his genial nature.

"Brought the O'Neills to their knees."

"I don't understand."

"You wouldn't have my cousin Declan. Too good for him, were you?"

It took Reason a moment to register. Then it struck her, "So, Declan *is* Wilder!" How excellent and awful to know she had found him. "And you're the cousin who broke your promise and joined the IR…"

"Sssh! Keep it down."

"Sorry. Obviously Wilder has told you about Colorado."

"*Declan* has mentioned it on a few occasions when he's been drunk."

"How long has he been in Belfast?"

Kieran paused to light his second cigarette. "Since last June."

"A *year?*" Reason choked. "What's he doing here?"

Kieran shirked and exhaled grey smoke. "Living."

"He certainly didn't seem surprised to see me."

"He knew you were in Belfast after reading that article in yesterday's paper about your work at the Gov." Kieran considered Reason slyly. "But Decky was surprised all right. Damn near took a stroke when he read you were here. You must have really killed him, love, cuz he hates you more than he hates the Brits."

Kieran's frankness stung. Reason opened her mouth to ask more, but Kieran put a finger to his lips as Jillie approached. "Another round, ladies?" He was already on his way to the bar.

Kieran McCartan didn't look like a terrorist. In white jeans and a rugby shirt, he looked about as IRA as Opie Taylor. His hands were clean, his jaw freshly shaven. He had straight, short hair and wore one gold ring in his left ear. As tall as Wilder, with cinnamon hair and Liam O'Neill's fevered blue eyes, Kieran was handsome enough to catch ladies' attention, he was strong and slim, but he'd lived a hard life. His body carried a series of scars. Most distinctive was his left cheek with its diagonal slash. He liked to boast it was the result of a rapier; in reality he'd had a broken beer bottle shoved into his face. He was pensive not shy, and his sense of humor was quick and black. But as fast as he could crack a joke, he could preach the precepts of freedom. His antipathy for the British was tempered only by his love of Ireland and life.

"Americans are health-conscious," he told Reason over his second Guinness and fifth cigarette, "but we Irish are life-conscious. Americans live like they'll live forever. We live each day like it's our last. Americans build for tomorrow. We Irish burn for today. We grab love and sex," he winked at Jillie, "when and where we can find it. It's dangerous here and life can be brief…and that makes living sweeter."

He was sporadically employed, taking manual work when work was offered, taking the dole when it wasn't, and he lived everywhere, never long having an address that could place him. He had few needs, fewer possessions. What little he owned he kept at his parents' house; a house that harbored his treasure, his five-year-old son Morris. Morris' mother had left Northern Ireland three days after Morris was born, before Kieran and she could be married, and Kieran hadn't heard from her since.

It was late. Wilder hadn't returned to the pub, and as Kieran and Jillie exchanged lingering kisses, Reason decided to leave. "Where's the bathroom?" she asked.

Without lifting her lips from Kieran's, Jillie waved towards a hallway beyond the snooker tables.

The hall led to what had once been a kitchen at the back of the house. Reason assumed the bathroom was off to one side, but it wasn't. She would have returned to the snooker room if a pantry door hadn't been unlocked and open a crack. Through the crack she saw a staircase. Ignoring better judgment, she climbed through the door and crept down two steps and peered into a cellar clogged with crates of liquor and sacks of coal. An unremarkable cellar, she concluded before noticing one of the crates slightly displaced.

Was she seeing things? Reason stepped down into the room. A ghost of a light seeped from under the box. Stooping to look through the slit, she discovered a manhole hidden in the floor; an old well. Pushing aside the crate, she tested the metal trap-door; a door that should have been bolted from below. On soundless hinges it dropped to reveal a ladder of jute descending into the earth. At the foot of the ladder a feeble light quavered. Quietly, holding her breath, Reason inched down the ladder for a look. She found herself deep in a pocket of earth where the air was thick, and off the pocket a slender tunnel threaded downhill; the ghostly light lay beyond. Along the dirt passage she crept; a claustrophobic little passage sized for one six-foot man. Peeking wide-eyed around the first bend, to her dismay, she saw Wilder in another dim pocket, seated on a bench, dressed head to toe in surgical greens. Seeing his clothes steeped in blood, Reason couldn't stifle a gasp, causing Wilder to lurch off the bench, spin and point a gun at her head.

"What are you doing down here? Jesus! I nearly blew your head off," he rouped in shock, still aiming his gun between her eyes. "What in the hell do you think you're doing?" he repeated this time in fury.

Reason gaped in horror. "I…I…why are you covered in blood?" Over his shoulder she saw another tight tunnel leading into darkness, and as Wilder glared upon her, she was terrified.

Viciously, he jerked her forward. "You forget you saw me; you forget you saw this place," he seethed.

"Are you hurt? Is that your blood?" Reason felt sick. How could this man, who once made tender love to her, now be furtive and bloodied and threatening to shoot her?

"Sit down and keep your mouth shut," he commanded, pushing her onto the bench. Scared speechless, she obeyed while Wilder stripped off the soiled garb and dressed again in the trousers and sweater he'd been wearing earlier. He combed his hair, checked his hands for blood, then punched off his flashlight. Seizing Reason's hand, he reeled her to her feet and shoved her back into the tunnel. "Go up the ladder, don't turn around, and don't say one damn word. *Hurry!*" he growled.

In a panic, Reason groped her way back along the passage in the darkest darkness she had ever known. Finding the secret ladder, up she scrambled, up into the cellar, up the stairs and into the kitchen. Without bothering to say goodnight to Kieran and Jillie, she fled.

Stealthily, Wilder followed. Once he was sure Reason was safe, he slinked up the ladder, bolted the hatch door, then raced back down the well and ducked into the tunnels. Within minutes, he entered Albie's through the front door and ran into Jillie at the bar.

"Here you are!" She noted his flushed expression then kissed his mouth. "What have you been up to?"

"Where's Reason?"

"She shot out of here like a bullet."

"You let her take off *alone?* She could get lost. Or hurt."

"She'll be fine," Jillie reassured and reached for Wilder's hand. "Come on, love, sit down and have a drink with me and Kier…"

But Wilder was out of earshot as he vaulted for the door.

"Why is he breaking his neck to catch Reason?" Jillie asked Kieran in disbelief. "I've never seen him pay that much attention to any woman…not even to me…and he doesn't even know her!"

Kieran's explanation was a couldn't-care-less shrug.

The night had grown squally. Wind brought fits of rain. Mist from the mountains drifted across West Belfast, and cold water pelted Reason as she dodged puddles and splashes from cars. The mood of the weather fit the mood on the street. The Falls was well-lit, but its side streets were fingers of darkness. Hurrying towards the Gov, Reason had a prickly sense of a thousand eyes recording her every move. She glimpsed over her shoulder every few feet and couldn't stop thinking about Belfast's invisible war. It was everywhere and it was nowhere; hidden bombs, hidden cameras, secret societies, secret police. It occurred late at night, down black alleyways, along less-traveled routes. Along the Falls Road.

And there was no denying the Falls after dark was a war zone. If the troops were daunting by day, they were horrid at night. Darting in and out of dark corners like machine-gun shadows, slinking along the sidewalks like uncoiling snakes, and pointing their rifles at each passerby, the young squaddies seemed more terrified than fortified; and their fear made them deadly. Reason worried if she made one sudden move, the soldiers would panic and shoot. And she had already come too close to that fate tonight.

Two helicopters parked overhead. In an effort to uncover the IRA sniper, the Falls Road was sealed off and crawling with security forces. All cars were being stopped and searched as were most pedestrians. Reason saw the policemen and soldiers hurling one young man after another up against the wall then forcing, at gunpoint, each one to lie spread eagle, face down on the sidewalk. As the men were searched and interrogated, they were alternately kicked and dealt rifle butts to the back. Reason prepared to be accosted and grilled, but the policemen and troops ignored her.

After what seemed like two hundred miles, the Gov came into sight. All Reason wanted to do was go home to Fiona's, take a long bath and a longer sleep. Her clothes were drenched, her head ached, her feet hurt…was there someone behind her? She checked once. No. She checked again, and before she could turn back around, a man covered her mouth and jerked her into the alley.

"Don't scream, Reas," he whispered and slid his hands around her waist. "It's me. Declan…Wilder. Promise you won't scream?"

Reason nodded, hoping her heart wouldn't shatter from fear. "First you want to shoot me, now you're trying to break my neck," she fumed and spun to face him in the rain.

"Keep your voice down! I'm trying to keep you out of trouble. You shouldn't be walking alone."

"A lot of the women here do it."

"Well, don't you do it. Where can we talk?"

"What's to talk about? I saw nothing, I know nothing, and you don't know me, remember?"

"For godsake, Reason, stop being difficult and let's get off the Falls."

Wearily, she assented. "My car's over in the physicians' lot behind the hospital."

Wilder leaned out of the alley to see if the coast was clear. "Let's go."

"You're acting like a fugitive. What have you gotten yourself into, Wilder?"

"Stop calling me that!"

"But, Wilder, you are Wilder."

"Wilder no longer exists."

"But…"

"I was born Declan Wilder O'Neill and that's who I am."

"But why?" Reason puzzled.

"Because I've come home."

"So how have you been, Mac?" Wilder slid into Reason's rented sedan and checked the view from the mirror to make sure they were alone.

"I've been fine. And you?"

"Couldn't be better." He melted a sidelong gaze from Reason's face to her ankles and wished he wasn't impressed.

"When did you grow the beard?"

"Makes me look distinguished, doesn't it?"

"Only if distinguished means looking like a badly-groomed goat."

"Still honest like a hatchet I see." Wilder looked insulted but quickly turned smug, "Last time I saw you your wedding had hit a little snag. Are you still madly in love with Reid?"

"How was I supposed to go on loving a man who couldn't stand the sight of me…thanks to you."

"See, Mac? I told you you'd thank me one day. Do you ever hear from him?"

"No."

"I talked to him last spring. He married a showgirl he met in Vegas."

"Goody for him."

"I suppose you're married now as well," Wilder sounded nonchalant.

"No."

"Have you missed me, Mac?" He smiled but his eyes were ice.

Yes! she thought. "Like a migraine," she said.

"And now here you are in Belfast; my humble home." Wilder stroked his beard in thought, running his eyes over Reason again. Visions of her naked astride him in bed seared his thoughts. He recounted, as he had recounted for two painful years, the ways she had loved him and loved him and made him kiss the sky. Then kiss the dirt. "Imagine a Wellworth-Howell coming to Ireland. How will you ever cope with the dirty Irish Catholics?"

Reason overlooked the gibe. "Why aren't you in Los Angeles reaming clogged arteries?"

"I came to Merry's funeral last summer and never went back to the States."

"*Merry's* funeral? Oh, Wilder, how awful." Her hand immediately flew to his arm. He shifted from her touch. "What happened?"

"She was a lawyer and had been speaking out against England's human rights abuses here. Some soldiers stopped her car down in Armagh, shot her sixteen times and left her lying on the road. She'd been on an Army hit list for months...the bastards finally got her."

"Oh my God. I'm so sorry."

"Another casualty of the Cure."

Reason gave him a blank stare. "The Cure?"

"The Crown Undercover Regiment. It's a special branch of the British Army trained to be assassins."

Reason couldn't bear the loathing that scorched Wilder's eyes. He looked mean, he looked hard. He'd come home to inherit eight centuries of conflict bequeathed him by his grandfather, his brother and sister. After years of avoidance he'd come to tilt the longest war. He could be Wilder, he could be Declan. He could be a physician or a Provo, but he couldn't be indifferent. Not this time. Not ever again.

"Are you in the IRA? Is that what tonight was about?" Reason dared to ask and received silence.

"I read about you in the newspaper. It sounds like you've made a success of yourself." Wilder considered the Gov fondly. "I was born on the third floor of this old hospital. What were you doing at Albie's?"

"Jillie invited me." Jillie…and Declan! Dinner and sex twice a week. Her heart sank.

"You have no business being in a place like that."

"I don't see why not. I was having fun."

"If you stay this ignorant, you're going to need a bodyguard, Mac. Albie's is in Catholic West Belfast, which means it's a target for Protestant gunmen and the Army. I about died when I saw you walk in. And then when you showed up in the tunnel…I see time hasn't taught you discretion."

"If it's so dangerous, what were you doing there?"

Wilder wasn't about to explain. "Next time you want a drink, go to the city centre. It's safer."

"Why didn't you come over to the bar when you saw me walk in?"

"I thought buying you a drink was more than enough," he sneered.

Reason couldn't look at Wilder. How he damned and despised her. "Why did you pretend you didn't know me?"

"Because I don't know you now. And don't call me Wilder!"

"You want me to call you 'Decky?'" she mocked.

"I don't want you to call me at all. The fact that you're here in Belfast means nothing to me. Nothing."

"Why are you so angry? I'm the one who got hurt. You caused all the trouble."

"Look, Mac, just stay out of my way. Nobody can grip a grudge longer than an Irishman, and I have one hell of a grudge against you."

"Then why are you sitting here in my car?"

"I had to make sure you understand that I want no part of you."

"Great," Reason pretended not to care, "because no part of me wants to be wanted by any part of you."

"Fine."

"Fine! Did you have anything to do with that sniper tonight?"

"So long, Mac. I'd say it's good seeing you again, but it's not." Wilder stepped out into the parking lot, stopped and sheepishly returned to the car. "Uh…I forgot I loaned my car to Kieran."

"So what?" Reason grumped.

"I missed the last bus, and waiting for a taxi with this weather will take hours. I have no way to get home." When Reason didn't offer, he appealed, "Will you drive me?"

"Belfast is a small city. I see no reason why you and your Irish grudge can't strut yourselves home."

"You'd send me out in this rain?"

"With pleasure," Reason smiled.

"But the police are searching pedestrians entering and leaving the Falls."

"Do you have something to hide?"

"Only myself."

"What have you done?"

"Can't you stop asking questions for one minute? It's been a long night, and I don't feel like being hassled by the cops, OK? Will you or won't you drive me home?"

"But if they're stopping cars…"

"You're an American and you're a woman. You'll slip right through the checkpoint."

"And what about you?"

"I stand a better chance sticking with you than I do on my own right now."

"What's your name?" the policeman asked when Reason pulled up to the checkpoint.

Reason answered nervously, alternately eyeing the policeman and the four soldiers behind him as backup.

"Where do you live?"

"Twenty two Duntroon Drive."

"You're an American?"

"Yes."

"What's your purpose on the Falls Road tonight?"

"I work at the Gov."

"Show me your driver's license and hospital I.D."

Reason did.

"Do you always work this late?"

"No, but I have a lot to do right now."

"Open your bonnet and boot."

Reason stepped into the rain and opened the hood then the trunk of her car. The policeman rifled through her drafting supplies and portfolios.

"What's this?" He studied the technical drawings then Reason's face then returned his suspicions to the drawings.

"Expansion plans for the Gov. I'm an architect."

"What are you going to do with these?"

Reason grew impatient and viewed the constable as if he were stupid. "What do you think I'm going to do with them, wallpaper my kitchen? I'm using them for the hospital's new wing."

The RUC man's eyes narrowed. "Do you have a problem, Miss McGuinness?"

"Yes, this is ridiculous. I'm tired and getting soaked standing here, and I've done nothing wrong."

"If you don't shut your goddamn fucking mouth, you'll be standing here all night." Without saying a word, the policeman detained her for twenty more minutes then crammed her drawings back in the trunk; purposely tearing some while letting others fall to the pavement. "Get back in the car," he snarled, stamping his mud-caked boots across her plans.

Relieved to be released, Reason peeled up her soggy drafts and returned to the car.

"Who's your passenger there?" The policeman bent to inspect Wilder with a flashlight, and Reason was certain Wilder would be the next man to be thrown into the street and beaten.

"Uh, he's…" she didn't know what to say.

"May I see some identification?" the lawman demanded. Upon scanning Wilder's hospital I.D., he talked into his walkie-talkie, listened to the RUC's information on Declan O'Neill, then motioned for two soldiers to assist.

"Step out of the car, *Duh*-clan," a soldier with an Irish accent ordered. "Drop your coat and take off those shoes." After Wilder complied, the soldier kicked the coat into the gutter and threw the shoes down the street.

Slam! The troops smacked him against the hood then kicked his legs out from under him. Dragging him up off the street by the hair, they heaved him against the car once more, frisked him with punches, then kicked his legs out from under him again.

"You're dirt," simpered one soldier. "You might as well lie in dirt." With their gun barrels pressed to his head, the soldiers kept Wilder face down on the street in the pouring rain. Reason protested hotly but was subdued when one of the soldiers smashed her left headlight with his rifle and screamed, "Fucking shut up, you bitch."

"You come from a long line of murdering assholes, don't you, *Duh*-clan?" the soldiers taunted, dumping the contents of Wilder's wallet and pocketing the cash. "Says here you're a fucking Fenian physician. Christ, what's the world coming to?"

Wilder twisted his head to glare upon the squaddie but he didn't talk back.

"You're still a murdering dickhead, *Duh*-clan." With his heavy black boot the soldier nudged Wilder's head back to the asphalt. "You shot that soldier up the road tonight, didn't you? That's why you're here on the Falls Road tonight, isn't it?"

"Oh, for christsake," Wilder groaned in disgust. "I just gave you guys my Grosvenor I.D. I'm over here to check on my patients."

"You're New Lodge gutter piss. Where do you live now?"

Wilder spit out the rain running into his mouth and recited his address, provoking howls of laughter and a kick to the ribs.

"My fucking ass!" the soldier brayed. "Where do you live, scum?"

Wilder repeated the upscale address and remained remarkably calm. "You have my wallet. Check my driver's license."

"What's a taig doing living out the Malone?"

"A lot of us physicians live out there," Wilder explained.

"Aren't you afraid the ULF will burn your fucking fancy house down?"

"The ULF knows everything about you, *Duh*-clan, and so do we. The last of the O'Neill Sinn Féin shits. Don't go out alone in the dark at night, *Duh*-clan. It's only a matter of time before somebody blows your motherfucking brains out."

Wilder didn't react. He'd heard it a hundred times before.

"You got a death wish living in Ulster, *Duh*—clan. They'll be digging your grave in Milltown soon. Right next to Brendan and Merry." The soldiers spit on Wilder and withdrew their guns.

"Did anyone come into the Gov with a gunshot wound?" the policeman resumed.

"I don't know. I wasn't on duty in the casualty ward."

"What are you doing on the Falls then?"

"I just told you, I had patients to see."

The two soldiers traded nods with the policeman then hoisted Wilder to his bare feet, once again by the hair. One soldier banged Wilder's head against the car a final time while the other poked his rifle to the back of Wilder's neck. "Can you say 'God Save Our Queen,' *Duh*—clan?"

"God Save our Queen."

"He's obedient as my damn dog," hooted the policeman to his chums. "Go home to your palace, shithead," he snorted, and with a last jab to the ribs, shoved Wilder into the car. "Miss McGuinness, find yourself a real man with a cock and forget this Fenian fucking faggot. And fix that headlight, darling. You ought to be more careful with your car. What is it you say in America? Oh yeah, 'Have a nice day.'" Fit to burst, the security men waved Reason through the checkpoint and swooped upon the next car.

"Welcome to occupied Ireland." Enraged, humiliated and hurting, Wilder avoided looking at Reason who was in tears.

"What about your coat and shoes?"

"Forget about them."

"Are you all right? Oh no, look at you! You're soaked. You're bleeding."

"I'll be fine." He wiped his split lip and gashed brow, and noticed Reason was as wet as he. The hint of a smile escaped him. She looked like she did the day she pulled him out of the river. "Will you watch where you're going? You nearly side-swiped that taxi."

"You said I'd slip right through."

"I was wrong."

"They're nothing but sadists," Reason raged and couldn't stop crying.

"Look, pull the car over and try to calm down."

"This is a nightmare!" Reason veered her sedan to the left and bumped into the curb. "Oh, Wilder, are you terribly hurt?"

"I'm all right. Will you stop crying?" Emotion pricked his breast. Reason should have been spared from this, and if he hadn't been there, she would have. "Come on, Reas, it's not as bad as it looks."

"I can't help it. First I see you out of the blue, then I catch you splattered in blood and waving a gun in my face, now this." She rested her head on the steering wheel and went on crying. "This city is too hard. I'm going to forget the damn hospital and go home. Tomorrow!"

It took awhile for Wilder to allow his hand to touch her. He'd spent 730 nights grinding Reason out of his system. Was he going to allow her feminine tears to dismantle his resolve and soften his heart? His fingers caressed her hair then her cheek. Her skin was still petal soft, she was wearing the same perfume she'd worn the night they made love, and she retained the magnetic allure that sucked him into temptation. But only fools were burned twice. He jerked back his hand. "There are a lot of people counting on your talents at the hospital. You'll let them all down if you leave."

"But," her voice grew small, "I don't want to be here when…" she couldn't say what she now feared.

"When what?"

She watched raindrops run down the windshield and said in a whisper, "When they kill you."

"Nobody's going to kill me," Wilder reassured.

"They killed Brendan and Merry. They'll kill you too."

"I'm not Brendan or Merry."

"*Are* you in the IRA?"

"Of course not!" he thundered. "Now stop asking me questions."

"OK, OK!" Reason winced. "I don't know how you managed to stay calm with those soldiers. I would have been kicking and screaming."

"You saw what happened when you mouthed-off to that jerk. I learned a long time ago it's useless to fight back when you're totally out-numbered. One smart word and they'd slap me in prison for assault and resisting arrest, and I can't be of much use behind bars."

"But why did they attack you? You hadn't done anything…had you?"

"You, more than anyone, ought to understand their motives, Mac." His voice hardened. "I'm an Irish Catholic."

She flinched at his rancor. "But how could they tell you're a Catholic?"

"The crown forces know everything about me. Because I'm Brendan and Merry's brother, I get hassled all the time. That was the third pair of shoes I've lost this month," he said with a cynical laugh.

"My God." Reason covered her eyes and ached to go home. "When those men were kicking you and making fun, I wanted to stop them from hurting you…I'm just so sorry I couldn't do anything to help you."

"That's funny coming from you, Mac. What's the difference between them tonight and you two years ago? Wasn't my crime the same both times?" Wilder reminded acidly. "Hell, I took a worse beating from you."

There was no communicating with his bitterness. Reason dabbed her eyes and started the car. "How do I get to your house from here?"

Neither spoke as Reason drove south of Belfast out the Malone Road past Christ Church College. In the rain it was hard to see, but even with limited visibility, she could see there were no rowhouses, no barracks, no tumble-down buildings. Large, detached houses with circle drive-ways and rose gardens graced quiet streets.

"I live on Grange Park Wood. Turn left at the next street. I'm in the last house all the way up the hill."

Reason veered left onto a sylvan street canopied in chestnuts and lush with rhododendrons. The broad lawns and woods and elegant homes reminded her of Connecticut. *If only this were Connecticut*, she moped. "I walked down to the New Lodge the other day. I can't believe you grew up there."

"And to think you fraternized with one of its filthy natives."

"I meant it's very sad."

Wilder stared out the window.

"I saw Tiger's Bay too. And I met a fellow from the Shankill. He got into a fight with some guys over in New Lodge while we were standing there. I about died…"

"Don't you have any sense?" Wilder barked. "What in the hell were you doing talking to a man from the Shankill? For that matter, you shouldn't be hanging around Tiger's Bay or the New Lodge."

"I didn't know he was from there, Wilder. I bumped into him, and he started talking to me. I don't even know where this Shankill place is."

"Keep it that way."

"What's wrong with it?"

"Would you walk through Central Park alone at night?"

"No."

"You don't walk through the Shankill day or night."

His reluctance to converse made Reason wonder why she bothered opening her mouth. Still she endured. "I heard you saying you work at the Gov."

"Yes. Here's where I live."

Hawthorns and holly hugged a wrought iron fence. A long, secluded driveway led to a two-story, red brick house with high gables and mullioned windows. Woodbine clung to the bricks and covered the chimneys, and five pristine rose gardens twisted here and there across the front lawn. The rounded front door was paneled in stained glass and flanked by brass lanterns.

"What a pretty place," Reason said. "Can I see the inside?"

"No. Thanks for the lift." Wilder eased out of the car.

"Let me help you," she jumped to assist.

"I'll manage."

"I could fix you some tea…"

"NO!"

"But…"

"I'm OK, Mac. Go home."

"I'm sorry those soldiers hurt you," she called as he walked away. "And I'm sorry I walked in on you at the pub. And Wilder, I'm very sorry about Merry."

"Goodnight."

"Maybe I'll see you around the Gov?"

"*Good-bye,* Reason."

"Wilder? Remember how you said you'd rather I hate you than forget you? Do you still feel that way?"

She struck a nerve. He strode back to her car. "Being remembered by you is about as appealing as being remembered by a hit man."

"Augh! I hate it when you're sarcastic."

"And you haven't changed a bit in two years."

"I didn't say a word!" She punched the dashboard. "I'm trying to get along with you, but you're determined to hate me."

"I *died* for loving you, Mac, and I'm only going to do that once."

"How could you die for loving me? It was only one day."

"Is that all it was?" That was like saying Pearl Harbor was only one day. "It only takes a second to shatter a world, Reason, but that doesn't matter anymore. I'm over you."

"My, haven't you become Dr. Heartless."

"You're right on that count, sweetheart. It took two years of hell before I gave up trying. But after you and Brendan, after Merry, I cut my own heart out and replaced it with something hard and cold." He tapped his chest. "I have a diamond in here, and there's nothing harder or colder than that."

Chills ran down Reason's spine. "Wilder, this is ludicrous. Why can't we act like adults and be friends?"

Wilder leaned back in the car with a scornful smirk. "A Wellworth-Howell be friends with a *taig?*" He clapped a hand to his jaw. "What would your mommy say?"

"I'm very sorry I called you that."

"You ought to be sorry. How can you sit there asking me to be your friend? Do you seriously expect me to pretend nothing happened two years ago?

"I saved your life! I fell in love with you!"

"No! You blew a hole through my life, Reason, or have you conveniently forgotten that part of the story?"

"I was hoping we could put that behind us."

"Haven't you ever regretted how you treated me? Your rejection was merciless."

"I can't repair the past, Wilder," Reason exclaimed in frustration.

"And I can't forgive it." He stormed away. "Maybe you and your chickenheart *should* go home tomorrow. I know I don't want you here."

There he was calling her a coward again. "You should be so lucky, O'Neill."

Later Wilder lay awake with his lies. It had been his torture and bliss to see Reason, he couldn't stand it if she had forgotten him, and he wanted to see her again. He had acted cold-hearted, but every second of the evening had been a struggle not to touch her as he had touched her before. He remembered every detail of her body, of their lovemaking, and to his bedevilment, he was still in love with her. But he refused to concede to his feelings after the last time when he spilled his heart all over himself and Reason passed him by. His passion beat for Ireland now. He vowed to distance himself from the woman he longed to reclaim. Reason, sweet Reason.

The rain clattered on like a symphony of hammers, and Wilder missed California. But he never considered going back, even when life in Belfast was hard. Reason had asked why he was here; because this was his home. He wouldn't forget his father's reaction when his last child announced he was leaving. Desmond turned grey with grief as another crevice broke through his heart. He refused to attend Merry's funeral and tried to talk Wilder out of attending as well. Wilder said he'd be gone a week. It had been a year. How could he walk away from everything Liam lived and died for, and now Merry and Brendan? How could he forsake his cousin again? Wilder had thought it would be uncomfortable seeing Kieran after so many years, but Kieran greeted him with wide-armed fraternity as though they had never parted. He had known for years Declan O'Neill would come home. And when Wilder met Kieran's young son, Declan Morris McCartan, he saw another lad growing up Catholic and hurtling headlong into the Troubles. Things had to change before Morris followed Liam's course. But it was Merry's funeral that cemented him to Belfast. Everything changed that June morning.

A Tricolour had draped Merry's coffin. A lone flutist played, children carried flowers, and scores of women and men embraced Wilder with sympathy and tears. Drizzle dripped from windy skies, yet hundreds of mourners braved the cold and trooped behind Wilder and Kieran and four other cousins hoisting Merry's casket up the Falls Road to Milltown. Glancing over his shoulder as he walked, Wilder had seen the marchers forging up the Falls like a battering ram. He hadn't been certain what propelled their steps, bereavement or belligerence, but their spirit was a formidable force; a spirit obsessed with its heroes and remembrance of death; a spirit that wouldn't submit. And Wilder had seen the troops and tanks surrounding the cortege like jackals. Two helicopters had hovered loudly and low; still the piper piped, the Tricolour flapped, and the force tramped on.

As the crowd marched into Milltown, Wilder couldn't miss the RUC station built beside the cemetery. With prying eyes and fine-tuned ears, it monitored West Belfast. Its oversized Union Jack unfurled in the wind like a heil to the British empire and a punch to the Irish. Bunkered behind a soaring metal wall, with cheerless slivers for windows and armed with spotlights, cameras and guns, the station could have been a prison. Wilder wondered who the prisoners were, the Brits within or the Irish without, and it was ironic to view the two opponents side by side; one alive behind bars and the other dead beyond bars. And he had decided the RUC kept watch over Milltown fearing the Irish Catholics might rise from the dead. If anyone could muster a rebellion beyond the grave, it would be the Fenians.

Milltown Cemetery. A jungle of headstones. Wilder had forgotten its distinctive disorganization. Hundreds upon hundreds of marble Madonnas, urns and Celtic crosses jutted skyward in chaotic rows squeezed into a grassy lot rising above the M1 motorway. Merry, like Brendan, had chosen to be buried in the family plot. Far back in the cemetery, it faced the republican monument where the IRA chronicled its dead in a grim roll of honor. Two hundred years of Irish republican names were carved into austere grey stone; names Wilder recognized as family and friends. He had raised his eyes to the hills above the Falls and prayed Merry's spirit would rest. In doing so he noticed the sleek Celtic cross made of rose marble marking a nearby grave. Its inscription shone in the rain.

Michael Patrick McGuinness

Bí mo leannán, is mo leannán sa amháin.

Saor Eire, grá mo chroí.

Wilder had wished the helicopters would cease for even ten seconds of silence to honor his sister, and to his amazement his wish had been granted. The helicopters vanished. Even the soldiers and police quietly, eerily receded. Looking down at the motorway, he saw a blue van parked at the foot of the cemetery. He assumed it was a curious tourist. But then he saw a black-hooded man in camouflage gear pop out of the back of the van. Up the hill he charged, and as he grew closer to the graveyard, he screamed, "Eat this, you Fenian fucking bastards!" Before anyone realized what was happening, the assailant pulled an automatic rifle out of his jacket and opened fire on the crowd.

Bedlam ensued. Where were the troops, the tanks, the police *now?* People crashed together in panic, some ducked behind the tombstones for shelter, others ran screaming through the cemetery. All the while the sniper shrieked obscenities and emptied his weapon on the helpless flock. Briefly the gunfire had ceased only to be replaced by two lobbed grenades that exploded amidst the dead and dying. Then the gunfire resumed, and after what seemed an eternity, the assassin retreated down the hill with a pack of hundreds on his trail. Over the fence he vaulted, into the van he dived, and off he was whisked down the M1 to safety.

Seven people were dead; scores were wounded. Ambulances crashed into the cemetery in droves. Screams pierced the wind, and horror blasted into Wilder. *Goddamn them,* he kept cursing as he tended the injured. *Goddamn them.* Who masterminded this ambush while the Army and RUC were suddenly and mysteriously absent? Later, as he and the priest finished the burial, Wilder pitched all hesitation into Merry's grave, and his heart crystallized with resolve. He had plodded into Milltown a Yank. He marched out a republican.

Protestants from the Ulster Liberation Force claimed responsibility for the shootings, but the gunman and his driver hadn't been found, and the police expended little effort to find them. There was a rumor the security forces had arranged the whole thing, but it wasn't investigated. The RUC denied allegations. Desmond O'Neill had hired dozens of lawyers, and each one hit the same walls of no comment, no cooperation. The RUC and Army would handle the matter. That was twelve months ago.

Wilder had then offered his services, not as a Provo, but as a physician. When summoned he would go to one safe house or another around Belfast to give care or counsel to republicans and their families. He was a marriage counselor, a mediator, a psychiatrist and bearer of solace, and in limited time with limited resources, he did what he could for men wounded on active service. He could suture lacerations, set fractures and stem certain gunshot wounds, but if a Volunteer was too badly injured for outpatient treatment, it was up to that person to seek care at a hospital. To ensure his own safety and the security of his patients, Wilder never requested a name or a reason for seeking medical care, and he didn't want to know who or what was going on in the movement. Over the months a rapport formed. Declan O'Neill, like his siblings before him, was dedicated and could be trusted.

And every time he encountered the crown forces he became more committed to doing his part. Since his arrival in Northern Ireland he had been harassed almost daily by the soldiers and police at checkpoints and on the street. Working at the Gov, being a physician, being an American gave him no remission. He was perceived as a taig like any other taig, and he was pegged by the security forces as the last bad seed of the O'Neills come home to sprout. But he wasn't like his siblings who loudly voiced their views. He lived quietly out the Malone and shunned all things political, giving the illusion he was neutral and uninvolved.

Uninvolved. The word stuck in Wilder's mind. He hadn't realized until tonight how uninvolved he was. With everything. For two years he'd allowed nothing to touch him. Then he saw Reason, and all the dangerous emotions awoke. Suddenly he was aware of the silence, the empty hours, the nights alone. He got out of bed and walked to the window. He stood watching the rain, thinking of Reason, how he'd loved her and hated her and missed her. And he wondered what would happen now that she was here.

Chapter Eight

Reason awoke to Fiona tapping at her door. "Reason love? There's a gentleman here to see you."

Wilder! Reason flew out of bed, brushed her hair and teeth, splashed on cologne and tied on her silk robe. She swept into the parlor to find Cain Cromwell seated on the sofa. But her eyes weren't long disappointed. Dressed in pale trousers and a sage linen shirt, he looked like an ad for Jamaican rum; cool, composed, confident.

"I'm sorry to wake you," he said, rising to his feet, "but I have an errand in County Down this morning. I thought maybe you'd like to come with me to see the country."

"I'd like that a lot. But how did you know where to find me?"

"Do you mind my having found you, Reason?"

She liked his smile; ingenuous and warm, a little shy. "Not at all."

"Are you related to Oliver Cromwell?" Reason asked as they drove south of Belfast.

"Probably, but what a vile relation to claim, especially here in Ireland."

"Why?"

"Haven't you heard? The old boy decimated the Irish in 1649."

"I knew he did a lot of damage in England, but what was he doing over here?"

"He came to crush 'the racially inferior Irish.' He and his armies slaughtered entire towns and cut the population of Ireland in half. He seized millions of acres of land and gave it to his English pals who set up a Protestant aristocracy, and then he declared Catholicism illegal and forced the Irish to become serfs on their own estates. No wonder his name's still a curse in Ireland."

"And what brought you to Ireland? Are you here to plunder or just to teach at Christ Church?" Reason teased.

"A little of both. My family owns land here…some poor Irishman's stolen estate no doubt. And then last summer I was offered the position at CC. But compared to England, I prefer living in Ireland."

"Really?"

"I'm the despair of my family you see. I fell in love with the wrong women, fought the wrong causes, adopted the wrong vices, and chose the wrong profession. I have three older brothers, all solicitors, all Tories, all pretentious pricks, and I'm the mad, bad son who hasn't the sense to conform. So I came to Belfast where misfits fit nicely. I keep an eye on the Cromwell estate and stay out of my family's way. It works out well for everyone."

"Don't you miss England?"

"Why would I when I'm in the Six Counties? Ireland beats an impassioned heart. People are hot-blooded and fighting for freedom here; so am I."

"How do you feel about the British Army being here?" Reason braved asking.

"It's way past time the Brits give Ireland back to the Irish," Cain replied sharply. But the subject made him uneasy and he was quick to change it. "Have you ever seen a prettier country?"

Reason gazed across emerald fields of tall grass and low brambles. Bluebells bloomed in profusion. She saw long-maned ponies, black and white cows, and clumps of black-faced, fuzzy sheep. In the distance the Mourne Mountains looked blue as Irish eyes, and beyond the blue, below billowing clouds, lay the sea.

"I've been in Manhattan for the last two years so this seems like paradise. I especially like those puffy sheep. They look like Q-Tips. What are all those yellow-flowering bushes? They're tangled on everything."

"Those are whin shrubs. You'll see them all over Ireland. We'll walk through a field of it this afternoon and you'll think you're in Hawaii because the flowers smell like coconuts. County Down is St. Patrick's country, you know. He's buried around here somewhere."

"Someone told me the other day that St. Patrick was English, is that true?"

Cain nodded. "The Englishman who brought Catholicism to Ireland only for other Englishmen to persecute Ireland for being Catholic."

"Say, do you by any chance know where the term 'taig' comes from?"

"I only know this because I have this comedian friend who makes jokes about Irish slang. It's from the Irish names Tadgh or Teague. The Protestants began using it as a derogatory term for the Irish natives." Cain directed Reason's attention to the right. "Look at those bluebells! They make the grass look purple. This is my favorite part of the island. One minute you're at the beach, the next in the Mournes, and in between are all these pastures the color of jade."

"Did you grow up in the country in England?"

"Yes, but it wasn't wide-open and rural like this. We had a few gardens and the obligatory horses for hunting, but we were so close to London I always felt like an arm of the city. I like County Down because I can drive for miles and see more sheep than cars."

"What errand do you have to run down here?"

"I bought a pair of Connemara ponies in Galway and they're arriving today. While I get them settled you can roam around My Lady's Leisure…that's the name of our estate. It's just beyond the mountains near the border. I hate to brag, but it's a glorious old place. It's up on a cliff above the Irish Sea, and it has gardens and woods and pastures and a grand view of the tides. I built the gardens myself…I'm terribly proud of them."

"My Lady's Leisure. What a romantic name."

"I have some of those Q-Tip sheep and a few cows and a goat, well, the estate is a small farm really. I think you'll enjoy it."

"You must show it off whenever you can."

Cain shook his head. "I rarely bring anyone down here. It's my retreat. Every artist needs one. But you're an artist and I wanted to show you how impressive the North of Ireland can be."

"You said you chose the wrong profession. Why doesn't your family approve of you being a professor of art?"

Cain viewed Reason uncertainly. "You have honest eyes, I like that," he complimented before deciding to tell the truth. "Up until a few years ago I practiced a different art form. By day I studied at Oxford, by night I was a thief. I could slip in and out of the tightest security and steal just about anything. My specialty was jewelry. Considering I was raised in a family of self-righteous lawyers, my genius for grand larceny amused me. I was a criminal to spite my father and brothers, and yes, it was terribly juvenile, but it was also terribly exciting, and I was the best."

"I'm surprised you aren't in prison."

"I broke in for the thrill not the treasure. I never kept the jewels. Returning them to their owners without getting caught was as challenging as stealing them in the first place."

"You broke in twice?"

"I told you, I was good. I'm not in Strangeways because my father found out about me a day before Scotland Yard, and he cut me a deal. He asked that I be allowed to do intelligence work for the British Government in return for no prosecution. I didn't like the idea of prison, so naturally I agreed."

"What sort of intelligence work did you do?"

"Surveillance on Arabs," Cain replied, looking away. "But there's no fun in crime when it's legal. After finishing my doctorate, I applied for a position at CC and promised to retire my sticky fingers."

"And are you retired?"

"I'm not a thief anymore, if that's what you mean."

"Do you still work for British Intelligence?"

Cain pointed ahead. "Here we are. Welcome to Eden."

Thirty five miles south of Belfast, perched on a chalky cliff, My Lady's Leisure was one of the few places in Ireland that hadn't been deforested.

Ensconced in pine, the estate was its own realm. The moment Cain drove under the wooded gateway, Reason felt worlds away from Belfast. Nature and serenity dominated the gravel road that wound up the hill to the manor; a three-story Georgian mansion of grey brick. Six chimneys swallowed in woodbine capped the hip roof. Pink roses, wildly blooming, rimmed the manor's first floor and spilled over the doorway.

Cain parked in front of the unassuming entry; a pair of rosewood doors with a beveled fanlight. "So? What do you think?" he turned to Reason, unable to hide his pleasure.

She considered the gardens and pastures. Fertile earth. Long, silken grass. Birds only birds to hear, and yes, she smelled the sea. Ireland's Eden. "Oh, Cain, it's wonderful."

"The house has fifty rooms and every one of them is a work of art. Come on, I'll give you the grand tour."

Hopping from the car, Reason heard the sheep and roosters, the wind off the sea...and *Bap, Bap, Bap.* "I thought we were away from all that," she grimaced up at the helicopter.

"You really are new here, aren't you, love? Do you like this sculpture? I call it *Unforgiven.*"

The bronze sculpture resembled a train wreck; jagged, twisted metal with dangling parts. A closer look revealed its inscription: **The world's depravities wrap around us and we wonder, is this a reflection or a vision?**

Reason expected a house full of servants and priceless possessions. She stepped into a house of empty rooms. No tables, no chairs, no paintings; nothing but marble floors, bare walls, and pediment doorways. Draperies had been stripped from the windows, leaving naked glass and unobstructed views of the estate's grounds. While there was electricity, there were few modern comforts. But the manor wasn't dour, at least not when Cain came home. He introduced Reason to the house with such affection, the rooms radiated his spirit. Beginning with the year 1700, he explained where every inch of wood, every square of marble, every panel of glass originated, and who had lived on the estate over the years.

"I sent most of the furnishings home to England," he said as he guided Reason into a two-story library with hundreds of books and no chairs. "Furniture diminishes the beauty of these rooms. When I want to read, I sit on the stairs or up against the wall. Notice the way that oak banister curves and how those mahogany walls tell a tale of two hundred years. And see how the hawthorns outside the window cast shadows on the floor? Now here is art as art should be; unadorned. I consider the house, not what's in it, the masterpiece."

Reason wholeheartedly agreed as she looked around. Prisms and crystals were hung in high places, casting rainbows across the walls. Sextants and compasses and maps and globes were tucked in the corners. "You have a telescope." She pointed up the library stairs.

"I don't get to use it much. The skies are cloudy so often, I sometimes wonder if heaven still exists above Ireland."

"Oh, but just think how much more you appreciate the stars when you do see them. It makes them all the more special."

"Aha! You're an optimist!"

"Is that bad?"

"It's good. Maybe you'll find something redeeming about me. I'm such a wayward man."

"I prefer wayward men," Reason smiled. This off-center man and his off-center world intrigued her. He lived without furnishings but was an aristocrat. He exalted nature but created surreal metal sculptures. He was confident yet self-effacing. His name promised infamy while he appeared to tread gently, and his contradictions made him the more appealing.

"Pop up the stairs and go through that door in the paneling. You see it up there? It's a secret passageway in and out of the master bedroom."

Into the wall and up a slim spiral staircase Reason climbed. "Oh wow!" Stepping into the suite, her feet sank into soft carpets. The room had a trio of floor-to-ceiling windows overlooking the sea. Two of the windows flanked a marble fireplace; the third window was really French doors that opened onto a balcony. A large four-poster bed piled deep in down dominated the room. Above the bed the ceiling was painted with an erotic scene of naked nymphs frolicking with satyrs.

"I thought the estate deserved at least one room that lived up to its name," Cain joined Reason in his bedroom. "When I entertain at My Lady's Leisure, I entertain here."

Reason looked at the view of the sea, the ceiling, the fireplace and bed. "I know I wouldn't mind being entertained here."

Cain met her eyes briefly. What would she be like? He appeared vexed to be attracted to her and pointed to the door. "I'll show you the gardens."

While Cain attended his ponies, Reason hiked up the hill to a walled garden. Seven-foot walls sheltered two hundred roses. There were bird-baths and fountains and more of Cain's ponderous sculptures. The walls were so high, Reason could see nothing but sky above them. She could hear sheep and cows and singing birds, but the helicopter had gone. Soaking up the tranquillity, she leaned back and welcomed the flood of the sun.

"How do you like my retreat?" Cain joined her.

"I could sit here all day, it's so peaceful. You really built all this?"

"Every stone, every rose. I've been coming to My Lady's Leisure every summer since I was eighteen, and now fifteen years later the place is complete."

"It's so romantic in here, like a place Byron would have had a tryst with one of his secret lovers."

"You like Byron? Me too." Cain wandered amidst his roses, checking the stems, brushing the leaves, caressing the buds. He pretended to be interested in the plants, but with each soft petal he stroked he imagined illicit trysts. With Reason. Button by button she would divest him and sink to her knees in the sun, up against the wall he would have her... "You know, I think I'm going to enjoy making art with you."

"You'd better," she laughed, "we'll be making it for months."

"Did you know the Victorians gave symbolic meanings to flowers? Like these camellias mean, 'Go away! I don't love you.' And these lilies say, 'It's heaven to be with you.'"

"And what do those carnations say?"

Cain gathered a handful of carnations and took them over to Reason, giving them to her color by color. "Red means, 'I burn for you.' Pink means, 'I can't get you off my mind.' And white means, 'You're beautiful and sweet.'" For a moment he stared down into her face and she smiled up at him in the golden sun. If she were any other woman, he'd kiss her. But this alliance was trouble begging to happen. In silence he turned away. "There's a path behind the manor that leads down to the beach. Let's walk along the shore before heading back to Belfast."

"Oh, I hate to think of leaving."

"You'll be back. I do all my artwork down here."

"Making art in a garden with two hundred roses," Reason sighed, taking a last look around. "I'll look forward to it."

Cain thought the same thing but he didn't say it. He tossed Reason another red carnation and led the way down to the sea.

"Would you like to drive back to Belfast through Armagh?" Cain suggested as they left the estate. "It has beautiful cathedrals, and if we go a little into the South, I can show you a Celtic dolmen…or maybe you want to get home."

"Oh no, I'm enjoying this," Reason said. Settling back in her seat she watched Ireland roll by. Small towns with stone churches, brambly hedgerows and sheep, fields of bluebells, fields of buttercups…then a helicopter landed and two dozen soldiers jumped out, trampling the flowers, scattering the sheep. Such a paradox this country of beauty and Brits. She watched the soldiers disappear into the woods, and she was thinking about Wilder and the previous night. How heavenly to have seen him and how hellish it became. She wondered if he was hurt, and would she see him soon. It was amazing that he was here, and she was here. Wilder had changed but his effect on Reason hadn't. One look and she was in love, but this time she wasn't afraid. One look and she remembered his skin, his scent, his kiss, his sex, and she wanted to know him again. She laughed at the thought, recalling Wilder's cold eyes. All she'd know of his passion was hatred.

"I should warn you about the checkpoint," Cain said as they drove into Armagh and neared the border. "It may be hard for you to take."

"Why? Can't you just drive from North to South?"

"Well, there are some unauthorized crossings into the Republic, but if England has its way, one day the periphery of the North will be fortified."

"Fortified?" Reason chuckled, thinking Cain was kidding.

"There are guards and gates at the border on all the main routes into the South, and the ones on the tourist track are tame. The Brits keep the truth hidden in the countryside, off the motorways. But out here is where the truth is told, where the war lives. And the deeper into the North you go the meaner the scenery gets."

Reason envisioned a border checkpoint to be like a weighing station for trucks on an American interstate; a little house with a little gate where people had to stop before passing through. But then she saw what Cain meant. Towering walls of corrugated metal ran as far as she could see in either direction over the grassy terrain, and there was a watch-tower that rivaled those along the Berlin wall; fortified high in the air, caged and armed, ready to shoot to kill. A traffic light allowed one car at a time to pass; other cars waited in line. A sign read, "**Security Forces regret any inconvenience or delay. Blame The Terrorists.**"

"But it's England's checkpoint, they built it," Reason didn't understand. "There'd be no inconvenience if Ireland wasn't partitioned." She gaped around at a loss. "Why are the walls here? Who are they keeping in, who are they keeping out?"

"The walls are what it takes to keep Ulster British. They're fortified because the IRA is determined to blow them down."

It was Cain's turn to enter the checkpoint. He had to drive slowly through the walls and over speed bumps. Sandbags lined the route; a route at all times in view of the green-glassed tower. Once inside, Reason could see nothing but grey walls and white cameras and barbed wire atop the walls, and because the walls were staggered, she couldn't see what lay ahead except more walls. It was like being in a metal maze; narrow and claustro-phobic. Finally, two soldiers appeared below the watchtower. One kept his rifle focused on the windshield. The other checked Cain's identification. Hearing Cain's compatriot accent, the soldier smiled and was polite. And he acted like being in this fabricated cage was normal.

"Oh sure, the guard was friendly," Cain said when they were cleared to pass. "I'm English, 'one of them.' But if I'd been Irish, they'd have pulled me from my car and treated me like a 'fucking, Fenian foreigner.'"

Too well Reason knew that scene. "I just can't believe this is happening here. I mean, when I think about England and Ireland it's certainly not this." She looked back at the walls, built like a dam. They cut in half a land, a people, and any semblance of love between the North and her Southern twin.

"The border is nothing but fuel for the Troubles. The IRA blasts one checkpoint after another. Unarmed men have been shot by soldiers while crossing from the South to the North, and it's open season on Provos down here." Cain glimpsed across at Reason, "These are the killing fields."

She turned to see the checkpoint receding. On the wall between the two lands someone had painted **IRISH OUT** in red, white and blue. "Irish Out," Reason shook her head sadly. "In Ireland."

"I told you those checkpoints are rough. They make you feel like a strangling bird."

"Or a tangled bird," Reason said softly. She thought of Wilder rushing into the river to save the waxwing, and the way he'd looked last night on the ground in the rain with the Brits. The same defiant face, the same passionate spirit determined to be brave. But the odds were against him, this time the river knew him, and the river had arms. "It's just that when I came here I had no idea things were so brutal. Suddenly I'm really homesick. And I miss my old friend."

"You won't be homesick for long, love." Cain gave her a smile. "I'm your new friend. You'll like me."

Reason smiled. But he wasn't who she wanted to see.

*   *   *   *   *   *

"It's Saturday, Declan. Don't you ever take a day off?" Kieran had come to the Gov to see his cousin's new office; a storage room with a metal desk and two folding chairs squeezed between peeling green walls.

"I'm always behind on my paperwork."

"A regular palace you have here, mate," Kieran joked.

"A far cry from Beverly Hills, isn't it? But I needed a place close to the critical care ward. Was there something you wanted?"

"Can you keep Morris next Friday? I'm going out of town on business." Provisional business he meant.

"No problem. We'll watch the World Cup."

"Thanks." Kieran swung Wilder a fond punch. "Sometimes I still can't believe you and I are together again."

"I'll be finished here in a second. Want to shoot over to the pub for a pint?"

"Not wise, Dec. Your being seen at Albie's last night was bad enough. I can't believe you hung around there so long before taking care of that lad's leg."

"What did you want me to do? Stand on the Falls with my medical gear and tell the cops I was waiting to patch up the sniper they shot? I did what I was told. The woman who contacted me said to go to Albie's and wait. I was far more worried about taking care of the gunshot wound than I was about being seen playing snooker with a few locals."

"I know. But for your own safety you should keep a low profile around West Belfast and not be seen socializing much with me. Guilt by friendship is enough to bury you, Declan."

"Everyone knows you're my cousin, and being Bren and Merry's brother I was guilty before I got here. If someone's going to shoot me, they'll shoot me."

"Nice life we lead, eh? I couldn't join you anyway. I'm meeting Jillie for a run. Christ, I hate jogging."

"That smile of hers talked you into it I'll bet."

"It wasn't her smile, Dec," Kieran said with a laugh.

"Pure sex, isn't she?"

"I've never had it so good. But if you mind me seeing her…I mean, you and she have been going at it awhile."

"I don't mind," Wilder insisted. "I won't be seeing her anymore."

"But I thought you and she…oh, I get it. You still have the Yank in your blood."

"I don't give a damn about Reason," Wilder bristled. "I told her to stay out of my life…what did you think of her? She looks good, doesn't she?"

"Nice body, sweet smile, but she's just another powderpuff, Brit-loving Yank who hasn't a clue what's going on in the Six Counties. You're too good for her, Declan. Too bad she showed up here in the first place."

"Yeah," Wilder concurred wryly, "of all my rotten luck."

Arriving home Saturday evening Wilder realized someone had bypassed his alarm and broken into his house. Nothing was missing, but everything had been touched. His medical journals and books were thrown on the floor, his closets were open, his drawers had been searched. And a sweet odor hung in the air. Patchouli. His worst fear curled along his backbone. He had been stopped on the Falls Road last night. Had he been visited by the RUC today?

It was understood in the Six Counties that the Royal Ulster Constabulary was a Protestant police force. While it insisted Catholics were free to join, few Catholics did. Its name said it all; the *Royal, Ulster,* Constabulary. The officers were required to swear allegiance to the British Queen. The British Anthem was played at RUC functions, and the Union Jack waved above RUC barracks. Many of its members were loyalists with an anti-nationalist bent, and there was nothing Irish, nothing Catholic about it.

The RUC had a reputation for covert surveillance and brutality, and the last thing Wilder wanted was to be arrested and interrogated. He was just a physician doing his job. He'd committed no crime other than aiding republicans injured in the line of duty. He laughed at the notion, knowing the truth. Aiding the IRA was a capital offense guaranteeing years in prison. He promised himself to be more cautious.

Chapter Nine

Declan and Kieran were Jillie's favorite topic Monday morning. "Och, Reason, yesterday was brilliant. We went to Decky's cousin's wedding. There was an Irish band, Declan bought everyone champagne, and the *craic* was fantastic."

"'Crack?' You mean crack cocaine?"

Jillie staggered with mirth. "Lord love us, no. *Craic* is Irish. It means good conversation. Did Decky find you Friday night by the way? He was upset we'd let you leave Albie's alone." She eyed Reason with envy. "What on earth did you do to him to make him so chivalrous?"

"I have no idea." Reason had sworn to herself she wouldn't pry into Jillie's affairs, still she had to know, "How long have you and Declan been going out?"

"About a year. Before I fell for Kieran, he and I would get together every night…we were *very* creative in finding ways to amuse each other," Jillie winked with bad intent. "Maybe you ought to give him a whirl. He's a dream machine on the waterbed. But I'll warn you, he has this thing for poor sex."

Reason was sorry she'd asked but couldn't resist, "'Poor sex?'"

"You know doing the business outdoors. He keeps trying to convince me making love in long grass would be heaven. When he first suggested it I thought he meant smoking grass, so I turned up one night with a few joints. Turns out he literally meant long grass, like cows eat! And then he started talking up some sort of rain, happy rain or something like that. Well, I curtailed that notion pronto. Gillian Paradise will do many, many things in bed, but nothing outdoors. I'd feel like a peasant!"

"Long, soft grass and tappy rain," Reason said. "Has he seduced you in the back seat of a Rolls Royce?" She was kidding.

"That's exactly what he did in a traffic jam in London last winter. Now how did you know he'd do something like that?"

"He just looks like a back seat sort of guy." Reason turned to her sketches and lined up her pencils in meticulous order. "How did you meet him and Kieran anyway?"

"Oopf!" Jillie gave her forehead a knock. "Now there was a day. It was last summer. I'd only been here a few weeks, and I was half-daft with infants. I was tending my neighbor's two babies and I didn't know I wasn't supposed to flush their nappies down the loo. My plumbing backed up from here to New York. The little ones were screaming, I couldn't find their spare nappies or their bottles, and I was desperate for a plumber. So I hoisted one baby under each arm and marched up the Falls to a pub near the Gov. I figured the best place to find a handy man on a hot day was on the other end of a Guinness. I walked right in with two buck-naked, bawling babies and put it to the boys, 'Is there a man around here to help me?' That's when Decky and Kieran came into my life. Kieran knew about plumbing and Decky knew about babies. I took them both home with me, fixed them a meal, and the rest is erotically ever after."

"How romantic," Reason commented glumly, thinking this was her comeuppance for having been cruel to Wilder. "Speaking of romantic, I met Cain Cromwell. He's the mosaic man."

"Och, magic! We'll be seeing a lot of him then. That's happy news."

"Isn't it? I can see why you had a crush on him." Reason checked the time. "I'm due at a meeting in the ER. Send those revised drafts down to neuro-trauma and set up a meeting with pathology, would you please?"

"Is it true you're hiring Ruairi McKee?" Jillie called after Reason.

"Yes."

"Did you know he's Kieran's cousin? Belfast is such a small world."

Reason spotted Wilder in the emergency room and waved to catch his attention.

"Oh, great," he grumbled. "Just when I thought the day couldn't get worse." He glanced up then back down at his charts. "I'm busy, Mac."

"Good morning to you too, Dr. O'Neill. Why didn't you tell me Ruairi McKee is your cousin?"

"He isn't my cousin. He's Kieran's cousin."

"Even so, isn't it odd that I'm here in Belfast while you're here, working where you work, and staying with your cousin's cousin?"

"That's right, you're staying with the McKees. Poor Fiona and Ruairi."

"Can't you be nice for one minute?"

"I told you I'm busy." But Wilder laid aside his pen and tapped his watch. "You have one minute. It's a pleasure to see you, Miss McGuinness. Fine weather we're having. What can I do for you?" he put to her insolently.

"I want to know if you have something to do with my being in Belfast. Do you?"

"*Me?*" Wilder scoffed. "Why would I want *you* here?"

"Did you know I was coming?"

"If I'd known, do you think I'd still be in Ireland?"

"I'm supposed to believe this is some sort of coincidence?"

"Believe whatever you like, Mac, but I had nothing to do with it."

She finally noticed. "What happened to your beard? You look almost civilized."

"I shaved it off."

"Why?"

"Because you didn't like it," Wilder answered tongue-in-cheek even though it was the truth. And after his encounter with the police, he preferred to change his appearance. "I hear I have you to thank for my spacious new office."

"Don't you dare complain, Wilder. That was supposed to be my store room. Dr. Thunder asked me if I would give it to you, and being terribly generous, I did. You're lucky I didn't have him stick you in the boiler room."

"I wasn't complaining. I'm grateful for an inch of privacy in this pandemonium. Thank you for helping me out. But I know the truth behind this story, Mac. You let me have the room because it's right down the hall from your office and you want to be near me."

"I see you still think you're cute."

"I see you still think I'm cute," Wilder smiled. "Your minute is up and I'm due in the OR."

"Wilder…" Reason snagged his sleeve.

"That's Dr. O'Neill to you."

"I was just wondering if you're all right after Friday night."

"You mean after being with you?"

"You know what I mean."

"Of course I'm all right. Don't mention it again."

Chapter Ten

Wilder had had a grueling Thursday. Trudging up the stairs, he turned right towards Reason's office instead of left to his own. He hoped Jillie hadn't gone home. Her warm Irish smile would brighten the day.

"Is Jillie around?" Wilder poked his head through the door to Reason's office and was surprised to find his friend sitting with his feet crossed atop Reason's desk. "What are you doing here? You hate hospitals."

He sported the *Westside Story* look; plain white t-shirt rolled up over his biceps, blue jeans cuffed over bare ankles and black Converse shoes. He was folding origami birds out of Reason's tracing paper.

"Jillie's long gone, sport." Cain held up a bird and pretended it was flying over the desk then crashed it down on its beak. "That was a sea gull diving into the ocean," he explained, smoothing the squashed bill.

"Where's Reason?"

"Down in radiology."

"You aren't waiting for her, are you?"

"As a matter of fact," Cain flung three paper cranes into the air, "I am."

Wilder's reaction was immediate. "Aw hell, Cain, you did it, didn't you? You couldn't stand it. You had to come up here and meet her."

"It wasn't like that. I'm the Gov's new artist and Reason's my fearless leader. I only met her last week."

"Oh yeah. I heard you won the competition. Congratulations. Wait, that means you'll be working with her. Swell."

"And that's all we'll be doing, Wilder, is working. I promise."

"Hey, did you check my house? I told you someone broke in the other night. Were there any bugs?"

"No. The place is clean. Whoever was there just wanted a look around."

"Who do you think it was? The ULF, the RUC?"

"Don't go getting all paranoid," Cain said with a shrug. "It was probably just a punk looking for something to steal."

"No punk could bypass that alarm. This is how it began for Bren and Merry…" Wilder shuddered. He didn't want to think about what could happen. "Nice flowers." He referred to the pink irises in a vase on the desk.

"They're from my garden. I'll plant you some this fall if you'd like." Cain folded another origami bird. "Here's a skylark…'Hail to thee blithe spirit.' Splat!" He sent it winging off the edge of the desk.

"You're bringing Reason flowers and you just met her?"

Cain glimpsed up sheepishly. "I'm trying to make a good impression." He fashioned another paper creature and proclaimed it a blue-footed booby. "You know, you had me believing she was a bitch, but she's nice. You also failed to mention how pretty she is."

"Don't go getting ideas, Cromwell, she's not the woman for you."

Cain batted the booby between his palms then crushed it with a clap. "Why? You don't want her."

"You've got that right, ace. But I don't want you wanting her either. Who's side are you on anyway? You saw what that woman did to me."

"Will you relax? I have no intention of getting involved with her. But the art competition was announced months ago, before Reason came over here, and you know how much this project means to me. I won't give it up just because it means working with your old flame."

"I'm not asking you to give up the mural. I'm just asking you to keep your distance from Lady MacBeth."

"I will, I will," Cain laughed.

"It's not that I'm jealous. I mean, I don't give a rip about her. It's just that I know what she's like. She gets off on making men want her. She'll turn you on then tear your heart out. I'd hate to see you get hurt, and I sure as hell don't want her coming between us."

"Don't worry, she won't. But maybe one night with her wouldn't be so bad."

Wilder knocked his palm to his head. "She's already started on you!"

"Hey, what do you expect? I'm a healthy man and she's a beautiful woman. What's the big deal, Wilder? I'm just wondering how she'd be, that's all."

"She's a cold fish."

"She doesn't seem cold to me."

"How would you know if you just met her?"

"I took her to My Lady's Leisure last Saturday…we had the best time. Tonight I'm taking her to my class at CC." Cain looked guilty again. "Strictly business."

"Look, Cain. Either you're friends with me or you're friends with her, but you can't be both. Your seeing her outside of work is fraternizing with the enemy to me, and it's suicide to you. It's your call."

Cain rolled his eyes at Wilder's inflexibility. "She's not worth risking our friendship, Wilder. I won't touch her. I swear."

"There are plenty of other good-looking women here at the Gov."

"Yeah, I know. Hey, wait until you see my mural. It's going to rival a Chagall."

"You're a genius, Cromwell, of course it will. Well, if Jillie's gone, I guess I'll head home."

"Shall I tell Reason you were here?"

"Why?" Wilder sounded perturbed. "I didn't come to see her."

"Of course you didn't," Cain made fun and folded another bird. "Look, Wilder, it's a vulture."

"Leave that one for Reason."

Wilder found Reason and several radiology technicians discussing the CAT scanner.

"May I speak to you a second?" He didn't give her a choice and pulled her aside. "Cain Cromwell is up in your office."

"Is he here already? Tell him I'll be right up."

"I'm not your messenger."

"Why are you looking so rattled?" Reason smoothed and straightened Wilder's necktie. "You're not jealous, are you, Wilder?"

"You wish. Cain's a good friend of mine, and I hear he's going to be working with you. Don't pull any of your crap on him, Reason. He's a decent man, and he's fragile." Wilder was adamant. "Don't you dare hurt him."

Seeing Wilder perceived her as some sort of monster, Reason was insulted. And she now understood why Cain had said she didn't look like a 'blood-sucking witch.' "He knows all about us, doesn't he? Oh, I can just imagine what you've told him. You are such a jerk! What do you mean Cain's fragile?"

"Just keep your claws out of him, Mac."

Reason held up her short, manicured fingernails. "Perhaps you'd prefer my fist in your eye?"

Wilder laughed at her. "Cheerio, Mac." He pushed out of radiology just as Bernard Thunder and the Chairman of the Board walked in.

"Ah, Declan, here you are," Bernard acknowledged Wilder with a clap on the back. "We've been looking everywhere for you and Miss...why there she is! You two have heard the news then?" He ushered Wilder back to Reason's side. "Well? What do you two think of the plan?"

Wilder and Reason traded a blank expression. "Plan?"

"About the new wing, about the new wing," the Chairman spoke up, thrusting forward his fingers to Reason. "I'm Hunter Cromwell, Chairman of the Grosvenor's Board. I've met my good friend Declan here, but not our pretty little architect. Pleased to meet you, pleased indeed."

"I'm pleased to meet you too, but what about the new wing?" Reason questioned the distinctive gentleman.

"Then you don't know? Didn't I tell you?" Hunter turned to Dr. Thunder, "I told you they hadn't heard. Reason, the Board and I have chosen Dr. O'Neill here to be the newest member of our design team.

"*What?*" Reason and Wilder exclaimed in one shout.

"I knew you'd both be pleased. Because of your expertise in cardiology, because you're so sharp and up to date, and because your father is the new wing's patron," Hunter addressed Wilder, "you're to be Reason's liaison to the medical staff…"

"What do you mean *his father?*" Reason interrupted in shock.

"You didn't know Sumner Steed is our patron? Wake up, Miss McGuinness, wake up!" Hunter sniped, not appreciating being interrupted. "Where was I? Ah yes, we want to make sure we build the best equipped, most modern and functional, not to mention beautiful new wing in Ulster." He exuded perfect-toothed grins. "We knew you two Yanks would enjoy working together on such a meaningful, marvelous project."

"I'm a surgeon not some idiot designer," Wilder protested. "I'm way too busy to be screwing around with Frank Lloyd Wrong here."

"*Screwing around?*" Bernard Thunder flinched. "Declan, our new wing is serious business. As you well know we're Belfast's busiest hospital. And surely you're aware of how desperately we need more space. We're only requesting a few hours a week."

"Yes, I know, but…"

"I can't work with him!" Reason joined the debate. "He knows nothing about design, nothing about construction, nothing at all. He's a goof and he'll get in my way."

"Oh, and I suppose you know everything about medicine, huh, Mac?" Wilder countered hotly.

"Stop it! You sound like two-year olds!" Hunter snarled. "I thought you two would be thrilled to work together. This is non-negotiable. I've told you the reasons for choosing you, Declan, you're a top-drawer surgeon, and our choice of you as our medical liaison seems damn sensible to me. You two wouldn't want to compromise your jobs just because you refused to cooperate, would you?"

"No," they muttered.

"Good, good. Declan old man, you're part of our team then." Hunter pumped Wilder's and Reason's hands again. "Nice finally meeting you, Reason. I'll be back in Belfast next Friday morning. I want preliminary sketches, an updated budget and a construction schedule on my desk by ten."

Long-limbed and lean at fifty eight years, with wavy chestnut hair brushed back off his high forehead, Hunter Cromwell carried himself with potency and pomp; shoulders back, chin up, brown eyes peering down his nose. Being a lawyer, his smile was trained to appear on command, and his forceful voice blandished uppercrust English. A high-boned face with a sharp nose and pouty lips gave him a princely air. He thought he resembled Laurence Olivier, and being so impressed with his looks, he behaved like a Hollywood heartthrob; everywhere he went he expected an audience. Without an ounce of fat padding his middle, in his chic, hand-tailored clothes, he was hale and fit; the portrait of success and self-satisfaction.

"Mr. Cromwell, you're Cain's father, aren't you?"

"Hunter, call me Hunter. Cain's my youngest boy. What's he done this time?"

"Nothing. I'll bet you're proud of him."

"Why?"

"For being selected as our artist in residence."

"Oh that. He'd better do a damn good job if he's going to put the Cromwell name on it." Hunter gave his lapels a jerk and shoved out the exit.

"And you said you had nothing to do with my being here!" Reason railed the instant the doors closed behind Bernard and Hunter.

"It was my father's bright idea, not mine," Wilder defended. "For some insane reason he thought I'd like to see you again."

"But how can your father be the Gov's patron? The funds for the new wing were donated by a company called *Sonas Ort* in Manhattan. Isn't *Sonas Ort* a strange name?"

Wilder shot Reason a look like she knew nothing at all. "If you spoke Irish, you'd know it means 'happiness to you.' *Sonas Ort* is my father's non-profit organization to aid the Six Counties. They donated $20 million to enlarge the Gov and requested Morrissey and Yeats be given the architectural contract with you serving as one of the architects. Then old Des arranged for you to stay with Fiona."

"You said you didn't know I was coming!"

"I didn't! The first I heard about your involvement in this was the article in the newspaper last week, and by then you were already here. Will you quit glaring at me? I'm not any happier about this than you are. I'd like to throttle my dad."

"Why did he want me here?"

"He thinks I have a death wish. And in his mad mind old Des thinks you'll lure me away from Ireland and save my life, again."

"Oh, he is insane. And here I thought it was my shining young talent that won me this job," Reason said, disappointed.

"If your bosses didn't think you could handle it, Reas, they never would have sent you," Wilder encouraged, sounding surprisingly nice. "But this is never going to work. I'm in the OR for hours, then I have my rounds and paperwork…I spend eighteen hours a day here as it is."

"Trust me, Wilder, I won't prevail upon you. I need your advice like I need a fork in my eye. But there's nothing I can do to change things. As Chairman, Hunter controls the funds for the project and that makes him my boss. You can complain to anyone you please, but whatever you do, will you at least be tactful? Please don't screw this up for me."

"Relax, Mac," Wilder smirked, "my lips are sealed."

"You're a monster!" she exclaimed with a sour smile, and thinking of Hunter's strutting manner, simpered, "I think Hunter looks like Liberace, don't you?"

"He's a bastard."

"Well, thank you for your eloquent opinion, Dr. O'Neill." Reason's hands flew to her hips and she stared Wilder in the eye. "You know, *Declan,* you get on my case for being biased, but you're just as bad. Not all Englishmen are bastards. Is Cain a bastard?"

"Of course not, but he isn't like his father. Reason, Hunter Cromwell is part of Ireland's 'glorious' British machine, and every loyalist politician in Belfast sucks up to him. He's a bigot, he's mean, and he's dangerous. Watch your back around him."

"You don't have to like Hunter's politics to appreciate what he's doing for the Gov and the community."

"What's he doing besides spending my father's money?" It irked Wilder just thinking about it. "He's such a hypocrite. He knows all about Bren and Merry, calls them 'murdering scum' Cain tells me. And when my dad was trying to get information on Merry's death last summer, H.C. was the first to denounce him. He got on the BBC and called my dad 'a blathering loony.' But when it came down to accepting my father's money, suddenly the O'Neills were Hunter's best friends."

"I'm sure he's not all bad, Wilder."

"You're only siding with Hunter because you're hot for his son."

"I'm not siding with anybody…and I'm not hot! I knew working with you would be impossible."

"Do you realize this arrangement means I can reject any or all of your designs?" Wilder taunted. "I can make your life hell."

"Any design you reject will be because you and the other team members gave me bad advice. Just tell me what you want and you'll get it."

"Right now I want to go home. It's been a long day."

"Hasn't it though." Reason gathered her sketchbooks and pencils. "Start thinking about operating room traffic flow and what sort of space you and the other surgeons would like to work in. And consider where you want the new lab and X-ray in relation to the OR and think about…"

"I'm too tired to think about that tonight, Mac. I'll catch you tomorrow and we can coordinate our schedules."

"Fine. Oh no! I'm late for my date with Cain." Reason shot to the door.

"What do you mean 'date?' I thought it was work."

"Goodnight, Wilder."

"*Declan!* Get it right, would you?" he mouthed sullenly, thinking Reason didn't need to be so bloody eager to join Cain Cromwell.

"I thought you'd like to see the city centre before we go to my class." Cain opened the front doors of the Gov for Reason. "The rain has stopped for now so we can walk. Straight down the Falls Road and you're in the heart of Belfast."

"Sounds good. Does it always rain this much here?"

"Sadly the North is no friend of the sun's." Like he wasn't sure what to do with them, Cain sunk his hands in his pockets. He kicked a stone along the sidewalk as he walked. And he kept stealing sidelong glances at Reason. "How is the Gov's addition coming along?"

"We're working night and day to get the project rolling, but no matter how fast my associates and I work, the Board keeps pressuring us to get the construction started. Hey, why didn't you tell me your father is Chairman of the Board?"

"I want you to like me," Cain said simply.

Belfast's city centre was a wheel of cobbled streets fanning from a large city hall. Broad streets and sidewalks entwined with no discernible order and were jammed with people frequenting a wide array of shops. Some of the stores were modern, some succumbed to time, melting down brick by brick, but most buildings stood staunchly reminiscent of the early 1900's; red-brick Georgian facades with gargoyles and stone faces leering over the roofs.

"To me Belfast looks like every old city in Europe. But it does have something unique and that's why I brought you down here." Cain led Reason through the crowds, down a cobbled tunnel through a brick wall. He continued winding her through the congestion until they came to an old church across from the docks. "Well?" he finally stopped and smiled expectantly at Reason.

"Well, what?"

"Don't you see it?"

She stared around. She saw the church snarled in ivy. She saw Belfast Lough, the shipyards, and a Victorian bridge across the River Lagan. "I'm not sure what I'm supposed to see." Cain tilted her chin skyward. "Oh wow!" Three copper sailboats with billowing masts seemed to float towards the Irish Sea. With each gust of wind, the sails flipped and rocked like a sloop under sail. "Did you make that?" Reason cried.

"I wish. See how it plays in the wind? It's mounted on springs. Isn't it great?" Cain motioned her over to the side of the church and scraped aside the vines. "It was made by a sailor named Michael Patrick McGuinness. Who knows, maybe he's your long lost relative."

"Maybe." For once Reason didn't take exception at an Irish connection.

"Michael Patrick is such a strong name. Sounds brave and proud…and cheerful, very cheerful."

"What's the name of this church?"

"The Laganside Church of Ireland; one of the oldest churches in Belfast."

In a sudden gust the rain resumed, and Reason raced around to the church's front doors. "Let's go inside."

"Some other time, love. I'll be late for my class." Cain captured Reason's fingers only long enough to pull her into a run. "If we hurry, we can see the monument to the Titanic before we catch the bus. I hope you don't mind getting wet."

"Have you been studying art all your life?" Reason wondered as she and Cain hopped the city bus.

"Against the odds, yes. My parents disapproved of it, thought it was vulgar. I might have given it up if there hadn't come a time when art was my salvation."

Reason would have pursued the comment but Cain turned away. "I can't wait to see your paintings."

"The reason you're coming to my class tonight is to strut your stuff, remember?"

"Strut your stuff?" Reason made fun. "You sound like an American. How do you know Declan O'Neill?"

"You mean Wilder? His father introduced us two years ago. Wilder came home to Malibu, it was a few months after you stiffed him, and he found me living in the guesthouse. I stayed there a year then got the job at CC and joined Wilder over here."

"I didn't 'stiff' him, Cain! I never set out to hurt him."

"You did hurt him though, and you weren't gentle about it. Do you know after you dumped him he went on a three-month drinking binge and nearly blew his residency? He adored you, and you killed him."

"I had no idea…I know what I did was wrong. But Wilder was just so intense. He wanted too much too fast, and I was about to marry another man."

"Maybe so, but you committed the worst deadly sin. You attacked him for being Irish and he'd had a lifetime of that."

"Look, Cain, if you have hard feelings towards me because of what Wilder has told you, we'd better settle them before we start working together. I did a bad thing, but I'm not a bad person."

"How could you be with those angelic blue eyes? Don't think I can't see your point of view, Reason. The truth is, I've always thought your trashing him…"

"Will you stop using words like that? I already feel bad enough."

"Sorry. You showed you had integrity when you…" he tried to think of a nice way to put it, "…unplugged Wilder's respirator and left him to suffocate in a lingering excruciating death, is that better?"

Reason frowned then laughed.

"A lot of women would have married him for his money and Hollywood connections, then divorced him and taken half of all he owns. At least all you wanted was sex, and he didn't have to hire a lawyer for that."

"Wilder never knew in breaking his heart I broke my own."

"Why did you do it then?"

"I was afraid of loving him," Reason answered quietly. "What were you doing in California?"

"Getting away from England."

"Did you like it?"

"No," Cain shrugged.

"Then why did you stay there a year?"

"California just seemed like a better place to call hell than London."

"What did you do in Malibu?" Reason chatted naturally, not knowing her questions were taboo.

"Painted. All I did was paint and paint and paint…hoping the colors dripping off my brush would bleed me."

"Bleed you of what?"

"I had all this blackness…I thought painting would release the demons inside me." Cain turned his eyes to the sidewalks passing beyond the bus. "I expected my works to be grotesque like Goya's, but they kept coming out clean, like Monet flowers pushing through the forest floor after a fire…I hated it…I hated myself."

"Does Wilder know you worked for British Intelligence?"

"As unforgiving as he is, I'd have to be crazy to hide that from him." With a stare saying Reason had asked a question too far, Cain fell silent.

And Reason regretted having pressed. "I'm sorry. I don't mean to be nosy, it's just that I want to know all about you."

"If you want to like me, Reason, it's best you know nothing about me."

Severe in its Tudor architecture, an uninterrupted sweep of red brick beneath a fat Union Jack, Christ Church College covered several blocks and was campus to eight thousand students. A flawless green stretched beneath its towers and mullioned windows; windows guarded by fiendish gargoyles. Cain ushered Reason through the university's arched foyer into a garden quadrangle. The roar of the Malone Road disappeared abruptly, like dropping off a cliff into calm. Suddenly. Silence. The clock above the quadrangle tolled seven times, then the only sound was the rainwater tapping the oak trees.

Reason scanned the courtyard. "Is your studio somewhere in this quadrangle?"

"See the last two windows on the right over there? There lies the lair of genius."

"Cubism in the Nude" was the topic of Cain's lecture. A young man and woman disrobed and twisted through a series of poses for the students to paint. Reason fiddled behind an easel, but Cain, not the models, had her attention. Charming and relaxed, he sailed in the rhythm of his brush while he instructed the class.

"Last week I told you that part of your grade will be to define water." Cain finished shading a thigh. "I didn't mean tell me water is H_2O! *Show* me water. Show me it's cool and purple rushing, hot red and crushing. *Show* me from water we're born and beyond the womb we rust, we're dust. But don't *tell* me it's H_2O…what in the hell does that mean?"

How attractive Reason found him. His confident brush strokes, the light in his eyes and lift in his speech as he employed his fingers on the canvas made her curious to know his fingers employed upon her. She studied him from his honey hair to his bare toes. He was six-feet solid and taut, not too thin. Working his land at My Lady's Leisure had given him muscles and an aura of health; he brought to mind power as quickly as he brought to mind passion. Reason loved his astute hazel eyes and slender fingers and the way he used them like a sorcerer to conjure art from his mind. Unlike his father, the self-proclaimed idol, Cain's unassuming smile said there was nothing false about him. His gentle disposition dominated the studio like a steady, soft glow; like a casual god, he put his students at ease and made himself impossible to resist. No wonder Jillie had left his class enamored. Everything about the Englishman promised intellect and sensitivity, romance and sensual adventure, and Reason imagined his prowess in bed. How he might undress and caress…

"That's an intriguing nude you have there," Cain came back to see what she wasn't doing. "It looks exactly like a bare canvas."

"Huh?" Reason jerked back to attention. "My mind was on your artwork not mine. You're so passionate…about your work."

"Art is making love to the mind, Reason. What are you going to paint for me?"

"To be honest I'm not in the mood. I spent the day up to my neck in graphics. You be the artist tonight, all right?"

Cain shook a Prussian blue finger at her. "You're a terrible student."

"I'll show you my art some other time."

"I'll look forward to it," he smiled, and there he was undressing Reason in his head again. No, no, Wilder was right. The woman was poison. Patting her on the shoulder, imagining his fingers stripping off her silk shirt, he moved on to another student.

"I feel cheated. The whole point of your coming tonight was to paint for me." Cain locked his studio and steered Reason down the hall. "I never intended to impose two hours of Picasso on you."

"I enjoyed you and your art, and I think we're going to have a great summer together."

Her words drove Cain's eyes away and he grew edgy. "I have a little flat up the Malone, a few blocks from here. We'll go get my car and I'll drive you back to the Gov."

Cain walked with Reason in silence. She assumed he was savoring, like she, the sights and scents of a golden-sun evening, but Cain was thanking heaven Reason couldn't read his mind. Her rapt attention all evening had flattered and aroused him. She had watched his every move, every expression, and she liked everything she saw. He fought to convince himself he was reading too much into those provocative glances, but no matter what they suggested, he had to ignore them. If she was as attracted to him as he was to her, their desire burned towards one damning conclusion. He had made a promise to Wilder, and tonight would be the last time he saw Reason outside the hospital. He had shown her My Lady's Leisure, his art and the best of Belfast. Enough. He would see her safely to her car and push her from his thoughts.

Compared to My Lady's Leisure, Cain's Malone residence was modest. One half of a Victorian duplex on two floors met his needs. Reason figured since the evening was young, Cain would invite her in. Instead he grabbed his car keys and trotted her to the garage. Once in the car, he drove to West Belfast without speaking. Tonight was the last time.

His haste mystified Reason. "Is something wrong?"

"No, no," Cain smiled at her.

"Are you upset I didn't paint anything during your class?"

"Of course not," he assured cheerfully. At the Gov, he said, "I'll see you next month. When you're ready to see my designs give me a shout." Unable to face Reason for fear lust would melt his resistance, he stared straight ahead and waited for her to get out of his car.

"A month is too long." Undaunted by the rush, Reason smoothed a hand up Cain's chest, tipped his chin to her and lightly kissed his lips; not seductively, a little kiss. Just enough to teach him the sweetness she could offer. "I had a wonderful time with you," she said. "You're the nicest thing to happen to me since I came to Belfast."

If Cain had parting thoughts, he did not impart them. Once Reason was in her car, he drove on. But he kept looking back. A kiss, a simple kiss. Forbidden fruit tastes sweet. Risks taste even sweeter. He would see her again.

Chapter Eleven

Duggie Knack read the typewritten note delivered to his Shankill rowhouse. **Horsetail Inn. Midnight. Friday.—Mad Hatter.**

Folding the paper, Duggie popped it into his mouth and ate it.

The day Reason met Duggie Knack in Tiger's Bay she had no idea she was face to face with Brendan O'Neill's killer. A member of the Ulster Liberation Force, Duggie had one goal; to keep Ulster British. He was Her Majesty's soldier. But he hadn't always been.

As a boy growing up in West Belfast he played with all the children around his parents' flat, and the terms Catholic and Protestant were rarely mentioned. His British mother could remember him singing Irish songs and learning Irish words from the Catholic boys. Ireland, England were one in Duggie's mind. His early years living up the Falls Road were happy times until the civil rights marches began in 1969. For reasons he didn't understand, his family began to feel threatened. There were rumors of Protestant men losing their jobs to Catholic rebels, of Catholics murdering Protestants in their beds, of priests taking over the world. In one summer Duggie's grey world cracked into black and white. Suddenly lines were being drawn, there was talk about equal work and equal power, and "Protestant" and "Catholic" became battle cries. Overnight, Duggie's friends became enemies. They refused to speak to him except to call him names. Often they hurled stones instead of slurs, and when stones weren't enough, the larger Catholic boys attacked him.

Everything changed. Nowhere was safe, no one was trusted. In the riotous summer of '71, Duggie's father was shot by Provisionals during a gun battle on the Falls Road, and Duggie's mother never forgave the murder. In her mind all Catholics were in the IRA, so Catholics killed her love. From that day forward she instilled suspicion and hatred into her susceptible son. The final schism came that Christmas when a gang of angry Catholics forced the Knacks out of their flat. Duggie came home one night to find his family's belongings in the street, and when he tried to enter his house, his way was blocked by a man with a rifle. "You don't live here anymore. Get out, you British bastard," he had blared, giving Duggie a kick.

At seven years old, Duggie was driven from the Falls Road into the fist of prejudice. He had lost his home, his friends, his father, his faith in a fair God...all because of Catholics. After he and his family moved to the Shankill, he attended segregated schools and never again rubbed elbows with papists, except to get into one bloody brawl after another. Over the years, as the IRA grew and thrived, so did Duggie's loathing. At sixteen he joined a loyalist paramilitary group, the Ulster Liberation Force; a 500-member sect of Protestant extremists who worked to keep Roman Catholics in their place through intimidation and murder. Following a motto of "If you can't kill an IRA man, kill a Catholic," the ULF roamed the streets of Belfast seeking out victims like vultures. Duggie burned Catholic houses, threw bombs into Catholic pubs, forced Catholic men out of their jobs at gunpoint, and once clubbed an elderly nun. By the time he was twenty he had murdered four Catholic men to keep Ulster free, and he hadn't spent a day in jail.

But Duggie's *piece de résistance* was Brendan O'Neill. The great crusader for equal rights. Duggie pulled the trigger that night after he employed a dull knife to hack off Brendan's manhood. Cramming it and a rosary into the republican's mouth moments before his death was a career high. "That ought to shut you up, you loudmouthed piece of shit," he had said before aiming his gun.

And just when Duggie thought he couldn't top Brendan's murder, the Cure enlisted him to ambush the mourners at Milltown. The fact that the funeral was for another Sinn Féin-loving O'Neill made the attack all the more rewarding. A British agent called "Mad Hatter" had driven Duggie to Milltown and handed him a machine gun and mask. "That's Brendan O'Neill's sister they're burying up there. Do what you do best, eh, Knack?" the Cure agent had laughed, giving Duggie a push out of the van. Duggie had hit the hill like a Marine hitting the beach. Though remaining anonymous to his victims as he opened fire, in his own mind he'd become a legend. After the Milltown slaughter he called himself "the Knack" knowing he was fearless, feral and expert at all things. His Protestant peers revered him; the Catholics feared him. There was nothing he wouldn't do for the Queen and her Cure.

To loyalist men like Duggie, Cure agents were heroes. But to the Catholic community they were known for one thing; their policy of shoot-to-kill. The Crown Undercover Regiment had two goals; to protect British interests in Northern Ireland and to eradicate the IRA by any means. Trained in the African desert to be ruthless, agents of the Cure were masters of disguise, assassination, and penetration deep within the enemy's camp. Their most insidious, ingenious skill was blending in with the locals then attacking when and where it was least expected. A single Cure agent could ambush a handful of republicans given one opportunity, and once on the inside, opportunity frequently knocked. But the Cure didn't always act alone. Sometimes it used Northern Ireland's sectarian politics to do its dark work. A Cure agent killing a Catholic man caused an uproar, but a Protestant killing a Catholic was an acceptable level of violence. So, if Mad Hatter needed a murder to serve England's purpose, Duggie Knack was employed. And when was murder an option? When Catholics spoke too loudly for equal rights, when they fought too hard for a unified Ireland, when they decried English torture and abuse; whenever rebels needed to be punished or suppressed.

"Do you have another job for me?" Duggie asked Hatter when they met Friday night.

"I want you to get a job at the Gov."

"OK, but why?"

Hatter pulled out an envelope and passed it to Duggie. Inside was a computer print-out of names. Men's names and the names of their children and wives. Duggie perused the list, looking blank. "Seamus McCabe, Sean Doherty, Michael McManus...who are these scums?"

"Well, Michael McManus is a plumber from Ballymurphy. And Sean Doherty is from Whiterock," Hatter said with a devious smile.

"West Belfast taig plumbers. Taking Protestant's jobs..." Duggie began to understand.

"Get a job then do your work, Knack. Now, what's this rumor I hear about you gunning for Declan O'Neill?"

"I got his brother, I'll get him too."

"That's not in my plan," Hatter said in a smooth English accent.

Duggie looked confused, "But you wanted me to kill Brendan, you gave me his address and schedule...I just assumed you wanted me to shank Declan as well."

"I wanted Brendan's death to look like a ULF job. But I took out Merry O'Neill, and I'll take out Declan." Hatter downed a shot of gin. "It's like shooting rats. The whole damn family's a scourge."

"And what about Kieran McCartan?"

"He's mine too," Hatter smiled. "The O'Neills have been my project for five years. I started the job and I'll finish them." Hatter noted Duggie's disappointment. "Just because Declan's off-limits doesn't mean I can't use you. Kieran thinks he's untouchable, and for now he is, but that doesn't mean we can't hurt him."

"What do you have in mind?"

"We'll go after his family and friends. He has a best mate named Aidan Duffy who's about to meet a bad end..."

Chapter Twelve

"Where's Jillie?" a little voice peeped.

Turning from her table, Reason beheld a miniature version of Declan O'Neill inching into her office. A shock of inky curls, a hint of a grin and startling blue eyes prompted Reason to say, "I'll bet you're Morris McCartan."

"How did you know that?" he peeped again.

"I know everything," Reason teased.

"Who are you?"

"I'm Reason."

"Reason? That's a silly name." Morris glanced furtively left and right. "Where's Jillie?"

Reason checked her watch; it was after seven. "She went home two hours ago."

That answer provoked an impatient huff. "She promised she'd be here. I have something to show her. She always breaks her promises."

"You can show it to me."

"I'm not allowed to talk to strange women." Morris reached into his trousers and pulled out a small, plastic bluebird anyway. "It came in my cereal. Isn't it beezer?"

"It sure is," Reason nodded. "Where's your dad?"

"Gone."

"Who's taking care of you then?"

"Decky!" Morris frolicked and carefully tucked the bluebird back in his pocket. "Are you one of Decky's girlfriends?"

"He and I are old friends."

Proudly Morris stated, "Decky's my uncle...well, he's not really my uncle, but I call him 'uncle' and he calls me his nephew cuz he'll never have any real nephews cuz Brendan and Merry are dead. We're having pizza at his house. Do you like pizza, Reason?"

"I love pizza. Where's Decky now?"

"Yelling at somebody on the telephone...you're an American," Morris appraised Reason's face in earnest, "all of Decky's other girlfriends are Irish."

"I'm sure they are."

"What are you drawing?" He inched closer and rose on his toes for a peek.

"A people flow chart." Reason held up a chart comprised of arrows and bubble diagrams. "What do you think?"

"All those arrows will pop the balloons and the people will fall out." Morris made a face. "Are you going to draw here all night?"

Wearily, Reason nodded. "I'm afraid so."

"Here you are! Hi ya, Mac." Wilder walked in. "Are you driving Miss McGuinness crazy?"

"Och no. She likes me."

Wilder gave Morris a rub on the back. "And here I thought she couldn't appreciate good men. I'm sorry I didn't get a chance to speak to you earlier, about the new wing I mean." He studied Reason's drawings briefly. "We had a woman blow an aneurysm at six this morning, and I'm only now getting out of the OR. Shall I call you this weekend or what?"

"Ask her for supper, ask her for supper," Morris urged, tugging on Wilder's wrist.

"I'm sure Miss McGuinness has other plans."

"No, she doesn't. She said so. And Decky, Decky, she loves pizza."

"You do? You wouldn't touch fattening stuff in Denver. Letting yourself go, are you, Mac?"

Reason returned to her work. Clearly Wilder didn't appreciate Morris' suggestion. "Your uncle is right, I have other plans."

"Na-uh," Morris shook his curls and flung his knuckles on his hips. "She said she was drawing all night, didn't you?"

"Do you have other plans, Reason?"

"Well...just work."

"Would you like to join us?" Wilder asked with a sigh of inconvenience. "Sooner or later we have to talk about this design team nonsense. We might as well get it out of the way tonight."

Wilder made the evening sound like living hell, and offended, Reason declined. "No thank you. I'm..."

"Here's your coat," Wilder plucked it off the door hook. "You can meet us at my house. Come on, stop looking like you're marching to the gallows. It will make Morris happy."

As Reason belted her jacket she asked the small boy, "Why do you want me to come home with you and your uncle so badly?"

"Decky and me likes the girls," Morris bragged.

Driving past Christ Church College and out the Malone, Reason marveled anew at the extremes between posh South and poor West Belfast. And she could understand the wealthy loyalists' fears of the IRA and British withdrawal. Their way of life was idyllic, clean and serene in multi-story, single-family homes with two car garages and gardens set back from arcadian streets. Settled atop hillsides or nestled in valleys, the views from their Georgian windows were of the green hills. No helicopters, no Land Rovers, no baby-faced soldiers, no young women with hungry babies, or idle men collecting on corners; just roses and songbirds and a lifestyle that made squalid inner-Belfast seem like an illusion. Here pink-cheeked girls in fine English saddles cantered ponies around paddocks, men in Izod played golf, women played tennis, and they looked well-fed, well-heeled, well-rested, clean and safe. And all this pampered Protestant privilege was built upon centuries of subjection of Irish Catholics.

But as Reason cruised along this peaceful path to Grange Park Wood, she knew if she were one of the privileged, she too would look the other way and pretend she didn't see. She would convince herself the Catholics in the New Lodge or up the Falls Road were responsible or somehow deserving of their privation. If the Catholics didn't like Ulster, they could leave, or it was their own fault for not accepting the generous British hand, or if they didn't want to be hungry, they shouldn't have so many babies. The Protestants too had inherited the longest war. Generations of oppression was their legacy, moral superiority their curse; it was all they knew and thought they deserved for remaining loyal to England. Hundreds of years of service had made them villainous victims at the mercy of the Crown. If Her Majesty withdrew her wallet and troops from the North, England would walk away unscathed while its faithful loyalists would be left holding one pernicious bag. Many Protestants did have a halcyon lifestyle, and they lived every day knowing, fearing equal Catholic rights and a unified Ireland would snatch their privilege away. And how could they not fear the huddled masses; masses they had huddled with their own clubs?

Wilder's house sat atop a knoll and overlooked a wooded park and the River Lagan. His garage sat back beside the house, and the walkway between the two afforded Reason an unobstructed view of the hills which actually did look greener on this other side of Belfast. As she walked to the front door, she inhaled the evening air scented with peppermint and lemon thyme climbing up the bricks of the house.

"Come in," Wilder called, echoed by a similar welcome from Morris.

The house's decor was California comfortable; white leather sofas on red oak floors, a scattering of Indian rugs, clay lamps, a bulky stone fireplace with a sleek oak mantle, and Cain's watercolor paintings of Malibu. Besides its main family room there was a large study and bath, an oak-paneled parlor, and a fully-equipped kitchen. Three bedrooms and two bathrooms completed the upstairs. And off the family room was a broad deck.

Morris said the menu was pizza, and Reason assumed he meant something delivered hot in a box. When Wilder called her into the kitchen, she was surprised to find him and Morris cooking. "You're *making* the pizza?"

"We're eating healthy like dudes in L.A.," Morris explained.

"Tell Reason our rule."

Morris held up four fingers. "We prefer chicken and fish, we don't fry, we love fruits and vegetables…Decky *makes* me say that part…and we drink our milk until we see Peter Rabbit on the bottom of our cup."

Everything Morris said amused Reason. "Smart rules."

"I'm bound and determined to teach Morris there's an alternative to heart disease." Wilder tossed Reason a green pepper and told her to chop it. "The way Kieran's mother cooks for this kid he'll be having bypass surgery before he's eighteen."

"What sort of pizza is this?" Reason peered into the bowl where she was tossing the pepper. "I don't think I've ever seen…or smelled meat quite like this…that is meat, isn't it?"

"It's an old family recipe," Wilder claimed. "Cheese and eel pizza on a soda bread crust."

"Did you say…*eel?*" Reason gulped.

"Don't you like slick and chewy eel?" Wilder arched a smile. "Morris and I love it."

"It's like ant-chovies only better," Morris said. "It comes from Lough Neagh."

Reason eyed Wilder disparagingly. "If you think I'm too chicken to try it, you're wrong."

"Och, you have to try it!" Morris exclaimed. "Around here we eat what we're served thankfully. You two don't like each other, do you?"

Wilder kept his eyes on Reason. Neither spoke.

"Everybody's always mad at everybody else," Morris stated without emotion and left the kitchen to go watch TV.

"He's so sensitive," Wilder commented after Morris had left. "Sometimes he picks up on things that no one else does. My aunt Nora, that's Kieran's mother, swears Morris has a sixth sense. I think it's because Kieran tells him absolutely everything. The little guy is five years old and knows more about the Troubles than I do."

"Liam O'Neill seeps into another generation."

"History is our fiercest heirloom," Wilder agreed, almost apologetically.

Morris chattered throughout the meal, which made the evening easier. The eel and cheese pizza tasted like rubber bands and French fries to Reason, but she ate every piece Wilder served her. After three pieces she figured he was trying to kill her.

"How's the eel, McGuinness?" Wilder goaded.

"Slimy. But I can understand why you like it. You are what you eat."

"No sir, Mac," he actually smiled, "you haven't changed a bit."

"Well, neither have you," she rejoined.

Morris goggled Reason awhile then announced with his mouth full, "You're much nicer than that old Jillie."

"Jillie's nice," Wilder defended.

Morris shook his curls. "She has eyes like an owl. But Reason has eyes like a dog, and dogs are nice. Are you going to sleep here with Decky tonight, Reason?"

Reason turned red. "Uh…no."

"Jillie sleeps with Decky sometimes. She sleeps with Daddy too. I think she sleeps with everyone."

"Reason and I aren't like Jillie and I. Why don't you go put the kettle on for our tea."

Morris pushed away from the table, gathered the dishes and loaded them in the dishwasher. After plugging in the tea kettle, he returned to the table to stare at his companions, hoping to catch more adult conversation.

"My goodness, Morris, you're a big help around the kitchen. No wonder Decky likes having you over for dinner."

"I don't have a mum, so I have to clean up after me," Morris quoted what Kieran had preached a hundred times. "I take care of me too."

"Morris, it's almost ten. You need to go upstairs and get ready for bed. You can watch the match wrap-up." Morris bounced an imaginary soccer ball off his forehead and ran from the room. "That will keep him occupied while we work." Wilder checked his watch. "I assume this won't take long."

"You know, Wilder, if you try any harder to offend me, you're going to hurt yourself." Reason rose from the table. "I left my sketchbook in the car. I'll go get it."

"Take the garbage out with you, will you?"

She extended her hand to Wilder. "Where would you like me to put you?"

It was the first time in days she had seen Wilder laugh. He looked much nicer that way. He snapped her hip with his napkin. "Go get your book."

Before going to her car, Reason stood on the deck, enjoying the view. Wilder's gardens were nothing like Cain's Eden in Down, but they were colorful and fragrant, especially beneath June's swollen moon. It was a mild night, gathering clouds foretold rain, but until then the sky shone. Behind Reason, beyond the house, sunset cast a golden glow. Before her the lights of Belfast shimmered. A chorus of birds sang farewell to the day.

"Nice night," Wilder said from the doorway.

"Your roses are pretty."

"You can thank Cain for that. He takes care of my yard. Whether I want him to or not. He has this habit of showing up here anytime he feels like it."

"Did you buy this house when you came back to Belfast?"

"No. Everything you see, the house, the furnishings, even the roses were purchased by my dad in an attempt to seduce Merry away from West Belfast. She never set foot in this place."

"Your poor father. How is he anyway?"

"Pulling his life together. He's into directing now and seems to be staying sane."

"I wonder what Liam would say about him now."

"That he's a rat's ass in the limelight," Wilder quipped.

"And what do you say, Declan?"

He ignored the question.

"Look at that moon. I always think of you when I see the full moon. Do you remember the moonlight in the gazebo?" Reason turned to Wilder wistfully. "How different you and I are beneath June's moon tonight. We're reduced to handshakes and stiff conversation."

"That's fine with me."

"Do you remember what you were doing two years ago?"

"Surgery." Wilder burned in recollection. He remembered drinking himself numb every night and dying alive for the love and hate of Reason. He remembered her perfume lingering like poison. He remembered lying awake in a sweat of desire and rage.

"I was returning wedding presents. What a gruesome task that was. It wasn't easy telling two hundred people I backed out of my wedding. I really hated you then."

Wilder appeared not to care.

"That seems like a lifetime ago."

"Thank God," he exaggerated a sigh of relief.

"And now it's you who's involved with someone else. Jillie's pretty, she's smart, and she's Irish. Does she know about us?"

"Us? There was no 'us,' remember?" Wilder reminded coldly. "But no, Jillie doesn't know…I never thought you were important enough to mention."

"You certainly told Cain an earful. I believe your exact words for me were 'blood-sucking witch.' How juvenile."

Wilder just laughed. "How was your evening with Cain last night?"

"I dragged him into my web and ate him," Reason smarted.

"When do you two start working together?"

"We're already working quite well together."

Wilder couldn't miss Reason's infatuation. "But you aren't seeing him, you know, like *seeing* him, right?"

"What does it matter to you?"

Wilder shifted, caught off guard. "Well, it doesn't."

A raven cawed from a treetop. Clouds darkened the dusk.

Reason smiled an appealing smile. "Do you know what my favorite memory of you is?"

"No, and I don't want to know." But Wilder knew she would tell him anyway.

"It's of you playing the flute for me after we made love. Those songs were gorgeous just like you were. Do you play the flute for Jillie now?"

"No. I haven't touched it since…I don't have time to play anymore."

Reason noted Wilder's hostile expression. "I never meant to hurt you, Wilder…if I had it to do over again…"

"But you don't, do you? The damage was done. Let's just get on with our lives and forget about Denver."

"I can't forget about it. Can you?"

"I already have, Mac."

"Even though we're together again?"

He avoided her eyes and wished the moon wasn't rising behind her; rising like it had over the gazebo; rising like his desire and thoughts of making love in soft Irish grass and slick tappy rain. "We aren't together. Your being in Belfast changes nothing."

"You're lying, Wilder," Reason saw through him. "I didn't forget one thing about you over the past two years, and you haven't forgotten a thing about me. My being here changes everything."

Turning aside, Wilder knew she was right. "As usual, you're wrong."

"Do I still remind you of a jack-o-lantern?" Reason asked to break the silence.

"Yeah. Everything about you reminds me of Halloween."

"And you say I haven't changed? I'll go get my sketchbook."

Paying attention to the moon instead of where she stepped, Reason missed two downward stairs and pitched headlong into a cluster of black-thorns at the base of the deck. Thorn-torn and mortified, she wrestled herself free and groped for her shoe that was snagged beneath the hedge. She touched cold metal. To her amazement, deep in the blackthorns she found a miniature camera now toppled lens-first into the mud. Beside the camera glistened a dime-sized coin. Unable to discern its letters, Reason tucked the coin in her shirt and retrieved her shoe.

Having heard the commotion, Wilder bolted outside.

"So help me, Wilder," Reason staggered to her feet and plucked twigs from her hair, "if you ask me if I had a nice 'trip,' I'll scream."

"The thought never crossed my mind." He rushed to assist her. "Are you OK?"

"I think so." She spat a leaf from her mouth.

"Can you walk? Does anything feel broken? Shall I carry you inside?"

"Helping me up the steps will be fine."

"I feel terrible, just terrible. I've been meaning to get lights out here for months." With one arm around her middle, Wilder limped Reason back to the house.

"Um, Wilder," Reason said in an undertone, "did you know there's a camera in your hedge? It was aimed at your house."

"Oh no," he moaned, disgusted but not surprised.

"I hit it when I fell. Its lens is now buried in mud."

"How thoughtful of you to disarm it for me," Wilder smiled.

"Aren't you upset someone is watching you?"

"Sure I am, but this isn't the first time. Last fall the RUC had a car with a camera in the headlamp parked outside my house for a month."

"Why?"

"Because I'm an O'Neill. Look at your poor hands and legs, and your clothes got all muddy." Wilder seemed to forget himself and cinched Reason tighter. "Oh, Reas, I am sorry."

"Careful, Decky, you're acting like you care about what happens to me."

He buffed a smudge off her chin. "Come sit down in the kitchen and let me check out your legs and…wipe that grin off your face. You know what I meant. It's not like you have the greatest legs in the world or anything."

"Then how come every time you see me at the Gov you about break your neck watching me walk?"

"I do not…how do you know what I'm looking at?"

"Still make you weak in the knees, don't I, O'Neill?" She patted his jaw and headed out of the room. "I'll check my own legs, thank you."

"You don't want my professional opinion?"

Reason glanced back. "If you don't think these are the greatest legs, your opinion lacks all credibility."

"What happened?" Morris appeared in the bathroom.

Reason perched on the tub. "I fell down the steps behind the house."

"Och, I've done that too! Decky has *Snoopy* plasters." Morris slid open the top drawer of the vanity and produced a box of band-aids. "See? I'll put one on your knee."

"You are without a doubt the cutest little boy I've ever seen," Reason complimented as Morris carefully pressed a Charlie Brown bandage to her leg.

"Why don't you like Decky?"

"I like Decky."

"You don't act like you do."

"Well, we don't always agree on things." Reason finished dabbing the last of her cuts while Morris watched her every move. "We need to get you to bed so Decky and I can work. Which is your room?"

"I sleep with Decky."

"Then run and jump back in his bed."

"Watch me. I'm Suuu-per-man!" Morris took a flying leap towards the mattress and landed in giggles. "Did you see me? Did you?"

"You were brilliant."

"Och, Reason, listen! Thunder! It's raining hammers and tongs."

"Really? It was clear just a few minutes ago."

"My daddy says rain comes faster than lightning here. Let's light the fire and tell stories." Morris pointed to the bedroom's cold hearth.

"It's too late for a fire, don't you think?"

"No, no. We'll get all snuggly." Morris jumped to light the coals then jumped back into bed. "The fire's lovely, see? Decky is taking me to the park tomorrow. You come too."

"Sweet of you to offer, Morris, but I can't."

"But the birds by the lake are swans! Come see!"

Reason took a seat beside Morris and petted his haphazard curls. "Has your uncle ever told you how he nearly drowned trying to rescue a bird?"

"Och no. Tell me! Tell me!"

"Why don't you lie back and…"

"There's someone knocking at Decky's back door! Did you hear it? Let's go see who's here."

Murmurs could be heard downstairs.

"It's probably one of the neighbors."

"Our neighbor opened his door one night and these ULF Prods in masks shot him. Right in the face. Decky and my daddy won't let me open anybody's door, and they won't let no one inside unless they know them."

Morris' offhand statement appalled Reason. A man being shot dead was an every day part of his little boy world. War seethed around him; it was all he knew. "Now where were we? I was telling you about your crazy uncle…"

Minutes later Wilder stuck his head through the doorway.

"Decky, Decky, did ye save the wee waxwing, did ye?" cried Morris.

"Huh? Oh, Reason's telling you *that* old story, is she? Actually, the bird saved herself. I need to go out for awhile." He looked to Reason, "Would you mind staying here with Morris until I get back?"

"No problem."

"We'll tell ghost stories!" Morris clapped.

Wilder noted Reason's knees decorated in *Snoopy* patches. "I see Morris showed you his band-aids. Are you sure you're not hurt?"

"Wasn't it just a week ago tonight I was asking you the same thing? These Friday nights are dangerous."

Wilder smiled faintly, absorbing the sight of Reason propped up on his bed beside Morris. Memories of her undressing him then herself in the moonlight flooded his head. How appealing she was then...and now. How easily she seduced him. "I won't be gone long."

Wilder hadn't a taste for adventure. Reason home by his fire, home on his bed, warm mesmerizing and spirited Reason, and not just in his dreams Reason, occupied his mind. He brushed the rain dripping through the car's window off his cheek and coat sleeve.

"Nice work, Kieran. Where did you get this cheap heap? It leaks like a fountain."

"We hijacked it in Turf Lodge. You might as well get used to being wet, Dec. We're leaving the car a mile down the coast and running to the bank."

"You're taking me to a bank robbery? I don't want any part of that."

"Aw, don't worry, Declan, the dirty work's done. None of the sticky sin will taint your hands. And if it does, ten Hail Marys will clean you right up."

"Just fill me in on what we're doing and skip the jokes."

"Oh, you're in a fine mood. The Yank's wound you up, has she?"

"Don't start," Wilder muttered, making Kieran laugh.

"I'll have you back to her in no time, Dec. The bank's in Portclare, and here's the beauty; it shares a wall with a law office. The office is being renovated and its back is covered in scaffolding. We used it as a ladder to get up to the second floor and through an open window."

"What about alarms?"

"The windows and doors of the bank are wired to alarms, but the walls aren't wired to anything. Our plan was we'd break through the wall from the law office into the bank, no sweat. Tonight's perfect weather for it. No one would be walking about, and the noise of the storm would drown out the noise when we smashed through the wall and blew open the safe. Three of us went up there expecting it to take a few minutes. But everything went wrong. It took forever to break through the wall; solid brick. When we got through, the door on the safe was a bitch to blow."

"How did you keep from blowing up the bank?"

"This one Volunteer is the surgeon of semtex. He knows exactly how much to use for jobs big or small. We figured this would be easy money cuz it's a little bank with a little safe, but hell no. Well, we finally got the fucking door off and Dr. Semtex tears his glove on a piece of metal and bleeds everywhere so we had to clean that up. Then the RUC arrived to check on the bank. And now this other Volunteer's near death and we can't just leave him. The minute the peelers drove off, I got out and came for you. Talk about operations gone bad."

"Will the RUC be back to check on the bank?"

"Probably." A mile down the coast from Portclare, Kieran grinned across at his cousin and made the sign of the cross. "Welcome to a life of crime, my son."

The night raged along the shore. Salt water flung from the ocean stung their eyes, the rain softened the sand making the hike to Portclare slow, but Wilder and Kieran pressed on down the coast. Lightning lighted their way, thunder followed each flash. But Kieran had been right, no one was out in the storm. Portclare was deserted. The adrenaline clawing Wilder's chest rivaled a heart attack as he and Kieran, both in dark coveralls, hugged the shadows and slinked along the city streets. Sneaking down the alleys, ducking beneath lighted windows, Wilder swore the streetlamps were getting brighter as he grew hotter and shorter of breath. At any moment his life and career could crash into the nozzle of a loaded gun. Only the thunder muffled his heart thudding against his ribs. Was that a face in the bakery's window? Were there witnesses he couldn't see? Was the RUC around the next bend? He sucked in his breath, his muscles tensed as he stole across each of six side streets and tiptoed on exploding nerves.

The bank and its companion law office stood at the end of a cul-de-sac. To the left of the bank was a library, to the right a park, and on all fronts, for the moment, not a soul was in sight. In a lapse between lightning, on the last leg of his guts, Wilder climbed up the scaffold, trailed by Kieran. One after the other they swung inside the back window of the law office and drew on balaclavas to hide their faces. Inside the bank, Wilder surveyed the premises; an electronically-locked door led downstairs, ominous cameras guarded the safe. Even if the cameras recorded their moves, their faces were hooded, and they would be gone before anyone saw what the camera had taped. And as long as they didn't tamper with the door, the alarm wouldn't sound. Wilder noted the ravaged safe and the second anonymous Volunteer, then he knelt to assist the unconscious third man.

Kieran relayed a series of symptoms. "It happened really fast. We blew the safe and cleaned up and were ready to leave when suddenly the kid fell down and started talking nonsense like he was drunk."

"The big lad was totally confused," the second man added, peering over Wilder's shoulder.

"He couldn't stand up and he sort of had a seizure, and then, *bam*, he passed out," Kieran said.

"We think he took a stroke. He looks like a corpse."

Wilder checked the young man's eyes, his pulse, his respiration, his breath. "Did he run all the way from the beach to get in here then help break down the wall?"

"Aye."

"Was he wearing a coat?"

"It's over there on the chair."

"Check its pockets for a candy bar or some kind of sugar."

Kieran found several sugar cubes. He tossed one to Wilder. "How did you know he'd have that?"

"He's probably a diabetic. All that exercise lowered his blood sugar. We need to get his glucose level up." Wilder lifted the man's head and placed the sugar cube under his tongue. "After the sugar melts, he'll be better and we can get him out of here."

"But...that was so simple," Kieran uttered, feeling stupid. "We shouldn't have dragged you up here. It's just that he looked dead."

"Nah, you did the right thing."

Once his patient was stable, Wilder examined what Kieran and his cohorts had pillaged; ten thousand pounds stacked in bundles and two safety deposit boxes. One box held silver and jewelry, the other box was empty.

"What was in there?" Wilder pointed to the empty box.

"This pouch and ledger." Kieran pulled both from his backpack and tossed them to his cousin. "My genius companion over there got blood all over them so we have to take them with us."

"Get a load of these." Wilder poured the contents of the pouch into his gloved hand. "They're some sort of stones."

"Shit!" Kieran hissed. "The peelers are back."

Just when Wilder thought his heart could stop pounding, he leaned to the window to see the RUC Land Rover parked in back of the bank. "Now what?"

"We wait.

*   *   *   *   *   *

Wilder had been gone for hours. Reason knew him well enough to know he wouldn't leave her and Morris without a good reason, but what was taking so long? She tried to believe he had been called back to the hospital, but she knew better. One look at his face before he left belied covert purpose. She wondered what he was involved in, she abhorred this new side of his life, and she wanted no part of it. But tonight she was stuck. There was nothing to do but pace the halls, watch the clock, pace the halls.

*   *   *   *   *   *

Two hours later the police remained parked at the back door of the bank.

"The bastards are here for the night," Kieran concluded, "so we're just going to do it. We're going to slide down the scaffold behind the Land Rover and hit the road running."

Wilder and the other two men thought Kieran was joking. He wasn't.

"We have two choices. Wait here and whoever opens the bank can let us out the front door for twenty years in Long Kesh, or we can bail out now and take our chances." Kieran spiked the cash into his back pack. He adjusted his balaclava, pulled out a revolver, as did his peers, and moved through the hole in the bank's wall.

Wilder stuffed the velvet pouch and ledger into his pockets before he ducked out of the bank. "How are you doing?" he detained the young diabetic.

"Other than being scared shitless I'm OK."

"I know this is going to be hard, but try to take it as easy as you can getting out of here. Don't push or you'll be hypoglycemic all over again."

"Yeah, I know." He popped more sugar in his mouth and shook Wilder's hand. "I hope to hell you didn't save me just to get shot."

Like an accomplice, the deluge had intensified with gale force winds until the storm masked and swallowed stray sights and sounds in the night. In the law office the foursome drew a collective breath of courage then headed out the window. The Land Rover was nearly invisible as four black shadows slinked one after the other like a chain unlinking along the scaffold. Rung by rung, prayer by prayer, they dropped. One man, two men, three and four men on the ground, against the wall, inching away, breaking into a run. Into the driving downpour, back along the side streets and alleys and out to the beach they dodged and darted and parted in pairs. And sick with dread and self-preservation, Wilder remembered little of their escape.

"Looks like it's going to rain all night." Kieran rubbed his fingers as he and Wilder galloped back through the wet sand. "I'm freezing, aren't you?"

Wilder didn't feel anything.

"Listen to that ocean thrashing. I can't tell where the ocean begins and the rain ends."

Wilder wasn't listening. His fear stirred a tempest more ill-natured than the thrashing sea. He sprinted faster.

"Lord love us, that was better than sex!" Kieran caroused as they dived into the car and stripped off their coveralls, gloves and masks. "That's £10,000 for the IRA and a slap in the face for the Brits. We were a foot from the little shits and we got away. "

"That was too damn much fun for me, Kieran," Wilder panted. "It's a miracle they didn't see us."

"Aw, fuck 'em if they did. Prison's not so bad." Kieran had been through the system so many times, interrogation, arrest and imprisonment were just another facet of everyday life. "It's all part of living the Ra."

Reason awoke beneath Wilder's stare. "You're back!" She jumped up from the couch. "I've been worried sick."

He motioned her into the kitchen. "I know you're ready to kill me. I never intended to disappear."

"It's all right, Wilder. Would you like me to fix you some tea?"

Reason's accommodating manner made Wilder question if he was in the right house. "I've been gone for hours. C'mon, I know you want to give me hell, so give it. I deserve it."

"I'm sure you had a good reason to be gone. I'm just glad you're back in one piece."

Exhausted and stressed, Wilder slumped into a chair at the table and buried his face in his hands. "I'll take the tea but put some Scotch in it. There's a fifth above the stove." He yanked off his shoes and socks and sodden shirt. And seeing him shiver, Reason left the kitchen and returned with a bathrobe and towel. Wilder stripped off his clothes in haste and slid into the dry robe. Reason toweled off his wet hair.

"I can dry my own head," he groused and grabbed the towel.

The half-tea, half-whiskey delivered, Reason paused behind Wilder. He left her speechless. She deplored his having committed God only knows what mischief, and she feared for his life. She wanted to scream sense into him; she wanted to cradle him in her arms. In compromise, she laid her hands on his shoulders. "Are you in trouble?"

He pinched his thumb and index finger together. "I came this close to getting shot by the RUC tonight."

Reason's heart all but stopped, but she knew not to pry. She kneaded Wilder's tense neck and thought of all the times in two years she had ached to touch him again. Now here he was. Still virile and vital; still her heart's thief.

"I feel like I just got off one of those rollercoasters that goes roaring around and around through loops upside down." Reason's soft hands seduced the cold from his flesh. She was heat and benediction, all things soothing and chaste, within arms' reach. And Wilder's drought of 745 nights could be relieved by her kiss, her caress, her body and mind. He glanced back at Reason's blue eyes. Yankee eyes freely roaming his face. Sweet woman eyes. Wellworth-Howell eyes of false promise and ice. He shrugged off her touch. And Wilder was Declan again.

Reason drew back. "What's wrong?"

"You're wrong, this night is wrong." He stood up abruptly and crossed the kitchen to replenish his cup with Scotch. "You have to leave," he pointed Reason for the door.

"I'm not your enemy, Wilder."

"You *are* the enemy." He turned his back. She could scarcely hear him. "I'd forgotten how nice you can be."

"Then give me a chance…"

"You don't belong here, Reason. Go!"

As Wilder wished her away, Reason felt hapless as the tide leaping towards her master moon; leaping to be received and sucked into his light. But he wanted no part of her. She could leap high, higher, touch the sky and not reach him; yet he would impel her. She looked to Wilder. And like the moon luring her with his power and distance, Wilder coolly stared back.

"I do appreciate your staying with Morris," he said before she left the room. "And thank you for not asking questions."

As she tied on her coat Reason remembered the coin she'd found in the garden. In the light she saw it was a gold charm depicting a winged sword. **Fear Nothing and Prevail** was inscribed on its blade. Whoever lost it had been lurking deep in the hedgerow behind the house. Replacing the charm in her pocket, Reason decided not to show Wilder. He had enough on his mind for one night. She found him out on the deck waiting for sunrise to brighten the rain.

"You know, Reas, as I was running down the beach tonight I kept thinking a cause is really a curse. To fight is to die, and not to fight is to die. Bravery and cowardice are just two forms of suicide."

"Oh, Wilder, please forget that cause before it destroys you."

He wheeled toward her. His palm grazed her cheek. And for an instant his heart beat on his sleeve. "I can't believe you're really here...I thought I'd never see you again..." he stopped. "You have to get out of here." He couldn't watch her leave.

The next morning as they drove back to West Belfast, Morris talked to Wilder about his "brilliant new friend." Reason did this, Reason said that, Reason knows everything. When Wilder explained Reason wouldn't be coming around again, he thought Morris was going to cry.

"My daddy should marry her. Then she could live with me forever."

"That's an interesting proposition, Morris, but I don't think your dad is her type."

"Are you her type?"

"No."

"Why don't you like her? I like her with all my life!"

"*I love you, Wilder. I love you with all my life!*" "Reason taught you that saying, didn't she?"

"Yes...is it naughty?"

"No. It just reminds me why she isn't my type."

Wilder awoke at midnight to the music of Chopin. Trudging downstairs he saw Cain on a ladder in the kitchen. "Cromwell, do you know what time it is?"

"Time for you to get rid of this depressing off-white," he said as he rolled fresh paint onto the wall. "Aren't you sick of it?"

"No, I liked it."

"You'll like this color better. Tahitian Dawn." Cain showed Wilder the paint can. "It says here it's the warm color of sunrise with just a hint of rose."

"It's yellow! I hate yellow."

"You'll like it when it dries. If she's such a cold fish, why did you pursue her?" Cain segued glibly and jumped from the ladder.

"What?"

"Reason told me how you spent months coming on to her. You seduced her less than a week before her wedding. Chivalry is dead," Cain sighed. "And I have to wonder why you'd expend so much energy on a 'cold fish.'"

"I didn't know she was cold until I tested the waters," Wilder yawned. "I got hijacked to Portclare last night." He recounted the tale. "I don't ever want to come that close to getting caught again."

"Aah, an evening after my own heart." Cain went about searching the cupboards and making himself a cup of tea. "Leave it to a Yank to have nothing but tea bags. You ought to try bulk Ceylon-Darjeeling from Harrods. Next time I'm in London I'll get you some." He extended a mug to Wilder then foraged through the refrigerator. "Do you have any biscuits? I like those little lemon ones. Geez, Wilder, you really need to go to the market more often. There's nothing to eat here! Look at this cupboard door." He opened the cabinet, closed the cabinet, opened it, closed it then turned to Wilder proudly. "Well?"

Wilder looked at his friend without a clue.

"It doesn't squeak anymore. Bloody thing sounded like a rutting cat. It was merely a matter of re-hanging the door on its hinges, out of alignment they were."

"Cromwell, you're a wonder. Hey, come here. I have something I want to show you." Wilder emptied the velvet pouch on his table. "Kieran left me in charge of these. What do you make of them?"

Cain turned a chunky stone over and over, held it up to the light, sniffed it, squeezed it, scratched it, and gave it a taste. "It's an unrefined emerald."

"Seriously? How much is it worth?"

"This rough stone could be worth half a million pounds."

Wilder counted the gems and his mouth dropped. "That means we have about five million pounds here. Amazing."

"These were in Portclare?"

"Obscure place to be keeping emeralds, don't you think?"

"Not if you don't want anyone to know you have them. Maybe the owner was going to smuggle them untaxed, unseen, and sell them on the black market. What are you going to do with them?"

"I have no idea. I just want to be rid of them."

Curiosity seized Cain. "Don't you want to know who owns them?"

"Nope."

"I'll send them back to the bank for you."

"Yeah, all right." Wilder trusted his friend. "Just be careful."

"What's this ledger?"

"I haven't looked at it. It was in the safety deposit box with the emeralds."

Cain flipped the pages. A smile inched across his lips. "May I have this too?"

"Sure. What's in there?"

"Standard accounting; numbers and names. See?"

"I wonder what that's about."

"I'm not sure, Wilder, but I think opportunity has knocked."

Chapter Thirteen

Because she knew little and assumed much, Reason convinced herself Wilder had committed a crime and become a wanted man. All day Sunday she anguished over his fate, and when he walked into her office Monday morning, she was elated to see him. "How are you?" She closed her office door and prepared for the worst. "I was awake all last night worrying."

"What are you worried about?"

"You know. The other night."

"Oh that." He could laugh about it now. "All's well that end's well."

"You mean you're safe? Really? Oh, Wilder, thank God."

"Until next time."

Reason did a double take. "What did you say?"

"I said until next time."

"*Next time?* You nearly got shot and didn't learn a thing?"

"In this game there's only winning big or losing it all. This time we won."

Reason slapped down her pencil and sprang from her drafting table, grabbing Wilder by his necktie. "Your *life* isn't a game, Wilder."

"Yo, Mac, my tie isn't a toy. Knock it off!"

"I'll knock it off all right." Twenty four hours of raw nerves and two years of rancor boiled into a rage. She swung a punch to Wilder's arm, he ducked, and she blasted his eye.

"Ow! What did you do that for? What's the matter with you?" He dodged another swipe.

"You're going to be dead soon, and you ask what's the matter with *me?*" Reason wound up her fist only this time Wilder caught it.

"One more punch and you're going to the psych ward. I mean it, Reason, get ahold of yourself." With that warning, he pushed her away.

"After all my worrying…my heart *bled* for you…and now you say 'next time?'"She clapped her hands to her temples. "You…you stupid…I *prayed* for you! GET OUT OF MY OFFICE!"

"Fine. *Fine!* I'll talk to you when you calm down and grow up."

Reason responded by hurling her T-square at Wilder's head.

"Have you seen what you did to Decky's eye?" Jillie asked that afternoon. "Everybody's talking about it. What did he do to make you so mad?"

"He was born," Reason sulked.

"Seriously, what did he do?"

"It's his casual attitude. He's living as if his life is a movie, like there are sets he can walk on and off of anytime he wants without repercussions."

"Reason, you hardly know him. What makes you say that?"

"Oh, forget it. Let's get back to work. Hunter wants to break ground on July third, so that gives us two weeks to get organized. I need you to keep track of who's been hired."

"I'm already doing that," Jillie assured.

"Oh, great. Ruairi McKee will be in tomorrow. I think he'll be a good employee, don't you?"

"He's reliable, easygoing, and smart. He'll be cracker."

"Jillie, have you ever met a person you don't like? I swear you're friends with everyone."

Jillie found that funny. "Oh, poor dear Reason, nobody likes everybody. There are scads of people I'd rather see dead than alive."

"Or tarred and feathered," Reason joked. "Take Declan for instance."

"Och no, the best way to see him is stripped naked in bed."

Reason averted her eyes, looking down on the Falls. The police were stopping cars again. "Tell me something, Jillie. Are the cops here as vicious as I've heard?"

"What have you heard?"

"That they torture confessions out of people, that they leak information on Catholics to loyalist assassins, that they plant spy equipment around Catholics' homes, that they shoot unarmed men...things like that."

"If all that were true, it would make them bloody despicable."

"Is it true?"

"Uh oh," Jillie cocked her head. "I hear Hunter Cromwell out in the hall."

"He's in London until next week."

"Sorry, pet, but I met him in the elevator when I came in. Rumor has it he's out for your hide after your fist fight with Declan. I'll be at my computer if anyone needs first aid."

"Good morning, Reason." Debonair in a pinstriped suit, Hunter swaggered in. "How are those preliminary plans coming?"

"They'll be on your desk Friday."

"Excellent. Excellent. But I'm here to discuss another matter." He rested his hip on the corner of Reason's desk and folded his arms.

"I know you're thinking the worst of me, Hunter. There's no excuse for my behavior, and..."

"No need to apologize, Reason. We all make mistakes. It's not that I dislike Americans, I love Americans, but you're not what Mrs. Cromwell and I have in mind for our son. Granted, Cain's no prize, but we'll protect him nonetheless. The truth is, the boy's mad as a hatter. In the past he's had an odious penchant for Irish girls...he's so susceptible to the wiles of you foreigners. Certainly you're a step up from Irish...or are you Irish as well? With a name like McGuinness..."

"McGuinness is a nice name," Reason justified, surprising herself.

"But a Catholic Irish name," Hunter reminded.

"Hunter, what's the purpose of this conversation?" Reason was as perplexed as she was offended. "Are you telling me not to see Cain?"

Reason's outrage warned Hunter to mind his tongue; he might be the next one she popped in the eye. "No, no. Just don't get any notions about becoming a Cromwell."

"I wouldn't dream of being a *Cromwell,*" Reason scoffed.

"I'm glad you understand your place. Now, I expect you at my Solstice Fete."

"My *place?* Your *what?*"

"The Solstice Fete. My annual fund-raising ball for the Grosvenor at Bernard Thunder's estate up in Portclare. It's strictly black tie." Hunter passed a scornful eye over Reason's skirt and blouse. "I assume you can manage the proper attire." He strutted back to the doorway. "I'll see you Saturday. And Reason," he faced her sternly, "assaulting the medical staff will not be tolerated. Have you *no* breeding? Disgrace this hospital again like this morning and both you and Declan O'Neill will be wearing a lawsuit. We begin our team meetings next week, and you two will work together. You *will.*"

"So, Reason love, what do you think?"

Cain sneaked up behind her in the emergency room, causing Reason to drop her notes. "Oh! Cain! I didn't see you come in."

"That's why I made such a good thief." He collected her papers and handed them to her with a bow. "How does this sound? You and me alone in a candlelit ballroom with a little wine, a lot of music, and one hundred dancing bigots."

"You must mean your father's solstice thing."

"Has H.C. already talked to you about it?"

"In a way, yes."

Cain could tell by Reason's expression, "Did he accuse you of scheming to marry me?"

"Actually, he did. Did he talk to you about it too?"

"I should have warned you. It's standard procedure. I've asked him not to do it, but it only makes him do it more. The old coot's convinced my sole salvation is a good Englishwoman of sterling pedigree. So, will you endure the Fete with me?"

"That isn't a very appealing invitation. Ask me like Byron would ask."

Cain's fingers teased an errant blonde strand from Reason cheek, her skin was soft like he had imagined, and he bent his request to her ear, "Hold me, make love to me, come with me, say yes."

"Are you going to take me home in a rush at the end of the evening like you did last week?"

"No. I'll take you slowly," he promised, unable to recall his eyes from her smile. A sensuous smile on lips too briefly kissed. On impulse he pulled Reason into his arms, bent her back a little and kissed her with desire, causing her to drop her papers again.

Reason lost her breath, her heart raced. She hadn't been kissed like that in two years.

"Until Saturday night, love."

*   *   *   *   *   *

Wilder had been home from the hospital less than an hour before Reason knocked on his door. "Did you see the nine o'clock news?" She charged into his foyer. "That's what you were up to Friday night, isn't it?"

Still repelled by her behavior the day before, Wilder stared coldly upon her. "Come to blacken my other eye?"

Reason tipped Wilder's head towards the light. "I'll be darned. Looks like growing up with brothers came in handy."

"I'm in no mood for you, Mac. What do you want?"

"Have you seen the news?"

"No."

Reason turned on the TV. "The local news will be on in a second."

"**IRA terrorists masterminded a heist over the weekend,**" began the lead story. "**Using sledgehammers, the Provisionals broke through the bank's wall and blew open the safe…**"

Reason flung her arms skyward. "You *robbed* a bank?"

"I didn't rob anything!" Cain had promised to send the gems back so Wilder was telling the truth.

"You weren't afraid of being shot because you were innocent, Wilder."

"Who in the hell do you think you are barging in here demanding I explain myself?" he erupted. "I don't give a damn what you think about me or how I choose to live. It's *my* life! What do I have to do to convince you to leave me the hell alone?" he roared.

"It's just that I'm so afraid for you," Reason replied meekly.

"You didn't care if I lived or died two years ago. Now suddenly you're Florence Nightengale," Wilder's comments shuddered in sarcasm. "Go away, Mac."

"All right."

"Reason, wait." He slapped a folder full of papers into her hand. "Here are my recommendations for the Gov. This should take care of any business we might have together for awhile."

Reason's face fell. Her feelings bled. He hated her.

"Don't slam the door on your way out," he jeered.

"That's it!" Reason swung her arms in an X like an umpire. "I give up trying to make peace with you. I cannot believe for the last two years I've tortured myself thinking you were the kindest, most intelligent and romantic man on earth. I actually thought walking out on you was the biggest mistake of my life. Thank you for proving me wrong." She stamped down the walkway to her car. "And I'm glad I pounded your eye, Declan O'Neill. Compared to a bullet, you got off easy!"

Chapter Fourteen

It was several days before Wilder made it up to Andersonstown; a neighborhood atop the Falls Road. On Friday afternoon he found time to consult one of the old historians. Albert "Albie" Coogan and Liam O'Neill had been friends. Both grew up in Belfast. Both fought the British for independence. Both were pillars of republicanism. But outlasting Liam, Albie had lived to be ninety.

"Declan!" Albie hailed his young friend from his doorway.

"How's it going, Albie?"

"Not bad, not bad." With a pat on the shoulder, he welcomed Wilder. "Let's see the eye then. A wee woman smacked you a smacking I hear. Have time for a cup of tea?"

Wilder touched his bruised eye. "I'll give the girl credit, she has a nice right hook. No time for tea today, Albie. Do you know who Michael Patrick McGuinness was? I saw his grave at Milltown."

"Michael Patrick McGuinness? Aye, the name's familiar." Wilder could see Albie scanning the years. "Aye, there's his wee face. Grew up here in West Belfast so he did."

"What were the circumstances surrounding his death?"

"To tell you the truth, lad, I can't recall. Let me ask some of the other old boys."

"Did he have a wife, any family?"

"Och no. He was an only child and never married."

"Are you sure about that, Albie?"

"Aye," Albie nodded. "Michael was the son of a sailor, passed his youth on the sea. Why are you so keen on him?"

Michael Patrick had died just months after Reason's third birthday. Probably a coincidence, Wilder figured. But it was no coincidence that she knew the word *taig*. She had to have learned the distinctly loyalist curse from someone who had experienced Ireland's sectarian war. "I'm just interested in people named McGuinness."

"Rest easy then, Declan. Old Albie will find out what he can."

*   *   *   *   *   *

At four o'clock Jillie stepped into Reason's office. "There's a fellow here to apply for a job. He insists he knows you. His name's Duggie Knack."

"Buzzed red hair, bullet earring?"

"My God, it's true," Jillie gasped. "You do know him. But he's so...so scary."

"I met him by accident. Has he filled out an application?"

"Oh yes," Jillie groaned. "Under past experience he wrote, 'I done it all.'"

"Tell him when he gets serious to come back."

Jillie glimpsed over her shoulder at Duggie scuffing his feet in the hallway. "The city is full of his sort, and they cause nothing but trouble when they can't find work. Maybe you should give him a chance to be productive."

"It can't hurt to talk to him I guess."

Duggie sashayed into Reason's office like the pleasure of his presence had been requested. He wore Swiss-cheese-looking jeans and metal-toed boots. A sleeveless t-shirt flaunted his hard-muscled chest and biceps. And Reason noticed both his arms, like his hands, had tattoos; the right with King Billy on a horse, *Remember 1690*, the left with a Union Jack, *No Surrender*. He flopped into the spare chair and greeted Reason with a thumb's up. "Never fear, the Knack is here. I've come for the job."

"Hello again, Duggie. What sort of job are you looking for?"

"Maybe I oughta be a brain surgeon," he clowned. When Reason failed to laugh he straightened up in his chair. "Any construction work. I'm as talented as I am good-looking."

That coaxed a smile from Reason. "Well, I don't need any more laborers right now. If you come back in August maybe…"

Duggie burst to his feet. "But I gotta have a job here. I gotta."

"Why?"

"Why?" That stumped him. He couldn't reply, because Mad Hatter told him to. "I need the money."

"Doesn't everyone in West Belfast? Why should I hire you?"

"Why shouldn't you? I work as good as anybody else." He hung his head and stared at his feet. "I've been looking for work for two years. I have a mother and two sisters to tend. I thought you, knowing me so well and all, would give me a chance."

"I know nothing about you except the last time I saw you, you were throwing garbage at Catholics."

"Oh, I don't do that anymore. I'm reformed."

"You are?"

"Oh, yeah, yeah." He licked his lips nervously, glanced out the window then dropped to his knees beside Reason's drafting table. "Please give me a job, pleeeeez. I'll be a right decent spud for ye so I will."

Reason leaned on her palm and observed Duggie in wonder. He was the picture of pathos and punk rebellion, and while he was unlike any man she had met, he was persuasive. He seemed down on his luck; she felt sorry for him. "Have you ever worked construction before?"

"Sure. I'm good with a hammer. Give me a chance, OK?" He remained kneeling and begged with his squinty, green eyes.

The design team had hired competent foremen, and Duggie was too eager and obsequious to ignore. "For crying out loud, Duggie, get up off your knees."

"You're going to slag me off, aren't you?" he cried.

"No, I'm giving you a job. Go down to the trailer on the lot next to the hospital and they'll assign you to a team."

"Lord fuckin' love ye!" He rebounded with a whoop. "The Knack is back!"

"Duggie, do me a favor?"

"Yeah?"

"Don't make me regret hiring you."

"Hey, I'm an angel." With a wink, he hurried away.

Chapter Fifteen

"Unseasonably hot and dry," promised the weather, and Saturday evening brought eighty degrees and fair skies. As demanded, Reason wore the proper dress; alabaster, off-the-shoulder satin, fitted like an hourglass, beaded in sequins and pearls.

"That length looks nice on you, pet, shows off your lovely legs. With all those sparks and spangles you look like sunlit snow," Fiona flattered when Reason came downstairs. "Ruairi," she summoned from the foot of the stairs, "come see our Reason."

"Don't disturb him, Fiona. You're going to embarrass me."

"He needs to be disturbed. God only knows what he's doing up there in that attic of his. I don't ask…it sickens the heart out of me…and he thinks I don't know what he's up to? His brother Vincent used to fiddle about up there, and Vincent is dead," Fiona clicked her tongue and called to Ruairi again. "He's up there with his cousin and Declan."

"Declan's here?"

"Aye, he and Kieran have been here all afternoon."

"I didn't see them come in."

"They came in through the door in the back garden wall. Those two sneak around like a couple of rats."

"There's a door in your garden wall?"

"It's hidden beneath the ivy; built during the second world war. A lot of the gardens, even some inside walls of the rowhouses connect to each other around here."

Ruairi then Kieran appeared at the top of the stairs; both cheerfully disinterested in Reason.

"Brilliant so she is," Ruairi complimented dutifully.

"Magic," Kieran added before trailing Ruairi back to the attic.

"Regular poets," Fiona muttered. "Nevermind them, pet, you're pretty as a princess."

"Thank you, Fiona." Reason bent to kiss her cheek.

"I didn't see Declan come down, did you?"

"No," and Reason didn't miss him. But she returned to her room to find him stretched out on her bed. He didn't compliment her as she walked in, he didn't have to. His eyes said it all.

"Gee, Wilder, come in and make yourself at home. I see your black eye is looking better. Too bad. I rather liked you that way."

"What time does Prince Cromwell arrive?"

"Seven." Reason went on getting ready like Wilder wasn't there.

He had confronted Cain about taking Reason to the Fete, and Cain had sworn he had no interest in Reason beyond being her artist. But even if Cain was sincere in his desire to remain platonic, Reason was doing her best to undermine his good intentions. It was Denver all over again. Reason and another man. Only Wilder wouldn't care this time. He would not. "You look too good, Mac."

"Thanks." She combed her hair and lined her lips and drizzled perfume along her throat, between her breasts.

"Out for Cain's soul tonight?"

"And his body. Why aren't you going to Bernie's? You were invited."

"None of the Catholic physicians ever go."

"Oh, for heaven's sake, it's a social party not a political one," Reason said impatiently.

"You have a lot to learn, Mac. Anyway I'm on-call, and I always get called, so I never make plans." Wilder swung his legs off the bed to sit like *The Thinker*. He watched Reason in silence awhile then asked, "What do you want from me?"

"Nothing."

"The other night you said you're afraid for me. What am I supposed to do about that? I didn't invite you back into my life. I didn't ask you to worry about me. Are you expecting me to give up what I came home to achieve?"

"What did you come to achieve, Wilder?"

She asked all the hard questions. "I couldn't stay in America doing nothing, could I? And now that I'm here, I can't go home. This is home."

"Do you hear yourself? You've become like your father. He denied his old home and he denied his new home and he had nowhere left to be except miserable."

"This is different! I'm not miserable...or at least I wasn't until you showed up."

"That's not my fault. Blame your father."

"Before now I had nothing to lose...well, except maybe my life and that didn't scare me. But then I saw you again. Damn it, Reason, you've complicated everything."

"So shoot me and put me out of your misery."

"Shooting is too good for you," he smiled.

"All I want is for you to be careful. Is that too much to ask?" Reason met Wilder's gaze in the mirror. "Don't die for loving Ireland."

"You prefer me dying to love you instead, right?"

"You take nothing seriously!"

"What do you want me to do, Reason, *what?*" he exclaimed in frustration.

"Live a long life, that's all."

Wilder pushed from the bed to stand in the evening sunlight streaming into Reason's room. The familiar red chains of chimneys and black roofs beyond the window reassured his eyes. Then he looked back at Reason. Before she came to Belfast, life was a game. He never cast his eyes back as he ran. And he never worried. About anything, especially himself. He drank with friends and slept with Jillie and worked for his country and cause. He risked all with his diamond heart. Now life was still a game, but its prize had changed. It had become more valuable. And harder to lose.

"This is unreal, isn't it, Reas? You and I, together but not together, here, now, remembering all that was and wasn't between us…did you really think you made a mistake leaving me that night?"

"Yes."

His eyes rested upon her, but like she was a beam too bright, he looked away. "I'm standing here wondering who in the hell we are. I hardly know you, you hardly know me, you never met Merry or Bren, you've never met my dad, yet here I am sharing this country, this war with you. It's like you've become part of the war."

"The only war I'm a part of is the war in your mind, Wilder."

"If my mind's at war, it's because you're making me nuts! Wait a minute, I know why you're driving me crazy; it's because you saved my life. Well, hear this, Reason, I release you from being responsible for me. I can take care of myself."

"You don't need to shout." She stared at herself in the mirror, glossing her lips. "I'll let you drown this time."

"Free at last!" Wilder waved his hands, then seeing Reason ignore him, passed one final glance over her curves. "Equipped with rocket-launching legs, machine gun hips, and breasts men would die for, the temptress prepared to conquer the knight. I'll let you finish grooming your weapons, ace. I only came in here to convince myself that you don't look as deadly damn gorgeous as the night you ripped my heart out."

"And?"

"Cain Cromwell is a dead man." Wilder headed back upstairs to the attic. "Hope you have a rotten time without me, Mac. By the way, you were wrong about one thing," he called from the landing. "You say I never take anything seriously. I took *you* seriously…look where it got me."

"Holy hell! What a gorgeous woman!" Cain exclaimed when Reason walked downstairs. "You're looking some kind of *wild*."

Startled by Cain's interpretation of formal attire, Reason returned his stare. "Talk about wild, I had no idea I was spending the evening with a Musketeer."

Prince Charming Cain was not. At least not where the Solstice Fete was concerned. More the image of Captain Blood, he arrived with his hair tied at his nape in a pirate's love lock; he was clothed in black jeans, huaraches and an ivory poet's shirt open at the neck. "I make a habit of looking improper amidst British propriety."

"Won't you feel out of place?"

"I'm always out of place with my father and his friends."

"Then why are we going?"

"Because it will provide you the rare privilege of meeting the stars supporting the Gov. Guaranteed to be an evening you won't forget."

As Cain held the front door for Reason, Wilder thundered down the stairs.

"Oh look, the McKees let their lunatic out," Reason joked as Wilder streaked by.

"Gunshot to the chest," he said and bolted out of the house.

"Where?" Cain and Reason asked together.

"Up the Falls." Wilder vaulted into Fiona's car. "Yo, Cromwell, don't fall for the old gazebo line," he called out the window as he left. "The lady won't respect you in the morning."

"I guess we know where he'll be spending his Saturday night. What's 'the old gazebo line?'"

Reason raised her bare shoulders. "Who knows?"

Each June the Solstice Fete occurred thirty miles north of Belfast, just outside Portclare, at the seaside estate of Dr. and Mrs. Bernard Thunder. Tudor half-timbered with a Union flag flying high, it was a wee bit of England overlooking the Irish Sea. But with its electronic gates, barbed-metal fence and ten-foot wall, the manor seemed more like a penitentiary to Reason.

A tuxedoed butler led her and Cain through one opulent room after another until they reached the ballroom; a magnificent hall of mirrors and chandeliers reflecting off a pink terrazzo floor. Four grand doors opened onto a terrace facing the water. For a moment the room smelled of Givenchy perfume and sea air. Then the gunpowder fragrance of power and wealth permeated the clear summer air, and everywhere skulked Ulster's patricians.

To Reason the gathering resembled a beauty pageant where the fairest of them all paraded good breeding and affluence like high-fashion dolls. The women shopped in London. The men preferred Milan. Not entirely the grey-hairs Reason had imagined, the ages in the ballroom ranged from fifteen to eighty. No face lacked authority, no voice temerity, every opinion was gospel, and no other race existed beyond this mecca for the imperial and perfectly correct. Here were God's chosen landlords in the country of riches and rags.

Reason expected critical sneers when she and buccaneer Cain were announced. Instead everyone exulted to see him.

"Our hero," one woman welcomed with several pecks to Cain's cheek.

"Here's our boy," cheered another.

The men pumped his hand. "Damn good to see you again, Cain old man, damn good."

And patted his back. "We need you in South Down, son. Any plans of coming our way?"

All the while Cain returned the hearty greetings and introduced Reason around the room.

"Why do all these people keep calling you their hero?" Reason wondered and accepted a goblet of wine from a sterling tray.

"Because I dared not to wear a tuxedo," Cain confided facetiously.

"Stop kidding."

Cain downed his goblet of burgundy in one gulp and peered over Reason's head across the glittering ballroom. "Only amidst my father's tribe could a Cromwell ever be considered a hero in Ireland."

"I see you're up to your old tricks. Hello, darling." A tall, beige-haired woman in black chiffon hooked Cain's arm and kissed his cheek.

"Mother, this is Reason McGuinness."

"Charmed," Emily Cromwell smiled but ignored Reason's hand. "You're the architect. Such interesting work architecture, tearing down history to replace it with mirrored glass. Don't you miss America?"

"Yes, but I'm liking Belfast more and more every day."

"Leave it to an American to find Belfast likable," Emily smiled.

"Oh, I think it's beautiful here."

"Your people are from Ulster then?"

"My people?" Reason echoed.

"You don't look Irish, but then anyone can be a blonde these days," Emily smiled pleasantly again. "Our Cain was in the States, had a delightful time, didn't you, darling?"

"Best damn days of my life," he quipped.

"But, oh! You women are so pushy over there. Poor Cain was chased by one young thing after another. All after his money of course."

He glanced mordantly at Reason. "It was hell."

"And what does your family do, Reason?"

"My stepfather…"

"A broken home? Poor child. I thought Romans couldn't divorce, but then in America everything is easy and free. You have multiple brothers and sisters I presume?"

"No." Under fire and disliking it, Reason looked to Cain to intercede, but he didn't.

"Our Cain has three brothers, all solicitors in London, all married to fine English ladies. Only Cain is left for some gentlewoman to catch."

"Excuse me. I see some of my associates coming in," Reason concluded with her own version of the forced smile.

*   *   *   *   *   *

"What have we got here?" Wilder asked as he scrubbed his hands before shoving into the operating room.

"Aidan Duffy," said the nurse. "Thirty one years old, shot three times in the chest. I'm surprised he's made it this far actually."

Wilder was too. "Where was he when he was shot?"

"Walking home to Turf Lodge. He'd been at the pub celebrating his new job here at the Gov. Miss McGuinness hired him only this afternoon."

"Any idea who shot him?"

The nurse leaned beneath Wilder's ear. "I heard it was the Cure."

"Were there witnesses?"

"Several, including his mum. She says two men in a Mercedes drove through Turf Lodge, one fired three shots at Aidan while the driver made a U-turn and headed back towards the city centre. Mrs. Duffy says an hour before her son was shot the area was crawling with troops, but when her Aidan lay bleeding in the gutter there wasn't a soldier in sight. Och, his mother is shattered. One of her other sons was shot by the Army in the New Lodge two years ago."

*   *   *   *   *   *

Animated conversation moved the evening from dinner towards the auction. Antiques, paintings and jewels were being sold, and everyone was particularly excited about Hunter's emerald necklace; a genuine Cromwell heirloom from nineteenth century England. Its sale alone would generate at least £50,000 for Grosvenor Hospital. And after the guests had emptied their pockets for Hunter's good cause, the dancing would begin.

Being a benefit for the Gov, Reason assumed everyone present had some connection or at least familiarity with the hospital. But she found the majority of people hadn't visited the Grosvenor and never would. After all, it was in *West* Belfast. Reason made the mistake of asking one woman if her children had been born there.

The woman jerked back and plugged Reason with indignation. "I wouldn't be caught within a mile of that place."

"Why are you donating money to it then?" Reason asked, bewildered.

"Well, we have to have it. Someone has to take care of those people."

Cain found Reason humorous.

"What's so funny?" She didn't understand what she had said to offend.

"You are so innocent."

"Are you making fun of me?"

"No. I'm enjoying you."

"What am I doing wrong? Every time I mention the Gov I get a blank stare, a huff or a wisecrack."

"Take a walk in the garden with me." Cain led her by the hand out to the terrace, down its brick steps, onto the lawn. "The Gov is a pauper's hospital."

"But it has an excellent staff and modern equipment, and what about our emergency services…Belfast couldn't survive without our blood bank and thoracic surgeons."

"These people can't relate to that. All they see is a dreary old eyesore slumped in a bad part of town. They have private physicians in private clinics with private rooms. To these folks the Gov is known for bullets and bombs, and they don't want that element oozing into their side of life. Gladly they'll donate money to keep the untouchables where they belong."

"If our hospital is so undesirable, why is Bernard Thunder its chief of staff?"

"Bernie has been at the Gov for twenty five years, and I doubt he'd consider working anywhere else. He was born in the Shankill, you know, worked his way up. He may have risen above the Gov's clientele socially, but he'd never turn his back on them, at least not the loyalist part of them. He's proud of his staff and the work they do. Think of him as Ulster's Mother Theresa," Cain said with a laugh.

"That makes some sense, but why does your father come all the way over from England to head the Gov's board?"

"H.C. does it as a favor to Bernie, they've been friends for years. But considering he dislikes the Irish so much, I'm surprised he's lasted this long."

Reason glanced back at the ballroom. "But these people aren't Irish, they're British."

Cain clapped his hands together in delight. "Oh, Reason, you are a gem." He pulled her down to join him on a stone bench. "You may think those highbrows in there are British, and they'll tell you they're British, but ask anyone from England who those people are, and they'll tell you those loyalists are Irish. The fact is, if you aren't born in England, if you're born anywhere on this Emerald Isle, then in the eyes of the English you're Irish. And Irish means second class."

"But...how can your father not like these people when he's so friendly with them? They treat him like he's royalty."

"He adores being adored. But trust me, Reason, he considers those people in the ballroom to be fools. That's the history of these two countries. England will always see Ireland as its poor-relation and whipping boy."

"England holds Ireland in contempt, but its Army is here to maintain British rule." The irony baffled Reason. "It's like they're over here punishing the Irish for not being British, but not allowing the Irish to be British even when they want to be."

"Ah, Cain, there you are," Hunter waved his son inside. "We need your opinion."

Cain cocked a dubious eyebrow. "This ought to be interesting."

"There's only one solution for a unified Ireland," stout, bald Dr. Thunder said as Cain and Reason joined his circle. "The South needs to give up this Irish malarkey and rejoin the United Kingdom. Ireland would be unified once and for all under our queen."

Hunter drew Cain forward, briefly noticing Reason. "Hello, Reason dear. Marvelous presentation yesterday, marvelous."

"Indeed it was." Bernie patted Reason's head. "She's quite the little artist. Now, Cain, tell us if you think the Cure can stop the violence in Armagh. A lot of us think we should be increasing our agents down there."

"I say kill as many of the IRA bastards as we can," Hunter jumped in before Cain could speak. "They're nothing more than animals; let's hunt them down. Hell, we should blow those bloodthirsty murderers in two and mount their heads on the wall."

"What a conversation piece that would be," Bernie guffawed, leaning on Hunter's shoulder. "Sign me up for the safari, H.C. What do you think of the idea, Cain?"

Cain had nothing to say.

"Forget this nonsense about a political solution," Hunter continued. "We have tried for years to make peace, but the Roman Catholics refuse to cooperate."

"We wouldn't be in the mess we're in today if the Catholics weren't always wanting more," added an unidentified member of the circle. "They had everything they needed. We took care of them. Even now, they're sitting fat and sassy under British rule."

"St. Patrick should have left the snakes and driven out the Paddies," someone kidded.

"Lose them all in prison I say," declared another voice.

Hunter commanded the discussion again, "Prison's too good for terrorists. The only language they understand is right between the eyes. And the only way Ulster is going to know peace and prosperity is to take out every Roman Catholic gunman once and for all."

"Kill them before they have a chance to cause trouble," agreed Bernie. "They'll never sway us with their bombs. We will hunt them and hunt them and hunt them until the end of their days," he pledged.

"And what if you shoot an innocent man on your hunt?" finally Cain spoke.

"Bah! Roman Catholic and innocent isn't possible," Hunter fleered. "If I had my way, we'd let the Army shoot every Catholic on this island who stands in the way of peace."

"Oh, bravo, H.C., bra-vo!" Dr. Thunder rallied.

Like he was making a speech to thousands, Hunter rattled on, "We English are committed to wiping out the IRA at any cost. If the Fenians want to play big boys' games, they better be prepared for big boys' rules. Bring on the Cure and let slip the dogs of war!"

Revelers within ear-shot gave Hunter impromptu applause. But Reason had drained white. Her eyes were wide as they shot from Hunter to Bernie and landed accusingly on Cain. She opened her mouth to object.

"Reason love, why don't you go get us more wine." Cain gave her a nudge and she bolted outside.

Taking refuge in the gardens, she stared out at the sea stained copper by the setting sun. Burn the Catholics, hang Irish heads on the wall, hunt them and hunt them; more frightening than the words was the applause they invoked.

Catching Reason drenched in the twilight, Cain whirled her around to face him. "Did my father's friends shock you?"

"They make me sick."

"You have just heard the most powerful voices in Northern Ireland."

"Do you agree with them?" she demanded to know.

"They're absurd."

"You think they're *funny?*"

"Reason, their self-importance is ridiculous. No surrender!" Cain was laughing then slammed to serious, "They're dangerous men. A lot of them belong to secret societies like the ULF that have no purpose other than keeping the Catholics down, better yet, dead. Brute force is their solution for everything."

"And nobody blames them for the war?"

"Bite your tongue! The loyalists have this country by the balls, and the English government allows them to get away with it."

Reason sighed in exasperation. "Is this all anyone talks about here? I don't want to get involved. I don't want to care!"

"Sooner or later you will care, Reason. It's impossible to be in the Six Counties and not choose one side or the other."

"And what side did you choose, Cain? Those men called you their hero."

Cain kept his eyes on Reason. "I'm no hero."

"Are you a Cure agent?"

"I'm an artist."

"I want no part of you if you're one of those killers. Are you, Cain? Bernie asked your opinion on the Cure like you were an expert. Do you hunt Provisionals?"

"No. People ask me those questions because I worked for MI5."

Reason searched Cain's face for clues as if his expression would divulge an assassin behind his mask, but Cain's brown eyes were kind. His face was honest. "Did you know the Cure killed Wilder's sister?"

Cain cast his eyes to the sea. "Yes. Listen, Reason, if you want to get away from this, I'll take you home."

"Not yet. I want to see the auction. Gee, your mother certainly took a shine to me."

"The old cow dished you a dose of the prejudice the Irish have been served for centuries." And thus Cain had let his mother speak. Reason had tasted the tip of her own sword; wasn't that precisely the prejudice her own mother would have directed at Wilder? "Hey, look. A fairy tree!" He pointed to a hawthorn cloaked in white blossoms. "Did you know it's unlucky to bring a hawthorn's flowers into a house? Some say it's because the Crown of Thorns was made from a hawthorn. Others say it's unlucky because fairies live in them."

Reason took a closer look. "Do you suppose there are any fairies in there tonight?"

"Undoubtedly there are several." Cain filled his hands with flowers from the hawthorn. "Let's go inside."

*　　*　　*　　*　　*　　*

It never got easier. Each time he endured his own little death. "I'm sorry, Mrs. Duffy, but your Aidan has died." Knowing his words shattered this woman's world, Wilder felt more reaper than surgeon.

But a typical Irish mother, Mrs. Duffy sank with quiet dignity. "Aidan was a good boy. He wasn't involved in politics." Suffering too hot parched the tears in her eyes. "I just don't get the point. What did they shoot him for? I don't get the point at all."

*   *   *   *   *   *

Minutes before the auction, Hunter summoned Cain for a meeting. Cain declined, but Hunter hauled him into the library anyway.

"Would a tuxedo have killed you?" he berated when Cain closed the door. "Look at you. You're a goddamn disgrace. Didn't I tell you to show up looking decent?"

"I'm far more decent than your friends out there," Cain fired back.

"This is a formal affair, Cain. You're damn lucky these people think you're a star, otherwise they wouldn't have let you and that woman through the door."

"Reason looks beautiful, doesn't she?" Cain said, smitten.

"Set fool's gold in platinum and it's still fool's gold, Cain; the woman is common. What is the point of your showing up looking like some sort of hoodlum? To insult your mother and me? Must you insist upon being the rebel everywhere you go?"

"I am the rebel everywhere I go."

"Now you listen to me, boy, I'm not going to ask you again to behave like the Cromwell you are. What you do and say affects me directly, and I have assets and interests to protect over here. You are an *English* man and you will remain an *English* man."

"That's my life sentence," Cain sniffed.

"You belong in the asylum! I had hoped you'd come back from California a man, but you remain the spineless ninny." Without warning, Hunter delivered a slap to Cain's face. "Be a man! Don't humiliate me again."

"That's what it takes to be an *English* man, isn't it, H.C? A decent image and a ready fist." Cain nursed his jaw and laughed at his father. "Is this interrogation over?"

"No. I called you in here because I need you to do a job for me."

"What sort of job?"

"I lost some property in that bank robbery here in Portclare last weekend. I need you to find it."

"What were you doing using a bank in Portclare?"

"That's my business."

"You're off your head, pops. That was a Provisional job. Whatever you had is gone daddy gone."

"Get it back for me, Cain," Hunter's tone was ominous.

"How do you expect me to do that? You think I can just stroll into a republican club, find the fellows who robbed the bank and ask them for whatever you lost?"

"You'll find a way."

"What did you lose?" Cain already knew but played along.

"Ten uncut emeralds and a ledger."

"Where did you get uncut emeralds?"

"Just return them to me."

"Impossible."

"Do it, Cain, or I'll tell Reason the truth about you. You'd never see her again after that."

"You just said what I do affects you directly," Cain chuckled. "You wouldn't want to tarnish the family's good name by telling Reason the truth."

"Try me," Hunter smirked. "Or I could sell My Lady's Leisure to the highest bidder."

Cain fell silent. "I can't guarantee I can find your gems. They're probably out of the country by now."

"Try."

"You're insured. Why can't you just say the stones were stolen?"

"Or what if I were to discharge Miss McGuinness and send her back to the States branded as an incompetent, worse yet a thief?"

"Blackmail is ugly, H.C."

"But effective. Get me those gems, Cain."

"Suddenly it seems you're awash in gems. Where did you dig up this hundred-year-old emerald necklace you're hawking tonight? I don't recall our family having heirloom jewelry."

"The Cromwells have always had a fine collection of jewels."

"Well, that 'fine' old necklace you're peddling is a fake."

"Nonsense," Hunter gruffed.

"Give up the act, daddyo. You can fool those suckers out there, but you can't fool me. I didn't spend four years in the jewelry business without learning about jewels. Your £50,000 heirloom is a sham."

Hunter froze tight-lipped and waited for his son's next move.

"I couldn't care less if you swindle your dear Ulster friends, but be careful trying to blackmail me, H.C. I'm a Cromwell like you're a Cromwell. I can lie, cheat and steal with the wizards."

"What's your point?"

"You say one word to Reason about me, you hurt her or slander her work, and I'll crucify you."

"All right, all right." Unable to meet Cain's killing stare, Hunter dismissed his son with a wave, "Go enjoy the party, boy. After all, that's what you do best."

Catching Reason's hand, Cain dashed from the ballroom.

"But what about the auction?" she protested as they fled.

"Take off your shoes. Take off your shoes!" he ordered on the terrace with such impatience Reason kicked off her heels. "Now keep hold of my hand. Don't let go," he whispered and took off running. Dodging willows and birch trees, they pounded down a sidewalk, over the lawn, across the gardens, down fifteen steps and through a gateway of security cameras until the Thunder's house fell from sight and the sea rushed into view. And still Cain kept running until the sand grew deep and flooded their feet, until the air grew salty and damp and the wind frisked through their hair, until the cold, black water splashed up their shins. Standing still at last, Cain flung wide his arms and screamed to the darkened sky.

Unamused as the sea wet her white dress, Reason streaked back to dry sand. "Why are you screaming?"

"Because I feel like it!"

"You're crazy."

"You're right." He flung his shirt then his slacks and underwear to shore and dived deeper into the waves. "Come swim!"

"Oh sure, Cain, I'll jump right in in my dress."

"Forget your dress," he cavorted. "C'mon. Where's the wild in you?"

"I'm going back to the auction."

"Want to watch them salve their consciences? And they say the Catholics bought indulgences."

Reason paused to watch Cain. There he was floating in water the temperature of Greenland like he was one of the glaciers. "Aren't you cold?"

"Feels warm as the womb. Try it!"

She had never met a more mercurial, inscrutable man. "See you later." She hiked back to the house.

But the auction had lost its appeal. As the auctioneer held up *objets d'art* and the bids soared, all Reason could think about was West Belfast and the good-hearted people she'd met at the Gov. And here were Ulster's rich supporting the untouchable old hospital at arms' length like their pet disease. As she slipped from the ballroom she heard the word, "Sold!" and turned to see Dr. Bernard Thunder clasping the antique Cromwell emerald around Mrs. Thunder's neck.

Stopping to pick up her shoes, Reason returned to the shore. "I grabbed a towel for you," she called to Cain as he waded naked out of the sea.

"That was a quick auction," he gibed, catching the towel.

"I'd rather be out here with you. They just sold your family's necklace by the way."

"How much did it raise for the Gov?"

"£65,000," Reason said to which Cain just laughed.

"Now you'll come for a swim?"

"I don't think so."

Cain leapt to her side. "Be un-Reasonable tonight."

"I'll take my night warm and dry, thanks."

"Do you have something to hide under all these white beads," he skated wet palms up her arms, "or are you just shy?"

"That water is freezing."

"Stop playing it safe. Come baptize your soul in Irish waters, come crazy with me." He leaned close to her ear, "I dare you!" Tossing aside the towel with a whoop he skidded back to the pitch black tide.

No sight but the stars. No sounds save the water and Cain's voice bumping in on the breeze. "Aren't there things in the water at night?" Reason worried.

"Only the sails of a thousand souls. And Loch Ness monsters."

"Isn't the tide too strong?"

"You can see for yourself the tide is out. Stop making excuses, Reason; come experience life."

"Oh, all right." Carefully folding her clothes as she shed them, Reason followed Cain's lead to the water. "I can't believe I'm doing this." She greeted the inky deep bravely and lunged to join Cain. But she only made it thigh-deep. "Oh my…God!" The cold sucked her breath, socked her heart. "You really are deranged!" As fast as she rushed in, she rushed out.

"You big chicken, don't give up so fast." Cain seized her wrist in fun. "Stand still for one second, and I'll show you how to forget the cold."

"The only way to forget it is to get out of it!"

"Play along."

"OK, OK. Just hurry up and show me before I drop dead."

With hands clamped on her hips he moved her against him and held her there as a wave surfed over their legs. Reason would have insisted she was freezing if Cain's eyes weren't so hungry upon hers, if his hands weren't so caressing, if his body wasn't addressing hers. He raised her palm to his lips and watched the water filter down her wrist and drizzle over her breasts. He then mimicked the drizzle with one deliberate finger. And he waltzed her round and round in slow steps, round and round in the brisk, shallow water. As another wave approached, his lips met hers, and with Reason locked in his arms, he sank to his knees into the sand and let the wave wash over their embrace.

"Are you still cold?" His hands stroked her body. He kissed her again.

Reason requested Cain's lips with her answer, "Desperately." Simmering in his kiss, she assumed he would make love to her on the beach. That certainly appeared to be his desire, hers as well.

But Cain scrambled to his feet. "Come on, darling, let's get you dry then." Splashing ashore with Reason in tow, he wrapped the bath towel then his arms around her. "Now don't you feel electrified? Wasn't being cold and erotic better than being reasonable, Reason?"

"Much better," she agreed through chattering teeth.

"We'll get dressed and go back to the party. I want to dance with you."

Reason pushed back her wet hair. "I can't go back looking like this."

"Like a sensuous, sexual woman you mean? You look better than heaven to me."

"Maybe so, but…why are you smiling?"

*She's not worth losing Wilder's friendship. I shouldn't do this…*Cain peeled open Reason's towel and used it to belt her body to his. "Because," he kissed her bare shoulder, "I feel so bad about feeling so good with you."

"If we were in front of a roaring fire, I'd love to pursue this, but if I don't get dressed, I'll die."

"Will you give me one dance?"

"I'll dance anywhere in the world with you, Cain," Reason dived into her clothes, "except back in that house. I don't want to see those people again."

Cain shivered into his trousers. "Aha! You *have* been baptized in Irish waters!"

"Maybe so."

"You'll dance with me anywhere?"

"Yes."

"Then I'll take you to our own private ballroom."

Leaving the beach, Cain turned to see Reason's face, looking for what? Traces of love. Traces of Wilder. That Reason and the Irishman still shared strong feelings was obvious. Cain had seen the way Wilder's eyes laid claim to Reason and how she lived to capture and torment those eyes.

"What is your relationship with Wilder these days?"

Reason stepped back. "We have no relationship at all."

"Back there in the water were you thinking I was the wrong man? Were you wishing I was him?"

"Wilder is the wrong man, Cain."

"He's never gotten over you. He keeps pictures of you in his desk drawer, did you know that?"

"No."

"Are you still in love with him, Reason?"

She glanced away, and Cain didn't press to confirm what he already knew. He headed her up the steps leading to the manor. "Next time I kiss you, Reason, I want you thinking of me, not him." And he didn't want to be thinking of Wilder either.

Reason had no idea where Cain was taking her. All she knew was they needed the flashlight from his car. He steered her through the Thunder's gardens only to descend to the beach again down another flight of stairs.

"See? The house is built on a point," he showed Reason from the bottom of the steps. "We were on the other side of the point before. If we walk back this way, to the foot of the cliff, we'll be directly below the house. Hear how the music filters down?"

Reason heard clarinets keeping pace with percussion. "How do you know about this spot?"

"This isn't my first Solstice Fete. I've spent years perfecting escapes from the Thunder's manor. I found this particular ballroom in 1980.

I've never shown it to anyone before." Through shallow sand onto rocks they walked. "You can only see this place when the tide is out, otherwise you wouldn't know it existed."

Reason thought Cain was talking about a cove. What he showed her was a grotto, carved by the sea into the rock. Bolted into the chalky cliff was a thick wooden door. Its latch was an iron claw gripping an iron ring; it required the blow of Cain's fist to unlock. On squeaking hinges the four-foot door opened to reveal a cloister.

"Mermaids come here for shelter when the sea is rough." Cain handed Reason the flashlight. "Step inside."

Reaching far back and far up into the cliff, the grotto was larger than it appeared from the beach. Its walls were chalk; its floor sand. Fist-sized holes punched by the surf allowed a breeze to spiral through and whistle out the low door.

"I wouldn't want to get caught in here at high tide."

Reason made for the exit. "When is that?"

"Relax, love. Not for hours."

"Does Bernie know about this place?"

"Yeah, he let's fishermen use it. There's a ring for securing a boat down at the shoreline."

"Listen." Reason stood still. "They're playing 'Always.'" She recalled Wilder playing it for her on his flute. "*That's you and me, Mac,*" he had said. "*I'll be your lover after always comes and goes. I'll love you that long…*"

*   *   *   *   *   *

Bap, Bap, Bap beat the music of two helicopters scouting the Falls; they would play until dawn. Wilder slumped down in his office and listened to the night beyond the hospital. A slow, sure crank of retribution charged the air. Aidan Duffy wouldn't go unavenged. Melancholia filled Wilder's mind, and he wished daylight would bring a reprieve. But there was no peace between twilights; it was a 24-hour, open-all-night war. Tomorrow and tomorrow he would be suturing the traumas the Troubles inflicted. Aidan died like Brendan died like Merry died. God, damn the Union Jack.

The Gov was quiet; loneliness made rounds. It was hard to remember a normal life. Wilder wanted someone to go home to, someone he could tell how sad he felt, someone who would curl around him and shield him from the Belfast dark. He thought of Jillie. But no. He wanted what he didn't want. Reason. By now she would be home. He picked up the telephone. What if she was still out? He didn't want to know. He put the phone down. But she wouldn't still be out. What would she and Cain be doing at two in the morning? He picked the phone up. On this warm, starry night he knew what he would be doing with Reason. He put the phone down and went home alone.

*   *   *   *   *   *

The tide rolled in, rolled out, rolled in, rolled out to a hypnotic beat. Reason swayed with Cain to the tune of the Irish Sea. Round and round they drifted like little boats on a breeze.

"You're enjoying yourself?"

Without lifting her head from Cain's shoulder, Reason nodded. "I think you're secretly a prince."

"Aren't all English men?"

"Or maybe," she considered his clothes, "you're a pirate pretending to be a prince."

"That's it! I'm the mad marauder of Tintagel."

"I think that's who you were last Thursday after your class. One minute you were nice, the next you couldn't get rid of me fast enough. Is it because you knew your family wouldn't accept me?"

"Good God, no." Hugging Reason closer, Cain answered with effort, "It's just that I have so much to hide and so little to share. You're a good person, Reason. I have no right complicating your life."

"How could you complicate my life?"

"If I touch you once, I'll touch you always. You'll hate me for that one day."

Reason stroked Cain's cheek. "It's too late now. You've touched me."

"And one day you'll be sorry."

She checked his eyes again, still benign, still without guile. "Are you always so mysterious?"

"Better to be mysterious than notorious. The tide's rising, love. It's time to go." He led Reason out to the beach. "Look up at those stars and tell me you can say goodnight to me."

Reason looked up at Cain. "What would you prefer me to say?"

"That you'll come home to My Lady's Leisure with me."

"And what?" She imagined becoming his lover in that enormous bed by the fire.

He pulled her against him until she could feel his body harden. And he kissed her. "And watch the sun rise over the sea with me. We'll wrap up in a blanket, and I'll read Byron to you on the beach. Would you like that?"

She smiled up at him newly confounded. "Yes."

Chapter Sixteen

"Take a look at this." Ruairi handed Wilder a music box.

"Good God!" Wilder lifted the works to uncover a half-inch machine-gun shell.

"That cartridge penetrates flak jackets. The Brits will never be safe again."

"What gun uses this?"

"A 'Light Fifty' sniping rifle. So far we have three."

Wilder fingered the bullet, thinking of Aidan Duffy's chest wounds. "Do the Brits know you have this?"

"They don't know how many we have or where they are, but they know we have our hands on a deadly new weapon."

"How did they find out?" Wilder answered his own question, "Touts."

"A Volunteer in London turned informant last summer. The son of a bitch told the Brits the rifles were being moved into Belfast and he'd sell the Cure the details. Luckily another Volunteer in London took care of him before he leaked more than that; killed the Cure agent in the process. Cain set the whole thing up."

"Cain...Cromwell?" Wilder stammered. "What's he got to do with anything?"

"He was friends with the Cure agent who died."

"And Cain set him up?"

"Yeah. He told Cain he was meeting with the tout and Cain told the Provos where the meeting was. And it's a good thing. If that tout had talked, Kieran and I would be in jail. You know, for once your dad did something right. We can't thank him enough for recommending Cromwell. Cain's a gold mine of inside information, and if it weren't for him, the rifles wouldn't be in our hands. He got them for us in Berlin and keeps all three at his estate in Down. Have you been to My Lady's Leisure?"

"A few times." Wilder had no idea Cain was so involved with the war. It was a subject they rarely discussed. "How did he get a hold of guns?"

"Cromwell can get anything."

"He wasn't in the Cure, was he?"

Ruairi laughed, "If he had been, the Ra would have killed him by now."

Though he knew Cain provided Ruairi and Kieran with information on MI5, Wilder was stunned. "Cain never seemed the sort to deal friends, or arms."

"Nobody needs friends in the Cure, Dec."

"How long has he been helping you?"

"Since the day he got here. I thought you knew…hey, did Kieran tell you I'm quitting the Ra?"

Wilder was further dismayed. "You've always said you were in it for life."

"I joined after the Brits threw me in prison…I was really angry back then. But now I have a job at the Gov. And I don't want to spend another day in jail or die like my brother. And when Aidan died last night, I said, 'That's it.' I still support the cause, but as for being in the army, I want to quit while I'm alive."

"But very few people know you're involved in the IRA."

"Aye, but it's time I move on."

"Can any of us really move on, Ruairi? We'll always be targets."

"Yeah, well, I want to try." Ruairi pointed to the cartridge in Wilder's palm. "What do you think of our acquisition?"

Wilder dropped the bullet back into the music box and tossed it to Ruairi. "Not much."

"You should see your face," Ruairi started to laugh. "You're pale as plaster. I didn't ask you to use the gun for christsake. All I did was show you its bullet."

Wilder considered his friend with mixed emotions. "And all I see is the damage it will inflict."

"You'd better toughen up, Declan. You can't be a spectator in this. If you support the war, you have to support the casualties of war."

"Part of me can live with that, the part of me that grew up here, the part that gets kicked around by the Brits every day. But part of me is appalled by the violence. I don't want to condone it."

"You want to condemn it?" Ruairi scorned.

"I work on the other side of the casualties, Ruairi. I bust my butt every day trying to keep people alive. I took the Hippocratic oath for God's sake…"

"Your man Hippocrates also said extreme diseases require extreme remedies. England is Ireland's extreme disease."

"All I'm saying is my role here is to help not harm. I'll help you guys but that doesn't mean I want to know what you're doing. And the only time I'm interested in bullets is when I'm cutting them out of a wound."

"You'll never keep your hands clean, Dec."

Wilder didn't say anything.

"The minute you became our physician, you became a soldier, Declan. You and the Ra are the architects of change in Ireland." Ruairi caught Wilder by the chin to stress his point, "You're a *soldier* with a justifiable cause, and you may have to do harm to help one day. No matter what side of our struggle you're on, your convictions have to be strong enough to give you the confidence to kill someone without hesitation, without regret. Remember that, live and breathe that, or get the hell out of the war."

And Wilder knew what Ruairi was thinking. That he was like his father, that maybe he belonged in Malibu. He looked Ruairi dead in the eye, not ashamed to be Desmond's son. "Speaking of architects, where's Reason? I didn't see her when I came in."

"I was looking for her earlier myself. She hasn't come home yet."

Wilder double-checked his watch. "She must have come in and gone out again."

"Her bed hasn't been slept in. I checked."

"You don't suppose she was in an accident or something?"

"Nah. I'm sure she's having too much fun to come home."

"It's three in the afternoon! I don't want her having that much fun."

"You know, Declan, ever since Reason came to Belfast you've been preoccupied. I'm beginning to wonder which armed struggle you're committed to."

"I am *not* preoccupied! I'm just looking out for the woman."

"Face it, Dec, she's getting nailed by Cain," Ruairi said without care.

"Oh, will you relax? She's in good hands with Cromwell."

Wilder's heart twisted. That's what concerned him.

"No leads on the men who murdered a Catholic man in Turf Lodge last night," said the anchorwoman while the TV camera focused on people dropping flowers at the site of Aidan's murder. Reason watched the grim tribute and couldn't believe the strapping young man she had hired was dead. The RUC and Army denied the Cure had been involved, stating officially that the killing was the work of the Ulster Liberation Force. But the ULF wasn't taking credit, and word on the street never lied; the Cure *had* visited Turf Lodge.

"The RUC reports a rifle found at the scene belonged to Aidan Duffy. An anonymous eyewitness reports Duffy was aiming the gun at the Mercedes moments before being shot…"

Reason glanced up to see Wilder joining her in the McKee's family room. "Cinderella has finally come home from the ball," he said, taking in the sight of her freshly bathed, in her silk robe with her hair damp and loose on her shoulders. She looked beautiful.

Reason cleared a spot beside her on the sofa. "Have a seat. I'm surprised you're over here this late."

"You know I never let sleep interfere with my night life."

How well she recalled their intimate, into-the-night conversations in Colorado. "Here to see Ruairi?"

"Yes. What they're saying isn't true you know." He referred to the murder being described on TV. "Aidan wasn't carrying a gun. Aidan Duffy hated guns."

"Why are the police saying he was armed then?"

"If they ever admit the shooter was with the Cure, the RUC and Army will say the agent shot Aidan in self-defense. All the security forces have to say in disputed shootings is that they fired their guns because they thought their lives were in danger, and the case is forgotten."

"Don't they have to prove there was a gun at the scene?"

"No. The burden of proof is on the defendant; guilty until proven innocent. If Aidan had lived, it would have been up to him to prove he wasn't carrying a gun. Poor Kieran is taking the news really hard. Aidan was his best friend. I wish we could have done more in the OR."

"I'm sure you did your best to save him."

"Three shots to the chest? There was nothing to save, and it makes no sense. Aidan had no connection to the IRA, so why did the Cure single him out? The Cure never does anything without a reason."

"Aidan had one connection to the IRA, Wilder," Reason observed shrewdly. "Wouldn't the Cure go so far as to murder Kieran's best friend to send a warning to Kieran and others like him?" Having heard the conversation at Bernie's, she knew this scenario wasn't just possible but likely.

Wilder stared at Reason in surprise. "You're catching on to the politics here. You could be right."

"How does everyone know it was the Cure? It could have been the ULF like the police are saying, couldn't it?"

"Yes, but the ULF always claims responsibility for the Catholics they kill, and nobody has owned up to Aidan's death. And the details of his death are contradictory. When there's talk of the victims having guns when there were no guns, when the eyewitnesses tell a different story than the police, you can pretty much be assured the Army or the peelers are involved in something dirty. This was a neat, methodical hit in broad daylight. One minute there were soldiers all over Turf Lodge, the next minute there wasn't a squaddie in sight; they knew something was up. Then suddenly a Mercedes arrived in a poor section of West Belfast; a Mercedes with mud-covered license plates and dark windows, in no hurry to leave the scene of the crime. That's too fancy a car for the ULF to be using. Plus a sophisticated military rifle was used to deliver three dead-eye shots to the chest just to the right of the heart to ensure Aidan would squirm in his own blood long enough to terrorize the natives…all calling cards of the Cure. On top of all that, Aidan's mother told me Aidan had been receiving threats from the Army. She said the soldiers had been harassing him on the streets for weeks, telling him his days were numbered and calling him 'Dead Meat' Duffy. She also said Aidan thought he was under surveillance. My sister was saying the same thing a few days before she was killed."

Cain's murky connections to the Cure haunted Reason. "How can you tell if someone is a Cure agent?"

"You can't. The Cure is famous for its ability to blend with its targets until it's time to kill them."

"How awful," Reason gulped. Cain was a Brit. A Brit who had worked for British Intelligence after giving up a penchant for robbery. A Brit Hunter's friends embraced. A Byron-reading Brit of docile soul and tender touch she had fallen hard and fast for. Reason debated disclosing her suspicions to Wilder, but there was nothing about Cain that suggested he was a killer. And she feared one word to Wilder, and Cain could wind up dead. "What happens if a Cure agent is uncovered by the IRA?"

"He'll be shot."

Unsettled by the conversation Reason jumped up. "I have a seven o'clock meeting tomorrow. I'd better get some sleep."

"Hold it, Mac." Wilder drew her back down beside him. "You haven't told me about Hunter's Bigotry Ball. How was it?"

"Fine, but you were right about Hunter. He really is a jerk."

"And what about his son?"

"Cain was," Reason sighed to remember, "stupendous."

"*Stupendous?* He's not that great, Reason." Wilder crossed his arms, frowning. She had never called *him* stupendous. "Where were you all day?"

"Out."

"I could see you were *out*. Were you at work?"

"No."

Wilder drummed his fingers on his thigh, gave the television a glance then pegged Reason. "So, where were you? I've been trying to find you since noon."

"Why?"

"Must you always answer a question with a question? I wanted to make sure you got home safely, that's all."

"I was with Cain."

"All night and all day?"

"We lost track of the time."

Wilder hated her answer. "A night and one day is your style, isn't it, Mac? Did you let him fall in love with you then ax him at sundown?"

"Heavens no." Reason patted Wilder's cheek. "I only do those things to you."

"I can't believe you spent the night with Cain." Wilder followed Reason to the stairs. "You just met the man! Now suddenly he's *stupendous* and you're falling all over him.

Seeing Wilder's jealous reaction, Reason couldn't hide her pleasure. "Keeping pictures of me in your desk and all, maybe you wish I were falling over you."

"How do you know what's in my desk?"

"Cain told me."

"I have lots of pictures in my desk, Mac; all of them past tense. I've been meaning to throw them out for months. I can't believe he's snooped through my drawers."

"He asked me if I'm still in love with you."

"And what did you tell him?"

"That I preferred him to you."

"You lied, didn't you?"

"Good girls don't lie," Reason laughed.

"You must be a great liar then," Wilder laughed back. "Leave it to Cromwell to mention those photos. You know, Mac, one of these days I really do have to get you out of my life."

"You'll never do it, O'Neill."

"Is that a challenge?"

"It's a *fact.*"

"Sorry, sweetheart, you're history."

"In that case, Wilder, I'm yours forever because the one thing you Irish prize above all is your history."

He couldn't win, and admiring Reason two steps above him, he didn't want to. "What was your father's first name?"

"Why do you suddenly want to know that?"

Wilder rubbed the headache Reason had given him. "Can't you *ever* answer a simple question?"

"Kent."

"*Kent* McGuinness? Sounds like an Irish cigarette," Wilder snickered en route to the attic.

"It's an old Connecticut name...Wilder? Are you really going to throw out your pictures of me?"

He viewed her from the third floor landing. Silky woman with upcast eyes. Yes eyes, yes mouth, "*Yes,*" she had sighed. White breasts, parting thighs, "*Now,*" she had sighed. "No picture does you justice, Reas."

Chapter Seventeen

"Jillie, what are you doing?" Reason asked when she walked into work.

"I lost my necklace." Jillie crawled out from under her desk. "It was a gift from my granny."

"What does it look like?"

"It's just a wee lucky charm on a chain. I never took it off because it kept me safe. Och, I'll be cursed if I've lost it." She scrambled up. "Hopefully it's at home in my closet. How was your weekend with Cain?"

"So wonderful I was sorry when it was over."

"Did he make love to you?"

"No."

Jillie rolled her eyes. "I'd ask for my money back. I spent my weekend trying to console Kieran. He was there when Aidan was shot. I saw him right after it happened. He had blood all over him, but he didn't say a word, not one word. He just took my hand and wouldn't let go, and we came here and sat in the waiting room until Declan came out…Kieran and I took Aidan's mother home. Honestly, I thought the night would never end. Now listen to this, today Kieran got a letter at his parents' house. It had a bullet in it from the gun that was used to kill Aidan, and it said, 'We'll kill everyone you care about. Morris is next.'"

Reason dropped into her chair, aghast. "Oh my God. Who was it from?"

"The Cure I suppose. Isn't that just the most evil thing? Who would hurt wee Morris?"

"Oh, you don't think they'd really hurt him, do you? He's just a little boy!"

"Kill the weed before it flowers…or so the Cure would say."

"What's Kieran going to do?"

"What can he do? The RUC would laugh at him if he asked for protection. Being a republican, he deserves what he gets…well, that's what the RUC says." Jillie touched up her lipstick and smiled at herself in her mirror. "Can you believe it? I've seen Kieran every day since that night at Albie's when you and Decky abandoned us. Do you think Declan has found someone else? He hasn't called me in weeks."

"Really?" That made Reason's day.

"He says he hasn't been seeing anyone, but I think he has. Do you know he won't even kiss me now? I should be jealous, but then I've always been more interested in Kieran. Oooh, knowing the Cure is skulking around here makes my flesh crawl. Those English bastards terrify me."

"Me too. I know if I ever saw one I'd drop dead from fright."

*   *   *   *   *   *

When Wilder slipped inside his house after midnight the scent of patchouli slapped him seconds before the nozzle of a revolver butted the back of his head. Without removing the gun, the intruder marched him through the dark into the kitchen.

"Sit down." On flickered the overhead lights. "Wilder!"

"What in the hell are you doing, Cromwell?"

"You scared me to death!"

"I scared *you?* For God's sake put the gun down."

Irreverently, Cain tossed the revolver over his shoulder. "Good thing it didn't go off," he joked as the weapon hit the floor. "There was somebody in your house awhile ago. I was asleep on the sofa…by the way, I found 60p under one of the cushions, and dust! Don't you ever dust?"

"Will you just tell me what's going on?"

"Right. I woke up when I heard the front door open. I thought it was you, but when you didn't turn on any lights, and you were sneaking around, and I smelled that stinking patchouli, I knew it wasn't you. I got off the sofa quiet as a cat, and I saw this man, a tall man, in a balaclava sneaking into your living room. I grabbed the butcher knife from the kitchen here. Did you notice I finished painting? What do you think? See, it's not yellow."

"It's stunning, Cain. Finish the story."

Cain helped himself to a banana. "You know what sounds good right now? A peach. Do you like peaches? I'll bring you some. I followed the man into the living room," he went on alternately using the banana as a prop and a snack. "'Drop the gun, you son of a bitch, or I'll blow your brains out!' I yelled." Cain flourished the banana in the air. "I about brought the roof down. The sheer volume alone was frightening. I was louder than..."

"Cromwell!"

"In the dark the fellow couldn't see I didn't have a gun, so he dropped his gun which is what I just threw over my shoulder. Then I hurled the butcher knife like a magician throws knives in a knife act." Cain spiked the banana peel across the kitchen. "It breezed right through the bastard's shadow, into the wall. 'Next time it's your face,' I yelled, and the guy bolted. The knife landed right in the heart of the Hollywood Hills. You know that watercolor I did for you? The knife is stuck in the O." Seeing Wilder growing impatient, Cain hastily finished, "I tried to grab him, but he took off out the front door. When you came in I thought you were him, back for more."

"Was it the ULF?"

"Could be. But by the make of gun he had I'd say it's more likely it was the Cure," Cain added with his mouth full of another banana. "I heard about Kieran's bullet in the mail. Obviously it's open season on his family and friends. You just can't beat a banana from Honduras. I've tried the ones from Ecuador and..."

Wilder yanked the banana out of Cain's hand. "You act like this is a goddamn joke!"

"What do you want me to do? Cry?" Cain jerked back his snack. "I don't think the guy was here to hurt you, at least not tonight. You're being checked out. Probably because you're related to Kieran."

"That explains why I keep smelling patchouli. They've been in here before, going through my stuff. You don't wear patchouli, do you?"

"I don't want to smell like an old hippie! Apparently it's your intruder's calling card. They want you to know they were here because they want you to be scared."

"Well, it's working," Wilder admitted.

"Ruairi tells me he told you about the sniping rifles. It's information you could regret having. The Brits are desperate to find those guns and they might haul you in for interrogation."

"Oh, more good news," Wilder groaned. "How did you manage an arms deal?"

"I have connections from my intelligence days."

Wilder drew his arms across his chest; a chill pricked his neck. "Did you really have a friend killed in London last summer?"

"He wasn't a friend. He was a Cure agent and knew everything about Kieran and Ruairi," Cain replied, growing nervous.

"Would you have done it yourself? Could you shoot a British soldier?"

"There's the difference between you and me, Wilder. I would in a second. You wouldn't in a lifetime."

"You weren't high on coke when you set him up, were you?"

"No! I've stayed clean since leaving the clinic in L.A.," Cain growled, losing his breath, looking away, inching for the door.

"If you were watching Arabs for two years, how did you come to know a guy in the Cure? It's about as clandestine an organization as you can get."

Cain wiped sweat off his lip. "We…met at a covert methods of entry course."

"How did you find out there was an IRA informant in the first place?"

"I stopped by the agent's house for a visit one day. I was gathering information for Ruairi," Cain leaned outside and took several breaths of cool air. His hands shook, his heart pounded. "The agent asked if I wanted to go with him to meet a 'real IRA bastard,' and I said 'yes.' But before I went with him, I contacted Ruairi and set up the hit. Look, Wilder, I don't regret doing it, but I don't like talking about it."

"Sorry. I just had no idea you were so involved."

Cain leaned back into the kitchen. "Do you know who those emeralds you bagged in Portclare belong to? My father."

Wilder let go a laugh. "Seriously?"

"Classic, isn't it? Mr. Holier-than-thou smuggled them out of Colombia to sell on the black market in Zurich, and now he wants me to find them."

"Didn't you send them back?"

"Not when I learned who they belonged to. I have plans for the old man."

"There's another commandment I've broken then. If I ever go to confession again, I'll be in there a month. Speaking of confessions, what's going on with you and Reason? She came home from Bernie's head over heels about wonderful you. You swore you wouldn't get involved with her."

"All I did was take her to the party. We danced and I read her some poetry. Big deal."

"Reason's word for the night was 'stupendous.'"

"Wow," Cain liked that.

"Did you make love to her?"

"Of course not! I enjoyed her company. Come on, Wilder, you don't mind me seeing her as a friend, do you?"

Wilder smiled at the justice. He had said something similar to Reid when he had every intention of stealing Reason. "I can't stop you."

"If you don't want me to go on seeing her, just say so."

"I said so weeks ago."

"Oh yeah, you did. But, considering I'm 'stupendous,' I owe it to Reason to see her again," Cain laughed.

"We all have our ghosts, Cain. Yours is a man in London, mine is Reason McGuinness. I don't want to watch you fall in love with her."

"We'll sneak around like Capulets and Montagues then. I'm kidding! You worry too much, Wilder. Uh oh, it's after midnight. I have to get out of here. I have work to do at home."

"Don't you ever sleep?"

"Sleep is for people with clean souls." Cain stooped to retrieve the intruder's gun. "We'll donate this to Ruairi." Giving it a gunslinger's twirl, he snapped the barrel to his temple and pulled the trigger. When nothing happened he laughed out loud, "Must be my lucky night."

Horrified, Wilder tackled Cain and slammed him to the wall. "What in the fuck was that?" he blared. "Don't you *ever* do that again!"

Cain scratched his chin, puzzled. "I wasn't doing anything, Wilder. Is there something you'd like me to do? I do topiary. Would you like that?"

"Cromwell, you're *nuts.*"

"We're all nuts." Cain saw himself to the door. "I'll be over to fertilize your roses next week. Can you do this?" He tap danced in a circle then removed an invisible top hat with a majestic bow. "You learn all the best steps in Hollywood."

*   *   *   *   *   *

The crowd on the street reminded Reason it was Tuesday. Braving ceaseless rain and the presence of tanks and helicopters and policemen in droves, hundreds of people marched up the Falls Road below Reason's window at the Gov. Six men in black hoisted the coffin towards Milltown; a coffin draped in a Tricolour flag and wreathes of flowers. One tin whistle sweetly defied the dark day and tweetered on the north wind. The horde of mourners, like a black tide flooding up the Falls, were the portrait of Belfast to Reason. They could have been Catholic or Protestant. In grief both sides looked the same. And grief was nothing more than a terrible tide. It swept in, it swept out, things changed, things stayed the same. Grief was Belfast's consistency. Turning away,

Reason returned to her drafting table overcome by the heartbreak of Ireland's most beautiful city.

"You paged me?" In surgical greens and a hurry Wilder darted in to see Reason.

"Why aren't you at Aidan's funeral?"

"I have surgery in ten minutes." He checked his watch then passed his eyes over Reason. "You look nice today. Was there something in particular you wanted to see me about, or did you just want to see me?"

"You missed the design meeting yesterday." She dabbed her eyes. "I need your approval on the blueprints for the atrium."

"I'm free after three. I'll come up here and take a...what's the matter?"

"I was watching the funeral and listening to the music. Sometimes this city makes me so sad."

Wilder watched the cortege passing below, his own heart feeling sick. "I keep thinking about Aidan's mom burying two sons in two years...kind of like my mom. In the end, who really dies for Ireland? The mothers."

"If you open the window, you can hear a tin whistle. It always makes me cry. There really must be Irish in me somewhere."

Wilder could have been sarcastic. Instead he was tender. "I've always believed that's the best part of you, Mac. I'll see you this afternoon. And you really do look great today."

Chapter Eighteen

"You're invited to the McCartan's party tomorrow." Wilder caught up to Reason in the hospital parking lot Thursday evening. "Morris is turning six. He called me today to ask if you would come."

"I'd love to."

"You aren't booked with Cromwell?"

"I'm seeing him Saturday. He's going to show me his designs for the mural."

"You really like him, don't you?"

"Yes. He makes me glad to be in Belfast…unlike other men I know."

"No need to get catty, Mac. About tomorrow night. It's just a little party at Saint Joseph's starting at seven."

"Is that a church?"

"Yes, off the Antrim Road not far from Fiona's."

"Do you think it's safe for you and me to spend another Friday night together? After the last two I'm not so sure."

Wilder didn't miss the chance to steal the upper hand. "I didn't say we'd be together, Mac. Morris invited you, not me."

*   *   *   *   *   *

"Is Reason here yet?" Morris pestered Jillie.

"For the millionth time, no. Quit bothering me." Jillie went on plugging candles into Morris' cake. "Where's your dad?"

"Over there behind the bar with Uncle Ruairi, see? Hi Daddy, hi Ruairi." Morris skipped in a circle and caught Jillie's wrist. "What time is it now?"

"Seven ten." Jillie shook free her hand and gave Morris a shove. "I have a splitting headache, Morris. Go away."

"OK, but if you see Reason, tell me, tell me, tell me."

"You'll be the first to know, you little monster."

"Have you seen Reason?" Wilder sneaked up behind Jillie and kissed her neck.

"Not you too! You'd think Reason was the Queen of Sheba."

"Morris has asked me where she is at least a thousand times. I just wondered if you knew what's keeping her."

"She had a late meeting with the pathologists about the new morgue. She'll be here, don't worry. My stars, Decky, don't you look pretty, all poshed up. Ooh, you smell nice too." Jillie looked around the gymnasium for a spare woman. "If you tell me you're here alone looking this fantastic, I'll eat my heart out."

"*Me?* Alone on a warm summer night in glamorous Belfast?" Wilder cracked a smile, "Yeah, I'm alone."

"You should have called me before I made plans with Kieran. We could have had an erotic night."

"Nah, I'm on call again this weekend, and you know what that means. I'll be outta here in an hour."

"You really don't mind me seeing your cousin?" Jillie asked, annoyed that Wilder had never acted jealous or begged her to come back.

"From what I've heard it's too late for objections. Kieran's crazy about you."

"And poor Decky's alone. All work and no play. Give me a call sometime and I'll fix that."

"I'm sure you would." Wilder kissed Jillie's nape again. "Cheerio, love."

Reason walked into the old church hall and beheld the Irish conception of a "little party." Every McCartan, McKee and O'Neill mother, father, brother, sister, grandparent and child for three generations was on hand to wish Morris well. Six musicians filled the stage with fiddles, flutes and banjoes. Men and grandchildren danced. Women and women danced. Young men clustered at tables far from the ladies and pondered black pints of Guinness while the ladies congregated merrily elsewhere, and children ran giggling in between. And only conversation was thicker than the cigarette smoke choking the windowless hall.

"Whoa, McGuinness, look at you!" Jillie approved of Reason's smoky leather mini-skirt, lemon charmeuse blouse and matching spiked heels. "I thought you'd never get here." She grabbed Reason's hand. "Morris honey, look who just arrived."

Morris skidded towards Reason too fast and tripped into her knees. With frosting-smeared fingers he used her ankles to pull himself up. "Lucky you sure got a whole lotta legs, Reason, or I'd of never gotten up," Morris tittered giddily. "I got a hamster for my birthday, a *real* hamster. Wanna see him?"

Reason stooped to brush the frosting off her shins then gave Morris her hand. He was dragging her across the room and talking faster than Reason could listen, when a slim, pepper-haired woman interceded.

"Morris love, we're going to cut your cake soon. Hadn't you better go help Kieran with the plates?"

Birthday cake being even better than Reason, Morris zoomed away.

"He's full of beans our Morris. And you must be Reason. Hello, love. I'm Nora McCartan." Wilder's aunt hugged Reason hard. "Fiona has told us all about you, dear. Och, you're a lovely girl. Come meet the rest of the family."

A far cry from Cain's frigid mother the week before, Nora tucked Reason under her wing and introduced her around the room. Without reserve every granny, husband and cousin welcomed Reason into the clan.

"She's practically an O'Neill," they cheerfully agreed though Reason didn't know why they'd say that; she assumed Wilder had never mentioned her to the family.

After making the rounds, Nora, her husband Eamonn, Fiona and three other female cousins sat Reason down at their table and ordered her a "wee glass of whiskey with a wee brandy chaser." She wanted nothing to drink but quickly learned she couldn't "just say no" at this Irish celebration. It simply was not done. Every time she declined, instead of bringing her nothing like she requested, someone brought her two more drinks. The more she resisted, the more they insisted, and the drinks piled up before her. In less than no time she was a "wee bit punctured."

Kieran had come over, as had Ruairi, but Reason hadn't seen Wilder. She had hoped he would be playing his flute, but he was nowhere in sight. Someone said he had been called back to the hospital, someone else said he was outside playing football with the kids, but as the spirits muddled her head, Reason didn't care where Wilder was or wasn't. His family was more entertaining.

"Why aren't more of the men and women sitting together?" Reason noted the segregation.

"The sexes are worlds apart, love," Eamonn McCartan explained, nudging Nora's ribs. "The men are talking about football and what they did at the pub last night; the women are talking about work and wee babies."

"Well, they must get together sometime…look at all these children."

"Most couples meet when they fall on top of each other in the pub on their way to the loo," one cousin cracked. "I met my Sean at the Rotterdam down by the docks so I did. He reached for me instead of his Guinness…that was his first mistake!" she crowed.

"Don't couples talk and enjoy being together?" Reason questioned further.

"Only time an Irish woman talks is to argue or nag, which is *all* the time," an uncle at a nearby table joked.

"Och no, Frank O'Neill, you devil. Your Bridie is a saint," Nora chaffed.

"See what I mean? Arguing! A wee pint never talks back."

"Until the next day!" cried Eamonn.

"But what about romance?" Reason pursued.

"*Romance?*" Everyone at the table laughed. "Guess we never think of that."

"Washing, cooking, cleaning, feeding the wee'uns, who has time? I'll take a good sleep before I'll take a man," another cousin proclaimed in jest.

Nora wore an impish grin and tapped her chest, "I tell my Eamonn I'm going to find me a boy toy and run away. He shapes right up so he does. 'Who's going to cook me dinner?' he howls. Romance, ha!"

But eventually separate spheres entwined. The men and women slid to their feet to meet in the middle of the room and dance. And when the Guinness made the men sentimental and the ladies bold, romance had its way. Just like religion in Belfast, love was all right as long as it stayed in its proper place on its side of the room.

"Not all Irish men are unromantic, my dear," a grandfather from County Tyrone clarified as he trotted Reason about the dance floor. "But too many of our lads have spent hard years in prison, and in prison young men think about freedom and foreign places not love here at home where the war is."

That sobered Reason, but Morris arrived to lighten the mood. "You said you'd come see Leonard." Clamping Reason's fingers, he pushed through the crowd to the side of the room.

"Who's Leonard?"

"My hamster, silly. Do you like the name Leonard?"

"Oh yes."

He showed Reason the cage sitting on a bench. "I wanted a dog, but we can't have a dog cuz we don't have a yard. Leonard has his own wee sock to sleep in and a wheel to run in…he came with his own yard you see."

Reason watched the hamster running in his wheel. "Gee, Leonard's almost as cute as you, Morris."

"Aye, but I don't sleep in a sock why doesn't Decky like you?" he said all in one breath.

"Did he say he doesn't like me?"

"Uh huh."

"Well," Reason took a moment to think above the brandy fog in her mind, "I wasn't very nice to your uncle when I knew him in America."

"You saved his life, that's nice."

"That's about the only nice thing I've ever done for him."

"Are you sorry you weren't nice?"

Reason's voice fell. "Terribly."

Morris sat down on the bench and peered up at Reason glumly. "Do you think my daddy is going to marry Jillie? He goes to her house all the time."

"You'll have to ask him about that."

"I don't like her."

"How come?"

"She's a Brit."

Reason covered a laugh. "She's as Irish as you, Morris."

"She could be a Brit," he fussed.

Reason took a seat beside Morris. "Jillie was born and raised in Dublin."

But Morris wouldn't be swayed. "But what if she's bad? What if she kills my daddy?"

"Morris, Jillie is on your side. Isn't she nice to you?"

"No, and she's not like us..." he stared into his small hands "...I don't want my daddy to die."

Reason wished she could guarantee Morris wouldn't lose his father, but Kieran lived in harm's way. Looking into Morris' face she saw worry and fear too severe for a little boy. And she knew in no time the fear would congeal. Before long Liam O'Neill's fire would torch Morris' soft eyes.

"You shouldn't be worrying on your birthday." Reason petted Morris' curls sympathetically.

"I worry everyday."

The cutting of Morris' birthday cake couldn't have come at a better time. When Morris noticed his father motioning him up to the stage, like magic his worries took flight and joy sent him skipping up to blow out his candles.

"Make a wish," the relatives cheered when Morris inhaled a great breath.

As Morris blew out his candles, Reason guessed what he was wishing. If only birthday wishes came with a guarantee.

Cousins and uncles from each of the North's six counties pranced Reason up and down the dance floor until her feet knew every dance step in Ireland. She had planned to stay one hour, she had work to finish at home, but after three hours she had lost all ambition. The party was better than working, and after all the "wee" drinks she had accepted, she decided she was more likely to be in the morgue than re-designing one tonight.

"Shall we jig another ring around the floor or have a wee brandy?" an uncle from Armagh City asked Reason before the next song.

"Oh, I'd better sit down." She wavered atop her tall heels. "I'm not much of a jigger."

"If you wouldn't wear hooker high heels, you could jig with the best of them. Hello Uncle Niall."

"Decky! How's it going? How's Dessie? You're looking super, lad. Have you met Reason? Reason, this is my nephew Declan. Declan, this is Reason. She's from your side of the world."

"Really? And here I thought she was English...or does she just prefer English men?"

Feeling the tension as Wilder and Reason stared eye to eye, Uncle Niall excused himself. Neither noticed; they stood in the center of the room and the party swirled around them.

Wilder caressed Reason's curls before sliding a hand of possession down her back. "I heard you were only staying an hour. It's been three."

"I heard you were called back to the hospital." Her fingers stroked his jaw. "You're still here."

"You've had too much to drink."

"You haven't had enough."

"I'm on call."

Reason smiled up at Wilder sincerely. "Then all of Belfast is safe."

"Has anyone told you you're lethal in that skirt? Lady, you sure got a whole lotta legs."

"I wanted to get your attention."

"It worked." Wilder captured her in his arms. "Want to dance?"

"No, it's a jig," Reason resisted with a hand to his chest.

"You might hear a jig, but I hear the prelude to a waltz." He held her firmly.

"You'd better lead then." She welcomed his body closer. "Where have you been all night?"

"Around."

"I didn't see you around."

"I planned it that way. I wanted you to get to know the family. What do you think?"

"What was that you once said to me? 'To know the Irish is to love the Irish.' They're all so friendly; they treat me like I'm one of their daughters. Wilder, we're not dancing to the music at all. I think we ought to sit down until there's a slower song."

He tightened his arms around her. "I like it this way."

"I thought you wanted me out of your life."

"Oh, I do, I do, but I couldn't be the only O'Neill here tonight not to dance with the glorious Yank."

"Did you just call me glorious?" Reason laughed.

"Yeah, I did. Do you have a problem with that?"

"It's better than being a jack-o-lantern."

"Tell me, Reas, two years ago you said you saw good-byes in my eyes...do you still?"

She searched Wilder's blue, Irish eyes, and felt a shiver. "Yes. But I'm not afraid anymore."

"Good. I heard you talking to Morris awhile ago. He really likes you."

Reason wouldn't look up. "Unlike his uncle."

"Ah yes," Wilder didn't contradict but was droll, "unlike his uncle."

Hurt, Reason broke from his embrace. "I don't want to dance with you anymore."

"Come on, Reas, don't run away from me." Wilder swiped a playful fist to stop her and missed. "I was only joking."

"You could have fooled me." She marched back to the McCartan's table, and Wilder let her go.

The party played on, another day faded. Gazing around the smoke-fogged hall, Reason saw everyone laughing, drinking in excess, and singing with great animation. Again she marveled. Belfast was a whirlwind of extremes; extreme violence and wrath, extreme gaiety and self-abuse. It was all so intense, so unquenchable like a wildfire determined to consume itself with pleasure and pain. But not being one of these durable souls, she said goodnight and decided to walk the few blocks back to Duntroon Drive.

"Where do you think you're going?" Wilder joined her leaving the church.

"Home."

"Why don't you let me drive you?"

"I prefer the company of the stars," she declined, still hurting.

But Wilder refused to leave her. "I'll walk with you then."

She was glad he said that. After so many dances and drinks she never would have made it up the Antrim Road if Wilder hadn't braced his hand on her back to ensure she kept moving. "You called me glorious…but I'm not glorious. Those stars up there are glorious. Belfast's stars are as pretty tonight as Denver's stars were two years ago."

The sky was spotless, the night calm; no roar of traffic, no barking dogs, no midnight choppers, shootings or bombs, just blessed, docile stillness. And the air smelled of coal fires and diesel, damp grass, fish and chips, and sweet piquant smoke from the pipes of men scurrying home from the pubs. Not a bad scent just the Belfast scent.

"The first time I saw this neighborhood I thought there was little reason to look up." As Reason passed the New Lodge rowhouses she revised her first impression. "But when the clouds disappear, it's a different world above your old home." She encouraged Wilder to look skyward. "The stars are beacons of hope. You see, if you tear back the drizzle and turn out the lights, there's peace in the sky above Belfast."

"Or maybe it's just because night hides the sores."

Reason gave Wilder's arm a punch. "Have you no poetry left in you?"

"*You're* the artist. I'm the scientist."

"Scientists, bah!" She anchored her arm around Wilder for balance. "You're the first to tell the world stars don't fall for wishes and princes don't come from kissing fishes. You'd take the magic out of Houdini if we artists would let you."

There was such passion in her, such energy and youth. Tonight Reason shielded the Belfast dark and showed Wilder the stars. "Thank God for you artists then."

Stopping on the outskirts of the New Lodge where Duncairn Gardens met the Antrim Road, Reason turned to Wilder excitedly. "Say something funny."

"Something funny."

"No, no, tell me a joke."

Wilder reached into his repertoire, and on cue, Reason held out an imaginary cap for donations and pretended someone had dropped in a coin. Grandly she bowed. "Thankee, thankee, gods bless ye."

Only once before had she astonished Wilder; when she called him a taig. This was happier awe. "How do you know about that?"

"A woman just knows these things," Reason larked.

"Wow. I haven't thought of that in years. My dad and I…on this very corner through all hells of weather. We'd stand here together, partners in puns." He repeated the blessing, "Thankee, thankee, gods bless ye. Wow."

"I read that in the sixties the New Lodge didn't have indoor plumbing and families had to sleep four to a bed…is that true?"

"I didn't know what indoor plumbing was like until we moved to California. But it wasn't so bad. We didn't know any other way." The memories softened Wilder's voice. "I slept with my granny and Merry until I was six. I thought it was great fun because my grandmother was quite a large woman and wore layers upon layers of flannel. I was never cold sleeping beside her…and she smelled like cherry cough drops. To this day when I go to bed alone, and the sheets are cold, I think of the old days when I was warmer."

"You need an electric blanket."

"Electric blankets are for Yanks," he joked. "Memories of the cold keep me humble…and Irish."

"Is there any Yank left in you, Wilder?"

"Only when it comes to dealing with you."

Reason pondered the heavens again. "Why do you keep coming near me when you don't want me around? Why are you walking here beside me?"

"I couldn't let you stagger home alone. Liquor and those long legs court disaster."

"I'm serious, Wilder. If you don't like me, why won't you leave me alone?"

"OK, OK, so kill me for being a gentleman."

"You know what I think?" She tiptoed her fingernails up his spine and swirled a circle around his ear. "I think you can't resist me even when you try."

"You might be right."

"With your arm around me like a thousand welcomes I wish we could walk together all night." Admiring her old friend, Reason asked herself if Wilder could ever be anything but her wrong man, as she had told Cain. Wilder the Irish Catholic. Having met his family, those terms defined wisdom and wit, courage of spirit, generosity and an indestructible passion for life. Tonight everything Irish shone. Especially the wrong man, the only man.

Too quickly they reached the McKees' door.

"Did you have a good time tonight, Reas?"

"Oh aye," she sounded Irish. "I love your family. They made me laugh…just like you used to…and don't spoil things with your smart remarks, OK?"

"OK. I know Morris enjoyed seeing you again." Wilder glanced up at the constellations then down at Reason. Glorious. "I heard you telling him the only nice thing you ever did for me was save my life. That's not true."

"It's not?"

"What we shared…maybe it was only one day, but it was one perfect day."

From his eyes simmering upon her, from his fingers wandering over her skin, Reason expected Wilder to kiss her, but he didn't. He was considering how her eyes, her lips, her body played havoc with his mind. He swore in that moment he would sell his soul to strip Reason bare and take her to bed, to surrender his grudge and confess how vital she was to him, to ask her to share the rest of his life. But the devil wasn't buying souls, and Wilder was silent. "I'll see you Monday," he said.

But Reason didn't let him leave. She nabbed him by the collar. "There's no reason we can't enjoy a lifetime of perfect days and nights, Wilder." In her tall shoes it was easy to steal a kiss, which she did. Ardently.

Wilder was slow to react. The midnight boiled and constricted around him as Reason's lips delighted his. Reluctantly he kissed her, but her mouth was warm and open, and her breasts grazed his chest, and pulling her against him, he kissed her hungrily, repeatedly. And he was thinking he could lose his life, he could lose his freedom and not care half as much as if he lost Reason again. Oh, why did she have to come back? He didn't want to risk another heart death, but he loved her and loved her, and all he felt was anger to be so endangered and enslaved. "Don't do this to me, Reason, not again." He broke away and turned his back.

"Turn me off, turn me on, turn me off. I am not a light switch! What is the problem with you, Wilder?"

"Nothing. Don't give me a hard time."

"I don't think I could give you a hard anything! Have you become gay or what?"

"Hardly," Wilder disclaimed arrogantly, "though around you that might be an easier option."

"You are so unforgiving! How long are you going to punish me for Denver?"

"Until it doesn't hurt anymore." He strode away.

*　　*　　*　　*　　*　　*

Friday night's perfection dissolved into Saturday's torrent. Whipping winds rushed down the mountains, rain blasted in off the sea, and My Lady's Leisure was hidden in clouds.

"We won't be seeing the stars through your telescope tonight." Reason rested against the wall in the library and sipped her wine. "But this is nice too."

"Are you sure you're warm enough?" Cain worried before joining Reason on the floor. "I can put more coal on the fire."

"I'm fine. Do you know I'd never seen coal before I came here? When Fiona showed me a piece of it, I stood there staring at this hard and heavy *rock*. And it burns so hot! One night I sat too close to the fire, and it melted part of my shoe. And it's noisy." She listened. The fire rumbled a windy whirring sound. The coals sizzled, the coals popped. And graceful shadows pulsed on the walls of books. "It's amazing such a hard lump can produce such a soft light. It makes the room cheerful and," she focused on Cain and ran her finger around the rim of her glass, "romantic."

Cain stared into the fire trying to avoid staring at Reason. But he saw her; seductive in the firelight, wanting his mouth upon hers. She would think him cold-blooded not kissing her, but he was in flames like the coal. Flames licking between the coals, over the coals, rolling around and around in delirious heat. He had been insane promising Wilder he wouldn't love her.

"Does My Lady's Leisure have ghosts?"

"Dozens. The souls of the Irishmen the Cromwells robbed and ravaged roam these rooms at night. I'll bet there's one in here with us right now, perhaps sitting there beside you. Watching you. Wanting you. Touching you. Taking your soul with bony fingers. Maybe I'm a ghost," Cain rasped and beckoned Reason to him like the Reaper, "and the real Cain lies dead out in the ranting, panting rain. Am I making you nervous?" he laughed at Reason's wide eyes.

"Only a little. I don't believe this place is haunted…well, at least not when you're here. The ghosts have made peace with you."

"Maybe because as much as I love this estate I'll never think of it as mine. This land belongs to Ireland not an English landlord…sometimes I think I ought to burn My Lady's Leisure to the ground and free its hostage spirit."

"Oh, don't ever do that, Cain! This is a treasure."

"An illegitimate treasure."

"But you're a pirate and pirates pillage," Reason suggested jauntily.

"Aye aye, matie, it's true. I'm the pirate from Tintagel." Cain refilled Reason's wine glass then his own. "When I was little we spent our summers in Cornwall, and I wanted to be a pirate. I ran around with a stick, telling the fishermen I was Cap'n King Arthur from Tintagel Castle, and I'd sneak outside our house at night and stand on the cliff overlooking the ocean. I swore I could see tall ships flying skull-and-crossbone flags. I'd wave my arms and holler into the wind and wish they'd come take me away, but of course they never did."

"I wanted to be an astronomer," Reason revealed, "and to me the Empire State Building was a rocket. I imagined getting to the top floor and touching the stars. Something that tall had to reach outer space, right? One evening my mother took me up there, and all I saw was

Manhattan. The sky still seemed forever away. But just when I thought there were no rockets, my mom pointed out the Chrysler Building with its crown of pearly lights. I decided the building couldn't get to the stars so the stars came to the building."

"So I became a jewel thief and you became an architect. Seems we got what we wanted in round about ways. But then life's round about. There's always a twist."

"That's the truth. I was supposed to be on a site in Louisiana, then out of the blue my boss sent me here."

"Are you sorry you came?"

"Oh no. This is much more exciting than New Orleans."

"Is that because Wilder is here?"

"I wish you would stop bringing him up. I don't care if I ever see him again."

"Come now, Reason, he's a very nice man."

She folded Cain's hand into hers. "You're a nicer man. And a special man."

"Special how?"

"You're the first man ever to read poetry to me."

"I'm not."

"You are. And you're the first man I've ever swum nude with."

"I'm not."

"You are," Reason frolicked. "And you're the first man I've ever been out on a first date with who didn't try to get me into bed."

"Oh God, surely I'm not!" Cain moaned.

"Surely you are."

"Oh, that's real damn flattering to know," he complained, chagrined.

"You don't rush things." She tucked Cain's hair behind his ear and softly spoke, "I like that. I like it a lot." Her fingertip outlined his profile then brushed his lips to open his mouth, to suck her touch. "I like you a lot."

Drowned in desire, warned not to swim. Cain debated. Whether to do what he wanted or do what was right. His knuckles grazed Reason's cheekbone, and turning her to face him, he paused. Then seized her lips. One kiss soul-deep. That's all he wanted. To know again once, only once, her soft, warm mouth. Two kisses two, lingering, two. His hands moved along her shoulders. Three kisses she tied her arms around his neck. Four, four kisses more. He slipped his arm about her waist not to pull her closer but to hoist her to her feet. "Let me show you what's truly amazing about My Lady's Leisure."

He palmed a silver candlestick from the bookshelf and led the way to the foyer's great marble staircase that swept up to the bedrooms. "Grand old stairs, aren't they?" He leaped up the thirty curved steps. On the second floor, he said, "We're now in the center of the house," before turning left and proceeding toward what had once been a music room. Off the music room, through a pediment doorway was one of the smaller bedrooms, and off the bedroom was a dressing room. Inside the dressing room Cain stopped. "Look around."

Reason turned in a circle. There was nothing to see except bare, cedar walls, a hanging brass light fixture and a small round window. "It's an interesting little space," she said.

"But there's nothing remarkable about it, right?"

"Well, I like the window."

"Watch this." Cain pulled the light fixture to the floor, and as the lamp descended, the back wall of the dressing room rose in one piece into the ceiling like a drawbridge. All without a sound.

"Whoa!" Reason clapped with surprise and saw another hidden staircase, but unlike the one above the library, this one led down.

Cain lit the three candles on his candelabra. "Follow me and be careful. These stone steps are shorter than your foot and can be slick." Holding the light before him, he and Reason wound down a steep, corkscrew staircase. Other than the flickery candles the descent was dark as blindness. Step by step the stone walls grew cooler and danker, and the smell of mildew was replaced by the smell of the sea.

"You're taking me down to the water." Reason could hear the waves smashing into the cliff. "Secret caves and secret stairways…you are *so* incredible!"

The wind met their legs, drops of rain whirled on the cold, rushing air. Abruptly the staircase melted into a cavernous dungeon cluttered with rowboats, garden tools, wooden crates and metal boxes. A low iron grate like clamped teeth barred the outlet, and beyond the grate stood towering boulders lashed by the waves of the Irish Sea.

"Behold the Cromwell's escape." Cain lit an oil lantern on the wall and walked over to the grate. "This opens, but I doubt you want to go frisking along the seashore in the storm. You see the grate is only tall enough and wide enough for one of these rowboats to slip in and out. The great thing is, from the outside, this little exit is completely hidden by the boulders. No one knows it's here."

Captivated, Reason gaped around. "Do you think your ancestors actually used this escape?"

"Oh, many times. After Oliver Cromwell's visit to Ireland no Englishman on this island was safe. Whenever the Irish peasants waged an uprising and attacked the estates, which was every few years, my fearless family fled north to Protestant strongholds near Belfast. They would leave the youngest son and the servants to defend My Lady's Leisure. Naturally the servants took the brunt of the battles."

"Are any of these the original boats?"

"Who knows. Some of them are certainly rotten enough. My father wants to burn them, but I like keeping them around. I like to come down here and lie in the boats and listen to the surf. Sometimes I sleep here just because it's close to the sea."

"Look at the birds and fish carved in that old bow. Imagine the stories these boats could tell."

"I'm afraid most of them only know Cromwell treachery." He noticed Reason rubbing her arms. "Let's come down here again when it's warmer."

But Reason dallied, strolling back to the boats, fiddling with the oars, revering the nautical realm. "I like the sound of the sea. It's the music of life and passion." She cast a glance back at Cain. "Do you have a girlfriend?"

"I have women friends who come see me in Belfast. They bring me meals, they pose and I paint them, some make love to me…but I go to sleep alone." Cain watched Reason as she walked around the dungeon, allowing his eyes to do what his hands couldn't; explore her body. He loved her legs, her breasts, the smooth texture of her skin and hair, the graceful sway of her hips, her dimpled smile and eyes of strength. "I spent my twenties madly in love. But times changed. I changed." He cleared his throat and stared up the dark stairs. "Now anything I touch, I taint. I'm a nice man, but I'm not a good man."

"That's not true. I know a good man when I see one."

"You think I'm good?" Cain mocked.

In the pale lantern light Reason could see him. "I know you are."

He held out his hand for her, and when she came, he took her fingers and raised them to his lips. "Let's go back to the fire."

Hiking upstairs Cain related his favorite Cromwell tale. "This route wasn't always used for cowardly retreats. In 1789, one of the Cromwell daughters, Julianna, fell in love with an Irishman; her father's groom. Andrew McGuire was his name. Disgusted by his daughter's choice of lovers, her father forbid her to see, much less marry, Andrew, and when Julianna refused to obey, he arranged to have the Irishman hanged. But with the help of the local farmers, minutes before his execution, Andrew escaped from the gallows and raced on horseback, with the jailers hot on his trail, to join Julianna. Andrew had told her to wait for him in the dungeon until midnight, and if he hadn't come by then, she'd know he was dead. Down these very steps Julianna raced, back and forth across the dungeon she paced, and then she heard a whistle. Rushing to the grate she saw Andrew waiting for her on the moonlit beach. They stole a little boat and rowed along the coast far, far away from My Lady's Leisure."

"And they lived happily ever after?" Reason hoped.

"No. Andrew joined the Volunteers and was killed during an uprising against England in 1798. But he and Julianna had three sons."

"Oh, those stupid Irishmen," Reason moped. "Poison to happy endings they are."

"I suspect Julianna would tell you Andrew was worth every risk. She raised her sons to be as Irish as their father…she's the only Cromwell I can be proud of."

"Here's your tea, love."

The library glowed in firelight. Cain kept his attention on Reason while keeping his distance across the room. Reason settled before the hearth.

"I've never drunk so much tea in my life," she chuckled. "Everywhere I go here, any time of day, people offer me tea."

"We can't live without it. It might be one of the only English things about the Irish…or is it an Irish thing about the English? They go back so far together in history sometimes it's hard to say who dreamed up what."

"I made the mistake of telling Wilder once that I thought the Irish and English were the same people, just living on separate islands. He about had a nervous breakdown," Reason recalled, laughing. "Needless to say, I got one heck of a lecture. Oh, but that was ages ago. He's told you terrible things about me, hasn't he?"

"Your name was a curse around the O'Neills for awhile. But now everyone's glad you're here. They all say they've seen Declan smiling more in the past month than he has for a year."

"It's not me making him happy," Reason assured. "How on earth did you wind up being his gardener?"

"When I got here last summer Wilder's yard was a mess; he was letting his roses die because he had no time, or desire, to tend them. You can't let roses die! I spared their thorny little lives and have been tending them ever since. I live so close to him in Belfast it's no trouble to drop by."

"That's really nice of you."

"It's my privilege, love. A gardener is the curator of God's art. Even if Wilder fired me, I'd be back."

Reason couldn't miss the fondness in Cain's voice whenever he mentioned Wilder. "He's lucky to have a friend like you. How did you meet his father?"

"I met Sumner at a class in Los Angeles. He liked my paintings, I had nowhere to live, so he invited me to stay in his guesthouse in Malibu. He got me through a very bad time. I owe the man my life. Then Wilder and I met and became friends as well."

"Why does Wilder think you're fragile?"

Cain made a face. "Where does he come up with these things? Sometimes I think his head is screwed on too tight. I'm a pirate and pirates are men of steel."

"Seriously, why does he say that?"

"I suppose because when he first met me I was addicted to cocaine and wanted to die. My life was a real horror back then, and don't ask why. Wilder is afraid I'll return to my suicidal vices if life gets too tough. But he's wrong. I'm fine."

Chilled, Reason scooted closer to the fire. Something shifted in her shirt pocket. "I forgot I had this." She examined the gold coin in the fire-light. "Have you ever seen anything like this before?"

Cain poured Reason a fresh cup of tea, and upon seeing the charm, nearly spilled the tea on her head. The winged sword with the slogan, **Fear Nothing and Prevail** was the exclusive badge of the Cure. At first thunderstruck, he deftly recovered his smile. "Where did you get that?"

"I found it." She tossed him the coin. "What do you think it means?"

Cain rubbed his fingers over the burnished metal with familiarity; the past blasted his mind. *"Damn good show, Cromwell! Damn good show! Here's your medal…a piece of the bastard's skull. God bless the winged sword; God save the Queen."* Blood clots and bone shards, the suffocating stench of wet hay and sheep dung, the screams turned moans turned silence exploded into his head…"I have no idea," he replied, losing his breath. "Where did you dig this up?"

"In the hedge behind Wilder's house."

"What were you doing in there?"

"I fell into it."

Cain caught Reason's eye. "Did you show him this medal?"

"I probably should have, but I didn't. It hardly looks like something he would have. Then again, maybe it is his."

"No, somehow I don't think he'd have anything like this."

"There was a camera in the hedge as well. Whoever planted the camera probably lost this medal. Do you think it was the RUC?"

"That's a mystery indeed." Cain offered the charm back to Reason.

"You can keep it. I've no use for the thing."

Gone was Cain's happy demeanor. His mood grew as dark as the storm. He clenched the medal as if to crush it, then flung it into the fire. Slamming the doors of the fireplace, he pulled Reason up and pushed her out of the library.

"Where are we going?" She accepted her raincoat which Cain thrust upon her. He'd gone white as one of the Cromwell ghosts.

"I'm taking you back to Fiona's."

"But…you haven't shown me your designs for the mural yet."

"Another time," he snapped.

"What's the matter?" After Wilder's turning away last night and now Cain withdrawing in much the same manner, Reason began to feel like a leper. "Did that medal upset you? Does it mean something?"

"No, no," he rouped, loosening his collar and ripping off his shoes. "I just need to rest, to get away, to get away."

Reason didn't understand Cain's need to flee. "But I thought My Lady's Leisure was your retreat."

"Tonight the world found me. I'll go get the car." Like a toreador with a mad bull on his heels, Cain threw open the door and ran into the slanting rain.

Chapter Nineteen

Duggie shadowed Michael McManus off the hospital site at quitting time. "Yo, mick," he tapped Michael on the shoulder in the men's locker room. "Got a light?"

"The name's Michael." He offered Duggie a match, and seeing Duggie's "King Billy" tattoo, moved across the room.

"They call me 'the Knack.' Maybe you've heard of me." Duggie sucked his cigarette through a devious smirk. "How do you like working at the Gov, mick?"

Michael jerked off his muddy boots and slipped on his sandals to walk home. "I've no complaints."

"Feeds the wife in Ballymurphy I'll bet. Is she pretty? Her name's Emma I hear."

Michael shifted with misgiving and noticed the locker room was empty. "How do you know that?"

Duggie glanced around with a shrug and blew smoke in the Catholic man's face. "A little bird told me. You got three kiddies too. Joseph, Sean and Mary Louise."

Michael jumped to his feet and grabbed Duggie by the collar. "What do you want?"

"I have a message for you from the ULF, mick." Duggie withdrew a switchblade from his jacket and poked Michael's chest. "We don't want you working at the Gov."

"Look, Knack," Michael backed off, "I was hired fair and square. I have a right to this job same as anybody else."

Duggie twisted his knife to Michael's Adam's apple and inflicted a nick. "Come back to work tomorrow and the ULF will cut your wife's fucking tits off and shove them up your ass. Then they'll slit your kids' throats. Ear to little ear." Duggie wiped Michael's blood off his knife and pointed to the locker room door. "Have a nice life, mick."

*   *   *   *   *   *

As demanded by Hunter Cromwell, on July 3, on schedule, the groundbreaking ceremony was held at the Gov. With a triumphant wave of a shiny new shovel, Hunter was the first to crack the mud. In spite of heavy rain a crowd of medical personnel and neighborhood residents was on hand, and everyone cheered from beneath their umbrellas as their venerable old hospital's addition officially began.

"Today is a great and wondrous day for you, my dear friends of Belfast," Hunter declared grandly as his shovel slopped into the ground. "There is no higher priority for me and my medical associates than assuring your continued good health and well-being. Our Grosvenor Hospital is already the pride of Belfast, but as of this day, it's going to be even better. I am honored and deeply touched to be on hand for this tremendous, joyous occasion."

Hurrah, hurrahs rose above the downpour. It *was* a great day for the people and prosperity of Belfast.

"Where's Dr. O'Neill?" Hunter grunted as he kicked the mud off his Italian loafers.

"He's in surgery," Reason replied from beneath her umbrella.

"What the deuce is he doing in surgery at a time like this? He's part of the team. He should be here."

"I'm certain Declan is here with us in spirit, Hunter," Reason comforted staidly.

"Spirit, hell! It's disgraceful!" Hunter pitched his shiny new shovel into a puddle and motioned for his chauffeur. "Not at the birth of his own damn baby."

"Aren't you staying for the groundbreaking party the medical staff is having?" Reason called to Hunter who was leaving.

"Don't be daft. I've important things to do in London. Good day, Miss McGuinness."

"You can't seem to get enough of this place." Wilder appeared after nine p.m. and found Reason, as usual, bent over her drafting table. "Don't you ever go home?"

"Great works require great work." Reason smiled up at Wilder despite her frustration with him. His face was more rumpled and weary than his baggy blue surgical scrubs, but to Reason he shone.

"Here," he handed her a white rose.

"For *me?*" she recoiled in disbelief. "From *you?* "

"I hurt your feelings the other night and I didn't mean to. I'm sorry."

Reason was glad to hear him say that. Thanking Wilder, she put the rose in water and returned to her work. "You missed the groundbreaking. It was fun."

"I hear Hunter was looking for me at the ceremony. I wanted to be there, I know how much this project means to you, but I couldn't make it."

"Forget Hunter," she mumbled with a pencil in her mouth. "Come look at this. It's the new morgue…pretty cool, huh?"

Wilder surveyed the technical drawing over Reason's shoulder. "Nice perfume," he commented, bending closer to her neck and thinking her jasmine scent contradicted the deathly spaces detailed below. "I see they had you add six more drawers. Didn't I tell you last week we needed more?"

"The body count around here sure doesn't speak well for you surgeons," Reason kidded.

"We save a hell of a lot more than we lose! You think you can do it better?"

"Oh, calm down, Declan. It was a joke. Geez, you prima donnas are touchy."

"You picked a lousy day to be funny. I had a six-year-old girl die on the table this afternoon."

"Oh, I'm sorry."

"So am I." Wilder sighed and tilted against the drafting table so he could see Reason's face in the light. Pale hair, soft as whipped cream, swept off her shoulders, her midnight magic eyes melting blue upon his, the sensuous mouth outlined in cherry…red, white and blue. Miss America. "Tomorrow is the Fourth of July." He had been planning to ask her all day but wanted to sound spur-of-the-moment. "Say, I have an idea. Why don't you spend the day with me?"

"Why, look, it's Dr. O'Neill and Mr. Hide-His-True-Feelings." Reason pretended to pluck petals from her rose. "He loves me, he loves me not…no, I do not want to spend another wishy-washy minute with you."

"What's the big deal?" Wilder felt like an ineloquent teenager. "I'm only trying to be a considerate host here in Ireland. Tomorrow is America's greatest holiday. And you're alone in a foreign country. I figured you might be homesick…I don't think there's a lonelier day to be a Yank in the Six Counties than Independence Day."

"*You* wouldn't be homesick for America now would you, Wilder?"

"It's you I'm worried about."

"I'm too busy to be homesick."

"The Fourth of July is my favorite holiday. I'll be thinking of barbe-cued beef and beer on the beach, windsurfing, and weather so hot my bones turn to pudding, won't you?"

"Until you mentioned it I hadn't thought about it."

"You won't miss your family and the fireworks?"

"If I spend the day with you, I'll be thinking of fireworks every second; all the dud ones that no matter how hard I try to light them, they just sit there cold and lifeless."

Wilder tilted further back, folded his arms upon his chest and gave Reason a look of derision. "You just can't stand it that, this time, I'm not burning myself alive for you. Don't blame the candle for not turning on when the match is all wet, sweetheart."

"Don't be ridiculous, Wilder. I could seduce you again in a heartbeat. You know it, and I know it." She traced a question mark on Wilder's thigh with her finger. "But I don't want to seduce you."

"What do you want?" he wondered bassily, already half-seduced.

"I want life and passion, and I'm not going to find those with you."

Wilder left Reason's side and peered down at the Falls Road. "Do you know how long it's been since I've had an entire day off?"

"I have no idea."

"Well, neither do I. So, as of tonight, I'm taking my phone off the hook, disconnecting my beeper, and I'm not going to wear shoes. God bless Independence Day!"

"What are you going to do tomorrow?" Reason asked as she arranged her colored markers in rows and carefully covered her sketches.

"I'm driving up the Antrim coast to the ocean. Then I'm going to run barefooted down the beach until I fall down in sunburned sand and think of nothing, blissful, silent nothing."

"I'm sure you'll have a great time."

"I'm sure I will."

"I hope it stops raining."

"It wouldn't dare rain tomorrow. Did you see Ruairi around the hospital today?"

"He's in the Republic until tomorrow night. One of our steel orders was shipped to Dublin by mistake, and I sent him down to take care of the problem."

"Oh well, I'll catch him later this week. Are you sure you wouldn't like to come see the north coast with me? It's the prettiest part of Ireland."

"If you aren't going to burn at my feet, why bother?"

"You know, Reason," Wilder rubbed his chin with displeasure, "you're a difficult woman."

"Only because you are a difficult man."

He gave her a brisk salute, "See you Wednesday then," and he returned to his office, beset with unwelcome solitude. Before Reason had come to Belfast he enjoyed time spent alone; now he was acutely aware of an empty place growing wider beside him. Reason. Her name was his curse and incantation. One year he had yearned to get her into his life. Two years he had burned to get her out of his life. Now he yearned and burned, like sawing a sword in and out of his heart.

"Are you Dr. O'Neill?" A young girl appeared in his doorway.

"Yes." He knew why she had come.

She made sure they were alone. "There's a wee pint waiting for you."

"I'll be there." Swinging his jacket from the back of his door, Wilder ran for the stairwell.

Reason was coming out of her office when she saw Wilder shooting down the corridor. Having changed her mind about going up the Antrim coast, she ran to catch him. She could hear him jumping down the steps. He didn't hear her calling for him to wait, so she wound down three flights behind him. As she hit the fourth floor and Wilder reached the first she thought he would exit into the lobby, but she heard him keep going. At ground level the metal door opened then clanked shut. He was headed for the morgue, Reason thought. But she found the morgue locked tight.

"Hullo, Miss McGuinness," hailed an elderly maintenance man. "You be needing into the morgue then?"

"No, I was looking for Declan O'Neill. Have you by any chance seen him down here?"

"Aye. But moments ago over in the Deadlands, locked out so he was."

What was Wilder doing in the Deadlands? "Was he going to the reagent room?"

"No, he headed straight down the stairs."

"Is the door over there still open?"

"Och no, miss. T'is rules to be locked. Security you see."

"Will you let me in as well? Dr. O'Neill and I are working on a design for the new wing, and silly me, I forgot my passkeys just like he did."

"Aye, missie," the custodian waved Reason towards the concrete tunnel, "but you mustn't say it was me who let you in. No one is allowed in the Deadlands after dark. T'is rules you see."

The Deadlands was its own separate building connected to the back of the Gov via an underground pass. Once three floors of housing for medical students and nurses, the old bricks now preserved cabinets filled with fifty years of patient records and X-rays. The first floor was the hospital's reagent room. The basement, where Wilder had gone, had once been the morgue; now it was morgue to wheel-less gurneys and foot-less carts, and beds too weak to hold the sick.

"If you two are snooping in and about the old rooms, you'll be needing torches," the janitor said as he allowed Reason into the Deadlands. "You'll find several on the far wall aside the stairs. Not one word to anyone, love? Off you go then, there's the good girl."

Flashlight before her, Reason hurried down the stairs into the dead, dull corridors of the past tense morgue. She called Wilder's name; deathly quiet replied. Weaving through a maze of broken wheelchairs and boxes of chemicals, turning on and off lights, she leaned into each of seven autopsy rooms; open drawers, metal tables and weighing scales for organs revealed themselves, but not Wilder.

The eighth room had lost its light bulb, but using her flashlight, Reason could see stacks of microbiology media and laboratory reagents in boxes. The room's aged dumb waiter distinguished it from the previous seven. Long ago the little lift was used to ferry specimens between the clinical and anatomical pathology departments. Now it was a shaft of dead air behind a corroded metal door. Shining her flashlight up the old elevator, Reason could see the first floor. In order to do maintenance on the cables there was a passage on either side of where the dumb waiter had hung, and down the passage, far to the left, was a boarded-up hole.

Reason glimpsed around the windowless room and realized other than the main stairs there was no way out of the morgue. Hiking up her skirt, she climbed into the shaft and sidled along the passageway to the hole. Pulling the board aside she saw another pocket in the earth. And another tunnel; a tunnel like she had seen behind Wilder that first night at Albie's. Unless he vanished into thin air, he had to have passed this way. Determined to find out what business Wilder was into, Reason squeezed under the boards and sneaked into the black.

The Gov was notorious for its labyrinth of underground tunnels. Legend said the tunnels were dug around the turn of the century to smuggle wounded Irish rebels in and out of the hospital. During the World War Two Blitz, the passages were used again to shuttle staff and patients on stretchers safely between places on the Falls Road such as a Catholic church, a pub and a funeral parlor. Over the decades some of the tunnels had been bricked up and forgotten, and only a few people knew or cared which routes were still passable.

Beyond its opening, the musty tube was tall enough for Reason to stand and wide enough for her to extend her arms. In noiseless darkness, mitigated only by her flashlight, she proceeded through the tunnel warily. The way was damp and the way was uneven, twisting snake-like into the unknown. Every few meters she stopped and considered her folly, where did she think she was going? But curiosity lured her on. After several minutes she came to a junction, and trying to imagine the Falls Road above her she decided turning left led to what was now a women's resource center. Turning right led to the funeral parlor, and the funeral parlor was connected to Albie's pub. She veered right, and after five minutes of a gradual rise, unexpectedly, the pathway swerved and split again. To the left was a ramp. To the right the tunnel continued. Pausing on the ramp, she heard voices above.

Switching off the flashlight and reaching over her head, she groped for what must be a door into somebody's floor. Yes, there was heavy wood about two feet above her head, but beneath whose floor had she arrived? When the voices faded and footsteps paced away, Reason tried to push up the trap door, but it was bolted shut from the other side. In trying to open the hatch, she knocked loose a hail of dirt which showered her mouth and eyes. Spitting, choking and stumbling back to cover her face, her presence became known. When the dust cleared and she opened her eyes, she greeted the barrel of an AK-47.

"If you move an inch, I'll kill you," a man's voice growled down at her.

Reason froze.

"Climb up here. Slowly."

She dared to look up at the man peering down at her through his opaque balaclava. Keeping his gun aimed at her head, he called something in Irish, and another hooded man appeared with his rifle also directed at Reason. In terror she hiked up the ramp, and as she stood in the opening of the floor, one man grabbed her while the other cocked and fine-focused his weapon. The masked man slammed and bolted the trap door with his boot, patted Reason down to make sure she was unarmed then pushed her into a chair. The second man kicked a rug then a chair over the floor door and resumed his post behind Reason. The only thing she noticed about the room in that instant was a third hooded man covered in blood and mud, moaning in pain, and laid uncomfortably on a blanket against the cold linoleum floor.

"Who are you?" the first man in the mask demanded to know.

"Reason McGuinness," she scarcely squeaked.

"What were you doing down in the tunnel?"

She didn't know what to say. Who were these men? Where was she? Her stunned silence brought a gun beneath her chin and a repeat of the question. "What were you doing down there?"

"I...I..." she was too terrified to lie, "...I was looking for someone."

"You just happened to be in a tunnel this late on a rainy night *looking* for someone? Why the fuck were you down there?" he screamed in her face.

"It's the truth. I...followed him."

"You followed who?"

"A friend." The gun nudged her Adam's apple. "A ma...man from the...Gov."

"Why?"

"I...wanted to tell him..." she stammered between gulps of fright, "...I'd go with him to...up north...and when I thought he had gone into the tunnel...I was curious...and followed."

"*That* was immensely foolish."

"Please don't kill me," she sputtered in tears. "I didn't mean to come here...I don't even know where here is...I won't say anything, I swear."

"Did you find your friend?"

"No." She lost her voice.

Four eyes seared upon her and there was more discussion in Irish.

"Sit there and keep your mouth shut," one of the duo barked, to which Reason avidly nodded.

As one of the men left, Reason heard him locking the door. The remaining man took a seat and tracked Reason's every move, still aiming his gun at her throat. Daring to look around, she saw she was in a tight, windowless room, and from the wet, deep smell, concluded she was in another cellar. White medicine cabinets hung on white walls. Plastic trays and steel instruments cluttered the countertops. Overhead a naked light bulb made the room all the more bleached and glaring, and other than her chair and her keeper's, there was no furniture. And there was no heat. It was hard to sit without shivering, but with that rifle fixed upon her, Reason tried. She could hear movement in a room next door, and music. Handel's *Messiah*. Now and then she smelled chemicals. Formaldehyde. Alcohol. Ether. This had to be the funeral parlor, and beyond the ramp must have been the pathway to Albie's.

The door opened and the masked man who had left minutes before reappeared with a blanket which he draped over the injured man on the floor. Leaving once more, he returned yet again with hot tea in two badly chipped mugs. These he presented without a word to the armed guard and to Reason before leaving again.

Other than Handel's oratorio the room was silent, silent, too silent...until the man on the floor began coughing and spitting up blood. Reason could see his balaclava was soaked, and rivulets of red trickled down his neck to stain his shredded grey shirt. From the man's inability to react, Reason realized he couldn't raise his arms or his head. She looked to her keeper who was looking to her.

"I think we should raise his head," she suggested timidly.

The armed man held his gun to her and motioned for her to proceed. Kneeling beside the injured man, Reason gently lifted his head and could see his nose was bleeding. Even the slightest movement of the man's head made him squirm in pain. "If you have some scissors," she spoke hesitantly to her guard, fearing the wrong words would get her shot, "I could cut the mask away from his nose and mouth."

"You can't do that," the gunman snarled, trying to protect the patient's identity.

"But he can't breathe…I only want to help him…please, find some scissors." Drawing back the blanket, she loosened the wounded man's collar and unbuttoned his shirt. At the other end she removed his wet shoes and socks. There seemed to be no place on his body that wasn't trembling and leaking droplets of red. Shuddering at the sight of so much blood, she tucked the blanket back around him.

Keeping his gun aimed, her keeper backed up, and after searching several drawers, withdrew a pair of surgical shears. After brief indecision he handed them to Reason then steadied his gun and warned, "Don't pull any shit."

Obediently, Reason nodded. "I think you've broken your nose," she said as she cut away the wool now soaked and sticking to the injured man's cheeks. "Could I have a cold towel?" she asked her guard. Peeling off her linen jacket and rolling it into a ball, she slid it under the injured man's head then took the cold cloths and pressed them to his mangled face. Besides his nose, his mouth was gashed and oozing. "Is there any gauze?"

The guard handed Reason gauze to pack in the man's nostrils and under his fat upper lip. She then pinched the wings of his nose. As the bleeding stopped, she soothed and cleaned his face, and Reason could see she was tending a boy, seventeen, eighteen years tops.

"Did I lose any teeth?" he mumbled, barely conscious.

"I don't think so."

"I hit my head when I landed…it really hurts…can I have a drink of water?"

Reason turned to the guard who passed her a cup. "Only one sip, all right?" She tipped the cup to the boy's mouth and water spilled over his bloodied lips onto her sleeve.

The youth noticed Reason's red-spattered hands and skirt through frightened brown eyes. "Am I bleeding to death?"

Rubbing the boy's forehead, meeting his soft dark eyes, Reason felt sorry for him and took his hand into hers. What Fiona said to her all the time sprang to mind. "You'll be all right, love. You'll be all right."

The boy had serious abrasions, particularly on his arms and legs. His grass-and-mud-soiled pants were ripped and had been cut open from shin to thigh revealing knees embedded with gravel. His palms were pocked and ripped as well. His restricted movement suggested fractured shoulders and ribs, and it was Reason's guess he'd been trying to escape on a motorbike and crashed. And she further deduced somewhere in the funeral parlor Wilder was tending another injured rebel. Stunned to find herself in the company of Provos, she gaped down at her shaking fingers. They were red. Baptized in Ireland's waters. Now its blood. Her first instinct was to flee, to cry, to scrub herself clean. She swabbed blood and sweat off the Irish boy's face. Her guard adjusted his rifle, and *The Messiah* chorused on. Cold so cold this moment. On the Fourth of July.

An hour passed. Reason wanted to know what they were going to do with her but was afraid to ask. There on the floor she sat with the wounded boy, there she waited. Before the end of another hour she heard the door unlock and expected the second armed man to appear. In walked Wilder looking much like the night she had discovered him at Albie's; in gory green scrubs. Clearly he had been informed of her presence, he showed no recognition, no surprise to find her waiting.

"I hear you've taken care of this man," was all he said, but his voice was furious as were his icy blue eyes. He spoke to Reason's guard in Irish, and the guard jumped to help carry the young man out of the room. "You," Wilder meant Reason, "sit down on that chair. If you move one muscle, you'll be shot."

She thought they were leaving her alone, but before the door shut, the second masked gunman arrived. Not just pointing his gun at Reason this time, he stood stonily beside her with the barrel of his rifle screwed into her ear. Another hour like four hundred years sweated by until Wilder returned, dressed once again in the crumpled blue scrubs he'd worn earlier. For a full five minutes he stood before Reason without speaking, staring her down, seeming not to notice, nor care that she had a Kalashnikov rifle pressed to her head. Paralyzed, she stared back at Wilder in mortal fear with tears streaming down her cheeks. Then, after more Irish dialogue, the masked man withdrew his weapon and left the room.

"Don't say one word, not a goddamn word. You just sit there and listen," Wilder's voice shook with wrath. "You are in *serious* trouble, and you know why. You've jeopardized me, the others, the work we do here, and, damn it, worst of all yourself. *You idiot!*" he blasted. "You've just committed a crime on both sides of the game. You aided and abetted. You snooped around and know too much. What did you think you were doing?" He slammed a bottle of saline against the wall and it shattered and bled like Reason's tears. Then he grabbed her by the collar of her blood-smeared blouse and backed her up against the wall. "You are not to mention this night. You *saw* nothing, you *heard* nothing, you weren't here. If you ever, *ever* say a word about this to *anyone,* first they'll kill you then they'll kill me, do you understand? DO YOU UNDER-STAND?" he screamed.

Too terrorized, humiliated and overpowered to answer, Reason could only nod a weak nod and sag back onto her chair.

"Wash your hands." Reason seemed unable to move, so Wilder forced her up again. "Wash your hands!"

She did.

"Now take off your clothes," he ordered imperiously.

"Why?" she cried in alarm and raised her eyes to Wilder to spare her.

He softened his voice, "Nobody's going to hurt you. But you can't walk out of here covered in blood. Now hurry up and strip." He turned his back. "We have to get out of here. Speed it up!"

Reason unbuttoned her blouse then her skirt and let both slide to the floor. "Now what?"

Wilder tossed her a pair of scrubs. "Put these on."

When Reason finished, Wilder unbolted the floor door. Back through the darkness they stole, Wilder first then Reason. Reason had surrendered her flashlight hours ago, and Wilder didn't need one. Neither spoke. Overwrought, Reason wished she could evaporate and not have to face Wilder. The reality of what she had done crashed upon her. Her capricious behavior had damaged Wilder's credibility in the movement that was his life. To be followed by a woman! She had made him look foolish, careless and untrustworthy in the eyes of those he served. What had been harebrained adventure to her could have assured Wilder's banishment from his compatriots, not to mention his execution...and her own. Fear possessed her every heartbeat as she comprehended, really comprehended for the first time since arriving in Belfast, the deadly seriousness of these underground matters. The Provos were formidable, their war was their blood, and foolhardy young women were but paper dolls on the bonfire of their crusade.

"Will you be punished?" Reason asked meekly as they neared the Deadlands.

"I had to do a lot of fast talking," Wilder replied angrily. "Why in God's name did you follow me?"

"I saw you leaving and...I wanted to know where you were going..."

"Goddamn it, Reason!" he cut her off savagely. "You're driving me out of my mind!" He ground to a halt, and in the dark Reason smacked into his chest. "How many times do I have to tell you, this doesn't concern you?" He took hold of her shoulders. "Stay out of this part of my life."

"I will. I promise I will," she whimpered and melted into fresh tears. "Stop yelling at me...I couldn't possibly feel any worse. I know it's too late to say this, but I'm sorry, truly, deeply, wretchedly sorry." She tried to back away from him, but Wilder held her fast.

"Sorry just doesn't cut it right now." He drew Reason closer. "They could have killed you for your stupidity."

"Why didn't they?"

"Because they trust me…because you're so bleeding naïve. Helping that wounded kid didn't hurt your case either." His voice grew gentler as did his touch. "Sweet Reason…how am I supposed to protect you?"

"*Protect* me? You let that man hold his gun to my ear," she wept. "Was that your diamond-hearted idea? Was that *fun* for you?"

"God, Reason, no!" Wilder's hands dropped from her waist and flew to his throbbing temples. "That was living hell! When I walked into that room I saw my worst fears coming true."

He was glad the darkness covered his face. Light would have revealed his passion and frantic mind. In those five eternal minutes he had stood before Reason and the gunman, he loved her as he had loved no other. With all the frothing madness of his soul. But he couldn't help her, it was because of him she was sitting there tortured, and she tortured him. And he died again for loving her and for fearing the loss of her, and he lost part of himself. And he hated her with all his soul for causing him to die and to lose and choose sides between her and his cause. For five hideous minutes, heaven dangled over hell, and Reason, not Ireland, owned his life. For five minutes he had made his choice. The *wrong* choice.

"I would have spared you if I could, Reason, but witnessing your punishment was my punishment. I honestly didn't know if he was going to blow your head off. Jesus!" He swung Reason into his arms again, gripping her to his heart. "Please tell me that taught you a lesson."

"I won't sleep well at night for a long, long time," Reason cried.

"Good." Neither would Wilder.

Back in her office, Reason hoped Wilder would leave, but he stood waiting for her in Jillie's outer room.

"You don't need to walk me to my car," she called.

"I'm not going to. You're coming home with me."

She thought he was kidding, "Oh, I don't think so."

But Wilder needed to keep Reason close. To prove to himself she was safe. That he was safe. "I want to keep an eye on you overnight."

"Why?" she panicked. "Do you think the Provos are looking for me?"

"No. I just want to make sure you're all right."

"Wilder, go on. I'll be fine."

"Because you'll be with me. Please, Reason, don't argue. Not tonight."

She walked out belting her coat. "Oh, wait. I forgot the rose you brought me." She lifted the flower to her nose. "At least one nice thing happened tonight."

"Go on up to my room." Wilder let Reason in his front door. "You can wear one of my shirts to bed if you want. I'll be up in a minute."

Reason trooped on to the bedroom. She brushed her teeth and combed her hair and washed her tired face. Three normal bedtime habits but she didn't feel normal. Fear rang in her head, and she wondered if after this horrific night, she could ever feel normal again. Or maybe this was normal, for Belfast. She knew she wouldn't sleep, but she made down the bed and placed the rose Wilder had given her on the pillow. Pulling the first shirt she saw out of the closet, she undressed in a hurry, and buttoning the shirt up to its top, dived under the bedcovers. For a moment she relaxed, then Wilder appeared in the doorway. Sinking deeper into the bed, Reason avoided looking at him and hoped he wouldn't stay.

"If your nerves feel like mine, you must be desperate for this drink."

He placed a snifter of cognac on the nightstand then gazed down at Reason. "Does that shirt bring back any memories?"

She checked the red-striped cotton beneath her chin. "No. Should it?"

"That's the one you took off me in your gazebo."

Reason managed a small smile. "No wonder it feels so good."

Wilder moved away from the bed. He was as ill at ease as Reason. "Are you warm enough? I can light the fire if you like."

"No, the bed is plenty warm. If not, this will do the trick." Reason tipped the cognac to her lips and didn't even taste it. She downed the contents in a gulp.

"Would you like some more?" Wilder asked, taken aback.

"Yes."

Jogging back downstairs, he returned with a bottle which he set beside Reason. He took a drink then yanked off his shoes and socks. "I'm going to take a shower."

"Wilder? What language were you speaking tonight? It sounded like a cross between German and Japanese."

"Irish. Liam taught me and Kieran to speak it."

"Do the security forces know about those tunnels?"

"Some they do, most they don't. The troops used to go down in them looking for Provos, but too many soldiers got lost, some were shot. Now if they find a tunnel, the soldiers brick it up, but as fast as they seal one, the locals open another."

"Was that boy I took care of all right?"

"He will be eventually."

"Something about him reminded me of Aidan Duffy…his eyes."

"Reason, you never saw his eyes!" Wilder skidded over to the bed. "You're scaring the hell out of me. You cannot be this careless! They weren't kidding when they said they'd kill you, then me for one slip of your tongue. What went down tonight was *major league,* and the RUC will be looking for someone exactly like you who talks too much. You have to swear to me this night never happened. *Swear it!*"

Humiliated anew, Reason raised her hand. "Tonight never happened."

Wilder glared at Reason unconvinced. "Am I crazy to trust you, Mac? You know enough to bury me."

With a cry of protest she scrambled over the covers and captured Wilder's hands. "They'll have to bury me first before I'll ever hurt you again, Wilder. I swear it. If you believe in nothing else redeeming about me, believe I'm your friend."

She was passionately sincere, easing Wilder's fears a bit. But she was willful and curious and dangerously bold. "Did it ever occur to you not to follow me tonight?"

Guiltily Reason wagged her head.

"But you won't do anything like that again, right? You'll mind your own business, you'll think twice?"

"Absolutely, yes," she vowed.

Wilder freed his hands from Reason grip. "I never wanted you to be involved in this, Reason. You do understand how dangerous it is?"

"I do now."

"I'll be in the shower if you need me."

Reason watched Wilder empty his pockets and peel off his shirt. She looked at his bare shoulders and back, and she remembered the way she had slid her hands up his backbone and encouraged him to go deeper, slower, harder, and the way those arms had wrapped around her and tenderly, fiercely held her. She wanted to touch him and be touched, kiss him and be kissed, love him and be loved. But he wanted to be left alone. "Do you remember the shower we took together in Denver? Now that was the night I'll never forget."

"Vaguely," he shrugged. Vaguely hell. They'd hit the wall so hard they knocked the tiles loose.

"You don't think about me…about us…like that at all anymore, do you?"

"Oh no, Reason, never," was Wilder's sarcastic reply.

As she lay listening to the shower, Reason wondered why Wilder had insisted on bringing her home. Like his adverse-mindedness on everything lately, it was like he wanted to keep his eyes on her and never see her again. But maybe he, like she, had seen in one stunning flash how easily they could lose each other, and how viciously that would hurt. For whatever reason, she was relieved to be here. Wilder's bed was big and warm and smelled of her favorite vision; each time she smelled Wilder's cologne the memory of their lovemaking steamed to mind. No wonder his sheets felt erotic rubbing her skin. And she felt safe here.

One snifter of cognac hadn't calmed her. Two had worked wonders. Outside the rain stopped, or had Wilder simply turned off the water? Reason switched out the light. Wilder's aftershave wafted into the bedroom. Yes, this was better than sleeping alone. Would he be joining her in his bed? No. Still this was nice. Closing her eyes and cuddling Wilder's pillow, she craved sweet dreams, but the memory of the rifle barrel jammed to her head forbid sleep. Like loud music leaves a ring in the ears, terror left a buzz. What if her guard had pulled the trigger? But he didn't pull the trigger. But what if he had? And God in Heaven what had she inadvertently been accessory to?

Softly saying Reason's name through the darkness as he came out of the bathroom and receiving no reply, Wilder went about the business of preparing for bed. Reason listened to her name soft from his lips, wishing its sound would cling to her ears for all time. And in the light from the bathroom she watched Wilder's every move. How he tightened his bathrobe, how he combed his curly wet hair, how he brushed his teeth, how he contemplated himself in the mirror. Did he see the love of Reason's life? And she saw how he turned off the light and stood in the doorway watching her. Was he thinking that tonight had proven them vulnerable and their vulnerability made every second priceless? No. Reason was certain Wilder's grudge was burning her in effigy by now. She had complicated everything.

Wilder approached the vacant side of his bed, and Reason watched him draw back the covers. Unable to sleep, she would welcome his company, but he was only retrieving a pillow. Now that he knew Reason was near and out of danger he could sleep. Across the hall. Across the hall might as well be across the Atlantic. Midway to the door he had second thoughts, turned back and paused at the foot of his bed. He was dying to hold her, be warmed by her, to sleep by her side like a husband fulfilled. God, it had been so long. But no. She was safer out of his arms than in them.

"You aren't leaving, are you?" Reason murmured.

"No."

"Wilder, I am so sorry about tonight. With this transgression on top of all my other transgressions, you'll never forgive me." She pushed the rosebud away and hid her misery in her pillow. "I just can't do anything right around you," Wilder could hardly hear her say, "and you mean everything in the world to me."

"You are kind of like Dennis the Menace," he said, moving to Reason's side, sitting on the bed, rubbing her shoulder, peeling the pillow from over her eyes, bending low to smooth away her tears. And he considered forgiveness and petitioned his heart, but it was too soon.

Mortified to be graceless, to be crying, to be the woman unrequited, Reason turned away and didn't speak again. But Wilder remained seated on the bed like a Catholic school boy seated in his confessional. Unable to forgive, praying to be forgiven. For all he refused to feel.

Chapter Twenty

Reason ran downstairs to get the morning paper. She found what she was looking for plastered across the front page; what Wilder had meant by "major league."

Three British soldiers shot dead in shoot-out with IRA. After a twenty minute gun battle with Provisionals on the outskirts of Belfast last night three soldiers were killed and two seriously wounded, Reason's eyes skimmed the article. Two hooded men were seen escaping on a motorbike...the IRA, in claiming responsibility for the killings, said, "No member of the Imperial security forces is safe in Northern Ireland as long as the British Army remains on Irish soil. The recent ruthless murder of Aidan Duffy proves once again the British Army is a pernicious force that must be driven out by extreme and peremptory means."

Reason tossed the paper aside and covered her eyes. She wanted no part of this, she did not want to know! But the Falls, New Lodge, the Malone, the Cure, through Wilder and Cain and Hunter Cromwell, she had seen it all too clearly, felt it all too dearly. Oh, to retreat and never glance back. But it wasn't knowing she had tended a Provisional that made her wish to flee. It was the unexpected shock of feeling sympathetic. When she had looked into those dark eyes last night she hadn't seen a terrorist or a murdering bastard. She saw a frightened young Irishman willing to die for his country.

Outside birds sang as they always sang. The sun was strong, the sky blue as it had been blue for a billion years. Still life shed its old ways around Reason, and allegiance to Wilder's world sprang from yesterday's ash. Something had been born inside her; some ebullient seed that made certain she would no longer be neutral. She hadn't fumbled her way into one night's misdemeanor; she had intercepted the 800-year-old war.

Wilder found Reason leafing through an album of photographs in his den. "This must be Merry," she said without looking up from the curly-haired, blue-eyed woman. "She was pretty."

"Yes, she was. Why are you wearing your coat? Are you still cold?"

"You confiscated my clothes, remember?"

"I kind of like seeing you in nothing but a trench coat," Wilder said, yawning. "Give me a few minutes, and I'll drive you back to the Gov for your car."

"You were right. It isn't raining on the Fourth of July."

"Like I said, it wouldn't dare."

"Are you still planning on driving up the coast today?" Reason noticed his casual attire; shorts and a Dodgers' t-shirt.

"You bet."

"Isn't it rather late? It's nearly noon."

"It's a short drive and the day is long."

"It's a perfect day to go to a beach," she hinted, wanting to join him.

"Sure is," Wilder yawned again. "Did you make any tea?"

"Yes." She trailed Wilder into the kitchen. "I don't know what I'm going to do today...I guess I could go to the Gov this afternoon."

"Did you get the morning paper?"

"It's on the table."

Wilder pulled out a chair and read the news, not mentioning the front page. "Did you get something to eat?"

"Yes, thanks. Gee, going to work doesn't sound like much fun, does it?"

"Not to me," he snapped the paper up to his face.

Reason marched over to Wilder and punched the paper down. "Aren't you going to ask me to go up north with you?"

"I already did. You said 'no.'"

"I changed my mind."

"Did you now? Imagine that."

Reason slunk back across the kitchen. "I'll be outside whenever you're ready to leave."

But Wilder didn't drive to West Belfast. He took Reason up the Antrim Road to Fiona's. "Go get dressed. You have twenty minutes."

"I can come with you?" She was already out of the car.

"Did you honestly think," Wilder was laughing, "I would leave Belfast without you on the Fourth of July?"

Along Ireland's rugged north coast, miles of immaculate, ivory beaches collared steep ivory cliffs jutting into the wild Atlantic.

"Look at that sapphire ocean." Wilder never tired of seeing Antrim's coast. "We've left the world behind and come to heaven."

Beneath a sky blue as forget-me-nots Reason saw a scene God created in a generous mood. To the left as far as she could see were green velvet pastures dotted with brambles. Shaggy ponies and Q-Tip sheep stood bewildered in the heat. An old man in a horse-drawn wagon waved from the field. The breeze rushing in the car window smelled of coconut whin and mist from the sea, the sounds whispered peace, and there wasn't a helicopter in sight.

To the right shimmered the Atlantic, flinging its waves into the air like a show of jubilant hands.

"I think the ocean's glad to see us," Reason said as another wave flared high and hailed hello.

The austere beauty of the cliffs hundreds of feet above restless shores was made the more profound by the lack of humanity. Other than the farmer and four passing cars, Wilder and Reason hadn't seen another soul.

"I know I'm glad to see the ocean." Wilder turned off the highway onto a dirt road. "I came up here last summer whenever I could. It made being away from Malibu easier."

"So, you *are* homesick." Reason had thought so.

"More than I want to admit. I think about California all the time."

"Do you ever go home?"

"I've been too busy. But I'm going home for Christmas. How about you? After a month, are you homesick?"

"Only a little, but you know what I miss the most? American accents. Everywhere I go the speech is so foreign, and no matter how familiar the scenery becomes, the language reminds me I'm an outsider."

"Aye, you sound like an outsider. But then that's what you want to be. You aren't Irish, remember?"

Reason poked Wilder in the ribs. "Be nice. That's the cool thing about the ocean," she continued. "It doesn't have an accent. It sounds familiar wherever you meet it." She watched the waves crest and curl and slide into froth. "I love the ocean. It's so sensuous the way it moves, the way it glides over your skin, touching every place, and the way it sounds like life, breathing in, breathing out. When I was little we went to the Caribbean a lot, and I'd cry every time we had to go back to Connecticut."

"It's not like Connecticut is far from the ocean."

"No, but my parents were. They went to the islands for the sun not the water. When they discovered Palm Springs they thought it was Mecca. It's amazing how I love the sea and my mother hates it."

"Your mother hates the Catholics, the Irish, the sea...does she *like* anything?"

"She likes me," Reason said happily. "This road looks like it's heading over a cliff. Where are we going?"

"Somewhere that's going to make you fall in love with Ireland forever."

The road was heading over a cliff but not before stopping at the brim, and there on the brim stood the skeleton of a castle whose moss-covered walls had been tumbling into the Atlantic for 600 years. Like uneven, arthritic fingers, matted in whin and sinking into the chalk cliff, the scattered remains loomed, prey to time, sport for the wind. Chimney columns, semi-circles that once were round towers, and broken walls stood like sagging bags of stone awaiting the whacks of surf and storm. A precarious wonder, it reminded Reason of chessmen on a dustpan being swept, piece by piece, into the checkmating sea.

"It's beautiful," Reason exclaimed as the castle grew closer.

"I'll bet you've never built anything that could last 600 years."

"It's that old? I wonder who lived there."

"Pirates. The inhabitants of this old palace used it to lure ships into the coast. The water is shallow below, and the unsuspecting ships would run aground on the rocks, then the natives would race down the cliff and plunder the cargo."

"Is it all right to go over there and look around?"

"Sure. Castles like these are crumbling all over Ireland. People see them rather like tree stumps."

Leaping from the car, Reason ran through the ruins. "This is the most beautiful place I've ever seen! There's a huge waterfall rushing off that cliff over there. Do you see it? And look at all the grottos along the coast." Her feet sank into foot-long, windswept grass; grass deep and yielding as a featherbed. "Wilder, look! It's the long soft grass." She bounced on the spongy mounds, and just to see if it was as soft as it looked, she lay down and filled her fingers with the long blades, and smelled the fresh earth and stared up at the cloudless blue sky. "Oh, yes! It's just like I imagined. Like a mattress. It's soft from cushions of moss."

It hurt to see Reason there in that grass; that Irish, made for loving, long soft grass, grown thick and soft from tappy rain. If she had lain there in other times, he would have lain upon her, possessing her, taking her there, there in that soft, deep grass. But today he shifted his eyes to the raging waterfall.

"I see stairs down to the beach." Reason was on her feet again. "May I go down there?"

"That's exactly where we're go…" Before Wilder could finish, Reason had leaped from the castle to the stone steps, and running headlong down the cliffside, she vanished from sight.

It was seventy two degrees. "Perfect Fourth of July weather," Reason decided as she smoothed a place for herself in the sand.

"Too bad the water isn't warmer. Have you ever felt it? Pure ice."

"Aw, you big pansy." Reason thwacked Wilder's knee. "I've been swimming in it…at night…nude," she bragged without thinking.

"You have not. When?"

"With Cain at the Solstice Fete."

Wilder's only reaction was to peer down at her through his opaque sunglasses. Then he did what he said he would do, took off running barefooted down the abandoned beach. Reason made no attempt to run with him. She settled back in the sunshine and stared up at the castle and the waterfall, then over the rising tide and down the beach where Wilder was jogging. Last night had never happened, but today was real. Today she and Wilder were together and love tumbled over white cliffs.

Plink…Something bounced beside her. *Plink, plink.* It was raining daisies. Reason glimpsed skyward to see Wilder standing thirty feet above her on the ledge of a sand dune. Against the afternoon sun, waving his arms to catch her eye, he reminded Reason of Apollo preparing for flight. More daisies fluttered down then Wilder hiked down to the beach. "Did you like the flowers? I found them growing in the castle."

"They're great."

"We have to eat everything in here because I'm not hauling it back up the cliff," he said, dropping a cooler into the sand. He sat down beside Reason and opened the cooler. First he pulled out a red rose then a white rose and a handful of blue cornflowers. "These are for you. Flowers for my flower of the seaside. Happy Independence Day, Reas."

"Thank you," she said, enchanted.

"Let's see, I have champagne from Napa, hotdogs from Jersey, pickles from Pittsburgh." He kept pulling things out.

"Champagne, hotdogs and pickles? Are you pregnant?"

"Pregnant with *joie de vivre,* m'love. And for dessert?" Out came a small green book. "Yeats. Not very American, but very romantic."

"Wilder, this is wonderful."

"Better than going to work?"

"Much."

He wasted no time in popping open the wine which he poured into paper cups. "Consider yourself lucky." He referred to the cups. "In Malibu we drink it straight from the bottle."

"To 1776, and freedom," Reason toasted, "may it come to Ireland one day."

"You want to go swimming?" Wilder yanked his shirt over his head.

"No."

"You'll go with Cromwell, but not with me?" He gave Reason that look through his dark glasses again.

Before Reason could answer, Wilder had her by the foot. "No shoes allowed." He tossed her sandals into the air then grabbed her hand.

"Where are we going?"

Out of his pocket he withdrew his wooden flute. "For a wee stretch of the legs."

"You're going to play your flute for me!"

"Aye, love, just for you." Playing *Brian Boru,* he charmed Reason along the shore.

∗   ∗   ∗   ∗   ∗   ∗   ∗

"Is Reason here?" Ruairi peered around the corner at Jillie, who sat snapping her gum and typing at her computer.

"She took today off. Can I help you, love?"

"I just stopped by to tell her I'm back from Dublin and everything is sorted."

"Did you hear about the IRA battle with the Brits last night?"

"Aye. I'm glad I missed it. Life gets miserable around here when Brits get shot. I was stopped and searched twice walking up the Falls to the Gov this morning. Now, do I look like a killer?"

Jillie turned from her keyboard and reviewed Ruairi's appearance; red tie, clean white shirt, houndstooth slacks, honest smile, auburn hair. "A lady killer maybe," she flirted.

Ruairi blushed and modestly smiled. "Tell Reason I was here, would you?"

"I just made some tea. Want some? I've been up here alone all day and could use the company."

Ruairi tipped his watch. "Well, it is four o'clock."

Jillie led the way into Reason's office. "Do you have a girlfriend, Ruairi?"

"No one steady."

"Milk and sugar?"

"Black. Paltry office Reason has here. Must be a miserable inconvenience to be so cramped."

"Have you ever seen anyone keep a desk so neat? It drives me crazy the way she lines up her markers and pencils in perfect little rows. Where do you do your engineering projects?"

"In the attic at home."

"Do you like being an engineer?" Jillie chatted, checking Ruairi out head to toe.

"Aye. Do you like being Reason's assistant?"

"Sure. This job is a dream. Reason lets me do whatever I want, and," Jillie rolled her chair closer to Ruairi, "nearly every man in the hospital has been up here to consult on the new wing. I'm enjoying a world of propositions."

Ruairi looked at Jillie's sweet face and smiled, "I can see why."

She inched further forward. "Do you think I'm pretty, Ruairi?"

"I'd be blind if I didn't."

"Kieran calls me perfect. Do you see much of him?"

"Only at weddings and funerals."

"How come? You're friends, aren't you?"

"I should be going."

"Do you think I'm too tall?" Jillie laid her palm on Ruairi's thigh.

"I don't know. I've never noticed how tall you are really."

Dashing her empty teacup to the floor, Jillie popped to her feet. "Stand up!" She snagged Ruairi's elbow and yanked him up before her, causing his tea to splash down his shirt. "Well?" her violet eyes searched his.

"Does tea stain?" Ruairi tried to dry his shirt with a paper towel. But Jillie lifted his chin to regain his attention. "Do you think I'm too tall?"

At six feet she surpassed his height by three inches. "Well, you *are* quite tall."

Jillie kicked off her heels and fingered Ruairi's tie. "How's this? Better?"

"Yeah…yeah, I suppose." He glanced down at his stained shirt. "I have to go."

"No you don't." Jillie pitched herself into his arms. "Let's play."

Ruairi stumbled back in surprise.

"Make love to me," she requested before sucking his mouth onto hers.

"You're winding me up, right?"

"Was that kiss a joke? You do know how to make love, don't you, Ruairi?"

He looked insulted.

"Well, don't just stand there looking stupid then. Show me."

"What about Kieran?" He accepted Jillie's French kiss.

"I'm an equal opportunity enjoyer of cousins. I've been waiting for this chance to be alone with you for weeks."

"You have not," Ruairi scoffed.

"Yes, oh yes." Jillie unsnapped her skirt. "I've been with Kieran and Declan and now I'm dying to know how it feels with you." Her sweater and bra hit the floor. "I saved the best for last."

"Reason wouldn't approve of this."

"Reason isn't here." Jillie nudged the door shut then twisted the lock.

"Kieran won't be happy about this," Ruairi worried as Jillie loosened his tie.

"Kieran will never know," Jillie giggled, and with a broad swoosh of her hand, cleared everything off Reason's perfectly-arranged desk. "Oohee! I've been wanting to do that for weeks."

"You're a wild one, Gillian." Ruairi stripped off his clothes faster and faster, keeping his eyes on Jillie pirouetting nude and beguiling before him.

"Aren't I the greatest?" She leaned back on the desk. Her eyes consumed Ruairi's body. Paddy strong. Paddy white. Paddy hard and proud. "Come on over here, lover." She licked her lips, and her eyes flashed with purpose. "You're going to love what I have for you."

*   *   *   *   *   *

The tide grew tall and rambunctious, but the heat hung beneath the cliff, and the evening stayed mild. Moving back from the shoreline, under the wing of a dune, Wilder lay with his head in Reason's lap and smiled up at her, and Reason stroked his hair, smiling down. It was nine o'clock and still light enough to read when Wilder opened his book of poems and handed it to Reason.

"I thought you were going to read to me," she said.

"I want to look up at the sea dusk and the castle and you. Start here," he indicated a passage from *The Rose*.

Reason lowered her eyes to Wilder. "Is this another sad Irish poem?"

"It's a masterpiece. Read."

She did.

"This part is my favorite," Wilder interrupted near the end.

"*'And bending down beside the glowing bars,'*" Reason quietly read, "*'Murmur, a little sadly, how Love fled*
And paced upon the mountains overhead
And hid his face amid a crowd of stars.' Wow," she sighed.

"You approve of my taste in poems?"

"Oh, I do."

"Another bit of the Irish that isn't so bad. We might get that snooty Wellworth-Howell out of you yet," Wilder teased, plucking the book from Reason's hands and tossing it aside.

"Don't you want me to read anymore?"

"No. The book hides your face. You know, Mac, if you keep adjusting your prejudices, you just might leave this country a nicer person."

"I hope that's true." Reason looked down at Wilder with humbled eyes. "I owe you such an apology for the way I treated you in Denver. I did use you to get out of my engagement to Reid, but I still wish you hadn't told him about us. I wouldn't have gone through with the wedding."

"Would you have stayed with me if I'd said nothing?"

"No. I needed the last two years to grow up."

Wilder rubbed his palm over her cheekbone. "You could have grown up with me you know."

"I wouldn't have grown up. I would have grown dependent, trading one man for the other. You wanted to possess me."

"Yes, I did," he acknowledged without regret, still pondering possession. "Did you ever think of finding me again?"

Reason smiled, "I used to imagine running into you at the Plaza Hotel. I had this elaborate fantasy about seeing you in the lobby and…well, it was terribly sexy and terribly silly. But for two years I didn't walk by the Plaza once without going in just to make sure you weren't there waiting for me. Oh, I knew it was ridiculous. I just liked pretending the dream could come true."

"What happened after you saw me in the lobby?"

"Well, you were sitting there looking like a movie star in the Palm Court. You saw me walk in, and you couldn't take your eyes off me…because everyone else in the room ceased to exist for you…oh, this is stupid," Reason shook her head, embarrassed.

"It's fascinating. I couldn't take my eyes off you, then what?" Wilder slipped his hand around Reason's and raised her palm to his lips and didn't take his eyes off her.

"You jumped up and came striding over to me. Not just walking, you were striding like a man rushing to claim his dream. You didn't say a word to me, you just swept me into your arms and kissed me, and you carried me to the elevator and you were still kissing me. You held me in your arms and kissed me all the way up to your room, and you still hadn't said hello. Passion left you breathless you see," she laughed, feeling foolish. "Oh, I can't believe I'm telling you this. It must be the champagne."

"I like it. So then what did I do?"

"Let's see," Reason went on turning her thoughts inside out, "once we got to your room, oh it was a gorgeous big room, you carried me not to your bed but to a rug in front of the fireplace. And you undressed me and served me champagne and you never took your eyes off me, and then you lay down beside me and I took off your clothes and you made love to me…and it wasn't until you were deep inside me and holding me like you'd never let go that you whispered my name…'Hello, Reason,' you said," her voice dropped with sentiment, and she turned her eyes to the blackening water, "and I started to cry because I'd missed you so very, very much and couldn't believe I was with you again…but of course you were never in the Plaza and this must sound pathetic."

But Wilder savored the fantasy, employing the Irish glens not the Plaza Hotel; they lay in a forest on the grass in warm mist and sunshine. And Reason's mouth was on his as she wrapped her legs around him and he came deep inside her, loving her, only her forever. "Sounds like," his voice was dry, he cleared his throat, "I missed the chance of a life-time. If I'd known, I would have moved to Manhattan and spent every afternoon in the Palm Court."

"Instead I find you playing snooker at Albie's."

"At least you found me."

She met his eyes again. "And you said you didn't know me. You said you didn't want to know me. Did you get involved with anyone after I left Denver?"

"No. I was too busy. I'm still too busy. Did you get involved again?"

"No. All my friends think I'm going to be an old maid."

"What I don't understand is how you could have that fantasy when you didn't want me, when I simply wouldn't do."

"Oh, you are never going to forgive me for being confused!"

"After a few hours at the Plaza with you I'm sure I'd reconsider."

"What did I know, Wilder? I'd been with oatmeal Reid for years, and you were this spicy foreign food. I didn't know my own mind or what I wanted. But that night I wanted to be with you. And then when you made love to me it was so powerful...like an undertow pulling me somewhere I wasn't ready to go." Reason pondered the castle poised above like a blossom on the crag folding into dusk. "I knew nothing about Ireland...I knew nothing...except that I was engaged to Reid and in love with you, and I didn't want to be either."

"And do you know more now?"

"Not where you're concerned. And being here with you again doesn't help. The Six Counties and your involvement in them are hardly conducive to figuring out an already complicated relationship."

"Did you love me, Reason, or were those just words that night?"

Her eyes flew back to his. "I loved you."

"And now?"

"And now Wilder has become Declan and Declan has a diamond heart and I don't know him."

"And Reason falls in love with a Cromwell."

The surf hurled forth, sucked back. Forth. Back. Running to stay. Running to go.

"Did you really love me, Wilder?"

He stared up at the bright star of summer, brilliant white Vega; Vega the Falling Bird in the constellation of Lyra, the lyre. The lyre, symbol of Ireland. "More than you'll ever know," he said more to the star than to Reason.

"And now?"

"I've tried to sneak pieces of you back into my life, but you're already initiated into things you shouldn't know about, and I swore I wouldn't let that happen. And I swore to myself at Merry's funeral, Ireland would always come first. And I swore at my own funeral after you left me I'd never allow myself to get involved with you again."

"So why are we together tonight?"

"Because it's the Fourth of July."

"And what about the fifth of July and the sixth and Christmas and New Years Eve? Can the rest of our lives be special occasions?"

"Come on," Wilder rose from Reason's lap to his feet. "Let's go shoot fireworks at the stars."

"You're avoiding the issue like you always avoid the issue."

"I'm delaying it. Are you in a hurry to end our one day of freedom?"

"No, because tomorrow you'll tell me tonight never happened."

"Yeah, I probably will."

Reason accompanied Wilder out to where the ocean recalled itself. She took a sparkler from his hand. The sparks parachuted into the surf. "With all these nights to remember and nights to forget, I just hope the me in you and the you in me that mattered two years ago won't be dismissed."

Wilder flung his sparkler into the sky towards Vega in Lyra and thought about what Reason was saying. Dismissed. Like a bird, whose song is sung, falls from the strings of a quivering lyre.

The last of the sparklers expended, it was time to return to Belfast. "But not before we have that talk." Wilder guided Reason back to the dune, folded down and encouraged her to sit in front of him so he could wrap his arms around her waist. "You know what we have to do now," he murmured with his chin on her shoulder. Her curls tickled his lips. Her skin delighted his hands.

"Yes. Stop thinking there's something between us and get on with our lives."

"Reason, there *is* something between us. But last night was too close for comfort, and I'm not going to change my life."

"I never asked you to change, Wilder. All I asked was that you be careful."

"I am careful, and last night you jeopardized that. Whatever magnetism keeps throwing us together has to stop. I can handle being your friend but I refuse to go beyond that. Nothing is going to happen between us. *Nothing.* "

"Are you trying to convince me or yourself? Since that night at Albie's I haven't pursued you. Well, except for last Friday night when you limped away like an impotent monk."

"An impotent monk?" Wilder railed. "Excuse me, but I'm only looking out for your best interests! I'm trying to protect you."

"Well, whatever. You're the one who keeps coming around with your sentimental eyes, insisting you have no use for me."

"I know. I'm beguiled, enslaved, obsessed," Wilder laughed and lazed kisses along Reason's throat. "Will you keep seeing Cromwell?"

Reason tilted her face up to Wilder's. "Will you ask me not to?"

"Are you in love with him?" he asked lowly.

"I will be."

Arrow through the heart. Wilder hadn't expected her candor. "But you've known him only a few weeks…he's my friend…he's…" *not me.* He was cursing Reason's presence in Ireland again.

The waves rolled in. The waves rolled out. Rush. Hush. Passion. Peace.

"Are you ready to go?"

"Yes," Reason said sadly. "Just let me go wash the sand off my hands."

Soon it would be the fifth of July. Independence Day would be over for another year. At the shoreline Wilder came before Reason, and cupping her face in his hands, kissed her with all the longing he sought to deny; at first hesitantly then greedily until he nearly lost his resolve.

"You have to stop doing this," Reason sighed upon his lips.

"I will." Wilder watched the waves forsake the sands only to swoop to reclaim them. "I will."

*   *   *   *   *   *

"What in the fuck are you doing, Cromwell?" Kieran punched on the light and threw Cain out of bed. "You've been seen in the Shankill going in and out of the Horsetail Inn. You're dead if you're working with the ULF."

Cain blinked in confusion. It was the middle of the night, he was half-awake. "I'm working with the ULF," he admitted.

"You have ten seconds to explain that!" Kieran roared.

Cain crawled up off the floor and fell back into bed. "For the last year I've been trying to find out who killed your cousins. I'm using every loyalist contact I have to get information, and those contacts hang at the Horsetail. But these things take time and I have to be careful."

Kieran's glare darkened. "You're working with us *and* them?"

"I'm only working with them to help you."

"And what have you found out?"

"That Brendan and the Milltown funeral-goers were killed by the same ULF man. He works with the Cure and now he's out to take down the last O'Neill, namely Declan. I'm trying to prevent that."

"Do you know his name?"

"Yes."

"Speak up, Cromwell, who is it?"

"I don't interfere with your business, don't you interfere with mine." Cain stared Kieran down. "Either you trust me or you don't."

"Playing both sides of the fence is a deadly game, Cain."

"They're the only games I play. And I'm on your side. If you can't believe that, shoot me."

"What's your plan with this loyalist?"

"To use him to flush out the Cure agent who's after you. May I go back to sleep now?"

"Just remember we're watching you, and I want you to keep me informed. Do it, Cain, or you'll be getting another, less friendly visit."

"Yeah, yeah." Cain melted deeper into his covers. "No matter what I say or do you never forget that I'm English, do you?"

Kieran smiled, "Do I look stupid, mate?" He snapped off the light as he left.

Chapter Twenty-One

Early Thursday stormy weather returned. Rain pecked Reason's window like a persistent intruder, and she wished it wasn't five in the morning. Unable to go back to sleep, she got up and looked outside. Four policemen and six soldiers stood below in the street. Through dawn's gloom she could see them conversing and gesturing towards the McKee's house, then suddenly they kicked through Fiona's gate. Reason skidded out of her room just as the soldiers sledge-hammered through the front door and burst in screaming, "Wake up, you fucking Fenian bastards!"

The police and three soldiers stampeded up the stairs, smashing everything on the wall with their rifles as they ran; the family portraits, the mirror, the Sacred Heart. Downstairs the remaining trio of soldiers tramped room to room toppling Fiona's keepsakes. All the while the ten men shrieked obscenities whose volume alone terrorized Reason.

By now Fiona and Ruairi had run into the hallway. When Fiona realized the police had come for her son, she threw herself in front of him.

"Get out of my house!" she hissed and motioned the troops away with one outstretched finger. "My boy has done nothing wrong!"

"Get the fuck out of the way, you cow," the policemen blared and flung Fiona aside. Then they turned on Ruairi.

He had pulled on a pair of blue jeans but wore no shirt, no shoes, and the soldiers made certain their blows landed on his bare skin. The policemen pushed him against the bathroom door while one of the soldiers lunged screaming at Reason.

"On the floor!" he commanded and knocked her to the carpet. "Now on your knees!" Reason was too slow to get up and received a kick to the shins. "ON YOUR FUCKING KNEES, SLUT! Hands behind your back."

When Reason complied, the soldier bound her arms behind her with plastic strapping; left hand to right elbow, right hand to left elbow. "Keep your head down, bitch, and don't look at me. Don't look at fucking anything, or I'll blow your fucking face off."

The soldier similarly bound Fiona then entered Reason's bedroom like a dervish. He overturned her mattress, drained her drawers, smashed her mirror, and threw everything off her desk. Reason yelled in protest only to receive the butt of his weapon in her back.

"Suck me, bitch," he laughed as Reason fell forward. He gave Fiona a kick before racing up to the attic. Reason heard every inch of Ruairi's work room erupting.

"Can I at least put my shoes on?" Ruairi pleaded as the pair of policemen slammed him against the wall at the top of the stairs.

"Can you fucking hell," a policeman bellowed, stabbing Ruairi in the groin with his rifle, causing Ruairi to fall down the stairs. The constables and soldiers swooped down after him and hauled him to his feet by his ear. They banged him into the wall then shoved him down on his knees.

"You're a Roman Catholic dog and we're your masters. Crawl like a dog, you asshole," one policeman ordered and beat Ruairi about the head and neck with his fist. "CRAWL, GODDAMN IT!"

Ruairi crawled into the foyer. One of the soldiers then spiked his boot heel into Ruairi's spine, knocking him flat in the broken glass.

"Hail Mary full of grace look who's on his fucking face. Get up, pig!" Grabbing Ruairi's hair and snapping his head back, a policeman pressed his rifle to Ruairi's neck and snickered, "Now crawl out the door, bastard. You're going for a ride."

In helpless horror Reason and Fiona watched from the top of the stairs while the crown forces kicked and beat and insulted Ruairi as he crawled outside in the rain into an awaiting Land Rover.

"Get up!" Two soldiers thundered down from the attic and muscled Fiona and Reason to their feet. With rifles poked to their backbones and their heads jerked back by the hair, the women were ordered, "Downstairs!"

Neither woman could see where she walked as the soldiers shoved them forth, and both Fiona and Reason ended up missing the steps. Aided by squaddie punches, the women bumped on their backs down the stairs. Awaiting their graceless arrival were two RUC men who jerked the ladies up by their throats.

"OK, you dick-licking bitches, let's go."

Reason feared she and Fiona were going "for a ride" as well. Instead they were marched into the kitchen and told to kneel on the floor. Reason stared up at the soldiers now ransacking the cupboards and received a slap to the mouth. "I told you not to look at anything, you ugly whore."

Pots and pans dropped with earsplitting clangor. Cups, plates, bowls and silverware smashed to the floor. Glass was flying everywhere, pelting Fiona and Reason like shrapnel. Reason again glared up in outrage only to receive another brute smack. For ninety minutes she and Fiona remained kneeling with bowed heads while soldiers and RUC men ran in and out of the kitchen cursing and screaming insults. Finally, after rifling through every room in the house, the raiders prepared to leave.

Cutting off Reason's plastic handcuffs, the soldier who had repeatedly slapped her handed her a towel. "Your nose is bleeding the fuck all over." He grabbed Reason by the neck and pushed her face to the tile. "Clean up the damn floor."

"Kiss my ass, grandma," the sixth and last soldier cooed to Fiona with a squeeze to her breast as he ran from the kitchen and out the front door.

The instant the security forces were gone, Reason caught Fiona's sleeve in fear. "Where did they take Ruairi?"

Fiona could only wobble her head and delay a sob with her fist.

"Why did they arrest him?"

Again Fiona swayed her head.

"What can we do? *What?*"

Fiona's response was a wisp, "Wait…and pray."

"But what about calling a lawyer? What about Ruairi's rights?"

"Rights!" Fiona spat. "The peelers can detain anyone for seven days without charge, without access to a solicitor…" she considered her disheveled kitchen, "…there are no rights for Catholics here."

Reason staggered in shock, gaping alternately at Fiona and the ravaged scene. "Fiona, are you all right?"

"It'll take more than the boot of a Brit to hurt me. How about you, love? That soldier gave you a thrashing."

"I don't know…" Reason faltered again, too dazed to feel. Seeing Fiona's tears, she cinched her arm around the elder woman's shoulders. Beyond that sympathetic gesture she didn't know what to do, or where to begin restoring order to the house, to Fiona, to herself. It was all she could do to hold her nerves together.

"We've been through dawn raids before," Fiona rouped as she made her way into the parlor, "but this time I'm afraid for my Ruairi, desperately afraid." She burst into tears.

Reason scrambled for the phone. The second she heard Wilder's voice she started to cry. "Please come, please."

"If you think the downstairs is bad, you ought to see what they did to the attic," Wilder said, fitting the mattress back on Reason's bed.

"How's Fiona?"

"I cleaned up her cuts and gave her some Valium. She'll have a good sleep. Now what about you? Do you think anything is broken? Ribs, wrist, fingers?" He inspected Reason's bruised jaw. "You took quite a slap. Those fucking bastards."

Reason drew a deep breath. "I'm OK, Wilder, really I am. I think I'm too shocked to feel. I can't believe what happened here."

"I'll give you a sedative…"

Reason waved a demurring hand. "Valium can't erase what I saw. Oh, Wilder, it was hideous. We begged them to stop…that only made them laugh…and I kept thinking this is Ireland. Ireland with leprechauns and St. Patrick." She covered her eyes and slumped against her broken dresser. "Don't the security forces need a search warrant to enter a person's home?"

"No. They can search any house anytime."

"But they didn't even tell Ruairi why he was being arrested."

"They don't have to."

"Ruairi can at least call his lawyer, can't he?" Reason cried.

Again Wilder shook his head. "The police can keep him from contacting a lawyer for two days or more. Just enough time to beat out a confession."

"My God," Reason moaned. "What do you suppose the soldiers were looking for?"

Wilder raised his shoulders. Obviously they got wind of Ruairi's connection to the sniping rifles.

"Where do you think they took him?"

It took Wilder a moment to rake his thoughts back to Reason. "To Windsor Interrogation Centre."

"Do you have any idea what he's done?"

"No. We can only wait and see what happens. Reason, I think you should go home. As soon as possible. There's just too much going on around here."

Reason had been thinking the same thing, but now as Wilder folded her hands into his and looked into her eyes, home became Belfast. "I can't leave. I have a contract, obligations…"

"And your firm has other architects. I'm sure everyone concerned will understand if you leave this project. Will you go?"

Reason would never forget Wilder's calling her a coward. She'd prove him wrong. "It's only because I'm a woman that you're so concerned."

"You're the woman I care about."

"I'll be all right, Wilder." Brushing splinters of mirror off her pillow, Reason eased down on her bed. "You're right though, there is a lot going on. Every time I turn on the television or pick up a paper something terrible has happened somewhere in the Six Counties. Doesn't this ever let up?"

"No. Aw, Reason, look at your feet. They're cut from the glass."

Reason surveyed one foot then the other and sighed unamazed. "I hadn't even noticed. I'll go clean them up."

"You'll stay put." Wilder ran down to the bathroom and returned with a wet towel. Kneeling at Reason's bedside he pushed aside the folds of her robe and washed one ragged foot then the other. "You won't be dancing jigs for awhile," he said, giving her shin a rub. Patting away drops of water, he wrapped her feet in gauze. "Seems I should be sliding a glass slipper on your foot being your Prince Charming and all." He managed a smile as he applied the last bandage. "There you go, sweetheart. You'll be good as new in a few days."

"My first battle scars," Reason remarked grimly and swung her legs back up on the bed. "I'm so worried about Ruairi I feel sick."

"Me too."

Reason looked to Wilder for encouragement. "Now that they have him in custody they won't hurt him anymore, will they?"

She was so innocent. Wilder could have spelled out the truth, but Reason had been enlightened enough for one day. "Try to rest, love. I have to get to the hospital. I'll tell Jillie you won't be in today."

Reason considered Wilder's hands and wondered how he could hold them steady. But steady they were. Annealed. "Don't tell Jillie anything. I'll be there at nine."

*   *   *   *   *   *

Inside the police barracks two detectives took Ruairi off the soldiers' hands. Using handcuffs, they pinned his fists behind his back. One policeman pushed Ruairi forward just as the other policeman held out his leg. Skull to concrete, Ruairi hit the floor. Booting him over onto his stomach, the detectives dragged him by the feet down a corridor lined in metal doors and grey tile. Down a flight of stairs they descended making sure Ruairi's chin bumped over every step. Finally at the end of the hall the policemen shoved Ruairi into a cell. Overhead lights bleached the white walls bright and gleamed off the tile floor. A mirror at the rear allowed covert observation, and briefly, before being smacked against the wall, Ruairi wondered who watched behind the scenes.

"Welcome to Windsor Interrogation Centre, Mr. McKee," the older of the two policemen said while slapping an acrylic baton in his palm. "I do hope your stay with us will be memorable."

"I want my lawyer present."

"We'll get him for you," the older policeman smiled. "Eventually."

"Why have I been arrested?" Ruairi asked.

"*Why* were you arrested?" *Slap* went the baton into the policeman's palm. *Slap* louder, *slap* harder. "For the murder of those three soldiers Monday night, that's why, you piece of shit."

His irrefutable alibi made Ruairi relax. "I was in Dublin on business that night."

"The hell!" The older policeman banged his baton against Ruairi's skull in sharp, short hacks. "You know you did it, we know you did it, so let's cut the crap."

Blood oozed from Ruairi's head as he crumbled to the floor and lay dazed and panting. All he could see were the RUC men's black boots; boots that kicked his bare back and legs. The lights glared into his eyes, he couldn't breathe, and for a moment he thought the ceiling had crashed upon him. Pain drilled into his brain until he could no longer think, but *Jesus*, he could feel. *Feel. Jesus.* Sickening, shivering, crippling pain.

The second policeman, a pimpled stick-figure who Ruairi had heard someone call Harlock, grabbed Ruairi's hair and jerked him to his knees. Blood trickled into Ruairi's ears, over his eyes and nose until he could taste himself bleeding. Then *wham*, like a spiked ball, into the floor he cracked face-first again. He blacked out.

Stinging cold water mixed with ammonia splashed his head and assaulted his nostrils. His face seemed to catch fire as the detergent pooled in his wounds. Ruairi opened his eyes and ammonia blinded his sight. How long had he been unconscious? Not long enough. A portly, bald man in a sterile white coat, *a hospital coat like Declan wears,* was bending over him, probing his body with gloved fingers, counting his heartbeats, peering into his eyes with a penlight. A physician. Ruairi had seen him before. At the Gov.

"This one's strong as a bull," the doctor said before leaving the room.

"Get up." When Ruairi didn't move, Harlock yanked him up by the throat. "Take off your pants," he snarled through chipped teeth. "Take off your pants, shithead," he bawled, sniggering at Ruairi's cuffed and powerless hands.

It hurt to stand but not to defy his captors with silence. Ruairi hung motionless on aching bones.

"Look at this, ask him to do a simple task like drop his pants, and he refuses to cooperate," Harlock snorted to Franks, the elder policeman, and gave Ruairi a cuff to the jaw.

"Confess to the shootings and we'll go easy on you, son. Otherwise we're going to fucking cut your balls off."

Silence.

"Get Jaggars in here," Harlock grunted. "He'll make quick work of this scum."

Harry Jaggars, a hard-bodied athlete resting rubber-gloved fingers on his chest, strode into the cell. Proudly erect, shoulders square, a confidant man. A powerful man. Thirty years of swimming and tennis had brought middle age to him with strength and grace. His hair was wavy, jet black, slicked back above a sharp face with ice-blue eyes and a perpetual smile. A loyalist born in Belfast, he was committed to ridding the province of Provisional vermin.

"Can't remove your own pants, Mr. McKee? Come now, surely a tough Provo like you can manage a zipper. If you won't do it, we'll do it for you," Jaggars promised with that slight grin rippling over his lips.

Harlock offered one final plea, "Wouldn't you like to tell us what happened outside of Dungannon Monday night and save us the bother of beating the shit out of you?"

Ruairi posed stoically staring at the wall. The three policemen pounced upon him, crushing him to the ground as they clawed off his wet jeans. When he was naked they stood him up with rowdy amusement.

"How does it feel to be a Provo now, Ruairi boy?" asked Harlock, pretending to focus a magnifying glass while inspecting Ruairi's genitals. "You aren't much of a man without your bullets and bombs."

"Look at that sorry little flower," Franks prodded his baton between Ruairi's thighs, "might as well be a woman."

"They say," Jaggars eyed Ruairi's body with contempt, "the only thing smaller than a Provisional's dick is a Provisional's brain."

"You carrying any concealed weapons, Ruairi?" Harlock cleared the phlegm from his throat and spit it in Ruairi's face. As the mucus ran down Ruairi's cheek, the three policemen cackled in mirth. And, humiliated, embarrassed, hurting and hating, Ruairi stood.

"OK, men, bend him over," Jaggars further instructed, giving his gloves a snap. "You never know what they stow up their bums."

This Ruairi resisted with his last burst of venom, but the harder he struggled the harder they beat him. A knee to his groin settled the fight. Franks twisted Ruairi's hands further up his spine, Harlock snapped Ruairi's head forward until he was bent at the waist, and Jaggars stabbed an exploring forefinger into Ruairi's rectum.

"Look, I think he likes it," Jaggars taunted.

"What's that you're moaning, Mr. McKee? Do it harder? Harder?" Jaggars laughed as his finger forged its sadistic search. "I hear this is how Provisionals shake hands, is that right, Mr. McKee?"

Pain. Jesus. Degradation. Break my balls. I will endure. Jesus. I will...I will endure.

"OK, hoist him up." Jaggars withdrew his bloodied finger and waited for Franks to bend Ruairi erect. The wrath in Ruairi's blue eyes made Jaggar's smile all the wider. Such useless defiance, the bastards. "Now we check the other end. You never can predict where you'll find a weapon. Open wide, sweetheart."

While Franks continued restraining, Harlock pried open Ruairi's jaws, and Jaggars, using the same probing finger as before, swabbed Ruairi's mouth. Satisfied, he wiped his dirty finger on Ruairi's tongue. "Tastes good does it, Mr. McKee?" He stepped back with a sneer. "Now, let's talk about the three soldiers you gunned down in cold blood."

Ruairi stared Jaggars down. "I was in Dublin."

"Is that all you have to say in your defense?" Franks quizzed.

"It's the truth."

"Provisionals can't tell the truth. Tell me, Mr. McKee, have you ever smelled a testicle burning? Sweet as bacon." Jaggars motioned to his mates as he plucked off his gloves and marched for the door.

"We'll be back with matches, Ruairi boy," Harlock vowed with a malevolent smirk. "You'll confess, oh yes you will." He mashed Ruairi's nose back into the wall. Another chop to the head completed the round of interrogation.

But the respite was brief.

"Are you all right?" a new, soft-spoken policeman came in with a blanket to cover Ruairi. "Dear Christ, they really worked you over. You can't take much more, can you, son?" He clapped his jaw in dread, "You'd better cooperate, or I'm afraid those others will finish you off. Can you hear me?"

Lying still, hugging the restful cold of the floor, Ruairi could hear but gave no response.

"I'm on your side, son, and I don't want to see those animals going back at you." The policeman tucked the blanket tighter around Ruairi and stroked Ruairi's hair off his bleeding cheek. "I tell you what. Confide in me and I'll make sure those men never touch you again. I'll get you to a soft, warm bed and make sure your wounds are tended. Confess to me, Ruairi, and everything will be fine. I'm on your side, really I am. All you have to do is sign a few papers and then you can rest."

Ruairi closed his eyes. Revulsion chilled his flesh. The policeman leaned closer.

"I've never told this to anyone before, but I understand what you boys are fighting for. You have a genuine complaint, I mean that. And I'll help you any way I can when you confess to murder."

I'm a soldier. I'm right. Silence.

"If you don't confess to killing those soldiers, son," the policeman glimpsed over his shoulder fearfully, "I can't guarantee your safety. You're a young man, save yourself. Let me help you before its too late."

He is the enemy. The enemy is wrong. Silence.

"Your silence will be used against you, friend. It implies guilt. You're guilty, aren't you? Won't you trust me? We can get through this together. Come on, Ruairi, help me out here," the policeman wheedled with paternal concern. "I don't want to let those sadists back in here, but if you don't talk, you'll leave me no choice. Let me warn you, I've seen them do inhuman things to Provisionals."

Fuck you. Silence.

"I see," the constable huffed. "Silence is how you repay my kindness? Your attitude disappoints me." With the flare of a matador he whisked the blanket off Ruairi and replaced it with a kick. "Don't say I didn't try to save you, McKee. Obviously you have a death wish."

An hour passed before Jaggars and Franks were back. Franks carried a notepad. Jaggars twirled the acrylic baton. At once Ruairi was on his feet again, face to the wall, naked and shaking with trauma.

"Tiptoes and nose-tip, scum," Jaggars ordered with a clout to Ruairi's ear. He meant Ruairi should support himself against the wall using only his nose while leaning forward on his toes. This exhausting stance was to be maintained at all times. Each time Ruairi faltered out of position it meant a blow to the back of his head, and he faltered often.

"It says here you were seen leaving Dungannon on a motorbike Monday night," Franks read from his blank notepad.

"I was in Dublin," Ruairi mumbled, feeling increasingly cold and detached.

"Come, come, Mr. McKee, do we look like fools? We know everything," Jaggars grilled on. "We apprehended one of your cohorts an hour ago, names you as the shooter, told us everything about Monday night. If you'll admit your guilt, you'll make this a whole lot easier on yourself. Come on, let's sign some papers."

If they know everything, why are they still questioning me? They know nothing. "Like to…see my solicitor," Ruairi mouthed barely conscious and received a barrage of blows from both officers. Blood sprayed the wall.

"It says here you live with your mother. But if you're here, she must be alone." Jaggars clicked his tongue with worry. "A lot can happen to a woman home alone. I hear Franks here likes a piece of Catholic ass now and again. Is your mother pretty? Would she like the Franks Special, Mr. McKee? Does she need a fuck?"

Tears flooded Ruairi's eyes but no words leaked forth.

"Your confession might spare your old mum," Jaggars advised like a friend. "Think about it, Mr. McKee. Think hard. You're responsible for your mother's fate."

"Leave my mum…" he muttered in anguish.

Jaggars patted Ruairi's shoulder benignly. "Sign these papers, son, and we will."

Ruairi shook his head, and Jaggars drove his fist into Ruairi's chest. "Suit yourself." Pulling a handkerchief from his pocket and wiping his fingers, Jaggars pointed Franks towards the door. "We'll be back. Until then this is your home"

"No toilet. No water. No food. No clothes," Franks droned. "Wouldn't you rather talk to us and move to a more comfortable cell?"

Ruairi shook his head.

"You son of a bitch!" Franks shrieked and grabbed Ruairi by the testicles, squeezing until Ruairi collapsed.

Two hours passed. Jaggars returned with the pudgy, bald physician. Dr. Bernard Thunder.

"Sit up," the doctor ordered before realizing Ruairi had passed out. "Prop him up then," he directed with a groan of inconvenience. "Just lean him against the wall there. Make a damn handsome corpse, wouldn't he?"

Dr. Thunder approached Ruairi with distaste. Like a chicken pecking for grain, he touched Ruairi's flesh and bones with hurried, jerky plucks. The evidence of torture made no impression, but his stomach sickened every time he had to examine a Provisional. A naked sweating Provisional, no better than an ape. Still he had been told keeping the prisoners nude and degraded broke their resistance, and Bernie was for that. "You boys got a little frisky here."

"It's McKee's own fault for resisting our attempts to question him," Jaggars clarified solemnly. "He kept throwing himself against the wall and onto the floor."

"Many more hits and he'll commit suicide. Cracked some ribs I suspect, bruised kidneys, dilated pupils, moderate trauma to the head," Bernie related to his comrade dispassionately as he inspected Ruairi's bruised parts. "Hemorrhage behind left eye, dislodged jaw possibly fractured, definitely fractured his nose, two front teeth broken…surely the bastard confessed?"

"Not yet," Jaggars snorted. "Insists he's innocent."

"Innocent as Jack the Ripper." Bernie opened his black bag and began stitching the gashes around Ruairi's head with the same plucky, hurried hand. "I say, did you see the results of the races yesterday? Bet on White Flash, the wife's idea really, won a thousand quid I did. Jolly lucky, aren't I?"

*   *   *   *   *   *

When Reason heard on the afternoon news that a North Belfast man had been arrested on suspicion of murdering the three British soldiers, she knew it was Ruairi and marched up the Falls to the nearest RUC station. She could settle this matter at once.

"I've come about Ruairi McKee."

"Your name and address please."

She stated both. "Is he being charged with murder?" she put to the fresh-faced constable sent out to handle her.

"I'm not at liberty to say, miss. Your purpose here in Belfast?"

"I work at the Grosvenor Hospital. Where is Ruairi being held?"

"I'm not at liberty to say, miss. How long have you worked at the Grosvenor?"

"One month. Is he in prison? Is he OK?"

"I'm not at liberty to say, miss. Your connection with Mr. McKee?"

"I'm his boss. Ruairi was on business in Dublin that night," Reason pleaded to the unblinking official. "I sent him down there myself. Call the hotel where he stayed. They'll verify he was there."

"Dublin is less than three hours from Dungannon, miss."

"You think he left Dublin and drove back? That's nonsense!"

"Have you any proof he remained in Dublin, miss?"

"He phoned me around eight o'clock. I was in my office."

"Have you proof of that conversation, miss?"

"*I'm* proof. I'm telling you he called me. I'm sure the hotel has a record of the call."

"A call can be made by anyone, miss."

"I assure you it was him."

"He'll have his day in court, miss."

"But he's done nothing wrong! He shouldn't be in jail!"

"That's a matter for the police to decide, miss."

"You aren't listening to me. Ruairi is innocent!"

"Thank you for your interest, miss."

"Don't brush me off, please don't. This is a man's *life!*" Tears blurred her eyes. "May I talk to your supervisor?"

"I'll pass along your information to him, miss."

"Won't you please…"

"We'll contact you if we need you, miss."

"But please…"

"Good day, miss."

*   *   *   *   *   *

"Hunter old man! What brings you to Windsor?" Bernard Thunder greeted his friend as he walked out of the RUC station.

"I hear they have apprehended one of the killers, and he works at the Gov. Dreadful PR, dreadful."

"How true, HC. Dreadful."

"All of Belfast knows my abhorrence of terrorists…why, this is scandalous! A Provisional working for a Cromwell? Good God."

"I'm certain no one will blame you, HC."

"What's the bastard's name?"

"McKee, Ruairi McKee. An engineer working on the Gov's new wing."

"Bloody hell! He's one of that McGuinness woman's punks. I had my suspicions about her. Damn Provisional sympathizer. She has that look about her. Blonde hair, shifty eyes, damn sympathizer!"

Dr. Thunder wasn't sure he understood what blonde hair had to do with anything, but if Hunter said it, it must mean something. "Oh, but surely she had no idea…"

"Of course she had ideas. Insisted on that equal opportunity bullshit Yanks are always yapping about. I told her to hire good British men. Yes sir, I told her. Hire any Catholic and you hire the IRA."

Dr. Thunder stroked his hairless scalp and nodded, "How true, HC."

"Reason McGuinness will be dismissed tomorrow along with her band of henchmen. We'll make an example of her irresponsible hiring practices. Yes sir, Bernie, only a stern hand in this matter will save the Cromwell name. Bloody sympathizer she is."

"Perhaps she should be arrested," Bernie suggested off the top of his head.

"Arrested? Yes. Yes! That would put brimstone in her knickers. Back to America she'd run hidey ho. But first I want to see this McKee creature."

"Not much to see I'm afraid. Half-dead he is. Boys got a tad rough."

"That's what it takes, Bernie. Spare the rod, spoil the Crown."

Dr. Thunder clapped Hunter on the back and hurried on his way. "The missus has steak and kidney pie on the cooker. Join us for golf Sunday?"

"Love to, Bernie. Love to."

When Hunter stared through the observation window he beheld Ruairi curled in a crescent on the floor. "Rather like going to the zoo and finding the tigers asleep," he complained to the officer seated beside him. "Look at him lying there in his own piss. Filthy animals."

"It's not right beating a man like that," the young officer said quietly.

"Signed a confession, did he?"

"Refused to, sir. Maybe he's telling the truth." The young man glanced at Hunter skittishly. "What if he *is* innocent? We should let him go if he is."

"God's blood, boy!" Hunter reeled with incredulity. "You sound like my sissy son. What's your name?"

"Wright, sir. Ian Wright."

"How long have you been in the RUC?"

"A month."

"Why the deuce did a wussy like you join?"

"I needed a job to support my family, sir. I have wee children, and policing offered the best wages I could earn."

"Well, Wright, it seems you haven't the guts for this line of work."

"I have the guts, sir, just not the heart," and Ian was thinking it required the loss of his soul as well. "It's just that I'm a Christian," he explained simply, making Hunter laugh.

"Then lead the Crusade! Go in there and give that murdering devil a lesson."

"I can't, sir. Dr. Thunder said he's too hurt. We're waiting for the Cure to tell us how to proceed." The young man stared into his hands. "I'm afraid if he doesn't die, he'll be questioned again later."

"Good. There's no such thing as 'too hurt' when it comes to fighting terrorists, boy." Hunter cast a final glower at Ruairi. "Animals."

"Christ, they lost all control here. They weren't supposed to kill you!" Her infuriated voice fell upon Ruairi's ear as her warm hand touched his shoulder. "Ruairi? Wake up, wake up."

Ruairi's left eye was swollen shut, his right was a slit. The lights shot his head full of pain, his brain buzzed disconnected, and he wasn't sure who he was seeing. He gasped for air. "Water?"

"Not until you tell me what I want to know."

"I am," his breath rattled, "inno…"

"Of course you're innocent." Her impatient toe tapped. "You were in Dublin."

Ruairi knew he was dreaming, still he struggled to widen his eye. What shapely apparition stood amidst the glare? "You *believe*…?"

"Yes, I believe you. Who has the sniping rifles, Ruairi? You?"

So. They know. "Dunno." *I will survive.*

"Why must you Paddies be so damn pig-headed? You made it clear to me you're involved with the guns, Ruairi. You said the Brits would never be safe again. You know all about those rifles. That's why I had you arrested. Those cops out there seriously believe you're one of Monday night's shooters; fools believe everything I say. Naming you as one of the killers was a convenient way to wear you down, and by the look of you, I'd say it's time you start talking. How many guns have you gotten ahold of, where are they, and who's in charge? Are you in charge? Is Kieran?"

Go to hell, never tell. "Dunno." *I will…survive.*

"It's only a matter of time before we know everything anyway, so why don't you help me out? Who has the rifles?"

"Dunno."

A gold-tipped boot. Kick to the legs. Kick to the groin. Kick and kick and kick. "Tell me NOW!"

Defy or die. Endure! I will. "Dunno." Ruairi curled his body tighter, tighter until his chin met his knees, until he formed a circle of agony.

Kick the spine. Once. Twice. Fist to the chest. Bang his head against the floor. "Who, Ruairi, who?"

Never tell, go to hell. Suddenly, miraculously the pain drained from Ruairi's head and rose from his feet to gather in his breast like a fluttering chaffinch. Free. "Priest…" he moaned, closing his eye.

"Fuck your priests!" came the soulless response. "Who has control of the rifles? Who? McCartan? O'Neill? Tell me before you die, or I swear I'll tear your mother's house down around her head. And if I don't find anything that way, I'll go after Kieran and Declan even Morris. TELL ME!"

I will…will…survive… The bird flown to his heart had azure wings opening, stretching, gleaming, calling. Wings of water. Wings of sky. Graceful motion. Up. His mother's face. For a moment Ruairi opened both eyes very wide without difficulty and attempted to rise in recognition. "It's…*you.*"

She smiled. A ghostly laugh. "They call me Mad Hatter."

Heart beat. *Cold. Cold.* No heart beat. His chaffinch soul embarking, Ruairi fell back in fields of emerald. A wee soft wind. Feather rain, heather sweet. Whisper off the mountain tops, welcome. Death! Death. The rustle of a hard won tear. *I will…*

*   *   *   *   *   *

The telephone rang before dawn Friday morning. Reason awoke to Fiona's bloodcurdling scream. Ruairi had passed away in the middle of the night due to, the policeman explained, "self-inflicted injuries sustained while resisting arrest. And in his wild desire to die," the constable added to Fiona nastily, "your son assaulted two of our finest detectives."

"Self-inflicted wounds?" Wilder slapped the tears off his eyes. "You should have seen Ruairi's body."

"I just don't see how the police could beat him over and over until he died." Reason tried to understand as she sat in Wilder's office. "Why didn't they stop?"

"When it comes to the RUC, hatred overrules sense."

"And humanity," Reason said bitterly. "So now what happens?"

"There'll be an inquiry into the RUC's conduct by the RUC. But with the cops investigating themselves, everyone will tell the same 'self-inflicted injuries' story, and there will be no case, no prosecution. The police get away with murder and Ruairi stays dead."

"I hate this!" Reason clenched her fists to her chest. Her voice rose then fell. "I feel so helpless...and furious. Really furious."

Wilder could only shake his head sadly at Reason's first taste of official injustice.

Chapter Twenty-Two

"Ladies and gentlemen, we're beginning our descent into London."

Cain glanced out the plane window at England below then took a final look at his father's stolen ledger from Portclare. Everything in the book made sense; ordinary debits and credits involving large sums of money. So why did his father keep the figures stashed in an obscure safety deposit box? Hoping a visit to Hunter's office would clarify things, Cain tucked the ledger back in his briefcase and mulled the previous evening's dinner in Belfast.

"What's the word on that project I assigned you last month?" Hunter had quizzed through a mouthful of veal. "Come up with anything yet?"

"Nothing. Gems take time to track," Cain had lied. "I keep telling you that was a Provisional job. You might as well have asked me to bring someone back from the dead. It would be easier."

"I want my property returned to me, damn it!"

"You still haven't said where you got that property in the first place."

"Been in the family for generations," Hunter had explained lamely.

Cain found his father comical. "Funny you haven't reported them stolen then."

"You think this is amusing?"

"Immensely."

Blotting his lips, Hunter had glared across the table at his son. "Just do as you're told, boy. Is that too much to ask?"

"Aye, aye, Captain Bligh."

"Did you hear about the IRA bastard they lifted this morning? A sniper I'm told. Score one for our side," Hunter gloated over his trifle and tea.

"Who hasn't heard? It's blared from the headlines all day."

"He's one of your Miss McGuinness' rats, did you know that? Outrageous!"

"I've seen Ruairi at the Gov several times," Cain said of his friend.

"Now brace yourself, Cain. I'm firing Reason tomorrow. I might have her arrested as well."

"*What?*" Cain choked on his tea. "What's she got to do with this?"

"Isn't it obvious? She's a republican, and I will not tolerate her evil affiliations at the Grosvenor."

"Reason a republican? That's a good one, H.C." At first Cain had laughed then snapped to forbidding. "No matter what she is, you'll leave her alone."

"Don't you use that tone of voice with me!" Hunter had growled and slammed down his teacup. "Who do you think you're talking to?"

A viper's smile had coiled across Cain's mouth as he stabbed his father with ruthless eyes. "Who do you think *you're* talking to?"

"You listen to me, Cain. That woman is ruinous."

"Leave her alone," Cain had warned calmly, quietly.

"I have no intention of letting you…"

Cain aimed his finger like a pistol at his father. "Bang," he had whispered and retracted his smile. "Leave her alone."

Breaking into his father's office Friday night was easy considering Cain had copied the keys years ago. The Cromwell law offices were situated in an East End highrise with an impressive view of the Thames; from Hunter's desk the Tower of London could be seen. Seated behind that desk now, Cain recalled the times he had sat in disgrace before his father and wished he could condemn the old man to the Tower. One day in particular came to mind. Five years ago, June 12. A Friday. He could still hear Hunter's self-righteous voice,

"Well, well, Cain, you must think yourself jolly clever for being a thief all this time without getting caught. But your secret life of crime ends today. Being your father, I could have gone easy on you, had you exonerated and let you go free, but you'll be punished. The Cromwells have never been, never will be criminals. You have your choice between prison and the army."

Cain remembered finding both choices extreme. Everything he had ever stolen he had given back, and he had never, would never harm a soul. "What would I have to do in the army? Any foreign wars you can ship me off to fight?" he had joked.

"Yes, that is in fact the deal."

"Where?" Cain had tried to picture appealing wars. "Sri Lanka might be interesting. Burma perhaps?"

"Northern Ireland."

"*Northern Ireland?* Jesus, Dad, prison's better than that!"

"Take it or leave it."

"What would I have to do there?"

"Intelligence work. The terrorists are taking over the whole damn island."

"For how long? Just enduring your stupid Solstice Fetes over there is murder."

"Two years."

"Good God, that's forever!" At twenty seven, Cain recalled thinking his life was over.

"You brought this entirely on yourself, boy."

"But what about finishing my doctorate?"

"Belfast has Christ Church College."

"May I at least use My Lady's Leisure?"

"I suppose so. No one else in the family goes there."

"When would I start this assignment?"

"You leave for Tunisia Monday morning."

"What's in Africa that has anything to do with Northern Ireland?"

"Basic training."

"Which regiment are you drafting me into?" Cain had asked in alarm.

"A branch called the Cure. Guaranteed to make you a man."

The Cure. Cain stared at the floodlit Tower and wished he could go back in time, back to that June. He hadn't known it then, but everything changed that morning with his father's sentence. A passionate artist transformed to skilled assassin; all faith, all innocence, all grace would be spoiled. In looking back, how often he had regretted not choosing prison. But it hadn't all been bad. He thought of My Lady's Leisure and his unexpected love of Belfast and the Irish people. The Irish people. The enemy. The prey. *"Damn good show, Cromwell! Damn good show! Here's your medal...a piece of the bastard's skull. God bless the winged sword; God save the Queen."*

Shaking off dark memories, Cain began picking the locks on his father's cabinets. To his disappointment all he uncovered were briefs. Cain slammed the last cabinet and moved on to Hunter's desk. Top drawers, nothing. Middle drawers, nothing. Bottom drawer, a fifth of gin, another fifth of gin, pencils, pads, a locked box. Cain made quick work of its latch and threw back the lid. Passports. Hunter and Emily Cromwell each had three, all with forged names, all with exotic destinations. The elder Cromwells took several vacations a year to Málaga to touch up their tans, or so they alleged. The passports disclosed different ports of call; Monaco, Malaysia, Colombia, Caymans, Brazil.

Uncovering nothing else of interest, Cain was about to abandon his search. Then he looked down at Hunter's desk to find the answer staring him in the face; a ledger from the Grosvenor detailing the hospital's charity funds. Line by line, column by column, Cain compared one ledger to the other, and the figures in the ledger from Portclare began to congeal. Hunter kept two sets of books. From every charity benefit he sponsored for the Grosvenor, he siphoned three fourths of the contributions. He withdrew large sums to pay for nonexistent consultations, public relations promotions, catering, and entertaining donors; all paid to phony firms through offshore bank accounts. No wonder he kept the real set of books stashed in an obscure bank. And now Cain understood how his father came by the costly emeralds which, when refined, would be valued at millions of pounds. Greed and grand larceny had brought Hunter the riches he had lusted a lifetime to grasp.

Cain leaned back in his father's leather chair smugly. Thanks to Wilder he now had what he desired; a way to wreak vengeance on his father for consigning him into the Cure. He eyed the Tower of London. *I'd lock him up in White Tower for a hundred years,* he used to sit before Hunter wishing. Sliding both ledgers and passports into his briefcase, Cain thanked his lucky stars. He'd get his wish after all.

Chapter Twenty-Three

Ruairi had sworn to his mother he wasn't a Provisional. He had lied, just as Vincent had lied and died before him. Two sons. Two funerals. Facts of life.

"I've no choice other than getting on with myself," Fiona declared with forlorn resignation after Ruairi was lowered into the ground beside his brother in Milltown. The family urged her to join her daughters in Australia, but Fiona refused. Belfast was home. Her church, her work, her friends and ghosts were here. "I've lost my boys," she showed her back to the cemetery and plodded back to the Falls, "but I will *not* lose my home." God damn God bless Ireland.

The families congregated at St. Joseph's hall. Birthday. Deathday. The clans looked the same. "Have a wee whiskey and a wee brandy chaser." Reason accepted the drinks and circulated amidst the mourners. No one discussed how Ruairi died but everyone knew, everyone *felt*. Reason had seen it in the faces at the graveyard; blood of grief thickened by rage. Everyone kissed and hugged Fiona and shared good memories of Ruairi, of Vincent, of Fiona's late husband Sean. And despite the throes of sorrow, everyone found something to be thankful for, to go on believing in. Life burned on.

Aidan Duffy. Ruairi McKee. Reason saw Wilder standing with Kieran and tears blinded her eyes. Would he die as well? The possibility was too real. Maybe she ought to go home. Back to her uppercrust roots. Roots with no Irish earth to soil them. Peaceful, blue bloodlines. But what about Wilder? He would never leave Belfast, and she couldn't leave without him. Maybe she *was* responsible for him for the rest of his life.

"If he didn't kill anybody, why did the police arrest Ruairi?" Jillie drew Wilder to her in sympathy. "Was he hiding something?"

Wilder looked blank. "How should I know? Where did Kieran go?"

"Poor lamb went home to his mum's. Shattered he was."

"Why didn't you go with him, Jillie? He needs you right now."

"I didn't want to miss anything here. Personally," she confided, "I think Ruairi was up to his eyeballs in trouble. We were talking one day, and jolly out of yonder, he started laughing about the security forces never being safe again, especially now. What did he mean by that?"

"Beats me." Wilder watched Reason walk across the room. Seraph for sore eyes.

"He probably didn't know what he was saying. He was in a dizzy state of mind." Jillie appeared guilty and confessed, "We'd just had wicked sex on Reason's desk."

Before Reason had reappeared, Wilder might have cared. "You and Ruairi on Reason's perfect desk?" Today it was funny. "That's desecration!"

"Oh, it was. We sent her stuff flying. I thought I'd rearranged everything, but the next day Reason freaked to find the red pencils next to the blue pencils. 'Did I do this? Did I do this?' With palms to cheeks Jillie mimicked a flustered Reason. "'Did I actually put the reds next to the blues?' You would have thought life as we know it was over. Och, she was rattled."

Wilder couldn't help but laugh. "Did you fess up then?"

"Ha! I want to keep my job."

"My, my, on Reason's desk. Jillie, you're shameless."

"It was *Ruairi's* idea! He was so insistent. But I was in the mood anyway. Kieran won't see me as often as I want him…I have my needs. Ruairi fulfilled them."

Wilder put his arm around Jillie. "At least one nice thing happened to him before he died."

"Sickening how he went. They tortured him. I just cried and cried when I heard. Ruairi was terribly sweet, but oh!" she knocked a hand to her forehead, "so naïve."

"I think I'll head home," Wilder said absently.

"This party is dull, isn't it? Shall I come home with you and comfort you in the ways you like?"

Wilder viewed Reason again. His heart beat for her solace. *"Nothing is going to happen between us,"* he had said. "Yeah, OK."

Jillie smiled with delight. "I'll get my coat."

While Jillie collected her things, Wilder joined Reason. "Are you holding up all right, love?" he worried, stooping beside her chair.

"Yes, how about you?"

He shook his head and sought Reason's calm eyes. Her perfume still brought to mind the peace of a thousand flowers and inflamed his desire for her body warm and close to his. But no. "I'm not doing so well. I'm going home. But I wanted to make sure you'll be OK."

"Tough as nails I am," Reason pretended and laid her hand on Wilder's arm. "Is there anything I can do for you?"

He remembered hearing of Brendan's death. *What can I do to help you?* Reason had asked. She had rocked him in her arms, saved his life, rescued his heart. No fear of dying then, no fear of loving, losing. Touching her cheek as if she were sacred, as if she were forbidden, he gazed upon her then said what he didn't mean, "Nothing, thanks."

"It's early." She slid her hand into his. "Would you like to go for a walk with me in the tappy rain?"

Her fingers were electric velvet, soothing and scorching his skin. With one word, yes, she could be his and make everything right. But she could get caught in crossfires inching closer. With one shot she could be lost for having been too close to Declan O'Neill. Wilder freed his hand. "Not tonight."

"Will I see you at work tomorrow?" Reason looked crestfallen, her eyes begged Wilder to stay.

Sadness overwhelmed him. For all things loved and lost. "I have two bypasses. Probably not." He rushed to join Jillie.

The sight of Wilder leaving with Jillie tripled Reason's dejection. She wanted to run to stop them. *Choose me!* But why wouldn't Wilder leave with Jillie? She was one of them, part of the Irish tribe. Reason wondered if Jillie could please Wilder in ways she could not. Be more of a woman? Be less of a threat. Wilder had nothing to lose with Gillian. They would be lovers. They would share sorrow, answer need, grieve skin to skin. Forlorn homesickness gripped Reason as Wilder disappeared. She searched the mourners for a face to turn to and saw herself alone. The foreign accents taunted her ear. So much violence and woe to comprehend, so many strangers, and she hadn't a friend in the world to hold her.

Shoving out of St. Joseph's into the afternoon's soft rain, Reason didn't bother opening her umbrella. The mist touched her with tender hands. Dear tappy rain. She didn't turn right, she turned left and hurried down the Antrim Road towards the city centre. It felt good to run with the wind at her back. *Let the wind push me.* She headed for the docks. *Out to sea.* To see the ships. *Westward.* To see the sea. *Home.*

Every bed, every chair in the house was broken; cotton innards spewed corner to corner like popped corn. One week after Ruairi's arrest, mere hours after his burial, the soldiers had smashed their way back through Fiona's door to leave calling cards of chaos. Instructed to hunt for weapons, the troops sliced open every cushion and mattress, dismantled the toilet and sinks to search the pipes, and ripped up the bathroom and kitchen floors to inspect underneath. Finding the devastation when she returned to the house, Reason broke down on the stairs in fury and fear. Hatred shook her body. How, how could this be Ireland? And what *were* the security forces looking for? Surely they had found it by now.

"Reason?"

"Cain!" she vaulted to greet him in the doorway. "I'm so happy to see you!" She tossed her arms around him as he swept her to him. "I thought you were in London."

"I got home this afternoon. I stopped on my way in from the airport to see you and found this ungodly mess."

"As if poor Fiona isn't in enough pain. Wait until she comes home to this."

"She's already been here. I talked to her when I came looking for you earlier. She's in a complete state of shock, damn near a breakdown. Her brother Eamonn took her home with him…only to find the McCartan's house had been trashed by the soldiers as well. Why aren't you with Wilder? I just assumed he would…"

"He left me." Reason cried harder. "To go with Jillie. I needed him, and he just…left."

Infuriated that Wilder could be so heartless, Cain gladly consoled Reason. "Well, I won't leave you. Where have you been?"

"I went for a walk. Down to the lough. And I went back to that church with the sailboats on its roof. I thought maybe they would cheer me up," Reason buried her face in Cain's lapels, "but all I ended up feeling was lost."

"Now that I've found you, you can't be lost anymore." Cain smoothed Reason's wet hair and tightened his embrace. "Would you like to come home with me?"

Tearfully, Reason nodded. "I can't stop thinking about how Ruairi died."

"I heard all charges against him were dropped today…just in time for his funeral."

"I tried to tell the police he was in Dublin the night the soldiers were killed, but they weren't interested in listening to me."

"You know, Reason, Ruairi didn't kill anybody, but he was a Provo. He wasn't innocent, and the Army ripped this house apart for a reason. Ruairi had things to hide."

"That doesn't justify torturing him to death!"

"God no. It's just that, being in the IRA, Ruairi knew a lot of Provos come to bad ends. He made a choice with his life. Yes, he'll be a martyr, but he was also an infidel."

She broke from Cain's grasp. "The Irish are not *infidels!* Only your English bastards use terms like that!"

"I didn't mean to upset you." Cain came up behind her. "I liked Ruairi. He and I were friends…I'll miss him. A lot."

"I'm sorry. It's just that all this," she indicated the ransacked house and pictured the soldiers making Ruairi crawl on his knees, "is so gruesome, so brutal, so *unfair.* I want to make the meanness stop somehow…" she took shelter in Cain's arms again, "…but I can't."

"Come with me to My Lady's Leisure tonight." He pressed his lips to hers. "I'll make you feel better."

At the Down estate, Cain removed Reason's coat and steered her into the library. He served her tea and held her in his arms. And as the rain stopped and steamed off the fields, the old manor gave them its silence. And in the grey light of dusk Cain opened a bottle of Margaux and palmed two crystal goblets. Taking Reason by the hand, he wound her up the secret staircase to his bedroom and locked the door as if locking out the world.

He started the fire then threw open the French doors to the rising mist and sounds of the sea. "Do you hear that?" All damp and aromatic, the night rushed into the firelit room and quavered on the stretching flames. "Life! Reason, come listen." He pulled her to the doorway and stood behind her. "Do you hear what Life is saying? It's saying do this!" He flung wide her arms with his. "It's saying open your heart and release your pain. Go on, toss your woes to the night." He dispersed unseen cares like he was releasing a covey of birds and waited for Reason to do the same. "Now," he widened her arms again then hugged them back upon her, hugging her close to him as well, "embrace Life. Embrace Life with all your heart." He held her quietly a moment then whispered, "Did you do it?"

She banished thoughts of Ruairi, of Wilder leaving with Jillie. "Yes."

"And how do you feel?"

"Good," she replied.

"And the night is young." He returned to the fireplace and poured one glass of wine. "You're going to feel even better."

"How shall I entertain you at My Lady's Leisure?" Cain paced before the fire, never taking his eyes off Reason who leaned into the wind on the balcony. "Shall I juggle for you?" He launched three Wedgwood plates from the mantle up to the ceiling in succession, once, twice then caught all three in one hand behind his back making Reason laugh. "Or would my lady rather see me dance?"

"Please do," she urged.

Knocking an invisible cane to his loafers, he adjusted his invisible bow tie, donned his invisible hat and tap-danced across the floor to Reason. "Perhaps my lady likes me to work magic," he offered upon reaching her side. He pulled a silver coin from behind her ear, then another and another. "This is how the Cromwells made all their money," he joked and soft-shoed back to the fire. Spinning his imaginary hat into the air, he took off his shirt and unthreaded his belt. "Or perhaps my lady prefers a different sort of magic?" He lingered in the firelight with hungry sights upon her. There was no road back to platonic. Tonight he would satisfy temptation.

And Reason relished the current of desire he awoke in her. "She does."

Cain kicked off his remaining clothing and drew on a flannel robe, but not before Reason admired the powerful lines of his body. Having craved for weeks what he had yet to give, she awaited his love play. But he took his time, dallying before the hearth, savoring Reason head to toe in a leisurely gaze. Then coming to her gently, he turned her from the open window. His hands warmed her cheeks and wound through her hair, but there was nothing gentle or leisurely about his kiss as his mouth took hers fiercely. Nor Reason's as she kissed him with ebbing grief, flooding need. Gliding his hand up her thigh beneath her dress, eager to feel her, he pressed her tightly against him and seized her lips again.

And when she slid her hands from his neck to stroke him he said, "No. I want our first time to be special. I'll tell you when you can touch me." He flashed a lascivious smile. "Until then let me take your mind off the world."

His kisses teased her throat as he untied the sash of her dress and loosened the buttons up her back. "No more mourning for you, love." Cain lifted the dress off over Reason's head. "You're very much alive," he said in a low voice, rubbing his hands over her breasts, "and so am I." He opened his bathrobe and wrapped her to him until she felt his thighs welcome her hips.

Dancing her over to the fireplace, he tipped a sip of wine to her lips then drank from the goblet as well, and keeping one hand beneath her hips to hold her upon him, he further undressed her until she stood nude in his arms. First his eyes made love to her body. Then, sprinkling jasmine lotion into his palms, he closed his eyes and let his fingers massage her. And when his hands had finished, he tantalized her flesh with the sensual play of his tongue.

"Forget we exist beyond this room. Just think about Life and Passion sizzling between us, Life and Passion," he instructed hypnotically and produced a crystal vial from his robe's pocket.

"What's that?" Reason wondered as he opened the vial and dipped in one finger.

"Lotus oil, the vital flame, Life!" he murmured, touching his fingertip to her smile. Flame indeed. The oil torched her lips deliciously like cayenne and cognac, and when Cain claimed her mouth again, the pressure of his lips on hers made the fire the hotter, the richer. Stroking oil first like striking a match, his tongue then flickered flames along Reason's skin. And with each erotic caress, each lambent ploy, the heat of his touch intensified as did its pleasure.

"And Passion!" Cain dipped his fingers again, and cupping Reason's breasts in his hands, daubed each crest in lazy, stinging rings, once again fanning the fire with his mouth. And he continued his anointing genius lower, lower until Reason begged him to stop.

"Let me touch you," she sighed, filling her fingers with his soft, pale hair. He caught her disobedient fingers. "Not yet."

"But you're killing me," she moaned and scraped her fingernails down his chest.

"I'm Life-ing you." He crushed her to him impassioned, in love. "OK, OK, you win!" He handed her the vial of fire. "Ain't Life sweet," he laughed as Reason oiled her lips and slid onto her knees before him.

Troubles ceased to trouble. Two hearts pulsed and fought like whirling butterflies to entwine. No grief, *Life and Passion,* no injustice, *Life and Passion,* no fear. *Life!* He was already inside her when they moved to the bed, *Passion,* and holding her hips hard against his, Cain fell into the down blankets with Reason beneath him.

"Let's dedicate tonight to Ruairi," Cain suggested to Reason locked in his arms. "In tribute to the dead, we the living have a responsibility to burn brighter, love hotter, and fuel the splendor of life raging on. Reason?" She slept with her head on his pillow, her blonde curls crowding his shoulder, her hand still wrapped around his. A beautiful sight, she inspired feelings Cain had thought could not be reborn. She restored the buoyant soul in him, and in love he knew fresh innocence. His heart leaped. "I hadn't planned to be in love," he whispered and kissed her brow, "but I love you, Reason."

She awoke to the fragrance of roses. Deep-chested, full-lipped roses the colors of fire; amber-bright, ember-orange. Roses grown in Cain's walled garden, like he'd left a part of himself for her waking. **Until we Life again, I'll burn** he had written on the note attached to the flowers on his pillow. **You resurrected a part of me I considered forever lost. My soul. I love you, Reason.** She raised the roses to her nose. Cain's voice, his body and now his soul blossomed to mind. Pressing the bouquet to her breast, she inhaled deeply the fragrance of passion born from the wild heart of Ireland.

Chapter Twenty-Four

The day's end was cloudless and drenched in the scent of alyssum. Children played football in the street; shouts and pounding feet reverberated up and down the walkways. From the front steps of Cain's Belfast townhome, Reason watched life going on and felt much removed from its glee.

"What brings you here this late?" She spotted Wilder stepping out of his car.

"You," he said. Reason wore one of Cain's long flannel shirts over her nightgown, and she looked small and young and lost in that shirt, and she looked glad to see Wilder. But her smile was slow to find itself.

"I stopped by to see how you're doing. Having seen Fiona's house, it's a good thing Prince Cromwell took you in," Wilder said a little too harshly.

"At least Cain understood I didn't want to be alone. You, on the other hand, disappeared with Jillie."

Wilder took a seat beside Reason on the step. "I tried to find you last night."

"Why? Wasn't Jillie enough?"

"I was worried about you."

"Cain took me to My Lady's Leisure."

"He took good care of you I hope?"

"Cain works wonders."

Wilder's heart stopped short. It was in Reason's voice. The voice that had once spoken his name. Like that. Now "Cain" she said with knowing, with pleasure. They had made love. "Is he here?"

"No."

Wilder reached inside his coat. "I brought this for you. It's Ruairi's scale. I found it up in his attic and thought maybe you'd use it on your blueprints. It would be like a part of him is still involved with the new wing's construction."

Reason accepted the measuring tool and tried not to cry. "He was so excited about being an engineer."

"Will you use the scale?"

"Of course. Thank you." She regarded Wilder steadfastly, silently. "How are you doing? I felt so sorry for you and Kieran yesterday."

"I feel like hell."

"Me too."

Feeling Reason shiver as the damp crept up her shins, Wilder removed his coat and draped it over her knees. He drew her nearer to him with his arm securely around her. Shoulder-to-shoulder they sat. The alyssum bloomed, the stars burned, and night fell softly. They watched the children run home. The air rang with farewells. Doors banged open, doors banged shut. Quiet settled in. And the ghost town hush bid a gentler adieu. *Síocháin leat.* Peace. For Ruairi.

"Where is Cain?"

Reason shrugged. "He was here awhile ago, now he's gone. You're cold. Here put your coat back on. I'll go get mine." She hurried inside and Wilder followed her up to Cain's bedroom. Unable to find her jacket, she sat down on the bed. "Doesn't this bed remind you of something Henry the Eighth would have slept in? It's about that old."

Wilder considered the scene of the crime. Where love had had its way. "A bed is a bed," he said curtly.

"How was Fiona today?"

"Poor love is living on Valium and taking the hours one tick at a time. The whole family is afraid she's going to die of a broken heart, so Kieran suggested Morris go live with her for awhile. He thinks all that youth and energy will raise Fiona's spirits. Morris will be moving in once the house is cleaned up."

"Ruairi leaves, Morris comes." Reason's mood plunged. "I realized last night I haven't relaxed, really relaxed, since I got here six weeks ago. Soldiers shoot kids in the New Lodge and soldiers get shot on the Falls, the IRA blows up buildings in the city centre, the ULF kills Catholics for being Catholic…something happens every day…still life goes on like everything is normal…" she covered her face with her palms, "…I don't know how to turn it off."

"After awhile nothing shocks you anymore, and you'll get used to living on your nerves." Wilder offered Reason a sympathetic pat. "Once you're acclimatized, you won't realize how stressful Belfast is until you leave it."

"I had no idea it would be this hard." Reason rose from the bed. "I'm really tired, Wilder. You need to leave."

"You go to sleep." He trotted downstairs. "I think I'll wait for Cain."

"He might be out all night."

"I want to know what he thinks about Ruairi's murder. I'll be right here if you need me. Sweet dreams, sweetheart."

Sweet dreams. The words made her cry. Every night was a struggle against nightmares. Reason leaned into the wall, into the shadows. She found herself surrounded by foreign rooms, in the company of a man called Declan, and visions of Ruairi's broken body haunted her head. A great weight of homelessness and solitude crashed upon her, and she sank down on the top step. "Why did you go with Jillie after the funeral?" she whispered. "Why did you leave me alone? Is it because I'm not Irish?"

"You weren't alone," Wilder took exception. "My relatives were there."

"But you were the only other American…the only person I wanted to be with."

"I told you last week we couldn't see each other anymore," he tried to justify himself and failed.

"Wilder, I needed you as my friend yesterday…like you needed me when Brendan died. Is it against your rules?"

"I honestly thought I was doing the right thing for us both…I was wrong…but you weren't alone for long. Cromwell rushed to your rescue."

Reason turned her face to the wall to hide her tears and felt the more alone. "I know I can't waltz in after two years and be a part of your life. I was wrong expecting anything from you."

"The truth is, Reas, I took Jillie back to her place and went home alone. I didn't want to be with her…I only wanted to be with you last night, and my God, I needed you…but," steeped in grief and ambivalence, Wilder glanced up at Reason, "I just don't know what to do about us. I'm a danger for you to know."

Tears trickled down her cheeks. "All I wanted was for you to hold me, Wilder."

"Oh, Reason…" He leapt up the steps to her. Burying her head in his jacket as she grabbed him close, she broke down, and now only now did she feel comforted, did she feel hope. Wilder as well.

No words passed between them. They sat on the stairs in each others arms and listened to the stillness of summer. For now, for now, all was safe and soft and sane. For now they were home in their little Irish-American country of two.

Finally Reason stood up. "I have to go to sleep."

Wilder walked with her to Cain's bed. Stooping low in the darkness he kissed her. "God bless, love." And then he was gone.

Wilder arrived home to find Cain coming downstairs with his hands full of tools. Before either of the men could speak, a third man, wearing a balaclava and camouflage dungarees, slinked down the hallway behind Cain.

"Cromwell!" Wilder yelled just as the hooded man waved a rifle at Cain's back then at Wilder's face. Cain hit the floor, Wilder dived from the stairwell while the gunman strafed the ceiling and walls. Ceasing fire, the shooter bounded down the stairs and streaked out the front door.

"Oh no you don't!" Cain lurched to his feet, screaming expletives, chasing the intruder outside, leaving a trail of blood.

Wilder could hear Cain slinging obscenities all the way down Grange Park Wood to the Malone Road. Then his voice dwindled. Wilder stood bewildered in the calm.

"Well, there goes painting that masterpiece." Cain staggered back into the house, breathless and pale. "One of the bullets hit my finger." Daunted by the red mass that was his right hand, he fell against the wall. "Can you stitch it up? Damn it, I can't believe that son of a bitch got away again. "

"What were you going to do if you caught him?" Wilder examined Cain's index finger unzipped of its flesh. "You're lucky you aren't dead. Squeeze your hand as hard as you can around your wrist and elevate your finger." He pushed Cain's bloody hand into the air.

"Do you see the bone of my finger sticking out here? That doesn't look good."

"You'll need surgery to repair the damage." Wilder headed for his bedroom. "I'll get something to wrap around your finger then drive you."

"Where?"

"To the Gov to get you a hand surgeon."

"Can't you fix it here?" Cain gasped in dread.

"Not my specialty, ace. Keep squeezing your wrist and keep that finger elevat…Jee-sus!" Wilder's bedroom looked much like Fiona's house after the soldiers first visit; drawers and clothes strewn helter-skelter, the mattress stripped and thrown on the floor, books flipped open and tossed aside, lamps and photos smashed. "How did that guy manage this with you in the house?"

Equally astonished, Cain peered over Wilder's shoulder at the mayhem. "I had my Walkman turned up, I didn't hear a thing."

"What are you doing here anyway?"

"I was over in your other bathroom fixing the shower. Bloody drives me daft that steady drip, drip, gurgle, gurgle down the drain."

"You were up here fixing my *faucets?*"

"You really should pay more attention to home repair," Cain chided.

"You left Reason and came to my house to do plumbing? Right, Cain."

"I couldn't sleep, and I was making Reason nervous with my pacing, so I came over here. I knew you'd come home sooner or later, and I figured it was a good time to fix that damn drip."

"Why couldn't you sleep? A guilty conscience perhaps?"

"What do you mean?"

"You made love to her, didn't you?"

"After you abandoned her! You blew it royally this time, Wilder."

"You're right. I did." He kicked through the mess on his floor. "I can't believe you were here a second time when there was an intruder."

"Wilder, I practically live here."

"Yeah, Cromwell, I know. But if you're going to keep bringing trouble, I'm changing the locks."

"Locks!" Cain mocked. "There isn't a lock known to man I can't break."

Wilder flung several books on his bedsprings. "I'll worry about this later. Let's get you to the Gov." He retrieved a cloth from the bathroom and wrapped it around Cain's broken finger. "Are you experiencing a lot of pain?"

"Only if I move my finger."

"Then don't move your finger."

"What have you found out about Ruairi?" Wilder was anxious to know as he drove.

"Not much other than the security forces know he was connected to the Light Fifty rifles. So much for Ruairi's being unknown."

"Cromwell, how many times do I have to tell you to keep that hand around your wrist! Hold your finger up. It had to be the guns that got him arrested. The cops knew within hours that Ruairi was in Dublin the night those soldiers died."

"I've heard the Cure was involved in the arrest, and I know Ruairi told them nothing. That's why they tore up Fiona's house again after his death."

"What I want to know is who tipped off the security forces in the first place."

"Ruairi said the wrong thing to the wrong person."

"Ruairi would never be so careless, Cain."

"He would if he trusted the person he told. But whatever information the cops had did them no good. They're no closer to finding the rifles."

"So they killed Ruairi for nothing," Wilder spat. "Do you still have the guns?"

"They're safe and ready any…" Cain's grin slid off his lips. He could see the lights of the Grosvenor; sickly blue hues through windows black as hollow eyes. *Jesus Christ, don't leave me here! Let me out!*

"What's wrong?" Wilder noticed Cain sinking lower and lower into his seat.

"We're nearly to the hospital," Cain muttered, starting to sweat. "Maybe I don't need a surgeon. Maybe I can just go home."

"No, you can't just go home."

Cain opened his window and gulped the wind. He tried to think of other things. "That spook at your place tonight might have been a Cure agent."

Wilder's flesh crawled. "What makes you say that?"

"Reason found a winged sword medallion in your back hedge. It's a gold medal issued to every Cure agent."

"Yeah, I know. But this agent can't be real bright if he's leaving telltale signs of his presence like patchouli and military medals."

"The fragrance makes sense if it's used for intimidation; to let you know your 'territory' has been breached. But I'm sure he didn't mean to lose the medal. Some agents are very superstitious and carry the medals as talismans. You might say the winged sword is the St. Christopher of the Cure."

"How do you know these things?"

Cain resorted to sucking fresh air again and didn't say.

"No doubt the guy was in the hedge doing surveillance on my back door to see who comes and goes, or else he was planting that camera. How come Reason never mentioned finding the coin?"

"She had no idea what it was, and when she showed it to me, I didn't tell her. She worries enough about you as it is."

"So now the Cure's interested in me," Wilder wearily exhaled. "The perfect end to a perfect day."

"The Cure has been interested in you since you came back to Belfast, but it's not you they're after. They want to get to Kieran through someone close to him. Just like they arrested Ruairi, they could arrest you. Don't trust anybody, Wilder, not *anybody*."

"We both need to be careful, Cain. You're up to your skull in this as well. Come on," he opened his car door and motioned Cain towards the Gov's emergency room.

"This is going to screw up my hand." Cain balked as he walked. "Will I be able to do the mural? I have to do that mural!" He started back for the car. "There's no way I'm going in there. You can't make me go *in there*."

"You'll be able to do the mural only if you have this surgery." Like Cain was a stalled car, Wilder pushed him the rest of the way to the ER.

"Are you going to hang around for the surgery?" Cain hoped after Wilder signed him in and ushered him into a cubicle.

"I had planned on going home to bed. It's been one helluva night."

"Wouldn't you like to stay for the surgery? You know, make sure they don't give me a lobotomy or something?" Cain tried to be flip; fear betrayed him. "You know I'm not keen on hospitals. I'm always afraid once I go in, they won't let me out."

"Don't worry, Cain, they'll let you out."

"You'll make sure?" His fear was real and he gripped Wilder's arm. "You'll make sure they let me out?"

"I will indeed," Wilder reassured. "You'll be all right."

"Then I'll see you here and there, friend." Sitting alone on the examining table, Cain appeared lost. He tried to smile as Wilder departed, but he just looked sad, like a dog left at the pound.

Wilder paused in the hospital's parking lot and peered up at the clouds. Another foggy night with helicopters for stars. As he opened his car, he wondered if someone was watching, and as he closed the door, he wondered why he bothered locking the locks. There was no keeping out the forces of evil or good.

Cain was being escorted, more like coerced, out of his cubicle when Wilder came back. "Did you forget something, Wilder?"

"Yeah. I forgot to lock my car. Would I go off and leave you, Cromwell?" he kidded good-naturedly and took the place of the nurse walking Cain to pre-op. "I'll make sure nothing happens to you."

Cain was uncertain. "Swear to God?"

"Swear to God."

Nothing had been taken, Wilder concluded as he righted his bedroom, but then there was nothing to take where the Cure was concerned. He had nothing concealed. But the notion of British gunmen inside his house left him afraid. He was equally concerned about Reason. If someone was stalking him and saw him with her, they might think there was a connection. A republican connection. And pretty soon they would be investigating and harassing Reason. Reason who had shared Fiona's house with republican Ruairi and soon with Morris, and Morris meant Kieran would be seen around Fiona's as well. Inadvertent guilt. It killed Aidan Duffy. If they weren't careful, it could doom Reason as well.

*   *   *   *   *   *

Late Friday morning, Wilder stepped into Reason's office. "Hi ya, Mac."

She looked up, smiling, "I hear you spent most of the night in the OR with Cain."

"I don't know why but he has this thing about hospitals. I couldn't abandon him."

"That was really nice of you. How did he get hurt?"

Neither Cain nor Wilder wanted to worry Reason with the truth. "A plumbing accident. But he sailed through the surgery without a hitch."

"I know. I just took him to the airport. He insisted on giving his lecture in Glasgow tonight." Reason looked at Wilder expectantly, wondering why he'd come.

"Do you know what today is?"

"Friday?"

"It was four years ago today we first met."

"You actually remember the date?" Reason marveled.

"When I want to, I can remember everything that concerns you and me." He smiled a fond smile at Reason. "I meant it when I said I care about you." He drew a breath and hoped this would be easy, "That's why I don't think you should move back in with Fiona."

"Why?"

"Because too many things are happening around you. First you were living in the same house with Ruairi. Now you'd be living in contact with Kieran. The Brits will get the wrong impression."

"Like I'm a republican? Maybe I am now."

Hastily, Wilder shut the office door. "Don't even joke about that! You're in Belfast to work not to get involved in politics."

"Two years ago you practically begged me to share your politics."

"That was in Colorado where there's a constitution and a bill of rights."

"Jillie shares your politics. Why can't I?"

"Jillie doesn't know my politics," Wilder kept his voice low, "I don't tell her anything."

"OK, but I want you to know I'm on your side."

"What's that supposed to mean? You aren't Irish. You're an American, a *Wellworth-Howell*," Wilder stormed, understanding this could be disastrous.

What could Reason say? Her loyalty was suspect after her harsh disavowal of all things Irish. But that was before Aidan, before Ruairi. "Wilder, I've changed."

"Maybe you have, but there's no way I'm letting you get into things that will harm you. So far living at Fiona's has gotten you a beating, and that's bad enough. Now with Kieran coming around...what about the ULF, the Cure? You could end up like Aidan Duffy."

"So could you, but I don't see you changing the way you live," Reason reminded stubbornly.

"Damn it, Reason, this isn't about me. It's about keeping you out of danger. There are plenty of safe places for you to live. Hell, you've taken Cain as your lover, why not go on living with him?" Wilder tried to sound indifferent and failed. His jealousy was obvious.

"Why, Dr. O'Neill, are you encouraging me to practice safe sex?" Reason joked, making Wilder angry. "Look, Wilder, if I get hurt, what's it to you? What about your diamond heart? Where's that Irish grudge? And if you're so concerned about me, why did you leave me the other night when I needed you?"

"For the love of Christ, woman, I'm trying to protect you!" he yelled.

"It's too late for you to protect me!" Reason yelled back. "Ruairi's death changed everything. I saw too much, I *felt* too much, and this time you can't tell me it never happened. It *happened*, the Brits *killed* him, and I'll be damned if I'll let those bastards scare me away from taking care of Fiona!"

"Don't say things like that! Oh God, Reason, don't get lost in this." But how well he knew the Brits ability to recruit defiance.

Jillie tapped at the door. "Is everything OK? I heard shouting. You aren't punching Declan again, are you, Reason?"

"Everything is great, just *great*," Wilder fumed.

"Dr. O'Neill and I can't seem to agree on anything these days," Reason added sourly.

"OK, whatever," Jillie could feel the tension and bowed out.

Wilder waited for the door to close then turned to Reason emotionally, "Reason, please, *please,* for once, do as I ask. Moving into Fiona's will be like living on a land mine. Any association with Kieran can hurt you."

"I'll to do anything you ask, Wilder, if you'll ask me to do something I want to do. Fiona needs me, and I need her, and I'm moving back."

"You are the most difficult woman on this planet!"

"What do you expect with your glaring double standards? Why is it OK for you to be involved with Kieran but not me?"

"Because you are *not* going to be like Merry!" He could see she was determined. "I swear to God, Reason, you're going to be my undoing!" He threw up his hands and slammed out.

Chapter Twenty-Five

Morris filled Fiona's house with noise and motion. It wasn't that Reason minded his presence, but she realized working at home was no longer possible. From the moment she came in from the Gov at night, Morris was with her, asking questions, telling stories, demanding attention. When on hand, Kieran restrained his son, but Kieran often disappeared for days, leaving Morris to his own device, and Morris was determined. After dinner, Fiona would seat him sternly before the television. Morris would wait five minutes then sneak upstairs to find Reason, and Fiona was too busy to pursue the boy. He had become Reason's devoted fan.

Ruairi's death had taken its toll on Fiona. Once easy-going, she was now a whirlwind of nervous energy. She dragged herself into each new day, but once up, she rarely sat down. She was always cooking or scouring or tidying something she had tidied ten minutes before. Compulsively neat, she cleared away dishes and silverware the instant anyone finished with them. She wiped and re-wiped every counter and tabletop, jumped to sweep away each fallen ash or crumb, and constantly swept and vacuumed the rugs and hearth. She scrubbed every floor every evening and dusted the draperies and furniture several times a day. Keep busy, don't think, sweep and sweep, became her way of life.

Fiona tended Reason and Morris like their handmaid; washing their clothes, making them meals, cleaning their rooms, serving them tea. It wasn't that they expected her to do this, they simply couldn't stop her. Her insistent attention was nearly an assault, but she would burst into tears if anyone asked her to stop. No one asked. And when she wasn't cooking or cleaning, she was rushing off to work at the pastry shop or going to the market or clipping the lawn and tending the garden. Work had become the one thing she could control. Still she insisted everything was fine. "The Troubles have left me empty-headed that's all," she often explained with a distant smile. If Reason made any worried observations, Fiona would be surprised by the concern and act as if it were a mortal weakness to be depressed or confused or afraid; she had a duty to remain unscathed. So, in between cleaning and going to work, she smoked every cigarette down to the filter, drank every drink to the last drop, swallowed her Valium and struggled to sleep. Fiona had reached an acceptable level of suffering in a city normalized to marble. By summer's end Reason thanked God for Morris and his exuberant spirit.

At last the house was still. Fiona and Morris had been asleep for hours. Settling into the warmth of her bed, Reason tried to finish reading her mother's letter.

In your last note you mentioned loving the Irish Sea and going down to Belfast Lough whenever you can to see the ships. Honestly, Reason, I should think you could find more suitable distractions. Still, it's curious you should mention the sea at this time. A few days ago I was in the basement and came across an old Princeton sweater of your father's. In the pocket I found one of his nautical trinkets (I thought I'd thrown them all out). He used to wear this charm around his neck. It's made of tin, but I had it polished and lacquered to preserve it. I thought you might enjoy seeing it. I'm sure Kent would be thrilled to know you have it.

Reason examined the small charm sculpted into a dime-sized sailboat. Of all the peculiar materials to sculpt, tin. But the cheap metal gleamed pride like sterling, and she thought only a true artist could make the simple grand. Kent McGuinness must have had talent.

"You're awake!" Morris leaned around Reason's door. He was trembling and wearing his too-serious face again.

Good-bye quiet moment. Reason set the letter and charm aside. "I thought you were asleep."

"If I fall asleep and die…I'll to go to hell," quivered his tiny voice.

"Why would an angel like you go to hell?"

"Because of this." He hesitantly displayed an enormous cartridge.

"What is *that?*"

"A magic bullet," Morris expressed forlornly.

"Where did you get it?"

"I…I've had it…for weeks," he confessed in an agonized whimper.

"What's the matter?"

"I killed Ruairi!" he choked on a sob and dived into Reason's covers.

"You didn't kill Ruairi." Reason bent close to Morris' buried head and petted his curls. "Where on Earth did you get that idea?"

"I did kill him, I did!" he garbled.

"How did you kill him?"

"I took…his magic bullet," Morris' sobs intensified. He huddled face down in Reason's blankets, hugging her knees underneath. "Ruairi told me it has the power to drive the Brits away, and I wanted Jillie to stay out of my granny's house…so one day I sneaked upstairs to the attic and took the bullet out of Ruairi's music box…I was going to give it back, honest I was…but then the Brits came…if Ruairi had had the bullet…the magic would have saved him." His wail became snorts in the blanket.

"Oh, Morris," Reason pulled him off her knees and into her arms, "even magic couldn't have saved Ruairi. It's not your fault. Nothing is your fault."

He sobbed and sobbed into her shoulder as she wrapped him close. "But if he'd had the bullet…"

"No, Morris, nothing could have stopped those policemen and soldiers." Reason continued to embrace Morris while looking over his shoulder at the formidable cartridge. *The Army ripped this house apart for a reason. Ruairi had things to hide.* "Did Ruairi have a magic gun to go with the magic bullet?"

"A light fairy gun."

"He called it a light fairy gun?"

"Uh huh," Morris said.

"Have you shown the bullet to your dad?"

"Och no!" Morris whined in fear then loudly wept. "He'll hate me for stealing...for wanting to make Jillie go away."

"What do you have against Jillie, Morris?"

"She wishes I were dead. She said she'd like to stuff me with potatoes and boil me in oil."

On days when Morris prattled nonstop for hours, Reason could see where that might sound attractive. "I'm sure she didn't mean it, Morris."

"But what if she gives me poison apples?"

"Poison apples?"

"She said she has poison apples like in *Snow White*...she's a witch like that witch." Morris stared up at Reason through rainy blue eyes. "Are you mad at me for saying that?"

"No." Jillie's occasional Halloween hair and Zorro make-up might seem witchy to a six-year-old, motherless boy.

"You won't tell my daddy, will you?"

"I won't tell him anything, I promise. Have you shown the bullet to anyone else?"

"Not a livin' soul."

"May I show it to Decky?"

"Och no! He'll say I killed Ruairi," Morris shuddered and clung harder to Reason.

"No, he won't, Morris. He'll say, 'Och, Morris, you're a wee devil to be sure,'" she imitated Wilder's deep voice and Belfast accent, "'but you're my favorite wee devil in all the great, grand world so you are then.'"

Morris sprouted a giggle.

"May I show him the magic bullet?"

Morris bobbed his head weakly and started to cry again. "I didn't want Ruairi to die, Reason. Why didn't God stop them?" He meant the British forces.

"I don't know." Reason had wondered the same thing.

*   *   *   *   *   *

September nudged the late August breeze with hints of autumn. As Cain arrived at his father's Belfast townhouse, he saw yellow leaves on the maple tree and knew the short, dark days weren't long away.

"Cain! What brings you by?" Hunter called from the upstairs window.

"I finished that project you asked me to do for you."

"Did you get them? Did you?"

"Right here in my pocket, pops."

"Heigh ho bravo, son! Come in. We'll have a drink."

"So?" Hunter handed his son a tumbler of gin and leaned his elbow on the mantle. "Where did you find them?"

"Around."

"Well, where are they? Where are they?" Hunter rubbed his fingers and trotted in place.

"Before I give the emeralds back to you, we need to get something straight."

Hunter's glee slinked off his lips. "What?"

"I want in."

"On what?"

"Your scam."

"What in the hell are you maundering, boy? Scam, what scam?"

Cain tippled his gin, regarding his father fixedly over the rim of his glass. "Using embezzled funds from the Gov, you've flown around the globe and invested a tidy sum in raw emeralds. You purchased the uncut stones in Bogatá for a discount price then smuggled them out of Colombia, and now you want to sell them on the black market in Zurich for a fortune. I want in."

"That's rubbish! I've never been to Colombia, and those jewels belong to our family, have for years, simply years."

"This tells another story, H.C." Cain reached into his jacket and pulled out one of Hunter's forged passports. "Howarth Arrowsmith." He slapped it down on the coffee table like a blackjack dealer. "I want in."

Hunter began to take Cain seriously. "Where did you get that?"

"From your office in London. I have two more. Reginald Huxley, and my personal favorite, Rollie Orville."

Hunter scooped his passport from the table. "Give me the other two at once."

"I didn't bring them with me. I also have the Gov's books. Both sets. I must congratulate you, H.C. The way you've been stealing from the hospital is ingenious. You've covered your tracks like a pro."

"I'm losing my patience, boy. Give me my emeralds, goddamn it!"

Cain brought forth a single stone and Hunter snatched it.

"Where are the others?"

"Until you include me in on your scheme, they'll remain mine."

"Hoodlum!" Hunter snarled with a guzzle of gin. "Why do you want in on this? I thought you didn't care about money."

"I don't want the money, H.C., just the thrill of making the deals. Retrieving the emeralds made me miss the old days when larceny was my middle name. I want to be your partner."

"For what percent of the take?"

"No percent."

Hunter's suspicion deepened. "What's your game here, Cain?"

"Honestly, pops, I'm not trying to con you. I just want to be a crook again, only this time you won't turn me in for it."

"I'm not sure I'm keen on this. Not sure at all."

"Why not? We'd both get what we want. I want the danger, you want the cash."

"You're unbalanced, boy."

"The best criminals are. Wasn't I the greatest thief you ever encountered?"

"Well, you were quite good."

"And think of all the Cure has taught me since then. If you want to keep investing in emeralds, I could wheel and deal the Colombians' nuts off, then do the same thing in Zurich. I'll triple your profits. Better yet, I can invest your money…or should I say Ulster's money…in things that'll make you richer than emeralds."

"Like what?"

"The era is ripe with opportunity, H.C. With the Soviet Union in tatters, there's a deal a minute to be made. We can buy arms in Berlin and sell them in Baghdad. Arms are *big* money."

"Baghdad? You're mad!"

Cain had a sardonic smirk. "You're morally opposed to selling rifles to enemies, H.C?"

"Of course not, but it's too damn risky."

"The riskier the deal, the richer the payoff. Besides, if anything goes wrong, I'm the one who will be questioned. I'll flash a little I.D. and convince the authorities I'm doing business as usual for the Cure. Nobody's going to doubt that."

"I suppose not."

"Come on, Dad. I regret how I've behaved in the past, and I want to make up for it," Cain cajoled shrewdly and tossed the remainder of the gems in their velvet pouch onto the table. "Give me a chance to be your son again."

Touched, Hunter raised his glass. "By jove, you're a Cromwell after all!"

"The deal I have in mind begins in Germany. Sniping rifles and poison guns are what we're after."

Hunter smiled with excitement. "What are poison guns?"

"AK-74 Kalashnikov assault rifles; updated AK-47's from Russia. I'll need money for airfare, hotels, that sort of thing."

"You'll get whatever you need."

"I'll arrange the sale and transport of the rifles. You've already set up dummy bank accounts so laundering money will be a snap. I'll take care of every detail, and you can sit back and count your profits."

"You'll make this too easy."

"No, you've made it easy for me, H.C. The millions you've pilfered from your friends provide everything I need."

"Ho! By the time those Paddy suckers at the Grosvenor figure out what's going on, I'll be living in paradise like a king."

"What have you been doing with your profits besides buying emeralds and traveling the world?"

Hunter disclosed with satisfaction, "Dressing your mother like Imelda Marcos, furnishing the house with works of art, and I'm building a villa in Bimini." He winked at his son. "I've employed 'creative accounting' with my clients for years. You'd be amazed how many people have trusted me with their life savings."

Cain was taken aback. "Just how rich are you?"

"Rich enough, boy. Rich enough."

Hopping to his feet, Cain gave his father a smack on the back. "Nice to be working with you, H.C. I promise I won't let you down. We'll make more plans when you're here next month."

Hunter's eyes gleamed. "Welcome home, son. Welcome home." He went to shake his son's hand and only then noticed the cast up to Cain's wrist. "What happened here?"

"Just a little gunshot wound."

Undismayed, Hunter nodded. "No permanent damage I assume."

"I hope not. The cast comes off next week then I start rehab..."

Hunter didn't take time to listen. "Good. Good. I've no use for a gimp. You need a quick hand for grabbing the cash."

A spurious smile aimed at his father wound up Cain's face. "And the trigger."

Chapter Twenty-Six

"I'll give a full presentation to the design team next month, but I wanted to show you what I've done so far. I thought I'd do four panels. One for each season." Cain motioned Reason over to his easel. "Each mosaic will be a fantasy, like the flying sheep in the stars I did for the competition."

Reason loved his eager expression. "You're so passionate about this project."

"It means everything to me. These panels are the part of me I'll leave behind. See, here's my prototype for summer. It's not my best work. It's taking me awhile to get my hand back in shape."

In the manor's sunny library, Reason studied Cain's sketch. "I like this. It has playful energy yet it's spiritual." A red-sun sky with sheep for clouds whorled above a sea full of sailboats on purple water; water surrounded by pink roses. Gradually the water became an Irish garden with children riding azure stars. "It's magical. And full of hope. How did you dream it up?"

"Come with me to the walled garden and I'll show you. You know, Reason, today might be one of the last warm days of summer."

In the garden, Cain seated Reason on the grass in a circle of sunlight. "I want you to read Byron to me."

"Your inspiration is poetry?"

"Just read."

She opened the book of poems and held it before her, reading aloud, while Cain sat behind her with his arms around her waist. And he kissed her nape, her ears, her cheeks, her elbows, wrists and fingers. She kept reading. And as she read, he slid his hands beneath her shirt and rubbed her breasts with warm fingers, and kissed her throat, clavicle to chin, and if she stopped reading, he withdrew his hands. She read on. Raising one of her arms at a time, Cain removed Reason's shirt and unhooked her brassiere and slid it off and kissed each vertebrae in her back and massaged her shoulders and kissed her mouth and unfastened her shorts and slipped them off. She kept reading. He kissed her toes, her ankles, her shins and knees and thighs, and she kept reading in a circle of sunlight amidst two hundred roses on the last warm day of summer. And he undressed himself and she watched him between verses, and she was in sunlight and he was in love, and he sat facing her and wrapped her legs around his waist, and he held her upon him in a circle of sun, and he was inside her and sucking her and whispering Byron from memory because Reason was no longer reading. And a bee buzzed by, there were sheep clouds in the sky, below the sea simmered, Reason's heart sailed and Cain was a star to be ridden. In a walled Irish garden. On the sunniest of summer's last days.

"At what point do people become lovers? After making love one time or two times or three?" Cain wore nothing but a rose behind his ear. He filled his hands with petals and sprinkled them in Reason's hair then pulled her to him in the sunshine and kissed her savagely and kissed her softly. "We're lovers now."

"Yes, yes, yes," she kissed him in three places.

"I want you to know I won't expect you to stay with me. I know you still love Wilder, and don't deny it because you'll only end up making a liar out of yourself later. But I love you. And I lust for you. And as long as you're with me, I'll make love to you and I'll be your friend and you'll be my Muse, and together we'll make life nice, really nice. And who knows," he swept back Reason's curls, she gazed up, and the sun made her eyes Forget-me-not blue, "maybe you'll fall in love with me."

"You are so sweet." Reason was compelled to grab him, grab him very near for there was such sadness in his eyes. Yet such beauty in his garden, in his art, in his soul. And she wondered what suffering stoked his inspiration. "When you're so loving, how can you possibly think you taint what you touch?"

"You asked how hard coal can produce a soft light." His hands framed her cheeks, he pressed his lips to her brow. "To create the light, it destroys what it burns."

"It burns itself."

"And anything it touches."

"You and you're mysteries," Reason complained.

"You and your questions! Now how will you inspire me for autumn?"

Chapter Twenty-Seven

The last of the clouds scudded over Black Mountain. Children played in the gutters, stomping through puddles in front of the Gov. Beads of rain glistened making Belfast's sea of slate roofs shiver in golden dayshine. A nice day for a walk, Reason ventured up the Falls Road, which after twelve weeks had begun to feel like home. The helicopters made little impact now; she hardly heard them. She passed bricks of soldiers and didn't blink; she hardly saw them. The tumbling buildings no longer snagged her attention, nor did the idle young men or the IRA murals. When she walked up the Falls she saw the green hills, heard the lively chatter, and shared the craic with the Grosvenor's neighbors. She could no longer walk beyond the Gov without someone calling, "Where ye for?" and joining her for a chat.

"How's it going, Reason?" Happy as usual, Kieran came up beside her.

"Kieran! It's going great. The new wing's coming along. We're within our budget and everything is on schedule."

"It's a warm day, isn't it? Where ye for?"

"Nowhere, really. I'm just out for a walk."

"I hear there's a wee parade up by Beechmount."

A wee parade it was. Seven boys, about eight years old, carried six plastic drums and a tin whistle and marched along a narrow side street to a lively tattoo. An eighth boy brought up the rear waving a Tricolour flag and blowing kisses to anyone who caught his eye. By their outbursts of laughter and sidelong smirks it was clear the boys were clowning around.

"Entertaining their grannies," Kieran explained.

The youths capered up one side of the street, down the other, up again then down again until a small crowd had gathered to watch them drill. Reason was wishing she'd brought her camera when four soldiers stepped in front of the marchers.

"What's this shit?" bellowed one of the four.

"Move along, move along." Another soldier bullied the spectators away with the butt of his rifle while a third began recording names in his notebook.

Ignoring the soldiers, the boys marched on, drumming louder and harder, and rather than dispersing, a crowd began clogging the slender street. One of the soldiers grabbed the eighth boy and his little flag. He spit in the boy's face and tore the Tricolour in half. Grinning, he threw the orange, white and green pieces into the street. "Go home, you Fenian fuckhead," he gave the boy a shove. But the boy marched on.

"Why did he tear up that flag?" Reason spun to Kieran.

"It's illegal to fly the colours in the North," Kieran grumbled and started to leave.

"What do you mean it's illegal? This is Ireland."

"Aye, but it's against the law to be Irish. Come on, let's go before trouble starts."

But Kieran spoke too late. Someone hurled a rock at the soldiers, a cry went up, then a hail of rocks and garbage came flying down from rooftops and windows. The crowd grew larger as more soldiers appeared and more stones took flight. The situation exploded. Tanks sealed off both ends of the street. Helicopters circled and hunkered low. Soldiers and now policemen clubbed and kicked and dragged men out of the way, while women and children cheered and jeered and launched anything at hand. In disbelief, Reason watched as a soldier grabbed one of the marchers by the scruff of the neck and seat of his pants and flung him like a pail of water against a brick wall. Shots were fired into the air. Bottles crashed, flashed. Petrol bombs. More rocks, more shots. Flash. More breaking glass. Shrieks and curses. And then, just as she and

Kieran were breaking away, Reason caught sight of a policeman taking aim with a fat-nosed gun.

She grabbed Kieran's sleeve. "My God, what's that for?"

"Plastic bullets," he replied with his standard nonchalance.

"But that gun is huge."

"Has to be, love. Haven't you ever seen a plastic bullet? It's shaped and sized like the tube inside a roll of toilet paper only brick-solid and hammer-hard. They fly 180 miles per hour, can smash a skull so they can." Sardonically Kieran added, "A 'harmless' means of riot control so the RUC claims."

Boof, boof, the constable fired a round of the giant bullets at the rioters' legs. More rocks and blazing bottles. *Boof, boof,* he aimed higher, hitting an old woman in the stomach. *Boof, boof,* a young man was hit in the knee. A deluge of potato peels pounded the policeman. "I'll break your fucking heads!" he roared and jerked his gun straight ahead. *Boof, boof,* he shot one of the original marchers, still thumping his drum, point-blank in the shoulder. "You won't be beating your goddamn drum again, will ya, boy?" he shrieked as the boy's arm flew from its socket. Harmless.

Protests rang louder than shots. A gang of six men tackled the policeman, and the gang of six was tackled by a gang of twelve soldiers.

"Go ahead, shoot off his arm, you bastard," Reason heard herself joining the fray, "but he'll still find a fist. He and a hundred like him will be back to *bleed you white!*" She pushed forward to help the wounded boy, but Kieran clapped his hand over her mouth and dragged her the other way.

"Are you trying to get us fucking arrested?"

Tear gas fogged the sunshine, people scattered, and Reason was still swinging her arms as Kieran hauled her away.

"Oh my God," she gasped over and over as Kieran ran her back to the Falls Road now congested with curious bystanders and angry police.

"Are you going to calm down?" Kieran wondered, bowled over by Reason's emotional outburst. "Bleed you white? Jesus."

"I'm sorry...I completely lost it," Reason panted. "But I've never seen anything that...sadistic and...my God, I couldn't just stand there." She considered Kieran's face. Composed. Like he'd just taken a stroll through the park. "Didn't that upset you?"

"Happens all the time," he said.

"But that poor little boy..." she couldn't talk about it.

"Took a real pruning he did," Kieran's voice froze, and Reason noticed he clenched his fists until his knuckles turned white then gradually he unclenched them. "They were bouncing those baton rounds like fucking demons. Ol' Decky is going to be busy tonight patching up the victims."

"Won't they go to the Gov?"

"Not unless they're really hurting. Go in with a wound from a plastic bullet and they'll be arrested for rioting."

Reason throttled another scream. "The Army incited that riot! Why didn't they just let those little boys march? They weren't hurting anything."

"Didn't you know? Marching and flag-waving lead directly to terrorism," Kieran deadpanned. "Some people say the Troubles all began because a Catholic was flying the Tricolour and a Protestant minister tore it down."

"But the loyalists flaunt their Union Jacks. Just look at that RUC station over there. Aren't they provoking terrorism as well?"

"No, they're patriots."

Feeling sick, Reason took several deep breaths. Thank heaven the Gov was only a block away.

"Haven't you ever seen a riot, Reason?"

"I grew up in Connecticut," she concentrated on her unsettled stomach, "and we didn't have many kids getting their arms blown off by cops."

"Dickheads. I wish I'd had an Uzi to blow every one of those sons of bitches away."

Reason broke into a run the instant they arrived in the doctors' parking lot, and she kept running through the emergency room to the back stairs. Up six flights she flew without noticing the climb. Blessedly, it was the end of the work day, Jillie had gone, and she was alone. Alone with the replay of a savage bullet and such a little arm. *Took a real pruning...wish I had an Uzi.* Barely making it into her office, Reason locked her door and collapsed in tears against the wall. And when she had cried herself empty and thrown up twice, she grabbed the telephone to call British Air. Forget the Grosvenor. She was going home.

Waiting for a ticket agent, she envisioned everything she'd do upon reaching Manhattan. She'd go to her office on Fifth Avenue and look out at Central Park. She'd join her friends in Greenwich Village, visit the Museum of Modern Art, go to Lincoln Center...walk by the Plaza Hotel every noon. Wilder. He'd be glad to see her go. For weeks she'd been the pain in his neck. He could get on with his hard heart and secret life, answering to no one. And she could go back to her safe life of Anglo-Saxon Protestants and forget Irish Catholic Declan and his bloody war. She hung up the phone and wept. She didn't want to forget.

"...and in other news, one youth was slightly injured when he was hit by a plastic bullet after throwing petrol bombs at security forces in West Belfast this afternoon. RUC officials were unable to establish which police officer fired the shot that wounded the boy. Earlier, an RUC spokesman stated, 'We deploy baton rounds only in the most extreme cases when bodily harm to an officer is imminent and self-defense becomes necessary, and let me emphasize that we take great care to avoid causing personal injury to civilians...'"

Reason turned her radio off and fell back on her bed. The sun would set soon, still the day seemed endless. Come darkness she knew sleep would elude her. *Boof, boof.* How many times would that gun go off in her head? She eyed her desk and considered working, but she had stayed late at the Gov already trying to keep busy. How does one relax after violence? *Have a wee whiskey,* she thought with a sigh. Kieran had invited her along to the pub for the first time ever, but she'd endured enough sound and fury for one day. A walk beneath the moon might help.

A voice came from the foot of the stairs, "Kieran, are you up there?"

"No, he's not," Reason answered just as Wilder knocked on her door. "May I come in?"

After the riot, after having imagined returning home to live without him, Reason was glad to see Wilder and wished he wouldn't mind if she tackled him with heated emotion. She hugged her arms to her chest instead. "I thought you'd be out tending victims," she said.

"It's not my week. I'm not the only physician involved. There are quite a few of us; keeps us from burning out."

"If you've come to see Kieran or Fiona, they aren't here. Kieran's down in the New Lodge at a pub, and Fiona took Morris over to see your aunt Nora."

"Oh. Well, maybe I'll shoot down to the pub then." But Wilder lingered in Reason's bedroom. Trying not to be obvious he stole glances at her, appraising her appearance, making sure she was unhurt. He had heard about the riot, and Reason's reaction to it, from Kieran, and he figured she'd be packing to leave. But here she was, placidly seated, his beautiful Reason. Her hair was loose around her shoulders, blonde as the moonlight. She wore a soft angora sweater over soft breasts, her smile was sweet, and lifting her eyes, she fastened them upon Wilder like he was all she wanted to see.

"You can sit down if you like," she offered him a seat at her desk.

"I hear you managed to be at the wrong place at the wrong time again today." He smiled to hear himself sound casual when his heart was pounding and his blood was on fire. When he wanted Reason to take him into her arms and caress him, and undress him between slow French kisses and love him with wild abandon. He'd insisted nothing was going to happen, but it was happening, and it was getting harder to hold back his emotions. "Kieran told me all about it. He said you were shattered."

"It started out as an innocent little walk then suddenly all hell broke loose. Seeing that poor little boy get shot will haunt me the rest of my life. And that policeman did it just to be spiteful." Reason shook her head like she would never understand.

"Aye, this city pastes a scrapbook of specters into your head...I'm really sorry you had to see that, love." He thought to himself, if she had listened to him and not been with Kieran in a staunchly republican neighborhood, she would have been spared. But he didn't say it. "I'm surprised you didn't catch the first plane home."

Reason maintained a straight face. "The thought never occurred to me."

"Too bad the Gov isn't out the Malone Road. If you lived and worked over there, you wouldn't see this sort of thing happening."

"Sure, I could look the other way, but I don't want to."

"You really are changing, Mac. And it scares the hell out of me." But it also made her the more appealing.

She straightened the neck of her sweater and felt her father's tin sail-boat on a silver chain around her neck. Once she would have worn only gold. "The way I was before coming here is what's scary, Wilder." She looked around the room for her shoes. "Go ahead and go down to the pub. I was just getting ready to go out."

"With Cromwell?"

"'Cromwell' is in Zurich for two days. I'm going for a walk. Alone."

Wilder peeled back the curtains and looked out over the street. It was hard to accept Reason was sleeping with Cain, even harder to ignore. "Are you seeing a lot of him these days?"

"Yes."

"I suppose by now you think you're in love with him." Wilder hoped Reason would deny it, but she didn't. Her silence hurt. "Would you like some company on your walk?"

She slid one shoe on then the other and stared up at Wilder, loving the intoxicating blue of his eyes. "I don't want to keep you from going to the pub."

"I can go down to the New Lodge anytime."

She looked up at him again. "You didn't come here looking for Kieran. You came to see me. Admit it. You wanted to make sure I hadn't left Belfast, and you."

"Getting too cheeky you are."

"When are you going to face reality, O'Neill?" Reason breezed out of her room. "You can't resist me, never could, never will. I thought I'd walk over to the Somerton Road. And yes, I'd love your company."

"I think this is the most beautiful street in Belfast. Nothing but elegant houses with stained-glass windows and gardens smothered in roses. I come here all the time when I need to relax. It's like you step off the Antrim Road into the country," Reason said as they turned onto the Somerton Road, now dusk-dark with moonlight flickering through the tall trees. "It's so peaceful. And the air is the essence of summer. Flowers and freshly-mown lawns. I can smell the earth here. And look up. You can barely see through the trees, like we're wrapped in our own little tunnel of silence and leaves." *Bap, Bap, Bap.* Two helicopters cruised by. "Well, almost a tunnel of silence and leaves. I like the way the moonlight makes the leaves look like they have silver linings."

Wilder paid scant attention to the scenery. The warm night filled his head with nostalgia for slow dances and moonlit gazebos and Reason's body rising to meet his. If the air smelled like summer, it was the essence of Reason, and if the street was peaceful, it was because Reason was peace. And the moonlight was magic, and maybe there were silver linings beneath Belfast's sky. Maybe he could be in love, a lover, loved by this glorious woman wedded to his diamond heart.

"What were you looking for? Wilder? You aren't listening to me."

"Oh, sorry, love. What were you saying?"

"I asked what you and Kieran were looking for up in Fiona's attic after the soldiers arrested Ruairi. You two went through everything in that room."

"Nothing. Nothing at all."

Reason wrapped her jacket tighter as the damp roamed off the lawns. "You were both pretty upset about nothing then."

"Of course we were upset. The soldiers did a helluva lot of damage up there."

"Do you know what they were looking for?"

"No."

Reason ground to a halt before Wilder. "Stop lying to protect me! Today was living proof that you can't prevent me from seeing and getting involved in the war. It's everywhere I go! I made a decision after seeing that little boy get shot...I'm joining your fight."

"*NO!*" Wilder grabbed her shoulders. "You will *not* join anything, Reason."

But she was strong-willed. "I can change your mind."

"Not a chance."

She bent forward to whisper, "Light Fifty rifles."

Wilder staggered back, appalled. "How do *you* know?"

"Morris turned up with a 'magic bullet' he'd taken from Ruairi's workbench. I did some research and found out what Morris called a 'light fairy' rifle was really a Light Fifty. The Brits were searching the house for guns, weren't they?"

Wilder bobbed his head at a loss. "You shouldn't know these things, Reason. Where's the bullet now?"

"In my dresser."

"Good God!" he moaned and thought of a slogan of Liam's. *Help a republican, invite hell. One bullet for Ireland means ten years in jail.* "I want you to give it to me. Tonight."

"I've never seen a bullet that big before, have you?"

"Reason, don't say another word. You and I are committing a crime just talking about this." He gripped her shoulders harder. "Listen to me, *listen.* You've seen this can be a very cruel country, and I don't want you getting beaten by its secret police or murdered by the Prods."

She checked the deserted street, saying softly, "Look, I'm not asking to join the IRA. I just want to help you."

"If you want to help me, stay out of this. Please, Reason, if you care at all about me, *please* don't get involved. I thought I died two years ago when you walked out, but it would destroy me for real if anything happened to you. You saved my life...don't become the death of me."

All the day's intensity broke free. Wilder's impassioned pleas made Reason start to cry. "But I hate the injustice! A little boy had his arm intentionally blown off today and no one will be punished…Aidan died and Ruairi died and no one will be punished. There's no free speech, no free press, you can't fly your flag or be Irish…I just feel so useless standing by and watching the injustices stack up. I swear, if England were held accountable by the world for its brutality in Ireland, this war would have ended years ago." She choked back a sob, clinging to Wilder. "I thought if I could help you, I could save you somehow…I'm so afraid you're going to be like Ruairi."

"Third O'Neill's a charm, Reas. But," Wilder recoiled, his own eyes charged with apprehension, "if you want to save me, you have to stay out of this. I can't be looking over my shoulder and your shoulder at the same time. The more involved you get, the more likely both of us are to make a mistake."

"Then choose me over Ireland. Choose *me*," Reason implored.

"I can't do that."

"Then share Ireland with me. Let me choose you."

Jostled leaves moved the silence. Wilder clutched Reason to his chest. She wrapped herself around him. And all the distance he had struggled to maintain was lost, as was his resistance to that which he desired. She stroked his hair, his back, his arms. Oh God, how she unnerved him, controlled him and gave him pleasure like no other. How would he protect himself when, with a touch, she could pierce any armor? His kiss strayed to her throat, to her lips and remained there sweetly, too long. Each breath of wind smelled of woodland roses and Reason's skin, and with each sway of the overhead boughs, moonlight peppered the street in ethereal light. Reason, romance…*Bap, Bap, Bap*…reality.

Reluctantly, Wilder broke free. "I don't want you choosing anything."

"But, Wilder, I'm already involved whether you like it or not."

"Listen to you! You're still using my heritage against me. First you denounced my being Irish and wanted no part of me. Now you ask me to denounce my background and choose you over Ireland. And by asking to share my fight, you put me in the no-win position of endangering your safety to pursue my beliefs, which again demands I relinquish being Irish for you." He focused on the silver trees then looked Reason in the face. "I was willing to shed my skin for you once, Reason, but not twice. And you are not, I repeat *not,* involved."

"I wouldn't choose you, now you won't choose me." Reason brushed aside her tears and avoided Wilder's penetrating stare. "Once I condemned your being Irish and Catholic, and now I'm wishing I were both just to be near you."

"Could that be regret I hear in your voice, Mac?" How quickly he could regain his coldest depths and be Declan. "Aren't you the one who told me you can't repair the past so why regret it?"

But Reason hooked Wilder's hand with hers and continued along pretty Somerton Road. "The important thing is to learn from the past and not live to regret the present. It's a beautiful night and I'm with you, and as long as I'm with you, I'll have no regrets."

"I hate it when you're nice; it makes you impossible to fight," Wilder complained on edge, liking the feel of her hand and rebuking himself for liking it; how his heart danced while she was shooting his nerves. "I swear my father sent you over here to torture me. I had everything together. I'd gotten over you, at least I thought I had. I was a happy man, then you blew into Belfast. One look across Albie's, and I'm drowning all over again."

Reason nuzzled Wilder's fingers to her lips. "Poor tormented Declan Wilder. When we were in America you burned for me and Ireland. Now here we are in Ireland and you're still burning." Up slanted her woman eyes to provoke his. "But I'm only part of the flame. You're the match that keeps lighting yourself."

"I have never burned for you," Wilder denied and felt himself burning. "The clouds are coming in. We'd better head back to Fiona's before the rain starts."

Wilder tucked the bullet into his coat. "Now promise me you haven't seen a thing."

"I'm certainly seeing and hearing a lot I'm not seeing and hearing."

"Keep it that way, love."

"Are you involved with the guns?" Reason asked.

"No. I swear it."

"You shouldn't be carrying that bullet around," she worried. "What if you're stopped? You'll be arrested."

"I'm only driving home."

"But what if you get stopped?"

He pressed his finger to her lips. "I won't be stopped. Now, if that takes care of our business, I'll push off. I'm sure you'll be wanting to go to sleep."

"I'm not at all tired." Reason hoped Wilder wouldn't rush away, but he was already halfway down the stairs.

"Tell me something." He turned back to see her. "What if I *had* chosen you back there, said I loved you, asked you to marry me? What would you do about Cromwell? Dump him like you dumped me?"

"But you didn't choose me back there, did you?" she replied plainly.

"You make it all sound so easy, Reason, but it isn't. Cain's in love with you. For God's sake don't make light of that."

"I don't. But I can't forget he's not...you."

Wilder hiked up his summer's night smile. "You were right. I did come here tonight to see you. I honestly expected to find you packing to leave."

"And you wanted to wish me good riddance?"

"No, love, I wanted to wish you well."

"Looks like you're stuck with me, O'Neill."

"All kidding aside, Reas, are you going to be OK? You've been through too much lately."

Boof boof. "Seeing something like that changes you forever...but I'm not running home."

"Did you really use the words, 'Bleed you white?' I thought Kieran was making that up."

With a blush she nodded. "It just came out. I was furious."

"There's nothing tame about you, Mac," Wilder kidded but felt darkly afraid for her. "I swear there's a Fenian in you somewhere." With a last appreciative gaze at his friend, he hurried outside.

"Wilder?" Reason summoned from the doorway.

"Yes, dear?"

When he didn't retrace his steps she ran down the walk to catch him. "Maybe you won't choose me, but you said we could be friends." Her eyes melted upon his. "These past few weeks I haven't seen you and it's been awful. Please, Wilder, don't shut me out of your life."

"I haven't exactly managed to do that."

Her arms circled his neck. "Then kiss me again, won't you, friend?"

Such wicked sabotage he thought before seizing her mouth.

Wilder's departure was intercepted again at the curb by a pair of hands around his knees. "Decky!"

"Morris!"

"Declan, how nice to see you," Fiona slid her arm around Wilder's middle as he bent to kiss her cheek. "You aren't leaving, are you?"

"Actually, I was."

"It's not even eleven. Come in and have a wee cup of tea."

"Is Reason home?" Morris bolted in the front door.

"Morris, I'm sure she's tired," Wilder called after him.

"Nah! Reason never gets tired. I want to show her the birds I drew."

"Morris, get back here," Wilder ordered and Morris halted. "Give Reason a break tonight. I want you to go upstairs and get ready for bed. You can show Reason your pictures tomorrow."

"Look, I'm a flamingo." Morris flapped his arms and hopped up the stairs on one leg one step at a time.

"How does he know about flamingos?" Wilder turned to Fiona.

"Reason gave him a book about birds. Morris loves the wee things. Come into the kitchen. Are you hungry? Would you like a sandwich? I could fix you a meal."

"No, Fiona. Why don't you sit down, and I'll fix the tea."

"Wouldn't hear of it, love." She bustled to the stove, nabbed the tea kettle, scrubbed it, wiped the counters, straightened her canisters and finally turned the water on to boil. "I worry about Morris," she sighed, sweeping the floor. "He's very attached to our Reason. What's he going to do when she moves back to the States?"

"I don't know, Fiona. I worry about that myself. I wish Kieran would spend more time with him."

"Aye, you just try telling Kieran that. He's got his own life so he says. Lets me and his mum do the rearing of Morris. Now poor Reason finds the wee boy in her lap night and day."

"I'm sure if Reason didn't like him, she wouldn't tolerate it."

"Ought to be having her own wee babies, not tending Kieran's. She's such a lovely girl…I wonder why she's never married."

"She said 'no' to the right man, that's why," Wilder sniffed. "And everything would be so different now if she'd just said 'yes.'"

"What's that, dear?"

"Nothing." He stole the broom from Fiona's hands and led her into the parlor where he sat her before the hearth. "Sit down and rest, Fiona. I'll bring you your tea." She reached to dust ashes off the coffee table, but Wilder caught her hands. "Everything is all right tonight, Fiona," he insisted gently. "Have a rest."

"…and this is a robin and this is a hummingbird." Holding up the last of his drawings, Morris rolled back on Reason's bed and watched her brushing her hair.

"I like the hummingbird best, how about you?" she said.

"Me too. What do you suppose they hum?" Morris hummed a little tune. "I like them because they're little. Decky says he had lots of hummingbirds around his house in California. Have you ever been to California?"

"No."

"Me neither. Uh oh!" Morris shot off the bed and skidded into the closet. "Decky's coming!" He slammed the door.

"Come back for more?" Reason teased as Wilder came down the hall to her room.

He regarded her in her long silk robe. China white loosely draped around sleek, lotioned skin. It might as well have been transparent for his body's response. "I'm making Fiona some tea," he said, distracted, imagining he was untying Reason's robe and sliding his hands inside. "Come join us. Wait a second, where's Morris?"

"Morris who?" Reason laughed and motioned toward the closet.

"You know, the little boy who has a nose like a rhinoceros and ears like an elephant."

"I do not!" the closet giggled.

"You do too!" Wilder threw wide the closet door, grabbed Morris around the waist and tossed him over his shoulder. "And you're heavy as a hippopotamus. Tell Miss McGuinness goodnight."

"Goodnight," Morris tittered as his uncle bounced him across to Ruairi's old room.

Fiona fell asleep before finishing her tea, leaving Wilder and Reason in conversation by the fire.

"I made my reservations to go home for Christmas yesterday," Reason spoke lowly.

"Is home Denver or Manhattan these days?"

"Both. I'm spending a week in Denver with my family then flying off to New York to celebrate New Year's Eve with my friends. How about you? Heading straight for Malibu?"

"Absolutely. I'm planning two weeks of decadence and debauchery on the beach."

"Talk about culture shock. I don't see how you can go home to such a lavish lifestyle after being here for a year. Warfare and starlets are worlds apart."

"It'll be strange. I'm used to living with my eyes and ears behind me. Just think, no helicopters, no getting hassled for walking down the street, no hidden cameras or cops…my dad hopes once I come home I won't return to Belfast, but I'll be back. And he knows why I'll be back."

"Has the RUC ever found out who killed Brendan or Merry?"

"No. Both cases are closed."

"And you want to avenge them?"

"I want to improve the odds for all the other Brendans and Merrys. If I can help one Irishman further the cause for freedom, I'll call my work here a success."

"Will your work ever be done?"

"When England withdraws."

"That might be forever," Reason lamented.

"Forever is better than never, and I have nothing but time."

Reason concentrated on the fire's glow. Wilder was seated beside her within arms' reach, yet he dwelled light years away on his republican planet. She sneaked a wistful glance from the corner of her eye. *Oh! how I love you,* she wanted to cry. Noiselessly, she collected the tea cups and tiptoed into the kitchen to wash them. Wilder pursued her.

"Reason, don't look so unhappy with me," he coaxed, catching her soapy fingers, searching her eyes, stroking the silk of her shoulders. Resistance, insistence. He was kissing her again. "Sometimes the right thing is the hardest thing to do. It's easy to make the wrong decision but hard to make the right choice. Do you think I'm making all the wrong choices about Ireland…about you?"

She inched closer and pressed her reply upon his lips. A feather kiss. "No." Deeper. "Yes."

Wilder saw the roadblock in front of the New Lodge too late. He'd heard on the radio there had been a shooting, but he thought they said it was on the Crumlin Road. The security forces were sealing off the Antrim Road in both directions and searching all cars. He was third in a line and couldn't turn around without it looking like he was running away, which is exactly what he would be doing. He spied his coat tossed in the back seat and wondered what to do with the bullet. There was nowhere in the car to stash it, and there was no time to throw it away. Before he could do anything to save himself, two policemen were telling him to roll down his window.

Every so often Harry Jaggars liked to go back out on the street. He greeted Wilder with a smile, at once noting Wilder's Celtic t-shirt. A Roman Catholic. Even if it weren't for the shirt, Harry had a sixth sense about their kind. All in the eyes; a look of scorn and pride. He began the standard interview. Name. Address. Identification.

"What's your purpose here on the Antrim Road tonight, Mr. O'Neill?"

"I was visiting my nephew up on Duntroon Drive."

"What time did you leave Duntroon Drive?"

"Before midnight…minutes ago."

He surveyed Wilder's car. Powder blue, BMW, posh. "Fancy car you have here, Mr. O'Neill." With soul-chilling eyes, Jaggars perused Wilder's face. He already knew this Irishman. "Is it stolen?"

"It's *Dr.* O'Neill, and I paid cash for the car last summer."

Jaggars ignored Wilder's spite. "You're the rich one, are you, *Dr.* O'Neill?"

"Yeah," Wilder fired with condescension.

"It's a fucking miracle," Jaggars remarked to his colleague. "A mick who isn't on the buroo." More routine questions, then, "Step out of the car."

Wilder complied, hoping his knees wouldn't collapse beneath him.

"Are you related to Brendan O'Neill?"

"Never heard of him."

"Let me remind you." Jaggars shoved Wilder's head down on the top of the car. "He was your fucking Fenian asshole brother, *Dr.* O'Neill."

"Oh yeah," Wilder rejoined sarcastically and received a swift kick.

"So, finally I meet the last of the O'Neills. Over at Windsor we call you the 'suicidal taig' for coming back here. You don't look like Brendan, but then the last time I saw him he had a hole the size of plate in his skull. I wonder how you'll look with a hole in your head, *Dr.* O'Neill."

"I'll look dead," Wilder sneered, already thinking he was dead because of what was in his coat.

"Do you know anything about the shooting tonight?" Jaggars doubted Wilder knew anything about the incident but badgered him anyway.

"No," Wilder replied over the heart in his mouth.

"Open the bonnet and boot," Jaggars bossed his cohort, giving Wilder's head a whack with a thick plastic stick.

Wilder whirled to smack the muscle-massed lawman, but knowing it was only himself he'd be harming, he let the malice in his face suffice.

"Are you looking for trouble, *Dr.* O'Neill?" Jaggars thumped Wilder's curls.

The second RUC man, young Ian Wright, inspected the trunk and under the hood while Jaggars slammed Wilder up against the car and searched his torso with jabs.

"Nothing in the bonnet or boot, sir," Ian announced uneasily as he observed Jaggars' behavior. "Why are you hitting *him?*" Wilder heard Wright asking Jaggars aside.

"I'm making sure *Dr.* O'Neill isn't concealing a weapon." Jaggars spiked Wilder's face against the car's roof again and barked to Wright, "Don't stand there looking stupid. Check the inside!"

Wright scrambled into the car, and Wilder envisioned the foulest hells rising. This was it, the end of the line.

Grabbing Wilder's coat, Ian discovered the bulky bullet at once. *Thwap.* He heard Jaggars instilling more blows to Wilder's head and ribs, sniggering, "Would you like a broken nose, *Dr.* O'Neill?" Ian turned the bullet over and over in his hand reminding himself his job was to protect Ulster from terrorists. *Bang, bang, bang* went Wilder's chin upon the roof. Ian slipped the bullet back in Wilder's coat. With a cursory peek in the glove box and under the seats he bowed out of the car and scrutinized Wilder's emotionless face. "All clear," he reported.

"You sure?" Jaggars appeared disappointed.

"There's nothing in there but a coat."

"Sooner or later we'll get you, *Dr.* O'Neill. One of our bullets has your name on it." Jaggars patted a cut on Wilder's chin and grinned, "On your merry way then."

It had been a five minute inspection. It felt like five hours as Wilder accelerated away. The blood rushed from his head, his chest throbbed and throttled his breath, and once down the road, he swung to the curb. The bullet remained in his coat. Baffled, he drove on. Either the RUC was hiring blind men or that young policeman had let him go.

  ✻   ✻   ✻   ✻   ✻   ✻

It was hard to spot her at first. In her yellow hard hat and baggy grey coveralls she looked like one of the men, but the froth of blonde around her collar and grace of her walk gave Reason away. Wilder waited until she saw him waving outside the construction zone, then, mindless of the mud that splashed up the front of his scrubs, he low-hurdled over the red-ribbon barriers to meet her on the site.

"Well, McGuinness m'darling, you were right."

"I finally did something right?" Wilder's smile spread from his face to hers. At once she noticed the bruise on his chin. "What's this?"

"There was a roadblock on the Antrim Road last night. I got stopped."

"Oh my God!"

"Believe me, Reas, I'm lucky to be standing here admiring you," he quipped with a knock on her hard hat.

"You had that bullet and the police didn't arrest you?"

"The cop looked through everything and didn't say a word. Isn't that unreal? They've been tearing our houses apart to find the rifles, and that one bullet was enough to bury me."

"One of these days that Irish luck of yours is going to run out." Reason stroked Wilder's stubbled chin. "Hold it, what are you doing out here? You're not supposed to be on the site without a hard hat."

"I just came to see how we're progressing. Glad to see the steel going up." Wilder noticed the workmen leaving. "Do you have plans for tonight?"

"Of course I do."

"Change them," he appealed. "Have dinner with me. We'll talk all night. Like we used to."

She loved the invitation almost as much as she loved the heat in his eyes. "Have you truly forgotten the benefit dinner the medical staff is giving tonight at the Victoria Hotel? You paid £150 for a ticket, remember?" Reason laughed in dismay. "You're giving a speech on the new surgical services the Gov will be offering with the new wing."

Wilder slapped his jaw. "I completely forgot. Black tie, drinks at seven, dinner at eight?"

"Right." Reason guided him towards the side entrance of the Gov.

"Now I remember. I asked you three weeks ago if you'd like to join me, but you're going with Cromwell."

"I was. Cain needed to stay in Zurich an extra day."

"You're free?"

"All night."

Wilder raised suggestive eyebrows and slapped his arm around Reason. "Then tonight, you're mine."

"Oh goody, a date with Pat Boone. No thanks."

"What do you mean, 'No thanks?'"

"I'd prefer to go alone."

"And why is that, Mac?"

"We're nothing's-going-to-happen friends, remember? Why should I waste sexy blue velvet and French perfume on you?"

"I know what you're trying to do," Wilder responded with a laugh. "You're trying to provoke me. Sorry, Reas, it won't work."

"That's because you don't work. You're all crusty heart and rusty parts."

Wilder just laughed and chased Reason up the stairs. "Sometimes you're a brat."

"And you love it, Decky dear, cuz I'm beautiful when I'm bad."

"I'll pick you up at seven," Wilder turned left on sixth floor. Reason turned right.

"Make it six thirty. We'll have champagne."

Chapter Twenty-Eight

"You clean up good for a New Lodge kid, O'Neill," Reason smiled to greet Wilder. He wore a graphite tuxedo and black paisley vest. "You look great."

"You aren't hard to look at yourself, Mac," he countered, absorbing every inch of his old friend. Reason in velvet and organdy. A satin bow pinned her hair at her nape. Velvet the color of midnight flowed from her hips to her knees, and six cerise buttons fastened her filmy black blouse and led to a sash around her waist. The sheer black of her bodice veiled an alabaster bosom camisoled in lace, and her every breath was Wilder's temptation to see, to touch that which was almost revealed. He caught his breath, not forgetting the last time he took Reason dancing in black. "Where is everyone?" He continued into the parlor.

"Fiona and Morris are spending the weekend in Derry, and Kieran is upstairs waiting to borrow your car."

"That's right. He's taking Jillie to a horse fair in Armagh tomorrow."

"I didn't know Jillie liked horses."

"She doesn't. She goes to buy the equipment."

"But if she doesn't ride…"

"I didn't say she doesn't ride," Wilder said wryly, "she just doesn't ride horses."

"You mean she's into…really?" Reason looked shocked. "Were you into…"

"Whips and leather? Nah. Where's the champagne?"

"In the refrigerator." Reason settled back on the couch. "Go ahead and give Kieran your car. We'll take mine."

Wilder emerged from the kitchen with two glasses of wine, handing one to Reason and raising a toast, "*Sláinte.*"

"Sloncha?"

"'To your health' in Irish, though I must say your health appears to be," his attention strayed from her face to her body, "robust. It's high time you learn a few Irish words."

"So teach me."

"*Is álainn tú, a ghrá.*" Wilder toasted again, "You're beautiful, my love."

"How do you say 'forever' as in 'friends forever?'"

"*Go deo. Cairde go deo.*"

"Slipping her the mother tongue, eh?" Kieran walked in. "Lord fucking love ye, you two look gorgeous. Give us the car then, Dec."

Wilder flipped Kieran the keys. "Want some champagne?"

"Nah. Sissy stuff." Kieran considered Reason with interest. "I hear Morris gave you something magic. Do you know what would have happened to you if the Brits had raided the house again and found you with that?"

"I try not to think about it," Reason shuddered.

"You'd have been sent to prison for harboring articles connected with terrorism. Knowing that, would you do it again?"

"No, she would not!" Wilder intervened.

Flashing Reason his impish grin, Kieran continued to converse with his cousin in Irish. "I don't see why we shouldn't use her. She wants to help us."

"Absolutely not!" Wilder slapped down his wine and argued in the guttural language Reason couldn't understand. "Leave Reason alone."

"She could be a driver…"

"No! Drop it, Kieran. Take my car and go to Armagh."

"OK," Kieran yielded with a toss of his wrists. "*Slán go fóil.* That means 'cheerio for now.'"

"*Slán go fóil,*" Reason repeated cheerfully. "What were you two talking about?" she was dying to know when Kieran left.

"Safe sex," Wilder improvised. "Kieran doesn't understand the concept of protection."

Reason looked dubious. "I heard my name mentioned in that discussion."

"Kieran asked if I practice what I preach."

"And you said you were so out of practice all you could do at this point was preach?"

"Yeah, Reason," Wilder replied with a smile, "that's what I told him."

The Victoria Hotel had the look of a bordello; red velvet drapes, red velvet chairs, red carpets on buffed hardwood floors. The hazy, low light of cut-glass chandeliers made the Victoria the more antique, like the medical staff had come to an illicit rendezvous for two hundred.

At the benefit dinner, Hunter had expected to be sitting across from his son. He faced Declan O'Neill instead. "I thought you were coming with Cain," he said to Reason.

"He's still in Zurich."

"Zurich?" Hunter's face lit up. "Clever rascal that Cain."

"And he's a great artist," Wilder reminded. "Have you seen his mosaics for the new wing?"

"No desire to see the fool things. Leave it to Cain to use tile. Tile belongs in the toilet." Hunter enjoyed a swig of claret. "Seeing you and Reason here together is grand, simply grand. Does this mean you're working harmoniously?"

"Well, I wouldn't say that," Wilder smiled. "Currently we're at war over counter space in pre-op holding."

"Oh, but it's a harmonious war," Reason added, patting Wilder's hand.

"You know," Hunter clanked down his cocktail fork and spoke through a mouthful of shrimp, "I've just had a marvelous thought. Declan, perhaps you'd like to participate in a documentary film I'm financing for distribution in the States. He has the ideal face for cinema, doesn't he?" Hunter raved to the other couples seated at the table who agreed politely then returned to their conversations.

"What sort of film?" Reason couldn't imagine.

"Bernard Thunder has compiled a collection of videos." Hunter popped more shrimp in his mouth. "We have bombing victims. We have soldiers shot through the head, and policemen missing limbs blown off by car bombs...this is delicious shrimp. We have houses burning from IRA explosions, and naturally," he whispered, "we have mothers at funerals. Fabulous collection really. What do you think?"

Wilder looked at Reason. Reason looked at Wilder. "Why would I want to participate in this project?" Wilder asked.

"Declan, everyone knows you came back to compensate the good people of Ulster for the wickedness of your family. It takes guts to show your face around this town, boy, and by God, I respect you for it. So who better than you to be a spokesman denouncing the scourge of terrorism? And as a fine physician here in Belfast you see the plague of Provisional pogroms and could describe the traumas in gripping detail. Your being Irish and American would be very persuasive."

"What's the purpose of this film?" Reason pushed aside her shrimp salad, her appetite lost.

"To convey the heartbreak of Ulster of course."

"But it tells only one side," Reason objected.

"I might be interested in joining your project," Wilder humored Hunter, causing Reason to clutch her chest, "but I'd like to add some of my own material."

"Imperial! Imperial!" Hunter licked the last drop of cocktail sauce off his spoon. "What pictures can you provide?"

"Men imprisoned for twenty years on charges based on a confession that was beaten out of them by the police. Children maimed by plastic bullets fired by the police. Unarmed young men and women shot multiple times at close range by the Cure. Houses the Army smashed to bits. Victims of interrogation at Windsor RUC. Victims like Ruairi McKee and my sister. Victims of Her Majesty's force."

"No, no, Declan," Hunter tossed his head and snapped a bite of French bread. "You've missed the point. This is a film about the *good* guys. We mustn't give the bad guys the oxygen of publicity. We want to show America the savage Irish behavior England is combating. Do you understand what I'm saying?"

"Oh yes," Wilder eyed Hunter with disdain. "Perhaps I'm not the right spokesman for your project."

"Perhaps not, perhaps not. Maybe Bernie is a better choice, what do you think? He hasn't such a rough Irish accent."

"Let me tell you something, Hunter..." Reason couldn't take another gibe, but Wilder gripped her knee under the table.

"What's that, Reason dear?" Hunter waited for her to speak.

"I uh...think you look handsome in that tuxedo," she ad-libbed through gritted teeth.

He sat up proudly. "It was hand-sewn for me by the tailor to Prince Charles. By Jove, there's the real reason Cain isn't here tonight. A tuxedo would kill him. Aaah, now where is our meal?" Hunter clapped then rubbed his hands. "I hear it's leg of lamb. Superb choice, superb."

Reason assumed Wilder would remove his palm from her leg, but he didn't. He massaged her knee gently, absently. Like a man fondling a rosary. Comfort from a familiar place. She didn't mind.

After tea and speeches about the Grosvenor's expansion came the ten-piece band.

"I don't know how you keep your temper. One of these days I'm going to pop my fist in Hunter's face," Reason complained to Wilder as they danced in slow circles. "When do we get to tell the Hunters and the RUC and the Army to go straight to hell?"

"When we're boarding a flight to Manhattan."

"Be serious."

"I am serious. Merry spoke out and the Cure had her shot. Bren spoke out and the ULF shut him up. So much for freedom of speech."

"Augh! This place is worse than China! Sometimes I'm walking down the Antrim Road or up the Falls, and a soldier will point his rifle at me. And I feel like he knows what I'm thinking, like I'm going to be shot for my anti-Brit thoughts. It's hard not to be paranoid here."

"Aye, love, it is. How did you like my speech?"

"Oh, I've never heard anyone make angioplasty sound more thrilling. And certainly you were the best-looking speaker."

Wilder drew Reason nearer and talked close to her ear. "I'm glad we came together tonight. I wasn't looking forward to seeing you with Cain. Are you sorry you aren't with him?"

"That's a loaded question," Reason laughed. "It's nice being here with you."

"Last month you said you'd be in love with him. Are you?"

"Another loaded question."

"Are you?" Wilder repeated.

Seeing his anxious expression, Reason just smiled, "Don't ask questions you don't want answered."

"It's hard not to become fond of Cain. He's one of a kind. But I wonder how your passion for him would fare if I wanted you back."

"You never had me," Reason contradicted and drew back in Wilder's arms.

But Wilder waltzed her to him again. "You know I did. I think I still do."

He danced her a few more steps just to enjoy her body soft against him. "What do you say we cut out early and go back to my place?"

"I thought you'd never ask."

The wind was up, and the moon played hide and seek in the clouds. In then out it dashed, portending starlight and rain. And hints of autumn whirled down the hillsides, filling Belfast's valley with gusts of shivering mist.

Wilder showed Reason into his family room and took her coat. Tossing his jacket aside, he stooped to light the fire. "You choose the music. I'll choose the wine."

Reason chose Chopin and glided onto Wilder's white leather sofa. She kicked off her heels, stretched her legs along the cushions and melted back into the pillows. "There's something I've been wondering for weeks," she called toward the kitchen where Wilder had gone. "That night at Albie's funeral parlor you were listening to *The Messiah*. Why?"

"Aren't you going to make the obvious crack about me thinking I'm God?"

"You're hardly a god, Wilder," Reason scoffed.

"And here I've been thinking I'm the Apollo of the Gov. The truth is Albie Coogan likes his staff to listen to Handel while they're preparing the bodies."

"There really is an Albie?"

"Aye, he's been a mortician in West Belfast for fifty years."

"*Fifty* years?"

"He's ninety years old. Kieran and I have decided he's been around formaldehyde so long he's become immortal. He was a friend of Liam's. A real stalwart of republicanism. Anyhow, he believes *The Messiah* prepares the dead for their heavenly ascension."

"What a nice thought."

"I was playing it because that's all there is to listen to, and I like music while I work."

"Yes, I know. I've heard you have a penchant for the Grateful Dead in the OR. Sick choice for a surgeon, O'Neill."

"You look like a Renoir painting," Wilder complimented as he returned to the family room. "A succulent tribute to womanhood. I read that once in a review of a Renoir exhibition, and the image stuck with me. Succulent." His eyes sank to Reason's gauzed-in-black breasts as he delivered her wine.

"That makes women sound like something you pick up in the produce section!"

"It also describes the erotic abundance and roundness every woman possesses and every man desires to possess."

"And you're saying I'm succulent?" Reason made a face.

"I said you remind me of a Renoir painting. I didn't say which one," Wilder rallied, dimming the lights and pulling up a fireside chair. "Maybe you remind me of a haystack."

"That wouldn't be so bad. You could tumble down into me and stare up at the sky."

Tumble down, happy landing. Yielding sheaf beneath Irish sun. Yes, Wilder decided, Reason could be a haystack. Succulent harvest.

"Why are you staring at me?"

Wilder tipped his glass to his lips. "I'm thinking tonight feels good and you look good and it's good to feel good."

The room warmed. Firelight and rain on the windows. Reason held her wine out to Wilder, "*Cairde go deo.*"

"You're gorgeous when you speak Irish," he grinned, clinking her glass.

"I really did think your speech was good tonight. You're a natural in front of an audience. Maybe you should have been an actor like your dad."

"Forget it. Growing up as Sumner Steed's son was bad enough. Fame is a prison. We couldn't go anywhere without being swamped by Dad's fans or the press. I hated it."

"Did you go to work with your dad? Making a movie must be fascinating."

"It's tedious as hell. You spend most of your time standing around, waiting to do your scene. And once you've done it, you have to re-do it a hundred times. The only time I went to work with my dad and had fun was when I was fourteen years old."

"What happened then?"

"Oh, it was the best. Over the summer my dad took me on the road with him. He wasn't famous then and for eight weeks we played the West Coast, boozy club to boozy club. Of course at fourteen I didn't notice they were boozy clubs. All I saw were the showgirls. The best part was horsing around backstage. My dad and some of the dancers started teaching me to tap dance. Those girls were something else, tall and all fish net stockings, real temples of flesh, and such generous girls. They were always crushing me against their bodacious breasts and saying in their high, squeaky voices, 'Ooooh, he's soooo cuuute.' I had a *great* time."

"And did you learn how to tap dance?"

"Yes, but with those women teaching me I made sure I was a very slow learner. You've mentioned Cain's tap dancing. Just like me, he learned every step from my dad."

"Tap dancing suits Cain, but somehow it doesn't go with your sober nature."

"*Sober?* What a lousy thing to call me! Sober is the last gasp before dead. You really think I'm *sober?*"

"You didn't used to be, but you are now. Will you show me how you dance? Come on. It would be funny."

"Where there's tap there's laughter, at least that's what my dad always says. Can you believe it, he tapped his way through his nervous breakdown. I'm not kidding. He swears dancing heals the soul."

"So, physician, heal thy sober self." Reason swung from the sofa and tugged Wilder to his feet. "Prove you aren't one gasp from dead."

She was already laughing, and her laughter filled Wilder with happiness. Across the hardwood floor by the light of the fire he shuffled, one tenuous step then another and another, and Reason doubled over with mirth.

But Wilder was getting into it. "Did you ever see the old movie 'Holiday Inn' where Fred Astaire tap dances with firecrackers? Watch this. Or how about this move by Fosse." Wilder wasn't Fosse or Astaire, he stamped a frightful racket, but allowing the armor of solemn manhood to slip released the insouciant boy. And didn't insouciance feel good! Just like fourteen. "Come here and I'll teach you a few steps."

"Oh boy! Then, when we're tired of Belfast, we'll go on the road."

When Reason joined him in the middle of the room, he looped his arm around her shoulders. "Ready?" She was. "Watch my feet." He named every move, "Brush, hop, shuffle step, flap step, step, stomp. Got it?"

"I don't think so." She tried, failed, failed again and fell against Wilder fit to burst. "We're not going to make much money on tour. Oh! Look before it fades!" Reason ran to the window. The moon had unbuttoned itself from the clouds and made ghosts of the floating fog. "It's still raining, but there's moonlight on the lawn. Isn't it pretty?"

Pretty. Like Reason. How like the moon she wore the night. Pale skin beneath veils of velvet grey, showing herself partially, leaving Wilder wanting more. And racing into a blue shaft of light before the window, like she had created the lightness, she reminded Wilder of an angel's shadow illuminating his world.

"Sorcerer's smoke, that's what it looks like," Reason went on touting the enchanted moonglow now fading behind the rain. "Sorcerer's smoke conjuring…"

With his palm behind her neck, Wilder spun Reason around and tipped her lips to meet his. Intemperately he kissed and stroked her and fused her body to his, and wholeheartedly she kneaded her hands up his back and returned his desire. The scare of her encounter with a brutal riot, the scare of the roadblock the previous night left him ravening for life and relishing freedom. He loosened Reason's hair from its bow and smoothed it over her shoulders. Tonight the world was glad and dancing.

His tongue met hers in passion, he made agile work of her buttons and dashed the sash from her waist. His fingers balanced on the rim of her camisole and dipped now and then across the warmth of her breasts. After two years it took willpower to go slowly, Wilder longed to take Reason in one fevered pounce, but he wanted to savor this night. When she parted and pared his shirt over his shoulders, he stepped back to cherish her face in the firelight, but the fire had faded.

"Wait." Wilder jumped aside abruptly and slid across the room to recharge the flames. He intended to make love to Reason on the rug before the hearth's heat, but she misinterpreted his actions.

"What's wrong?" she strived to regain her breath.

"Nothing," he insisted as he added more coals, not wanting to spoil the romantic mood.

But Reason jumped to conclusions. "You're brushing me off again, aren't you?"

"No, I…"

"Come here, Reason, go away, Reason, right?"

"No!" Wilder sputtered off guard.

But Reason's ire not the fire ignited. "I knew it! I just knew it!" She impaled Wilder with a glare. "I knew you couldn't go through with it. I knew you'd go slinking away like every other time. Are you a man or a monk?"

"What? Wait a sec, I was just…"

"Don't say it! You were just going to tell me for the *billionth* time that Ireland is your choice not me and blah, blah, blah! Well, to hell with you, Declan!" She snapped her arms across her unbuttoned bosom and continued blasting him with her frown.

"That's not what I was doing at all…hey, get this straight I'm not a damn monk…you know, that's contemptible, Reason. You're condemning me for playing fair with you, for being a gentleman."

"Gentleman, ha! You're an embarrassment to your sex. *Real* men make love, Wilder. All you can make anymore are excuses."

Another jab in a twelve-week series of Reason's jabs to his virility. Wilder began to fume. Forsaking the fire, he whirled to face Reason. "You know I've been trying to protect you."

"From what? Your impotence?" she taunted, fastening her blouse with furious plucks.

"If I'm so impotent, how come you're desperate to have me? You've been coming on to me for months. And when I was kissing you a minute ago, you were praying I'd take you to bed."

"Even prayer couldn't get you up, Declan. And as for coming on to you, you have an amazing imagination."

"Liar!" He flung back her glare. "I'm the best thing that ever happened to you, and you want me to happen again."

"In your dreams!"

"I could have made your dreams come true if you'd kept your damn mouth shut, but can you *ever* keep your mouth shut? No! I was only coming over here to put more coal on the fire. I was planning on making love to you right here all night."

"Oh, sure you were. Another paltry excuse." She searched his face a moment. "Well, even if you were, I would have said 'no.'"

His eyes narrowed. "You would have said '*no?*'"

"Yes."

"Even after kissing me like you were just kissing me? Oh, there's no way you're ever going to say 'no' to me, Reason." He wasn't kidding.

"Try me!"

"Try you? The thought makes me cringe," Wilder reveled at his comeback and finished his wine. "But you could have gotten lucky. Tonight I was feeling generous. I was going to give you what you're dying for."

"I ought to punch you in the eye again," she raged, pushing past him to get her shoes.

"Do it and you'll be sorry."

"Oh, you really scare me, you big wuss."

"You know, Reason, I've had my fill of your nasty little digs."

"And I've had my fill of your sexual inadequacy." She snatched her coat from the closet.

"Don't you dare leave! We're not finished here."

Reason heaved open the door. "You can't finish anything."

Wilder had taken it from the Army. He had taken it from the RUC. And he had taken all he was going to take from Reason. He overtook her in the driveway. Grabbing her elbow, he spun her around. "Sometimes you're a real bitch."

She smacked his jaw. Hard. Again. Harder.

Instinctively, Wilder raised his hand but constrained his slap within millimeters of Reason's ear. Instead he caught her hair, jerked back her head, shoved her against her car and kissed her; roughly, insatiably, without consideration if he was hurting her, without pausing. And he kept kissing her up against the Volvo in the drenching rain. The wet streamed over their eyes and off their cheeks and sweetened the taste of their lips. Baptized in Irish waters.

Rushing his hands inside her raincoat he didn't bother with her buttons. With a sharp tug from her collar to waist, he ripped the front of her blouse open and slid his fingers under her camisole. And loving her breasts, he rubbed each nipple with his palm while his lips burned upon hers, now open and willing. And when her camisole proved restrictive, he snapped its straps and tore it off as well. Her arms slipped up his bare back, her fingers knotted his soaking hair, and when he sank his mouth to her throat, she encouraged him lower and delighted at his tongue's supple tease. Shirtless and barefoot, Wilder was freezing, but Reason was fire and making him too hot to care for the cold. His kisses hungered, hers tempted. Then gratified. And just as Reason decided he was going to undress her in his driveway, Wilder swung wide the car door and climbed into the back seat.

"Take off your coat," he instructed Reason still poised in the rain.

"But my skirt will get…"

He stripped off his belt, and with a kick, his slacks. "Take it off!"

She did then Wilder jerked her into the car. He tossed her coat into the front seat and ordered her onto his lap. "We're going to settle things, here and now."

His mouth was gentler this time but athirst, unrelenting. As his fingers ripped away the remains of her blouse, his lips sought her neck, her shoulders, her eyes, her cheek. For several minutes he kissed and caressed her and whispered her name. Never did his lips leave hers, deeper and deeper grew his kiss, shameless grew his fingers' advance. Without protest Reason returned his heated endearments, cinching her arms around his neck, responding to his touch. A cyclone of expectation excited her mind. Heat commanded her flesh. And all she heard was the roar of the rain like Beethoven's *Fifth* and Wilder's rapid breathing.

In time Wilder settled Reason beside him, peeled away her skirt and silk stockings then reeled her onto his lap again. "Now show me what you've learned in two years," he insisted with his tongue teasing her breasts, his hands wandering over and under her knees.

"What if I don't want to?" she resisted with pleasure.

"Oh, you want to. And I want you to…Jesus, how I want you…"

Wilder's intensity and force were all-engulfing, he overwhelmed her, and Reason found him frightening and exhilarating. She lazed her fingernails between his thighs and loved the feel of him hard in her hand. "And you insisted nothing was going to happen between us."

"It should have happened weeks ago. From the moment I saw you walk into Albie's I've been wanting to do this." Wrapping his arms around her, impatient to know her, he folded her down on the seat. "Is this *manly* enough for you, Reas?" he asked as he rolled on top of her. "Do I feel like an impotent monk?" He kissed and petted her then parted her legs.

"You're perfect," she moaned to feel his fit. "Perfect." It all came flooding back. The delirious, overawing power of love. And this time she wasn't afraid of losing her self. She had lost part of her self to Wilder years ago and only now regained it. To give it again. If he wanted every piece of her, she would afford it.

But everything changed after Wilder entered Reason's body. His mind rattled back two years; nobody grips a grudge longer.

"*I'm sorry, Wilder, but you simply won't do.*" Reason's disavowal, his scar. He remembered her eyes forgetting his face. "*You are the cruelest woman I've ever met.*" He despised her…

"*Today was living proof that you can't prevent me from seeing and getting involved in the war…I'm joining your fight.*"

"*NO!*"…and she was precious to him.

The deeper he stabbed the more detached he became. With every stroke he seemed to be disappearing; methodical and distant, he offered no part of his mind, no part of his heart to the act until Reason felt like she wasn't being touched. It was perfunctory, sex, an obedient lay, and the night was no longer dancing and glad. Sadly, Wilder realized all they were making was another bad memory. He detested the icicle part of himself driving a stake through his passion. Right after he applauded it.

Doing sex, faking love. It was like making love to metal. After two years of placing him on the altar of her idylls, Reason felt cheated, insulted, defiled. What had gone wrong? For weeks Wilder had been whisking her into his arms with desire. He had been undressing her with his eyes all evening, his hands had doted upon her throughout dinner, and when he said her name his voice belied affection. There had been nothing cool about his kisses or his body eager to take hers. But as Wilder withdrew like a man withdrawing a blade from his adversary, Reason grieved to realize Wilder was the one who had died. He had expended so much passion for Ireland and grudges, he was now bereft of those magic and potent intensities that drive a man in love mad. Yes, he could take her with lust like a man but not tenderly as a lover, not as a friend. Sweetness and light withered inside him 800 nights ago; she had come too late to touch him.

The rain drummed on the rooftop and raced down the windows like bars. The night air was stolid, sordid, stale. Neither Wilder nor Reason spoke. Self-consciously they inched apart. Wilder exhaled a breath of relief and drew on his slacks. Reason inhaled her impulse to cry and felt naked inside out. Time hung like thick, sticky weather and dripped down in minutes like hours. Disappointment. Regret. A trickle of tears. Retrieving her coat, Reason took flight from the car.

The fire had died and the family room was cold. Still Reason hugged the hearth for its last breath of warmth. Guiltily avoiding her downcast expression, Wilder darted upstairs. He returned with a bathrobe which Reason quickly donned in place of her wet coat. Barefoot and miserable, wet and wrinkled, he awaited her reaction.

"Thank you for that chilling introduction to necrophilia," she began in a voice too wounded to rise.

"I'm not sure what happened out there," Wilder uttered remotely, standing before her but staring away.

"It was awful, just awful," Reason sighed and moved to the couch; tears rolled off her blue eyes. "What were you trying to prove? Did you want to humiliate me? If so, you succeeded."

Wilder paced across the room. "I've explained things are different here, that *I'm* different here…for christsake, Reason, what more do you expect from me?"

"Tenderness, sensitivity…why did you bother making love to me in the first place…if you can call that frozen screw 'making love.' Why didn't you let me leave?"

"I didn't want you to leave. I wanted to make love to you…oh, stop shooting me with your eyes! Isn't sex what you wanted from me?"

"Yes, but I thought you still had feelings for me. Only hours ago you called me 'your love.'"

No less confounded, Wilder shrugged. "I do have feelings for you. My God, Reason, my head is full of you, and I wanted you like a madman tonight. But just when I started to feel really good I remembered the way you tore me in half. I told you I died for loving you and I did…I guess tonight was too soon."

"So you're never going to forgive me for hurting you?" Reason saw the bitterness in Wilder's face and shivered. "I totally botched things two years ago, didn't I?"

"All I know is that I thought I was over it and I'm not."

"Then I've been extremely foolish wanting you all summer and thinking we could be wonderful." Rain like shrapnel clattered against the windows. "Before I leave I'd like to collect what's left of my dignity and take a shower, that is if it's included in your stud service. I'm very cold."

"Of course you can take a shower," he said, feeling cold to the soul himself.

Reason couldn't help being wistful. "If things had been different, we'd be showering in each others arms…like before."

"Things became different the minute you walked out on me," Wilder muttered. "You changed both of our lives that night."

"Why can't we put that behind us?" Reason cried, but she already knew the answer. "Well, Declan, congratulate your grudge. You've repaid me in full. I couldn't feel any more used and discarded."

"I didn't use you! You think I *enjoyed* that?"

"Yes, I think you did. You satisfied yourself and degraded me in one shot. You've been burning to do that for two years."

"I have not!" He returned to her side. "It wasn't my intention to degrade you, Reason. For a few insane hours tonight I honestly thought we still had a chance…I thought I could love you without fear for you, for me…hell, I don't know. But I swear I had no idea it would feel like this; empty and godawful."

"But last night the way you kissed me…and tonight out by the car, you were so passionate." She rubbed his cheek shyly. "You can't tell me that was empty or awful."

"I don't want passion! Passion feels good for about twenty minutes and then it makes you bleed. If I let those feelings start, pretty soon I'll be dying. Hell, I'm already dying." He sighed to feel Reason's touch, fearing he was losing his mind. Forever never, forever never, he craved all and no part of Reason. "I hate you for coming here, for making me want you and need you and love you all over again, and now you know, you've *felt* the cold inside me. Cold you and Merry and Brendan inspired. Cold the war demands. Ruairi told me I was a soldier and I didn't believe him, but maybe he was right. In order to survive being surrounded by death part of me had to die. I'm drowning myself in numbness, Reason, and you can't reach me."

She regarded him haplessly. "I only want to love you."

"I don't want your love! Christ, Reason, don't love me!"

"I can't help it," she whispered, fitfully turning away. "Why is that so terrible?"

He cosseted her rain-soaked hair then pushed from the couch. "We aren't the same people we were two years ago, and this isn't Denver where all we had standing between us was Reid and your wedding. If only things could be that simple this time."

"Tonight seemed simple to me. We were together, and it felt good."

"Yeah, at first it felt good and then it felt like I was coming apart. I can't tell love from loss anymore…it's easier to feel nothing."

"So, if I were Jillie and you knew you could have me just for sex, there'd be no problem, right?"

Looking ashamed of himself he nodded. "I know I'm screwed up, but that's just the way it is."

"Maybe you don't want to feel anything, Wilder, but you do. You feel too much. I felt the same way in Denver. I ran out on you because I loved you so much it scared me. I thought in loving you I was losing my self and look where it got me? I lost you and broke my own heart. I've never forgotten your calling me a coward because I left you. Now you're the coward. You don't have the guts to give me a second chance."

"Only fools give second chances, Mac. If you're looking for a lasting relationship, call Cain."

"So tonight means nothing to you?"

"It means I lost all control where you're concerned, I made a mistake, and I'm sorry." He marveled to hear himself giving Reason the same lines she had given him two years earlier.

"Apparently I'm the mistake you love to make, Wilder, because you keep coming back."

"Damn it, Reason, I'm not Wilder! Wilder is dead."

"You made that clear out in the car."

"Stop messing with my head!" he blared. "Give your precious love to Cromwell! Be the death of him this time."

"All right, I will." Reason knew she was Wilder's loss. She climbed the stairs, saying over her shoulder, "If I make you so unhappy, *Declan*, let's see you never touch me again. Go ahead and try it. You'll never win this war."

Wilder stood at his bedroom window when Reason walked out of the bathroom. To her chagrin, the sight of him as she liked him best stabbed her heart. She liked him in his long black bathrobe. She liked his wet jet curls wild on his neck, and she liked his smile in that bathrobe; unguarded, boyish, a lover's smile. Wilder, always Wilder. But he wasn't smiling. And her eyes froze upon him.

"Are you warmer?" he put to her anxiously, feeling responsible.

Reason knotted the cord of her bathrobe with a jerk. "Not much."

"I made you some tea. It's there on the dresser."

"Thank you." She stood towel-drying her hair, contemplating her inscrutable Irishman. Passionate and heartless, loving and harsh, he was like Belfast, beauty and the beast. "I'll leave as soon as I'm dry. But it's still pouring, and I don't exactly have clothes to wear home."

"I'm sorry about that..."

"Don't apologize." Reason regarded Wilder with increasing disaffection. "You didn't see me objecting, did you? For awhile there I thought you were incredibly exciting. In fact, for the record, Declan, I was enjoying, really enjoying, being with you tonight. I liked it when you chased me, and I liked it when you kissed and undressed me. I liked your hands, I liked feeling your body on mine, in mine...it could have been spectacular if you hadn't ruined everything."

Wilder drew aside the curtains to ponder the rain, saying nothing.

"How can you be so unfeeling?" Reason seethed. "Aren't you the slightest bit sorry? You've treated me badly! You rejected me in the worst way."

"Did I really, Reason? Then I am sorry." The temptation was too great. Smugness hijacked his tongue, "I'm sorry, but you simply wouldn't do." Wilder had waited two years to grind it in her face, and it felt good to grind it. He started to laugh. "How does a dose of your own medicine taste, Mac?"

Reason hadn't seen it coming. Incensed, she spiked her towel to the carpet. "No doubt your revenge tastes sweeter."

"So what do we do, eh, Reas?" Wilder chuckled, still pleased with his comeback. "We still have to work together."

"What do we do?" Reason unbelted her bathrobe and let it slide slowly down her back to the floor. Stepping to Wilder's closet, she leafed through his clothes. "You loan me a shirt, I go home, and like you're always telling me, tonight never happened. *We* never happened." She turned, letting Wilder gaze upon her body. "There's just one problem. You're still going to want me like a madman and you can go to hell."

And he saw her smile a wicked smile. And suddenly he wasn't feeling smug, and victory tasted of defeat. Reason had his full attention as she sifted through his wardrobe. Lazily. Shirt by shirt. He loved her nude and she knew it, and used it, like salt in a wound. Too soon her skin slipped into a shirt. Like the moon had slipped into the rain. With each button she hid herself. And tonight didn't happen. *Fine!* Wilder simmered. But it wasn't fine. When he began the evening his intent wasn't to end it with Reason walking out in disgust. He opened his mouth to protest only to see himself painted into a corner by his own hand. He devised Reason's exile and she breezed out of reach.

Chapter Twenty-Nine

Only a pair of workers remained in the locker room; Kevin Murphy and Duggie Knack. Having had great success with his crusade to expel every Catholic worker on Hatter's list, Duggie swaggered with brazen prowess. Kevin Murphy would be number ten.

"How's it going?" Duggie sidled closer to Kevin's locker.

"I'm glad it's Friday. It's been a long week."

"Aye," Duggie puffed his cigarette. "Maybe you need a vacation."

"It's not that bad," laughed Kevin. "I've only been on the job two days."

"Maybe you need a vacation," Duggie repeated and produced his ready knife.

A big man, known for his strength, Kevin just laughed. "Aw christ, don't tell me you're the poor excuse the ULF sent to force me out of my job." Undaunted, he lunged at Duggie and slammed him by the throat against the lockers. Duggie's knife clattered across the room. "I'll crush your bones, little man, if you cross me again." Putting his face in Duggie's, Kevin roared, "I'm not Michael McManus or Joey Duggan or any of the others you thugs have driven out."

Of quick and stealthy hand, Duggie plunged a second knife into Kevin's gut. Kevin let out a howl, and before stumbling back, poked his fingers into Duggie's eyes. Unleashing ferocious slugs and kicks, Duggie flew at Kevin blindly, and raging with adrenaline, Kevin fought back, pasting Duggie several times in the face and neck with his enormous fists.

Wilder had come to consult an electrician, but he walked in on a brawl. Seeing blood spurt as obscenities flew, he jumped to separate the men on the locker room floor. At once he noticed Duggie's loyalist tattoos.

"He fucking attacked me," Duggie brayed as Wilder threw him off Kevin. "He attacked me for no reason!"

"The hell I did," Kevin panted, only now realizing the seriousness of his wound. He glanced up at Wilder, "You better get me to casualty."

"You fucking started it, you filthy psycho scum!" Duggie threw one last swing of his fist. "Look at me, I'm goddamn battered." He tottered woozily and dramatically fell against the wall. "Get me a surgeon before I die!"

"You won't get off this time, Knack," Kevin pledged.

"Wanna bet?" Duggie jeered.

"Shut up both of you! We'll sort this out later." Wilder nabbed Duggie by the scruff of the neck.

"You're taking me to a doctor, right?" Knack whined.

Wilder threw Duggie out of the locker room. "Get out and stay out!" Then he ran to help Kevin.

"I've talked to several of the workmen, and they say Knack has been threatening Catholic workers for weeks. I want him fired before he hurts anyone else," Wilder insisted to Hunter before going home the next evening.

"Do you have any proof or do you just have a grudge against Protestants?"

"Hunter, Knack is a known member of the ULF."

"Relax, Declan, relax. The matter has been settled. The RUC told me Kevin Murphy is a bully, a lager lout, and a suspected Provisional."

"Oh for christsake, Hunter, don't pull that shit. You know what's going on here. Kevin Murphy is being slandered and forced out of work."

"Here at the Gov we neither slander nor coerce," Hunter snapped. "We are equal opportunity employers and require only that our employees behave like humans. Mr. Murphy is a baboon, and Mr. Knack was defending himself. Dreadful, a thug that large picking on a poor little fellow like Duggie."

"Hunter, 'poor little Duggie' stabbed Kevin Murphy for being Catholic!"

"Mr. Knack has the right to protect himself. On the other hand, Mr. Murphy's attack was unprovoked; it was Murphy who brandished the knives and ended up stabbing himself. The RUC has already charged him with assault."

Wilder smacked his fist down on Hunter's desk. "And what about Knack? Was he charged?"

"Certainly not. He'll be back at work tomorrow."

"This is an outrage!" Wilder exploded.

"This is reality, Declan. Will there be anything else?"

"I came to thank you for saving my life, mick." Duggie leaned into Wilder's office several evenings later. "That big chimp woulda fucking killed me if you hadn't walked in." When Wilder didn't respond, Duggie went on, "I've seen you on the site with Reason McGuinness. Is she special to you, mick?"

Wilder stared upon Duggie in silence, but his blood ran cold at the mention of Reason. What if she ended up alone late at night with Duggie and his knife?

"Aw, don't worry, Decky, I won't hurt her. She's been dead nice to me," Duggie grinned, baring his brown teeth. "Is it true you're Brendan O'Neill's brother?"

"Get out of here, Knack," Wilder growled.

"The ULF says Brendan had a dick big as a horse. Is yours that big, mick?" Duggie plucked his upper lip in thought. "Aren't you afraid you'll be next?"

"Did you kill Brendan?" Wilder asked with deadly calm.

"Who *me?* I'm a fucking saint. But you better watch out, mick. We know where *you* live too." Duggie gave Wilder a one-finger salute and slinked from sight.

Chapter Thirty

It was late-September when Albie Coogan met Wilder on the Falls in the rain.

"Decky lad," he hailed, stepping up his gait to join his young friend, "I've that information on Michael Patrick you wanted. Come to my house and have a cup of tea. Miserable day. Bad for the joints."

"Are you still taking those tablets for your arthritis I gave you?"

"Aye. How's Fiona getting on then?" Albie puffed as he and Wilder hiked towards Andersonstown.

"Better. Morris is living with her now you know, and that helps. But she has a woman living with her who's helped most of all. You know how women are so able to console one another. She's been very good for Fiona."

"Aye, the McGuinness girl. Heard all about her at Ruairi's funeral so I did. Is she the reason you're interested in Michael McGuinness?"

"Yes. Any chance she's related to him?"

"None at all, lad. Like I told you, Michael had only his wee dad and mum as family. Both of them passed away years ago, and Michael died young."

"I'd hoped by some miracle she really was Irish," was Wilder's soft-spoken disappointment.

"We came up with everything we could on your man." Albie handed Wilder a mug of tea then settled himself into a chair by the fire. "He was born in County Armagh, but his parents moved to Belfast when his father got a job working the ferry between Belfast and Oslo. Michael's mother was sickly, so he spent most of his time smuggled aboard the ships with his dad. He skipped school for weeks at a time, finally dropped out at thirteen; education meant nothing to him or his da. The sea was their life. By the time he was sixteen, Michael could scarcely read or write, but your man was a born artist. Give him any material and he'd sculpt it into something magic. A friend of mine remembers Michael sitting in the park making wee sailboats of tin for him and his da to wear around their necks.

"When Michael was seventeen his dad lost his job, never sailed or worked again. He and Michael returned to West Belfast, and Michael got a job hauling coal. He used to come traipsing up the Falls Road looking black as a panther, and he'd be grinning at everyone he saw. He was a very nice young fella. He was also a republican. In the 50's and 60's the flame of the Ra was dying, but there were still a few die-hards determined to maintain the struggle, and Michael was one of them. He wandered back and forth between Belfast and Armagh, alternately sculpting and getting himself involved in incidents along the border. Apparently he taxied IRA men involved with the Border Campaign.

"As a driver he was mad they say, had no fear, and he was notorious for wild getaways. In any stolen car or lorry he'd go blazing through clouds of dust, and if the peelers were after him, all the better. I heard several tales of him being chased by the Armagh police through wee country towns, and he and his passengers always got away. But in '62 the IRA laid down its arms and all but disbanded. Nobody seems quite sure where Michael settled after that. Some say he moved to Armagh City. Others say he stayed here in West Belfast.

"One thing is certain, he remained an activist. If there was mischief along the border, Michael had a hand in it. But his luck ran out. He and two other lads were throwing petrol bombs at the barracks outside of Armagh City. All three were shot by the peelers. They threw the men's bodies out in the gutter to be picked up by their relatives. But nobody came for Michael. The old boys say Michael was brought home to

Belfast by a priest. His father was dead by then you see, and his mum refused to go to Armagh for Michael's body because he'd been involved with the IRA. Then the Church refused to grant Michael a Christian burial, his being associated with the Ra and all. He was laid to rest in Milltown without a proper funeral, poor critter, and nobody came to tell him good-bye. And he was only twenty seven years old. That's your man McGuinness, Decky."

Wilder shook his head, smiling at the notion that Reason and her blue-blooded mother could be so basely related. "No question about it, Albie, I was barking up the wrong family tree on this one. But who erected that cross for Michael in Milltown? It had to have cost a fortune. And what about the words written on the cross?"

"I haven't seen the inscription, son."

"*Bí mo leannán, is mo leannán sa amháin. Saor Eire, grá mo chroí.* 'Be my lover, my only lover. Free Ireland, my darling,'" Wilder translated.

Albie tapped his chin. "I couldn't tell you who's responsible for that, Decky, but old Albie will find out what he can."

Chapter Thirty-One

Sunday afternoon Jillie drove down the Antrim Road bending Reason's ear. "That Decky's a prince to loan me his car. Whenever I need anything, anything at all, he's right there to help me. Aren't I the luckiest of women? Both Declan and Kieran have made living in Belfast the best time of my life."

"I'm sure they have." From behind her dark glasses, Reason studied Jillie's naturally dark and thick eyelashes and shiny auburn ponytail. Was she really that pretty? Reason tried to convince herself the answer was no. But yes, Jillie was arresting with her classic features and haunting indigo eyes. But she was tower-tall and noodle thin. Maybe Wilder preferred that.

"I can't believe September is nearly gone," Jillie moped. "We won't see the sun again for weeks, and oh, how the north wind cuts through you in the wintertime here."

"Does it snow?"

"Now and then, and it makes Belfast beautiful; like it's wearing diamonds and ermine. I'm glad you could come today. I've been meaning to have you over for weeks, but it takes me forever to get organized...well, except when it comes to my work. I thought before heading over to the Falls you'd enjoy driving up to Cave Hill." Jillie pointed north as she sped around Carlise Circus and entered the Crumlin Road. "There's a lovely view of the city from up there."

Clifton Street was one of the arteries feeding into North Belfast out of the city centre. It was a short few blocks uphill that spilled abruptly into a congested roundabout called Carlise Circus and split in a narrow V into the Crumlin Road and the Antrim Road. Both roads continued over the hills into the pastures of County Antrim. Up, up, up the Crumlin Road climbed above Belfast, but other than being steeper, it looked the same as the Antrim Road to Reason. Jillie was quick to point out the difference. The Antrim Road was Catholic. The Crumlin Road was Protestant.

"It's another one of those subtle distinctions of tribe," Jillie explained. "They say you can tell a man's affiliations by which side of the Clifton Road he walks on. If he walks on the left, he's heading up the Crumlin Road, so he's a Prod. If he walks on the right, he's heading up the Antrim Road so he's a Catholic."

"Isn't the Shankill around here somewhere?" Reason remembered Duggie Knack mentioning the Shankill and the Crumlin Road.

"Yes. Do you want to see it?"

Reason wasn't sure. "I've heard so much about it…like it's the center of evil in this city."

"The center of evil is in the men not the neighborhoods, Reason, but I'll drive you down the Shankill to show you not only the Catholics are down and out in Ulster."

The Shankill was similar to the New Lodge only its cramped, treeless conduits of brick rowhouses were longer, rougher, bleaker, sadder. And not exclusive to the Catholic areas, the Shankill was blocked-up, torn down, abandoned and littered with trash. Tattered Union Jacks flapped atop a few shops, and in some places the curbs were painted red, white and blue. The graffiti touted victory to the ULF. **Fuck the IRA** was a frequent sentiment on scores of dead walls. And as Reason glanced right and left, the Protestants she saw looked the same as the Catholics. Same clothes, same dark hair and fair eyes, same smiles, same babies and young mothers, same dogs and pigeons and gossiping grannies. A Protestant fruit stand looked like a Catholic fruit stand, no better no worse. The butchers and bakers could have served either side, and the Presbyterian churches looked like any other churches to Reason. A rose garden could be seen here or there, and lace curtains softened the rowhouse windows.

But some things were noticeably absent. There were no prowling police and patrols of soldiers, no vehicle checkpoints, no surveillance cameras, no tanks nor Army barracks and watchtowers. No one monitored the Protestants and their violent marauders. And somehow to Reason, the young men in denim collected on the street corners seemed more frightening and fierce than the Catholic men. She'd heard the history of the Shankill residents marching up the Falls Road to burn down houses and terrorize Catholics. She knew the Shankill was home to the ULF, and weekly there was news of ULF men driving through Catholic neighborhoods, opening fire on the houses. As Reason stared around uncomfortably, blood-stains and death plots came to mind.

Like Jillie had read Reason's thoughts, she asked, "Have you ever heard of the Shankill Butchers?"

Reason had not.

"They were a gang of Protestant Jack the Rippers. For seven years they prowled the Clifton Road at night, bagging Catholics off the street and gutting them with a double-edged butcher knife. They could tell a Catholic by what side of the Clifton Road he or she walked on. All those years the Catholics in North Belfast lived in terror. But," Jillie continued in her silky deep voice, "the worst thing about the Butchers was what they called 'Rompering.' They'd drag a chap into the back of a black taxi, drive him to a pub, and torture him to death in front of an audience of cheering loyalists. Passersby reported hearing screams of 'Kill me! Kill me!' coming from those awful back rooms."

Sickened, Reason told Jillie to stop. But she had to know, "What happened to them?"

"The IRA got some of them, others went to jail. But there are still plenty of murderers living around here. Why just a few months ago, a wee man from Dublin wandered into the Shankill. When the loyalists found out he was a taig from the South, they stabbed him to death. Gosh, I wonder what the tourist bureau has to say about that?"

Reason looked at Jillie, perplexed. How casually the Irishwoman related grisly tales. Like mass murder was gossip. She seemed to relish the stories, telling them with the hint of a smile, like somewhere in the horror there was a punch line. And for an instant the cool hue of her eyes seemed cruel. Reason glanced away. The Shankill was playing games with her mind.

"Yes, it's definitely best to keep to your own turf," Jillie continued. "Lots of people here never leave their neighborhoods. I know Catholics who haven't been to the city centre in over twenty years. In fact, I know Catholics who have never even met a Protestant and vice versa. I suppose they prefer living apart. Other countries are tearing down walls; Belfast can't slap them up fast enough."

On the top of the Crumlin Road Reason could see all of Belfast, from Cave Hill to Bangor to Carrickfergus, and in the afternoon sun the old city shone. She especially liked the rays glistening like pinpoint flares on the lough. "I'll bet its pretty up here at night."

"Last Christmas a Cure agent brought three Provies up here," Jillie offered more local history, "shot all three of them point blank and threw their bodies down the hill. Hardly a lover's leap."

Jillie's house was number six in a red row near the bottom of the Falls and consisted of four rooms; kitchen, bedroom, bathroom, parlor. An earthquake of clothing covered the furniture. Reason wondered where to sit.

Jillie pointed to a stool in the kitchen. "Just push those newspapers off and have a seat. Care for some wine? You like Chianti? Me too." Before Reason spoke Jillie was slapping the wine into her hand.

"Ooh, what's this?" Reason spotted a little flask on the counter and twisted off its cap. "Mmmm, I love perfume. Is this some kind of bath oil?"

At first startled then smiling, Jillie plucked the bottle of patchouli from Reason and dropped it in a drawer. "It's ointment for the dog. Toby?" She called out the back door. "Toby, come meet our guest."

A bullet of wiggling white fired inside. Jillie's West Highland terrier plowed through the clutter into Reason's lap.

"How old is he?" Reason managed to ask over the whirling, wiggling dog.

"Ten. I've had Toby ever since I moved away from home. He's my best friend." Jillie lifted the dog from Reason and kissed his whiskers. "I love him so much I'd die without him."

Juggling an Italian dinner on paper plates, the women ate on the floor along with Toby who was served his own plate of gnocchi.

"Have you ever been in love, Reason?"

"Yes."

"Many times?"

"Twice. How about you?"

"I've never loved anyone, well except for Toby, but I suppose he doesn't count. I was born without a heart, or so I've been told by the men I've known."

"What about Kieran? You love him. And you care about Declan."

"Och, only a fool would fall in love with that pair," came Jillie's derision. "I adore Kieran. He always brings me flowers and tells the best jokes, and he's gentle, so many men aren't gentle," then her face fell, "but I don't love him. You know what love is for me, Reason? It's a luxury suite in hell; everything is perfect until I have to check out and pay the bill. No sir, I can't love Kieran or Declan; both will be gone in a year."

Reason thought Jillie was being fickle. "Where will they be?"

"Dead or in prison." Jillie grew fatalistic, "That's the thing about Belfast, you have to be half in love with death to survive it…nothing lasts here, nothing…except the rain and the British Army."

Her unexpected answer baffled Reason. "Why are you still seeing Kieran and Declan if there's no future with them?"

"For the sex. You really should do it with Decky. You'd be amazed by what he can do with his tongue. Or maybe you already know." She focused on Reason with great curiosity. "Have you slept with Decky?"

"I hardly know the man, Jillie. Why do you ask?"

Jillie smiled like she knew the truth. "I just thought maybe you had. Declan's been going out of his way to see you instead of me ever since you got here. You fascinate him. Haven't you noticed the way he looks at you?"

Reason shifted, ill at ease. "No."

"He makes love to you with his eyes. It's your legs and breasts; you've a nice set of both. Well, anyway you really ought to give him a go. I like seeing Declan because he's a cardiologist." Jillie made fun, "Surely *he* can find a heart in me."

"And what if he finds it only to break it?" Reason suggested cynically.

"Better to suffer than feel nothing at all."

Just then the paper boy arrived to collect for the newspaper, and when Jillie opened the front door, Toby shot outside. Down the sidewalk and into the street he bounded. Seconds later he collided with a Land Rover tank.

"Oh God, is he dead? *He's dead!*" Jillie tried to run to the dog then cowered in sobs. "I don't want to see him!" She retreated into the rowhouse, into her bedroom, and slammed the door.

Steeled for the worst, Reason trudged into the street where the dog lay motionless. But he wasn't dead. Gingerly she picked him up.

The Land Rover pulled to the side of the road. A young policeman jumped out. "I didn't see the wee dog, miss. Is he dead?" It was Ian Wright.

"No, but he's hurt. Where's the closest veterinarian, do you know?"

"There's a veterinary clinic open on Sundays near the city centre. Here, miss, give me the wee dog. We'll take him to the clinic."

Reason drew the dog closer to her chest, thinking she wouldn't trust the RUC with a dead dog much less a wounded one.

But Ian held out his arms. "Honest, miss, I'll do what I said. I'll take the dog and I'll be right careful and see to it he's helped. Come on, love, that dog is hurt and he'll bite you and then you'll be needing a doctor as well."

The dog whimpered and squirmed and let go a frightful howl, and tearfully, unsure what else to do, Reason thrust Toby into Ian's hands. "Just hurry."

Ian hugged the dog to his jacket and ran back to the Land Rover. As the police drove off Reason felt sick; she had entrusted Jillie's precious pet to fiends.

Two hours later Ian returned to Jillie's door. Jillie was still locked in her bedroom, crying. "The dog will be all right," Ian told Reason. "He's at the vet's on Hannah Street. You can pick him up in three days."

Reason looked shocked. Not at the news but that an RUC man had done something decent. "Thank you," she said grudgingly, inching away, shutting the door, fearing further discourse would incite her arrest.

Ian saw the contempt in Reason's face and walked away knowing any good deed he did as a policeman would be seen as a threat. And he wondered, as he often wondered, what he was doing in this line of work. The pay was extraordinary, but the price the pay exacted was exorbitant. He had this hopeless little hope that he could change things, that he could be moral amidst madness, but in his heart he knew all that would change was himself.

When Reason knocked on the door, Jillie cried, "Go away!"

"But Jillie, Toby is OK. He's hurt, but he'll heal."

Abruptly the sobbing stopped. Jillie slapped open her door and threw her arms around Reason. "It's a miracle! You're an angel…thank you…thank you, oh thank you," she sobbed and laughed. "May I go see him?"

"I suppose so. Tomorrow."

"Oh my, my, look at you! You're muddy and bloody…your clothes are ruined." Jillie began crying again.

"I don't care about that. I'm just glad Toby will be all right." Reason walked Jillie into the parlor. "Everything is going to be fine now."

Jillie shoved aside a mountain of books and pulled a fifth of tequila from the bookcase. "Want some, love?"

"No thanks."

Jillie sloshed the liquor into a cup and downed it in one shot. "You must think I'm mad," she said, still crying. "It's just that Toby and I have been through everything together…everything. He's always here for me and he likes me no matter who I am or what I do. I guess if I have a heart, it belongs to him." Quietly she laughed, "God, how pathetic. But dogs are so forgiving, you know? And now Toby's alive because of you." She raised a toast to Reason. "You're very kind. How can I ever repay you?"

"I didn't do anything, Jillie." Reason recounted what happened. Of the young policeman she said, "I didn't want to give him the dog, but I didn't know what else to do. Don't kill me for trusting the RUC."

"You and the peelers saved Toby's life, that's all that matters."

"This cop seemed genuinely nice. And so young, twenty at best."

"Poor baby. The RUC will eat him alive. And he'll get his ass kicked for helping a taig. Did you ask his name?"

"No."

Jillie poured herself more tequila, taking a thoughtful sip. "I'll have to find a way to thank him."

Chapter Thirty-Two

"Yo, Cromwell, got a minute?" Wilder signaled from the back of Cain's studio.

Cain peered up from his canvas and motioned Wilder to join his class. "Welcome to our phantasmal world of Salvador Dali. Care to try your hand?"

"Ha, you'd flunk me. I need to talk to you."

"Now?"

"I only have an hour before I need to be back at the Gov."

"Give me five minutes. I'm in the middle of painting the perfect leering eyeball. *Blood Shot* I'm calling it. Come see."

Wilder weaved through the students up to Cain's easel. "That's revolting!" was his reaction to the oversized eye drawn bleeding and staring through a pitch fork.

"Thank you," Cain bowed. "A good Surrealistic painting shocks and awakens the senses with its distortion and mutilation of form, rather like a very bad dream. Frankly, I despise Surrealism," he maintained behind his hand, "but it's a kick to teach."

"Did you dream this?" Wilder wondered, viewing the disturbing work as an insight into Cain's mind.

"I'd have to be bloody twisted to dream such things. No, no, I saw a man looking like this once," Cain disclosed matter-of-factly. "He had just been shot through the head. I thought I'd give it to Bernard Thunder to hang over his mantle."

"Is that supposed to be funny?" Wilder barked.

"Do you see me laughing?" Cain's eyes fell back on his canvas then he instructed his class, "You have ten more minutes to paint your secret fears. Now remember, have fun with this." He returned to his painting. "Just let me touch up this ruptured vessel, then we'll talk."

"How's your finger? I haven't really seen you since that night."

Cain displayed his finger and regarded Wilder with his Golden Retriever sort of sad eyes. "There was some nerve damage. Sometimes I can't feel my finger, and sometimes I can't move it, and I've lost some of my fine brush control. But the good news is I can still juggle."

Wilder inspected Cain's hand. "In time you should get sensation and coordination back. I'm really sorry this happened."

"What the hell, if Van Gogh could lose part of his ear, surely I can lose part of my finger. Is it still pouring outside? I was out at noon and nearly washed home to England."

"Yeah, it's bleak. It must be October in Belfast."

"You know, Wilder, we were damn cracked to leave California for this wrath-of-God weather. There now," Cain surrendered his paint brush and reviewed his gaping, gashed eye, "the finishing disgrace. Shall we go?"

"Did you really see that pitchfork scene or were you just kidding around?"

"I wasn't addicted to cocaine because my life was happy, Wilder."

"But where in London would you see something that gruesome?"

Cain looked away. "I've re-done my office since you were last here. I painted my walls heliotrope. Nice color heliotrope. Doesn't it sound poetic? Heliotrope."

Knowing it was useless to question Cain about his past, Wilder walked silently beside Cain down the old hallway. "I've always liked Christ Church," he said. "When I was a kid this place was out of my league. My school would bring us here on field trips, and I was totally in awe of the students. But never in a million years did I think I'd be college-educated."

"You're lucky your family moved to America." Cain ushered Wilder into his office and offered him a seat on a park bench. "Care for a drink?

I've some Scotch here in my drawer." Cain slapped his desk in high humor. "Finest Scotch money can buy. H.C. gives it to me every Christmas. I use it to clean my brushes."

Laughing, Wilder declined. "I like your purple walls."

"They aren't purple! They're heliotrope. Did you see I re-wired the light in your study?"

Wilder shook his head, he hadn't noticed, but then Cain moved through his personal life and property like the Invisible Man.

Noting Wilder's scowl, Cain exclaimed, "Well, there's just so much to fix at your house!"

"While you were in the den, did you take those three photographs from my desk drawer? That's why I'm here. I noticed they were missing last night and figured you..."

"Why would I want your pictures of Reason? I have my own vivid images of her thank you very much."

"Oh, this isn't good...who would want those pictures of her? Oh my God. That night at my house when you got shot...the Cure. Shit! How does this guy keep bypassing my alarm?"

"He calls the security company, has them shut off your alarm, then he picks your locks and walks in. Maybe you misplaced the pictures, Wilder."

"No. I'd just been looking at them. I should have thrown them away." Wilder jumped to his feet, cursing his carelessness. "I should have gotten rid of every trace of Reason. Christ, I wish she hadn't come here. How could my father be so *stupid?*"

Cain fiddled with a cluster of charcoal sticks. "Reason tells me you and she are barely speaking. Is it...because of me?"

"No. And no, she won't come between us now that you and she are involved." Wilder acted immune, like it didn't hurt. "It's not like I wanted her back. You're seeing a lot of her then?"

"Every day, and night," Cain said with pleasure.

"Lucky you." Wilder hoped Cain didn't detect it. The awful envy and frustration, and emptiness.

372 Reasonable Maniacs

But Cain was perceptive. "I swear to you, Wilder, I never meant to fall in love with her. I just wanted to get to know her, it was a game really…but then after Ruairi's funeral it got serious and it was too late to turn back."

"I don't blame you, Cain. I have to get back to the hospital."

"I'll be at My Lady's Leisure tomorrow if you want to come down. You haven't seen my Connemara ponies."

Wilder brightened at the prospect of the famed Celtic horses. "Won't Reason be there?"

"Not until tomorrow night."

"Tomorrow then. I'll be there."

"I want to see what you can do, O'Neill. Your dad tells me you were this hot shot polo player in Malibu. Dangerous sport. Not for the faint of heart."

"My parents had to tame the Fenian in me somehow," Wilder joked. "So they put me on a horse and gave me a mallet."

"Come down early. You can help me clean the stalls. You're laughing," Cain was as well. "Any horse lover knows a dose of manure nurtures the soul."

"Ah yes," Wilder nodded. Manure, the essence of heavenly horsedom. One whiff and his every whack of the mallet, every race round the bend, every rapturous slap in the saddle flooded back. "I'll know I'm dead in greener pastures when I'm face-to-face with the stars and there's the perfume of horses on the wind."

A sudden hush fell as Cain considered Wilder's words. "Spoken like a true Irishman," he said with unmistakable sorrow. "I'll always remember you said that."

*   *   *   *   *   *

Pea-sized ice mixed with the rain and pelted Reason's cheeks like gravel. A foul, frozen wind whipped her forward and pushed her down the Antrim Road. Of all the days to be meeting Kieran in the New

Lodge. In the four months she had been in Belfast she had never asked and Wilder had never offered to show her his former home. She knew it wasn't because Wilder was ashamed of his roots, rather because she remained a Wellworth-Howell in his eyes and wasn't Irish enough to share his past. So when Kieran offered to take her around, Reason jumped at the chance. Even now, as the north wind sent her reeling, she was anxious for the tour.

She met Kieran in a pub with no name. It was a box of four rooms attached to twelve rowhouses like their vacant caboose. Entering through a caged doorway, Reason noticed a group of men hunched before a fire, and there sat Kieran in their midst calling her to join them. Stools and captain's chairs circled pine tables, and through the smoke she saw a bar, that looked more like an altar, serving nothing but lager and stout. Beyond the bar stood a cooker piled in sausage rolls, and beside the cooker perched a young woman puffing a cigarette and tippling a Guinness in between attempts to master the flute.

"Not exactly James Galway, is she?" Kieran handed Reason a lager and positioned her close to the fire. "Brendan used to be a musician here. Decky and I would sit by this very hearth with Liam and listen to Bren play his flute. Decky learned to play the tin whistle right here at this fire. And Liam would sneak us each a wee shot of Guinness; aye, that was cracker. Old Liam was our hero." Kieran stared into the flames, enjoying the memories.

"The first time Decky came back in here after coming home, I thought he was going to cry. It was hard for him you see. This is the last place he saw Brendan and Liam alive. He still comes here sometimes, and everybody knows him from when he was knee-high. Can you believe he comes in here from the Malone? Whoever thought our Declan would live out the *Malone!*" Kieran smacked his thigh. "Decky would never tell you this, but when Liam wasn't looking, he used to sneak around in here begging for money for his family, and it never bothered him to be a beggar. He's always been practical that way, doing what he has to do to accomplish his goals. Yes sir, he'd slink man to man, and whether they gave him a shilling or a clout to the ear, he'd give 'em a grand wee bow and a handshake." Kieran downed the last of his pint and licked the blonde foam off his lips. "Come on then, love. Finish your drink and I'll show you around."

A dismal sunset hung over dismal circumstance as Reason and Kieran left the pub. Reason opened her umbrella. Kieran walked in the rain. The rain rushed in rivulets down the streets of the New Lodge towards the docks, washing rubble and litter over Reason's boots. And the odor on the wind announced it was Friday; fried fish. In the heart of the maze of red brick they came upon Upper Forest Street; a skinny channel of identical flats crushed together like a roll of pennies along a cracked, crooked sidewalk. The units were flat and the brickwork red-and-white-checkered making the row of downhill houses look like a ribbon of plaid. Each battered brick doorway was a narrow white arch with a ruddy keystone over the wooden door, and each of the flats had three slits for windows; one beside the arched entry and two like eyes too close together above the door. From the black roofs pot-bellied chimneys ran streams of smoke, and in the downpour, the smoke sank through the power lines overhead and filtered to the dirty ground.

Through the rain Kieran pointed, "Here's Decky's house."

Reason viewed the simple doorway through the sleet and deepening dusk. It looked like all the other doorways. "How can you tell?"

Kieran watched Reason's face closely, monitoring her reaction to the New Lodge and Wilder's austere background. Her eyes told of affection, loyalty and sympathy, and Kieran was pleased. "See that chip in the keystone above the door there?" He directed Reason's eyes. "Decky put that there with an empty bottle of cider when he was nine. That shows you how much progress has been made around here."

Through a sheer-curtained window Reason could see a sparse parlor off a steep staircase. The coal fire was small and helped light the room. The walls were plain and white.

"There's a wee back room and kitchen behind the parlor there," Kieran peeked inside over Reason's umbrella. "Upstairs there are two bedrooms. Hard to imagine all the O'Neills and McCartans fitting in there on Christmas and Easter, but we did. So what do you think of our Declan now?" Kieran inquired, pushing Reason further along Upper Forest Street.

Reason was thinking *Desmond* O'Neill was a remarkable man for aspiring beyond the New Lodge and making a name for himself in L.A. She thought Dessie not Liam was the hero. And she was thinking Wilder was extremely fortunate to have been lifted from privation to privilege. "I think he's done all right for himself."

"Oh aye, he's the pride of the clan so he is."

"Where did you and your family live?" Reason asked.

"Two streets over. It looks just like this, only our door didn't have a chip."

"Kieran, what did Liam do for a living?"

"He was like me, took odd jobs…window cleaner, carpenter, grave digger…did whatever he could for a few quid a week. Steady work has never been easy for us to find here."

"Was he nice?"

"Aye, if he liked you. But if you weren't fire and brimstone against the Brits, he'd have nothing to do with you. You've heard how he turned on his own son. Poor Dessie never belonged in Belfast. Liam used to insist Desmond was a changeling."

"Were Brendan and Merry ashamed of Dessie as well?"

"They loved him, but they sided with Liam. But not our Declan. He'd look Granda Liam dead in the eye and repeat Dessie's latest jokes, and when Granda wouldn't laugh, Decky would promise Liam that Des would make the whole world laugh one day. 'Can you do that, Granda, can you?' he used to nag. He's a loyal one our Decky. Stuck to his father like a Velcro fan club."

"And now here he is back in Belfast just like his brother and sister."

"That'll be killing Dessie to be sure. We were all fucking boggled when Des let Declan leave the States without a fight."

"Could he have stopped him?"

"No."

"Did Liam like Declan?"

"I don't think he wanted to. Decky is a lot like his father you see, irritated the bejeezus out of Liam, but Declan had a winning way about him that Liam couldn't resist. He loved learning our history and language. And he loved hearing Liam tell and re-tell his stories about the war for independence. Long after the rest of us had gotten bored, Decky was hanging on Liam's every word."

"And what did Liam think when Declan became a Yank?"

"It didn't bother him much. He knew Dec would come back." Kieran blew on his wet hands and drew up the collar of his coat. "I'm freezing. Let's shoot back to the pub." He bent to see Reason's face beneath her umbrella. "I forgot to tell you, my mum is expecting you to come home with Morris and me for a meal tonight. You'll come, won't you?"

Reason had never visited the McCartan's home up the Falls beyond Milltown. "I'd like that."

Nora McCartan kept a house like Fiona's. Clean, comfortable and decorated in trinkets. On one wall of the parlor was the obligatory row of photographs showing Nora's and Eamonn's seven children and ten grandchildren. On the opposite wall above the coal fire was a Sacred Heart and crucifix.

Reason had seen much of Dessie O'Neill's oldest sister at Fiona's. Nora O'Neill McCartan was a chatty, hopeful woman who bustled through life with good humor and pep. Her children, grandchildren and famous brother were her treasures, and despite the endless war and tragedies, Nora remained upbeat. Like Kieran, nothing could keep her down. In contrast, Eamonn McCartan was a tired soul; old too young, fifty five and faded. Of his four sons, two were in prison for bombing an RUC station, one was a Provo, and one, his eldest, was dead. Too many funerals, too many prisons, too many rampages had raged through his life, and he was the first to admit he had lost most of his mettle, much of his mind, and the whole of his heart. He couldn't remember the boy or the man within him, he could only feel the loss of humanity around him. But Eamonn McCartan wasn't bitter, just brittle with resignation.

"Got stopped on the Falls again today," Eamonn said as he joined his family at the table. "I was coming up from the shop with a bag of sweets for Morris. Two squaddies grabbed me and asked to see what I had in the bag. I showed them, and they told me the mint sticks were weapons."

Reason let go a laugh, "No way."

"Och no, love, it's the law. They call it the Prevention of Terrorism Act. The security forces can declare anything suspicious a weapon."

"And peppermint sticks are suspicious?" snickered Reason.

"Aye. The soldiers accused me of intending to sharpen the tips and use them as daggers. They kept me standing there in the rain for over an hour. And the whole time they were cuffing me about and threatening to blow my head off for carrying a concealed weapon. Finally they threw the candy onto the sidewalk and crushed it."

"You shoulda kicked them bastards in the balls!" Morris piped, waving his knife around like a sword."

"*Morris!*" Nora swatted his curls and glared at Kieran. "It's a fine language you're teaching your son."

Without further ado, Eamonn bowed his head and said grace. Fried cod, boiled potatoes, brussel sprouts and soda farls were served. The topic of the Troubles found its way to the table as well. Reason asked about an Irish harp with 'Long Kesh' carved in its wooden base resting on the mantle.

"My daddy made that in the Kesh," Morris proudly proclaimed.

"Morris, we have a guest!" Nora scolded again. "We'll have none of that talk at the supper table."

"It's all right, Nora." Eamonn McCartan pushed aside his finished meal and winked at Reason. "Reason knows about these things. She saw what they did to our Ruairi."

"Is Long Kesh a monastery?" Reason thought that sounded right.

"Just about!" Kieran quipped. "It's a prison south of Belfast."

"You were in prison?" Reason gaped at Kieran.

"I've been in and out of them all here. But Long Kesh was home for ten glorious years," Kieran offered his story freely. "I was eighteen years old and got arrested with two of my mates for possession of an AK-47. I'd be lying if I said we weren't planning on using it. We were off to ambush an Army patrol when we were stopped by the RUC."

"Och! You and your ancient history!" Nora jumped from her seat at the table and began clearing the dishes. "Sickens the heart of me, the very heart of me." Jerking Morris with her, she hurried into the kitchen.

Kieran struck a match to his cigarette. "Going to Long Kesh was a fact of life in the 70's and 80's."

His easy-going manner amazed Reason. "How can you be so casual about going to jail?"

"I joined the Ra knowing prison was inevitable. The way I saw it, I could live in Long Kesh or live in the prison of this occupied city. When I was fourteen, right after Decky moved to the States, I saw my brothers being dragged from our house during the Army's dawn raids, and by the time I was fifteen they were dragging me out as well."

"The soldiers wrecked our house three times in one year," Eamonn spoke up, his cheeks growing red, the cigarette between his fingers flicking ashes around. "They threatened to rape my wife and my daughters, and on all three occasions they hauled me and my boys to a barracks and beat us for four days. And they starved us. They spit in our tea and pissed on our food. When Kieran was sixteen the soldiers lifted him right off the Antrim Road, took him to the same barracks, hung him up by his feet and beat him with a whip. With a whip," Eamonn repeated mournfully, stretching a hand to rub Kieran's arm. "And the RUC wouldn't lift a finger to help us. 'Gettin' what we Paddies deserved,' they said. None of my four boys had done anything except be born Catholic, but the Army insisted they were Provos."

"The irony is, we weren't IRA men until the Brits provoked us into it," Kieran came back with his unshakable calm. "My dad here was forced at gunpoint twice to quit working at the factory so a Prod could have his job, and twice the RUC did nothing about it. My oldest brother was shot and beaten by Prods from Tiger's Bay, and my brother, not the Prods, was sent to jail for rioting. He died there. Starting in 1970, we were threatened and knocked about every single day by the Army, and the RUC went right along with the discrimination and abuse year after year. Just look at what happened to my dad today on the Falls; we're still being harassed." Kieran sucked his cigarette and spat back its smoke.

"I got tired of marching for peace and never being listened to in this city of big mouths and deaf ears. I got tired of marching for civil rights and getting shot at and clubbed and gassed. I got tired of being told to fucking know my place. And I realized no matter how many miles I marched or how many bricks or petrol bombs I threw, I couldn't beat the Brits unless I used force like they were using force. I mean, what other choice is there when you have no say in the government and the government refuses to listen? The Brits came to the Six Counties armed with machine guns and tanks, and they gunned us down in our neighborhoods; they ripped apart our houses; they threw us in jail. All because we were Irish Catholics daring to demand our fair share. And all we had to protect ourselves were our voices and fists, because in 1969, the IRA was dead."

"Listen to me, *listen*. In the early 60's the IRA was dormant, about to die," Eamonn contended in his soft, tired voice. "It had only a few die-hard members who had grown tired. They had laid down their guns and saw no reason to pick them back up. Then the Catholics started marching for equal rights, the Prods went berserk, and the Brits blasted into the North like your man Dirty Harry." Eamonn flung his cigarette into the fire with disgust, and before lighting up another, jabbed a finger eastward at England. "If England had stood up to the loyalists in '69, if England hadn't responded to the Catholic people's demands by shooting them dead in the streets, if England had listened to the peace marchers and worked to end Protestant domination in the Six Counties, there would be no IRA today. The IRA was dying, and England brought it back to life sure as hot air to embers."

"Aye, England is the IRA's best recruiter," Kieran agreed. "When I was seventeen, three British soldiers nabbed me from the New Lodge, threw me into their jeep and drove me over to the Shankill Road. It was summer and folks were out on the streets. The Brits pushed me out of the jeep in the middle of the Shankill and screamed, 'Here's a Provo bastard for you.' If I hadn't run like hell, I'd be dead. That's when I said, 'This is fuckin' it!' I joined the Ra the next day."

"His three brothers joined up right behind him," Eamonn added. "Nora was shattered, but I stood behind them, still do."

"I was young, but I wasn't full of romantic notions." Kieran inhaled his smoke, going on, "I knew I was a soldier and this was a war. I knew I wasn't going to get rich or be a hero, that I'd live on the run, that I'd probably wind up dead or in prison. But I also knew I had no other choice. I could have given in and lived with my eyes and ears closed like so many people around here have chosen to do, and that's fine for them. But I couldn't find peace in that. I knew if I surrendered without giving Ireland my best fight, I'd give oppression permission to advance. The minute you lie down for an oppressor you're under their boots forever, and I won't lie down. Let them call me a terrorist, let them call me a criminal and a thug, but *their* terrorism conceived the terrorist in me. I knew at eighteen, and I know now, there can be no peace, no progress for a partitioned Ireland."

"Aye, Reason love, there's only one thing you need to remember as you pass through this world." Eamonn tucked her hand into his and said, "Dissent makes good things better and bad things crumble. Plant that in your memory, love, plant that."

Reason's heart pounded as she pondered the drama of Kieran's life. Drawing her sweater tighter, she felt her father's little sailboat against her breast. What would Princeton-posh Kent say to find his daughter keeping treacherous company? "Why are you telling me all this?" she couldn't figure. Kieran was talking openly about a subject Wilder refused to discuss.

Before Kieran could answer, Morris escaped from the kitchen.

"Did you tell Reason about the Ra? Did you tell her about Bobby Sands? *Tiocfaidh ár lá, tiocfaidh ár lá,*" he zoomed around the dinner table chirping.

"Chocky are lah?" Reason parroted the Irish as best she could.

"It means 'Our day will come,'" Kieran translated before grabbing Morris by the elbow and ordering him to calm down.

"One day I'll shoot a Brit and go to Long Kesh!" Morris swaggered about.

"Morris, enough!" Nora put her foot down as she served trifle and tea. "I'll have no more talk of the Troubles in my house tonight."

"You were so honest about your lifestyle tonight," Reason told Kieran back at Fiona's. "Most men in your situation wouldn't say a fraction of what you've told me."

Kieran prodded the hearth coals with the tip of his boot. "I wanted you to see my point of view."

"I don't know how you stand your life. You're hunted, you're hated…"

"I'm not in this to be popular, Reason. Personally, I don't give a fuck what the world thinks…I know our struggle is the right thing to do. And I can't imagine living my life any other way."

"But don't you get tired of being abused, of life being nothing but conflict? Don't you want to give up?"

"Giving up isn't an option. All we can do is go on and fight the good fight. Try and try and try. Until we prevail."

"And what about Morris? Will this be his way of life as well?"

"One day England will withdraw from the Six Counties. Until then if Morris has to fight, he'll fight," the soldier decreed. "That isn't the way I want it, but that's the way it is."

Tears filled Reason's eyes. Lambs of God, sons of Eire. Oh, that terrible beauty! It was all so insane. So perfectly, logically insane. There was a justification for everything; a solution for nothing.

"I hear from Decky you've offered to help us." Kieran looked at Reason seated before him. "If you're willing, I have a job for you."

She regarded Kieran warily. "Like what?"

"Don't look so nervous, love. I won't have you doing anything that could hurt you. All we need is a driver."

She jumped to the first conclusion. "For a car bomb?"

"Don't be ridiculous," Kieran clucked with a roll of his eyes. "We need someone to deliver cargo across the border."

Reason's voice was barely audible, "Guns?"

Kieran copied her undertone, "No, men. You'll never know who they are or what they've done, and they won't know you so that keeps you safe. All you have to do is drive them one at a time to Dublin."

"Why me?"

"You're a Yank and you're a woman. Nobody is going to question your comings and goings."

"That's what Declan said the night we were stopped by the soldiers on the Falls Road."

"This won't be like that. You and your passenger will be tourists taking a lovely wee drive to the South."

"Are these men going down to the Republic to commit terrorist acts? I want no part of anything like that."

"No. They're to be smuggled out of Ireland before they get caught and are sent to prison."

One thought played through Reason's head; she could show Wilder once and for all she shared his passion. She could join his secret life. And never, *never* again could he call her a coward.

"This assignment would be less dangerous than harboring bullets or running through the tunnels. If you get stopped, you've done nothing more than give an Irishman a lift, and it's only four trips across the border. You'd be saving the lives of four young men, Reason. In your heart I know you want to help me and Declan."

"Is Declan involved in this?"

"He knows nothing about it. But he knows the four lads and wants them to be free."

"He wouldn't approve of this," Reason cautioned.

"Declan will never know. Will you do it?"

Reason glanced away to the water-striped windows. *"Can you say 'God Save Our Queen,' Duh-clan?"* The memory of Wilder lying face down in the rain with a rifle jammed to his head. *"He's obedient as my damn dog."* How she had cried that night on the Falls to see Wilder being beaten. *"You're a Catholic dog and we're your masters. Crawl like a dog, you bastard."* They dragged Ruairi away. *Boof boof.* *"You won't be beating your goddamn drum again, will ya, boy?"* *"Coward."* Reason turned to Kieran. "Yes."

Chapter Thirty-Three

By late morning the rain had become fog and a cruel wind lashed in off the Irish Sea. It was cold and damp with no trace of sun. Still Wilder headed to My Lady's Leisure, anxious to leave Belfast behind. The night before had been grueling. The IRA set off a bomb in the city centre. Wilder had been in the OR until dawn tending victims. And the irony didn't escape him, that the cause he supported came at a cost he abhorred. It was like he condoned the violence as long as it didn't bleed, and it filled him with anguish and rage and sorrow for his country. But driving into the hills helped. He stared up at the Mourne Mountains, regal and blue, and drove along the sea-hugging highway, and he wondered why he rarely visited pretty Down. His eyes moved over the open fields and up the brambly slopes, and he couldn't miss the Army garrison built atop the hill. Bolstered with towers of surveillance equipment it was one of the many eyes-and-ears forts monitoring the turbulent county. Then Wilder saw two helicopters bobbing over the rise, combing the farmlands. Pretty County Down.

Over 340 years ago, Oliver Cromwell gave County Down to his English peers. Now Wilder stood in the driveway of My Lady's Leisure. Gazing up at the elegant mansion, he wondered what an Irishman would have done with the land if a Cromwell hadn't seized it. He had to give the English aristocracy credit, the classical old estate provided a restful haven, and Cain kept it beautifully. Morning doves roosted on the rooftop and greeted Wilder with mournful cries. A cow mooed, a chicken ran by. There was a calico cat peeking around the side of the house, and the smell of horses and wet grain permeated the mist.

Wilder followed the calico's lead around the manor. Up the cobbled pathway leading from the back of the estate stood the stable and paddock and the little walled garden. Still trailing the cat, Wilder hiked to the stalls. He came upon Cain cleaning the hoof of a sorrel pony. Cain didn't say hello, but glad to see his friend, he handed Wilder a pick and pointed to the other pony. "Pissarro needs his hoofs cleaned."

Wilder gave both horses a pat, admiring their thick, flowing manes and feathery tails. A cross between an Arabian and an Andalusian, Connemara ponies were a small but hardy riding horse said to carry a thousand years of Irish strength within them. Having once run wild with the Celts along the rocky west coast of Eire, they breezed across hostile terrain with power and grace.

"These are fine horses you have, Cain." Wilder pulled up a stool behind Pissarro. "My father used to bet on the Connemara ponies whenever he was in Galway. More than once he lost our food money on the steeplechase," he said as he clasped the pony's fetlock.

"After you've cleaned Pissarro's hoofs you can help me soap the saddles and bridles."

"Is that why you asked me down here, to be your groom?" Wilder didn't mind, and it showed as he glimpsed sidelong at Cain.

"Gee, I like you, Wilder, but I don't want to marry you," Cain joked.

"You're a wise ass, Cromwell."

"There's an old horseman's rule, before you can ride you have to do your chores around the stable."

Wilder's heart leaped up. "We're going to ride?"

"Your Pissarro there is going to race my Gauguin," Cain challenged. "England against Ireland."

"You don't stand a chance, Cromwell." Wilder couldn't wait. "Did you know horse racing was the Celts favorite sport?"

"Why do you think I wanted you to see my ponies?"

"How long have you been a horseman?"

Cain arched a competitive grin, "I rode my first hunt when I was five."

Snowflakes whirled through the mist, and lowering clouds foretold rain. All the more reason to race. Wilder pitched his jacket onto a hay bail and shoved up the sleeves of his sweater before mounting Pissarro. On Gauguin, Cain led the way down a path behind the stable toward a field of tall grass dotted with hedgerows.

"We'll be racing church to church, that's from My Lady's Leisure to the borough of Pembroke. We'll canter to the top of that hill you see before us there," Cain described their course. "Below that is the first church. As soon as you can see the steeple of the church our race begins. From the churchyard we'll ride up and over the next hill, across seven pastures, and we'll keep going straight until we climb a ridge along the seashore. The very second you can see Southern Ireland across the lough, turn right. Ride straight along the ridge until you see the steeple of the second church. Our contest ends at the church gate. Did you get all that?"

Wilder repeated the directions to be certain. "You have the advantage knowing your way, Cromwell, but I bet I'll still win."

"Fifty pounds say you're wrong," Cain wagered.

"One hundred says I'm right."

"A fool and his money. You're on."

With the fervor of an Anglo-Irish war they contended across the rough country. Over hedge walls and fences, across farms and fields they raced, Cain in pursuit of Wilder, Wilder in pursuit of Cain. Up through the rain clouds, up to behold the green sea then along the windswept sea-ridge they galloped until their ponies were Pegasus, until their hearts were Daedalus, until the second steeple came into view. Then down the rolling knoll they plunged to the iron church gate. By a whip of Pissarro's tail, Wilder won.

"Well done!" Cain caught his breath. "How did you manage to beat me?"

"I'm an Irishman on an Irish horse in Ireland."

"Fifty more pounds says you can't beat me twice. I'll race you back to the first church. We'll walk the ponies home from there."

"Make it another hundred." Wilder gave his pony a nudge, and they were off again.

By the time they conquered the ridge again the rain had begun; at first drizzle flung off the sea then penny-sized drops then down splashed the sky. Used to inclement weather, the ponies didn't miss a beat as they hammered homeward neck and neck.

"Want to give up?" Cain shouted over the wind.

To which Wilder vowed, "Never!"

Triumphant as he skidded to a halt in the churchyard, Wilder raised his fists and cheered to have defeated his opponent twice. He spun to see Cain charging down the hill through black sheets of rain. "What happened to you?" he wondered as Cain and Gauguin straggled into the churchyard.

"Willful beast refused to go over that last hedge three bloody times!" Cain railed, shaking the water from his hair.

"The fairies got ye, lad. Put the evil eye on ye for trying to beat a Celt."

"It must have been the fairies who led you through this storm. I thought the rain would slow you down considering you don't know your way," Cain said as they trotted slowly home.

"But Pissarro here knows the way. All I did was ride the bends and let him run. You know I almost didn't make it down here today. The IRA bombed Castle Court last night." Wilder brushed the rain from his eyelashes and slicked back his dripping hair. "I spent most of the night reattaching a leg. It's nuts, Cain. It's all fucking nuts."

"You'll be needing dry clothes," Cain said as they crossed the foyer to the library.

"I have some jeans in my car, but I could use a shirt."

"This is my favorite room." Cain swung wide the mahogany doors like a king presenting his realm. "It's a model of the human soul. Look around, listen. Smell the eternity? The meaning of life, the secrets of the universe, the kingdom of God are all here in these books. And one day I'll have read every one."

Always impressed with the old library, Wilder turned in a circle. Hundreds of leather-bound books wall-to-wall beneath an ornately-coffered ceiling. As he scanned the shelves, the library's true marvel struck him. Countless books and not a speck of dust. Each leather volume had been cradled and cleaned. Wilder turned to comment and caught Cain gazing up at the ceiling like he gazed upon divinity. And Cain's undisguised love of County Down's farmland, of his ponies, of this room and each book affected Wilder deeply. He doubted any Irish native could revere the land more than this likable Cromwell. And looking around further, Wilder sensed the friendship Cain afforded him here in this sanctum sanctorum. The scholarly room wasn't a model of just any human soul. It was Cain's soul, and he welcomed Wilder inside.

"Do you think I'll ever read all these books, Wilder?"

"If you live to be a very old man."

"According to the Bible, Cain lived to be old as part of his punishment on Earth." Cain's long face appeared. "I'll be bloody well-read then. Come on." He trotted up the library stairs, through the hidden door in the paneling and up the corkscrew steps to his third-floor suite.

"This always knocks me out," Wilder said from the rear. "Hidden doors, hidden stairs…it's like being in a Vincent Price movie. Did you watch Vincent Price movies when you were a kid?"

"Wilder, living with my father was like starring in a Vincent Price movie."

In the master suite, Wilder saw the bed surrounded in candles and roses. "What's all this?"

"Are you truly so unpoetic?" Cain viewed Wilder with disbelief just as Wilder realized the props were for Reason.

And as Wilder contemplated what seemed to be miles of mattress upon which Cain and Reason would play, he was struck by the revelation that Ireland, his choice, made a frigid mistress on a deep winter's night. "May I go out on the balcony?"

"Sure. How's this?" Cain pulled a sweatshirt from his armoire and tossed it on the bed.

"Thanks." Wilder flung his leather jacket aside and ducked into the rain to lean over the balustrade and inhale the brisk, salted wind. The breath of the tide sighed like the breath of the storm, and he could scarcely see the waves through the dense, drowning mist. All he saw of the sea was its lacy white froth running like the hem of the fog along the hidden shore.

"*Give your precious love to Cromwell!*" It was one thing to demand it, another to live with it. Wilder stared back at Cain's bedroom. Reason *was* giving her precious love to Cromwell. He had seen little of her since the night of their disastrous lovemaking. She was on the site, he was in the OR, time flew. For two months they had spoken only when the design team dictated they meet. And during those meetings Reason was polite but cold. Every time Wilder recalled the back seat of her car, he was humiliated anew by his failure to feel, to give, to please and enjoy. But today, as their unhappy reunion revolved through his head, he realized the experience had been healing. The anger towards Reason he had nursed for two years had evaporated, and while his bitterness waned, his desire had tripled. Now as he stood in the downpour, memories of stripping Reason bare in the rain and making love to her scorched his mind. If only he had another chance. He smoothed the rain from his hair and face and ducked inside.

"I ought to be on my way," Wilder said, back in the library.

"Why are you always in such a hurry? Do you have to go back to work?"

"Not until tonight," Wilder stared out the windows at the hawthorns brandishing their thorns in the wind, "but I'm not comfortable being here with Reason coming."

"She won't be here for awhile. Damn damp, isn't it? This ought to take the chill off your shingles." Cain poured two highballs of whiskey. "To the victorious horseman." He hoisted his glass.

"Do you and Reason come down here every weekend?"

"No. But I wish she'd come live here with me for the rest of her life."

"Have you asked her?"

"Reason living happily ever after at My Lady's Leisure? With *me?* You're a mad Irish dreamer! It's you she wants." Suddenly Cain bounded across the library and pulled a flashlight from one of the bookshelves. "I'll show you something fantastic."

Reaching the dungeon, Cain lit the oil lanterns. "I used to come down here and pretend I was the Prisoner of Chillon."

"It reminds me of the Man in the Iron Mask. How come you haven't shown me this before?"

"I've always been more interested in showing you my gardens."

"How old are these boats?"

"Those green ones are at least two hundred years old. The others vary. Like that blue one has 1847 carved on its bow, and the red one is new."

Wilder surveyed the mossy green walls with their tarnished brass lanterns. "I *really* like this place. It makes me feel like a kid again."

"Isn't this the coolest hide-out? From outside you'd never know this dungeon is here."

"What's the story with this grate?" Wilder stooped to inspect the barred exit that led out to the beach. "Does it open?"

"Yeah. There's an old key. That's the romantic way of opening it. But there's also a motor that raises it. Look by your left hand. See the button that looks like a pebble? Push it."

Silently the grate rose. Wilder pushed the button again and the grate sank.

"There's another button outside so you can enter from the sea. It's hidden beside the keystone above the grate. Come over here," Cain directed Wilder to the far corner where there were three metal crates. "Here are the sniping rifles, and look at all these magazines. This ought to be enough ammunition to blow England back where she belongs."

Once again Wilder found himself perusing the weapon he had no desire to see. With a telescopic sight the Light Fifty was over five feet long.

"And that's only the beginning of this cache. You're going to love this," Cain went on with enthusiasm. "My father..."

Wilder seized Cain by the elbow. "*Hunter* knows about this?"

"Of course not!" Cain freed his arm with a jerk. "If you'd give me a chance to explain, I'd appreciate it. I just found out my father has embezzled several million pounds from his clients and the Grosvenor hospital. That's how he bought the emeralds. You know all those charity events like the Solstice Fete he holds? The old fart has been pocketing most of the money, and he's fooled every auditor."

"He's skimming funds from the poorest hospital in Belfast? What a bastard."

"Fortunately, the Gov will get most of its money back when I finish selling the emeralds. That's why I didn't send them back to Portclare. I convinced H.C. to let me hawk them. I'm unloading them one at time; makes them seem more valuable. At first I thought about turning H.C. in to the police, but then I reconsidered. I convinced him to let me in on his games. He thinks I'm re-investing his gems and cash in guns for Arabs, but I'm financing an arms deal for the Provos." Cain bent ruthless brown eyes to Wilder. "Not only will my 'noble' father be exposed as an embezzler, but also as a sponsor of the IRA. If he isn't shot, he'll go to prison."

"I know he's an ass, but why do you want to ruin your dad?"

"Because he ruined me."

Cain never spoke of his childhood, and only now did Wilder begin to comprehend the damage Hunter had inflicted upon his son. "How?"

Cain swiped a candle and box of matches from the workbench. Holding the taper before him, he plucked a strand of his hair and dangled it over the flame. "That's how," he replied and snuffed the flame between his fingers.

Wilder pressed no further. "OK, I can understand your contempt for Hunter…but why do want to help the Provies? Why do you store their guns and set-up their touts? Is it because of my family?"

"Wilder, this is your country, and England has to get the hell out of here. If it takes blasting them back to their own damn island, so be it."

But Cain's words didn't sit well with Wilder. He covered up the rifle and closed the crate. Then he slumped into the 1847 rowboat. "I don't know if guns are the answer to anything, Cain. Intellect tells me there can be a peaceful solution, but reality and history show me violence is the only force in Ireland that has changed anything in a hundred years. Violence accomplishes so much here because politics accomplish so little. What have we got to show for years and years of peace talks?"

"Three thousand funerals."

"I want the bleeding to stop, we all do. It's like feeding an 800-year-old fire," Wilder sighed. "We shoot a Brit, a Brit shoots a Provie, the ULF shoots a taig. The gun I see today is the victim I stitch up tomorrow, and it all seems so senseless and stupid, really stupid that we still negotiate with gunfire. But nobody listens to the priests and politicians anymore." He looked at Cain at a loss. "What other voice but violence is heard here? Aren't those sniping rifles just a louder voice? Kieran keeps telling me war can't have a face, it can only have a cause. But I see the faces, I see the wounds. And I wonder what the answer is. Why won't the Brits leave? They could give this country a chance to heal by withdrawing, that's all the IRA wants…but the Brits won't leave. They want the IRA defeated more than they want peace. And every year they fortify the border more, and dig their heels in deeper. I know I'm not supposed to think with my heart…after all, this is a war and I support the armed struggle."

"Do you really, Wilder?"

The vicious wind, the violent waves, the dulcet noise of nightfall. Wilder stared silently into his fists.

The warmth of the dungeon enticed raw breath off the sea. Snowflakes blew through the grate and chilled the room, but Wilder and Cain didn't notice.

"Have you ever seen the graves in the floor of Westminster Abbey?" Cain lay on the stone floor staring up at the ceiling. "Every few feet you're stepping on somebody famous. I'm seeing how it feels to be a dead poet."

"You're so weird, Cromwell."

"Crrraazy is the only way to be me." But then Cain grew solemn. "You really do have to watch out these days, Wilder."

"For what? Dead poets?"

"The Brits." Cain sat up and propped his head against a rowboat. "The Cure has spent the last year building a file on Kieran; they're determined to get him and the Light Fifties off the streets. Exactly how they connected him to the rifles I don't know. Maybe the same person who got to Ruairi got to Kieran. But now they're building a file on you, that's why they keep visiting your house. They want to know everything about you, and they're playing with you, messing with your head."

"Why haven't they arrested me like they arrested Ruairi then?"

"Don't think they aren't planning to do that, Wilder. But they're being careful. Ruairi's death was a monumental blunder. And they're worried about your father's connections with the press. He was a pain in the ass for the security forces last year when Merry died. The last thing they want is another story telling the truth."

"I doubt my dad wants to go through that again either. You saw how the Brits crucified him in the media. They tried to discredit and demonize him, called him a 'psychotic sycophant to IRA terrorists.' They did everything they could to ruin his health and his career."

"I don't know what will happen, Wilder. But the Brits are hoping Kieran or someone like you will slip up and lead them to this cache."

"They have their work cut out for them trying to nail Kieran. He's the master of this game."

"Maybe so, but you both need to be vigilant. The Cure is on to Kieran, and they'll be on to your work as a medic if you give them one chance. And they'll screw you to the wall for information one of these days. There's also the issue of Reason. Those photos of her are missing from your desk…"

"Reason has no connection to any of this crap and she doesn't know anything," Wilder interrupted. His eyes hardened with suspicion. "But how do you know all this, Cain? How do *you* know what the Cure is doing?"

"I have contacts."

"What contacts?"

Cain froze in guilty silence.

"Why won't you ever be up front with me about this, Cromwell?

"Wilder…be reasonable…"

"You be honest!" Wilder strode to the iron grate. "You breeze in and out of the Shankill. The ULF talks to you. And now you know about the Cure. You know too damn much, Cain, and it's giving me the creeps. Only the Cure knows what the Cure does. You know that and I know that, so who in the hell are you trying to kid?"

"Why does it matter, Wilder?" Cain stammered off guard. "You know I'm on your side!"

"Are you? *Are you?*" Hidden rifles, half-inch shells, the Cure, the RUC, the endless war, and Cain's averted eyes put Wilder on edge. Something in Cain's expression. Lies, he saw lies. "Maybe you're a Cure agent like the Cure agent you had killed last summer, maybe you killed Ruairi and Aidan…who knows," he charged, "maybe you and the RUC are planning a shoot-to-kill rendezvous right here at the manor to blow us Fenian bastards to bits!"

Shaken by Wilder's tirade, Cain staggered to his feet. His head swam. *"Damn good show, Cromwell! Damn good show! Here's your medal…a piece of the bastard's skull."* He pawed the neck of his t-shirt and fought for breath. "That's not…the way it…is."

"Then tell me how it is, Cain! Tell me how you know all you know!"

"I have connections, you know that. Stop yelling at me, Wilder!" Cain pleaded.

"It's not a good time to be a two-faced Brit, Cromwell." Wilder could tell Cain was hiding something by the way he refused to glance his way; by the way he panted and sweat and trembled and paced like a man hammered by guilt.

"Oh, now you too? None of you Irish *patriots* ever let me forget I'm a Brit. What do you want me to say, to do? I can't help being English, and I'm sorry to the soul for what my country has done to you! But how, how can you suddenly not trust me? All I've ever been to you is a friend." Unwanted tears embarrassed Cain as he finally met Wilder's eyes. "My Lady's Leisure is all I have in this world that matters to me," he said in a voice choked with emotion. "My books, my ponies, my gardens, these stupid old boats…this is my life. But I'd burn all this to the ground before I'd hurt you, Wilder…I swear to God Almighty that's the truth."

Wilder saw his friend's face and his eyes, such gentle brown, sad so sad eyes. "Oh God, Cain, I'm sorry."

"It's OK, Wilder." He blew out the lanterns and shone his flashlight up the stairs. "I'm going to check on the ponies. Want to come?"

"I'll be out to the barn in a minute. I left my coat in your room."

Reason was standing in the doorway of the balcony when Wilder walked into the bedroom. He watched her lean into the dusk with the wind sweeping her hair forward from her shoulders onto her cheeks. She looked Irish in an Aran sweater, and American in tight blue jeans. And Wilder recalled the night she had looked young and enchanting in the firelight and kissed him for the very first time. His heart had soared then. It skyrocketed now. *Give your precious love to me!* He imagined Reason turning to see him and opening her arms. She was taking his hand and leading him to the bed. She was drawing him down…sweetly, sweetly…

Preoccupied, Reason twirled a red rose beneath her nose and plucked its petals one by one before raising her hand in the breeze. For a moment the petals danced with the snowfall in candy-cane spirals then fired skyward like bloodstains on the wind. The illusion brought Wilder crashing back to real life. The mangled limbs, the burns and cries of last night's victims scarred his mind. Bloodstains on the wind. And he looked at Reason like she was all that was sane and wise in his world gone mad, and never had he needed the pure touch of a woman more to erase the obscenity of war.

Reason glimpsed back and wasn't surprised to see Wilder. She had heard him walk in and allowed him to enjoy a long look. "Hello, Declan," she greeted in her courteous-at-arms-length way. "Why are you here?"

"I came to see Cain's ponies." He joined her in the doorway. "Rough night."

"Like all the banshees of Eire are loose."

"You look pretty standing here, Reason." He raised his hand to touch her hair and she jerked away.

"Where's Cain?"

"Out in the barn." Wilder wished Reason would pay attention to him, but she stared through him. He pointed to the bed. "It looks like you have quite an evening ahead."

"Cain knows how to be a man," Reason said, still angry at Wilder.

He sighed with frustration. "I wish things had been different that night in your car, Reason. I wish I had it to do over again."

"Why? You'd still be incapable of making love. You're dead from the neck down."

"I certainly was that night. And you have no idea how much I regret my behavior."

"You should regret it, Wilder. You were a raving jerk."

He glanced at Reason, looking hopeful. "But the damage I did wasn't irreparable, was it?"

"As if you care," she said irritably.

"I want to fix this, Reason, I want you back in my life…"

"Yeah, sure, so you can have the pleasure of kicking me out of it again."

"Look, how can I make up for being a jackass if you won't let me?"

"You know, Wilder, you're a great cure for sanity. You told me to give my love to Cain, and I have. You can't have it both ways."

Wilder wouldn't meet Reason's eyes full of another man when it was easier to stare down at the sea. But even the sea screwed his heart. *"I'd rent a castle above the Irish Sea,"* he had once suggested to Reason. *"By day we'd sit on the white cliffs and plan our future. By night we'd lie in our bed and listen to the wind off the surf."* Now Reason was mistress in Cain's castle, and Wilder was alone.

"Oh, don't start with the sad looks! Wilder, Cain gives me his soul. You give me your anger. Which would you choose?"

"I'm not angry anymore, all right? I've been juvenile and petty, and I've done everything wrong since you came here. Can we at least go back to where we were? We were making progress at being friends again."

"No," Reason was adamant. She knew Wilder's game. He didn't want to want her, but he did. So he'd draw her near with that summer smile, and run his fingers over her skin, and kiss her with that soul-deep kiss, taking just what he needed to sustain his sex, then he'd slap closed his heart and shove her away. "I told you this would happen, Wilder, that you'd still want me, but I wouldn't want you." She handed him his jacket. "Good-bye."

He looked up at the ceiling with its sexually explicit scenes. And then he looked at Reason. "I won't give up on you. Last night as I was tending all those victims I was thinking how lucky I am to have another chance with you, and what an idiot I was wasting that night I had you right here in my arms. I got it wrong, like you got it wrong in Denver, and now I understand why that happened. It's damn easy to screw up when your feelings overwhelm you. Don't give up on me, Reason...I won't treat you coldly again, that's a promise. I don't want a diamond heart if it means losing you."

And Wilder saw what he wanted to see. For weeks Reason had kept it hidden, just like he'd kept it hidden, pretending not to care. The look of longing, loving, loyalty in her face. She turned to him like she didn't know what to say, what to do, but that she forgave him was obvious, and he smiled. On impulse he tossed his jacket over his shoulder. He caught Reason's hand and stared into her eyes. Lovely. Then he kissed her on the lips. Lightly. As a butterfly ruffles a flower. "When you close your eyes to kiss Cain tonight, think of me." He swiped his coat from the floor and made for the door. "See you later, Mac."

Chapter Thirty-Four

"You look upset," Cain said as Wilder drove away. "Did Wilder say something to you?"

"Everything that man says upsets me," Reason frowned. "But actually the problem is your father."

"What's he done now?"

Reason sat down on the foyer steps. "There's this man who works at the Gov and I think he's part of the ULF. He's been driving the Catholic workmen out."

"What's his name?"

"Duggie Knack. I knew he was bad news, but Jillie thought I should give him a chance…I should never have listened to her. I wanted to fire him, but your father refused to allow it. Then out of the blue this morning your dad called from London and accused me of making the Gov a safe haven for IRA criminals like Ruairi, and he told me to fire all my Catholic workers. He said if I didn't, he'd have me fired for contributing to terrorism"

"And what did you tell him?" Cain inquired icily.

"At first I was speechless. Then I got mad. I told him to go to hell."

"Oh, well done! I'll bet that fried the old goat."

"He got even nastier and called me an 'insolent bitch.'" Reason turned to Cain for guidance. "Now what? I don't want him to ruin my reputation or my career. But we can't have people like Knack lording over the workmen."

"Just go on with your work and forget every word the old man said." Cain's voice crystallized, "He won't harm you or interfere with you again."

"Are you sure?"

"I guarantee it."

"He is such a hypocrite, calling us his 'dear friends of Ulster' then pulling this crap. If the Irish Catholics are so contemptible, he should stay home! The Gov can raise money without him."

Cain agreed with a cynical smile. "The Gov would be better off raising money without him."

"There's something else about your father that concerns me. Back in July he asked me to print up a list of Catholic workers, and I did because I was naive and didn't know why he wanted it…but since then a lot of the men on that list have either quit or been killed or arrested."

"This list is in your computer?"

"Jillie's actually. She filed the work applications."

"How come you never mentioned this before?"

"I only remembered the list this morning. Do you suppose your father gave it to the ULF?"

"I'll see what I can find out. Has anyone at the Gov ever investigated these anti-Catholic incidents?"

"Oh, Cain, the design team brings it up to the Board all the time. Over and over I've asked for tighter security, and they tell us they're looking into it. But it's been months and we haven't heard a word. Nobody in authority seems to care. Aren't you cold?" Reason suddenly felt the winter chill. "I'm freezing."

"Follow me into the kitchen, my love, and I'll fix you an Irish drink called Liquid Paralysis. Guaranteed to warm the pith of ye."

"Sounds good, but," she detained Cain by his belt loops, "the problem is my feet. They got wet coming in tonight. I need a pair of socks."

"Hop on up to my room and help yourself. They're in the bottom drawer of the armoire."

Minutes later Reason skidded into the kitchen barefoot. She grabbed Cain at the stove and swung him around. "What is *this?*"

Cain's smile froze. "Where did you find that?"

She slapped the gold medallion into his palm and backed away. "It's yours, isn't it?"

He glared at her coldly. "Tell me where you found this."

She wasn't forthcoming.

"Reason, answer me!"

"I'm not telling *you* anything ever again!" Gaping upon Cain in horror, Reason backed towards the doorway. "Besides you should know exactly where you keep it."

He perused the winged-sword coin and read its inscription. **Fear Nothing and Prevail.**

"I saw you throw a similar charm into the fire, and you said you didn't know what it was. How many *Cure* medals do you have, Cain? Was it one of yours I found behind Wilder's house?"

His face went white. "Who told you about the winged sword?"

"I read about the Cure in one of Ruairi's books. You're one of them, aren't you? *Aren't you?*" she screamed.

"What if I am?" Cain snapped, weary of tirades.

"Then get away from me. Just get the hell away from me!"

"You're a republican now, are you, Reason?" he asked in a gruff voice and stared fiercely upon her. "You support the Provos?"

"Nobody deserves to be gunned down in cold blood like the Cure guns people down, Cain."

That provoked a guttural laugh. "And you think the Provos don't gun people down in cold blood?"

"It's *their country!* They're fighting for freedom. What are you English bastards fighting for, Cain?"

Cain tossed the medallion back to her and yelled, "Put this back where you found it! *Now!*"

Reason hurled the medal at Cain's feet. "Who are you going to hunt down next, you murdering pig? Wilder? Me?"

With a resounding curse, Cain slammed two mugs from the stove against the kitchen's stone floor. "What do you want me to say, Reason?"

"Say it's not true!"

The wind and rain whipping the night filled Cain's silence.

"Oh my God." Reason was petrified and inched away.

"You've left me no room to move here, Reason." He couldn't bear the way she looked at him, like he was monstrous. But then she was seeing him as he really was. And in that moment he felt his heart began to break. "If I admit I'm in the Cure, you'll despise me, and if I deny it, you won't believe me." He stretched his hand to her, "Just let me explain…"

"Don't you come near me!"

At full tilt Reason fled down the hallway, but Cain tackled her at the front door and forced her up to his bedroom.

"Sit down!" he blared.

Reason slinked into her appointed chair while Cain rummaged through his drawers. Madly he tossed clothes right and left, and Reason feared he was searching for a gun to kill her. Instead he withdrew what appeared to be a small ivory dish and pitched it on the bed. Back and forth he paced socking his fist into his palm. He looked at Reason, he looked away, he looked around the room, and when he muttered things under his breath he looked insane. Like they were too tight, he scooped off his shoes then his socks and loosened his collar. Then he ripped off his shirt and dashed it to the rug. And still feeling smothered, he threw open the French doors. In blasted the wind, and Reason cringed to think this crazed Englishman was going to throw her off the balcony into the Irish Sea. But rather than laying hands upon her, Cain bolted outside and leaned against the balustrade gasping for air in the pouring rain.

Appalled, Reason pushed from her chair and ran for the door.

"Don't!" Cain implored, stumbling to catch her. "Don't leave me." Drenched and shivering, he dropped on his knees before her and tugged her down to kneel with him. He wouldn't release her hands. "Reason, I love you." His voice trembled. "And it's because I love you that I never wanted you to know the truth…remember when I said you'd hate me one day? That you'd be sorry I touched you? Well, that day is today. I've only told two other people this story. One was a psychiatrist, the other was Sumner Steed."

"Then don't tell me," Reason cried, wishing she could escape. Cain looked so crazy and anguished she didn't want to hear what he would reveal.

"Now that you've found the medal, you have to hear it. But you can't interrupt me once I get started because every word is agony, and I'll lose my nerve if I don't get it out all at once." He kept hold of her hands as a sort of barometer. When Reason became repulsed by his confession she'd jerk her fingers away. He took a breath and began.

"I'm not now, but I was in the Cure. For two years. That's where my father sent me instead of prison, after he found out I was a thief. Believe me, I had no idea what hell he had condemned me to. After boot camp, I was sent back to London to learn intelligence-gathering techniques, and I studied every piece of surveillance equipment known in the modern world. They taught me how to use weapons; guns, knives, poisons, my bare hands, brainwashing, bombs…name any weapon, I learned where to find it, how to use it and how to dispose of it. Next I learned how to interrogate and torture information out of reluctant women and men. They taught me how to strangle a man, how to castrate a man, and how to beat and rape a woman without leaving a scratch of evidence. Here I was this peace-loving, twenty-eight-year-old artist being shown how to succeed as a sadist. After the first month of this insanity I pleaded with my father to get me out of the Cure, but he refused to help me. He said it would make me a man.

"After finishing training, I was assigned to duty here in Northern Ireland. They had me staking out Provos in Derry. For six months I lived, literally lived rain or shine, in a pasture and monitored the comings and goings at a horse farm. Eventually seven Provisionals were arrested and sentenced to life in Long Kesh for making fertilizer bombs, and the Cure called me 'brilliant' for preventing countless explosions. I knew I wasn't brilliant, but I believed I'd done the right thing. In the next year I went undercover as a postman, a grave digger, a house painter, even as a wino in the New Lodge. I learned how to look Irish, how to talk and walk and think Irish. All to fit in without being noticed. That's the scariest thing about the Cure; they're faultless chameleons. In two years of mingling, nobody ever foiled my cover, and they walked into every trap.

"I survived a year without having to hurt anyone, but in my second year my squad was sent to Armagh. Things are rough down there. They call it 'bandit country' because it's the heartbeat of the IRA. British troops have to be lifted in and out of the region by helicopter; soldiers would be blown up on any road in the county. We were assigned to border surveillance. 'Friendly guerrillas,' the Cure called us, and we were told there was to be no mercy shown to insurgents. If there was trouble, we were to shoot to kill. It didn't take long for me to see executions. There's always some shit going on along the border, so we were shooting often. We'd open fire on vehicles driven by suspected terrorists. Sometimes we'd obliterate a car with hundreds of rounds. It was all in the name of prevention of terrorism, and several men were killed by my squad. And if we happened to kill an innocent Catholic, the courts would rule the man hadn't actually committed any acts of terrorism *yet,* but he had been planning to do so, so the people of Ulster were spared his *future* evil. I really had no conscience about it. When you're nailing a car with two or three other men, you don't know whose bullet actually kills the occupants.

"But everything changed that April. Three other agents and I were assigned to monitor the activities of four suspected Provos who were stockpiling weapons in a barn. We were dropped into a forest near Crossmaglen before dawn and settled into location. We watched the men for a week, letting them dig themselves into deeper and deeper trouble. After ten days we had enough incriminating data and waited for the men to come back so we could arrest them.

"It was just before midnight when we saw the men enter the barn. I wasn't supposed to be part of the arrest team; my job was to cover the other three, but my teammates decided I should be in on the 'fun.' They handed me my rifle with a full magazine. Time for a little 'Pick your Paddy,' they joked as we moved in. I had no idea what they were talking about but followed them into the barn anyway. I wasn't prepared for what was about to go down.

"The instant the four men saw us, they raised their hands and didn't resist arrest, probably because we had automatic weapons and they were unarmed. One of the Cure agents made them lie face down in a pile of dirty straw, and then he and the other two made the four men eat sheep dung by pushing their heads into piles of it. They thought it was funny, saying things like, 'You are what you eat,' but I felt sick and wasn't laughing. Then they turned to me and told me to 'pick one.' 'One what?' I asked and they thought that was hilarious. 'Pick your Paddy,' they joked. What they meant was pick the one who'd be my prisoner.

"So I picked a young fellow with fox-red hair while the other three argued over who they were going to choose. Then without warning, they shot one of the men thirty times in the back and head and drove a pitchfork through his hair. All seven of us in that barn were drenched in his blood. The other three Provisionals started screaming, 'Don't shoot,' but their screams didn't last. The two other Cure agents opened fire and kept shooting their victims until their bullets were gone. Then they turned to me. It was my turn to shoot. The air was stale with sheep manure, it was pouring rain and ungodly humid, and I felt like I couldn't breathe. I remember blood dripping off my cheeks and into my mouth. I was sweating and coughing, and I remember thinking I was in hell. And all I knew was that I was an Englishman in Ireland killing Irish people, and it made no sense, no sense at all. 'Do it, Cromwell! Do it!' the three other agents were chanting and clapping and slapping me on the back. The young Irishman at my feet couldn't have been older than nineteen, and he looked up at me for mercy. He was crying and so afraid. 'I have a young son,' he said. God forgive me, he had eyes blue as the Virgin Mary's gown. The others were goading me on, 'Do it, do it, do it.'"

Cain focused on Reason, who gripped his fingers so intensely they hurt. She was ashen and holding her breath in the hope he'd done the right thing. Tears scalded his eyes before he looked away and shook free his hands. "So I did it," came his confession twisted in grief. Cain crawled to his feet and clawed at his neck where his skin felt too tight, too hot. He couldn't stop shaking. "I shot him in the head. I don't know how many times. Ten, twenty, fifty…the bullets kept flying, and the others were cheering and calling me a good sport, a real hero, one of the team. When it was over, I was covered in blood and sheep shit and bits of shattered bones. 'My, my, such a shame. Another case of IRA thugs resisting arrest,' the others cried, having themselves a laugh. I remember running outside into the rain, and all I felt was numb. That's how you feel the moment you forfeit your soul…the moment right before you begin your screaming deathfall. Numb. Then one of the agents came out and handed me a piece of the boy's skull like it was a prize. It's all part of the kill, to keep a souvenir. 'Damn good show, Cromwell! Damn good show! Here's your medal, ha, a piece of the bastard's skull. God bless the winged sword; God save the Queen,' he cheered in my ear. That's what I just threw on the bed…a piece of the bastard's skull. I keep it as my penance. Every time I see it, it reminds me I'm unforgiven."

Cain craned his neck backwards at Reason who still knelt on the floor. Rocked forward with her face in her hands, she refused to look up and said nothing. And nothing said everything to Cain. Silence like a death knell. He knew she was thinking about Merry O'Neill and Ruairi and Wilder…it could have been Wilder. And he knew she felt sick with loathing. By the movement of her head, he could tell she was crying, and it would only be a matter of moments before she raised cannonball eyes and blew him away.

"We were sent back to England the day after the ambush," he forced himself to finish the first half of his story. "The nationalists raised a furor, calling it a premeditated, shoot-to-kill blood bath, which it was. But we four agents were never charged or reprimanded for our conduct that night. As far as everyone in the RUC and Army was concerned we'd acted in self-defense and were cited for bravery. And yes, my father and his friends thought I was a hero. I'd finally done something like a true Cromwell." Cain drifted back to the open doorway. He could taste the north wind and smell the leaves losing their green. He could feel the frost hardening the fog. Cold crept down from Greenland tonight. Cold as God's eye upon him. Cold as Reason turning away. "Now you see, you've been touched by a monster, and you'll never forget I touched you or forgive me for it."

Cain's revelation assailed Reason's senses. The man was a fiend. For one season. But he was an outcast scarred for eternity; mark of Cain. The pain of living with what he had done, pain that kept him apart from his soul and his God, was far more fiendish. One look at Cain, and Reason could see his sorrow burned hotter than his sin, and while he might never see it, this fire was his redemption. He didn't hear her come up behind him, and when she touched his shoulder he flinched. "I don't want to hear anymore," Reason whispered and brushed the tears from Cain's face. She beheld another victim of the 800-year war.

He awaited execution. And received absolution. Instead of recoiling, Reason opened her arms. Three things raced through her mind. The Cure could murder Wilder anytime and her fear for him doubled. She was glad she had aligned herself with Kieran. And Cain was abominable in an abominable bonfire where everyone was a fanatic, and one fanatic was as bad as another, and all were damned and all forgiven for being right, for being wrong. And as she drew Cain's mouth to hers and closed her eyes, she thought of Wilder. Then she parted her lips and thought only of Cain.

He led the path to his bed, and when Reason reclined beside him, he locked her in a fervent embrace. And she curled around him like a rainbow curls around a storming sky, affording him grace.

Reason waited an hour before agreeing to hear the rest of Cain's story. She lit the fire and dimmed the lights, and filling her arms with Cain again, drew the covers around them.

"It only gets better," he promised as Reason braced herself. "I had just turned thirty when I left the Cure that summer, and I thought I'd be OK after I returned to a normal life in London. But once I got home, where the IRA are called terrorists and the Cure are called saints, I found myself coming apart. Nobody condemned me for murder, they praised me. I was diseased with shame and self-hatred. I started drinking and doing cocaine. It was the only way I could live with myself, and even then I couldn't stand what I'd done. Before the end of June I had a rip-roaring nervous breakdown; tried to blow my father's brains out with a .47 magnum. I didn't try very hard mind you, I could have killed him with ease if I wanted to, and he knew that. He still knows that. I ended up blasting the hell out of our house in London, but no one was hurt. And luckily the tasteless affair was kept under wraps...we wouldn't want to tarnish the Cromwell name.

"My father called me a coward, my mother called me psychotic, and they kicked me out of the house. Heroes don't have breakdowns. I was drugged and drunk and self-destructing, and I had no money and nowhere to go. So I just sat out in a rose garden behind our house for five days in the rain, and my parents ignored me. I sat there pretending it was my grave, and wishing I were dead. Finally my mother called an ambulance. Just like in the movies, a couple of men arrived and carted me away. My parents had me committed to a sanitarium in Dorset and refused to come to see me. They wouldn't even call. I asked them not to put me in there, but they ignored that too. I mean, if you have a reason to be crazy, are you really crazy?

"Remember me telling you there was a time in my life when art was my salvation? Painting kept me alive that summer, especially for those weeks I was locked in isolation. They took away my pens and pencils, but they let me have my paints and one brush. Finally, after spending a month in a stupor on Haldol, I called my father and begged, yes *begged*, him for money to go to a drug rehab center I'd heard about in L.A. He said no. I was utterly broken and desperate, and he kept telling me to 'Act like a man, act like a man.' I'll never forget his making me grovel.

Still in the end, he was glad to be rid of me and shipped me off to California hoping I'd never come back."

"I thought you said this story gets better," Reason fretted, unable to take much more.

"Have a little patience, love."

"Why *is* your father so cruel to you?"

"Hunter has two deadly sins, greed and pride. He'd rather die than be humiliated, and in his eyes I disgraced him; first by choosing to study 'sissy' art instead of law, then by burgling, and finally by rejecting the 'real men' in the Crown's Undercover Regiment."

"Did going to rehab help you? Did you recover?"

"I'll never recover, Reason. Don't you know by now I'm completely insane?"

Reason dismissed his claim and nuzzled him closer. "So what happened in L.A.?"

"I made it through the drug program without much trouble but remained beastly depressed. And that's when I took tap dancing lessons and magic lessons and juggling lessons trying to drag myself back to happy…and that's how I met Sumner Steed. He'd been a patient in the psychiatric center several times and came back every fall to teach a tap dancing class. 'Where there's tap, there's laughter' he told us loonies."

"And that's how you met Desmond O'Neill."

"I never called him 'Desmond,' and he never called Wilder 'Declan.' Those were names from a former life, he said. I'd be dead now if he hadn't come into my life. He's like a wheel of energy pushing toward a brighter tomorrow. I've never met a more positive, enthusiastic person. He honestly believes once we're given the right script we can all have happy endings. I'm still not sure I believe him. One day at the clinic he saw my artwork and liked it, and when he learned I'd spent two years in Northern Ireland he rather adopted me.

"After teaching me how to tap dance, he forced me out into the world again. He introduced me to his friends, which included every blonde in Hollywood I swear. He invited me to parties, touted my art about town, showed me the best of California, and encouraged me to visit his beach house in Malibu whenever I felt low…which for the first half of that year was all the time. By Christmas I was living there. You ought to see this place, Reason, the lair of lavish. How Wilder gave that life up to come here I'll never know. My living there worked out well for both Sumner and me. I got better, and Sumner enjoyed my company. I saw a lot of Wilder while I was in Malibu. He was finishing his residency but came home whenever he could; he was trying to get over you and failing miserably. For awhile he talked a lot about you, we'd sit on the beach and watch the sunset, and he'd think of something you'd said or done. Then one day your name was no longer mentioned, like you'd never existed."

"Go on, go on," Reason urged when Cain paused too long.

"During my stay I learned the history of the O'Neills, but mostly I learned about Wilder. Everything Sumner told me made me like him. He's such a good son and so dedicated to his father, and he's his father's pride and joy. Everywhere you look in Sumner's house there's a medal Wilder won or an award or a photograph. He has pictures of Brendan and Merry and all his brothers and sisters scattered around as well. Knowing about his family here in the North, I was afraid to tell Sumner the truth about what I'd done, but after accepting his help and hospitality for six months I felt like a fraud. One night I told him what I just told you. I thought it would end our friendship, but it didn't. After Brendan's death, nothing about Northern Ireland shocked him. He never mentioned it again. Then Merry was murdered by the Cure in Armagh in an ambush similar to mine, and Wilder bolted for Belfast. I thought Sumner was going to crack. First losing Merry then fearing he'd lose Wilder, he was frantic."

Reason could imagine. "Everybody here says they can't believe Dessie let Wilder leave."

"He did everything he could to convince Wilder to stay, but that Fenian blood in Wilder was not to be swayed. Suddenly after eighteen years, Declan O'Neill revived. But then this is something he's needed to settle. All his life he's been torn between two lives, and he has to decide once and for all, is he Wilder or is he Declan."

Reason already knew Declan had won. "Wilder is dead."

"As long as you live and breathe, Reason, Wilder will never be dead."

"I have no influence on him, Cain."

Cain just smiled.

"How did *you* wind up back here in Ireland?"

"I was in San Francisco when Merry died and Wilder left, and when I came back to Malibu, Sumner was losing it. It only took one look at him and I decided to move to Belfast. I promised him I'd take care of Wilder. I said I could use my knowledge of the Cure and the RUC to help prevent Wilder from being killed. Then I volunteered to help Ruairi and Kieran. I figured it was time I give something back to the Provos."

"That had to be hard for you coming back here."

"It was awful. But I love Ireland, and it was my chance to live here at My Lady's Leisure and teach at CC. And I love Wilder's father like the father I never had, and I love Wilder like the brother I never had. I wanted to keep both men alive and sane, and believe me it hasn't been easy. Sumner lives close to the edge these days, and Wilder is determined to get himself arrested or killed. He doesn't listen to a word I say."

"Can you blame him? You showed up out of the blue and took over his house, his yard, his life. That drives him crazy, you know."

"I know. I get infinite pleasure out of seeing his face when I tell him I've fixed this or that in his house. He gets huffy as an old hen about it, and it always makes me laugh."

"How do I figure in all this? Why did Desmond have me assigned to the Grosvenor project?"

"He knew how much Wilder loved you, and he thought if Wilder had something other than Ireland to live for, he wouldn't be so willing to die. Simply put, he sent you here to seduce his son and save his life."

"That notion certainly backfired." Reason nestled Cain closer and tenderly kissed him. "But then Wilder is lucky to have us as allies. Does he know you were in the Cure?"

"He knows I worked for British Intelligence. But, no, he doesn't know, and you can't tell him. If he knew, he'd have me shot, and don't say he wouldn't. It's the rule of the IRA; Cure agents are never forgiven."

"But what you did was in the past."

"There's no way Wilder or Kieran would believe I'm reformed. They'd think I was working undercover for the Brits. And there's no such thing as 'the past' when you're Irish. Even if it happened two hundred years ago, every transgression is current. Now maybe you can understand why the mosaic mural is so important to me. It's my chance to make amends here in Ireland. It's a tiny amendment, but it's the best I can give."

"Are you ever going to tell Wilder the truth?"

"No."

"What if he finds out? All those people at the Solstice Fete knew the truth about you, what if they tell Wilder?"

"Bernie's world and Wilder's world never mix, and even if those people were to meet Wilder, they would never expose one of their 'heroes' to a Catholic."

Reason lay listening to the storm. The wind thrashed the night and kicked the windows.

"That wind sounds like my autobiography," Cain said glumly. "Fretting and pacing the night, begging to come inside for a rest…but the wind never rests. It's cursed to chase itself around the globe forever." He paused, as did the wind, for a breath then both began again, "I'm not in touch with the Cure anymore, Reason. I don't know any other agents in Belfast, and they don't know me. But I have 'friends' in the RUC who work with the Cure, and I have 'friends' like Bernard Thunder who give me information because they think I'm their hero and will one day be convinced to rejoin the Cure. They trust me and I use them."

"Aren't you afraid somebody from the IRA will recognize you?"

"The IRA never knew who I was. Cure agents are as anonymous as carbon monoxide. So, if you ever get sick of me, just tell Wilder or Kieran the truth about me. I wouldn't last a day."

"Don't even joke about that, Cain. I'd never tell them!"

"I know you wouldn't, love."

"If you have an 'in' with the RUC, why couldn't you save Ruairi?"

"Unfortunately that's not how it works. The Cure knew Ruairi was guilty of terrorist offenses; if I'd gone to vouch for him, my cover would have been blown. How could I justify standing up for a known IRA man? I'd warned Ruairi repeatedly to be careful…and he wasn't. I honestly thought the RUC would let him go."

"What happened to the other Cure agents you were with that night in Armagh?"

"I only know what happened to the man who gave me that piece of the boy's skull…he and an IRA informant were shot by the Provos last summer in London."

Outside the storm raged. Reason had never experienced the wild gales of the North. Waves of wind, tides of rain, rolling, pounding, clawing at every cranny and crook. Fitting scenery for dark confession and drastic unction, she thought. And she thought she and Cain were mariners navigating this choppy night; two lovers huddled, clutching each other for solace, speaking softly, softly as though they feared something in the dark might find them. Reason didn't want to be found, only lost and tossed and twined around Cain. She traced a heart around his heart then stroked his bare chest. She recalled the note he'd written her in July, *You resurrected a part of me I considered lost forever. My soul.* Now she understood what he'd meant. "I want to help you find peace, Cain. I want to keep resurrecting your soul."

His voice was morose, "I'm way beyond peace and redemption."

"I don't believe that. I'll never believe it."

"I love you so much." He crushed Reason against him, losing himself to emotion.

"And I love you, Cain," she said with her lips warming his.

     *   *   *   *   *   *

She based her success as an agent on one premise; hide in plain sight. To be obvious was not to be obvious. Madeline Hatter gazed in the mirror and beheld beauty; lips full and rosy, regal cheekbones, a button nose speckled with freckles, innocent long-lashed, country-girl eyes. Languidly, she brushed her chin-length hair; hair she described as the color of champagne mixed with five drops of blood. Giving her head a toss, she admired herself again. No frenzied make-up, no ratted red hair. He liked her this way. She turned on the radio to drown out the rain. She despised the wind roaring outside, she despised Ireland, and she hoped the storm wouldn't delay his coming. He had called to say he might stop by after nine.

And she couldn't wait to see him. It had been seven days. Seven! Each time he seemed to make her wait longer before she could have him. When he walked in he would give her daisies, and she'd take his coat then his hand. He'd tell her how he'd spent his day; where he'd been, who he'd met, what they'd said. They'd discuss local news and trade jokes. He always made her laugh, made her happy. She would sip burgundy, he'd nurse a lager, and if she asked nicely, he would bind her hands in velvet ribbons and tease her with the tip of one red riding crop until she fell back on the bed in mirth. Then in one leap, he'd join her and wind her into his grip. And free her wrists with his teeth.

Tonight he'd promised to explain James Joyce. He made Irish literature compelling, especially with two fingers inside her and his tongue in her ear. As he talked he'd undress and massage her with rough hands, rougher kisses. Then he'd take her like a predator, voraciously. Without mercy. In a pounce he'd force her down and wedge his knee between her legs and bite her breasts and penetrate her by force; she liked it that way. Then he'd take his time, gently, pulling out, stabbing in, out, in, out, in, driving her higher and higher with urgent desire. "I'm teaching you patience," he'd tease when she tried to hurry his lovemaking; he'd go slower and make her beg for satisfaction. But she didn't mind pleading. He tormented and conquered and ignited her.

Madeline returned her attention to the mirror where three photographs of Reason taken in Colorado were propped. *So, she is the reason Declan no longer sees me.* She slipped the photos beneath her make-up tray for future use. She hadn't intended for Reason to get mixed up in this. She was the last person Madeline wanted to hurt, still Reason McGuinness could be enormously useful. To save his precious Reason, Declan might betray his Provisional cousin.

The door opened. And there he was. Wet with rain, windblown, smiling to see her.

"Kieran! Give me your coat. Oh, you sweet man!" she purred and held out her hands. "You brought me more daisies."

"Turn around and let me look at you." Kieran gave Jillie's shoulders a spin. "I never cease to be amazed at how gorgeous you are. I swear you look different every time I see you."

*   *   *   *   *   *

Reason picked up the bleached bit of bone. "I don't think you should keep this, Cain. It's morbid, and as long as you have it around you can't close the door on your ghosts."

"That door will never close."

"You have to forgive yourself."

"And how do I do that, Reason? How do I forget what I saw, what I did? I robbed a little boy of his father. I killed a nineteen-year-old man who might be getting out of prison soon if he'd had the opportunity for a trial."

"But nothing you say or do now can change what happened. It happened and it's over."

"I didn't have to pull the trigger. I could have spared the boy."

"But you didn't. You can't go on torturing yourself over what might have been. Look at it this way, if you hadn't pulled the trigger, you never would have gone to California and met Sumner, and you wouldn't be here right now helping Wilder and loving me. Maybe your calling comes from falling from grace. I don't know, I just think you need to let the past pass and stop nailing yourself to a cross." She held out the bone to him. "At least put this part of the nightmare to rest."

Cain was silent.

"I'm sure that young Irishman's soul isn't pleased knowing part of his skull remains in the hands of a Brit," Reason persisted. "Mystics would tell you by keeping a part of that boy's physical being you're keeping his spirit enslaved to the earth and that horrible night."

"What do you suggest I do? Pop the bone in the trash?"

"I think we should lay it to rest where his spirit longs to be." Reason sprang from the bed. "Get your shirt and shoes."

"Why?" Cain resisted moving from beneath the warm covers.

"We're going out where your ponies run."

"What for? It's like a hurricane out there."

"To send the Irishman home."

"There, there. Under the fairy tree." With her raincoat flapping, Reason ran ahead of Cain through the deep grass of My Lady's Leisure's meadow. Beneath a gnarled hawthorn she stooped. "This is where he would want to be."

"*I'll know I'm dead in greener pastures when I'm face-to-face with the stars and there's the perfume of horses on the wind*," Wilder had said, and Cain had thought of the young man he had slain. He tested the air. Yes, there was the perfume of horses. In silence he dug a hole in the wet turf.

"You're burying the past. You're closing a chapter and setting ghosts free."

Cain accepted the bone from Reason and pressed it into the black, Irish earth. He pictured the boy's blue, begging eyes. *Don't shoot.* Rain on his face hid Cain's grief. "I don't feel resolution. I just feel very, very sorry."

"Every resurrection begins from ashes, Cain."

Patting the soil around the fragment, he prayed to the sky, "Forgive us our trespasses as we forgive those who trespass against us." He buried the bone then buried his face in his muddy hands. "Forgive me. Forgive *me*," he implored under his breath and tilted his face to receive the rain. Blessed Irish rain had washed blood from his hands two years ago; tonight soil streamed from his fingers. But he didn't feel cleansed. He would never be clean again.

*   *   *   *   *   *

"I got stopped ten times on the Antrim Road today. That makes it a hundred times they've stopped me so far this year," Kieran complained to Jillie as he stepped out of their mutual bath. "I was walking up the Falls, and nine squaddies took turns detaining me in the rain. One would ask questions while the others shouted insults and spit in my face. They kept kicking my shins and poking me right here," he indicated the bridge of his nose, "and saying I was going to make 'an ugly corpse.' Then they'd take my coat and shoes and throw them in the gutter and let me go. I'd go get my coat and shoes, and a block down the road same thing; they'd stop me, ask the same stupid questions, then there go the coat and shoes. This went on for two fucking hours."

"What did you do when they stopped you?" Jillie hung on every word.

"I just stood there laughing at the bastards. They're pathetic."

"I wish you wouldn't go out in broad daylight," Jillie worried. "You'll be shot by the ULF walking around like that."

"If the Prods want to kill me, the Cure or RUC will make sure they find me. Just like they made sure the ULF found Brendan. I'm a target whether I'm on the street or in my bed. Do you have any cigarettes?" He opened the drawer of the nightstand. "Nice gun." He withdrew a .22-caliber pistol. "What's it for?"

"If the ULF breaks in here looking for you, I want to be ready."

"You'd probably wind up killing yourself." Kieran opened the barrel. It was loaded. "Do you even know how to shoot?"

"I'm deadly," Jillie smiled.

"Yeah, right." Kieran tossed the gun back in the drawer.

"Decky told me Ruairi's inquest was last Tuesday and nobody told Fiona or her lawyer about it. That stinks."

"The RUC claimed they couldn't find Fiona's address. Funny how they managed to find it the night they lifted Ruairi. May I use this towel?"

"Sure you can, love. Do you know what the jury decided?"

"That Ruairi died from self-inflicted blows to the head. Big surprise."

Jillie yanked the plug and watched the bubbles wind down the drain. "Won't anyone in the RUC be prosecuted?"

Kieran tossed aside his towel and strode back to Jillie's bed. "The Director of Public Prosecutions decided the evidence of Ruairi's 'suicide' didn't warrant prosecution."

"Did you ever find out what information the police were trying to beat out of him?"

Kieran briefly observed Jillie drying her thin, straight body then turned on the news. "I don't want to know."

"I'd like to know."

"Why? It won't bring Ruairi back."

"Well, he died to protect *something*, and I'm curious what sort of things men are willing to die for. What are you willing to die for, Kieran?"

"Most days a cigarette."

"I'm serious. Would you die before confessing a Provisional secret?"

"I hope I never have to find that out."

"I wish Ruairi hadn't died so soon. He had a lot to offer us…but then we all have to go sometime I guess. You must miss him terribly." Jillie slipped between the perfumed sheets, beside Kieran. From her bedside she produced a decanter of apricot brandy and poured two generous glasses.

"Of course I miss him. Ruairi and I had been friends since birth. I got another bullet in the mail today. This time the Brits said I'll be dead in six months."

"Oh God!" Jillie covered her face. "How can you say that so casually? Aren't you afraid?"

Kieran teased back Jillie's wet hair and stroked her cheek. "I'm afraid for my family more than for myself. Especially Morris."

"I know he means everything to you, love. Have you ever thought of quitting the Ra?"

"Never."

"You don't want to be like your cousins, do you?"

"Hell no. I want to go out in a blaze of glory," he said with a laugh.

"Don't say things like that, Kieran," Jillie whimpered. "I'd die if anything happened to you."

"Would you really?" From her overwrought expression Kieran thought she might be serious. "You shouldn't fraternize with republicans then."

"Oh, but you're the sexiest men alive."

"And how can you tell if a man is a republican?"

"By the caliber of his weapon." Laughing, she gave Kieran an erotic grip. "I like touching you here most of all, sucking you is even better." With a dip into her glass, she painted a brandy smile on Kieran's stomach and erased it with a lick. "Is Declan a Provisional?"

"No."

"What's the story between him and Reason?"

"They're Yanks."

"Ha! There's more to it than that," Jillie contended. "Declan would do anything for Reason. Haven't you seen the way he looks at her? I'd kill for a man to look at me like that."

"I look at you like that all the time."

"You do not!"

"Yes, Gillian," Kieran drew her mouth to his, "I do. You're gorgeous."

"And so are you. You have a face to launch a thousand hearts."

"The only things I want to launch are rockets. Right into Windsor RUC."

"Are you involved with rocket launchers now?"

"I'm only trying to be sexy, love," Kieran kidded when Jillie looked like she believed him.

She stroked brandy on her breasts and served him a taste. "Why do you stay here in Ulster? Why haven't you escaped to greener pastures like so many others?"

"Greener pastures than Ireland? There's no such place," he managed to gasp as Jillie glazed then sucked brandy streaks across his pelvis and inside his thighs. And she lazed brandied circles around and around his ribs, drawing a target.

"Did his brother and sister's deaths have anything to do with Decky's moving back here?"

"Jesus, I don't know, Jillie," Kieran gruffed, losing patience with her.

"Declan should have stayed in America. Why did he come back when Brendan and Merry both died such violent deaths?"

Snapping his arms around her, Kieran flipped Jillie over and stared down into her face. "Why are you asking so many questions?"

"Sorry." Her expression was sincere. "It's just that I don't see enough of you these days, and there's so much I want to know about you, and I worry about you and Declan all the time."

"Don't worry," Kieran soothed, lifting Jillie's hips to grind his.

"Oooh, now that feels magic. But don't be gentle this time. Hurt me a little…make me scream."

"No, love," Kieran tenderly kissed her, "I won't ever harm you."

Chapter Thirty-Five

Southwest of London, home sweet home. Cain hadn't visited the Cromwell estate since his parents disowned him. Two years gone, his life had unraveled, but little in his father's world had changed. Same aristocratic mansion. Same fine art and Hepplewhite. Home. Cold shoulders, marble hearts. Cain paced the halls. Old, so cold. Rooms upon rooms echoing catcalls of shame. *"What's the matter with you, Cain? Why can't you behave? The boy's not right in the head, not right at all."* Home. Run of the manor for good boys; bad boys play alone. Cain mounted the granite stairs and recalled being banished to his room. Now banished from home. Home. Act like a man. *What's the matter with you?* Sweet home.

His mother was in Paris, and the servants were off for the night giving Cain the opportunity to see his father alone. Hunter played chess at his men's club on Sunday evenings, and Cain had time to prepare. He lit the fire. He placed the box on the coffee table then patted his coat pocket. Did he know what to say? Yes. He sat down to wait.

When Hunter entered his study with his evening tea, he found Cain lounging on the sofa. "What are you doing here?" he stumbled in shock, spilling tea on his silk pajamas.

"Can't a son come home for a friendly visit?"

"Well, certainly…but you haven't been home in years."

"Now that you and I are partners I thought we should improve our relationship. Don't mind me. Sit down and have your tea. I'm just lying here thinking of the last time you and I were together in this room. Do you remember?"

"How could I forget?" Hunter positioned himself near the fire, keeping a watchful eye on his son. "You tried to kill me."

"Ah yes," Cain reflected amiably, "what fun we used to have. You thought I was crazy."

"Thought? *Thought?*" Hunter snorted. "There was no thinking about it, boy. You were a stark-staring psycho."

"Those were the days, weren't they, H.C.?" Cain examined his fingernails and blandly mentioned, "I'm still crazy, you know. My trip to Zurich in August netted £500,000. I received the final payment Friday and deposited it in Rollie Orville's off-shore account. I'll sell the last of the emeralds in a few weeks and we'll be rolling in cash. Everything's going exactly as planned. I've contacted my friends in Germany. We'll do the arms deal in Berlin then move the guns into Baghdad," he fabricated slyly. "I tell you, H.C., my wheeling and dealing is going to change your life. You'll applaud my Cromwell cunning."

"I knew you had it in you, boy," Hunter beamed and toasted Cain with his tea. "How does it feel to be a high roller, son?"

"Better than you could ever imagine. See that box on the coffee table?"

"What is it?" Hunter inquired happily.

"Fifty thousand pounds."

Hunter squirmed with interest. "Where did you get it?"

"I stole it. From your office safe," Cain grinned.

"Damn it, Cain, what's the matter with you? Why did you do a fool thing like that?"

"Just to be bad I suppose."

"I'll be taking my money back now if you please." Hunter hustled to his feet to reclaim and count his money. "It had better be all here or you'll repay every pence."

"It's all there. Why are you keeping so much cash in your office?"

"I haven't deposited it yet."

"Your latest withdrawal from the Gov?"

"No," Hunter told the truth, "it's a payment from one of my clients."

Cain closed his eyes and waited until his father finished counting the money. When Hunter attempted to sweep the box from the table, Cain whisked a pistol from his overcoat and shot the box out from under his father's grasp.

Hunter staggered aside clutching his heart and gaped upon Cain in horror. "God's blood, Cain! What in the hell was that?"

"That was a warning." He didn't get up from his repose and mildly glanced his father's way. "You broke the rules, H.C. How are we supposed to work together if you break the rules?"

"What rules?" Hunter stammered in a state of distress.

"Think, H.C., think. Didn't I warn you to leave Reason alone?"

"Well, yes but…"

"You didn't leave her alone, did you?"

Cain's tranquil smile under stiletto eyes gave Hunter goose flesh. "I only suggested that she…"

"That was a big mistake." Cain cocked his pistol and swung from the sofa. "*I suggest* you never suggest anything to Reason again. Tomorrow you'll call her at noon and apologize. I expect you to grovel. Beg her to forgive you for being a horse's ass."

"Yes, yes. All right."

"Call her promptly at noon, H.C., or I'll be back."

"I said I'd call her!" Hunter barked.

"Good. Then you're going to fire Duggie Knack. And after that, you'll make a generous donation to the Saint Joseph fund for the unemployed."

"What in the deuce is that?"

"Saint Joseph's is a church near the New Lodge."

"Go burn! That's a Roman church!"

With a resounding curse, Cain fired another shot into the wall above Hunter's head. "Damn!" Cain frowned at his compromised trigger finger. "My aim isn't what it used to be. I just put a hole in the Gainsborough. I never liked that picture. Now where were we? Ah yes, you were saying you'd love to make a donation to the St. Joseph fund for the unemployed. A thousand quid you say? Make it a couple thousand. What the hell, make it five."

"Five thousand pounds?" Hunter roared, but seeing Cain point his gun at the Matisse, frantically nodded. "All right! All right! Now put the gun away, Cain."

"What's the matter? You aren't afraid of me, are you, Dad?"

Hunter uttered something under his breath and tried to leave the room.

"You aren't leaving without your £50,000, are you? Pick up your money, H.C. Go ahead, pick up the box."

In the sight of Cain's pistol Hunter hesitantly obliged.

"Now toss it in the fire."

"*What?* You're mad!"

"That's me. Mad, bad and glad to know ya." Cain twirled his gun once then aimed at Hunter's face. "Put the box in the fire."

"What's the purpose of this depravity, Cain?" Hunter stamped in a fit.

"From now on every time you hassle Reason or her workmen it will cost you. This time it costs £55,000. Next time will cost you a limb. Come on, Dad, take your punishment, be a man. Put the box in the fire."

Hunter chucked the box into the flames and watched the money catch fire.

"There now, that wasn't so hard, was it?" Cain stuffed his gun back in his coat and hurried over to slap his father cheerfully on the back. "We can be best friends again."

"I never should have let you out of that asylum two years ago!" Hunter bawled.

Cain pinched his father's cheek, mocking, "Ah, but you did, didn't you?"

"If you're quite finished, Cain, I'd like to retire."

"There is one more thing. Tell me about the list."

Hunter wearily groaned, "What list?"

"The list of Catholic men you asked Reason to give you in July."

At first Hunter's memory was hazy. He scratched his dark hair. "Ah yes, I did ask her for a list of R.Cs. I suppose you'll be wanting me to send a check to the Pope now?"

"Why did you want the list?"

"I was setting up a scholarship fund." Hunter saw Cain's dubious scowl. "A fake scholarship fund, OK?"

"Did you give the list of names to anyone? The ULF perhaps?"

Hunter viewed his son with irritated confusion. "Why in blazes would I do that? I'm sure the ULF doesn't want to give Catholics money for college."

Was he telling the truth? Cain considered his father without conclusion. "Can you think of anyone who would give such a list to the ULF?"

"Hell, Bernie's in the ULF, he has lists all the time," Hunter blurted carelessly, his nerves overwrought.

Cain pounced on his father's slip. "Our esteemed Dr. Bernie is in a paramilitary organization? I knew he didn't like Catholics, but I had no idea he was killing them."

"Now look here, Cain, this is top secret. You keep your goddamn mouth shut."

"If it's so bloody secret, how do you know, H.C.?"

"Bernie has meetings once a month in his game room. I've only attended them twice, but I know he has lists of names. He and his men use them to hunt down terrorists. And don't be thinking I'm in the ULF. I only go to Bernie's for the food and drink."

"Who belongs to this group?'"

"Hells bells if I know or care, boy," Hunter grunted.

"Where does the ULF get its lists of names?"

"From the Cure and cops, where else? Good God, Cain, you better than anyone should know the security forces use the loyalists as their assassins."

"Interesting. Well, I'd love to stay and chat, H.C., but Broadway awaits." Swinging his arms and snapping his head to a soundless beat, Cain tapped across the study like a vaudeville veteran hoofing sideways off-stage. "Shuffle off to Buffalo," he referred to his dance steps and bopped out the door with a salute. "Be nice to me and I'll teach you to dance sometime, daddyo. Till then, goodnight, goodnight!"

Hunter slumped onto the sofa. His chest burned with tension; his ears rang from the gunfire. Blinking up at the Gainsborough his heart bled. How could Cain so carelessly damage a grand work of art? He stared into the fire, at the cinders of his money, and wondered what he'd done to deserve a deranged son.

Chapter Thirty-Six

Sneaking out of Nora's kitchen at sunset, running along the rowhouses, Morris boxed with the wind. It would rain soon. He squeezed his fist tighter and hid it in his coat pocket. Neither the dusk nor the weather would deter him. Kieran had entrusted him with a message for a man who would be waiting in Milltown. Knowing it was Provisional business, Morris was honored to take part. And to insure he got the message exactly right, insisting it was school work, he had asked Reason to write it down for him.

His heart sang as he skipped. He would make his daddy proud. Ten minutes too early he scampered into the graveyard. Even though the sun waned over creepy headstones and the wind moaned, Morris wasn't afraid. Milltown housed some of his favorite friends; Aidan, Ruairi, Merry with the red-gold hair. Kicking through the grass, he proceeded to Merry's grave to wait. He ran into Jillie midway through the cemetery.

"Morris!" she acted surprised to see him. "What are you doing here?"

"Uh....I came to see Merry's grave." He gawked up at Jillie with dread and tried to run away, but she grabbed his arm.

"Why aren't you with your granny waiting for your father like you're supposed to be?"

"I came to see Merry's grave," he stammered again and screwed his fist deeper into his coat. "What are you doing in the cemetery, Jillie?"

She'd been watching the McCartan's house and had followed Morris. "I was reading the names on the republican monument."

"Uncle Ruairi's name is on the memorial. Did you see it? Did ya?"

"Yes, I saw it." Jillie gazed upon the boy moodily. "Do you suppose Decky will have his name on that monument one day?"

"Decky?" Morris found Jillie's question queer. "He's a surgeon."

"But is he a member of the IRA?"

"Don't talk to Brits, lad," Granda Eamonn and Kieran always warned. And Morris knew Jillie was a Brit. He stared her in the eye and tried to hide a shudder as she leered back darkly. "Course not, silly. Why do you put red dye in your hair?"

"Because I like the color, silly." Jillie couldn't help noticing Morris guarding his fist in his coat. "What do you have in your pocket?" she asked with a pleasant grin.

"Nothing," Morris squeaked and tried unsuccessfully to escape.

"Are you up to mischief?"

Morris hid his face and shook his curls.

"Are you delivering items to be used for terrorism, Morris? Is that why you won't show me what you have?"

In fear, Morris kicked Jillie in the shin and repeated what he had heard his father say to the soldiers, "Mind your own fucking business, you English bastard!"

Jillie merely smiled and tightened her hold on Morris' arm. "You're learning the game early, pet. You want to grow up and be just like your daddy. I can see it in those big, brave eyes. Why do you think I'm a Brit?" she quizzed, maintaining her Irish accent.

Granny Nora called it intuition, and Morris wished he knew what Kieran would call it, but then, he had never told his father his suspicions. "I just know."

"Have you told this ridiculous story to anyone?"

"No, but I will."

"Will you, Morris love? It was a shame about your daddy's friend Aidan. If you go around telling lies about me, the RUC will find *you* dead in the gutter next. And then they'll find your daddy with his brains on the wall. Have you ever seen brains on the wall, Morris? Now," she fastened the boy by the shoulders firmly, "we can do this the hard way or the easy way. It's your choice. Show me what you have in your pocket, please."

Morris glanced desperately across the graveyard for the man he was supposed to meet. No one was in sight. He tried not to cry and failed. His tears joined the tappy rain. But he squeezed his fingers tightly and refused to submit.

"Why must you Irish always choose the hard way?" Jillie let go of Morris, and as he fled, she thrust forth her foot and tripped him. *Smack,* he sprawled in the gravel. "Are you going to cooperate with me?" she bent over Morris to inquire.

Morris tried to crawl away. "Nooo!"

"Have it your way, love." With ease Jillie grabbed the boy by the ankles and began swinging him around and around, his head and arms flailing over low headstones as she whirled him like a dervish. "If you don't show me what you're hiding, I'm going to let you go," she threatened with a laugh. "Are you going to show me?"

"No!" Morris wailed, wishing he and Jillie weren't alone amidst the dead.

Faster and faster Jillie twirled in circles, and when Morris refused to comply, she did as she promised. She let him go. Over three low graves he sailed screaming, crash-landing against a Celtic cross which gouged his ribs and knocked away his wind. He fell on the grave, limp as its sodden grass. Jillie had suspected Morris was carrying detonators or fuses, but all the little boy had was a note. She shone a penlight on the paper. **November 16. 10 p.m. Craig Station.** Pressing the note back into Morris' palm, Jillie pinched the boy's cheeks to rouse him.

"Morris honey? Morris? Wake up, sweetheart. You had a little accident. Come on, love, I'll take you back to Nora's."

Upon opening his eyes and seeing Jillie towering above him, Morris shrieked in panic. Jillie jerked him to his feet and slapped his mouth with the back of her hand.

"Shut up and stay shut up, Morris! You say one word to anyone about what happened here tonight, and I'll have your father shot dead just like

Aidan. And then I'll blow your granny's head off and Decky's too, and it will be *all your fault.* You see, it occurred to me you might be of more use to me than other members of your family."

With two fractured ribs, Morris was too hurt and dazed to walk back to his grandparents. Without protest he allowed Jillie to carry him the short distance to the McCartan's house. All the way up the road he cried, and Jillie soothed him like a mother.

"I don't know what he was doing in Milltown," Jillie said as she handed Morris over to Eamonn. "I'd been visiting a friend's grave and stumbled across Morris lying unconscious up against one of the crosses. I looked all around and didn't see anyone else in the cemetery, so who knows what he was up to." Jillie's eyes filled with tears and her voice cracked as she cuddled Morris' bruised chin, "Poor little lamb. I feel absolutely terrible. I just love Morris to death."

"He'll be all right, love," Eamonn reassured Jillie, thanking her for helping. "No doubt he's addled from his fall. Nora's calling Decky now. We'll get the wee boy to the Gov. Thank God you found him."

"Yes," Jillie agreed, dabbing her eyes before one tear smudged her mascara, "it was a fortunate meeting."

"Can you tell me what happened to you?" Wilder asked Morris in the emergency room as he shone a light into each of Morris' eyes.

"I don't remember."

"What were you doing in the cemetery in the first place?"

"I was helping Daddy," Morris whimpered.

"Kieran had you running a message?" Wilder asked angrily.

"Aye," Morris snuffled. "And I did everything wrong."

"Did you deliver the message?"

"Uh uh," Morris cried and covered his face in shame. "It's still in my pocket."

"You *wrote it down?*"

"I had Reason write it...I was afraid I'd forget something," Morris mumbled behind his hands. "Oh, please, Decky, please don't tell my daddy."

"Did anyone other than you see the note?"

Had Jillie read the note? Yes, Morris knew. A flood of tears dripped over his frown as he peered up at his uncle and yearned to confess. But his father would be shot. Decky and Granny too. And it would be his fault. "No." He hid his face again.

Wilder pried Morris' hands from his eyes and squeezed the little boy's fingers in moral support. "It's all right, Morris. If nobody read it, no harm was done." He pushed aside Morris' tears and warmly smiled. "You shouldn't have been on such a dangerous mission in the first place. I think you're very brave."

"Aye, and I'll be braver. One day I'll have a gun," Morris smoldered with hate and gripped Wilder's hand. "I can't wait until I blast a Brit."

Taken aback by Morris' vehemence, Wilder remembered himself as a boy. The best Fenian in the family. Can't wait to kill a Brit. Tears had streamed down his father's face when Wilder uttered those same acrid words. Liam had smiled. *What has this legacy done to us?* Wilder pressed Morris' curls to his chest and kissed the top of the boy's head. "Let's get you x-rayed and see about those cracked ribs, OK, sport?"

"Where's my daddy?"

"Out in the waiting room trying to calm down your granny."

"Is he mad at me?"

"No," Wilder comforted, helping Morris off the examining table. He swallowed the bitter knot in his throat. "He's grateful you aren't dead."

While Morris was in radiology, Wilder hauled Kieran up to his office.

"Are you out of your goddamn mind?" he seethed the moment Kieran closed the door. "Morris could have been killed!"

"But he wasn't." Kieran took a seat on the edge of Wilder's desk. "You said he's going to be fine."

"You sent a little boy as a messenger! He was attacked for God's sake."

"By Prods from the Shankill," Kieran assumed. "They've been in Milltown desecrating graves for the past few months."

"All the more reason not to let Morris go into the cemetery alone after dark!"

"Morris isn't any different than we were when we were kids, Dec. We were delivering *uisce beatha* for Liam when we were Morris' age, remember?"

"Yeah, but delivering bootleg whiskey to Liam's friends hardly matches Morris running messages for the Ra…I haven't thought about Liam's whiskey for years," Wilder smiled. "Remember the night we split a fifth and thought we could fly?"

"You're the one who decided we could 'leap tall buildings with a single bound.'"

"You and Ruairi both broke your ankles leaping over the wall," Wilder recalled, laughing.

"And you threw up on Aunt Fiona twice. Or what about the time those Prods beat the hell out of you and me over in Tiger's Bay because we wouldn't kiss a picture of the Queen? You wound up with a couple broken ribs yourself."

"They pounded my chest with a pipe." Wilder sobered. "That's why I'm saying Morris should be spared from the bullshit we endured."

"How?" Kieran fired back. "I don't see the Army withdrawing. I don't see the Prods giving Morris equal rights. Nothing has changed in over twenty fucking years. In fact, it's gotten worse."

"Morris is only six and already a republican."

"He was *born* a republican, Declan! I'm sorry the wee boy got hurt, but it's time he learns to be tough like you and I learned to be tough."

Wilder pressed his fingers to his brow in exasperation. "I don't understand how you can be so careless about your only child."

"Och, listen to you going on like your fool father," Kieran fleered, giving Wilder's ear a cuff. "Wimping out, are you, Yankee Doodle?"

"Cut it out, Kieran. I love Morris, and I'm not going to sit by and let you jeopardize his life. Your his father, act like it! Take care of him!"

"Listen, Dec, sooner or later he's going to be a soldier and not because I'm forcing him into it. He already wants to fight."

"Can't you at least wait until he's older before turning him loose on the Brits?"

"Yeah, I can wait. It's Morris who can't."

Chapter Thirty-Seven

A slow night at the Horsetail Inn made it easy to converse. Cain sipped a gin and tonic while his companion tossed back stout after stout at Cain's expense. Their introduction had been arranged by mutual friends in the ULF; at last Cain had sleuthed out the little man with a big reputation.

"You're a hero in my book, Knack."

"Hero, hell! I'm a legend."

Cain stared at Duggie with the forbidding dispassion of a practiced assassin.

"I hear you're a legend yourself." Duggie raised his pint. "Ulster is right, Ulster will fight." He smeared the creamy foam of Guinness off his lips and wished the Englishman would smile. Having heard tell of the man's record along the border, he made Duggie nervous as an apprentice to an idol. "Is your name really 'Mr. Good?'"

"To you it is."

"Why did you want to see me tonight, 'Mr. Good?'" Duggie smirked.

"Are you willing to work for the Cure?"

"Well, of course."

"Are you working with another agent right now?"

"Now and then, yeah."

He knew Duggie wouldn't say who the agent was but would perhaps reveal, "What does he have you doing?"

"The usual, keeping taigs in their place."

Cain took a methodical sip of his drink and let tension mount. "Taigs at the Gov?"

"I was doing that, but I got dismissed. Who gives a fuck? It was dead boring there. I'm used to the adrenaline kick, you know what I mean?"

"When you were at the Gov did someone give you a list of workmen to harass?"

"Aye. My handler in the Cure."

"And why did your handler single out workers at the Gov?"

"Cuz the new wing is being funded by that fucking Fenian O'Neill in Hollywood. The Cure doesn't want him thinking he can call the shots with his fortune and fame, ya know? I'd shank that dickhead Declan if I could."

"Why can't you?"

"The Cure wants him." Duggie finished another pint. "Do you have a job for me, Good?"

Cain raised his shoulders. "Maybe."

"Soon?"

Cain slapped £20 on the table as he rose. "Drinks are on me until we meet again."

"When's that then, Good?"

"I'll be in touch."

Outside the inn, Cain punched the button down on his recorder and rewound the tape. He had a meeting with Kieran. Soon the Provos would know everything about Duggie Knack.

Inside, Duggie marched up to the bar and ordered a shot of the best English gin. He was running with the big boys, and life was good.

Chapter Thirty-Eight

November had come. The leaves on the birches framing the physicians' entrance flashed orange through dwindling green. Against white bark they became tricolour trees, and as Wilder walked into the Gov at sunrise he smiled thinking God was an Irishman. He found Albie Coogan waiting in his office.

"Good morning to you, Decky. Brilliant day."

"Indeed it is. What brings you to the hospital this early? Are you sick?"

"Nah. I found out more about Michael Patrick. Now where did I put that note?" He patted his coat pockets and pants. "Ah, here it is." He slid a paper scrap across Wilder's desk. "There's a sculpture by your man McGuinness on the Laganside Church of Ireland. No doubt you've seen it? The flying sailboats?"

"Oh yes. My mom took me down there once when I was a kid."

"Now I've written it all out for you, see? There's an old priest who might know how the church came to have Michael's sculpture. His name is Father Leo."

"Thanks, Albie. I'll check it out." Wilder added Albie's note to a bevy of notes tacked to his office wall.

"I'm away then. Off to confession." Albie wagged his balding head. "At my age having something to confess would be downright exciting." Without explanation he picked up a pen and notepad from Wilder's desk and nodded Wilder's way. "God bless you, son. See you soon." Fitting his wool cap to his scalp, off he went.

Wilder read Albie's message, **10 p.m. Craig Station** then tore the paper into multiple pieces. Tonight, Kieran and fourteen other men would waylay the British freight train from Pembroke.

Reason let herself into Wilder's office to leave a series of blueprints, and as she laid her drawings on his desk, she spotted Albie's message tacked to the wall. **Michael Patrick McGuinness sculpture on Laganside Church of Ireland. See Father Leo.** She hadn't realized Wilder was interested in Michael Patrick's artwork. Being curious about the sailboats herself, Reason decided to go see Father Leo that afternoon.

Beneath its skin of woodbine, little Laganside Church was a square box of Gothic architecture facing the docks. Stained glass windows bearing Saints Michael and John flanked the arched wooden doorway. As late afternoon settled over the River Lagan and lough, Reason entered the small house of God. The overhead lights glowed lowly and the air was filmy with dust, and all ten rows of pews were empty. A candle burned on the altar, but other than its white flame, the church was unheated. Father Leo, on his hands and knees with a bucket, heard her come in. Sallow and rough-skinned, bent and bulging from seventy years of good eating, he resembled a bespectacled yam.

"Good evening, my dear," he waved his scrub brush in the air but continued cleaning the wood floor. "What can I do for you?"

Reason hugged her raincoat closer for warmth. "I came to ask about the sculpture on your roof."

"Remarkable, isn't it? Made by a young man named Michael Patrick McGuinness. It's not for sale, mind you."

"Oh, I don't want to buy it. It's just that since I first saw it, I've been wondering about Michael Patrick. Who he was, where he lived. Is he still alive?"

"Och, no, dear." Round and round Leo ground his brush, flooding the floor and himself with water. "He died years ago. Only a lad he was."

"Who was he? I mean, why is his sculpture on your church?"

"Why are you interested in a poor wretch like Michael?"

"I love his sailboats. Whenever I'm in the city centre I come over here to look at them."

"It's beastly cold in here." Father Leo plopped his brush in the bucket, dried his hands on his plaid trousers and struggled up to rest in the pew. "There's a tea kettle behind you, love; see it by the front doors? Plug it in and make us a cup of tea, will you?"

Her teeth chattering, Reason was glad to oblige.

"Sad story about Michael Patrick, terribly sad." Father Leo jammed his glasses up higher on his nose and leaned back. "I met him thirty odd years ago. I'd seen him walking to and from the docks. He had dreams of being a sailor."

"Did he study art?"

"Gracious, Michael had no time for studies. He quit school for a life on the sea. Och, he was a bold and striking young fellow with molasses-black hair and skin white as daisies and startling blue eyes. And he had this big, broad smile that unfolded like an accordion across his face whenever I saw him. One day…it was New Year's Day and raining like Noah…I looked out the church doors, and there he was standing on the lawn with a woman. Oh, she was bawling her eyes out and holding on to Michael for dear life. I asked if they'd like to come inside to get out of the rain, and the wee woman ran in fright. Both were Roman Catholics and afraid of coming into a Protestant church. I think they truly believed we Prods have horns and live in league with the devil. But I coaxed them in to get warm. Right where you're standing now, Michael Patrick stood with his lady love."

Reason brought Father Leo a mug of tea, and he encouraged her to take a seat beside him on the pew.

"Her name was Johanna MacBride, just a wee mutt of a girl, so pale and pitifully thin. But she had pretty blonde hair and eyes the color of the Irish Sea…not quite green, not quite blue but shimmering with light. And och, she was shy, kept hiding behind Michael she did. Michael said he'd heard that the Church of Ireland was almost Catholic only without the pope, and he asked if I'd marry him and Johanna. Seems their parents objected to the union, and their priest wouldn't marry them without their parents' consent. Michael had all the necessary papers, and he and Johanna begged me to help them be together. So I married them. Och, it was a lovely wee wedding, and that Michael had quite a heart. He stood there at the altar and pledged to Johanna before God she'd be his love, his only love forever.

"Months later I saw Michael on the docks. He said he'd been turned down for several jobs and had given up the idea of sailing. Brokenhearted he was. He had a job hauling coal, and Johanna worked as a maid; poor as dust they were. Johanna's family had disowned her for getting married, especially for getting married by a Protestant. Treated her like she was dirty, Michael said. His parents cursed the union as well and threw him and Johanna out into the street. Would you be very kind and get me more tea, dear? My joints get so stiff this time of year; hard to come and go it is."

Anxious to hear more, Reason hurried to the tea kettle, poured more tea into Leo's mug and hurried back up the aisle to her seat.

"I didn't see Michael again for over a year. He and his Johanna turned up here at the church with their baby daughter. I thought they'd brought her to be christened, but they told me she'd been baptized in Armagh and would be raised a proper Catholic. Now what was her name?" Leo scratched his head. "Can't for the life of me remember." He sipped his tea and gave Reason a smile.

"It was another year before Michael brought me the sculpture. To thank me for marrying him and Johanna. One of the wealthy ladies Johanna worked for had donated the materials Michael needed to sculpt, and he wanted his boats to fly in a place close to the sea. He and I rigged the sailboats up to the gable on those coils. It took most of the spring to get the thing positioned right, but we finally did it. Oh, Michael was proud of those boats!" Leo's face grew melancholy; his pale eyes watered.

"After that I never saw him alive again. That December, less than a week before Christmas, Johanna came to see me. She said Michael

Patrick was dead, and she asked if I could help her bring his body home from Armagh City. Apparently no one else would fetch him. I borrowed a lorry, and Johanna and I brought Michael back to Belfast."

"What did he die of?" Reason asked.

Leo wiped his eyes on his sleeve. "He was shot by the RUC. Seems he was an IRA man. Johanna was certain when I learned Michael was a republican I'd take his sculpture off the church, but I didn't. This house of God has no politics, and Michael was my friend. Sadly, his family and the Church weren't so generous; they abandoned him. Abandoned Johanna and her wee baby as well. Can you believe the Catholic Church refused to give Michael a burial? So, just like I had married him, I buried him. Johanna, her little daughter and I had a proper funeral up in Milltown Cemetery on Christmas Eve. No one else came. I played the tin whistle, and Johanna and her daughter put flowers on the coffin. We bid him good-bye in a foul, freezing mist. As long as I live I won't forget his wee daughter waving a little Tricolour as Michael was laid to rest. Only twenty seven years old he was."

"That's a horrible story," Reason mourned. "Where in Milltown is his grave? I'd like to go see it."

"The plot was unmarked for years. Then ten or eleven years ago a cross was added. I'm sure Johanna had it erected. Go to the center of the cemetery and look for the Celtic cross made of rose marble. It's magnificent, the most expensive headstone in Milltown. You can't miss it."

"What happened to Johanna and her daughter?"

"After the funeral I didn't see them again. Years later Johanna wrote to wish me well. Seems she had moved to America and remarried."

"At least she got a happy ending. But poor Michael Patrick."

"Aye, breaks my heart. Oh, look at the time, love! I have to get ready for evensong. Will you stay? It's a delightful service."

"I can't, but thank you." Reason shook the old priest's hand and left the pew. "Thanks for telling me the story," she called as she opened the front doors.

"My pleasure, dear. Come visit my church anytime. By the way, what is your name?"

"Reason," she said as she left.

"Reason?" Father Leo tapped his chin. "Reason! That's it! That was the wee child's name," he called. But Reason was gone.

Chapter Thirty-Nine

Three miles inland from the Irish Sea, thirty miles southeast of Belfast, Pembroke was a one-street, rural village whose train station was the central picking-up and dropping-off point for County Down. An informant had told the IRA the ten o'clock train would be carrying surveillance equipment bound for a security company that served the British Army.

The Volunteers had been over the operation many times. Everyone knew their role. When the train stopped at Craig Station, Wilder's job was simply to be on hand in case someone got injured. He was to remain in the shadows while two men boarded the train and shepherded the passengers into a single car. Eight other Provos were to unload the cargo, and five more Volunteers were to hold people living in nearby houses at gunpoint. After the shipment was destroyed, the passengers would be ushered to safety and the train tracks blown up. The men would then depart via carefully planned routes. All this was to go down in less than twenty minutes.

The night was restless, in motion. Gale force winds had been forecast; already the air paced across the farmlands. Withered leaves chattered on the elm trees, tumbletwigs and stalks rolled past. Occasionally the bleat of a sheep lilted in from the fields, and fog wafted off the bogs and swirled towards a moonless sky. Ensconced in darkness, the sixteen men in balaclavas lay in wait in the barrow pit below the tracks. No one spoke or smoked or dared breathe aloud, and other than Wilder and Kieran, none of the men were acquainted. For tight security, Volunteers met, completed their task, and anonymously parted. This way, if one was captured and interrogated, all he could confess was what he did, not who he did it with.

Wilder sat with his back to the hill and pondered the stark, naked stars. Orion the Hunter rose in the east chasing Lyra the lyre to the west. A sure sign of autumn. Wilder wasn't nervous. He had served as a medic on two other midnight train raids, both easy and neat. Each time he'd made it home before midnight, gotten a full night's sleep and gone to work the next day without a hitch. He was mulling his morning rounds as the train chugged into Craig Station. When all departing passengers had disembarked, the men split into their respective cells. Five ran for neighboring houses, the rest sneaked up the hill, across the tracks and into the station.

"Provisional IRA," they announced as they stormed the depot. The station master and three bystanders were frisked and ordered onto the train where the two Volunteers detained nine passengers. As instructed Wilder hung back. Meanwhile, Kieran and seven others raided the freight. They had come for cameras and listening devices and weren't disappointed.

Wilder stood watching the open doors of the train, alternately scanning the fields and the empty depot. Everything was going as planned. Right on schedule. He could see the hostages through the train windows, and he heard the Volunteers saying no one was going to be hurt, that this was a routine "reassignment of British goods." Yet the mood of the passengers' faces showed fear, and contempt. Wilder remembered being robbed by masked men on a subway train in Manhattan when he was fifteen…terrifying. But this wasn't Manhattan. This was the British railway. If they insisted on waging a war, let them be plundered.

"Why can't you boys behave?" Wilder heard an elderly woman scold. "What would your poor sainted mothers say?"

No one answered.

"If you were my boys, I'd see you tarred and feathered," she added, shaking her finger at the Volunteers.

Oh dear God! Wilder lifted his head and prayed his ears were wrong.An oncoming tank. Then another and another. Suddenly there was an eruption of shouts and a hail of gunfire coming from one of the nearby houses. Wilder turned to see two hooded men retreating towards the tracks with a swarm of soldiers running and shooting behind them. Within seconds both men were dead, and the planned routes of escape were blocked.

"Shit!" Wilder ran to the cargo hold where Kieran and the others looted. He grabbed Kieran by the arm to make sure they didn't get split up. "The whole fucking Army is coming."

As the soldiers closed in on the train with their weapons discharging, Wilder, Kieran and the nine other men dived out the sliding cargo door, rolled down the embankment and sprinted across the pitch dark field beyond the station. The terrain was uneven and muddy and littered with rocks and stone fences, and the renegades scrabbled over hurdle after hurdle, not sure where they were running, just running to stay alive. In less than no time a battalion of soldiers gave chase on foot and in Land Rover tanks. Flares, one after another, flashed and scorched the night. Wilder could feel a hundred rounds of bullets whizzing past his ears just as two of his escaping comrades were shot. Then *BLAM!* The earth convulsed, the darkness ignited. A volcano of metal and dirt blinded the stars. Precisely on time, the tracks blew apart then collapsed into a hole; the last four cars of the train burst into flames.

Nabbing Kieran and another man, Wilder jerked them left to plunge headlong through a stand of blackthorns, and reeling into obscurity, they careened down a steep knoll. *Splat,* they landed in a bog. Up through the muck they scrambled and continued running, running against a great wall of wind. Over the gale they could hear the tanks veering off to the right above them. For the time they hadn't been spotted, but *bang, bang, bang* shattered the night as the troops pursued the other six men on the lam. Across two miles of hilly, sheep-laden pastures and slick, shallow moors the threesome stumbled and fell through the darkness. In fear they hardly noticed the effort of flight.

"Where in the fuck are we?" Kieran panted as he shoved through rushes and slime up to his shins.

"Who cares as long as we're alive?" Wilder gasped, flinging aside his balaclava and wiping the sweat from his eyes.

"We can't be too far from the sea," the third man, a juvenile recruit named Hugh, figured as they fled. "Can't you smell it?"

"All I smell is sheep shit," Kieran griped.

The wind fired gusts flattening the fields at seventy miles per hour. Like the gusts worked up a steam, the fog deepened and drifted swiftly. There would be no consulting the stars for direction.

But Wilder smelled the ocean. Hugh was right. They were running east. "If we can make it to the coast without getting caught, we might be OK. Cromwell lives about five miles south of Pembroke. We can go there."

"Five more miles? I'm already shattered," Kieran rasped, discarding his hood as well, barely able to breathe.

"I know, I know." Wilder impelled his two mates by their jackets to keep pace through the mire. "Let's just get to the seashore and worry about it then." Dodging one of multiple sheep, he scanned the clouds nervously. "I don't think the helicopters can fly tonight."

"That's the only good thing about this fucking wind," spat Kieran.

Bang, Bang, Bang vibrated the far fields in their wake.

"We're going to be all right," Wilder hoped his optimism didn't sound as forced as it was. "Yes sir, we're going to be fine."

The bogs ended a mile before the sea. The land grew more and more arid and sandy with fewer places to hide. So the men crawled. And all the while they could hear the troops swarming and searching behind them in the fog.

"Maybe the mists are going to hide us," Hugh hoped with his chin dug into the sand.

"No, we have to make it to Cain's before the fog gets too dense or we'll end up stranded out here, not knowing where we are or where we're going. We'll be sitting ducks for the Army. Come on, let's run for it," Wilder prompted. "I can hear the tide so we must be close."

The wind-swept field they had been creeping across abruptly dropped to the seashore. In the fog and dark none of the trio saw the eight-foot ledge, and all three took flight over the rim, landing in sand. Wilder and Kieran were brushing themselves off when Hugh cried out. The fall had snapped his shin. The bone punctured his slacks and bloodied the sand.

"Aw fuck, that's it for me," Hugh writhed. "You two go on."

Wilder squinted through the night and saw they were at last upon the Irish Sea. The coastline was gentle, the beach passable and wide. "We'll get you down to the shore and stash you in the side of the hill."

"No!" Hugh cried.

"It's all right, mate," Kieran assured the frightened young man.

"For christsake, no. You'll be shot! Just leave me. Go!"

Here was one facet of the haywire night they could control, and grumpily the cousins barked in one voice, "We are *not* going to abandon you!"

Using their fingers, Wilder and Kieran dug like dogs into the chalky wall of the sea bank until they had formed a man-sized slot. With effort they fitted Hugh inside, out of the wind, out of sight.

"I'm sorry," Hugh mumbled, catching Wilder's wrist. "I'll be better the next time out."

"Yes, yes, I'm sure you will. OK, now let's dig another hole," Wilder instructed his cousin.

"Why?"

"Because you're staying here with the boy. He can't be left alone."

"*Me?* You're the bleedin' surgeon!"

"I'm the only one who knows how to get to Cromwell's estate."

"Great mother of God, Declan, I'm not a nurse!" Kieran cursed under his breath. "What am I supposed to do for him? How come he keeps passing out?"

"He's in shock. All you have to do is keep him quiet. Don't let him move a muscle, not a muscle. I need to immobilize that leg before he can travel. Look, the fog is getting thicker by the hour. Hopefully you two will be safe here until I can come back and get you."

"How are you going to find us again?"

Wilder scoped his surroundings. On a distant rise a radio tower with blinking red lights defied the fog. "Don't worry, I'll find you."

"It'll take awhile for you to make five miles on foot."

"I'm not going on foot. Stick your nose in the air. Smell that? It's manure."

Kieran helped Wilder dig the second hole. "What are you going to do?"

"Pilgrim," Wilder mimicked John Wayne, "I'm going to steal a horse."

The sleeping farm was a fourth of a mile down the beach. One lone horse grazed in a paddock; an Irish horse unperturbed by great winds. Careful not to spook the beast, Wilder eased over the fence rails and nabbed the horse by its halter. Gently befriending it with rubs on its nose, he checked the horse's hoofs and legs and shoulders to be sure it was healthy and could run. Opening the gate with stealth, he led the horse down to the shoreline. Then swinging up on its back, he gave a nudge and was off

Gusts off the sea kept the fog flying so Wilder could see far enough ahead to guide the horse. The tide was low and rough as he rode in the water's edge. As man and beast cantered south along a uniform strand, the coast wall grew taller so that in the haze and sea spray Wilder and his pony were absorbed by the night. He could no longer hear guns and flares exploding, the wind whipped the surf, and the beach was deserted. Still Wilder spurred the horse to a gallop. Sunrise was but hours away.

As he rode towards My Lady's Leisure, he was thinking of a story Cain once told about Irish Andrew McGuire. Andrew raced for his love, Wilder raced for his life; he envied Andrew his nobler cause. And he imagined Reason, like Julianna Cromwell, breathlessly waiting. *ReasonReason, ReasonReason.* Wilder's pounding mind kept pace with the horse's hoofs. *God, don't let me die without her. If I die tonight, I'll never see her again, and I'll die remembering her whisper, 'Choose me.' If I get through this night alive, I'm going directly to her. I'll pull her into my arms and kiss her till she grows old beside me. Sixty years, yes, I'll kiss her for sixty years. And I'll make love to her and hold her here against my heart. And we'll have a hundred children and travel the world, and for sixty years we'll stare isnto each others eyes and see the beautiful and the good. And for sixty years we'll sleep rolled together, and peace only peace will play through our dreams.* His visions amused him. *Is this what fugitives think about? Women and fairytales? It's better than thinking about getting caught...yeah, a hundred children from a hundred different love games...*

My Lady's Leisure loomed on its hill through the mist. Wilder veered his horse from the beach and thanked God to be halfway toward surviving the night. First he took the horse to Cain's pasture and turned it loose, then he sprinted down, down to the back of the manor where the grate hunched in darkness. Concentrating on every crack, Wilder groped to find the button by the keystone that unlocked the dungeon's teeth. He could see nothing through the grate and for a moment feared what might be lurking inside. Quietly the grate rose. Into the eerie old haunt Wilder ducked. All he could think about was getting back to Kieran. But first he had to call Cain to bring a car to My Lady's Leisure. Up the hidden stairs he flew. Giving the lamp string a yank, he opened the hidden door and skidded into the manor. Not daring to turn on a light for fear who might be watching from the woods, he blindly bumped through the black rooms and corridors down to the kitchen.

It was two in the morning. Surely Cain was home. "Answer, answer, answer," Wilder panted as Cain's line rang for the tenth, eleventh time. "Where the hell are you?" He slammed the phone down and dialed Cain's number again. "Damn it!" Wilder's mind flipped through alternatives and crossed his last resort. He slugged the wall in protest, but there was no other way.

When Reason picked up the phone, Wilder skipped formalities. "Come to the dungeon. Hurry." Throwing the phone back on its hook he was off again. Out the back door, up to the barn. Bridling Pissarro then Gauguin, forgoing their saddles, he led the two ponies into the fog. "Pissarro, old man," Wilder whispered to the pony as he climbed aboard, "you were lucky for me once. Do it again."

*   *   *   *   *   *

Two a.m. Was he being held hostage? Had he murdered someone? No, he lay mortally wounded on his deathbed. The scenarios blazed through Reason's mind as she dressed. That Wilder was in trouble was all she needed to hear. Five minutes after his call she was out the front door. Twenty miles out of Belfast she reached the roadblock. Like a surreal scene, six camouflaged, tar-faced soldiers stepped out of the fog and surrounded her car; each with his rifle aimed at her windshield. Four policemen hovered in the background, guarding the road.

The same tired questions. Reason answered by rote.

"...and what brings you out at this time of the morning, Miss McGuinness?" a pudgy soldier grilled as he shone a flashlight in Reason's face and bent to peer inside her car.

Reason rubbed her temples as if they were throbbing and let go a sigh. "Oooh, what a night! I just finished work, can you believe it? I had *no* idea the lighting in a morgue could be so complicated." She reached for a blueprint on the passenger's seat. "Look at this, just look at this!" She batted pretty blue eyes up at the Brit. "Forty, count 'em forty, different kinds of tract lighting made exclusively for use during autopsies. Let me tell you, I about died! Ha," she swatted the man's arm, "no pun intended."

The soldier stared at her without blinking but smiled. Another dizzy American. "What are you doing out here alone on the road?"

"I'm meeting a friend, Dr. Cain Cromwell, at his estate for the weekend. I'm taking tomorrow off and figured since I'm wide awake anyway I might as well get the drive to Down out of the way. How am I supposed to sleep after thinking about lighting up corpses all night? Is there some reason why I shouldn't be driving?" She grew apprehensive and gripped the soldier's hand upon her car door. "Am I in danger?"

He swayed upright. "Didn't you hear we foiled an IRA train robbery in Pembroke earlier tonight?"

Reason had not heard and her worries doubled. "Was anyone hurt?"

"Nobody that matters."

So Wilder was raiding a train and things went awry. Reason feared her heart could be seen beating through her sweater. "Did you catch the Provos?"

"No, but we will. There's a house-to-house search on all over this area. Be alert while you drive, miss. If you see anyone or anything suspicious, call the Newry RUC, would you?"

"Oh, I will, I will."

"Lock your doors and don't pick anyone up."

"Oh, I won't, I won't."

"On your way then." He patted her roof and waved farewell as the other five soldiers dissolved back into the mist.

*   *   *   *   *   *

On off, on off. The red lights of the radio transmitter marked the spot. It had taken less than an hour.

"You actually made it back." Kieran dived to greet his cousin.

"How's this for first class transportation?" Wilder tossed Kieran Gauguin's reins. "I have some makeshift splints for the boy's leg. How's he doing?"

"He's dead."

"*What?*" Wilder ran to Hugh's side. "What happened?"

"All of a sudden he got restless and said he couldn't breathe. He was flopping around, trying to stand up, and I was trying to keep him still. Then he started wheezing and panting and coughing up blood, and next thing I know, he keeled over. I told you not to leave him with me," Kieran chided dismally. "I'm sorry."

"There's nothing you or I could have done for him, Kieran. He must have thrown an embolus."

"Thrown a what?"

"A clot. It happens with fractures sometimes." Wilder swabbed Hugh's brow and brushed the mud from his lifeless cheeks. "At least now the poor devil doesn't have to ride back to Cromwell's."

"I found this rosary in his pocket." Kieran wrapped the beads around Hugh's fingers. "We'll have to leave him here."

"There are worse places to die." Wilder buttoned Hugh's tattered coat as if to break the wind off the cold Irish Sea, and the night seemed endless, senseless, vicious, sad. "Holy Mary Mother of God pray for us sinners now and at the hour of our deaths," he murmured to Hugh. Flares and the rumble of troops resumed in the distance; every second was a second closer to daylight. Wilder motioned to Kieran. "Let's go."

"They could find us anytime now. I've never come this close to dying before, have you, Dec?" Kieran admitted as he jumped onto his pony.

"Once. In a Colorado river."

"You know what I do to keep steady? I play a song over and over in my head."

Wilder gave Pissarro a kick and headed into the tide. Heavy mist hid the shore. "What song?"

"That old song Liam taught us. 'I'm a rambler and a gambler a long way from home, and if you don't like me, then leave me alone. I eat when I'm hungry and drink when I'm dry, and if moonshine don't kill me, I'll live till I die.'"

"I hate that song," Wilder grumbled.

"Sing it and you'll feel better," Kieran advised with amazing calm.

After five harrowing hours of evading capture and fearing death through miles of bone-biting fog, the simple tune became a mantra for perseverance. Over and over Kieran hummed and garbled the song; every other word being a profanity. And soon both men were mouthing the words like an incantation. *Bang, Bang, Bang from the west…drink when I'm dry,* flares flashing nearer…*and if moonshine don't kill me…*shouts carried on the wind behind them…*I'll live till I die.*

"They must be searching the coast on foot," Kieran heard the voices first. "How far back do you think they are?"

"It's hard to say with the fog, but if we can hear them, they can't be far. At least we're moving forward."

"If the soldiers catch us, they'll shoot first and ask questions later." Kieran uttered a low laugh, "Jesus, Joseph and Mary, what a night! Even if I'm shot down dead, just seeing that train track blow tonight guarantees I'll die happy. It'll be months before the Brits have that rail system up and running. And think of the thousands of pounds it will cost."

"And after they repair it, you'll blow it up again, right?"

"But of course. How far are we from the estate?"

"I don't know." Wilder prodded Pissarro to a faster gait. "I won't know we're there until I see the manor." He glanced back. "Are the voices getting closer?"

Kieran tried not to falter. "Aye, Decky. This time we might actually take our tea."

"We are *not* going to die!" Wilder refused to relent. "We'll be all right." *I'm a rambler and a gambler a long way from home…*

*   *   *   *   *   *

The back route to My Lady's Leisure was a skinny, unpaved road well off the highway and rarely traveled by anyone other than farmers. Reason kept checking her rear-view mirror. Since a mile beyond the roadblock a pair of headlights had shadowed her journey. Remaining discreetly behind her, the headlights made every turn Reason made. She tried to concentrate on the ribbon before her, but her eyes wandered repeatedly to the mirror. Curious, she pulled to the side of the road to allow the other car to catch up and pass her, but no car came. Through the mist she could see the headlights pulling aside as well. Terror knocked her heart. Another look back, was it the RUC? Intuition said yes.

Reason knew the route, every bend, every hill, and there were many hills. There were short cuts as well. Speeding up gradually she counted the rises and falls. On hill four a car going down was hidden by the hill from a car going up, and at the base of hill four was a dramatic turn left onto a tributary road that looked to be little more than skid marks through deep grass. But it ran to a barn and behind the barn were more tracks that led, via sixteen zigs and zags, to the stable at My Lady's Leisure. Cain had explained it was a trailer route between neighboring farms.

Up hill four she motored at normal speed but at the crest she accelerated. Not braking at the base of the rise she fishtailed left off the main road onto the farm path, and punching off her headlights, still speeding, plowed towards the barn. Just as she wheeled around the barn's corner she saw the shadowing headlights pop over the knoll. Yes, it was a Land Rover. She held her breath as the military vehicle reached the bottom of the hill. Would it detour as she had? Straight into the fog it sailed. Reason's legs went weak and her hands trembled as she sped across the meadow, but there was no time to be afraid. Reaching Wilder before the police was her only concern.

*   *   *   *   *   *

Despite fits of wind, the fog obscured everything except the palm of his hand before him. Wilder could no longer see Kieran, and finding My Lady's Leisure from the beach would be impossible. But before Wilder despaired, Pissarro bolted away from the seashore, up the chalky hillside and into the grass.

"What the fuck?" Kieran's curse cut through the clouds as Gauguin raced off-course to catch Pissarro.

"Just let him run," Wilder rejoiced to his invisible cousin. "The ponies know their way home."

Chapter Forty

The fog congealed into a seraphim. Hair of light, fair smile, all things beautiful and glad. She floated on fluttery wings. Wilder exhaled thanks to God to come upon Reason swatting through the mist to welcome the pair skidding up to the manor.

"Are you all right?" She glanced anxiously from Wilder to Kieran, both covered in grit.

"Now that we can finally get out of the wind we'll be fine," Wilder said, leaping from his pony.

"Reason, you are a holy sight!" Kieran jumped from Gauguin to kiss both her cheeks.

"Hurry up and get into the manor." She set Kieran moving toward the raised grate. "The police and Army are everywhere."

Wilder couldn't pry his eyes off of Reason and she looked back at him with grateful relief. "Thank God you're safe," she whispered. "I heard on the radio eight Provisionals were killed tonight, and I kept thinking they'd killed you after you called me."

"*Eight?* My God. Did you have any trouble driving down here?"

"I was stopped at a roadblock near Saintfield, and then I had to lose the police."

"I beg your pardon?" Reason's offhand admission blew Wilder away.

"They were following me in a Land Rover. I'm sure all cars on the road tonight are suspect, but I couldn't let them trail me here to My Lady's Leisure when I knew you'd be coming. So I took a short cut."

"Reason, are you *crazy?* If the police had caught you trying to lose them, you'd be strip searched and up to your neck in interrogation right now."

"I did what I had to do to protect you," she said, looking up at him with loyalty.

Her tender assertion filled Wilder with fear. What was that quality in her voice, in her eyes? Audacity? What had Ireland done to his smug Wellworth-Howell? Yes, Reason had been arrogant then, but safe so safe. Now one look at her defiance, and he regretted having gotten her involved in the maniac night.

"Did I hear you say you dodged the peelers?" Kieran gave Reason a thumbs up as she and Wilder entered the dungeon.

"Mind your own damn business, Kieran," Wilder hissed.

"I brought some dry clothes down here for you guys. And here are a couple towels to wipe the mud off your hands and feet."

"Afraid we'll dirty the dungeon?" Kieran cracked.

"No. But when you come upstairs you'll leave tracks. If the security forces show up, they'll figure out you're here."

"My, aren't you a clever girl?" Kieran piped up again and received Wilder's glare. But already unworking their buttons, both men were eager to shed their clothes.

"Well, um," Reason cleared her throat as both men stripped, "I'll just go take care of the ponies."

"Reason love?" Wilder detained her gently. "Thank you."

She stroked flecks of mud off his brow. "Anytime."

"What is your problem, Dec?" Kieran asked after Reason left the dungeon. "You're the one who spent a year bitching about her not being Irish, about her not understanding a thing about you and our history."

"I never wanted to convert her!"

"You asked for her help tonight, didn't you? Why can't you just accept it, Declan? She's one of us now."

"She is *not* one of us," Wilder argued as he pushed his hair off his face and slid down the stone wall to rest. "And she never will be. I only called her tonight because…"

"Because," Kieran filled in Wilder's blank, "we both trust her and know she can handle anything. And what makes her a jewel in our cause is that she's willing to die for you."

Wilder lurched to his feet. "Don't say that!"

"It's the truth."

"No! You're wrong!" Wilder's composure eroded. "Reason isn't going to die for anybody; not for me, not for you, not for anybody! This whole night, this whole country is fucking insane. What are we doing here, Kieran? What? I don't know, do you know?" He grabbed one oar after another and heaved them against the wall. "It's all bloody useless! *Useless!* I couldn't save Ruairi, I couldn't save Merry or that poor kid we left back on the beach…he was just a boy for christsake…and now Reason? The bastard's can't have her! No way, *never!*"

"Take it easy, Dec," Kieran clicked his tongue and calmed Wilder with a few trusty pats. "The troops are sure to find us if you keep yelling."

Wilder strode to the staircase. "I'm going to get us a drink."

Wilder was going through the kitchen cupboards when Reason returned from the stable. In the light she saw he was bog-splashed and bruised. He had one bloody gash over his left eye, and after tangling with the brambles, his face looked like an autographed baseball. For several seconds they stood on opposite sides of the kitchen.

"Are the ponies OK?" Wilder asked, drinking in every inch of Reason.

"They're fine," she nodded, already rushing to Wilder.

He opened his arms. She couldn't dive to him, run to him, fall head over heels to him fast enough.

"I've been praying for hours to stay alive just to see you again," Wilder sighed. "I kept thinking over and over that nothing mattered except seeing your face."

"I was afraid you'd been shot." Reason clenched her arms fiercely around him. "I've never been happier to see anyone in my life than I am to see you right now."

Wilder thought Reason would unleash her usual condemnation of his dangerous life, but she was silent. The last thing he wanted to hear. Unspoken camaraderie. "You've saved my life again."

"I know," she smiled up at him. "How's Kieran?"

"He's doing *Ave Marias* to be off the pony. Where does Cain keep his gin?" Reluctantly Wilder broke from Reason's embrace. "We all need a drink."

"In the library." She led the way. "Now what do you do? Hide out?"

Wilder frowned down at his watch. "I have rounds at nine."

"You're going *to work?*"

"What am I supposed to tell my patients? 'Sorry, I was out running from the RUC all night and can't take care of you today?' Luckily, I don't have any surgeries."

"I honestly don't know how you keep your sanity leading one life by day and another by night. You could be a comic book hero. Insurgent Surgeon."

"This is no worse than the 72-hour shifts I pulled during my residency."

"Those shifts nearly killed you." Reason recalled the Colorado mornings Wilder straggled in from his three-night, no-sleep rotations. "If I was at your house when you came home, I made you breakfast in bed, remember?"

"You cut the toast into stars and floated marshmallows in the orange juice. And you always put milk in my tea. I hate milk in tea."

Reason's knuckles flew to her hips. "You never told me that."

"I hated the milk but loved the hand that poured it."

"Oh!" She pressed her palm to her heart. "What a nice thing to say."

Wilder loved Reason's enamored expression, and in her eyes he saw all things beautiful and good. A moment's peace. And quiet. So quiet. Grand to be alive with her, only her, for sixty years. Flares erupted far beyond the window. The wind lashed. *She's willing to die for you.* "Come on, let's get the gin."

"I won't add milk in the future," Reason promised as she waved Wilder down the hall. "So we're going to go back to Belfast like nothing has happened?"

"The safest thing is for you and me to drive back alone. Someone will pick Kieran up later."

Reason was eager to enlist. "I can drive him."

"No."

"I have the day off, it would be…"

"I said no!" Wilder cut her off and wished he could fling her flying home to Manhattan, out of the dark side of his life. "All I need from you today is a lift back to the city."

His ferocity hurt Reason's feelings; her eyes slinked from his face.

"I'm only trying to help you." She walked into the dark library. "Here's where Cain keeps the gin."

At once Wilder reproached himself. "I didn't mean that the way it sounded." He lunged to stop Reason, pulling her back into his arms. "You've already done so much to help. Just knowing you're here for me is the greatest help of all. But today you need to rest, and not be seen with Kieran." He gazed upon Reason with affection and lowered his lips to hers.

"Stop!" she resisted, pinning her eyes on the library windows over Wilder's shoulder.

"Don't brush me off again, Reas. It's been so long…"

"Soldiers!" She shoved Wilder deeper into the shadows just as the first rap shook the front door. "Hurry! Back to the dungeon."

"How? I don't know the way. Every room upstairs looks the same."

Giving Wilder a whiplash, Reason crunched his hand and streaked across the dim foyer. Up the thirty curved steps she tugged him to the second floor. They sprinted past several doorways. Like casting a fishing line, she reeled him into the music room. "Go through the pediment door to the bedroom and into the dressing room. Pull the lamp. GO!"

Pound, pound, pound. Fists on the door. As she careened down the stairs, Reason noticed her sweater smudged with mud and sand.

Stripping it off, hurling it behind her in haste, she took a breath for composure and swung wide the front door.

"Sorry it took me so long, darling...oh!" She jumped back and ignored the soldiers reaction as they beheld her sheer nightgown tucked into her jeans. "I thought you were Cain. What's going on?"

The soldiers disclosed their purpose, and Reason allowed them inside. Drawing one of Cain's jackets out of the cloak room and modestly wrapping it around her, she escorted the four men flourishing rifles down the front hall.

How different the story when the security forces entered the house of a wealthy Englishman. No vile obscenities, no breaking through windows and doors, no punching Reason about. Decorously explaining they had come to ensure her safety, the soldiers scavenged room to room, asking Reason soft-spoken questions and worrying about her being alone in a huge, empty house with Provisional fiends on the loose.

"I'll be fine, really I will," she assuaged their every concern.

"Haven't you heard the IRA is notorious for torturing women and children?" one soldier said. "They're fucking animals. Rape a woman then blow her brains out if she squeals."

Reason's eyes simmered on the young man, thinking how a British soldier similar to him had bound her hands and made her kneel, had driven his rifle butt into her back, had slapped her face and called her a whore. "I've never heard that one before," she remarked crustily.

Animals. As she trailed the soldiers through the mansion and listened to their thick brogues, Reason realized if she met these men on the streets of Belfast in civilian clothing, she couldn't tell them from any other men in Northern Ireland. They were Ulster-born Brits, but underneath their green-mottled helmets and black-painted faces they looked the same and talked the same as their republican foes. But they weren't the same. Loyalist Prods, Irish-Brits, animals from the flip-side of the war.

"It's a lucky thing you guys happened upon that train robbery," Reason chatted. "Pembroke must be thankful you charged in to save the day."

"It wasn't luck, darling. We got a telephone tip an hour before the robbery. The stupid pigs were betrayed by one of their own."

Reason's heart tripped. "How do you know that?"

"Gave us a Provisional password. Only an insider knows the codes of the group."

"Foiled by a tout; serves them right," Reason mirrored the soldiers' gloating. "But if you knew they were robbing the train, how come you didn't catch all of them?"

"We got to Pembroke as soon as possible, miss," a soldier took offense. "There must have been twenty of them fuckers, and they scattered faster than niggers at a lynching. We tried to shoot as many of them as we could...hell, we plugged eight of them smack between the eyes."

Another soldier licked his finger and marked the air. "Brits eight, Provies nil. Not a bad score for one night."

"Not bad," Reason agreed with a churning stomach. But for the grace of God, it could have been Kieran and Wilder.

"Well, gents, we've taken enough of this young woman's time." The leader of the pack marched back to the front door and the other three trooped out with cordial nods. "Go back to bed, pet. Keep your doors and windows locked. All the best to you now."

"You can relax." Reason strode into the dungeon with pillows and blankets for Kieran. She handed Wilder the fifth of gin. " The soldiers have gone."

Wilder glimpsed up. "What happened to your sweater? They didn't..."

"Nah." Reason drew Cain's coat closed. "I couldn't exactly open the door in the middle of the night with fresh mud all over me."

Kieran gave her a nod. "You're a natural at this, aren't you, love?"

"Aye, so I am," she japed. "But you guys have a real problem."

"What do you mean?" Wilder and Kieran chorused.

"Do you know why the security forces were in Pembroke tonight? They were tipped off about the train robbery by someone in your organization."

Kieran and Wilder traded shrugs as their minds considered possible leaks. "Well, I know I didn't say anything to *anybody*," Kieran made clear. "I never do, never will."

Wilder checked the time. "I can't worry about it now. I'm going to take a shower. Kieran, you can sleep here all morning. Someone will pick you up after noon."

"Here are some cookies." Reason handed a bag to Kieran. "They're the only food I can find."

"You're the angel of mercy you are, Reason," Kieran expressed fondly. "I knew we could count on you."

Wilder peeled off his shirt and socks and fell back on Cain's bed. His body ached, he longed for sleep.

"I made you some tea," Reason walked in, "without milk this time."

"Oh, thanks. Caffeine's the only energy I have left."

Reason brushed the hair from Wilder's forehead and sat down beside him. "Your poor face and hands are so scratched. How will you explain this at the Gov?"

"Just like you did last summer, I tripped and fell face-first into the blackthorns behind my house."

"You look more like you shaved with the blackthorns. Wilder," Reason petted his curls again, "why were you in Pembroke? I thought you weren't a Provo."

Wilder wagged his head wearily. "I'm not. It was a dangerous operation. They asked me to go along as a medic. I thought it would be easy." He turned to Reason, seeking the affection her eyes afforded. "You should have seen the passengers. I mean, to the IRA it makes perfect sense to be raiding a train for British equipment, but to those passengers it was just another frightening violation. They had such hatred in their eyes. Have you ever seen anyone look like that? It goes clear to the bone."

"You. The night I walked out."

Wilder gave Reason's knee a rub. "You know, armed struggles make sense until the victims become real. And more and more all I see are the faces."

"Does that mean you want to quit what you're doing?"

"No. Because I know even if the IRA laid down its arms tomorrow, the problems would stay. The loyalists would still lord over the North, Catholics would still be oppressed, Ireland would still be divided, England would still be ruling, and sooner or later another IRA would spring up. Sometimes it takes being hated to change things that need to be changed, and it takes guts to be hated and go on." Wilder rubbed his neck. "Does Cain have any ibuprofen?"

Reason went into the bathroom and returned with the pills and a glass of water. "I can rub your back if you like."

"That would be great. Every muscle in my body hurts."

Reason knelt behind Wilder, massaging his shoulders, and he relaxed and listened to the tide crashing beyond the windows. "I'm sorry I had to call you tonight, Reas. Here I've spent five months telling you to stay out of my affairs, and now I pull you into the thick of them. I swear, if there had been any alternative, I would have chosen it, but I need a safe ride back to Belfast."

"It's OK, Wilder." Her thumbs glided up and down his neck. "Rescuing you, escaping police, it seems so unreal…who would have thought this could happen to an ordinary person like me?"

"Certainly not me," Wilder uttered grimly. "But last night was real, Reason, and it was violent and ugly. Eight men died, a ninth died in Kieran's lap…and as for your evading the police…Jesus, that stops my heart."

"What amazes me is how easily that sort of thing comes to me. I should have skipped architecture and majored in crime." Reason was kidding but she felt Wilder tense up. "Do you want me to stop?" She leaned around to see his face, not wanting to be rejected again.

"No, love." Wilder found peace in her hands sliding over his aching joints. "I'd like you to go on forever."

Reason's palms were tide-like, gliding in, gliding out along his clavicles, circling down, curling around his breastbone, drawing back, in, then out. She smoothed her hands down and across his chest. Her hair breezed over his shoulder, her fragrance lingered, her voice soothed. Back and forth swept her fingers, and her fingers were heat. Hot refreshing, hot transporting, hot and soft seducing.

"When I was riding over here I knew at any moment I could be shot, and all I could think about was you. I swore if I survived, I'd take you in my arms and never let you go." Wilder stared around Cain's room. Traces of Reason were everywhere; her books and lotions on the nightstand, her clothes in the closet, her toothbrush in the bathroom, her perfume on the sheets. Like she had become Cain's woman. He turned around to face her. "But that's not going to happen. I let you go months ago, and now you're in love with Cain." He wished she would deny it but she didn't. "I ordained it, didn't I? Give your precious love to Cromwell…and you do, right here in this bed."

Reason met Wilder's gaze and her heart caught fire like it always caught fire at the sight of him. She loved Cain but she was in love with Wilder and that was forever. "You asked me not to give up on you and I haven't."

"But I think you have. You and Cain are closer than ever, and I haven't seen you in weeks."

"Would I be here right now if I'd given up? But I don't know what you want from me, Wilder. You keep changing your mind. You seem to want me in your life just to push me out of it, and you seem to want me only when I'm involved with someone else."

"All I want tonight is to hold you. Can I do that?" Wilder cupped Reason's chin in his palm, stroking her cheek. "I'm dying to kiss you."

"Then kiss me."

He petted her hair and her face, keeping his eyes on her eyes, then he took her into his arms and lay down on the bed with her. And he kissed her softly, drawing back, smiling to see her smile, then he kissed her again with hunger and lust and all the force of his heart that had stayed alive to love her, only her. And his hands slid over her body, under her sweater, touching her skin, pulling her close, like he wouldn't let go. It was good to have survived, for this kiss, this woman. But passion got the best of him, he touched Reason too intimately, kissed her too greedily, and she stopped him.

She left the bed and stood staring eastward over the sea where grey dawn squeezed through droplets of mist. "We can't do this, Wilder. Not in Cain's house, not in this room."

"I know." He walked over to Reason and kissed her cheek. "But one of these times we're going to get this right." He disappeared into the bathroom. "I'll be ready to leave in ten minutes."

"You don't want me helping you any more today, but I will pick up Morris for Kieran after school."

"Good idea...Morris? Milltown!" Wilder skidded back. "My God, Reas, that has to be it. Whoever attacked Morris in Milltown last month must have read the note he was carrying and alerted the security forces about last night's raid."

"And Morris still remembers nothing about that night?"

"Nothing at all."

"So now what do you do?"

Wilder headed for the shower. "Who the hell knows?"

Beyond the car windows Down receded.

"I'm really looking forward to Christmas vacation. After this morning I'm counting the days."

"Me too," Reason agreed. "I've been over here so long I can't remember how it feels to be in America."

Wilder eyed the cloud-capped sea to his right and dreamed of Highway One up the coast to Carmel. "It feels free."

"I'll bet your father is planning a huge celebration for your homecoming."

"You'll probably read about it in the *National Enquirer*. He has several actresses he wants me to entertain."

Reason peered over her sunglasses dimly. "At your swank seaside house?"

"Hey, that's a good idea. We'll share a little wine, frolic naked on the beach, and have outlandish sex under the stars. How does that sound?"

"Sandy," Reason clipped.

"Aha! Look at those blue eyes turning green behind those Ray-Bans," Wilder teased. "You're jealous. So why don't you come to Malibu and be the one I entertain?"

"Sorry, I'm busy. I just want to see my family and relax."

Wilder looked disappointed. "Can I come see you?"

"I'd like that."

"You wouldn't be ashamed of me this time, Mac?"

"Wilder, this time I'd throw open the door and introduce you proudly."

Reason pulled up to the Gov before eight. "We must be living right. Not a single checkpoint or roadblock."

"Now if I can just stay awake, this ordeal will finally be over." Wilder slipped Reason's hand into his. "Thanks for the lift, Reas…thanks for everything."

"Anytime, Wilder."

"When will I see you again? Tonight? Tomorrow? Sunday?"

"I'll be with Cain all weekend. But I'll see you next week."

"Maybe you can find out where Cain was at two this morning."

"I'll try."

"How is the Prince of Peculiar entertaining you this time?" Wilder asked enviously. "The guy's a three-ring circus."

"He's going to paint my portrait."

"'He's going to paint my portrait,'" Wilder mimicked Reason's enthralled voice. "A sofa-sized nude on black velvet no doubt."

"Maybe that's your idea of art, Wilder, but Cain has taste. He's going to capture my essence."

"What's your essence?"

"I'm not sure. Cain says he'll evoke it from deep within me."

"Was he talking about your essence or your orgasm?" Wilder grumped.

Reason just laughed. "Hey, you haven't seen the necklace my mother sent me." She pulled the tin sailboat out from under her sweater. "My father made it. Isn't it nice?"

Aftershock of the earthquake night. Wilder gaped at the sailboat then Reason then the sailboat again. "Your...*father?* Your *real* father?"

"Yes. What's wrong? Wilder, why are you staring at me like that?"

Ecstasy and panic left him speechless. His wild hunch had been right. Reason McGuinness was as Irish as he. Daughter of an uneducated seaman and staunch republican shot dead in Armagh; heiress to 800 years and *tiocfaidh ár lá*. He would have to go see Father Leo for more details on Michael Patrick, and Reason mustn't know the truth as long as she remained on Irish soil. Already she was too involved in the war. The last thing he wanted was for another Merry to be born.

"Wilder, what is it? What?"

He couldn't stop staring at her. She was all he desired. Innocence, intelligence, sexuality, courage, compassion, humor. Irish. He searched her eyes, lovely Armagh eyes, then he kissed her mystified smile. "*Go dté tú slán, m'ansacht álainn Gaelach.* " Take care, my beautiful Irish darling. He bolted from the car before Reason could ask him what he'd said.

Chapter Forty-One

Reason arrived thirty minutes early at Christ Church. She saw Bernard Thunder enter Cain's office.

"Hello, Cain son. How's it going?" Bernie strolled through Cain's door Friday afternoon.

Cain looked up from behind his desk and extended the doctor his hand. "What brings you to the university?"

"You." Bernard closed the office door all but a crack.

"Have a seat." Cain pointed to the park bench.

"Why, this looks exactly like the benches in Lady Dixon Park."

"You're right. I stole it."

Bernard smiled uncertainly. "I have a favor to ask of you."

Cain folded a paper airplane and launched it over Bernard's head. "Ask away, mate."

"I was over at Windsor RUC this afternoon. Got called in to tend a prisoner with a fractured skull. Clumsy yob threw himself down a flight of stairs," Bernard gave Cain a wink. "Anyway, I ran into Harry Jaggars. He said to tell you hello. Decent fellow Harry. He can smell a terrorist a mile away." He lowered his voice, "He has a young constable in need of a mentor. A Cure agent here in Belfast has requested the young man be promoted into the Covert Methods of Force unit, but the lad is reluctant. In fact, he's thinking of quitting the RUC, which would be an unfortunate loss. I suggested to Harry that you talk to the boy. Who better to advise a pup on the joys of breaking a Provisional's balls?"

"I don't suppose Harry mentioned the name of the Cure agent?"

"No, but I assume it's a chap from London; he's successfully infiltrated the IRA I'm told."

"Good for him. But why can't this agent talk to the lad himself?"

"He has to remain anonymous for security reasons. Naturally, I suggested you could encourage the boy. Don't be modest, son. Everyone knows you're still the pride of the Crown when it comes to tracking terrorists."

"I am good with an SLR, aren't I? Yeah, I love screaming, 'Kneel, you son of a bitch!' Then *kapow!* Brains hit the wall." Cain aimed another paper airplane and watched it smack Bernie between the eyes. "Ten points!" he exclaimed with a laugh. "What's this policeman's name?"

"Ian Wright," Bernard grouched, disliking his face being used as a target. "Will you talk to him?"

Cain deliberated while staring into Bernard Thunder's stainless-steel eyes. "Have Harry send the boy over. If I think he's worth my time, I'll advise him."

"I knew we could count on you, son. You've always served our country well, but I still say we need you in Down."

"Never fear, Bernie. I'm taking care of the Provies in my own special way. That reminds me," Cain spoke in a hush, "I hear you're in the ULF. Isn't murder contraindicated for a physician?"

"I see myself as an antibiotic, saving lives by eliminating pestilence."

"Provocillin," Cain suggested wryly. "I'd like to join your group."

"Excellent! We'd be honored to have you as one of our members. Damn awful about the train robbery last night. Luckily eight of the little shits were shot."

"Eight more men who never had the chance for a trial." Cain considered Bernard somberly. "I'll expect Mr. Wright Monday morning."

"Good, good. Oh! Cain, I almost forgot to ask you. I'm going to London over Christmas, and I need the name of a jeweler. Your father said if anyone knows one, you would."

Cain arched a grin. "I've rather a passion for jewels. What sort of jewelry do you want?"

"I don't want to buy anything. I want to have your family's emerald necklace appraised. Its being a Cromwell heirloom, I'd best find out its true value and insure it accordingly. I paid £65,000 for it, but your father says it's worth twice that amount."

Cain all but choked on derision. The necklace wasn't worth 65 pence. "Well, if that's true, at £65,000 it was a steal. My father must have been mad donating it to the auction."

"He's a generous man, Cain. Now, who can you recommend in London?"

"There's a little shop called Bibelot on Bond Street. Do tell them I sent you. They remember me well."

"Imperial!"

"I say, Bernie, do you keep that necklace in a safe place? I'd hate to hear our family heirloom had been stolen."

"You needn't worry, son, I have a wall safe. It would take a magician to crack it; opens with a numerical code. If the code isn't punched in correctly, a hell-raising alarm goes off in the house plus another silent alarm rings at the security firm. But the scoundrels could never find the safe in the first place." Bernie leaned close to Cain's ear, "It's behind a two-hundred-pound mirror in the guest loo. Takes me and my sons to move the fool thing."

"Sounds challenging, Bernie." Cain fashioned another airplane as Dr. Thunder turned to leave.

"Always a pleasure seeing you, Cain. A good evening to you then."

"Good evening, friend." Cain spiked his aircraft into Bernard Thunder's back.

Overhearing the conversation, Reason feared Wilder was being set up. She fled the building to join the cold wind blowing away from Christ Church. *Kapow!* Blown away, blown away. She rushed to warn Wilder, to tell him the truth about Cain, but he wasn't home. So she waited. And she pictured Cain's face. All the Englishman had ever shown her was kindness. She thought of him revealing his past and trusting her enough to reveal it. No actor could play the pain that cracked Cain, and Reason had unconditionally opened her arms. And her heart. How now could she doubt him? Because even having renounced the Cure, the Cure lurked within him. He still had the heartless heart to kill, he still liked dangerous games. And Reason would do whatever she had to do to protect Wilder. But what about protecting Cain? *"If you ever get sick of me, just tell Wilder or Kieran the truth about me."* For Wilder she would sacrifice Cain?

Too nervous to sit, Reason explored Wilder's yard. The gardens were put to bed for the winter. How carefully each rose cane was mulched to survive Belfast's freeze. How perfectly tilled the soil for its sleep. Cain's hands had done this. God's curator. Reason continued around to the back of the house, up to Wilder's deck. The stairs down the hill into the blackthorns now had graceful black lanterns lighting each step. Little beacons; Cain's work. And there amidst the blackthorns Reason saw Cain's latest gift to his friend. Three birdhouses on poles; stucco white, thatched-roof Irish cottages for the sparrows and larks. Little secure places for wild things. And the birdhouses had one Irish word painted over their little round doors; *saoirse.* Freedom.

Tears blurred Reason's eyes. For one moment she had lost her head and lost her trust, and she would have cost Cain his life. It was she, not he, who had a Judas heart. The thought filled her with shame. And she realized how precious Cain was to her. She ran to her car.

Cain had waited for Reason for over an hour even though he knew she wasn't coming. He knew where she was. She had gone directly to Wilder. Wilder. Sumner's prize. Idol of Reason's eyes. Wilder who lived to risk everything and appreciated nothing. Trying to remain upbeat, Cain put on his jacket, snapped out the lights and locked his office. But walking down the corridor, hearing the wind howl, solitude shook him. He had thought of nothing all day except painting Reason's portrait. Tonight he would paint her from memory. Alone. And My Lady's Leisure would whistle and whine in quietude. Having contended all his life to be a solitary man, it was hard for Cain to believe Reason, Wilder's Reason, had become an integral part of his happiness.

He knew by now she had told Wilder everything. Wilder would know Cain had been a Cure agent and was conspiring with Bernard Thunder. He'd conclude Cain had deluded him, and he would sign Cain's warrant of death. *Kneel you son of a bitch. Serves me right. And Reason will side with Wilder and call me unforgivable and deceitful and slam the doors of her life. Why didn't she stay long enough to let me explain?* Because to her he would always be tainted. In her eyes he was a threat to Wilder. And Wilder always came first. But maybe it was for the best if Reason aligned herself with the Irishman. Cain owed his life to Sumner, and Sumner had been furious to hear Cain had formed a romantic liaison with the woman Wilder pined to possess. But Sumner was wrong. Wilder didn't pine. He overlooked. Forsook. Squandered Reason. And Cain wished Reason would walk into the room and see him; him as Cain Cromwell before the Cure twisted him mad. And he wished she believed in him enough to know his words with Bernie were lies. But no. For Wilder, she assumed the worst. And turned away.

She found him in the library, setting up his easel by candlelight. Preoccupied with his work, Cain hadn't heard Reason come in. He had the sleeves of his shirt pushed up, his vest was black cashmere, contrasting his fair skin. His wool slacks were pressed and well-fitting on taut legs, and his sunny hair was tied back in its short lovelock on his nape. How sturdy, steady his fingers cleaning a brush. How powerful his arms and wrists daubing his palette. And his face belied a lust for life. Unlike Wilder, who had grown solemn and hard, Cain was robust and rich with passion.

"Cain, I'm sorry I'm late," Reason burst into the room, charged with emotions she couldn't hide.

He dropped his brush in surprise. "You've come!" But had she come to forswear him? "Are you here to tell me good-bye?"

With his brown eyes mild as trade winds upon her, she discounted every ugly word she'd heard. "Why would I do that?"

"Because you heard my conversation with Bernie. How do I know? You broke the first rule of surveillance. Never wear a scent unless you want to leave a trace. I smelled your perfume."

"I didn't mean to eavesdrop, well, yes, I did...I thought you were conspiring with Bernie..."

"And now you think I've been lying to you about who I am, right?"

"You wouldn't lie to me, Cain."

"Did you run to warn Wilder? Is that where you've been?"

Thank heaven Wilder hadn't been home. Reason shuddered to think how close she came to betraying Cain. "No."

"But I thought your loyalties lay first with him always."

"So do yours, Cain."

"And what about your loyalty to me? Reason, if you and I are to have any sort of relationship, you have to trust me. I know that's hard knowing what you know, but if you can't do this, we have no future, *I* have no future."

"I trust you, and I'm loyal to you. And right now all I want is you."

Cain stared at Reason as if she were all he saw, all that mattered, all that was. He threw down his palette and ran to grab her, to fill his palms with her hair, to possess once more the softness of her lips. And zealously, Reason returned his passion. He undressed her quickly. She helped him tear off his vest and shirt and slacks. Entwined, they crashed up against the library wall. Books and papers toppled around them. Not removing his lips from Reason's, Cain tried to lead the way up to his bedroom, but there was no time. They stumbled up the stairs towards the library's loft, but that was too far. Halfway up the steps, Cain gripped Reason beneath him and they slid down the steps to the library floor. And there amidst Goethe and Schopenhauer they made love. And My Lady's Leisure whispered quietude. Beatitude. Evermore, evermore.

Naked and smiling, Cain returned to his easel. "And now I'll paint you."

"Oh not yet," Reason protested. "I want to brush my hair and take a bath and…"

"No. That would spoil it. I want to capture you in this moment with my touch, my life, my love still fresh upon you."

"But, Cain, I look…"

"You look sensuous, like Ariadne after Venus gave her an immortal lover."

"That would make you Bacchus, my immortal lover then." There stood Cain in his natural glory, and the idea of him and Greek mythology inspired Reason's fantasy. "Yes, I can see you as Bacchus; the youthful and beautiful god of drama and wine."

"Or am I Theseus, the dashing hero who Ariadne first loved and helped to escape from the man-eating Minotaur in the maze?"

"Oh, don't be Theseus!" Reason cried, for in Greek mythology Theseus ran off to be an Argonaut and broke Ariadne's heart. "Theseus abandoned Ariadne after she saved his life. You have to be Bacchus."

"Then Bacchus I'll be and love you forever. Now let me get you a glass of wine. Re-light the candles that have gone out, would you?"

"You're going to paint me by candlelight? How romantic."

"Candlelight is the twilight of genius, my love."

Reason accepted the beaujolais and kissed Cain's fingers as he served it. "How do you want me to pose?"

"Any way that's comfortable. I'll paint you as I see you no matter what."

Cain spread a carpet before the library's hearth. Reason settled back and was glad for the heat of the fire on her bare back. "Aren't you cold with no clothes on?"

Cain arranged tubes of paint beside his easel and primed his palette with colors. "After that phenomenal sex I'll be sweating for a month. Does my being naked bother you?"

"Not at all. It adds to the art of the evening. Besides, I like looking at you."

Cain tapped his paint brush on his canvas like a conductor alerting the orchestra. "Are you ready to be immortalized?"

"Can't I at least comb my hair?"

"Nope. Your hair is the result of passion. What's more beautiful than that? And now," he dipped his brush in hooker green, "a masterpiece dawns."

"There," Cain relinquished his brush after two hours and reviewed his work, "I'll call it *My Lady's Pleasure*."

Reason hopped to her feet and drew on her robe. "May I see it?"

"Not until it's finished."

"I'll die of curiosity!"

"No, we'll both be dead from starvation before that. It just occurred to me we haven't eaten. Toss me my bathrobe, would you? Thanks, love." He wiped the paint off his fingers and drew on the robe. "Let's go see what there is for dinner."

"I hope you have more food here tonight than you did this morning."

Cain gave her a funny look. "What do you mean?"

Cat out of the bag. Reason didn't know what to say. She turned away and concentrated on the fire.

But Cain came up behind her. "Reason, what did you mean?"

"Where were you last night?"

"I was at home. I talked to you, remember?"

"You said you were at home but you weren't. Wilder tried to call you at two this morning."

"Oh, did he?" Cain took Reason by the shoulders, forcing her to face him. "Don't tell me he got you involved in that Pembroke shit! He didn't, did he?"

"How do you know about Wilder's latest adventure?"

"I figured it out real fast last night. I went to his house, but he wasn't home. When I turned on the late news and heard there had been a train robbery, I knew right away that's where Wilder was." Cain threw up his arms in outrage. "The man is begging for catastrophe! So, when he couldn't reach me, he called you, and you rushed to his aid. Brilliant."

"I came down here and got him early this morning."

"Damn him! Here? You came here to the estate?"

"It was Wilder's only choice. You don't mind, do you?"

"I mind like hell him dragging you into this," Cain seethed.

"Will you just calm down? You don't know the whole story."

"Then tell me the whole story."

Reason related the details. "…and those phones are probably tapped, so you see there was no one else he could safely call."

"That explains the stray horse in my paddock. I thought it had wandered in out of the fog. And the soldiers came here?"

"They were quite civil actually."

"And you managed them?"

"I was a nervous wreck, but yes."

"Oh, Reason, Reason, what are we going to do about you?" Cain looped his arms around her shoulders. "I was sure Wilder would shield you from all of this. He and I agreed on that."

"Well, I didn't agree on it. No one has the luxury of staying uninvolved here, Cain. You told me that months ago and you were right. I want to help."

"Reason, don't do this!" Cain spun away. "You're begging for a bad outcome, and I've seen too many of those."

"All I did was drive down here!"

"To save Wilder! Your passion for Irish freedom is really your passion for Declan O'Neill."

Reason didn't disagree.

"You can always go home," Cain suggested tersely.

"How could I leave you? How would I leave Fiona and Morris and…"

"And your precious Wilder. You'd risk everything for him, even your life, even my life." Cain started cleaning his brushes. The blues swirled in turpentine, then the reds in droplets bled, and the greens ran like his jealousy. "Does he make love to you when you're with him?" he inquired, without looking up.

"No."

Cain raised brows of incredulity. "The man's a pillar of restraint. But you want him to, don't you? You'd let him take you in a second."

"I don't want to talk about Wilder!" Reason said fitfully.

"I'm your lover, he's your love." Cain slapped down his brushes and headed for the kitchen. He wished he weren't feeling jealous, and hurt. Sumner had Reason sent here to love Wilder, to seduce him and save him, so how could Cain protest her devotion? He had no one to blame but himself. He'd been warned, and he'd rushed to Reason like a man rushing into thin air.

Reason let him walk away. She couldn't say the words he wanted to hear. That she didn't want Wilder. Or that she could resist him. "Life would be easier if I didn't love him, Cain. Can you understand what that's like? To love someone you shouldn't?"

He held out his hand for Reason to join him. "Sadly, love, I can."

Chapter Forty-Two

"Drugs and alcohol, Cromwell?" Wilder didn't knock Monday morning. He whisked off his driver's cap and waltzed into Cain's office unannounced. "I should have known you'd be at my house last Friday. I got a phone call this morning from one of my patients. She called to thank me for the advice."

"Oh, you mean the woman with the sprained ankle? Yeah, she called your house that night. I recommended she put ice on her foot, elevate it, and take two ibuprofen with three large glasses of wine."

"You're hopeless…but she said your advice worked. Reason tells me you know the whole story about Friday."

"Thank God for your loyal Reason."

"Ah, cut the glare of daggers, Cain. I had no other choice than to call her."

"The hell you didn't! You could have stayed out of trouble in the first place. You're damn lucky it worked out. If you pull this shit again, Wilder, I'm going to rip out your tongue through your nose, and don't think I don't know how to do precisely that."

"Hey, if you'd been around…"

"If you had told me your plans…"

"It doesn't matter," Wilder backed off. "There was nothing you could have done to avert disaster. But thank you for letting us use My Lady's Leisure."

"Seems I had no choice."

"You didn't show me how to open the grate to the dungeon for nothing, Cain. Did Reason tell you the security forces were tipped off?"

"Yes, and she told me about Morris in Milltown." Cain noticed the time. The young man from Windsor would be arriving, and Cain didn't want Wilder seeing him with a constable. "Sorry to rush you off, but I haven't time to talk now. Is there a particular reason you're here?"

"I'd like to store some medical supplies at My Lady's Leisure, if that's OK with you."

"Sure. I'll bring you a set of keys when I return your golf clubs."

"You have my golf clubs?"

"Oh, didn't I tell you I borrowed them? Shot a seventy six last week at Portrush. Well," Cain hastened Wilder to the door, "it's good to see you alive. Next time let me in on your plans, and I'll be home."

Wilder opened the door and there stood Ian Wright. He recognized the young man at once as the policeman who had let him slip by on the Antrim Road. Wilder spun to Cain in suspicion.

"Hello, sir." Ian extended his hand, remembering Wilder. "Dr. O'Neill, right?

Wilder refused his handshake. "You two are *friends?*"

"He's my new student," Cain said and offered Ian his hand. "I'm Cain Cromwell."

"Ian Wright, sir."

"Sir?" Cain groaned. "Don't call me 'sir.'"

"Uh…sorry, sir," Ian nervously stammered and shied from Wilder's stare of aversion, and why wouldn't he be averse? Ian wished he could apologize for all the Harry Jaggars who preyed on Irish men.

Wilder glanced from Cain to Ian, but to Cain's surprise, he didn't say anything. He just tipped his cap and left.

"Sit down," Cain instructed, sizing up Ian who reminded him of a walking garden. Long and lank as a cornstalk. Hair the color of pumpkins, eyes broccoli green, cauliflower skin. And young as a sapling. "How old are you?"

"Twenty, sir…I mean, Dr. Cromwell."

"Call me Cain. How do you know Dr. O'Neill?"

"We met at a checkpoint on the Antrim Road last summer."

Cain rocked back and propped his feet on his desk. "So, you've come to talk about the CMF unit."

"I guess so," Ian shrugged.

"Do you know the name of the Cure agent who recommended you for CMF?"

"No."

"Do you know why you're being promoted?"

Ian had no idea it was because he had helped save Madeline Hatter's dog. "I'm embarrassed to say it, but no. I've only been on the force a few months and I'm nothing special."

"Have you any exceptional talents or experience?"

Ian shook his head. "I'm really quite ordinary. In fact, I'd say I'm a disappointment."

"Curious, curious indeed."

"Oh, but I'm likable and smart," Ian offered with the retiring smile of a boy.

"Ah yes, those qualities are prized by the RUC. Why did you join the force?"

"For the money."

"Being with the RUC, you're a Protestant?"

"Aye, sir. Church of Ireland."

"Are you a member of any paramilitary groups? The ULF, perhaps? Some policemen are."

"Och no, sir."

"As a member of the security forces you're at risk of being murdered. Do you worry about that?"

"Well, sir, I don't want to die, but I don't want my family to go needing either. The life insurance is good. I'm worth quite a lot dead."

"How do you feel about the IRA?"

This time Ian didn't answer quickly. He lowered his eyes. "I think they're very violent...and we'll never defeat them."

Ian's reticence didn't escape Cain. "Would you like to work along the border?" He pretended to aim and shoot a rifle. "Quite a few Provos have been defeated down there."

"The truth is, I don't like guns."

"You don't like guns, and the Cure wants you to be trained in covert methods of force?" Cain laughed out loud. "Is this a joke?"

"Well, I don't really want to do this, but Detective Jaggars is insisting. I said I'd talk to you just to get him off my case. He's very intimidating, you know?"

"That he is. Have you ever shot anyone?"

Ian's face grew a shade paler. "No, sir."

"Ian, the CMF unit is all about ambush and assassination. You'd be working undercover with the Cure."

Ian was quiet.

"Being a cop is more of a necessity than a choice for you, right?"

"If I had my choice, I'd be a veterinarian. But police work is the only job I could get and make enough money to support my family. I have three wee sons."

"Three sons and you're only twenty? You're a busy man."

Ian's cheeks flooded radish-red. "Got married at sixteen so we did."

Cain pressed his fingertips together beneath his chin and considered the young man. "Were you working at Windsor when Ruairi McKee died?"

Ian refused to look up. "Yes."

"Were you part of the interrogation team?"

"Och, Jesus, no."

"Who interrogated him? I can't remember."

"Jaggars, Franks and Harlock. Do you know them?"

Cain nodded and made a mental note of the names. "Terrible how Ruairi died."

"Sickening," Ian moaned. "He kept saying he was innocent of murdering those soldiers, and he was."

"Come now, Ian, can Provisionals ever be innocent?"

"I suppose not," Ian muttered. "But anymore are any of us innocent? We let the war grind on and do nothing."

"What can anyone do?"

"Stop living like it's fucking 1690! All I know is, if we demand that the IRA surrender and give up their guns, we'll only make them stronger. That's the problem, the loyalists and the British want to have all the weapons, all the power. The IRA will never go away or disarm, so we should deal with them."

"We don't negotiate with terrorists."

"Oh, for the love of God," Ian blustered. "And where's that gotten us?"

Cain couldn't hide his dismay. "Of all the people to send over here for me to talk to."

Ian figured he'd lost his chance for promotion, maybe even his job. He had nothing to lose and added, "I just think somebody ought to listen to the republicans for a change."

"What could they possibly have to say?"

"A lot of Catholic Ulster votes for republicans in the elections, so they must have something to say worth hearing. But the British government keeps having peace talks and either refuses to include Sinn Féin or kicks them out of the talks. We'll kill them, but we won't talk to them. Around here, murder is easier than dialogue. I know the Provos are bad, but the British are no better. Either both sides disarm or no one disarms. There'll be no victories here, Dr. Cromwell, just bloodshed."

Cain stared at the young man, dumbfounded. "Are you for real?"

"Hey, all Protestants aren't screaming loyalists," Ian defended angrily. "Some of us realize what's going on over here is wrong. Some of us are ready to try any sensible solution, including a unified Ireland, if it will end the damn war. And the truth is, I thought I could do some good in the RUC by being open-minded. But I was insane. The longer I'm on the force, the more contempt I have for it. And for myself."

"So why are you even considering the CMF?" Cain puzzled.

"I don't want to shoot anybody, I just want to stop the fighting. I want to change things, and the only way to do that is to become the change I want to see. I'm sure this sounds ridiculous to someone like you, but I thought maybe I could spare a man's life, maybe I could offer a shred of morality by *not* killing. The only way to change the RUC is to change the men within it."

"You're Ireland's Gandhi, are you? Just remember he was shot dead."

Ian stared down at the floor. "Oh, it's a stupid idea. I'm embarrassed I even suggested it. I may as well try to part the Irish Sea! I'm sorry, Dr. Cromwell, I don't belong here."

All the sweet scruples of an unblemished soul, all the absurd belief that virtue prevails. Cain saw himself at twenty, and he saw Ian as another tender virgin about to be lost. "If you pursue morality amidst ruthless men, Ian, all I can say to you is raise your hands so we can measure your palms for the nails. Nothing's more dangerous than reform." He produced his fifth of Scotch and poured two shots into glasses. "But that doesn't mean you can't do some good. Have a drink, and we'll talk."

*　　*　　*　　*　　*　　*

Jillie pulled the drapes and closed Fiona's parlor door to darken the room. "Come sit beside me, sweetie," she patted the sofa for Morris to join her. "We'll watch the movie together."

Seeing the closed drapes and door, feeling trapped, Morris bolted himself to his chair. "I hate *Fantasia*. I hate it!"

"Morris, it's your favorite movie." Kieran regarded his son, perplexed. "Jillie took the afternoon off and rented it especially for you."

Since his night of terror in Milltown, Morris had been unnaturally sullen, and he refused to tell Kieran or Reason or Granny Nora, not even his beloved Uncle Decky, what troubled his mind. Many nights he had wandered into Reason's bedroom as she worked, and his blue eyes brimmed with torment. His lips would part as if to disclose what tortured his heart, but each time he would turn and run back downstairs before a single secret escaped.

"I want to go upstairs to my room," Morris pouted, giving the rug a kick and glaring at Jillie.

"But Morris honey, I hardly ever see you." Jillie thumped the sofa again. "Come on over here; we'll have fun."

Morris would not forget the brigade note. **November 16. 10 p.m. Craig Station.** Eight men got shot, and he blamed himself for each fallen soul. Jillie had read the note. Jillie told. "No! You can't make me!" Morris blared and tried to run from the room.

Jillie wiped tears from her lashes and made sure Kieran caught her crestfallen look.

"Morris, get back here," Kieran ordered and Morris slinked back. "What's the matter with you? Where are your manners?"

Morris gazed up at his father with haunted eyes, and he prayed he would always have Kieran to look up to. "I'm sorry, Daddy."

"Don't tell me you're sorry. Tell Jillie."

Jillie smiled expectantly; a smile of gloating, of power and cunning. Pretty so pretty smiles blinding Daddy blind. One skinny tear escaped Morris' eye, but he stared back at Jillie. And he couldn't wait to be a man. With a gun. To fight back. "I'm sorry, Jillie," he croaked through gritted teeth.

She opened maternal arms to the boy; arms like a Venus Flytrap waiting, waiting...Morris ran to sit in his chair.

Kieran turned on the VCR and the movie began. "Tell Jillie what you're favorite part of the movie is, Morris."

"I don't remember."

Not understanding his son's mood, Kieran glimpsed at Jillie apologetically. "Morris likes the *Sorcerer's Apprentice.*"

As pink hippopotamuses danced, Morris watched the hemlock lady's fingers crawl up Kieran's chest...*Fingers like scorpions,* Morris cringed. Jillie stroked Kieran's cheeks and hair...*She's sharpening her claws,* Morris held his breath. Jillie whispered in Kieran's ear, and when Kieran smiled and kissed his love, Morris saw the sick, besotted smile of a man being patiently, purposely poisoned.

"Did you know Brits go to hell?" Morris announced. "There's no light or silence or sleep there. My teacher says hell is a hot, howling pit."

Both Kieran and Jillie turned to the boy in dismay.

"The devil hates Brits most of all," Morris continued desperately. "He roasts 'em alive."

"Morris, what is your problem today?" Kieran boomed in annoyance.

Morris let sing the top of his lungs, "This movie is stupid and you're stupid and Jillie is stupid and I hate her, I hate her, I hate her." Noting Kieran's reddening face, Morris took to his heels. Into the foyer he raced. In panic he heaved open the front door and saw Reason arriving. On fleet feet he galloped to greet her.

"Morris, what's wrong?"

"Let's go for a walk." He stole Reason's hand, not giving her a chance to decline.

Stomping through fallen leaves along the sidewalk, Morris tugged Reason down Duntroon Drive until they dipped into the day's last sunshine beaming through the bare trees. "Do you hear what the wind says, Reason, do you?" Morris pulled her into the center of the sunbeam where November's chill pretended to be May. "It says, 'Hallo, hallo,' and..." he dissolved into tears.

"Oh dear, Morris," Reason stooped to face him. "What's the matter?"

Morris gurgled, "Nnnothing," and didn't want to talk. But when Reason's arms tightened around him in the warm sunlight, he felt safe, so safe. Pinching his arms around her neck, he rested his head on her chest and allowed her to hug him. Her hair glistened and played like fragments of the sunset as it caught the wind and caught the light and tickled his cheek. Her touch on his brow was velvet, and her neck smelled like lilies. White lilies, the symbol of Irish freedom, and Reason set troubles free. He clung to her until his arms grew weak and his heart burst into song.

Chapter Forty-Three

Reason was finishing a last bit of work before going to bed when Kieran materialized out of nowhere. "Do you know where Our Lady of Lourdes Catholic Church is?"

"Isn't it the old brick church just up the Antrim Road from here?"

"Aye. Can you be there Wednesday morning at nine?"

Reason checked her calendar. "Yes."

"Good. Go around to the back of the church. A car will be provided for you. You'll be picking up a nun and driving her to Dublin."

Reason crinkled her brow. "A nun?"

Kieran offered no explanation. "She'll give you directions where to drop her once you get to Dublin. Understand?"

"Yes."

"Her name is Sister Mary Agnes. Be sure to ask her full name before you let her into the car. Goodnight then, love." As quickly as he appeared, he vanished.

Shadows cupped the alleyway behind Our Lady of Lourdes. Junipers rose like a pontifical cap on either side of the lane and blocked the morning sun. With misgiving, Reason walked into the alley where a red Volkswagen awaited. Despite the illicit circumstance, her loyalty to Kieran and Wilder prevailed. Before getting in the car she reflected upon what she was doing, and in American terms it was insane. But things kept happening to her in Belfast that weren't normal, but they were normal for Belfast. The city stirred madness in many a mind, and sooner or later the madness seemed reasonable.

It was twenty minutes before a priest escorted the nun out the back door of the church. Reason watched them conversing as they glided in their swarthy cassocks and fingered their long ivory beads. The sister slung along a tattered duffel bag; the priest carried a pint of bourbon. Upon reaching the car, the father patted the sister's shoulder and opened the car door, saying to Reason, "This is Sister Mary Agnes." The nun flashed a toothy greeting Reason's way, heaved her bag into the car like a forward pass, lit a cigarette and slapped the priest farewell on the back.

"Come inside with me please," the father then instructed Reason.

She drew back in alarm. "Why?"

"Don't worry, miss, it's only for your habit. A car driven by a woman and a nun looks suspicious," the priest said while whisking Reason into the church, "but a car carrying two sisters shall safely sail."

Primping in the rearview mirror, Reason found her reflection immensely amusing. A nun. "I was told to drive to Dublin via County Tyrone," Reason informed her companion, knocking the folds of her black cap away from her cheeks and starting the car. "Is that all right?"

The nun bobbed her broad cap and switched on the radio. Flipping through the stations, Mary Agnes couldn't decide between a sports talk show and the morning news. And as the good sister screwed the dial station to station, it was impossible for Reason not to notice the nun's hairy hand. Startled, she considered the sister's face. Not a hint of a beard, just a baby-soft chin, thin pale lips and rosebud cheeks. Finding the masquerade clever, Reason snatched glimpses of her passenger all the way down the Antrim Road. There was something familiar as the nun twisted his young face to Reason. Soft, dark eyes. She had met this boy. Another stolen glance. In Albie's funeral home the night she followed Wilder through the tunnels. The wounded young man with the broken nose.

"You make a brilliant nun. Prettier than any of the ones I ever had in school." The sister studied Reason's face. "And you've been in my dreams," he admitted. "I've never met you, but I've seen you in my head a hundred times. How can that be?"

"We have met, well, at least I think we have. Last summer you broke your nose among other things in a motorcycle accident, right?"

"Aye, but I don't remember seeing you."

"I cut your mask off and tried to stop your nose from bleeding. You were pretty hurt. The whole experience probably seemed like a dream."

Mr. Sister sat awhile then uttered brightly, "Well, thanks for tending me then." He peered up at the sun and rubbed his hairy hands. Then he unscrewed the bourbon. "Nice day for a journey so it is. Have a wee drink, will you?"

Reason declined. "Are you looking forward to leaving?"

"Oh aye. Can't wait to get out of this heart-of-stone country. I only wish my brothers had gotten out," the sister lamented with a drink.

"Maybe they can join you later."

The sister roughly chortled, "Hardly. They're dead. Did you know Aidan Duffy? He was my older brother."

"Oh, yes. I liked him. The RUC hasn't found who killed him, have they?"

"Hell, they know who killed him. They just don't fucking care. One less taig is all they think. Aidan wasn't a Provie you know. I wasn't either until the fucking Cure shot him. Enough is enough. Went and joined the Ra right after the fucking funeral I did."

A cursing nun. Only in Northern Ireland.

"Aidan's death destroyed my mum and dad," the young man continued acridly, tipping the bourbon to his mouth again. "First the Brits killed Paul then Aidan. And neither was a Provie. Neither."

"Paul was your other brother?"

"Aye. Some soldiers in the New Lodge mistook him for an armed terrorist, that's how they fucking explained it. They shot him outside our front door. Only thirteen he was, and there was no fucking inquest, no investigation. The Army called the shooting self-defense. Fucking case closed."

"That's terrible."

"Terrible." Another gruff chuckle. Another guzzle of bourbon. The nun went on, "Mourning by rote, that's what's terrible. Grief has become a fucking habit here. Terrible! Everybody stands in line to wail and tear their hair about the violence, but nobody ever does fucking anything about it."

"You're lucky to be leaving the Troubles behind. Maybe you can start a happier life in the South."

"Leaving the Troubles behind? That's funny," the nun had another hearty snort. "What do you think this is? A friggin' fairytale? I'm not going to Dublin to live fucking happily ever after. I'm going to catch a flight to Berlin."

"What's in Germany?"

"AK 74's."

Reason shook her head with resignation. "Do you think peace will ever come to this country?"

"Peace?" the sister crowed and slapped the dashboard. "That's a fucking farce."

Reason was taken aback. "What a pessimistic thing to say."

"Nah, love, it's realistic."

"Peace is hardly a joke."

"Do you know how many times we've been promised a peaceful solution over the last twenty five years? And every round of talks ends up being nothing more than a round of tantrums thrown by the fucking politicians. Nothing ever gets settled. So how else are we supposed to cope with the constant disappointment other than making a joke of it? See, what you're promised but never given is the thing you come to hate. Over and over we've been made to look foolish for getting our hopes up for peace, for believing the Troubles could actually be solved. The only sure thing in our lives is the war. It's the one thing we can hold onto; the one thing that will last and never disappoint us with its awfulness."

Reason sighed with discouragement. "That's depressing."

"Aye. I suppose that's why so many people here pound themselves daft with the drink and pop Valiums like candy," Mr. Sister stated without much care. "Were you in Belfast last spring?"

"No."

"Some folks out the Malone decided to have a peace rally. They came to the park and said they were going to release 3000 doves; one for every victim of the war. But only a handful of people bothered showing up, and the peace promoters didn't release doves at all. They released 3000 pigeons. Pigeons! That fucking says it all," he guffawed and swizzled more bourbon.

Crossing the border was easy. Kieran had routed Reason through an unauthorized border crossing deep in County Tyrone where there were no soldiers or checkpoints. Free as field mice, the nuns rolled through lush farmlands and cruised into the Republic.

"We slipped right through? We're in the South?" Reason's heart pounded. "I thought for sure someone was going to leap out of the bushes and pull us over," she said as the border dwindled out of sight in her mirror.

"Nah. We'll be all right now, love." The young man began removing the heavy wool habit to reveal jeans and a sweater. "Good-bye to the fucking British Queen," he rallied with a final wave to the North.

Later that evening Kieran joined Reason in Fiona's kitchen. He checked her up and down, and when he decided she was fit, he kissed both her cheeks. Everything that needed to be said of the day's mission was said in a nod. Kieran then grabbed his jacket and stalked into the game of the night.

*   *   *   *   *   *

RUC OFFICER GUNNED DOWN BY IRA, cried the front page of the papers Thursday morning. **Officer Clive Harlock of Windsor RUC died in a hail of bullets fired at his car late yesterday,** Reason read with her morning tea. **An IRA gang sprayed the Ford Sierra with bullets. Mr. Harlock was found sitting in the driver's seat.** She skipped several paragraphs. **"Clive was a gentle, peace-loving Christian who never raised a hand against another living soul,"** said a spokesman for the RUC. **"No doubt the Godfathers of terrorism who ordered this evil act are wringing their hands with glee."** Reason glanced up to find Kieran reading over her shoulder.

"He's one of the men who beat Ruairi to death," he stated casually as he tapped cornflakes into a bowl.

"How do you know that?"

"It's amazing what I can learn from Cain." Kieran bent close to Reason to be sure Fiona wouldn't overhear, "Officers Harlock, Franks and Jaggars kicked and clubbed and killed Ruairi. 'Three gentle, peace-loving men.'"

Reason perused the news article further. The RUC spokesman responded with tears in his eyes, **"History shall judge most harshly those brutal gangsters who chose to murder their fellow countryman..."**

Chapter Forty-Four

Thanksgiving Day in America, unsettled weather in Belfast. Every so often the sun popped out only to be quashed by fits of rain. Reason looked out her office window while water gushed down and smeared the view. Wishing for twelve hours of blistering sun, she dreamed of Denver's gleam below the glory of the mountains, of Manhattan's tiara of towers bursting towards heaven in magic and light.

"Rain's got you feeling homesick too, huh?" Suave in a herringbone blazer and black flannel slacks, Wilder claimed the chair at Reason's desk and seemed to read her thoughts. "I've been thinking about ninety-degree heat and blue margaritas all day."

"Ninety degrees sounds wonderful. I'd throw off my clothes and dance in the sun." Reason wheeled to Wilder happily. "How's our insurgent surgeon this afternoon? Recovered from last week I hope."

Catching sight of Jillie working at her computer, Wilder closed the door. "After I crashed into bed Friday night, I didn't wake up again until Sunday morning, and even then I felt wasted. I think I'm getting too old for those hours."

Reason traced the drizzle with her pencil. "Only twenty seven more days and I'll be home for three weeks."

"I have you beat. I'm on a plane to Malibu in twenty, count 'em twenty days."

"And there your nubile starlets await."

"Aye, but I'll be thinking only of you, Mac."

"Yeah, right," Reason japed. Her eyes were bright with the sight of Wilder seated before her. So handsome. "To what do I owe the pleasure of your visit?"

"What are you doing for dinner this evening? Being stuck here in Belfast I figure you won't be eating turkey...or are you seeing Cromwell tonight?"

Reason rolled her eyes but laughed. "You're kinda cute when you're juvenile, O'Neill. Tell me, why are you always coming in here at the last minute asking me to spend the evening with you? I have a life you know."

Wilder pretended to be offended. "I don't recall asking you to spend the evening with me. I just dropped in to wish you a happy Thanksgiving."

"Oh? Oh. Sorry." Reason inched back to her view overlooking the Falls Road.

"And as for it being the last minute, will you give me a break? I got out of surgery only an hour ago then I did my rounds."

"What are *you* doing this evening?"

"Right now I'm going to walk up to Milltown to visit Bren and Merry's graves before it gets dark. Great family reunion for the holiday." He stepped up behind Reason and placed his hands on her hips while resting his chin atop her head. "I was hoping you'd come to the cemetery with me...I was just winding you up a minute ago. I did come to ask you to spend the evening with me. I know it's the end of the day, and maybe you are busy...please say yes."

Reason turned around, laughing at the games she and Wilder played. "Of course I'm busy," she patted Wilder's chest pertly and slipped out of his reach, "but for you I'll make time."

"Making time? Sounds good to me, Reas," Wilder cracked, enjoying her long, shapely legs.

"Your time for making time ran out in August, ace," Reason corrected and tried to ignore Wilder's fascination with her body and face. "I've been meaning to go to Milltown all week."

"Why?"

"I want to see the grave of Michael Patrick McGuinness. Which reminds me, why did you have a note to go see Father Leo about him?"

"How do you…know about Michael Patrick?" Wilder stammered. "How do you know about Father Leo?"

Reason belted her raincoat. "Ever since I saw Michael's boats on top of the church I've wanted to know more about him. Then last week I noticed the note on the wall in your office. So I went to see Father Leo."

"And what did he tell you?" Wilder asked with his heart in his throat. How much did she know?

"The saddest story. If you went to see Father Leo, surely you heard it."

"Yes, I heard it."

"Why are you interested in Michael McGuinness, Wilder?"

His eyes feasted on Reason. A succulent tribute to womanhood. "Same reason as you. Because of the work of art he left behind."

"Magnificent, isn't it?"

"Flawless," Wilder agreed softly.

"Where are you two away for?" Jillie chirped, wondering again if Reason and Wilder were lovers. Reason avoided looking at Wilder…like he tortured her heart. Jillie shifted her sights to Wilder. Reason was the story in his eyes.

Wilder draped one owning arm over Reason's shoulder, and not lifting his eyes from her face, answered offhandedly, "Up to Milltown to cavort with the dead."

"See you later, Jillie," Reason called with her attention on what Wilder was saying in her ear.

He acts like I no longer exist. That, dear Declan, is a stupid mistake. Jillie tapped her fingernails on her desk. She had been putting it off for weeks, but as she watched Wilder amorously sweeping Reason away, she decided the time was right. She picked up the phone.

"What are you thankful for today?" Reason asked Wilder as they enjoyed the flash of afternoon sun that shimmered in puddles up the Falls Road.

"I'm thankful I have you to count on, and that I wasn't shot last week. How about you?"

"Believe it or not, I'm thankful your father had me sent here."

In silence, Wilder hooked Reason's hand, and he was glad when she held onto him. Tightly. Up the Falls as soldiers teemed and soldiers watched. Tightly. And as the rain gobbled the sun, and the wind dived off the hills, Wilder sensed he was taking Reason home. To Milltown. To Michael. To Declan.

While Wilder paid respect to his siblings, Reason stood before the cross that marked the grave of Michael Patrick. Spellbound, she was immune to the raw breeze biting her legs and the foul, freezing mist whipping her curls. Vividly, she reconstructed the scene Father Leo had described. A tin whistle had played for Michael Patrick. *Lonely, so lonely.* Reason remembered one night long ago when Wilder had taken her to hear Irish music, and the tin whistle had brought to mind a thousand farewells and sad separations; a whistle hauntingly familiar yet never before heard. Reason touched her heart with emotion and felt the sailboat necklace upon her breast. Smooth and pretty. Pretty Johanna and her little daughter. A linen Tricolour and white lilies in a foul, freezing mist. Dark, running mud, an open grave...*Don't die! Good-bye.* Michael's wee daughter waving the Tricolour. *Blue, Irish eyes...Good-bye, Daddy. Good-bye, good-bye...*

When Wilder came to Michael's grave he found Reason in tears. "What does that mean?" she pointed to the Irish inscription on the cross.

"*Bí mo leannán, is mo leannán sa amháin. Saor Eire, grá mo chroí.* Be my lover, my only lover. Free Ireland, my darling."

"Oh, that's so sweet, and sad. Do you think Johanna had this cross made for Michael?"

"Yes, I think she did."

"I don't know why seeing his grave makes me this upset. His story is just so tragic," Reason wept as Wilder put his arms around her. "Every time I think of him and Johanna, it breaks my heart."

Wilder fought the urge to tell Reason everything. How would she handle the fact that she, the haughty Wellworth-Howell, had been born in West Belfast? That she had been baptized in the Church? The Irish Catholic Church. Once it would have disgraced her. Now Wilder knew for certain it would give credence and fuel to the dawning Fenian already too headstrong within Reason. "I'm sure he appreciates your tears for him, Reas. But remember Johanna and her daughter moved to America and found a better life. Michael would have wanted that for them, don't you think?"

"Yes. But it just goes to show you falling in love with a republican is madness. A woman might as well put a shotgun to her heart." Reason peered up at Wilder whom she fervently embraced. Raven curls delightful to feel...*I love you with all my life, marry me, marry me...*brilliant blue eyes above that summer-night smile...*Jesus, Reason, don't love me, I can't help it....*madness. She stepped back to free herself from Wilder's clasp, but he refused to release her.

"We'll leave in a minute," he said over the wind then he raised Reason's right hand to his lips. He kissed each finger and caressed her hand to his cheek, to his heart. And when Reason least expected it, in the grey-lemon light between sunset and rain, in the foul, freezing brume that shrouded Michael's cross, Wilder slipped a gold ring on her fourth finger. A crowned heart cupped in two hands; the Claddagh. "This was Merry's. See, it has her initials. She would have admired you like I do, and I want you to have it," Wilder said, still claiming Reason's Irish eyes.

Flash went her arms around Wilder again. Then came the tears. "I'll treasure it forever."

"That's how long I want us to be friends, Reason. Will you wear it that long for me?"

"Yes," she pledged and pulled Wilder heart-to-heart.

"Yes, she said yes, and all the O'Neills and all the McGuinnesses sleeping here beneath our feet heard her say it. Yes!" Wilder danced Reason around on the grass of Michael's grave. "Now this old church-yard is the most special place on earth. Here, right here with Michael Patrick as our witness, my history lay claim to you, Reason, and as you know Irish history is the strongest bond known to man."

"Oh, Wilder…dear Wilder." Reason laughed and tears slipped off her lashes, and she hugged him close and thanked God for bliss on this Thanksgiving Day. Amidst Milltown's explosion of crosses.

"The heart means love, the crown means eternity and the hands mean friendship." Walking back to the hospital at dusk, Wilder explained the Claddagh. "Worn on the right hand like you're wearing it, with the heart turned outward, means love is being considered. If the heart were turned inward, it would mean your heart belonged to no one." He slid his arm around Reason's waist. "If I'd put it on your left hand with the heart turned outward, it would symbolize two loves that have become inseparable."

"Is there a story connected with this ring?"

"In Ireland there's *always* a story," which Wilder proceeded to tell. "Once upon a time in the wee Irish village of Claddagh, young Diarmuid O'Driscoll was captured and sold as a slave to the owner of a gold mine in Africa. He left behind his true love, who he was to have married in the spring. As the years passed, Diarmuid became friends with a goldsmith who trained him in his craft and promised Diarmuid his freedom. And having never forgotten his true love, Diarmuid spent years fashioning the Claddagh ring. The art kept his love alive. When he finally returned to Ireland fifteen years later he found his very beautiful and *very* patient love waiting. He slipped the Claddagh ring on her finger and they lived happily ever after."

"How can that be an Irish story if it has a happy ending?" Reason kidded. "Wilder, I do love this ring, and I'll wear it for the rest of my life, but," she didn't understand him, "you and I aren't lovers anymore."

Cain in her eyes, in her flesh and blood. Blue-hearted and so jealous he ached, Wilder understood Reason's reservation. Reservation he had recklessly sown. "I'm painfully aware of that, love. But last week changed things. I'm never going to forget how glad I was to see you waiting for me at My Lady's Leisure or how bravely you handled the soldiers that morning or how you cried for Michael Patrick today. *Everything* is different between us now, Reason. Friend or lover, you are now, have been, and will always be part of my life. I want to celebrate that."

Reason had her arms around Wilder again. And it could have been summer, warm and fresh and full of hope. The Falls Road was an island, and the soft rain fell like rose water and there was no war. Only the torch song of madness. And Wilder.

But paradise was fleeting. A Land Rover bumped to the curb, and in a flurry of rifles and profanity, four soldiers erupted out its back door. One soldier grabbed Reason by the neck and threw her backwards into the street. The other three tackled Wilder and pitched him headfirst into the tank.

"Nooo!" Reason screamed, running towards the Land Rover and slugging whatever soldier she could snag. "Leave him alone! In the name of God, let him go!"

"Get outta here, bitch," one soldier bellowed, and raising his leg, gave Reason a boot to the hip that sent her sprawling. Howling a war whoop as Reason hit the ground, the Brit piled into the Land Rover behind the others, and off they sped down the Falls Road.

Through tunneling vision, Reason struggled to reach the sidewalk while several people rushed to help her. "Poor girl, poor wee girl. Och, love, don't cry." But she was crying, and the rain pelted her face like thumbtacks, and the whirr of a thousand helicopters shattered her ears. All she could think, as the streetlamps along the Falls faded, was of the morning the Army lifted Ruairi. She never saw him again.

*   *   *   *   *   *

"So? What did you want to see me about?" Hunter strutted into Cain's studio at Christ Church.

"Hello to you too, H.C." Cain glanced around the room; a forest of easels, no chairs. "Have a seat."

"That's real damn amusing, Cain. What do you want?"

"How do you like my painting?" Cain called Hunter over to see his watercolor scene of a Victorian hospital with coal-charred turrets and barred, black windows. "Do you recognize this place?"

Hunter blandly shirked. "What is it, a prison? I've never seen it before in my life."

"Oops, I must be delusional again," Cain nudged his father's arm. "I keep forgetting you never came to visit me. That's the sanitarium at Seton Close. If you look closely, you can see me clawing the windows." He pointed to one of the gloomy turrets. "See, there I am behind the bars. They've just released me from the bed I've been strapped to for three days." He raised his voice to squeaky and made fun, "Let me out, let me out!"

Hunter exhaled in repugnance, and tapping his toe, checked his Rolex. "I have a plane to catch, Cain. Tell me what was so almighty important that I had to skip tea and come all the way over here."

"Bernard Thunder is going to London soon."

"Bully for him. So what?" Hunter twitched to be on his way.

"It seems you've convinced him that the heirloom Cromwell necklace he purchased at the auction last summer is worth £130,000." Cain clicked his tongue with disapproval and went back to painting the sanitarium. "You really should be more discreet, old man."

"For God's sake, boy, make your point, make your point!"

"Bernie came and asked me for the name of a reputable jeweler in London so he can have the emerald pendant appraised."

Suddenly Hunter wasn't in such a rush. His cheeks lost their color and his mouth drew taut. "Oh. Oh dear. That is awkward. Well, I'll say I had no idea the necklace was a fake."

"You could do that." Cain concentrated on his brush strokes. Up, slowly up like a rising ax. Down, quickly down like a chop. "But you'll only make matters worse by lying twice. I plan on telling Bernie I told you the necklace was worthless the night of the auction. The night you let him pay £65,000 for a green lump of glass."

"Now why the devil would you do that?" Hunter whined, agape.

Cain gave his father an angelic smirk. "Because, unlike you, I'm an honest man."

"You're honest like I'm a virgin! I know that look, Cain. You're up to something fiendish. What is it you want from me *this time?*"

"Poor, long-suffering Hunter having to endure his twisted son." Brush up, gently up. Down brush, chop. "I'd like to strike a deal with you that will be beneficial for us both."

Nervous and pacing beside Cain, Hunter was all ears.

"In exchange for the title to My Lady's Leisure, I'll retrieve the fake necklace from Bernie's safe thus saving you from going to jail. I'll also be protecting your holy reputation in Ulster."

"God's blood, Cain, that's not an even trade!"

"I'm giving you the same opportunity you gave me, H.C. You can go to prison for fraud, and disgrace the family name, or you can pay your debt to society with the title to the manor. Take it or leave it."

"I'll damn well leave it, you worthless pirate."

"Fine with me, but just remember you brought on your downfall by yourself." Cain painted a silver cloud over Seton Close then added a flock of ravens.

"Goddamn you, Cain!" Hunter exploded and grabbed his son by the neck. His eyes bored into Cain's and his saliva spattered Cain's cheeks as he raged, "You're a wicked, ungrateful, conniving little shit! Useless, you're useless!"

"Like father like son," Cain laughed it off, knowing he had his father cornered. "Come on, H.C., you can't stand My Lady's Leisure. You haven't been there in over ten years. Don't make me turn you into the RUC. Just think, they'd do a thorough investigation of you and your finances, and with all those missing funds from the Gov and fake passports...which I have records and copies of by the way..."

"ALL RIGHT!" Hunter screamed so red-faced and bloated he looked like the breast of a robin.

Cain was wildly entertained as he pushed his father's hands off him and returned to his painting. "When I have the title, you'll have your heirloom."

"You'll have the title when I have the necklace." Hunter scurried for the door before Cain demanded anything else. "And if you blow it and get caught at Bernie's, I'll let you burn, you monster."

"Oh, H.C., one more thing. I have everything arranged for my trip to Berlin over the holidays. This useless little shit is going to deal you the fortune of a lifetime."

"At least you're good for something," Hunter growled and smoked away.

"Let me out, let me out," Cain joked in his father's wake.

*   *   *   *   *   *

"So, *Dr.* O'Neill, we meet again." Harry Jaggars stared down into Wilder's bleeding face. "I'll bet you thought since your father is a big star, we'd leave you alone. But your father is a faggot, asshole lunatic, and he wouldn't dare come crawling back to Ulster to save you, now would he? You're ours, *Dr.* O'Neill."

Stripped of all clothing except his underwear, Wilder lay on his back staring up at a white bulb in a white room at Windsor RUC. His hands were cuffed behind him. His feet were shackled as well. After having been dragged and punched and hurled down two flights of stairs he was glad to be at rest on the floor. He knew he'd been arrested because of Kieran and the rifles. "I want to see my solicitor immediately." He licked the blood from his mouth and tried to sit up but was stopped by a silver-tipped boot on his neck.

"You're a fucking door mat. You don't move until we tell you to move," a second policeman simpered and stooped to spit in Wilder's face. "I don't even want to see you blink. Blink, you son of a bitch, and I'll break your motherfucking balls."

Willfully, Wilder blinked and paid the consequence with a steel toe between his thighs.

"You don't need a lawyer, *Dr.* O'Neill," Jaggars continued placidly, pulling a plastic baton out of his back pocket. One side of the baton was flat like a strap, the other round like a bat. "We're detaining you for routine questioning, as is our legal right."

"And I…" Wilder writhed, "…have the right to…see a lawyer."

"Romans don't have rights," Jaggars corrected with a slap to the top of Wilder's head. "Under your robes and crosses you're all terrorists. I told you I had the unhappy privilege of meeting your loud-mouthed brother and bitch sister. Both Sinn Féin, murdering scum. Do you remember the last time you saw them, *Dr.* O'Neill? No? Let's refresh your memory." He whipped forth an envelope. "Perhaps you'd like to have these framed."

Jaggars tipped the photographs Wilder's way; photographs of Brendan and Merry. Both were bereft of faces from gunfire. And Merry had been beaten. Beaten before violent release. Horror scalded Wilder's brain, his heart burst into tears, his soul replied in flames, but he didn't close his eyes. He stared Harry Jaggars down.

Disappointed by the Irishman's restraint, Jaggars smacked his baton against Wilder's shoulders and chest. "We got rid of them and we'll get rid of you. Are you going to follow the family tradition and go down the hard way, *Dr.* O'Neill?"

"No," Wilder moaned and tried to concentrate on something other than his body's suffering.

"I don't know about that." Jaggars scrutinized Wilder. "You're a member of the Provisional IRA, aren't you, doctor?"

"I'm a thoracic surgeon. I don't have time for that crap."

"My, my, a thoracic surgeon…but you're still a gutter-sucking, Fenian pig." Jaggars gave a short snort of derision and paced in foreboding silence. "Oh gracious me!" he clapped his palm to his jaw. "How rude, we're making the good doctor lie on the floor." He motioned to the two other constables in the room. "Get *Dr.* O'Neill a chair. Perhaps, being a *thoracic surgeon,* he'd prefer a throne. Would you prefer a throne, *Dr.* O'Neill?"

Wilder dignified no response.

Seconds later the pair of burly policemen returned with a small table. "Get up," one ordered and prodded Wilder with a kick.

Wilder refused.

"GET THE FUCK UP!" the policeman shrieked and hauled Wilder to his feet by the hair. "Now sit down." He forced Wilder onto the table by ramming a fist into his abdomen.

"You ever heard of the crab position, *Dr.* O'Neill?" Jaggars wanted to know.

Wilder managed to nod as he doubled over, hurt and windless.

"Good. Do it for us. *Now.*"

Wilder stared up at Harry Jaggars intractably. "No."

"Oh, for christsake!" Jaggars motioned impatiently to his two assistants. One man grabbed Wilder's head, the other his shackled feet. Together they arched him backwards across the low table until his hair and toes nearly touched the floor. "Comfortable, are you?" Jaggars noted the tears of agony staining Wilder's cool facade and smiled. "Now, let's talk." He marched alongside the table, tapping his baton in the air like he was conducting a tune. "You say you aren't a Provisional, *Dr.* O'Neill, and sources tell me that's probably true. But just like your filthy siblings, you're up to your neck in republican shit. How did you get those scratches on your hands and face? Robbing a train perhaps?"

"I fell off my deck," Wilder groaned.

"Clumsy slob," Jaggars sniggered behind a tight smile. "Did you have a hand in the death of Detective Clive Harlock?"

"Of course not!"

"What about the rifles, *Dr.* O'Neill? Are you involved in that business?"

Wilder ignored the question, and Jaggars slammed his baton down on Wilder's stomach. "You know here in Ulster there's no such thing as a right to silence," he bellowed in Wilder's ear. "As far as the court is concerned, your silence is the same as a confession." Then he whispered, "I like you, *Dr.* O'Neill, really I do, so I'll give you another chance. Are you involved with the sniping rifles?"

"No," Wilder choked on the pain ripping his unnaturally bent body. "I know nothing…about…any…guns."

"I see." Jaggars circled around and around the table. The only sound was the *click, click* of his metal-toed boots. "Is Kieran McCartan your cousin?"

Breathless and sweating, Wilder croaked, "You fucking know he is."

"You're right. I already knew that." *Click, click, click.* "I know everything about you, *Dr.* O'Neill. We've been watching you. But this evening I'm more interested in your cousin. Quite the villain he is. Was Mr. McCartan a participant in the train robbery last week?"

"I don't…know."

"He killed Harlock, didn't he? And now he's involved with the rifles. Who's working with him? You, that's who. You're his right hand man, aren't you, *Dr.* O'Neill?" Jaggars fired questions without taking a breath.

Wilder squinted up at Jaggars with bewilderment.

"Oh, very clever to pretend you don't know." *Whap, whap,* the baton met Wilder's shins. "*Is* your cousin the keeper of the guns?"

"How the hell…should I know," Wilder barely managed to pant. The two men holding him wrenched his back backwards more and more across the table until he felt like a horseshoe. "I don't know…about…any robberies or killings or rifles! I swear to Christ, I do not…know!" he yelled and momentarily blacked out.

Wham to the gut, *slap* to the head, *smack* to the chest, to the knees. *Click, click, click.* "Let's try again. Where is Mr. McCartan keeping the rifles?" Jaggars repeated mildly. "We know all about the Light Fifties, doctor, so there's no need to be coy. Tell us where they are and we'll let you go."

"If you know…so much…why are you…asking me?" Wilder hissed as pain stabbed up his ribcage and down his spine.

"Oh, I am disappointed, *Dr.* O'Neill." Blows to the abdomen like a drum roll. Pound and pound. "You aren't being cooperative. If you would answer my questions truthfully, you could go home. Otherwise, we're going to keep you here in this position all night, maybe all week." Jaggars never faltered, never wiped the thread of a smile from his lips, never blinked his glacier grey eyes that drilled into Wilder's like ice picks. "Be a good man now and tell me all you know about your cousin and the rifles. Does Mr. McCartan have them? Where? How many does he have?" *Click, click.* "You might as well be honest, *Dr.* O'Neill, because no matter what you say or don't say I'll make it known you leaked us damaging information about the IRA. You'll be named as a tout, and touts don't last long around here…unless we protect them. Won't you let us protect you, *Dr.* O'Neill, or do you prefer a bullet in the back of your skull?"

"Fuck you," Wilder spat and misery flooded off his eyes into his hair.

"Oh dear, that wasn't a nice thing to say," Jaggars said with chilling composure as he threw aside his baton and withdrew a pair of stainless steel pincers from the table's drawer. Clawing Wilder's underwear down savagely, Jaggars applied the pincers to Wilder's testicles and squeezed until Wilder screamed, until he passed out.

*   *   *   *   *   *

Reason came to and saw Jillie seated beside her. "Where am I?"

"Och, poor love, this is Grosvenor casualty. You took a nasty fall. You have a concussion." Jillie dabbed Reason's brow with a cold cloth and petted her hair. "How do you feel?"

"Awful." Reason sat up slowly. Her head felt like it had its own heart, throbbing loudly, excruciatingly. "What about Declan? Has anybody heard from him?" she questioned Jillie anxiously.

Jillie shook her head. "I just talked to Kieran. He's heard nothing. We might not hear a word for a week."

"But, but…oh God," Reason covered her face in fear and tried in vain not to cry. "I don't know why they arrested him, Jillie. He hasn't done anything wrong."

"Maybe he's in the IRA."

"No! He's not!"

"Maybe he shot that policeman Harlock or knows who did."

"No, no," Reason wept.

"Maybe Decky knows more than you think, love."

"No, he's not involved in anything."

Jillie focused on her friend. "Are you sure?"

"I'd stake my life on it."

"Och, don't stake you life on anything in this city, love." Jillie handed Reason a tissue for her tears. "Now don't you worry. Our Decky will be all right. If he's innocent, they'll only hurt him a little. No serious harm will come to him."

"Ruairi was innocent and the RUC killed him!" Reason fretted. "Jillie, you should have seen it. We were just standing on the Falls Road talking, and all of a sudden these soldiers attacked us. They were beating Declan and kicking him and…"

"Oh!" Jillie noticed Reason's new gold ring and interrupted with a grin, "Did Declan give you this? You weren't wearing it when you left the Gov."

"Yes," Reason replied miserably. "Isn't it pretty?"

"It's gorgeous. Does this mean you and Decky are involved? You know, in a clandestine romance or something deliciously sexy like that?"

Reason frowned in vexation, finding Jillie's questions ill-timed. "You know perfectly well Declan and I are friends. Where's the doctor taking care of me? I want to go home." She kept checking the clock and rubbing her aching head. "Is anybody ever going to come in here and check on me so I can leave?"

"He's in love with you, isn't he? Are you two lovers?"

No longer listening, Reason crawled from the bed and smoothed her rumpled blouse and skirt. "I'm leaving."

"Oh, I don't think that's wise. You're bobbing around like a dingy."

"I am not. I feel fine. Thanks for being here for me, Jillie. I'll see you tomorrow morning."

"Tomorrow! Don't be silly," Jillie caught Reason's sleeve. "I already canceled your appointments. Take tomorrow off and rest."

"I'll see how I feel in the morning. But right now I have to find Kieran." Scraping aside the curtains of her cubicle, punch-drunk and swaying, Reason used the wall for support and shuffled to the nurses' station to be released. She was told she would be staying the night for observation.

"This is ridiculous. I refuse to let a little concussion stop me," Reason protested as an orderly marched her back down the hall. "I'm all right. Really, I feel fine, just fi..."

Luckily this time a nurse was on hand to catch Reason before she could crack her head again.

*   *   *   *   *   *

"I'm going for a cup of tea with the others. You want to come, Ian?"

"Nah. I'm not much in a mood for the craic."

The fellow constable gave Ian Wright's pumpkin hair a pat. "Be a sport and cover for me then. See if you can get the scum in room six to wake up."

Ian despised going in to rouse the detainees. They were always disoriented and disgraced and wielding hatred in their eyes. He took a deep breath and stepped into the cell. A nearly naked man lay on his back on the floor. Slinking closer, Ian came face-to-face with, *"Dr. O'Neill!"*

Wilder stared up at him with screaming, wordless acrimony.

"Aw, my God, sir. You shouldn't be here. Oh God, I'm sorry," Ian dithered, alternately patting Wilder's shoulder and using his sleeve to remove the blood on Wilder's lips and head. "Are you really hurt?"

Wilder laughed bitterly and turned his face away.

"Now listen to me. Listen." Ian leaned down to whisper, "You just lie here and pretend to be unconscious if anyone comes in. Jaggars and them are off having tea. I promise, sir, I'll help you. OK? OK?"

Another RUC tactic. Wilder hardly heard him. Pain, scalding pain was all he knew.

"Don't give up, sir. I'll hurry." Ian sprinted for the nearest telephone.

An hour later, Jaggars marched in and tossed Wilder his clothes. "You're free to go, for now."

His body protested each movement, but Wilder grabbed his shirt, coat and slacks and stiffly dressed. All the while Jaggars stood in the doorway watching him, and Wilder nailed loathing to Jaggars.

"No hard feelings, I hope?" Harry was sardonic.

"Go to hell."

"We'll see you back in here soon, doctor. If not, we'll see you in the morgue. What a pity if the ULF gets you. All of Belfast will grieve the loss of such a fine *thoracic surgeon*." Jaggars observed Wilder a moment longer then cranked on his boot. "Someone will show you out."

Stepping outside Windsor, Wilder inhaled the fresh air; air brisk with mist and the lingering scent of turpentine. A car sped out of the parking lot. A racing-green Jaguar. Cain.

Chapter Forty-Five

His fingers caressing her cheek woke her. "Wilder!" Reason cried as she sat up in her hospital bed.

"Don't grab me!" He flinched when she threw wide her arms. "Every part of my body hurts. How are you doing? You must have a rip-roaring headache."

"It's more like a dull ache." Reason reached up to turn on the light and Wilder caught her wrist.

"You don't want to do that, love. I look pretty bad."

"Oh no," Reason started to cry. "They beat the hell out you, didn't they?"

"Yeah. But compared to what they did to Ruairi this is nothing."

"Why did they arrest you?"

"For information. They didn't get it." Wilder slid his hand over Reason's fingers and eased down beside her. "After they let me go I went to Fiona's and heard you were here." His eyes wandered over her in humility and heat. His knuckles grazed her cheek again. Cool so cool and yielding her skin. He longed to be held, to feel like a man, to be loved. "I signed your release papers. Will you come home with me?"

Wilder said nothing as he drove along the Malone Road at midnight. His mind was a fist of humiliation and rage. The police had rendered him powerless, degraded and unnerved him, and they had made him stronger, harder. The RUC's brutality ratified his defiance, and now more than ever he would resist their subjugation. Still his mind ached and was glum. He felt violated and vulnerable, caught between valor and disgrace. He wanted to feel esteemed and potent, and he wanted to be safe and rocked to sleep like a boy. He gazed across at Reason. She was the antidote, the answer. Instant pleasure would negate searing pain. But, while his mind begged to be coddled, his body hurt too much to be embraced. He looked down at his hands, which had been spared the torture. He could touch her.

Reason helped Wilder into his living room. In the light, in horror, she saw his contusions. And the tears streamed down her face. She hated that he had suffered, and she loved that he was alive. "Can I fix you something to eat? Should I make up the fire? Do you want some aspirin, a cold cloth, a shot of whiskey? I could rub your feet."

"Reason love, you're injured yourself, you need to rest. I brought you here to look after you, not to have you serve me."

Seeing Wilder trying to bend down and failing, Reason stooped to remove his shoes and socks for him. "There must be something I can do for you, Wilder."

"Will you let me touch you?" he requested in a low voice.

She let her coat drop to the floor. "Do whatever makes you feel better."

Drawing Reason to him, Wilder untied the ribbon around her collar. He ran his hands over her shoulders and hair and unbuttoned her blouse. With each opening button he swirled his fingers over her skin, and closing his eyes, shut out the abuse his own skin had endured. Her warmth sucked the cold of Jaggars' eyes from his mind. Her breasts were soft against his hand, and the silver-toed boots and plastic baton ceased to crack inside his skull. And when Reason's blouse fell to the floor, Wilder led her up to his bedroom.

"Will you take off your skirt for me?" he asked and she obliged. She wore white lace and red satin but not for long. "I don't think I can be clever with lingerie either," Wilder smiled ever so slightly, and Reason further disrobed. And when she was nude, he moved her against him with care until the splendor of her body nursed his sore flesh. His lips hurt too much to kiss her; his fingers were his kiss. Touching, stroking, and pain was receding.

"I have to wash the scum of the RUC off before going to bed. You can help me with that."

Gently, Reason undressed Wilder, and she saw the sickening signs of abuse; welts, like he'd been whipped, bruises, like he'd been kicked. "Oh my God, what did they do to you?" She stared helplessly at his torso then into his face, and she burst into tears again. "Oh, Wilder…I can't stand this. I *can't.*"

"That's a great way to greet a man's body," he didn't miss the chance to be funny. How endearing and damning Reason's tears. "Don't cry, Reason. Please don't cry." He crushed her to him. It hurt, but it was a pain he could live with again and again. "I hate it when you're this unhappy."

"But you're so hurt…let's leave Belfast," she suggested on impulse. "Tonight. We'll spend Christmas together; we'll go to Malibu and fall in love. Please, Wilder, let's go home."

"No," he resisted harshly, unmoved. "If I go home, the Brits win."

Reason recoiled in despair. "But one of these days…"

"Let them fucking kill me then! I will *not* run away this time."

"And what about me?" she cried. "You keep saying you won't let the Brits hurt me, but there's nothing they can do that would hurt me as much as losing you."

"I don't want to have this conversation," Wilder's voice was tired, sad. "Just come here. Come here," he sighed, extending his hand to Reason.

He took her to his shower and pulled her under the water with him. And the warm, healing stream washed over him as he held Reason against him. Away went the sweat and blood and fear, but nothing dissolved the rage. Rage was a weapon, a mandate. Onward to victory. And rage was a thirst. For freedom. For blood.

But for now, pleasure. The water made Reason's body slick. Wilder slid his hands over her slowly, tenderly, and she caressed him and licked the water running down his chest, and touched him where he requested. Lightly they kissed, it hurt, but Wilder jerked Reason's mouth to his and kissed her harder. The desire to come together was electric but ungratified, which made it all the more erotic and intense. Answering Wilder's desire, Reason knelt down, and seeing the damage where the pincers had been, leaned forward and bestowed her lips. With a moan Wilder caught her hair and fell back against the tiles, and she kissed him again. And again. With a flickery tongue. Fight fire with fire, torture of the police, torture of a woman. He begged her to stop.

"Did I hurt you?"

"You're giving me a heart attack," he barely caught his breath.

"Didn't that make you feel good?"

"Too good." He rubbed his palms up Reason's back and slid them down her front. "I want to make love to you, Reason, but I'm just too hurt."

"It's OK, Wilder. But one of these days," she stroked him intimately, "I want more. I want everything."

"And I'll give it to you, love. But for now just take me to bed gently, and hold me in your arms."

Chapter Forty-Six

He stood at the foot of the bed while his eyes adjusted to the pre-dawn grey. He couldn't see her, but he knew she was in the room. That perfume betrayed her every time. And he wished the pain in his heart would kill him because he didn't want to see, didn't want to know. But there was Wilder asleep, propped up against a pair of pillows. And loyal moon to her sun, there was Reason. Why did she have to come here? Wilder must have called her. And she had rushed. To soothe him. To love him. Always. Cain dug his hands into his coat pockets and backed out of Wilder's bedroom. He had come to the house to see how his friend was doing, but he hadn't expected to find him naked with Reason asleep in his lap.

Cain fell against the stairwell and tried to stop his heart from breaking. *Wilder. My good and true friend. You warned me about getting involved, but it's too late. I love her…more than you ever will, ever could.* Without a sound, he returned to the bedroom and prepared the hearth and lit the fire so the room would be warm when Reason and Wilder awoke. He watched them sleeping then stole away.

Wilder pried up his eyelids to greet the day. Frost on the windows softened the steel light of dawn. Darkness released itself in jaundiced rays and the morning rose in gloom. He watched Reason beside him. So tranquil, sublime. How thoughtful it was of her to have lit the fire. The room basked in heat which made the sore day brighter. He looked down at his chest with a fury not tempered by sleep. Jaggars was expert at his job; he could beat a man without leaving a lasting mark. Last nights welts had receded, and only bruises colored Wilder's body and face. His head had a chain saw buzz, and his neck was stiff, but worst of all was his back. Every breath and movement hurt along his spine. He reached down, and waking Reason, pulled her into his arms. "How's your head?" he asked.

"It's nothing compared to how bad you must feel."

"Remember that scene in the *Wizard of Oz* where the Tin Man rusts and can't move?"

Drawing the covers up over them, Reason nestled closer to Wilder. "I'll bring you breakfast in bed then."

"I'd rather you be my breakfast in bed." He wished he felt well enough to make the love to Reason he was dying a thousand deaths to make. "But I'll have to settle for toast and tea. You needn't hurry away though, love." His hand skimmed up her thigh. "This is a great way to start the day."

"Usually I wake up to find Morris and his Teddy bears on my head." Reason brushed the wrinkles from the sleeves of Wilder's shirt she was wearing. "After two and a half years, do I still look good sleeping in your shirt?"

"No."

"No?"

Wilder opened her shirt and slid his hand inside. "I like you better without it."

"Ooh, I think I like it better too." She petted the bruises on his chest and allowed him to touch her in any manner that pleased him. "You don't have any broken bones, do you?"

"Our creative police know how to torture a man so he's bent not broken," Wilder's sarcasm rattled with enmity.

"You're going to file a complaint against the RUC for use of excessive force, aren't you?"

"Sure, but it's a waste. The RUC will investigate itself, and it'll be months before they reach a conclusion. And they'll conclude I was resisting arrest. Truth is, Reason, I'm lucky I wasn't charged with assaulting an officer. I got off easy."

"You're still awfully hurt."

"True." Wilder lay back in the pillows and rolled Reason on top of him. "But what the hell, let's see how far we can make it anyway."

"How did your mother meet Wesley Wellworth-Howell?" Wilder asked as Reason helped him dress.

"At a lawn party on Long Island. Wesley saw her across the crowd and fell in love with her."

"Your mother was a guest at this party?"

"What else would she be," Reason cracked up, "the *maid?*"

"What was her maiden name?"

"Rousseau." Reason wiggled one sock then another over Wilder's toes. "Anna Rousseau. Isn't that the coolest name?"

"So cool it sounds made-up. How old was she when she married Wesley?"

"Twenty three. OK, now step into your pants one leg at a time."

"Did she work?"

"Work? A *Rousseau?*" Reason mocked. "Wilder, the Rousseau's idea of work is tying their own shoes."

"Uh huh. How did she support you two then?"

"From her inheritance," Reason explained as she drew Wilder's slacks up his shins. "I told you, the Rousseau's are old money."

"So your mother inherited big bucks. Right. Before she met Wesley where did you guys live?"

"We stayed with a friend of hers. Mrs. Tillysburn had a little guest house no one used. We lived there about two years, until Mom met Wesley."

"You had all that money and didn't live in a palace?"

"Well, there was only Mom and me. We didn't need much room."

"What did you and your mother do all day if she wasn't working?"

"Oh, I hardly ever saw her. She had lunch and tea parties with different women every day. I spent my time terrorizing the teachers in a nursery school."

"You didn't have a nanny like other rich girls?" Wilder couldn't believe how masterfully Johanna MacBride McGuinness had deceived her daughter. And for so long.

"I was too wild for a nanny, at least that's what I was told."

"I'm afraid wildness is in your blood, Mac. Did your mom ever go to college?"

"Oh, yes." Reason handed Wilder his shirt which he buttoned over his ribs. "She was in her late twenties before she started school though. I remember our chauffeur driving her to class every day, and she was so excited about learning. You should have seen her crying at her graduation. When they handed her her degree, she was sobbing."

"What was her major?"

"Fine Art. Then five years ago she finished a Master's degree in Modern Art. Now she dedicates her time to helping struggling young artists."

"And let me guess, she likes sculptors best."

"That's true. Good guess."

"How old was she when she had you then?"

Reason fed Wilder's belt around his middle and kept her arms around him a moment. "Eighteen. Her parents refused to see her after she and Kent eloped. I think that's one of the reasons she doesn't like talking about him. She hates to be reminded of her foolishness."

"She considers her marriage to 'Kent' foolish?" Wilder wondered where Johanna came up with that name; so unworthy of the spirited Irishman.

"I'm not sure. I gave up years ago trying to get her to tell me anything about him. I don't even know how they met."

"Did you ever meet your grandparents?"

"Never. You want to wear these loafers? Give me your foot. Even though they left us their money, my mother's parents wanted no part of us, and Daddy's parents were dead."

"That's the first time I've heard you call your real father 'Daddy.'"

Reason drew her hand to her mouth. "I haven't ever called him that before. It just sort of…slipped out."

"Do you remember anything about him?"

She thought awhile. "I vaguely remember his funeral; it was raining and cold. And he had beautiful blue eyes, like yours. There now, I think you're dressed." She stepped back, and straightening Wilder's tie, appraised her valet-work. "Och, you're magic, love! I'll get ready and drive you to the Gov. Where are my clothes?"

"We sort of left them everywhere, didn't we?" Wilder laughed.

Reason spotted her skirt and blouse, underwear and shoes neatly folded on Wilder's dresser. "Did you put my stuff here?"

Wilder shook his head. "I thought you put them there when you started the fire."

"I didn't start the fire."

They exchanged puzzled faces, then Wilder cursed and Reason grew pale.

"What in the hell was he doing creeping around here?" Wilder damned Cain for spoiling the intimate morning. "I'm sick to death of him invading my life!"

"I'm sure he meant well, Wilder," Reason defended with a loyalty Wilder despised. "What's he going to think? This isn't at all like it looks."

"It's not?" Wilder could still feel the curves of Reason's body where his fingers had had free reign. He could still hear her moan as he stroked and aroused her. He still tasted her lips and felt her hands that had touched his body since daybreak. "If it wasn't like it looked, what the hell was it?"

Reason played with the cord on her bathrobe. "It was perfectly innocent."

"You call what we were just doing 'innocent?'"

"Nothing happened, Wilder."

"If I weren't hurt, it would have."

"But it didn't."

"Damn it, Reason, will you quit acting like we've committed adultery? You aren't married to the man!"

But maybe in spirit she was. Reason had a bond with Cain Wilder didn't understand. They were erotic companions stitched together by something covert. Something profound. And this wasn't like Reason's lame love for Reid from whom Wilder had easily led her astray. This affection danced from its heat and gained momentum every time Reason surrendered herself to Cain's arms. And she had surrendered herself to Cain many more times than she had ever surrendered to Wilder. A realization that pierced his breast like a flaming volley. He wanted to throttle Cain for weaving his sorcery upon Reason, but how could he denounce the eccentric master who complemented his life?

"There's the phone, Reason. Go ahead. Call him and explain things. Tell him you didn't have an orgasm when I had my tongue inside you, tell him you didn't like my hands on your breasts, tell him you weren't down on your knees with me in your mouth, yeah, tell him how *innocent* we are. Then tell him when you touch me it means nothing. And when I touch you it means even less."

"Wilder, don't be that way!"

"How should I be? You're doing it to me again. Just like with Reid. Suddenly you're all worried about Cromwell and I'm invisible. What we did, what we had is reduced to 'nothing happened.'"

"Something happened, Wilder. We hurt Cain. You're the one who told me he's fragile, and he is."

"It's his own damn fault. He shouldn't have walked in here!" Wilder barked, but he didn't mean it. He felt as guilty as Reason.

"I know that. I'm sure he knows it too. Look, I'll talk to him later. Right now let's concentrate on getting to work. Are you sure you feel up to going to the hospital?"

"I can feel just as miserable there as I can here."

"I'll come back tonight and help you…"

"No," Wilder declared in a worsening mood and handed Reason her shoes. "You've helped me plenty, thanks. Go fix things with Cain." With that he walked out of the room.

Reason trailed him to the stairs, thinking he validated once more what she had said last month; all he seemed capable of giving her was anger. She paused halfway down the steps. "Why are you so angry? Cain didn't hurt anything."

"He didn't? We were having a terrific morning, and suddenly there he is stealing you away."

"He didn't steal me away, Wilder. I'm standing right here."

"But you're thinking of him."

"No, Wilder, I'm thinking of you. I'm thinking of your touch, your taste, the smell of your skin, the feel of your arms…and how much I love you."

Wilder continued to the front door. He had seen Reason forgetting his presence the second she knew Cain had found them together in bed. "And what about Cromwell? You've been in love with him from the moment you laid eyes on him."

"I don't know. I just know last night we were closer than ever and I don't want to blow it with you again."

"And I don't want to be blown away again. Come on, it's getting late. Let's go."

But Reason wouldn't budge. "Don't walk away! Talk to me. Tell me what you're thinking, what you're feeling."

"The only thing I'm feeling right now is frustrated. I just want to go to work."

"If you're jealous of Cain, why can't you tell me? Why can't you tell me to forget him and come back to you?"

Wilder didn't answer.

"Why can't you tell the truth, Wilder? Why won't you turn around and tell me you love me? Isn't that why you gave me Merry's ring?"

"Would it make any difference if I said I loved you?" He backed up and cast doubt upon her. "Would it change your feelings for Cain?" He pointed to her black-and-blue forehead, and his voice was soft, "Would it keep you safe from me? Yeah, last night we were close, too close. You got hurt because you were with me, Reason. And so did Cain."

"Wilder, I hurt when I'm *not* with you! I miss you, I ache for you." His silence exasperated her. He was slapping the walls up, retreating. "Don't you do it! Don't become Declan and disappear. How do you feel about me?" She awaited his reply. He refused to comment. "Damn it, Wilder, for once, just once, tell me how you really feel!"

But Wilder stood at arms' length, reading the volumes of Cain usurping Reason's body and soul. "The way I see it, Mac, it's too damn late for me to feel or say anything."

"That's not true! Don't shut me out, Wilder, please."

"I'm not shutting you out." He palmed his car keys. "May we go now?"

"Let me spend this evening with you then," Reason persisted. "Last night in the shower was wonderful and waking up with you was wonderful and wearing this Claddagh ring is wonderful. Please, Wilder," she pleaded, "say you'd like to see me tonight. It's not too late. Let's keep falling in love again."

But Wilder wasn't listening. He was remembering the times Reason's peace and safety had been violated over the months because of him. Maybe love and Belfast were mutually exclusive. He didn't know what to say, what to think, and suddenly the stress of the week felt like a rampage from which he needed relief. "Not tonight, Mac. Maybe next week."

Reason did a double take. Wilder had chosen once more to slam her open-book heart. "Here I am *begging* to be near you, and you're telling me *next week?* Just forget it, Wilder! You'll see me after Christmas...if you're lucky." She strode to the car. "And don't call me Mac!"

Chapter Forty-Seven

Jillie nearly pitched the phone against the wall. "You *let him go?*"

"A source of influence convinced me O'Neill's interrogation wasn't necessary at this time."

"What do you mean? I'm your fucking source!" Jillie raged. "This is my assignment! Who is this source? I want to talk to him!"

"Now, now, Maddie, settle down and let me take care of this."

"What sort of person would stick up for O'Neill, Harry, except another terrorist?"

That made Jaggars laugh. "He's a colleague and I owed him a favor. I also trust his judgment."

"What about *my* judgment? You can't go against my orders!"

"This is Ulster, not England, Madeline." Harry laughed again, patronizing, "You go back to your typing there at the Gov, sweetheart. I'll handle O'Neill."

Cain sat at Reason's desk but hadn't heard Jillie's conversation. "Reason is coming in to work today, isn't she?" he called when Jillie hung up the phone.

"Cain! I didn't know you were here." Jillie caught her breath. "Reason called to say she'll be in. Poor lamb was up in the neurology ward for observation most of the night."

"Reason was *hurt?*"

"Those Army psychos attacked her and Decky last night." Jillie strolled into Reason's office, smiling Cain's way.

"Good God! I had no idea she was involved in that altercation."

"She took a frightful fall; about split her head like a melon." Jillie patted her teased and sprayed hairdo and checked her make-up in her compact mirror. "She was supposed to spend the night here at the Gov, but Declan came like Lancelot and swept her away."

"And how is Declan, has anyone said?"

"He handled himself well I'm told," Jillie replied. "Took every blow like a man. But then what did the RUC expect? He's Irish."

Cain cocked his head. "Are you wearing bells?"

"I have a little bracelet with ten gold bells around my ankle, see? It's a gift from an older gentleman. Reason would wring your neck if she saw you moving things around on her desk. I made love on her desk once. On the Fourth of July. Reason was gone all day."

"While the cat's away the mice get laid, huh?"

"I get wild urges sometimes," Jillie giggled. "I just shoved Reason's markers and pencils aside and threw off my clothes. It was utterly sudden and sinful. We did such naughty things. I'd be glad to show you what I mean."

Cain smiled faintly and considered Jillie's punk-rock style. An attractive woman exuding adventure and heat. But she had an aura that scorched. Like the Sahara scorches a lost and thirsty soul. Too hot, too bright. The Cleopatra make-up and cool, violet eyes, that sphinx mouth and sultry voice were a mirage, and he wondered what she was trying to hide. "Were you with Declan?"

"No. Ruairi McKee." Jillie smiled at the memory of the naive Fenian. "I gave him the mother of all memories to take to his grave." She applied a dark circle of scarlet to her lips and puckered a kiss at her reflection. "How long have you and Declan O'Neill been friends?"

"A few years."

"You know him quite well then."

"As well as anyone knows him."

"He's the catch of the day around here. There isn't a single woman in this hospital that hasn't slung her hook in his waters."

"Does that include you?"

"No. It's his cousin I'm after. Besides, I couldn't catch Decky even if I wanted to. He only has eyes for Reason."

Cain noted Jillie's every blink, every breath. "You and Kieran are friends? I didn't know that."

"We're much more than friends, Cain. It must be awkward with both Decky and you seeing Reason."

"Not really. Reason sees little of Declan and lots of me."

"I can't believe that suits Declan."

"It's rather like Androcles and the lion," Cain managed to smile. "Reason is the thorn in Declan's paw, and I am plucking her from his life."

"I hardly think I'm a thorn!" Reason arrived and saw Cain looking upon her coldly.

"How's your poor head?" Jillie mothered Reason's bruised brow. "Oooh, that looks dreadful, and how it must ache. Augh! Those soldiers are pigs!" Taking a cue to get to work, Jillie hurried out to her desk, and Reason closed the office door.

"I didn't know you'd been hurt. How are you feeling?"

"I'm fine." Reason wished everybody would stop asking her about her head.

"So fine you spent the night with Wilder," Cain taunted. "Misery loving company, was it?"

"I knew you were going to be upset, but nothing happened. Wilder and I helped each other out, that's all."

"You certainly helped each other out of your clothes. Was that really necessary, Reason?"

"Wilder was hurt and he seemed so alone...oh, for heaven's sake, Cain, you shouldn't have been sneaking around his house in the first place!"

"If I'd known I was going to find him naked with you in his lap, I wouldn't have come."

"Are you here to give me grief? If you are, you can leave. I'm in no mood for a fight. You shouldn't have been at Wilder's."

"I know. And I've known all along you and he weren't finished. So am I the next man to be discarded, Reason? Are you going to dump me now that Wilder's made love to you?"

"Cain, it wasn't like that."

"How the hell was it then?"

Guiltily, Reason turned away. She deplored having hurt him. "You're so angry."

"Of course I'm angry!" Cain spun her into his hands. "I thought we had something special."

"We do. But that experience with the soldiers last night was more than I could stand. I was so afraid and Wilder was hurt. Please, Cain…you promised you wouldn't ask me to justify my feelings for him. He's my friend, he needed me and I…needed him. And yes, I still love him…but I love you too, and this is totally not what I wanted to happen!"

"Just don't forget about me, Reason." Cain kissed her hesitantly, afraid she wouldn't want him. "Don't toss me aside like I don't matter."

"Oh, Cain, I won't, I couldn't. But I can't toss Wilder aside either."

"I didn't ask you to, did I? But he's never going to love you as much as I do."

Reason feared Cain was right. And it broke her heart and made her angry. Wilder was a fool. And so was she, for trying to grasp what refused to be reached.

"Are you sure you're feeling OK?" Cain interrupted Reason's thoughts.

"If one more person asks me that, I'll scream. I'm fine!"

"Then come with me to Donegal. Now, right now."

"I can't. I have so much work."

"Forget work!"

Reason turned to see Cain sweeping everything off her desk. Pencils and papers sailed. Markers and scales bounced to the floor. "Stop!" she cried, but Cain just laughed.

"Let's run away," he flipped a triangle over his shoulder, "and steal each other's hearts." Up in the air went a roll of tracing paper, unwinding as it flew. He threw erasers at the frost-glazed window. "Surrender to spur of the moment. Surrender to me."

How this man surprised and enchanted. How his flesh and fresh spirit pleased her. Cain didn't hide from his feelings, didn't lie, didn't make her cry; he made her forget the war, the war of Wilder. He opened his arms. Reason stepped to fill them. "I surrender."

"Let's go to Donegal then."

"Tonight. I'll go tonight."

Through a smile he kissed her, and she returned the smile, the kiss. And she hugged him, he made her life nice. He caressed her face, she stroked his chest and rested against him. He leaned into her, their lips weren't long apart. The kiss lingered and grew impassioned, impatient to heal, to allay and forgive. Cain locked the door.

"Tonight is too long to wait," he said with his hands in Reason's curls. He pulled her over to the desk, folded down backwards, and fitted her on top of him. "I was dying when I saw you with Wilder this morning."

"We didn't make love, Cain."

"You saved that for me, right? Prove it now, right now."

What Wilder denied her, Cain offered freely. Wilder inflamed her like a craving she couldn't sate and left her burning for the more he wouldn't provide. Reason felt cheated and defiant and so in need of something to last more than one kiss. Outside it was raining, and the helicopters hovered. So sullen the day, and there was Cain's smile. A smile she drank in like summer. And she thought as she touched him, after having touched Wilder, *This war makes us do terrible wonderful things.*

Wilder stuck his head in the door and caught Jillie's attention by shooting her in the neck with a water gun. "OK, ya dirty rat, gimme alla yer dough, or I'll hafta snuff ya."

"You're the dirty rat!" Jillie squealed and slapped aside the trickle on her neck. "It's pediatric cardiology day again, isn't it, Dr. O'Neill?" She twirled around on her chair, but Wilder's bruised face didn't surprise her. In fact, he looked better than she had expected. "Good God, Declan, you look like something belched up from the morgue."

"Yeah, too bad it's Christmas and not Halloween. I had a date with the Windsor goons last night. So, doll," he raised his pistol to Jillie's eyes and put his finger on the trigger, "what are ya gonna gimme before I blast ya?"

"Don't point guns at me, Declan," Jillie warned without smiling. "You might not like what I give you."

"Well, aren't you a spoiled sport," Wilder huffed with disappointment. "You're supposed to promise me anything, like the women in the movies. I guess I'll have to point my gun at Reason." He jerked a thumb at Reason's closed door. "Is she here?"

"Yes, but you don't want to go in there right now."

"Why, what's she doing?"

Jillie resented Declan's smitten preoccupation with Reason and enjoyed breaking the news. "Remember me telling you about Ruairi and me on Reason's desk?"

Wilder didn't understand. "Yeah, so?"

"So Reason's in there making it with Cain on her desk. Either that or they're doing it up against the wall."

"No way," Wilder refused to believe it, but seeing Jillie's confident nod, he faltered, "Oh, but she wouldn't…not here, not after we…now? Right now? On her *desk?*"

Jillie bobbed her head again and gloated to see Declan redden. "Everything crashed to the floor then one of them locked the door. Too bad the walls aren't thinner. I'm sure we're missing a ripping good romp." And seeing she had hit Declan where it hurt most, she added, "Reason says Cain's good, very good."

Wilder took aim with his pistol and fired three shots at Reason's door. Then blowing off the nozzle and twirling the pistol around on his finger, he turned to Jillie and blackly smiled. "Too bad it's only water."

"Is there a message you want me to pass along to Reason when she's done doing Cain?" Jillie laughed, enjoying the pain in Wilder's eyes.

"No." Enraged, with his heart in pieces, Wilder strode down the hall.

Two hours later he burst into Reason's office. "You don't waste any time, do you, Mac?" Wilder ran his eyes up then down her. She looked too damn happy, too damn pleased and appeased. Her hair was neatly combed on her shoulders where Cain's fingers had played, her blouse was re-buttoned where Cain's lips had strayed, and her skirt was sleek over her hips where Cain had had his way.

"Get out of here, Wilder."

He checked the time. "Four hours ago you were in bed with me, and now you've had Cromwell for lunch." He stepped forward and touched Reason's arm only to jerk back his hand as though she sizzled. "Yeow, you're one hot little number."

"Wilder, I'm busy."

"You sure are. Have you no self-restraint at all?" he blasted.

"Have you ever heard it's none of your business?"

"If you're going to lie down with me like my lover, then you bet it's my business. You want me to be honest with you? First you be honest with me! What man in his right mind is going to profess undying love for a woman he knows is in love with someone else? A woman who has already trashed his life once."

"The same kind of man who says he'll see a woman next week after she's poured her heart out. The same kind of man who's *crippled* by his fear of intimacy." Reason shoved a stack of papers into her briefcase. "I'm leaving."

"How could you do this, Reason? How could you go from me to him in a matter of hours?"

"Cain and I are lovers, Wilder. We enjoy making love." He viewed her with scorn and she lost her temper. "You don't want me, you jerk, so let me get on with my life! If you'd told me how you felt four hours ago, this wouldn't have happened!"

"You want to know how I feel? Hell yes, I'm jealous of Cain, and I'm burning alive to make love to you, and I'm frustrated by the bedlam around us. But mostly I feel betrayed by you all over again." Wilder swung his fist forward and hooked Reason's arm. "I came here earlier to tell you I'm in love with you, that I'll always be in love with you, and I find out you're making it with Cromwell on your desk!"

"Then tell me not to do it," she challenged, looking Wilder in the face. "Commit to me now, choose me now, make love to me now, marry me."

He answered her glare with his own and flung back her arm. "Damn you, Reason!"

Grabbing her briefcase, she stormed out.

Chapter Forty-Eight

Wilder sat at the back of the lecture hall where Cain paced behind a large desk and lectured a captivated audience.

"…you have to tear down tradition," he exclaimed and jumped up on the desk. "Art is insurrection!" he pounded his chest, making everyone laugh. "Be ye a warrior unto status quo! And don't sit there asking me how to paint, how to think, how to rebel. What use the artist who seeks to be told how to paint? The moment you're told how to be creative, you stop being creative…"

Insurrection. Be ye a warrior. Wilder thought of his wild week. Trains and evasion, incarceration and Michael Patrick's daughter; love between the fist and perfect kiss. Today, as every bone, muscle and joint in his body hurt, he wasn't sure he wanted to be a warrior.

"Wilder, is that you lurking in the shadows?" Cain boomed from his elevated post.

A hundred eyes screwed Wilder's way.

"Now there, ladies and gentleman, is a fine example of an artistic traveler who's defied status quo. Dr. Declan Wilder O'Neill gave up a movie-star life in Southern California to return to work here in his home town of Belfast. That's what I mean by insurrection. To be a warrior you have to be brave enough to throw off what's comfortable and seek what's difficult. There are no comfortable geniuses, my friends. You aren't comfortable, are you, Dr. O'Neill?"

"You know I'm not, Cromwell."

"Genius! There's an artist of destiny."

Wilder screwed his eyes heavenward. He wanted to punch Cain, especially after this morning, but that would be akin to punching the puppy that followed him home.

After his lecture, as the room emptied, Cain wound his way back to join Wilder. "Man, you look awful. The RUC played hell with you."

"What do you expect? I'm a warrior. What were you doing at my house this morning?"

Cain scratched his head sheepishly. "A bloody nuisance, aren't I? I stopped by on my way to work. I have an early lecture on Fridays. Well, I just wanted to check on how you were doing after last night...I was only trying to help...I had no idea Reason would be there. If I'd known, I wouldn't have come."

"Don't you *ever* ring a doorbell or knock before you barge in?"

Cain deliberated before lifting his shoulders. "I don't think so."

"I suppose Reason told you this morning was perfectly innocent."

"It was, wasn't it?"

Facetiously, Wilder nodded, "Sure it was."

"So, what's up? I have to leave in a few minutes."

"I want to know how you pulled it off last night. How did you get me released from Windsor?"

"I had nothing to do with it."

"Come on, Cain, I saw you driving away."

"Did you now?" That he had interceded for Wilder was apparent when he squeezed Wilder's shoulder and smiled with friendship. Still Cain insisted, "You can thank Ian Wright for your release."

"You mean he was serious when he said he'd help me? And how did a young recruit like Wright convince a detective to let me go? He didn't. He called you and you came to Windsor. Obviously you have friends in high places at the RUC."

Cain steeled himself for Wilder's barrage of questions. None came.

"You're a good friend, Cain," is all Wilder said. "Thank you."

Seeing the fraternity in Wilder's eyes, Cain couldn't stem the happiness in his heart. He accepted Wilder's palm and clasped it firmly.

"*Semper fidelis,* Wilder. Did you know that detective beating you is one of the men who killed Ruairi? His name is Harry Jaggars."

"Is that right?" The enemy had a face and a name now. "What are you doing with the likes of Ian Wright, Cain?"

"I should think last night answers that question. He's on our side."

"The RUC is never on our side," Wilder fleered.

"Ian is. That's the second time he's helped you. Last summer he searched your car on the Antrim Road and uncovered a bullet. He didn't say a word about it to anyone, did he? He's a good lad."

Wilder was far from convinced. "How did you find him?"

"Bernie Thunder introduced us."

"Thunder is a snake in the grass! Why did he introduce you to a cop?"

"Ian was interested in my art."

As always with Cain's explanations, Wilder could tell there was more to it than that. "And you just happened to find out he's willing to be a tout?"

Cain tapped a finger to his head. "I knew the right things to ask."

"What's in this deal for Wright then?"

"A clear conscience."

"Well, Cromwell, I don't know how you do what you do, but I'm grateful for your help. You rescued me from hell last night. But when are you going to stop looking out for me?"

"When you go home to L.A."

"I wouldn't be much of a warrior if I did that," Wilder kidded, not taking Cain seriously.

"You're a warrior all right," Cain sat down backwards in the seat ahead of Wilder, "but your battle isn't about a border; it's about who you are. Are you Declan or Wilder? The two are racing in opposite directions."

"I don't have multiple personalities, Cain. I'm Declan Wilder O'Neill."

"No, you're Declan. Wilder. And both of you are running away from your feelings."

"We are...I am not!"

Cain viewed Wilder at a loss. "Then why are you letting me take Reason away from you?"

"Hey, you're all she sees, all she wants," Wilder responded angrily.

"Yes, but I have to work magic to get her attention; all you've ever had to do is walk into the room. It's you she really wants, and you know that. But you keep running away from her. You're afraid she'll leave you alone again, you're afraid you'll get hurt. You'll take on the Brits, and you're willing to die, but you're scared to death of loving Reason." Cain shook his head as if Wilder were pathetic. "Look, Wilder, if you love her, then *love* her and stop fooling around. Tell her how you feel, don't lose her again."

"Oh, this is priceless crap coming from the man who only hours ago screwed Reason senseless in her office. You had to make sure you staked your claim on her after I'd been with her, didn't you? How can you sit there with a straight face telling me to love Reason when you want her yourself?"

"I'm only trying to fight fair, Wilder. Your father didn't send her over here to fall in love with me."

"My father has no sense!"

"Don't you think Reason belongs with you and not me?"

"Of course I do!" Wilder blared, finally being honest. "But last night is an example of how her life would be with me. She'd get hurt, and you'd get hurt, and I'd get hurt."

"And still you took her to bed! One minute you're swearing you'll protect her by staying away, and then she's in your arms. You are so damn inconsistent!"

"Show me something around here that is consistent, Cain. And don't you criticize me. You have the luxury of being English, of being left alone. I can't walk down the street without getting jumped on. I never know what's going to happen or if I'll survive. I'm just trying to live my life, and I can't seem to live it with or without Reason. All I know is she makes me happy and she tears me apart."

"You don't know what in the fuck you're doing!"

"I know what I'm doing moment to moment, Cain. There's no point planning beyond that because nothing goes the way I expect."

"Well, your moments have consequences for all of us, Wilder. Why did you give Reason Merry's ring?" Cain asked, his own voice rising.

"Why did you take her home with you last night? Why the hell did you call her to come get you at the manor last week? If you want to protect her so goddamn badly," he yelled, "why are you knocking yourself out to see her?"

Wilder shrugged like he had no other choice. "Because life hurts so much when I don't see her. And this is what she wants, Cain. She comes to me willingly."

"Damn it, Wilder, make up your mind! Either commit yourself to Reason, or let her go. Do you or don't you want her back?"

"Cain, don't you see? Reason's not going to let anything happen to me without it happening to her as well."

"Then take her home to Malibu! Save her, save yourself. And save me as well because I love her, and every time she goes to you I die a little. Don't kill me by inches, Wilder."

Wilder didn't know what to say.

"If you're not going to love and care for Reason, to hell with you!" Cain blew up. "I'll marry her! And then you can't have her, ever!"

"Marry her then!" Wilder yelled back.

At once Cain regretted his outburst. "I don't want to be at odds with you, Wilder. You said Reason wouldn't come between us, you said you didn't want her, and I believed you."

"You aren't at odds with me. You're right, I'm at odds with myself. I wish life were easier to live here." Wilder composed himself, speaking quietly again, "I don't know what to tell you, Cain, except all's fair in love in wartime and nothing in love and war makes sense."

Cain gave the Irishman a nod. "Then it's every man for himself."

"Yeah, I guess it is."

Cain collected his papers and drew on his coat. "I have to go."

"Where are you off to this time?"

"Sheephaven Bay."

"What for?"

With his fingers pinched together, Cain brought them to his lips. *"Amore,* baby, *amore."*

"Reason's going with you?"

If he asks me not to go with her, I won't. All he has to do is ask. Silence. "Why else would I be going? *Slán,* Declan or Wilder or whoever you are."

"Hey, Cromwell," Wilder paused on his way out, "thanks again for helping me. And about Reason and me? What you saw this morning was exactly like it looked. There was nothing innocent about it."

*   *   *   *   *   *

"But you won't come back!" Morris screamed when he spotted the overnight case. He ran crying from Reason's bedroom.

"Morris! It's only for two days." Reason dashed after him and caught him by the belt. Into her hug he melted. "I'll be back Sunday night."

"No, you won't. Nobody ever comes back! You're going away. My daddy says you live in N'York City. I asked Decky, and he…" Morris choked, "…and he said it was true."

"Yes, but I won't be moving back to New York for months. Well, I am going home for Christmas, but, Morris, I'll be back. I'll be back this Sunday night, and I'll be back after New Year's." She kneeled and kissed Morris' deluge of tears. "I love you, Morris, and I will come back."

"What if you don't?"

"But I will. Won't you please have a little trust in me?" *Trust!* Reason squeezed Morris tighter. To a motherless boy in a city of paranoia and deceit, the word was unknown.

Morris sucked for air. "Pppromise?"

"I promise."

At once Morris cleared up and allowed hope back into his eyes. "Why aren't you going to Donegal with Decky?"

"Decky didn't ask me to go to Donegal. Cain did."

"Cain's nice, isn't he, Reason?"

"Yes, he is."

"Is he really a Brit?"

"Yes."

"He asked if I'd like to come ride his ponies, and I said 'yyyes!'"

"You see, he and I must be coming back if he invited you to ride the ponies."

"Oh, but now Decky will be sad," Morris decided gloomily.

"Because you're going to ride Cain's ponies?"

"No, silly. Because you're leaving. Maybe he could go to Donegal with you."

"Believe me, Morris, Decky won't be sad, and he wouldn't enjoy himself."

"Why not?"

"Well…he's been through a lot lately and needs to rest."

"Couldn't he rest with you?"

Reason stood up and kissed the curls atop Morris' head. "No, he couldn't…and he wouldn't want to. Now why don't you come help me pack."

Chapter Forty-Nine

Wilder had come to My Lady's Leisure early. To walk the ponies in tappy mist, to smell the turf fires on neighboring farms, to hear the doves and sea call. And he had come to leave medical supplies. He was stocking the shelves in the dungeon when Kieran arrived to prepare one of the Light Fifty rifles.

Neither spoke as they went about their business. Wilder unloaded sutures, splints and painkillers while Kieran donned leather gloves and slid bullets one by one into an eleven-round magazine. Today, what Ruairi died to protect, congealed. Today brought the IRA a deadly new tool. Wilder dared not reflect upon the tolls. He could hear Ruairi admonish, *"You're a soldier."* A soldier, like a surgeon, wanting to keep clean his hands.

"Now a sniper plies our craft," Kieran announced as he readied the gun for transport.

"You?"

Kieran didn't say.

"When?"

"Soon." Kieran helped himself to a bottle of Cain's Scotch and sat back on his hands. "This is going to heat things up. You'll probably be seeing Windsor again soon, me too. The Brits are just waiting for one of us to fuck up. Mind yourself every day now, Dec."

"I will. And, Kieran, I swear to you, no matter how often they arrest me, I won't say a word."

"I know you won't. I won't either." Kieran raised the whiskey to his lips, drank then handed it to Wilder in solemn communion. "Until death do us part, Dec."

Wilder took a drink. "Until death."

Kieran lit a cigarette and flipped the match in the air. "So, Cain and Reason are in Donegal? Must be nice to be able to get away. Did I tell you we got Malachy Duffy out? Smuggled him to Dublin dressed as a nun. He's in Berlin now."

"Setting up the arms deal?"

"Yeah. Good of Cromwell to provide us with the cash and connections."

Wilder gazed around the dungeon at Cain's rickety treasures and wondered about Cain's unexplained clout with the RUC. "I just hope he doesn't double-cross us."

Kieran shrugged as he blew smoke into the breeze off the sea. "It's his funeral if he does."

"Somehow I doubt Cain cares much about that. The guy's nuts. I can't figure him, Kieran. How could he set up that assassination in London? It was so cold-blooded. And still I think he'd rather hammer his own heart than hurt another living thing."

"None of us are what we seem, Dec. Thick skin masks cold blood."

"I'd still like to know his story." Wilder swigged another drink. "One day he shows up out of the blue in Malibu like a long lost brother."

"An English brother? Great Mother of God, I hope Liam didn't hear that! We'll have him back from the grave. Ah, this is living," Kieran delighted in Cain's aged Scotch. "And what about Cain and Reason? Do you think they'll get married? She's a prize worth keeping. You were fucking daft to give her up, Dec."

"I think I'll go blanket the ponies. Want to come?"

"Nah. I'll stay here and finish my work."

Buoyed on savage winds off the sea, the rain was horizontal and hit the windows like a fist. It eclipsed the world beyond the glass. Rather than brave the storm, Wilder wandered into the library. But it wasn't the old books that intrigued him on this wintry day. It was the large oil canvas. Shrouded beneath a gossamer veil was Reason unclad and imbrued with a mantle of flowers. Like a Titian Venus, she lay on a damask chaise in pink-pearl sand with the sea curling skyward at her back. Her fair hair cascaded over her shoulders and tangled into leis of cream gardenias and crimson hibiscus and melted into a bosom seductively full and white. Across her hips fell a swathe of lilies which swept over her thighs to merge with the sand. At her feet lay a chest of gold coins, a pirate's stolen treasure, and in her left hand, she held Forget-me-nots; blue as the ocean behind her, blue as her ocean eyes. This delicate blue was the brightest hue on the canvas, and Cain had only used it three times; eyes, sea, English flowers. His message was clear. *Forget me not.*

To stare at Reason through Cain's loving eye was painful, but Wilder couldn't tear himself away. Yes, Reason was a tantalizing subject, but Cain's artistic power was the wonder. Cain had lamented the summer's gunshot wound had impaired his technique, but all Wilder detected from Cain's hand was beauty. Inspired by deep, erotic pleasure, Cain's genius gleamed in his vision of Reason, who appeared glorified in the warmth and light of her nakedness. Guiding the wise tip of his brush, he had captured Reason's jack-o-lantern radiance. Her true self. Cain had seen it and felt it and made it immortal. From Reason, he created a masterpiece; Wilder had created nothing but heartache. He covered the portrait, both sorry and glad he had seen it.

*   *   *   *   *   *

Cain and Reason kicked along the white-sand strand of Sheephaven Bay which fed into the Atlantic. The horseshoe-curved bay was surrounded by craggy hills red with heather. Clouds settled on the hilltops but drifted over the ocean when the wind blew, and as the clouds drifted, the sun filtered through. Occasionally fine rain formed in the sunlight, and the bay would fill with rainbows.

"It's nice to go for a morning walk with songbirds instead of helicopters. I didn't realize how stressful Belfast was until I left it." Reason soaked up the tranquillity around her and savored the mist tapping her cheeks, and even the mist seemed softer on this side of the border. "I don't have to worry about getting shot, there are no soldiers, no bombs, no ULF...I feel like I'm out on parole."

"All that 'normalized' insanity seems pretty abnormal now, doesn't it?" Cain agreed. "And think how nice America will seem when you go home for Christmas. You might decide not to come back."

"Oh no. I have too much invested in Belfast to leave it behind now."

They wandered further down the beach. The tide swept in. Clouds raced up off the sea, the air glimmered rainbows, and Cain was whistling *Greensleeves*. And he looked regal in the sun, and charming, Prince Charming. Smitten with happiness, Reason tackled him, and he crashed to the sand. Laughing, she crashed down with him and threw her arms around his head.

"What's this?" Cain cried, not disliking her affection.

"I just wanted to kiss you. Because when I'm with you everything feels safe and right, and I'm having such a nice time," Reason rejoiced in the Donegal glory far removed from Belfast and her Fenian sons. "Hey, let's build something in the sand. A skyscraper."

"You can't have a skyscraper in Donegal."

"You're right." Reason surveyed the site. "A boat then. Let's sculpt a curragh and line it with shells."

It took less than an hour.

Cain patted a handful of seashells into the stern. "In a few minutes the tide is going to crush our boat."

"No, it won't. It will send it sailing. It's the cargo not the vessel that matters."

"What can a sand boat carry?"

"Wishes," Reason said in a whisper. "Make a wish and put it in the boat, and then when the tide comes in, your wish will sail around the world and finally come true."

"How long does it take a wish to sail around the world?"

"That depends on the weight of the wish."

"OK," Cain got into the spirit, "I have mine. Do you have yours?"

Reason did. They clutched their wishes, awaiting the tide. When it rushed in to collect the canoe, they tossed their petitions into the bow. The boat melted beneath the wave, and its sandy remains tumbled out to sea.

"Now what?" Cain watched his wish sail away.

"We wait for our wishes to come true."

The damp had penetrated Cain's shirt and slacks, now his muscles and bones. He pulled Reason to her feet. "I'm freezing. Let's go back to the hotel and have a drink."

Reason preferred to commune with the vast, shining waters. "I don't want a drink."

"Come on. I have something to show you."

The little hotel overlooked Sheephaven Bay and the rolling, rocky pastures partitioned by stone fences. The houses along the one-lane road were stucco white with roofs colored black, red, blue or green. Bright doors red, yellow, blue were seen as well.

"Wilder once told me not to see Donegal is not to see Ireland. Now I know what he meant. This is beautiful, Cain."

"Right now I want you to see this." He flipped through the pages of the book he'd brought to show Reason. "I'll never forget this handwriting. It committed me to the Cure and then to the sanitarium." He glanced up with a forbidding smile. "This belongs to my father. It's a second set of books for the Gov's charities." Cain nudged the ledger across the table.

Reason read the first few pages in dismay. "Your father has been embezzling the hospital's funds for *months*." She looked at Cain with misgiving. "Why are you showing me this?"

"Read on."

"Oh no! He's been into the new wing's funds from *Sonas Ort!* Look at the names of these engineering and construction firms he's paying...I've never heard of any of them."

"That's because they don't exist."

Reason skimmed Hunter's transactions. "How much has he stolen from us?"

"A few million pounds. He's siphoned from every fund he could get his hands on."

"Have you told Bernie?"

"No. I have plans for my father."

"Cain, this isn't a chess game! The last thing we need is your father bankrupting the Gov."

Cain poured Reason more wine and encouraged her to drink it. "I've known my father was up to something since last summer." He related how he had come to unmask Hunter. "...but I'm also keeping two sets of books. The real one, and the one I show H.C. He steals from Bernie, gives the money to me, and I buy weapons which I'll give to Kieran."

Reason stared across the bay into the red light of evening, knowing her life couldn't get much stranger. "How are you accomplishing all this?"

"Same way my father is embezzling from the Gov; through a maze of phony companies and off-shore accounts, all listed under pseudonyms that H.C. uses on his fake passports. Every illicit transaction has been recorded."

"Unbelievable," Reason muttered and downed her wine.

"My father curses the IRA, and now he's their generous sponsor. Once we get our shipment of arms this spring, we'll alert the auditors, and the truth will be told." Cain leaned back in his chair and folded his arms. "I'll bury that son of a bitch."

"But, Cain, you're spending the Gov's money! And to have the Gov linked to the IRA would be disastrous. It's the Gov's reputation you'll sink."

"No, Bernie will be a hero after he discovers to his horror my father's shocking embezzlement and even more shocking investments. He and the ULF will go after the old crook with a vengeance."

"But how will the hospital recoup its losses? How will we finish the new wing?"

"Relax, love. I've replaced most of the *Sonas Ort* funds through the sale of the emeralds. As for the rest, Bernie and the other members of the board will sue my father for all he's worth, and he's worth a lot. But I thought you should know about the fiddled figures in case there's a problem or I need your help."

"What do you expect to gain from this?"

"H.C. sent me to the Cure. I want to repay his kindness."

"Cain, revenge is poisonous."

"No, it's a reason to live."

"And what if your father wants revenge and takes away My Lady's Leisure?"

"In two weeks my father will no longer own My Lady's Leisure. I persuaded him to deed it over to me."

"How did you accomplish that one?"

"Thumb screws and sweet talk," Cain joked.

"And what if this arms deal goes wrong and you get arrested?"

"I'm just the catalyst, Reason. I haven't carried out any of the business myself and every transaction leads to my father. One thing I learned in the Cure is how to be dirty and stay clean."

"I don't want to know about this, Cain. Just tell me when it's over. Will it ever be over? If revenge is your reason for living, who's next?"

Staring our the window, Cain didn't answer. He was thinking about Jillie. Something about her eyes had left him unsettled. The quality of cunning. She did reconnaissance on every face. He'd seen eyes like that before. In the mirror.

Chapter Fifty

Outside Letterkenny they crossed the border. *Bap, bap, bap* into Derry. Metal walls, fanged wire, watch towers and guns replaced rainbows and mountains and sand boats for wishes. When Cain stopped for petrol, Reason saw the headlines.

Four soldiers shot dead. New terror weapon unleashed. The soldiers were literally blown off the road by a sniper firing from less than 150 yards. The shots were the result of a high caliber sniping rifle recently acquired by the Provisional IRA.

"*Déjà* violence," she turned to Cain, feeling depressed, "we're back in the British North." And part of her wished she'd never seen Donegal. If she'd never seen its freedom, she wouldn't regret giving it up. It made the chains around Ulster all the more glaring, and coming back to Belfast all the more bleak.

Reason walked into Fiona's and found Wilder reading on the sofa. After Friday's bitter quarrel she wasn't sure what to say to him or what he might say to her. She inched into the firelit room. "What are you doing here so late?"

"I'm the babysitter." Wilder didn't take his eyes off of Reason. He was glad to see her after what seemed to have been a year-long weekend. He pictured Cain's portrait and thought Reason was even more radiant in real life. "Where's Cain?"

"He headed straight for Down to check on his ponies."

Reason regarded Wilder shyly, he looked back and shyly smiled. The conversation lagged.

"You looked rested," Wilder spoke up. "Any problems from the concussion?"

"None. How about you? Are you still in so much pain?"

"Nah, it's not so bad."

Another awkward pause.

Reason tried again, "I read about the soldiers who were killed yesterday. I guess Ruairi's been avenged. Or maybe this was to get even for Pembroke." She thought Wilder would elaborate.

He didn't. He clapped his medical journal shut and swung to his feet, preparing to leave. "Do you know it's after eleven? I was beginning to think you'd never get home. Morris has been watching the clock for hours and driving me crazy asking about you. I think he thought you weren't coming back. He finally fell asleep in front of the window waiting for you."

"Poor little guy."

"Fiona is over at Nora's, and Kieran…God alone knows where Kieran is." Still unable to bend at the waist, Wilder stooped down with effort to retrieve his shoes then pushed up with a groan.

Reason jumped to assist. "Here, give me your foot. I'll put your shoes on for you."

"Well, this is embarrassing," Wilder muttered but allowed Reason to help him. "How was Donegal, or did you get out of the hotel long enough to see it?"

"It was gorgeous."

"Romantic, huh?"

"Very," Reason nodded and went on tying Wilder's shoes.

"Made for lovers."

"That's for sure."

"I'll bet you and Cromwell had a regular honeymoon."

"Oh, for Pete's sake, Wilder, what are you trying to say? Cain and I didn't make love, if that's what you're dying to know."

"Really?"

"Really. I was too tired." Reason helped Wilder slide on his coat and lifted his hair over his collar. And when he turned to her unable to hide his relief, she flung aside Donegal's peace. She couldn't shed it fast enough.

"For awhile there…well, I had myself believing you and Cromwell had gone off to get married."

"*Married?*" Reason tapped Wilder's nose. "You and that wild imagination. But it was good to get away from Belfast for awhile."

"I'm sure it was. Unfortunately your being gone was tough for Morris."

"I know, but sooner or later he has to face the fact I won't always be here."

"The problem is he's grown so fond of you. He's used to seeing you every day and having you to talk to, to count on when he needs you…he realized this weekend what the world feels like without you in his life."

"He doesn't have to worry for a long time," Reason declared, not guessing Wilder referred to himself as well as Morris. "My leaving Belfast is months away." She watched Wilder walk for the door. "Well, I guess I'll see you around."

"Yeah, I guess. Oh, this is ridiculous!" Finally, Wilder said what both of them were thinking, "Look, Reason, about last Friday…I was an idiot. I'm sorry I reacted so badly."

"No, I'm sorry, Wilder. I was totally insensitive. What I did was spiteful and mean, not to mention indiscreet."

"I could have told you what I was feeling instead of acting like a jerk again. You wouldn't have turned to Cain if I'd been honest."

"But I shouldn't have gone to Donegal when you were hurt."

"I should have asked you not to go."

"I would have stayed."

"I wished you had."

"Well, I'm back now, and if there's anything I can do, anything at all, let me know."

"You can give me one more chance to get it right."

"You're going home soon. You'll have to make me your new year's resolution."

"I will. And, Reas, next time you're indiscreet? Do it with me."

She rolled her eyes. "That was a one time fling, Wilder."

"There's just one more thing. From now on, total honesty. I'm going to tell you what I think and feel. This will be a challenge for me, mind you, but I'm going to take the risk and do it. You know what I'm thinking now?"

Reason drew back, afraid to guess. "No, what?"

"You tied my shoes too tight."

"Oh, sorry."

"And you know what else I'm thinking?"

"What?"

"That it's really good to see you."

"It's good to see you too," Reason chuckled.

"And here's another thing. I'm thinking if I weren't hurt, I'd back you right up against the wall and go crazy on you."

Reason just laughed.

"And, Reason? I hated every minute you were gone." Wilder walked out the door then turned back. "And I do love you. I never stopped loving you and I never will." He tossed her a kiss. "Until we're indiscreet."

Before going to bed, Reason went to check on Morris. He was asleep but she kissed his forehead anyway. Up batted his eyelids; a sleepy grin followed.

"You came back," he garbled half-asleep and extended his fingers to touch Reason's nose to be sure she was real.

"You see, good things happens when you have faith, Morris."

"Aye. Didya see Decky?"

"Yes. He just left."

"He watched the clock all evening waiting for you to get home."

"He said you were watching the clock."

"Och no, it was Decky. Every five minutes he kept asking me when you'd be home; about drove me crazy so he did. I think he was afraid you weren't coming back."

"That uncle of yours is hard to figure."

"He bought me a lovely wee bike for Christmas," Morris yawned. "Och, it's brilliant." He kicked off his covers. "It's outside! I'll show you."

But Reason rested a palm on his shoulder and encouraged him to lie down. "You have to go back to sleep, or you'll be so tired you'll fall face-first onto your desk at school tomorrow."

"OK, but...um, Reason..." he turned his face to the wall so she couldn't see him, "...I think I knew you'd come back, but I wasn't sure...and Reason? I'm glad you came back."

"I am too, sweetheart."

"And Reason?" Morris' voice was hushed and pressed to the wall. "I love you."

Reason ducked back to kiss Morris on the cheek. "And I love you too."

Chapter Fifty-One

"Last week the murdering sons of bitches killed four soldiers," Bernard Thunder stumped around his game room, addressing his ULF peers. "They kill four of ours, we'll kill four of theirs. Harry Jaggars has given us files on a number of men. We know where they live, and we'll pay them a visit. It won't be Father Christmas who comes down their chimneys this year," Bernie smiled. "It'll be the Ghosts of Christmas Present, ghosts like Duggie Knack."

Cain sat in the back. His eyes passed over the heads hung on the wall; bears, a cougar, a fox, a wolf. And scanning the faces in the room, he saw clergymen and constables, businessmen and generals. As these men around him plotted, he wondered if there was a conscience or soul among them. They seemed as bereft as the mounted heads. All he sensed in the room was malice. And the limitless fuels of war; hatred and vengeance and the need to be right. As right as the IRA with their bullets and bombs. He thought of life in the psychiatric hospital, where madness was kept behind bars. Yet in his time at Seton Close, he'd never heard such sinister maundering or felt the absence of God more than he felt in this room. This was the asylum where the inmates ruled. Our day will come, no surrender; the cries of their little war. It was all so psychotic and so fiercely, fanatically real.

Cain closed his eyes and heard Bernie reading the names of future victims like they were winners in the lotto. Making mental notes, he would give the names to Kieran so the targets could be warned. But in such a small country there was nowhere to hide. With the police helping the ULF, even those who took shelter could be found.

Chapter Fifty-Two

"What's new?" Cain popped into Wilder's bedroom at dusk.

Wilder whirled with a start. "Once just, once I wish you'd use the doorbell."

"But you might not let me in. Didn't you hear me downstairs? I've been here for over an hour."

"You have? What have you been doing?"

"I caulked the windows over the sink. There was a draft in your kitchen. Here, I brought you some tea. What are you doing?"

"What does it look like I'm doing? I'm packing."

"Don't tell me it's time for you to go to Malibu already? Good God, it's December!" Cain clutched his shirt and fell comically against the door jam. "'Gather ye rosebuds while ye may, Old Time is still a-flying: And this same flower that smiles today, tomorrow will be dying.'"

"You know, Cromwell, you're wasting yourself at CC. You belong in Vegas."

Cain threw wide his arms. "Art *is* the stage. Now drink up. You'll need the caffeine." He waved the mug of tea under Wilder's nose. "We have a busy night."

"What do you mean 'we?' I have a lot to do before my plane leaves tomorrow."

"Yes, yes, there's plenty of time for that. But first we're going to a Christmas party."

"Forget it, Cromwell. I don't want to go."

Cain raced back downstairs and up again. "I rented you this tuxedo." He ignored Wilder's protests and laid out the black jacket and trousers. "I think you'll like the green cummerbund, looks very Irish…classy too."

"There is no way you're getting me into this, Cain." Wilder checked Cain's attire; black cashmere jacket, black t-shirt, black jeans with holes in the knees, and yellow running shoes. "I like your tuxedo better."

"I don't 'do' formal wear." Cain double-checked the clothes on the bed and sifted through Wilder's armoire for the right socks. "There, that's everything. Now all we need are your bulletproof nerves and a pair of gloves so there won't be fingerprints."

"No!" Wilder pulled Cain away from the armoire. "I'm not going anywhere tonight. Look, Cain, I've already been through too much in the last few weeks. I just want to go peacefully home to L.A. and enjoy Christmas with my dad." He stuffed the formal wear back into its box.

Cain pawed the clothes out again. "You won't get hurt. You'll have fun."

"I'm not going. No, no, NO!"

Cain sighed and hunched away to the window. "After all I've done for you…"

"No!"

"It's not like you owe me anything," Cain moped and flaunted his lost-hound expression. "I only do the plumbing, the pruning, the negotiating to get you out of Windsor…"

"Oh, all right!" Wilder relented. "What is it you want me to do?"

"Holy hell, you're a pal!" Cain broke out his smile and bounded back to Wilder. "Has your body healed enough that you can help me move a two-hundred-pound mirror?"

"Probably. Why?"

While Wilder continued to pack, Cain explained his scheme to plunder Bernie's safe in exchange for the title to My Lady's Leisure. "…and it will be hours before Bernie realizes he's been robbed."

Cain's motive captured Wilder's fancy. How could he not help Cain keep his beloved manor? "You know what puzzles me in all this shady business is how you turned out to be such a nice guy with Hunter as your father."

"I'm the bright spot in a dark line," Cain quipped. "Thanks for helping me out, Wilder." He leaped to shake Wilder's hand. "You're the brother I never had."

When Wilder opened his mouth to joke about not being brother to a Brit, Brendan came to mind. A true brother. But Brendan never tap danced, and Brendan didn't watch out for him or caulk kitchen windows or paint rarefied portraits of Reason. And Brendan was dead. Forget me not. From the corner of his eye, Wilder stole a glance at Cain reeling around the room. Brother.

"How's the tuxedo? OK? It looks good."

Wilder fiddled with his bow tie and cuffs as Cain shifted into third gear on the two-lane road north to the Thunder's. "Actually it fits pretty well. If there's a party going on, how are we going to get into Bernie's safe?"

"How else?" To Cain it was obvious. "We're going to walk right up to it, take what we need, and go back to the party."

"Why can't we be like regular burglars and climb through a bedroom window…but then, you never do anything that's regular, do you?"

"Too easy."

Wilder peered out the window at the Antrim Coast. Cracking sea wind, sea waves like cymbals, sea gulls sailing, but no helicopters. Farmhouses festooned with Christmas lights flashed through the bare trees. Pretty innocence, peace on earth. It was freezing under layers of clouds, and the air was thick with droplets; tappy rain would fall soon. Wilder drew his overcoat tighter. "Will you go home to England for Christmas?" he asked.

"No." Cain tightened his grip on the steering wheel. "But I'm going skiing in Switzerland for a few days next week." *"We got a live one, boys, there are a couple of fellows in that yellow Ford. License plate matches the one the RUC gave us."* "Christmas means nothing to me."

"What's that shining in the back seat of the car? I think they've got rifles. Hold it, one of those terrorists is a woman." "I always spend Christmas alone at My Lady's Leisure." *"Probably the Virgin Mary, hahahaha. If we approach them, they'll open fire."* "I prefer it that way." *"Then we won't approach them. What do you want to do? Tomorrow's Christmas, let's give them a break. Shut up, Cromwell."* "I put up a little tree, never decorate it though." *"We can't let terrorists drive away."* "If you decorate a tree, you have to undecorate it." *"Let's send 'em home for the holidays."* "It always depresses me to undecorate a Christmas tree." *"Happy Christmas, fuckers!"* "All that magic and glitter gone for another year." *Bangbangbangbangbang.* "But I always have a plum pudding, can't imagine Christmas without it." *"Open the car door, carefully, carefully! Jeeezus Christ, there's blood everywhere! Yeah, they're definitely dead. But wait, those weren't rifles we saw."* "And I always get a present for myself." *"Well, I'll be a son of a bitch, the back seat is full of presents."* "Last year I bought a kaleidoscope." *"What shall we do with them? Leave them?"* "Maybe this year I'll buy a music box." *"Hell no, let's divide them up, take them home, might be something nice for the kids."* "One that plays 'Greensleeves.'"

"What's the matter?" Wilder turned to Cain who had abruptly swerved to the side of the road.

Instead of answering, Cain bolted from the car. Over the retaining wall he hurdled and stampeded down the hillside to the beach. At first Wilder thought Cain was being funny, then he saw Cain ankle deep in sand, slapping through the rising fog and stripping off his clothes as if they were in flames. Wilder sprinted after him. "What in the hell are you doing?" he demanded to know over the wind.

"Can't breathe, can't breathe!" Cain was in tears and clawing at his neck to remove an invisible collar. "I have to get the blood off. It's in my eyes. Oh God, it's in my eyes!"

"Stop it! Look around, Cain, you're all right!" Wilder grabbed Cain by his naked shoulders and with a forceful shake prevented him from further undressing and lunging into the frigid water. "That's rain in your eyes, Cain, rain! There's no blood, no blood." And, as he gaped into Cain's face frantic with terror and grief and pain so much pain, Wilder realized the Englishman was wounded; deeply, darkly wounded on a level below the heart, below the soul. On a level where man met God. A level where men were no longer men but rather specters doomed to roam eternity in chains. And all Wilder could do was tug Cain away from the grasping shoreline, as though he were tugging back Cain's spirit, back through catcalling pulpits of madness and shame. Madness and shame frothing and flooding up from Cain's soul, up from his heart to become tears. Like blood in his eyes.

"You can let me go. I'm all right." Cain struggled away from Wilder, weakly laughing. "Aren't you going to tell me I'm not right in the head? Aren't you going to run away?" he chuckled, collecting his clothes.

"No," Wilder reassured and took Cain's arm. "You can dress while I drive. 'Old Time is still a-flying,' and we have a safe to rob."

Cain stumbled in the sand, casting his eyes to the open sea. He could breathe now, and there wasn't a trace of blood. Yes, that was rain in his eyes. No, tears, baby tears, smearing his sight. *"Only babies have tears, boy, babies have tears! Act like a man!"* He wished he weren't crying for Wilder to see. But sometimes it hurt so awfully. So meanly. To remember. *"Jeeezus Christ, there's blood everywhere."* Oh God, God, God. His voice eked forth, "Listen, Wilder, I…"

"You don't have to explain anything, Cain." Wilder filled his palms with sand and watched the wind magically suck it from his hands. Fluttery, soundless ascension. Like releasing a shower of stars. That's life, let it go. He turned to Cain kindly. "We're *all* nuts."

Arriving at the Thunder's estate, Wilder marveled at the metal walls and barbed wire corralling the house. "Bernie's not paranoid or anything, is he? He lives in a fortress."

"And all we have to do to break in is announce we've arrived. You aren't nervous, are you?" Cain asked as the electronic gates swung wide and Wilder drove in.

"After the Pembroke train fiasco, I'll never be nervous again. Shot every synapse to hell that night."

"This is the first time I've ever gone into a house to nick a piece of junk," Cain remarked tartly. "Imagine going to prison for stealing fake jewels."

"Do you have any idea how you're going to get into Bernie's safe?"

"Nope."

"Oh, that's comforting to know."

"Hell, Wilder, there isn't a safe known to man I can't crack."

"Where did you learn all these dirty tricks?"

"I'm a Cromwell, remember?"

Walking up to Bernard's front door, Cain brushed the last pellets of sand off his jeans, adjusted his shirt and coat and combed his fingers through his wet hair. "Now remember, at nine o'clock sharp the men will retire to the study to smoke. The women will sit around in the dining room. That's when we'll shoot up the back stairs. We'll have about forty five minutes to get in and out before dessert is served. Are you ready?"

Wilder shadowed Cain up the steps. "Yep."

"As your dad would say, 'Where there's tap, there's laughter.'" Cain did a little two-step. "On with the show." He let the brass knocker drop.

The butler peeked through a porthole.

"Cain Cromwell and date," Cain announced, making Wilder laugh.

The butler's eyes darted left and right, right and left. He closed the peep door and ushered the two men into the foyer. But before reaching the ballroom, Cain encountered his father amidst a group of men.

Hunter appeared startled then up swung the forced grin. He shook Wilder's hand like they were best friends then hugged his son. "Delighted to see you both, delighted." But once out of earshot, Hunter grabbed Cain by the ear and hauled him aside. "What are you doing here? Good God, you're dressed like a damn priest."

"Deeear, H.C., have you forgotten Bernie's oh so *faux* gems?" Cain waddled away from his father like Charlie Chaplin. Twirling an invisible cane, he wobbled back. "If you aren't glad to see me, I'll leave and let you retrieve the necklace yourself."

"Why the hell did you bring Declan up here with you? He's out of place as a nigger in the House of Lords with this bunch."

"Bernie invited all the Gov physicians. Do you like his tuxedo? The finest money can rent. I charged it to you."

"Just get the goddamn necklace and get out!"

"Yeah, yeah, I catch your drift, daddyo," Cain made fun and kissed his father's clean-shaven cheek. A kiss Hunter hastily wiped and dashed to the floor.

"Don't make a spectacle of yourself, boy." With a final lour of warning, giving Cain a knuckle in the back, Hunter threw wide the ballroom doors and announced with flourish, "Look who just arrived!"

While Cain performed juggling feats and hat tricks, Wilder made his way around the ballroom, meeting the guests. It was an easy room to work, and he enjoyed the craic. Unlike Hunter predicted, Wilder fit in well. He had mastered social panache; say a few clever opening lines, pass out free medical advice, quote holiday poetry through a boyish grin, clasp everyone's hand, and be sure to kiss the ladies. "Happy Christmas, Happy Christmas." *Thankee, Thankee, gods bless ye.* In the days he scampered man to man in the pubs of the New Lodge, begging for money or bites to eat, he never dreamed he'd find himself in the company of Ulster's elite. He gazed around the crowded room and beheld the North's most powerful men. The loyalists, changeling heirs of Ireland.

Wilder's eyes stalled upon Harry Jaggars. In suave evening attire the detective shone, but a tuxedo's finesse only added to his air of cruelty. Harry Jaggars, polished and beaming like a switchblade. Even wearing a smile to be greeting his friends, his face was a memory of violence. Watching Harry extend his manicured, soft-palmed hand to his peers, Wilder felt every blow of the man's baton, every squeeze of the pincers. And how Harry's peers welcomed him; men in tuxedos lauding their trusty sword.

Striding across the ballroom to the table where Harry helped himself to canapés, Wilder confronted the constable. "Hello, Harry."

It took Jaggars a moment to comprehend who addressed him. The instant he recognized the Irishman, he scanned the room for back-up. "You're out of place here, O'Neill."

"Relax, Harry, I come in peace." Wilder brushed a piece of lint off Jaggar's shoulder and brandished a dangerous smile. "Bernie and I are associates."

"Bernie would never invite you here."

"And why is that? Because I'm behind enemy lines?"

"Tread carefully, Dr. O'Neill."

"Or what?" Wilder derided. "You'll beat me up again?"

Harry chilled Wilder with his chrome smile. "Crawl back to your gutter, Declan."

"My gutter is your gutter, Harry. You and I are neighbors. I can see your house from my backyard. And here I thought I'd moved above the rabble."

Harry drew back. "How do you know where I live?"

"How did you know where my brother lived, Harry?"

"Don't push your luck with me, doctor. Your days are numbered as it is." Jaggars shoved Wilder aside.

"Maybe you'd like to come over for a drink some evening. Or do you prefer getting to know me through the cameras you plant in my yard?"

Harry helped himself to a stack of oysters and smiled like he was enjoying the game. "I say, Dr. O'Neill, where's Reason McGuinness tonight? Is she home alone?" He lowered his voice, "She's a pretty piece of ass, Dr. O'Neill. Is she a good fuck? Does she suck your filthy Fenian balls off?"

Wilder wanted to blast his fist into Harry's smirk. But one hint of a lover's distress from him, and Reason would become Harry's hostage. And then Wilder tried something, just to see its effect. "Those questions can be answered by Cain Cromwell. She's his woman. Why don't you go ask him?"

His perpetual smile faltered, and briefly, Harry looked daunted. "Does Dr. Cromwell know you're giving it to his woman?" he regained his stride. "You were all over her in Milltown last week."

Wilder stared at Harry like his words meant nothing. "Reason and I are friends, obviously you know that. And yeah, Cromwell knows, but he's very protective of Reason. He'd rip my 'filthy Fenian' balls off, yours too, if either of us laid a hand on her."

"It would be wise for her to return to America then. Beautiful things get hurt here, Dr. O'Neill."

Wilder's blood ran cold. "You'll commit suicide if you touch her, Jaggars," he said in a voice too gruff.

Harry screwed his metal eyes to Wilder. "Is that a threat, Dr. O'Neill?"

"Say those same words to Cain and you tell me."

"One more word out of you, Declan, and I'll have you arrested for assault." Harry started away.

And Wilder couldn't stand it. He got in the last words, "Kiss my ass, detective." No longer in a festive mood, he stood apart from the guests. He watched Cain dancing a cha-cha and juggling Mrs. Thunder's Waterford goblets. Always the clown, Cain collected Bernie's friends around him. Especially the ladies. They found Cain irresistible. It was his muscular body, his buccaneer hair, the pirate prince of revelry. Life was his joke, the joke at his expense. Wilder knew the truth. Behind the laughs lorded the beast that chased Cain into freezing water and put tears of blood in his eyes. And Wilder wondered what monster so preyed on Cain's mind it inspired hideous visions and hurled him howling into the dark.

Curious to see more of Bernie's mansion, Wilder left the ballroom. He walked through the first door he came to; a study with oak walls dotted with the heads of wild game. Turning in a circle, he saw one dead-eyed, rigid animal after another. Then he clapped eyes upon Cain's painting. *Blood Shot.* The leering, surreal eyeball gazing through a pitchfork. Wilder had thought Cain was kidding when he said he was giving the grotesque work to Bernard, but there it was hung among the heads. Why was Cain giving gifts to Bernie in the first place?

After-dinner mints were being served in the dining room when Wilder and Cain slinked up the back stairs, down a deserted corridor and through the last bedroom on the left. With a penlight leading the way, they came upon the rococo mirror bolted above a marble counter in an immense dressing room off an equally immense bath. A formidable red siren hung above the top shelf of the dressing closet. Upon seeing the mirror, Wilder and Cain exchanged scowls of aversion; two hundred pounds of baby pink and baby blue-painted roses carved on a garish gold frame.

"I hope we don't crack the thing," Wilder tried not to laugh. "Break a mirror this ugly and we'll have seven years of bad taste."

A surgeon of thievery, Cain removed the bottom bolts of the mirror. In a matter of moments, he motioned for Wilder to lift and help him lower the monstrosity to the floor. As Bernie had confided, behind the mirror was a small safe in the wall beside a recessed metal cabinet which housed the electronic brain of the alarm. Beneath the door of the safe was an illuminated key pad where Bernard's secret code could be typed. Unconcerned, Cain produced a professional lock pick set. Trying different picklocks, he had no trouble cracking the metal cabinet and popping open its door. Like he had done a hundred times before, he traced the routes of the alarm's wires and cut the circuit that led to the siren. But he didn't cut the power to the key pad. The only way to get into the safe was to punch in the right four-digit combination.

"You know the code, right?" Wilder assumed confidently.

Cain rubbed his gloved fingers over pursed lips. "No...but we have until dessert to figure it out."

"Oh, this is good news." Wilder gave a Jack Benny slap to his cheek. "We should have no trouble. There are only about four thousand possible combinations."

But Cain wasn't fazed. He settled back to think. "If we were Bernie, what numbers would we use? The date of the Battle of Boyne? Punch in 1,6,9,0."

Wilder did. The key pad blinked on and off as the numbers made little beeps, but nothing happened.

Cain rattled off Bernard's birthday and his wife's birthday and their wedding anniversary. Blink, blink, beep beep, nothing.

"How do you know all these dates, Cromwell?"

"Research, son, research. Try 1,3, 5,2...that's one of his son's birthday." Wilder typed in the numbers to no avail, but he cocked his ear and hit the numbers again. Listening intently, he went through the numbers on the key pad one through ten. He wheeled to Cain in revelation. "Do you hear that?"

"You mean the beeps?"

"They aren't just beeps, Cain, they're...what was that?" Wilder punched off the penlight and dived deeper into the closet. Hushed, rushed murmurs came from the bedroom.

"I'm sorry I'm so late. We don't have much time...oh God," came an impassioned gasp.

"Time enough for this and this," seduced a reply.

A man and a woman. Groping, kissing, undressing, falling on the bed in a furious heat.

As the couple's lust soared into transported pants and moans, Wilder figured what the hell, and shining the penlight through his fingers, punched four numbers into the key pad; 2,1,7,1. The safe opened. He reached in and pulled out a black velvet box which he opened and showed to Cain. Astonished by Wilder's sleight of hand, Cain nodded and pushed the necklace into his pocket. Closing the safe's door, Wilder lifted his end of the mirror and Cain lifted his. Soundlessly, they replaced the baroque barricade.

As the couple's passion wound up, Cain gave Wilder a nod towards the closet door. Dessert would be served in the dining room soon. Having no time to be timid, out through the bathroom they scrambled on their hands and knees. Into the darkened bedroom, past the foot of the bouncing bed they crawled. And cantering on all fours through piles of discarded clothing, Wilder wondered whose hearts were beating hotter, the lovers' or the larcenists'.

"Faster! Faster! Oh, God, oh!" the woman was moaning and beating her fists on the bed.

Faster, faster Wilder and Cain loped across the room towards the door. If his heart hadn't been ready to launch from his chest, Wilder would have burst out laughing.

"Oh, Harry! Oh, Harry!" the Englishwoman panted in ecstasy peaking, "I heard 'God Save the Queen!'"

Upon the threshold, Wilder broke into a run and streaked down the abandoned hallway. He didn't stop running until he hit the back stairs, blazed through the music room and skidded up to the dining room doorway. On Wilder's heels, Cain shot from the bedroom as well, but not before hearing the tinkle of bells. Little gold bells around a lady's ankle.

"OK, how did you do it?" were the first words out of Cain's mouth when he dropped into the driver's seat after the party. "How did you open the safe?"

"Elementary, dear Cromwell. Didn't you hear the beeps? They were musical notes. Number one was C, two was D, three was E...numbers 2,1,7,1 are notes D, C, B, C. Once I heard the scale I figured 'God Save the Queen' would be Bernie's choice for a song."

"By jove, that's brilliant! You're becoming an admirable ne'er-do-well, Declan."

"On the road to ruin so I am, and what a glorious road it is. I have to tell you, Cain, I thought you were off your rocker when you first suggested it, but tonight has been great. It's the first time in weeks I've truly enjoyed myself." Wilder viewed the countryside streaking past. The tappy rain had materialized softly and drifted across the hills. Tiny beads of rain rolled down the windows. Tiny beads of Irish water the fairies would pluck from the trees and string into rosaries, or so Reason once said. "I especially loved the look on both the Thunders' faces when you were tossing those Waterford glasses into the air. But do you know what the best part of tonight was? Robbing Bernie's safe under Harry Jaggars' nose. Here's a top cop, and he can't stop a robbery. He can beat the crap out of a man, but he can't stop a robbery."

"And aren't you glad he didn't stop us? Do you suppose he's the Harry of," Cain mimicked the throaty exclamation, "'Oh, Harry, Oh, Harry, I heard 'God Save the Queen?' As far as I could tell he was the only man named Harry at the party."

Wilder clapped his hands and relished the notion. "Now wouldn't that be beautiful? We're crawling out of the bedroom, getting away while he's getting off. 'Oh, Harry, Oh, Harry!'" he did his own moaning imitation and snorted with hilarity. "I'm never going to forget that one."

"Who do you suppose the woman was?" From the bells, Cain wondered if it could have been Gillian Paradise. Surely other women wore ankle bracelets with bells. And what would a dizzy secretary from the Gov be doing at Bernard Thunder's super-elite party? Why would she be cooing, "Oh, Harry, oh Harry," with a refined English accent? The answers to those questions sent prickles up Cain's neck.

"I don't know, but she sure was loving it."

Jillie had said her ankle bracelet was a gift from an older gentleman. "How old do you think Harry Jaggars is?" Cain mused. If it was Jillie, she arrived at the party after dinner, but why hadn't she appeared for dessert? Because Harry warned her not to? Because Wilder was at the party? Because it might blow her cover?

"I'd say he's about forty. I wonder if that woman knew she was making love with a monster."

"Perhaps the lady prefers monsters." Cain's would have to confirm his suspicions, quickly.

"If the lady likes Jaggars, the lady's a monster as well."

Chapter Fifty-Three

"On the first day of Christmas my true love sent to me a Catholic strung from a tree. On the second day of Christmas my true love sent to me two murdered dickheads...park here, park here," Duggie stopped singing long enough to command. He and another man slouched in the back seat of a black taxi while the third man swung to a stop midway up the Antrim Road. "According to the RUC, the man we're after walks this way every night at twelve."

"We're just shooting him and driving away, right?" The driver wanted to be sure he understood.

"I dunno," Duggie shrugged and handed his friends bottles of lager. "Let's see what sort of mood we're in when our man comes along." He withdrew a knife from his jacket. "Sometimes shooting is too good for 'em."

*   *   *   *   *   *

Wilder had put off asking until Cain turned onto the Malone Road, "Why is Harry Jaggars afraid of you?"

Cain let go a laugh. "What?"

"He was giving me a hard time about Reason..."

"What was he saying about Reason?" Cain interrupted.

"He wanted me to know he knows about her. He suggested she could get hurt."

"That son of a bitch."

"I told him she was your woman, and he backed off, like that made a difference. Does it?"

"Maybe," Cain replied.

"He's afraid of you, isn't he?"

"I have a flexible conscience, Wilder, I know how to ignore it. That's what scares Harry."

"How do you even know him?" Wilder knew Cain wouldn't answer. "Let me guess, you met at a surveillance class." He had suspected for months, "You were one of them, weren't you? Were you involved with the RUC? Is that how you know all you know and do what you do? Is that how you got me released from Windsor?"

Emphatically, Cain shook his head.

"Truth is, Cain, I don't care who you were or who you are. Just keep Jaggars away from Reason. He could use her to destroy us all."

"I'll do what I can," Cain muttered.

"Why did you give that painting to Bernie?"

"You went into his game room?"

"Yes, and there was your art splattered on the wall like somebody's guts. I can't believe Thunder wants that thing hanging around." Wilder stared expectantly at Cain. "Well? Why did you give it to him?"

"To make a point," Cain answered remotely. "But Bernie didn't get it. He never gets it."

"What's the point of a pitchfork and eyeball?"

"That killing is pointless; that all you get from a kill is a lot of blood and wide-staring eyes."

"You mean like the eyes in those dead animals on his walls?"

"All the eyes..." "*Do it, Cromwell! Do it...another case of IRA scum resisting arrest,*" "*...open wide, very wide, so the souls can get out...*"

The hell hounds snapped at Cain again, and seeing the tears on Cain's lashes, Wilder regretted mentioning the macabre work. "I saw another painting of yours recently," he said to ease the tension. "Your portrait of Reason."

"Did you like it?"

"Oh yeah. You captured the angel in her so perfectly, she could hang in the Sistine Chapel…well, except that she's nude."

"Why, thank-you. I'm going to hang it in my library." He listened to the rain splashing off the road as he drove; such a swift, clean sound like flight. "You should see what I got her for Christmas. An emerald necklace."

"Whoa. Nice gift, Cromwell. An emerald to remember you and the Emerald Isle." Forget me not.

"I wanted to give her something immortal, something dramatic, like a gift from Bacchus."

"*Bacchus?*"

"Ariadne's immortal lover…Reason wants me to be Bacchus, but she doesn't realize it's me she's freeing from the maze."

"What, do you two stage Greek mythology in bed or something?"

"Oh, but life is mythology, Wilder. There's always a Minotaur to slay and a maze to escape and hearts to be broken…and we're all demigods, aren't we?"

Partly human, partly divine. "Yes, I suppose."

Cain pulled up to Wilder's house. "Well, I'm away, old man. I've an early class tomorrow. More warriors to mislead you know. What time does your plane leave in the morning?"

"Ten."

"I'll bet you're anxious to see your dad. You're lucky. You love him and he loves you. I hate my father and he hates me. The two are the same really, love and hate. Both bind you forever. Well, have yourself a happy Christmas, Wilder, and tell your father hello."

"Why don't you come to Malibu for Christmas?"

"That's a nice offer, but I'm going to St. Moritz in a few days, and I can't leave the ponies alone on Christmas. They'd be lonely. Now get out of my car and let me go home," Cain nudged Wilder out the door.

"Happy Christmas to you, Cain."

"Wilder?" Cain called. "Thanks for giving me a hand tonight…and thanks for not asking me why I was acting crazy."

Wilder waved from the doorway. "You always act crazy, Cromwell. It's part of your charm."

*   *   *   *   *   *

Duggie pondered the graffiti across the street. **Brits Out.** "Do you think England will abandon Ulster?"

"Nah," answered one accomplice. "We've been loyal to the Queen, we've fought and died for her. England owes us. Owes us big."

"But what if England did pull out?" the other accomplice suggested the unthinkable. "We wouldn't be British anymore. And we wouldn't be Irish…who would we be then?"

Silence shook the car until Duggie comforted, "We won't let 'em leave us. We'll fight the British to stay British. And if they give one fucking inch to the taigs, we'll strike back. They taught us to fight, let them fight us."

"Do you have any new year's resolutions?" the driver asked Duggie.

"Aye. I'm gonna blow that last asshole O'Neill in half right in the lobby of the Gov. I've been watching him, know everything about him. After Christmas, that fucker's dead."

"But the Cure said he's off-limits."

"So? They don't run the ULF. We take out who we want to take out."

"Yeah. I hate it when some English motherfucker tells us a Fenian's 'off limits.' This is our country, not theirs."

At eleven-thirty the victim came around the corner and headed up the Antrim Road. Duggie and his mates tugged on their balaclavas and chugged their beers.

"Shit, he's got somebody with him. A woman," the driver said.

Duggie belched and rolled down his window for a better look.

"Are you sure this is the man we're supposed to slot? It's not midnight yet," the second man put to Duggie. "He doesn't look much like his picture. The guy in the picture was fat. This fellow's thin."

"Yeah, yeah, he's the one. Peter Devane, a New Lodge taig. You two grab the bastard and pull him into the cab. I'll take care of the bitch."

Hand-in-hand, the unsuspecting couple swayed up the sidewalk. They didn't notice the black taxi. But too soon the three hitmen sprang upon them. The man was beaten about the face with a pistol and wrestled into the cab while Duggie dragged the terrified woman into an alley.

"Are you a good Catholic girl, pet?" Duggie quizzed with the tip of his knife to the woman's throat.

She tried too late to hide the crucifix around her neck. "Please don't hurt me or my boyfriend. We aren't involved in anything…we aren't on anyone's side…please…"

"Shut up," Duggie spat. "You shouldn't be walking up the Antrim Road late at night, especially with a motherfucking mick. Lie down." When the woman didn't immediately obey, Duggie pushed her face-first to the ground. "Lick my boot. Lick it!"

Tearfully, she did.

"You got sisters, pet?"

In horror the woman nodded.

"Then this will teach them to stay off the streets of Belfast."

"Please, don't hurt me," the woman whimpered.

"Say 'God save our queen' and I'll let you go."

"God save our queen," came her quick, frail reply.

"Good girl." Duggie produced a semi-automatic pistol and shot the woman in the head. Then he ran back to the waiting taxi. "There's one less cow in Ulster." Off he and his friends peeled with the Catholic man held at gunpoint on the back seat's floor.

"Good job, Knack," the driver congratulated. "What's next?"

"For now," Duggie polished his knife on his pant leg, "just drive around."

*   *   *   *   *   *

Wilder poured himself a drink, but as he sat down to reflect on the evening, Reason walked into the family room. She wore a black jacket, faded jeans and running shoes.

Wilder jumped up, delighted to see her. "How did you get in here?"

"Kieran let me in. I hope you don't mind."

"Of course I don't mind. Join me for a drink? A patient gave me this bottle of champagne. I was in the mood to celebrate Christmas."

"How nice." Reason slumped onto the sofa and freed her hair from its ponytail.

Wilder detected the stress in Reason's voice. "What's wrong?"

"Nothing." She looked away. "You're going home tomorrow. Lucky you."

Wilder handed her a flute of wine. "In eleven little hours."

"Weren't you going to tell me good-bye?" Reason downed the champagne and requested more. "Weren't you going to wish me Merry Christmas?"

"I tried to call you several times today. You've been gone. And then I was going to come over to see you this evening," he refilled Reason's glass, "but I was unexpectedly called away."

"To a party?" she noted Wilder's tuxedo. "What have you been up to?"

"No good and good fun."

"You had a date?"

Reason's envy charmed Wilder, and playfully he kissed her. "Yeah. With Cain. And how about you? Where have you been all day?"

Reason didn't have to say anything because the doorbell rang. A young man delivered a message, "All clear." He gave Reason and Wilder a nod then vanished into the night.

Wilder recognized the boy as one of Kieran's messengers. "What's he talking about?" He threw aside his glass and pulled Reason to her feet. "What did he mean, 'all clear?'"

Wilder's shocked expression and harsh grip left Reason tongue-tied.

"Reason, tell me what's going on. Answer me!"

"Don't yell at me!"

He let her go. She sank back onto the sofa. "I'll tell you everything when you calm down."

Passing a hand over his face in dread, Wilder guessed what had transpired. "You were out on some sort of errand, weren't you? Weren't *you?* Have you lost your fucking mind?"

"How can I explain if you're going to go ballistic?"

"What's to explain? You were helping Kieran after both Cain and I have begged you not to get involved. Jesus! What in the hell is the matter with you?"

"Are you going to stop screaming at me?"

Fit to be tied, Wilder nodded. He stood before her like a firing squad. "Just tell me what you did."

"I drove a man to Dublin." Reason paused, expecting Wilder to blow up, but he remained quiet, staring impassively upon her. "I don't know who he was or what he'd done. We drove south through Armagh." Again she paused only to be slapped with silence. "Outside of Crossmaglen, the guy thought the police were following us. He told me to speed up, which I did. He knew the county and kept telling me to turn here and turn there. We drove through pastures and forests, and then we changed cars in some farmer's barn. That was a little scary. I've heard stories of people getting shot by the Cure in remote places like barns. But we were all right. I don't think this man thought I could handle it, but I did. You would have been proud of me, Wilder."

Another chance for his input. Not a word. He didn't even blink as he stared her down.

"When I got back to Belfast, I met Kieran at a safe house. He said I couldn't go home yet. The ULF killed two people up by Fiona's tonight, and Kieran didn't want me going home alone. I didn't want to come here because I knew you'd flip out, and you were never supposed to know about this, but Kieran insisted. He had someone drive me over here. And now that it's OK to go home, now that I've explained things to you and you're furious with me," Reason concluded matter-of-factly, "I'll leave."

A whopping hush crushed the room. Wilder maintained his stance in front of Reason, tapping his fingers together methodically, like a ticking bomb. His face had drained of color, and his eyes wouldn't release hers. With his heart bleeding in horror, he beheld Michael Patrick's daughter, disastrously, beautifully, foolishly fearless like her ill-fated father. His emotions short-circuited and caught fire as he delved into Reason's blue, bold eyes. He felt everything; awed, proud, enraged, terrified, soul-sick and wildly in love.

And as Wilder's senses collided, Reason remained self-assured and patient in his sights. "I hoped when I got involved in this that maybe, just maybe, you'd allow me into your life, that maybe you could see me as worthy of your respect, and when you gave me Merry's ring I thought you'd accepted me." She hoped Wilder would respond but he didn't. "Apparently no matter what I do, in your eyes I'll always be a Wellworth-Howell...but never again can you call me a coward."

Wilder didn't know what to say or what to do. He was too angry and appalled. He walked out of the room and headed upstairs.

"You know, Wilder, if you think about it, this must be how your dad feels about your being over here. He doesn't want you to get hurt like you don't want me to get hurt. But you're here, and there's nothing he can say that will deter you, is there? Because you believe with all your heart in what you're doing. And just what were you and Cain up to tonight? Something illegal, something dangerous? Before you tear into me for doing what I think is right, think twice." Reason raised the champagne to her bittersweet smile; how Wilder despised the taste of his own lifestyle.

Tearing off his clothes, Wilder grabbed his robe and slammed into the shower. He resented Reason's acumen. She played him against himself, using his dedication to justify her own. OK, yes, his father had cried when his last child left California, and yes, Desmond had begged him not to get involved, and yes, Wilder had ignored every plea. And yes, he and Cain took risks. *But this is different!* How? *I don't know!* he raged. Because Reason was a woman and she was precious to him...but he was precious to his father...*but I'm Irish*...so was Reason...*shit.* She would follow him into hell and prove she was tough enough to take it.

But he wasn't tough enough to take it. He'd face down the Brits alone but not with Reason. No. The bastards couldn't have her. She was his weakness, and there was the difference. If she died, he wouldn't survive the loss of her. And to save her he'd risk everything and sell everyone out, including Kieran and himself. If the Brits knew that, they'd use it. They'd taken her pictures from his desk, Harry knew her by name, they knew it already. All they needed was an excuse to arrest her and she seemed determined to oblige. She wanted Wilder to love her, and he did, and she wanted to be Irish for him, and she was. But if she thought he'd praise her courage, he couldn't. All he saw in her republican quest was the woman whose ransom demanded his soul.

"Feeling better?" Reason asked when Wilder returned to the family room.

"Just tell me one thing," he spoke tensely, sharply. "Did Kieran force you into this?"

"No, I volunteered. I *wanted* to do this, Wilder."

"Because you'll do anything for me, right? Go to prison for me, be beaten by the RUC for me, *die* for me? What you've done makes me *sick*. Sick to the soul. Maybe you aren't a coward, Reason, but you're fucking naive! Is this the first time you've done this?"

Reason shook her head. "Last month I drove Aidan Duffy's brother to Dublin."

"Oh, that's real goddamn great!" Wilder lurched away. "So where do you want to be buried, Mac? Cuz, bang, bang, baby, in this game you're dead."

"'Let them fucking kill me then!' Practice what you preach, Wilder," Reason came back crossly. "I've said the same thing to you a hundred times, I've begged you to give up Ireland and choose me, and you haven't listened. You're as determined to fight back as I am. And every day the Brits add to that determination. We both have the bruises to prove it."

"I have a hundred reasons for being involved, but you have no reason for getting into this mess other than stupidity!"

Finally unnerved by Wilder's relentless, loud temper, Reason's tears welled. Whether Wilder liked it or not, he was her reason, and searching his eyes, which assailed her, she perceived nothing stupid about loving him and his country madly. Unintimidated by his anger, she slipped her arms around his neck and filled her hands with his damp hair. Wilder's expression was surprised as she caressed him. Had he expected her retreat? He was her reason. She parted her lips upon his in an ever-faithful kiss. Kiss like communion. He was her reason. She opened his robe, and tears from her eyes tapped his bare chest, and she retrieved her tears with her mouth, kissing his shoulders. Then sliding her hands down the lean of his body, she untied his belt to pay further homage to her love. Kneeling before him, she ran her fingers over his thighs and up his hips and backbone as she rose again, slowly, kissing and stroking and loving his sex, his soul. He was her reason. She recaptured his lips and hugged him to her. "Is that reason enough for you, Wilder?"

Exasperated to have been sabotaged sweetly, he gaped upon Reason at an impasse. He wanted to shake her and knock sense into her head. He wanted to sweep her up and love her. And he wanted her to disappear forever so she couldn't break his heart. She tried to turn away. He put his hand on her shoulder, as if to decide whether to pull her to him or push her aside. A whisper was all the voice she had left him, "Promise me you won't do any more errands for Kieran."

Reason regarded Wilder with affection and stroked her thumb along his jaw. "You're hating yourself for loving me right now, I can see it in your eyes, and you wish I'd make this easy for you, but your Ireland is my Ireland, Wilder, and nothing's easy between you and me, but I love you, I love you with all my life," she murmured, stealing a kiss from his frown.

His eyes wandered over her. Why, why did she make life so hard, him so hard? *God,* to be inside her. He touched her hair, his hand slid down her cheek to her chin. She kissed his palm. This was the beginning, the end, the loss of his soul, it took to its wings, his heart was hers, she had all the power, he tugged her closer, and wished her away, and bent his mouth to hers with desire burning out of control. There was no stopping his need to have her. Already he was undressing her; already his touch, his tongue, a man in love was taking her. She tore open his robe to thread her hands up his chest, up his cheeks, into his hair, and she yanked his lips atop hers. "Hurry," she sighed. Stripping off Reason's shirt, Wilder found she wore nothing underneath. His heart thundered.

He backed her into the hallway and ran with her to the stairs, he was breathless, thinking, *hurry,* and he kissed her all the way up to his room. Beyond the windows tappy rain fell. The bedroom was warm and illuminated by the fire's glow. Dropping to one knee, with hands and fingers eager to rip, to tear, he unbuttoned her jeans and smoothed them down her thighs, he kissed her thighs and higher, down her knees, he kissed her knees and higher, and down her calves. For a moment he sat back and savored the sight of her body, then he jumped up, lifting Reason into his arms. "Wrap your legs around my waist, slide your arms around my neck."

Happily, she consented and drank of his lips with her lips; thirsty kisses, kiss of a starveling, of a zealot. Up against the wall they smacked eye-to-eye after what felt like eternity's separation. Wilder's hands slid up Reason's ribs, caressing her, cupping her breasts. She searched his face, his aroused preoccupation, his eyes penetrating hers, his lips smiling a lover's smile. Beautiful, so beautiful her Irishman hard with lust, hard for her, soon hard inside her. His body was hers now, hers to enjoy. His hands slipped beneath her, holding her against his chest. In the fire-glow Reason's skin was golden; Wilder was in shadows, dark and light. Her legs tightened around him; he grazed his mouth over her breasts and circled his tongue around and around until her nipples grew firm and fat and slid between his teeth. With her fingers lost in his curls, Reason held Wilder's head to her heart and he tongued her and sucked her, up against the wall. What he was doing to her, God, it had been too long.

"I've been out of my mind not making love to you all these months." Wilder sank to his knees to part Reason's thighs. "How could I have denied us both for so long?"

"You and your diamond heart." Reason slid down to hold him. Her fingers teased and squeezed him, pleased him and made him sigh. She stroked his smooth-shaven face. "Don't be Declan tonight," her voice was soft, her kisses softer as she opened her mouth upon his.

Wanting her gentle and willing beneath him, Wilder swept Reason to the bed. He pushed his suitcase and clothes aside. There was a fifth of *Blackbush* on the mattress, a gift for Desmond. He twisted it open and took a drink, just a sip to wet his lips, then he kissed Reason and licked the taste of Ireland from her lips. He tipped the bottle to one finger and stroked whiskey over her chin and throat, around and under each breast, across her stomach, between her legs, and he licked the whiskey away, and folded down on top of her so that her skin burned into his skin. He owned her and idolized her and surrendered to her and begged for her favors. And this time he wasn't Declan, and this time he simply would do. He pressed Reason down. She lifted her hips to meet him, and gripping his backbone, she urged him deeper and deeper and wilder and Wilder. And he loved her like he had first loved her, with abandon, and two years of distance took flight. There was no past to hinder, no future to fear, just now and now. And this was forever. With Michael Patrick's daughter.

"Did I redeem myself this time?" Wilder asked with a kiss.

Reason lay back and exhaled with pleasure. "When I said I wanted more I had no idea just how much more you had to offer."

"Do you know how many nights I've lain awake dreaming of this moment when I could hold you after making love to you before making love to you again?"

"Surely Declan never dreamed of this. Oh, I wish you'd stay Wilder forever."

"I'm Wilder until after Christmas, love. My dad will kill me otherwise," Wilder said with a laugh.

"And what about those women he wants you to entertain?"

"You're my only woman, Mac."

"Gee, you've come a long way from that Irish grudge you were holding against me." She slid her hand between his legs. "I like you holding this against me better."

"Wait a sec, before cranking me up again, OK? We need to talk."

"I don't want to talk. I know what you're going to say."

"What am I going to say?"

"You're going to start in again about Kieran. Not now."

"When should I start? In an hour, tomorrow? I'm lying here now, lost in you, loving you, and I'm afraid for us both. I'm not as strong as you, Reason. You've managed to cope with my involvement in the struggle, but I can't handle yours. I lost my brother and sister to this war, I lose patients, and sometimes I think I've lost myself, and sometimes the only thing that makes sense to me is seeing your face. I've been letting people go all my life, and I want to hold on. I want to be held onto. I'm tired of letting go and grieving for the love and loss of you." He lifted her hand and kissed the Claddagh ring on her finger. And he stared down at the sailboat necklace around her throat. "Don't be like Merry, don't leave me to live in love with a memory of you. Please."

"I won't leave you. I promise."

"Will you stop helping Kieran? Promise me that."

Reason turned her back and watched the rain falling beyond the window. "I don't think it's fair that you expect me to do what you refuse to do. I can't shut my eyes and pretend this countrsy hasn't happened to me. All I'm doing is driving some men down south, it's not like I'm smuggling guns or planting bombs."

"See what I mean? You're frighteningly naive. Those men are fugitives from the crown, Reason. If the Brits see them, they'll shoot first and ask questions later."

"All the more reason to get them out."

Wilder clapped his palm to his forehead, astonished by Reason's blind dedication. "Kieran is using you, Reason. You're just another resource, and to him everyone is expendable. Hell, he let Morris deliver that message in Milltown and look what happened there? Morris got hurt, and the message ended up with the Brits. I nearly died, Kieran nearly died…no more errands, Reason. Say it, swear it, now."

She couldn't do it. In compromise she said, "I was done doing what he asked me to do anyway."

But Wilder wasn't satisfied. He couldn't forget Michael Patrick's refusal to relent. And now here was his daughter, as pugnacious, and persistent. And wasn't that the history of Ireland? His history as well. In Reason's eyes he saw his own passion, his own troubled destiny. And he thought of how Reason had once said in his eyes she saw sad good-byes. The terrible beauty, the fanatic hearts, oh, Ireland of the welcomes and the warriors. There was a rage and sorrow this country inspired, and once awoken, it burned beyond the heart's expiration, from generation to generation, blood to blood. This country got into the soul of anyone who saw its wounds like the wounds of a beaten child. How could he ask Reason not to react?

More than frustration in this moment he felt resignation. To the force of his heritage, to the urges of war, to the terrible knowledge that the lust for justice could impel even the most logical to larceny. Defy or die but never submit. *Goddamn the British.* And there he was thinking of Merry's funeral, of his own conversion to subversion, of the day he traded the American dream for the Irish wish. He sighed, "And I suppose you won't give up Cromwell for me either. So this leaves me wondering if you're going to die or just make it with another guy whenever you aren't with me." Wilder rolled out of bed and began getting dressed. "I can't live this way, Reason. I can understand your need to do what you do, I just can't watch you do it. So you go do what you have to do. Do it for Kieran and do it with Cain, just don't expect me to pick up your pieces when it all blows up in your face."

"Damn it, Wilder, you want all the control and none of the risk of loving me and me loving you."

"You have all the control, Reason. And that's what scares me."

"If I have so much power, why can't I get you to commit yourself to me? Why do you *always* have reservations and conditions? You're just looking for another excuse to keep your distance from me."

"You're right. I know that now. You want me to be Wilder, well, here I am. The guy who lost you two years ago and fell apart. The guy who drank himself to sleep and cried like a jerk and saved your pictures and loved you nonstop to this moment, to the moment of his last breath and beyond. Yeah, that's me. And you're the one risk I'm not willing to take, the one thing so precious I'm not willing to lose. And maybe this is why my dad moved to America, because it was easier to leave and not look back than witness his world's destruction. Heartbreak is worse than death, Reason, and that's why I prefer Declan." He looked back at Reason, and his heart caught fire and found wings and a sword to fall on. He loved her with a tremendous love and a dreadful love. Her face, her pretty face, his heart's desire, his heart's demise. "I knew the minute I saw you walk into Albie's last summer you were going to destroy me again. God knows, I love you, Reason. God knows you have me, body and soul, and God, how I wish you'd never come back." He took a seat on the bed and watched Reason gather her clothes.

She was crying. It was all too painful trying to love Wilder and loathe the Brits and mourn Ruairi and help Kieran and build a hospital amidst murders and bombs yet stay sane and strong and hopeful. Oh, that's what Belfast killed best. Hope. "How can I fix this, Wilder? I won't see Kieran, I'll tell Cain good-bye, I'll do whatever you want…just don't send me away from you."

"What's the alternative, Reason? I can't give up my work here. They don't need surgeons in Malibu, but they need them desperately here. And you can't give up your work. My God, this city needs architects like sutures to close wounds. And really, as much as I want it, how would you break up with Cain? I warned him not to get himself into this, I knew he'd love you and that you loved me, and he acts so crazy sometimes I worry about what he'd do without you, and this is a fucking mess."

"Can't we just go on the way we are? Can't we be in love and make love and be together and just let the future be what it will be and not worry?"

"And what, we string Cain along, knowing one day one of us will lose? Don't you want a settled life, a family, a home? All the things I can't offer. Why postpone the inevitable, Reason? Every time we're together, it's harder to be apart."

Reason cried harder, thinking about Cain and his past. She didn't want to hurt him. She loved him. And she loved Wilder. And it was Wilder who had betrayed them all by swearing he didn't want her when he did, by forswearing love when he loved eternally, by risking his life but never his heart.

"You know what, Reas, we have tonight. We lived life in a day in Denver, we can do it again here. Don't leave me until tomorrow," he requested softly, going to get her, taking her back into his arms. He unbelted her robe and slipped his hands around her, and he imagined how he would feel if he never saw her again. Void of volition and life. And he had a terrible sense of foreboding. Like this was the last time they'd meet. "We aren't going to part in anger this time."

The next morning Reason drove Wilder to the airport. They listened to the news of the previous night's murders. Innocent lovers stabbed and shot. The ULF claimed their victims were travelers with the IRA. Any excuse for a killing. And neither Wilder nor Reason spoke of the crime. Both were thinking the same thing. It could have been them or anyone like them. And sometimes Belfast was too hard.

"I am so ready to go home," Wilder said as he kissed Reason good-bye.

She handed him his ticket and his passport and the morning paper. They stood in the soft rain. He kissed her again. And again.

"You'll come to Denver for New Year's?" Reason asked.

"Absolutely." Fear crept up Wilder's spine. He couldn't shake his feelings of doom. He shouldn't be leaving. "Be careful, Reason. At least promise me that."

"I will, I swear."

Waiting for his flight, Wilder read the details of the murders. **ULF kills Catholics in Overnight Horror Spree. Harrison Weller, 26, and Cynthia Mahoney, 22, both from North Belfast were found slain. RUC officials confirmed Mr. Weller's throat had been slit. Despite confirmation that neither victim had terrorist ties, the ULF remained unrepentant, "If republicans and their fellow travelers in nationalism persist in their hopeless crusade for British withdrawal, funerals for family and friends will be their reward."**

Wilder crumpled the newspaper. He let it fall from his hand and didn't look back as he boarded his plane for America.

Chapter Fifty-Four

Strands of haze roamed the hills like lost souls wildering in from the ocean. Daylight dwindled over the Atlantic and scattered its mustard hue across the incoming tide, upon the beige, barren sands, and over the heathered moors of Donegal; southern Donegal this time where they hadn't been. The sea wind lay bitter siege to the coastline, but the view from the precipice made the elements worth resisting. With their coats bundled around them, Cain and Reason walked along the rocky, black cliff above the waves crashing, below the sun sinking. The tourists were long gone, lobster pots and fishing nets lay deserted along the shore, the natives had sense to stay by their fires now, and only Q-tip sheep shared the cliffside with the rovers.

"Day after tomorrow you'll be in St. Moritz." Boxing with gull feathers flung skyward on the wind, Reason danced backwards in front of Cain.

"Skiing alone, missing you, making love to you in my mind. You're sure you can't come?"

"I wish I could, Cain, but since I'm going home next week I have a lot of work to finish. Oh, but I'm glad you talked me into coming here with you today." Reason spiraled around, drinking in the Irish country-side. Countryside without trees, without fences, without fetters or bounds. Far as her eyes could see. Gleann Cholm Cille on the wild west coast of Eire. Down a narrow dirt road, across heather mountains, through the peat bogs, and over the heaths they had ventured. To see what they could see; eternity where a ribbon of violet on the horizon joined the dark of the ocean and the light of the day. Reason opened her coat like wings, and fluttering sport to the wind, chased her shadow along the precipice pass.

"After tonight I won't see you for four weeks. I'll die," Cain complained, running with Reason who was three steps ahead.

"You won't die. I'll call you and you'll call me. We'll make love on the telephone. It'll be very erotic."

"But words can never replace fingers and flesh. No doubt you'll be talking to Wilder while you're both in the States."

"No doubt."

Cain had thought long and hard about Wilder. He had given the Irishman every chance, every warning to take Reason back, to commit to her. All's fair in love in wartime, Wilder had said. Cain watched Reason frisking before him. Spirit, sprite, lover, mother, woman, wife. The time was right. He caught Reason and waltzed her into his arms. "Do you love me?" Sea gusts pushed Cain's hair around his face and his words were his heart. "I love you, forevermore you." He had kissed her in the sea, in the rain, in the dawn and dusk, now in the whipping wind. His palms lifted her mouth to his. "Say I make you happy," he murmured on Reason's ear.

"You make me happy!" she cried, exhilarated by Donegal's savage seashore and Cain's savage kiss.

"Now hold out your hand. I wanted to give you this at sunset in the most Irish place in Ireland." He placed a satin box in her palm. "Happy Christmas, Reason. And no, I didn't steal it."

Deep shamrock green glowing in the topaz sun. A one-carat emerald hung on a string of diamonds took Reason's breath away. "Cain, it's gorgeous!"

Wilder had perfectly said it. "An emerald to remember me and the Emerald Isle; it's in the shape of a teardrop and a flame. Here, let me put it on you." Turning Reason to face the sunset, Cain fastened the necklace around her neck then glided his hands around her waist. "I brought you here because I want this moment to be unforgettable. I love you so very much, and you love me. I know I'm not Wilder, but I'm willing to dedicate my whole heart and self to you. You can waste your youth and passion on a man who refuses to choose you, or you can choose me." The wind paused as if to listen. Cain smiled and was sure. "Let's get married."

Reason spun about-face. "What did you say?"

"Be my wife, Reason. Stay with me. Marry me."

She looked back at the ocean shaking down the cliffside. "Oh, Cain, no. I'm not ready."

He hushed Reason with a finger to her lips. "Live with me at My Lady's Leisure then. Live with me and I'll paint you in a thousand lights. And love you. Always you."

Reason broke free and stared across the black Atlantic westward, Malibuward, Wilderward. He was her reason. Her frustration. Her life.

"I know you love Wilder, Reason, but life is short, and he's unwilling to give you what you need. Time after time he has pushed you away."

"Because he's afraid for me. Are you?"

"When you're with him, yes. When you're with me, no. Remember the wishes we put in our sand boat? This is my wish. Prove I don't taint what I touch. Give yourself to me."

Reason fiddled with the Claddagh ring on her hand. Wilder would ever be Declan. She would never be Irish. And nothing would change. West the gulls sailed. The sky closed upon itself in patches of grey-blue twilight. The moors were bathed in silken mist, and the air was charged with tappy rain. *"God knows, I love you, Reason…you're the one thing so precious I'm not willing to lose."* She turned her face to the rain. What was that Wilder had said years ago? *"Silly girl, you just saved my life. Now you'll never lose me."*

"Reason? What do you say? Will you stay with me?"

She took Cain's hand and walked on along the precipice. "It wouldn't be honest, Cain. I do love Wilder, I'll always love him, and I'd feel bad that I wasn't giving you my whole heart."

"You love me too, Reason, and whether you want to admit it or not, Wilder's your past. He has been from the moment you and I met. I don't care if you're dishonest, let's try it. Live with me until the roses bloom, until the days are long, and if you don't think I'm the man of your dreams by June, I'll vanish."

"I don't want you to vanish."

"Say you'll try it."

"Let's see what happens in the next few weeks, OK?"

"Oh no, look at that worried expression! I've pressured you like a bad salesman." One, two, three five-pence coins Cain pulled from behind Reason's ear. "Here's your money back, madam, sorry to have troubled you."

And Reason laughed at his magic. He always made her laugh.

Chapter Fifty-Five

When Morris skipped out of the school building Jillie appeared beside him. He let go a yelp, but she whisked him into the front seat of a brown Mercedes before he could make a fuss. *Snap,* the doors locked, and Morris couldn't get out.

"Would you like a biscuit, Morris?" Jillie offered him a package of vanilla cremes before she started to drive.

Petrified, Morris managed to twist his head in refusal and cower lower, lower into his seat.

"Don't be afraid of me, sweetness. Oh, you aren't still upset about the cemetery, are you? Heavens! That was weeks ago. Surely you've healed by now. I know you're anxious to go outside and play, so let's get down to business. I need your help again."

Though he tried to be tough, Morris started to cry and turned away from Jillie's all-knowing eyes. Wordlessly, humming along with the radio, she drove him over to the Shankill and parked in front of the Horsetail Inn.

Morris peered up then down the Shankill Road and squealed in terror, "You aren't going to leave me here, are you?"

"Maybe I will, maybe I won't. I don't want to hurt you, Morris, and if you cooperate, you'll be all right. Now then, there's a rumor two of your father's friends are being smuggled out of Ireland before Christmas. And rumor has it these two very bad men killed three soldiers in County Down last year."

"I'm glad they killed them!" Morris declared and received Jillie's slap across his jaw.

"I suspect your daddy knows when and where this escape will happen," she continued calmly. "I want you to find out the details for me."

"No," Morris sulked.

"Morris, use your head. You don't want us to arrest your daddy and beat him at Windsor, do you? Did you see your uncle Decky after he visited Windsor? He was hurt, wasn't he? Your daddy wouldn't get off that easy. Remember Ruairi? Your daddy will be next, and you'll have to bury him for Christmas. That doesn't sound like a happy holiday to me, does it to you?"

"But I...don't want...to help you!" Morris sobbed into his fists.

"Morris love, in this life we can't always do what we want to do. Maybe you don't want to help me, but I'm sure you want to keep your daddy alive."

"But he won't tell me anything," Morris argued frantically. "How am I supposed to find out anything?"

"Your father is going to a pub tonight. I don't know which one. I want you to follow him and tell me who he meets. That's all you have to do is tell me who he meets."

"Why can't some of your goons follow him?"

"Some of my goons?" Jillie giggled and ruffled Morris' hair. "I can tell you've been talking to Decky. I don't have any goons, Morris. And why should I risk my beautiful neck when I can have you do things for me? I just hope you can keep track of your father. He's clever."

The truth was Jillie had tried to follow Kieran, but it proved futile time after time. During the day she could find him here and there along the Falls Road, but at night, Kieran lived like a phantom. Wherever he went after sunset, in any moment, he was darting in and out of buildings and doorways and clambering over rooftops and garden walls and running through a maze of tunnels and alleyways Jillie didn't know existed. When she first started trying to trail him, she was convinced Kieran could vanish into thin air. She had called in soldiers and constables to help without success. The man was a master, a challenge, and Jillie loved that about him. And arresting him had proved fruitless too. He had been beaten and starved and locked in prison, and not once had he divulged more than "Fuck you."

And Kieran knew as much or more about surveillance equipment than Jillie did. She had tried every undercover device the Cure had to offer, but invariably Kieran found and destroyed it. And unlike Ruairi, Kieran was guarded, even with his friends. Jillie had hoped liquor would make him glib, but Kieran rarely drank more than a pint at the pub, and he never mentioned Provisional business. Ask one wrong question and he wouldn't say another word for the night. And while sex had long been her most persuasive weapon, Kieran outsmarted Jillie at that as well; starving her for his affection, giving her ecstasy in small doses, determining when and where and how often they would make love. It was his way or no way, and Jillie wanted his way in all ways. After months of frustration, she accepted the fact she had met her match. But sooner or later Kieran would trip, and she'd win.

"You're a goon." Morris sneered up at Jillie and didn't care if she hit him. "I hope the Provies blast your brains."

"I love you too, Morris dear," Jillie said with a smile. "Well, I think we've sorted things. I'll meet you after school tomorrow, and you'll tell me what you've learned. If you don't show up, you won't see your daddy or Decky or Reason or your grandparents ever again. And if you say a word, I'll have them all killed and then I'll kill you." Jillie unlocked the car doors and motioned for Morris to get out. "Run along now."

Morris couldn't budge. "But this is the *Shankill*. I don't know my way home." He twisted to Jillie in panic. "It'll be dark soon! Please, Jillie, take me back to the Antrim Road. *Please!*"

"Hurry up and get out of the car, Morris. It's been a long day and I want to go home."

"But...but..." horror filled his face when he realized Jillie was deserting him.

"You'll be fine...as long as you keep running."

Morris sat open-mouthed, goggling the notorious Protestant neighborhood, too scared to cry. "But…what about the ULF?"

"What about them?" Jillie leaned across Morris, opened his door and gave him a shove. "Out you go, little rabbit. Maybe this will teach you to be nicer to me. See you tomorrow, love…if you survive tonight." Off she drove and left Morris huddled on the curb. In his Catholic school uniform.

Right and left were Protestant school children getting off the buses in droves; there was nowhere to hide. Morris knew his only chance was to make a mad dash in any direction. Headlong he charged down the Shankill Road, not knowing where he was going and too terrified to ask. He felt a thousand enemy eyes focused upon him. Maniacs and killers lurked behind every window and door. He knew if the Prods caught him, they would string him up and whip him and burn him and pluck out his eyes and….*crash,* he bowled into a small shopping wagon. Knocked flat on his back, gawking up at a hunchbacked, old woman, Morris could see she had blue, watery eyes that looked loose in her head, kind of rolling around and around. As she bent to see him clearly, Morris saw her flat nose was blistered and infected, and like a rickety old witch, she had a blackthorn cane and a wiry, wee dog that ran barking in circles.

"Lord love us! Are you hurt, dear?" she asked and stooped to collect her potatoes and apples rolling away from her tipped wagon.

Morris was dizzy and struck mute.

"Och, poor lad, you've torn your wee jacket. You must be feeling poorly. Where do you live, son?"

Morris wouldn't say and scrambled to his feet in dread. Oh no! The sun was setting! Darkness would snatch the light soon, he'd lose his way and then…and then all fiends from the shadows would be on the prowl looking for him in particular. Morris didn't know what to do or where to run or where to turn. He stood trembling and dumbstruck, thinking he hadn't a prayer of surviving the night.

The old woman recognized Morris' Catholic uniform and shook her head with concern. "By the look of your clothes I'd say you're a lost little critter. Are ye lost, son?"

Morris nodded and awaited immediate death.

"Come along then. You'll be all right." The old woman took him by the hand and nearly had to drag him back up the Shankill beside her. The little dog ran alongside them, yapping and nipping at Morris' pant leg. "I have a great-grandson about your age. Och, he's a bold one."

Morris didn't hear a word the woman prattled as she hiked him past rows upon rows of Protestant houses with Union Jack flags and ULSTER LIBERATION FORCE. KEEPING ULSTER BRITISH graffiti. In his head a song played; a song the Prods sang every July when they marched through Belfast celebrating King Billy's triumph.

"If guns were made for shooting
Then skulls were made to crack
You've never seen a better taig
Than with a bullet in his back."

"Here we go, wee one." The woman led Morris up to her doorway in the middle of thirty identical doorways in a long strand of brick.

Morris gaped at the houses and thought they looked the same as the ones in the New Lodge, but as the woman led him inside her tiny flat, his mind howled, *She's taking me in to boil me in water. Taig soup I'll be!*

"Have a seat on the sofa, dear. Would you like a nice cup of tea?"

Morris flattened against the closed door. *She's boiling the water!* Daring to look around the parlor, he could see the old woman had no pictures of the Blessed Virgin, no Sacred Heart or crucifixes, but she had a pretty picture of Jesus. Morris felt a little better seeing that. And she had a brilliant canary with a song like a song from a meadow, and Morris felt a little better hearing it sing. The wiry dog ran around and around in circles with a ball in its mouth, asking Morris to play. Morris threw the ball timidly, and when the dog brought it back, he felt a little happier. And the woman had an afghan blanket like Granny Nora's only

Nora's was purple and this one was blue. He pulled it over his knees because he was cold, and he felt a little safer.

"Here you go, pet." The old woman brought Morris a mug of black tea.

Apparently she hadn't boiled *a lot* of water. Just a little red kettle full. Fiona had a red kettle. "May I have some sugar please?" Morris ventured, feeling rather courageous.

"Och sure, love." She brought him a bowl from which Morris helped himself, and she brought him the same chocolate biscuits Fiona always served.

He thanked her and sipped the comforting tea from his perch on the woman's lumpy sofa. "Who's that wee man on your wall?" Morris referred to a large photograph.

"That's my grandson Martin. He was killed by the IRA last spring."

"I'll bet you were sad. My uncles were killed by the Brits, and I was sad."

"Aye, pet, I was very sad. Now we have to get you home for your supper. You don't have to tell me where you live, love, just tell me who I can call to come for you."

He thought of his father. Oh no, he mustn't ask his father to come to the Shankill. He might be shot dead. Decky would come to the Shankill, but Decky had gone to America. Fiona would die of fright before coming to this area, and Granny Nora and Granda Joe couldn't drive. That left Reason. Morris smiled to think of her. Reason wasn't afraid of the Shankill. He had memorized her phone number at the hospital and prayed she'd still be there.

"You can call my mum." Somehow saying Reason was his mother made Morris feel better, like she was his slayer of demons, like she would always be there to hug him, like she wouldn't let anything terrible happen.

By the time Reason got to the neighborhood, Morris was laughing because the old woman was letting him hold her canary. He was glad to be leaving, but he shook the old woman's hand before Reason led him out to her car. For a moment as they motored away and the old woman waved from her doorway, Morris believed the Shankill wasn't so awful with its melodious birds and playful dogs and gentle, old women with watery, loose eyes.

"How on earth did you end up way over here?" Reason put to Morris as they merged onto the Crumlin Road.

"I got lifted," Morris mumbled and avoided Reason's stare.

"Lifted by whom?"

"The Brits."

Reason felt like a crowbar trying to pry the truth out of Morris. "What Brits?"

"Just Brits. They were playing a joke. They thought it would be funny to drop me in the Shankill. They did that to my daddy and Decky too. They do it to everybody."

"You must have been terrified."

"Me?" Morris patted himself on the chest. "Och no. I was ferocious."

The old woman had told Reason the true story. "My, aren't you brave then?" She reached across and took hold of Morris' hand. "Are you sure you're OK, sweetie?"

Morris faced Reason in that same fit-to-burst manner, like he had something profound to confess. The words hung on his tongue. His face was pinched with conflict and desire for help, and tears stung his eyes. But no sound came out. He glanced away.

"Daddy? Did three soldiers get killed in County Down last year?" Morris wanted to know if Jillie had been telling the truth.

"Aye, Morris, they did."

"Did the men who did it get away?"

"I don't know."

"Hmmm, I wonder how they could get away. In a boat maybe or on a plane. How do you think they could get away?"

"On the back of a winged pony," Kieran replied absently and continued reading the paper.

"No," Morris giggled, pressing on, "how do you think they'd get away?"

"Why do you want to know, Morris?"

"Because I heard at school these squaddies died, and I want the Provies who did it to get away."

"Don't worry about it."

"But how would they get away?"

"Somehow."

"But somehow how?"

"Morris, I don't know how."

"Are you going to the pub tonight, Daddy?"

"Aye."

"Which one?"

"A new place off North Queen Street."

"I wish you'd stay here with me…Daddy, do you have to go?"

"I'll stay with you tomorrow, OK?"

"Take me with you tonight then!"

"Not tonight, Morris. Besides you're too young to be hanging around pubs."

"You and Decky used to go with Liam."

"And we always wound up in trouble. You've had enough excitement for one day."

Morris' heart sank. He knew if his father were going to the pub for the craic, he'd take Morris with him, but when Kieran went to the pub "on business" Morris was never allowed. "Do you have 'business' tonight, Daddy?"

"No more questions."

Morris hung his head and debated telling his father the terrible truth. But Jillie had promised to kill Kieran and Decky and Reason. Staring across Fiona's parlor at his father and revering the sight of him, Morris turned on the television. Already haunted by the souls of the eight men gunned down the night Jillie learned of the Pembroke robbery, Morris prayed God would save the two Irishmen the Brit-witch now hunted.

Kieran tucked Morris in. "I'm sorry you landed in the Shankill."

"I wasn't scared, Daddy, I wasn't."

"I know you weren't. Like father, like son, eh?"

"Aye," Morris yawned and rubbed his eyes then grabbed his father's sleeve. "Don't go tonight, Daddy. Stay here. Tell me about Liam, OK, OK?"

"Tomorrow night we'll talk, I promise. Tonight you go to sleep."

Fitting a cap to his head, Kieran slid on his jacket and set out through the back door. Morris had already made his way out the front door and around to the back of the house when Kieran took off through Fiona's garden wall. Following his father's footsteps came naturally to Morris. He'd been Kieran's shadow for years, and Kieran had taught his son well. The route was a maze, full of dodges and darts around rowhouse corners and trash bins, down muddy alleyways, through abandoned buildings and Mrs. Holloway's secret garden door, but at least tonight there were no thorny hedges or metal fences to climb.

After prancing foot to foot outside the pub for forty minutes, Morris slinked through the front door, and keeping close to the wall, strained his eyes through the smoke to locate his father. There he was wearing dark glasses and playing snooker with a man Morris didn't know. Morris crept up to one of the patrons and made covert inquiry about the unknown man. The chap had introduced himself only as "Beezer," and he had never been seen in the pub before. Feeling like Judas Iscariot and begging God for forgiveness, Morris took to his heels and sprinted back to Fiona's.

As he slinked into the house and back to bed, he tried not to think about what the IRA did to informants. One shot through the skull. But if he told the Provies now he was being forced into grassing, they would forgive him, protect him…but one word and Jillie would kill his father and uncle. Catching a wail before it shattered the darkness, Morris erupted from his bed and ran to sleep with Reason.

*   *   *   *   *   *

"You're amazing, Knack," Cain said over the Horsetail din. He had come to meet Duggie one last time. "I'm told you're totally without fear. No wonder the Cure likes to use you."

"Aye, there's nothing too tough for me."

"Tell me, Knack," Cain played his hunch, "is your handler with the Cure Gillian Paradise?"

"Yeah, but she calls herself Mad Hatter. Do you work with her too?"

"No," Cain said without emotion. "But she has quite a reputation. I hear she's infiltrated the IRA."

"Ha, is that right? Well, wouldn't the Provos shit to know Hatter's behind the deaths of the O'Neill's and the Milltown Seven then?"

"I thought you did those on your own, Knack," Cain said in surprise.

"Hey, I did them perfectly," Duggie defended testily. "It's just that Hatter arranged things. She sure put you big boys to shame when she offed O'Neill's sister. Man, it took balls to shoot that bitch so many times." Duggie quaffed his Guinness, chuckling, "I'd sell my soul to be there when she blasts McCartan."

Gillian Paradise had killed Merry O'Neill and arranged the mayhem at her funeral. Jillie, close to Wilder, closer to Kieran. "Is she easy to work with?"

"Hell no! Thinks she's the goddamn queen. I'd rather work with you."

Cain cracked a smile. "I'm flattered, Knack."

"Are you here with a job for me?"

"Sadly, that will be impossible now," Cain had gotten what he came for and planned never to see Duggie Knack alive again. "Knowing you work with Hatter, well, I can't interfere."

"We'd make a good team, Good."

"I'm sure our Miss Paradise will keep you busy with meaningful projects."

"It won't be the same. Hatter's just an upstart bitch from London. But you...you're like Mel Gibson. Maybe you'll have something for me next year."

"Perhaps. Until then I'm just glad to say I met you, Knack." Cain raised a toast and finished his drink.

"Remember I'm available, Good. I'll do you right proud if you use me."

Cain stood up and shook Duggie hand. "Good-bye, Mr. Knack. Good-bye."

After learning the IRA knew where to find him in the Shankill, Duggie had been living at his aunt's house. He figured he was safer in Tiger's Bay. He put the key in the front door and slipped into the dark house. He stood a moment in the foyer, listening intently, like a weasel listens for the wolf. His aunt was out; the house stood still. But he had a prickly feeling, like somewhere eyes had found him. Pressed to the wall, he slipped into the dark parlor, shut the door, drew the curtains aside and peeked out at the street. Nothing stirred. But reaching for the lamp, he stopped, his ears pricked up; the door knob twisted. Before the lights came on, before the intruders said one word, in panic, Duggie hurled himself full tilt at the parlor window. It was an incredible sight; a bullet of flesh penetrating the panel of glass. Sound as a roach, he hit the ground as the shooting began. *Thwap, thwap, thwap,* the shells bounced around him, and Duggie fled for his life.

The Provos didn't chase him. Their attempt on the ULF man's life foiled, they made haste out of Tiger's Bay.

*   *   *   *   *   *

Knowing there wasn't a second to lose, Cain rushed to find Kieran. But neither Nora nor Eamonn had seen him.

"Would Morris or Fiona know where he is?" Cain inquired.

"No, love. Kieran tells none of us his business. Och lord, sometimes that man's gone for days," Nora chided.

"Do you think he's with Jillie?"

"Nah. She's in Dublin with her family for two weeks. Kissed her good-bye this morning I did." Eamonn furrowed his brow. "Why, Cain, you're pale as a parsnip. What's this about?"

Cain figured he had two weeks to tell Kieran about Jillie. In the meantime, any damage that had been done was too late to repair. "I'll be in Switzerland for the next few days, but tell Kieran I have to talk to him. It's extremely important. Happy Christmas to you."

Chapter Fifty-Six

The operation wasn't supposed to be until after the holidays, but on this grey December eve, Kieran had come to Reason asking for help. At first she refused then relented. She was to drive one man to Dublin; at the last minute it changed to two. And now the men she was meeting were an hour late. Growing restless, Reason waited in a Toyota behind a row of bombed-out buildings off the Antrim Road. It was seven p.m. on the solstice. The longest, darkest night of the year. She had been instructed by Kieran to abort the mission if the men hadn't shown up in an hour. She was preparing to leave when the pair skidded up to the car. They were supposed to be dressed in business suits. They wore torn jeans and denim jackets. There had been no time for disguises. Both plunged into the sedan, shaking and sweating profusely.

"That was too fucking close," one puffed and wiped his brow on his sleeve. "They nearly had us."

These men weren't cool-headed and composed like Malachy Duffy or the fellow she escorted through Crossmaglen. These were men on the run in a desperate way, in a desperate hurry.

"We can't go near the motorway. They'll find us for sure if we do," one said to Reason. "We have to go through County Down into Armagh…do you know the way?"

Kieran had given her every detail. "Yes."

"If we don't get out tonight, we don't get out at all. The RUC is hunting for us this very second…they'll kill us if they catch us," the man panted and repeatedly craned his neck to the left and right. He turned to Reason, "You'd best hurry up and drive, love."

Reason had driven this remote stretch of road between Belfast and the border once with Cain. It meandered across rolling farmlands into the deserted interior of Down. The road was wide enough for only one car in some places and much of the way was unpaved so the driving was choppy and knocked the three travelers about which set them the more on edge. But Kieran had insisted this way would be the safest on this particular night, and Reason trusted his word.

There was scant conversation as they drove. One of the men lay trying to sleep in the back seat. The other sat stonily bidding his homeland good-bye. Occasionally the two men would converse in undertones and curse every time they glanced at the clock. Time was of the essence. *Hurry, hurry,* the roadway urged. Tension electrified the journey, and after twenty rough miles, Reason began to get a bad feeling.

As they snaked back and forth through the inland corridors of Down, fog began settling in; gradually coiling itself around the trees and farmhouses in milky strands, making Reason and her charges claustrophobic. It spiraled around the headlights and windows as if to bind the car. In some of the lowland meadows they couldn't see more than five feet in front of them. And the night was motionless and voiceless and waiting for something. Something to come out of the fog. But onward the trio forged, trusting Kieran's plan. By nine o'clock they crossed into Armagh. The fog hulked oppressively for miles and played tricks on the brain. Reason began to imagine faces peering out of the mist, and every quaver of fog looked like a specter, worse yet a soldier-at-arms. *Crack,* the car hit a boulder, but it sounded like a discharging gun. The startled threesome grabbed their chests where their hearts roared, and they laughed at their overreaction. There was nothing to fear. It was only a rock they didn't see in the fog. Only a rock.

Five miles from the border, the fog fragmented into thick and thin pockets. Reason scanned the emerging fields and saw nothing except brambly hedges and sheets of grass. The trio was progressing on schedule but they weren't complacent. A growing feeling of dread spread over the car as they plowed blindly through tunnels of white. The men loosened their collars and opened the windows for air. Reason concentrated on her driving and felt sicker and sicker with misgiving as they sped across Armagh. Armagh where the Cure slinked through the pastures on their hands and knees. Waiting, waiting to strike. Who watched the little sedan through the fog? Who waited? The trio had come too far to turn back. This was the men's sole chance for freedom. They had no choice but to entrust themselves to the solstice. The longest, darkest night.

Two miles from an unsanctioned crossing into the Republic, the threesome encountered a barricade of boulders piled high across the road. Moving forward was impossible. Tributary roads ran to the left and right.

Reason stopped the car and deferred to the men. "Which way do we go?"

Left led to a farmhouse and over a hill. Right led to the village of Ballyhanna less than one mile from the border. The men argued heatedly, and Reason's flesh rippled over her bones. She was terrified. She wanted to vault from the car and run as hard and as far as she could. Dear God, what lay beyond the suffocating fog? And what trailed them at the rear? Had she seen lights flash on then off in the rearview mirror?

"There are barricades down here all the time," one man insisted, constantly peering ahead and over his shoulder like he feared Something would choose now to drift out of the mist.

"Nah, there's something wrong. I can feel it. That barricade wasn't supposed to be here."

"What in the fuck are we supposed to do at this point? Fly? Either we go left or we go right, but we have to choose one way or the other."

The man's voice shook and his cheeks went white. "I tell you something's not right."

"We don't have time for this! Kieran knew what he was talking about. He wouldn't steer us wrong."

"Well," the fretful man took a moment to reflect, "the truth is, I'd rather die out here in a blaze of bullets than rot like a corpse in Long Kesh."

Die in a blaze of bullets? Reason's bravado evaporated. *Bang, bang, baby, in this game you're dead.* She didn't want to die.

They decided to head for the village; right they proceeded. The one-lane road dropped steeply downhill into a meadow where the clouds crushed upon them and immersed them for three nerve-smashing miles. Was there something behind them? Reason kept checking. What was that she saw out of the corner of her eye?

"We shouldn't have come this way," the man fussed on. "Something is terribly, terribly wrong."

Reason swallowed hard. Her knuckles were white on the steering wheel. God almighty, what was gathering around them that they couldn't see? She had grown cold and numb, but sweat stung her eyes and her breath was shallow and quick. Something *was* terribly wrong.

Through phantasmal vapors they could see a score of buildings and a cluster of houses. The extent of Ballyhanna. Nothing moved. There wasn't a sound. The shops were dark, the streets abandoned. Dim lights lit little houses with curtains drawn tight. Was the village sleeping? Or holding its breath?

Beyond the village in a depression where the fog was a cloak, the man who fretted ordered Reason to stop.

"Why?" She was afraid to stop for fear of what might catch them.

"What is your problem?" his cohort objected frantically.

"Shut up both of you! Stop the fucking car!"

When the Toyota came to rest, the man told Reason to get out.

"Are you crazy?" she recoiled aghast.

"I said *get out!* I don't want you driving us anymore."

"But...but why?"

"Scram!" The man gave Reason a rough slug in the arm. "Keep your head down and don't stand up. Go!"

Reason opened her car door and tumbled out in sheer terror.

"Don't go back to the village," the man advised hastily as he bounced into the driver's seat. "Crawl until you're in the tall grass. Stay close to the earth, then run like hell!" He shoved the car into first gear. "And pray for our souls, love." Off he and his mate fishtailed into the fog.

Less than two minutes later the Something made itself known. Like a grim marquee, one headlight after another flared and closed in to block the road. As she reached the tall grass and scrambled up a hill, Reason spotted hordes of soldiers converging on the narrow roadway below and surrounding the Toyota like the jaws of a trap. The soldiers made no attempt to apprehend the fugitives. They gave no chance for the men to surrender. They just opened fire with automatic weapons and pummeled the car with a steady stream of bullets.

Diving to the ground, Reason covered her ears and still the gunfire shredded the darkness. It sounded like she was in the front car of a rollercoaster in a pitch-black tunnel brattling over rough, steel tracks. *Whap-whap-whap-whap-whap-whap.* Precise, staccato eruptions plugging the sedan in succession, in slick, hypnotic rhythm; like a rollercoaster plummeting and soaring, plummeting and roaring *whap-whap-whap-whap.* The machine gun fire went on for over ten minutes until the Toyota juddered and danced on its tires and resembled a colander.

"Nice one, nice one," voices rose on the wind after the shooting stopped. After the kill.

"How many are there?"

"Two."

"Are you sure? The dispatch said there were three."

"See for yourself. Two. Hahaha. Two dead ducks."

"Where the hell is the third one then?"

Like Providence had punched a hole in the fog for Reason, from her crouch on the hillside she could see everything happening below. She didn't want to look as the soldiers swarmed around the car. It was too horrible to watch. But she couldn't tear her eyes away. Several men, some in balaclavas, dragged the bodies from the car and heaved them on the ground like carrion. Sagging masses of crimson goo was all that was left of the fleeing men. The soldiers kicked the corpses face-down into the grass and fired a *coup de grâce* at close range into each of the victim's heads. Then they patted each other on the backs and swayed about with success. So there would be no physical evidence of their extreme method of assassination, a team of men began collecting the hundreds of bullets, the bodies were removed, and the car was set on fire.

Dropping her head into the wet grass, Reason wept in fear and revulsion and wondered if she would get out of this sane and alive. The fretting man must have sensed what was coming. He forced Reason out of the car to save her life. But she wasn't safe. As the Army and scores of policemen teemed below, she didn't know what she was supposed to do. Run like hell. But where? Anywhere out of the line of fire. Run like hell. *This is Hell.* Run.

Thankful to be dressed in black, she merged well with the night. Keeping her head down, all but kissing the dirt, Reason made her way over the hill on her elbows and knees then dived downhill. She found herself in another field of tall grass, in another pocket of smothering fog, in God knows where. Other than the lament of a distant cow, there wasn't a sign of civilization to be seen or heard. *Don't shoot me, don't shoot me,* she panted over and over to herself and softly wept in shock as she pawed her way through the longest, darkest night of her life. Run like hell. She dared another jump forward, and to her dismay, out from the mist pounced two soldiers in camouflage gear and balaclavas. One pinned Reason's arms behind her while the other raised his automatic rifle to her nose. Taking note of her dark attire and wild panic they concluded the obvious.

"I knew there was a third one!" rejoiced a raucous Brit. "And a bitch at that. You were in that car, weren't you, bitch?"

"What are we going to do with her?" asked the soldier behind Reason.

The gunman considered in silence then growled, "Shoot her dead like the others."

Reacting on instinct, catching both men off guard, Reason punch-kicked her foot into the groin of the man with the gun in front of her. As he stumbled back in a fit of profanity, she stomped as hard as she could on the foot of the man holding her arms and broke from his grasp. Praying for a miracle, she hurtled across the pasture at a break-neck pace. Through the knee-high grass she leaped, knowing at any moment she would be shot in the back. *Let them fucking kill me then!* But by God she would go down fighting.

After running awhile and hearing no footfall behind her, she dared a backwards glance across the misty farmland. She snapped her head to the left, to the right. No one was there. Had she lost them in the fog? Taking a chance, she slowed her gait to catch her breath; at once the two soldiers lunged out of the grass from both sides and tackled her roughly. She landed on her stomach with both men on top of her, and this time they held her fast.

One soldier stripped off Reason's coat and tied her arms behind her back with nylon cord. "Shut her up before the whole damn village hears her!" he grunted to his comrade. "There's some tape in the car."

Using duct tape, the other man plastered Reason's mouth to stifle her cries then added a slap for good measure.

"You can cry us a river, sweet thing, but nothing's going to save you," the soldier promised and yanked up Reason's head. All she could see of the man were his eyes, and his eyes shivered her soul. Executioner, no remorse. "You run with the Provos, do you?" He pinched Reason's chin in his leather-gloved hand and forced her to look at him. "Provos are made to be hunted. Provos get their fucking heads blown off. Did you know that when you decided to become their bitch? Did you think you'd die like a dog?"

Tears streamed down Reason's face and she jerked her head away.

"Do you want to kill her or shall I?" the second soldier was anxious to know.

"I thought we'd both unload a few rounds." A harsh, low laugh. "We'll shoot until her guts come out."

612 Reasonable Maniacs

Reason's eyes swam in panic as the leather-gloved gunman hauled her to her feet only to knock her to the ground with a slug. Back across the pasture to a waiting car the two men dragged her like a sacked doe. Her face and hair and clothing mopped the turf and mud, and the fog, the hellish fog masked sight, strangled sound. Stopping at last beside a car parked deep in the night, the soldiers stared down into Reason's face then jerked her up by the throat and ordered her to kneel. Then and only then did she realize she was in the hands of the Cure. *"Yeah, I love screaming, 'Kneel, you son of a bitch!' Then kapow! Brains hit the wall."* She thought of Cain in Switzerland and Wilder in California and understood she was in this drama alone. She considered pleading for mercy but knew the Cure wouldn't afford it. A wicked silence ensued. The soldiers leered down at her laughing, and Reason stared back at them in fright and contempt. They took aim with their rifles.

Bang, bang, baby you're dead. She should have listened to Wilder, to Cain, to reason. She never dreamed she'd be the one to die. She thought of her mother receiving the news at Christmastime that her daughter was a terrorist...a dead terrorist in Armagh. *Michael Patrick McGuinness died at Christmastime in County Armagh.* Why was she thinking of him? *Blue, Irish eyes...Good-bye, Daddy, good-bye.* And Reason regretted not getting married and having a child, not being able to finish the Gov's new wing, not seeing her family or Cain or Wilder again...*oh, Wilder!* Kneeling with a shattering heart and a cloudburst of tears, Reason wished the men would pull their triggers and get it over with. It was a pain worse than death pondering all the things she would never do...all the faces she wouldn't see.

"Wait." One of the soldiers eyed Reason in a different manner. "Let's fuck her. I know the perfect place for it." The men hoisted Reason to her feet. And so she couldn't easily run, they took her shoes and socks and tossed them across the field.

Icy fog wrapped around Reason's bare arms and feet, and both soldiers sniggered to see her shiver. "Makes her tits stand up pretty," one guffawed, giving Reason a fondle. Then they hurled her into the trunk of the car.

"She won't survive long in there," said the cohort.

"Who the hell cares?"

Down crashed the lid of the trunk, it was hard to breathe, and Reason knew she was lost. She thought of Merry O'Neill shot dead and lying for hours steeped in her own blood. But at least someone found her. As the car she was stowed in drove away from the carnage, Reason realized she was going to be murdered, and no one would know of it for months, even years. She would vanish. Without a trace.

Reason had been in the trunk for thirty minutes when the car stopped. She heard the driver get out and stride back. Was this it? Was he coming to kill her, to rape her, to demand unspeakable acts?

The trunk opened, and the soldier dragged her out and threw her into the back seat of the car. "Move one fucking toe," he threatened, "and your face will be splattered all over the inside of this car." Those were the last words spoken for an hour.

As the driver cut across County Down, the scenery became recognizable to Reason. They were drawing closer and closer to the sea. She expected the men to pull off the deserted road any second to torture and then shoot her, and she felt she would go insane with fear. It was a cruel thing these men were doing. Prolonging her agony, keeping her in suspense, making her anxious for them to kill her and not hurt her anymore. She just wanted the nightmare to be over.

Now the road was eerily familiar. The driver sped towards My Lady's Leisure. Closer and closer they grew to the Cromwell estate until the driver swung into the little lane to My Lady's Leisure, continued up to the driveway, and parked the car. Floodlights on the corners of the manor glowed through the fog; the manor was dark and tightly locked.

"Welcome to party headquarters," the driver proclaimed. "The fellow who owns this place used to be in the regiment; some of us boys use the stable now and then for 'special occasions.' I'm sure Cain wouldn't mind." Both men hopped out of the car. The driver ran to open the stable and chase the ponies into the pasture; the other soldier opened Reason's door. "OK, slut, your time has come to fuck." At gunpoint, he motioned her to get out. He removed the cord from her wrists and ripped the tape off her mouth. "I want a hand job then a blow job." His hands slid upon her crudely, obscenely. "Come to daddy, sweet thing," he urged.

Reason poked the man's eyes and wrenched free of his grope. She understood if she ran, the men would hunt her down, but she bolted anyway. Gunfire, she heard gunfire in her wake. One shot. Two shots. Three shots. Four. Death raced to claim her. Madly she sprinted through wraiths of fog around the manor and down, madly down the cliff, hoping to reach the dungeon in time. She could open the grate with its covert switch and hide on the secret staircase.

Oh God, oh God, she thought, running hard. Almost there. Footsteps thudding nearer, near. From behind a man brutally grabbed her. She spun around. "Oh no, God no," Reason moaned, delirious with fear. It was a soldier. He dragged her forward towards the manor. More footsteps. Gunfire like rockets. The soldier shoved Reason to the ground. She tried to flee, but he tripped her, commanding her to, "Fucking lie down!" He dropped to the earth as well. Horrified, Reason saw the other Cure agent streaking towards her with his rifle cocked, then dropping to one knee, he took aim to unload a killing volley. This was it. But in a blur of rapid motion the hooded man on the ground beside Reason raised his own revolver and fired. One shot. Between the eyes precisely. The agent keeled backwards into the fog, and silence strangled the night. The hooded man then jerked Reason up and flung her towards the grate. Then a third soldier appeared and waved his arms. Reason all but fainted. How many of them were there? Relinquishing Reason, the man who had chased her bolted back up the cliff and ran towards the soldiers' car.

Open, open, open, Reason begged upon reaching the grate, and the grate granted her wish. Into the dungeon she lunged in a frenzy. Down went the grate. Were the agents behind her? Had they seen her skid inside? She stumbled through the maze of rowboats and lurched up the secret stairs. Halfway up, in the darkest dark, she sagged onto a step and crouched as stilly as her terror allowed. Her breath was nearly as loud as the sea; her heart louder. Where were the hunters? Still out combing the fog? Had they entered the house?

Eternity passed and still Reason cowered without moving in absolute darkness on the frozen stairs. She hoped eventually the soldiers would stop searching for her and leave. She would hide for days if she had to. A frigid wind blew down the stairwell, and despite hugging her arms and drawing her knees to her chin, she couldn't get warm or stop shaking. Something tickled the side of her neck. She swatted the air and hoped it wasn't a spider. Worse yet a rat. There it was again. Something on her nape. She reached behind her head again, and this time she touched a cold hand. Losing herself to a shriek, she plunged forth, swinging and slapping at whoever pursued her until she missed the last slick step and wound up in a heap on the dungeon floor. Moaning and pleading and crying as the hand now grabbed her by the leg, she blacked out.

Chapter Fifty-Seven

"No, no, no, no, no," Morris ran howling and waving his arms. Midway down Fiona's steep stairs, he launched himself at the soldier's back and grabbed his khaki collar, toppling the soldier over backwards at the foot of the steps. Morris then booted the Brit in the head; a head protected by a helmet so dense Morris bruised his bare toes. But, undeterred, he continued kicking and hitting and hollering until one of the raiding policeman jerked him away and slammed him face-first against the wall. In tears, Morris lay watching the soldiers and RUC drag his father away by the heels.

Picking himself up, with no one home to console him, he wandered through the house in a daze; what to do, who to call, where to go. Fiona and Granny Nora and Granda Joe were in Ballymena. Decky was in America. He had no idea where Reason was. Trembling with chattering teeth, he went to close what was left of Fiona's axed front door. Droplets of Kieran's blood shimmered on the floor and continued like a connect-the-dots puzzle down the walkway to Fiona's gate. Morris touched his father's blood and stared down at its sheen on his fingers. Smearing the blood over and over his face, smearing it through his tears and over his lips, he huddled on the stairs and writhed in a fear and fury so penetrating, so savage and corrosive it changed forever the shape of his soul. And in the sudden stillness of the long, darkest night, hatred devoured his heart. He had told Jillie...the Brit.

*   *   *   *   *   *

Hooded and handcuffed, Kieran was driven to Windsor. Other than the initial beating upon being arrested, he was unscathed. Being informed that he had been detained for routine questioning, he was marched into a sweltering room and seated on a bench. Kieran had no idea what they were going to do to him, this treatment was new, and he steeled himself for the worst. Fluorescent lights buzzed, and the room harbored a nauseating, wet smell, like rancid fat and putrefied eggs and feces-fouled water. The lights buzzed like flies. The room grew hotter. Louder, louder buzzed the lights until the room seemed to vibrate and shudder in heat; until Kieran began to sweat and get prickly skin.

"Hello, Mr. McCartan." A man in shoes that clicked entered the room. Harry Jaggars. "I'm sorry we had to awaken you so rudely, but we have a matter of importance to discuss. It's about tonight's escape attempt through County Armagh. Does that ring a bell?"

Kieran shook his head. The lights buzzed. The heat seared. A chill crawled up his spine.

The door to the room opened and closed again. Someone of docile footfall had entered the room, and Kieran could sense the person bending before him to stare into his hooded face. Madeline Hatter motioned for Harry to proceed.

"It grieves me to report your Provisional friends ran into an unfortunate accident. You say you're winning the war, but we're shutting down the IRA's reign of terror, Mr. McCartan."

Kieran knew nothing about the ambush. All he knew was Reason had been driving the car.

"One of your thugs, a pisspot scab named Beezer, says you're involved in abetting wanted criminals, Mr. McCartan. Would you care to explain?"

Kieran knew that wasn't true. Beezer didn't know him, and Beezer couldn't identify him. Beezer's knowledge was limited to the escape route and the names on the fake passports. But the fact that Beezer had been arrested proved once again there was an informant. Kieran had nothing to say.

"Shall I take your silence as an admission of guilt, Mr. McCartan?" Harry clicked in circular steps around the bench, and had a voice smooth and dry as gin. "You're so guilty, sin sweats from your pores."

The sanctimony in Harry's remark made Kieran simper. "And you're a fucking saint I suppose?"

Madeline covered a laugh. Dear, defiant Kieran.

"Have it your way, Mr. McCartan, but tonight is a preview of your fate. Think of me as your ghost of Christmas Future." Jaggars jerked Kieran to his feet and told him to kneel on the floor.

Kieran refused.

With a snicker and *click, click,* Harry kicked Kieran's legs out from under him and sent him sprawling face first into a puddle of jelly so obscene smelling, Kieran retched and coughed and rolled away gagging. He tried to stand up and was kicked in the neck by soft, silent shoes. Shoes that leisurely departed. Open, shut went the door.

"Leave the cuffs on. Take the hood off," Jaggars ordered then clicked from the room, saying smugly, "The wage of sin is death, Mr. McCartan. One of these times it will be you who dies."

As the hood slid off his eyes, Kieran discovered himself lying atop the clotted pulp of his two dead comrades. The brown stuff of their limbs and guts was smeared on his arms and legs, on his face and chest, and what was left of their skull-less eyes leered upon him. Their mouths gaped with fragments of teeth. And as he frantically scrambled to his feet and doddered back vomiting, he remembered seeing Merry O'Neill looking much the same way. Great God, Reason! The corpses were so dismembered by gunfire it was hard to tell if she was one of them. But he saw no blonde hair, just tufts of black sprung from unraveling brains.

Panic urged him to flee, to wail, to crawl and beg on his hands and knees to be released from the room. The buzzing intensified as did the heat and stench of festering flesh. The naked, white lights bored upon him from all sides. The only place he could look without blinding his eyes was on the corpses. Kieran slid down the wall of his cell, still retching and weak in the knees. Insanity threatened his mind. The incessant whirr of lights like flies and the sight of violent death shook his soul, but he refused to submit to the horror and hysteria seething up from his humanity. This was a grotesque British ploy to spur him into betraying his comrades and cause.

He had seen dead bodies before. A body was just a shell, like a sleeping bag, and now, unzipped, his friends' spirits had flown. The dead couldn't hurt him. The British could. He said an Our Father, and pinching his eyes together, clenching his fists, he chanted the doctrine of war. He was loyal to the IRA; he would die before betraying his peers. He was deeply committed to a free Ireland. He was a revolutionary with a noble and justifiable cause, and the men holding him prisoner were morally wrong. He knew he was superior, and one day, one day, all the deaths and tortures, even his, would lead to liberation. *Tiocfaidh ár lá.* And the hours dragged by and by and quietly he sat. Chanting, praying, staring a hole through the faces of death.

*   *   *   *   *   *

Reason heard her name. In the dark of the dungeon she immediately started to struggle. But his hand was covering her mouth, and he gripped her firmly around the middle. "Reason, it's me. Stay quiet."

Frantic, she jabbed her elbows into his ribs and tried to get up off the floor.

He pulled her against him. She smacked his head with her fist. Still he held her. "For God's sake, Reason, it's really me. I didn't make it to Malibu. I'm here, right here."

She couldn't believe her ears. "*Wilder?* It's you? It's really you?" she whispered in the darkness.

"It's really me. And you're safe. But the manor is full of Brits. We have to stay down here awhile."

Spinning to grab Wilder, Reason smothered her cries against his shoulder. "Don't let them hurt me anymore. Please, don't let them hurt me."

Resting against a rowboat on the floor, Wilder stroked and rocked Reason and crushed her to him and thanked God he wasn't in California. And tears streamed down his face. "I won't."

"You won't leave me?"

He raised Reason's hands to his lips and kissed each palm gently and caressed his cheek with her fingers. "I'll never leave you, love."

"You're crying," she whimpered.

He touched her tears, a sort of communion, like he and Reason had received the sacraments of hell.

Despite Wilder's tenderness, Reason sobbed and shivered and questioned her sanity. Her thoughts had grown fuzzy. Was this a dream? She felt weak and unreal and terrified and lost. Why had she lived, why had they died? *Pray for our souls, love...* "Oh God, oh my dear God...Wilder?" She no longer felt his arms. Her head nodded, heavy with sleep. "Wilder, are you here?"

His kiss convinced her. He was warm and wrapped around her and whispering her name.

"Did you shoot...that soldier?"

"Yes."

"I nearly died..." she drifted off.

"No, love. I won't let you die and leave me alone," he promised with all the power of his heart.

"I can't...can't move." Reason desperately tried to ask Wilder why. But she was too groggy. Her fears were blessedly fading, and the blackness of the longest night withdrew.

Chapter Fifty-Eight

"...and the IRA duo were killed by an Army patrol. Timothy O'Shea and Patrick McCann died after the car in which they were fleeing was sprayed with automatic gunfire. A spokesman for the army said, 'Our armed forces have once again demonstrated their extraordinary ability to take out of circulation the murdering IRA terrorists who are waging a campaign of blood in our province...'"

The radio woke her...or was she still dreaming? Reason awoke in her bed. The cuts on her hands from crawling through the rocks and grass had been cleaned. Her face, chafed from the duct tape, had been salved. Her hair had been washed, and there wasn't a trace of the Armagh mud on her skin. She gazed around at the miracle and hadn't a clue how it came to pass.

Carrying a cold compress, Fiona poked in her auburn head. "I thought I heard you moving about in here. I've been worried sick! How are you, dear? Och, you've had a good sleep."

Muddled, Reason rubbed her head. "How did I get back here?"

"A young man brought you home early this morning. You were sedated."

"*Sedated?*" Reason checked the time. Midnight. Over 24 hours had passed since she was hiding on the manor stairs. She remembered nothing after that.

"Aye, love. The lad said you'd had a scare and went a bit mad. Och, don't cry, pet." Fiona applied the compress to Reason's brow and added a kiss. "It happens to us all now and then."

Whap-whap-whap. Reason lay still, listening to the rollercoaster rampage. Yes, she felt a bit mad. Dropping her head back into the pillows, she hoped to find rest for her mind, but all she could see was the Toyota convulsing in a hail of bullets. Sorrow filled her eyes. Nausea and relief rushed in where terror had tread. How close she had come to dying. How gruesome the deaths she had seen. And like Cain, she would live the rest of her life with the night's preview of hell. It had all seemed so reasonable when she agreed to drive men to Dublin, and the first two trips had been painless. But it seemed insane now. The only time the war had made sense was when it was going in her favor. And what of the men who apprehended her in Armagh?

Reason expected the worst. "Was I raped?"

"Great Mother of God, I hope not! The young man said you weren't hurt."

All Reason could remember was that she was chased and shackled and grabbed in the dark. And now she was home as if it had been a grisly illusion. How had she survived? "I'm so confused. Fiona, I don't know what happened." Her voice cracked. Tears followed. "Who was the man who brought me home?"

"I'm embarrassed to say I don't know, love. He was just a boy really, not more than twenty, with hair the color of carrots. Does that sound familiar?"

Reason shook her head.

"Och, it was all very strange. He showed up on the doorstep with you in his arms. He was awfully nice, had a grave concern for you, but he was vague. I asked him a hundred questions, but all he said was he found you at Cain's estate, and you were in need of a rest."

Reason peered down at her nightgown. "Where are my clothes? The clothes I was wearing last night?"

Fiona shook her head blankly.

"How was I dressed when I got here? Wasn't I covered in mud?"

"No. You were clean and wearing that nightgown and a man's rain-coat. Cain's I presume. I thought you'd had too much of the drink at first." Fiona surveyed Reason with curiosity but didn't pry. Reason's mysterious comings and goings of late were none of her business, and she knew Reason was a good girl. But casually she mentioned, "The craic is two Cure agents were shot dead near your Cain's manor last night. Killed not long after the shooting in Ballyhanna they say."

Reason jolted up. She had witnessed one of the shootings. "*Two* agents were killed?"

"Aye. Of course the security forces are denying it."

Dazed, Reason stared into her palms. It was like a dream, but it wasn't a dream. "Fiona, was Declan here this morning?"

Fiona gave Reason a funny look. "He's in America, love."

"Well, of course he is." But Reason wasn't as sure as she sounded. She sensed somehow it had been Wilder who saved her, and he'd said, "*I won't let you die and leave me alone.*" "Oh Lord, what's happened to me? Nothing makes sense. Where's Kieran? Maybe he can explain all this."

Fiona's eyes watered, her lips quivered. "He's been lifted. The soldiers came and took him last night. Poor wee Morris was alone here in the house for hours. Scared to death he was. Found him curled up under the Christmas tree. He had blood all over him."

Reason didn't bother swatting her tears, and Fiona gathered her up in a hug. "You'll be all right, pet."

"Was Morris hurt? Where is he now?"

"If that wee boy grows up without being mad, it'll be a miracle. He's seen so much in six years. He's staying with Eamonn and Nora. Praise God, he didn't see you coming in this morning. He'd have thought you were dead and had a conniption. Don't worry, you'll see him before you leave."

"That's right. My vacation started today. Oh, thank God," Reason wept. "I'm going home." She hugged Fiona harder and through her black, bleak visions saw one guiding light. Her family. The family only hours ago she had feared never seeing again. Cowering on Cain's secret staircase, she had sworn, if she lived, to resign from the Grosvenor project and never return to Belfast. And she didn't care about Wilder or

Cain or Kieran and *tiocfaidh ár lá*. Let them dance in their flames of obsession. Let them be the reasonable maniacs wildly rushing to their destruction. Reason hadn't the lust to fight another day.

Fiona sensed Reason was saying good-bye. "That's the thing about you Yanks," she said, not hiding her disappointment. "You come over here, you see us like a three-ring circus, and you leave. You can get on a plane. All we can do is get on with our lives…"

The racket jarred Reason and Fiona from the bed to the window. The deafening roar hammered along Duntroon Drive, rattling the panes and doors. Reason could see the helicopter, settling low above the streetlamps, so low she could see the face of the pilot. How big the chopper looked up close. Much bigger than it looked in the sky. An enormous green dragonfly. Was it landing on the roof across the street? No, just harassing. Just jolting the Fenians awake. Two Cure agents had been shot dead in Down, now all taigs would pay. The soldiers had to be laughing on board the aircraft as the Catholic neighborhood snapped open its eyes. Wake up you fucking Fenians. Wake up. Reason turned her face to the wall and sank to her knees in tears. They had won.

*   *   *   *   *   *

The plane would be cleared for landing soon. How sane Malibu would seem, and how safe. Beyond the jet's windows clouds clustered and darkened the Pacific below. Wilder wished he could pitch his memories of the past week into those black, churning waves. And yet, thank God Harry Jaggars had prevented him from leaving Belfast. If he hadn't been arrested and had come to Malibu, Reason would be dead. And thank God he was released from Windsor in time, and Ian Wright had told him of the ambush. He covered his eyes and saw again the scene. The sight of the Brits dragging their quarry from the car to fire *coups de grâce* was a memory he'd carry till death. It was all too obscene.

He could see Reason running; he could hear his gun open fire. *Why in the hell were you out there? Don't say for me!* In the dungeon, he had given Reason morphine so she would sleep; she wouldn't recall her savior. *One day I'll tell you what I've done...killed a Brit, lost my soul.* Wilder stared down at the ocean. He called himself a healer, and he'd shot a man dead. In that split second, the physician had met the soldier, and seeing the warrior within him, he was amazed by his indurate power. Declan had killed and killed well, and Wilder had no regret. And that was hideous; the hideous nothingness of numb. He should feel *something*.

But Ruairi had foretold this dispassion. *"You're a soldier, and you may have to do harm to help one day...your convictions have to be strong enough to give you the confidence to kill someone without hesitation, without regret."* And now Wilder understood what Ruairi had meant. A soldier wasn't clemency; a soldier was a cause, an anger, an implement of protection and change. A soldier was an animal, and the animal lay beneath the surface of every man, and having once seen its teeth, a man would never be a man again. He would be a griffin; head and wings of an eagle, body of a lion. And what war had transformed him? A woman, woman of light. *Oh, why was she out there?* God alone knew what the future held. Wilder had heard rumors a ceasefire might be declared. But that wouldn't stop men like Harry Jaggars from hurting Reason, and the Brits' dirty tricks would continue. *Sweet Reason, be safe from me...never return to Ireland...but soulmates can't say good-bye. They're bound. Forever. Oh, Reason. My sweet, Irish Reason...*

*　　*　　*　　*　　*　　*

"Reason, Reason, Reason," Morris burst into Fiona's parlor at tea time. "Lookee what I...why are you crying?"

Welcoming Morris into her arms, she told him the truth, "Because I'm leaving Ireland tomorrow."

"Don't cry! If you cry when you leave Ireland, it means you'll never come back. Don't cry, Reason, don't cry." Morris wound his hands around her and hugged her as hard as he could. "I brought you your

Christmas present. I made it at Granny Nora's. I'll go get it." He darted from the room then darted back. "Close your eyes."

Reason accepted the piece of construction paper. On it Morris had cut and pasted his own squiggly version of a hummingbird and dusted its wings with blue and silver glitter.

"It's our favorite bird, see? It's for your desk at the Gov. I made one for Decky's desk too. Oh, but his has gold wings. I think gold wings fit Decky, don't you? I made my daddy a lark with red wings. But you're definitely silver and blue." Morris admired his artwork then admired Reason. "Silver and blue. Like the Christmas star! I'll bet if the Wise Men saw you, Reason, they'd follow you to N'York City."

His every word made Reason cry harder. How could she abandon this lost, loving child? *Whap-whap-whap.* "*Nice one, nice one!*" "This bird is beautiful, Morris. I'll put it on my desk and keep it forever."

Sliding to her, Morris flung his arms around Reason's knees. "When are you coming back?" he quizzed, staring up at her with complete trust.

"I have a lot of work to do in New York…"

Morris interrupted hoarsely, timidly, "Do you think my daddy is coming back?"

"I don't know. I don't know anything!" Reason cried.

"I know he'll come back, cuz you said good things happen when you have faith, and I have faith, Reason," Morris said bravely, looking up at her for assurance.

But she had no assurance, she had lost faith. Reason broke away from Morris and ran up to her room. In tears, she gathered her belongings. She packed away Ruairi's scale, not forgetting how Ruairi died. Was he a martyr, or a fool? And she was thinking of Wilder. Of Kieran and Cain. Of gentle, green mountains and deep, savage kisses. "*When are you coming back?*" She glanced up and saw Morris watching her, but he wasn't upset to see her packing. He believed she would return. The sight of his trusting eyes and sweet smile were more than Reason could bear. Grabbing her coat, she raced back down the stairs, out the door. It was her last night in Belfast, she couldn't wait to escape, and it was breaking her heart to leave.

Outside the rain fell softly, but sunset came like a foe. In every shadow Reason saw the Cure. It was hard to breathe, impossible to relax, and she wondered if she could ever face the dark again without fear. She wanted to bolt back into Fiona's and slam the door. Instead she stepped into her car and drove down the Antrim Road to the docks.

She walked along the River Lagan. All misty and gold, the old river shone. In the distance the lough ran roughly to embrace the Irish Sea. And Reason found herself standing on the lawn of the Laganside Church, staring up at Michael's boats. Even now, with her heart aching, those sailboats made her smile. She was about to leave when the doors of the church opened. Father Leo stood bidding his evensong flock farewell. He caught sight of Reason and called her name. It was like seeing Johanna out on the lawn, but unlike Johanna, her daughter didn't run away.

Reason walked over to Leo. He could see she had been crying. "Whatever is the matter, my dear?" he inquired, patting Reason's arm. "Come inside where it's warm."

It was good to go into a church, close to God. Reason felt safe here. "I'm leaving Belfast tomorrow," she said, brushing tears from her eyes. "I feel like such a quitter, and a coward, I should stay and finish my work, but terrible things have happened…I don't belong here, Father. I never did."

"Your mother said the same thing," Leo said without thinking.

"What do you mean?"

Father Leo flushed red and looked flustered. Declan O'Neill had been to the church and asked Leo not to reveal Reason's past. But that wasn't what Michael would want; he'd want his daughter to know the truth. And he'd want her to stay in Belfast. Leo broke the news quickly, "The day I told you the story of Michael Patrick and Johanna, I couldn't remember their daughter's name. It was Reason because she was Michael's reason for living, and you're that Reason."

"What?" Reason laughed out loud, "Oh, I don't think so."

"It's God's truth, dear. I know this is a blow, but Michael McGuinness was your father and Johanna MacBride is your mum."

"But...no...my father's name was Kent, and my mother is Anna Rousseau and she's not Irish...she doesn't look Irish or sound Irish...she hates the Irish!"

"And why wouldn't she when everything Irish betrayed her? You were born in Armagh City, and you lived in West Belfast. Michael made that wee necklace you're wearing and gave it to your mother on their wedding day. His initials are carved on the back."

Reason jerked the necklace up to her eyes and saw "MM" scratched in the tin. She gaped at Leo in awe. She had thought nothing more could shock her, now here was another blast. In an instant she was transformed, she was lost. She was *Irish*. Irish as Wilder, and she *had* learned the word "taig" from her mother, and Michael's bold heart beat within her. Sagging into a pew, her heart not knowing whether to shatter or sing, Reason broke down and wept. "My whole life has been a lie. Lies my mother taught me. There was no Kent McGuinness or Anna Rousseau, and we aren't old money...and I was there the day Michael was buried. You played the tin whistle, and I had a little flag...I was there...in Milltown...and I swear my heart broke when he left me..." *Blue, Irish eyes. Good-bye, Daddy, good-bye.* "And Michael, my *father* was a republican and the RUC shot him..." "*Nice one, nice one!*" Reason's voice dissolved into sobs.

"If your mother told lies, I suspect it was to protect you from her unhappy past."

"Protect me? She made me a snob and a hypocrite!" Reason thought of Wilder who simply wouldn't do. "She deprived me of my heritage, she said the Irish were no better than apes, she made me a *Wellworth-Howell!*" for the first time she spoke the name with shame. "That must have broken Michael's heart."

"You need to ask your mother for the whole story, Reason. I only know what I saw here. Your parents suffered awfully, they were shunned and discarded. But there was nothing about you that could have broken Michael's heart. You were his Reason. And the fact that you're here now, in this place where he married your mother, must make him happy indeed."

"This explains so much; why I was afraid of Wilder, why I love this country and couldn't stay uninvolved, why I was out there the other night…at least now it doesn't seem so crazy. Maybe Michael called me back here to put his spirit at rest, or maybe to awaken mine."

In an instant Reason's world was destroyed, and in an instant it was restored, in a form she'd never dreamed. She was an immigrant, born to privation, daughter of a rebel and a maid. A rebel shot dead by the Brits. Candles flickered on the altar. She flashed back to Armagh and the car in flames. Two men had died, like her father had died, like Merry and Brendan and Ruairi had died, for the crime of being Irish. And she remembered asking Wilder how the IRA could hate the British when the British were so decent. *"We'll shoot until her guts come out."* *Whap-whap-whap.* They faced the world with their seemly speech and told of a commitment to peace. Peace as they slapped up their barracks and threw down their gauntlets; as they terrorized Catholics and succored the Prods. They didn't want concord or talks between tribes. They wanted dominion, at any price. And there would be no mercy for the Irish. If one little car inspired a thousand bullets, how many bullets would Her Majesty spend for a kingdom? But the Brits *hadn't* won. The Wellworth-Howell perished in that ambush, and up from those killing fields where Michael had died, the McGuinness was reborn.

From the beginning Reason had said she didn't want to care, and from the beginning she'd had no choice. Wilder and his country possessed her. Michael laid claim to her soul. She could run away, she wanted to, but surely as the shore recalls the sea, she would come back. For Wilder. For Morris. For Kieran and Cain. For Michael Patrick McGuinness. And even as her courage stumbled and her heart felt weak, she knew there was no solace in retreat, no life in America apart from her work and the men she loved. Taking a breath, as if she were about to dive in too deep, Reason thanked Father Leo and left. She looked up at Michael's boats on the roof, happily sailing to nowhere, adrift on the whims of the wind. This was her home, here was her life. Her fate had been sealed from birth.

Back at Fiona's, Reason unpacked Ruairi's scale and placed it on her desk. How fitting to have a measuring tool in memory of a man who wouldn't give an inch. *"Giving up isn't an option,"* Kieran had said. *"All we can do is fight the good fight."* She touched her father's necklace around her throat. There too hung Cain's emerald teardrop and flame. *"Live with me until the roses bloom."* It was a lovely notion. But she wondered if Cain had looked at his victims like the soldiers in Armagh had looked upon her, like she was less than human, like she deserved to die. Would she be able to look at him now without seeing the Cure? Dear God, how Armagh would haunt her. She had no idea if she would recover. She was afraid of the future, and peace was a thing of the past. But she had survived, she was alive. To be Michael Patrick's reason. And Wilder's Reason. Wilder was never going to let her into his life or out of his life. Two hearts inseparably bound. She slid Merry's Claddagh off her right hand and placed it on her left with the heart pointing out.

Printed in the United States
92357LV00003B/22-39/A